W9-ANE-042

THE
CRIMSON
CAMPAIGN

BY BRIAN McCLELLAN

Promise of Blood
The Crimson Campaign
The Autumn Republic

THE
CRIMSON
CAMPAIGN

THE POWDER MAGE TRILOGY:
BOOK 2

BRIAN MCCLELLAN

www.orbitbooks.net

Copyright © 2014 by Brian McClellan
Maps by Isaac Stewart

All rights reserved. In accordance with the U.S. Copyright Act of 1976, the scanning, uploading, and electronic sharing of any part of this book without the permission of the publisher is unlawful piracy and theft of the author's intellectual property. If you would like to use material from the book (other than for review purposes), prior written permission must be obtained by contacting the publisher at permissions@hbgusa.com. Thank you for your support of the author's rights.

Orbit
Hachette Book Group
237 Park Avenue, New York, NY 10017
HachetteBookGroup.com

First Edition: May 2014

Orbit is an imprint of Hachette Book Group, Inc. The Orbit name and logo are trademarks of Little, Brown Book Group Limited.

The Hachette Speakers Bureau provides a wide range of authors for speaking events. To find out more, go to www.hachettespeakersbureau.com or call (866) 376-6591.

The publisher is not responsible for websites (or their content) that are not owned by the publisher.

The characters and events in this book are fictitious. Any similarity to real persons, living or dead, is coincidental and not intended by the author.

Library of Congress Cataloging-in-Publication Data
McClellan, Brian
    The Crimson Campaign / Brian McClellan. — First Edition.
        pages cm. — (The Powder Mage Trilogy : Book 2)
    ISBN 978-0-316-21908-2 (hardcover) — ISBN 978-1-4789-7945-6 (audio download) — ISBN 978-0-316-21909-9 (ebook) 1. Kings and rulers—Fiction. 2. Imaginary wars and battles—Fiction. 3. Betrayal—Fiction. 4. Imaginary places—Fiction. I. Title.
    PS3613.C35785C75 2014
    813'.6—dc23
                                                                        2013024412

10 9 8 7 6 5 4 3 2 1

RRD

Printed in the United States of America

For Michele,
My one and only
My friend, my collaborator, and my love

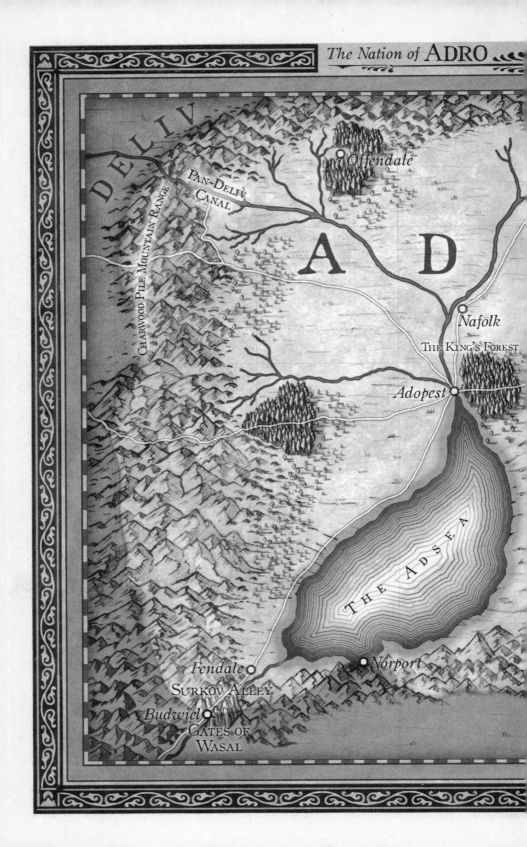

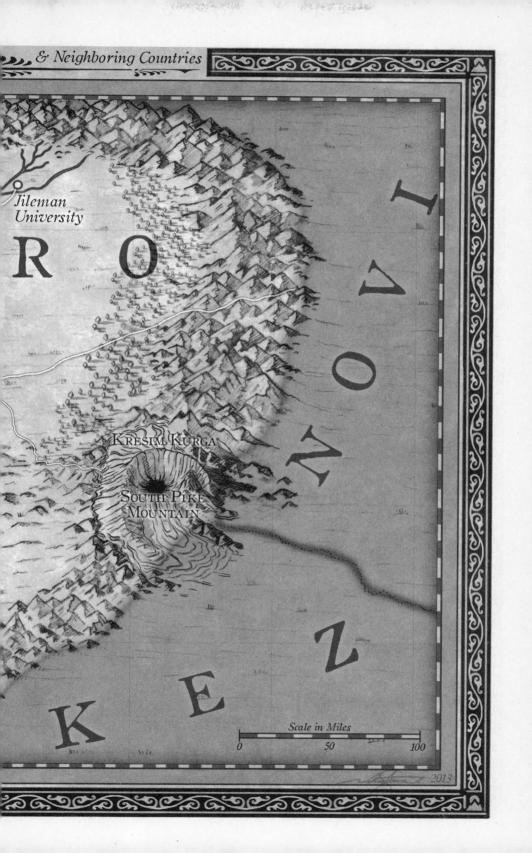

Jileman
University

R O

N O V I

K E Z

KRESIM KURGA

SOUTH PIKE
MOUNTAIN

Scale in Miles

0   50   100

2013

CITY OF

ADOPEST

AND SURROUNDINGS

1. Kirkamshire
   Adopest University
2. Adom's Wall
3. The Samalian Market
4. Samalian District
5. Lighthouse of Gostaun
6. Dwightwich Belltower
7. Kresim Cathedral

8. Baker's Town
9. The Routs
10. Elections Square
11. Public Archives
12. Centestershire
13. Black Street
14. Hrusch Ave.
15. Skyline Palace

16. Union Headquarters

HIGH TALIEN

NEW CITY

FACTORY DISTRICT

WEST LADEN

OLD CITY

THE ADSEA

Scale in Miles

0   1   2

2013

THE
CRIMSON
CAMPAIGN

CHAPTER

1

Adamat stood perfectly still in the middle of a deep hedgerow outside of his own summer house and stared through the windows at the men in the dining room. The house was a two-story, three-bedroom affair sitting by itself in the woods at the end of a dirt path. It was a twenty-minute walk into town from here. Unlikely anyone would hear gunshots.

Or screams.

Four of Lord Vetas's men milled about in the dining room, drinking and playing cards. Two of them were large and well-muscled as draft horses. A third was of middling height, with a heavy gut hanging out of his shirt and a thick black beard.

The final man was the only one Adamat recognized. He had a square face and a head that was almost comically small. His name was Roja the Fox, and he was the smallest boxer in the bareknuckle-boxing circuit run by the Proprietor back in Adopest. He could move faster than most boxers, by necessity, but he wasn't popular with the crowds and did not fight often. What he was doing here, Adamat had no idea.

What he did know was that he feared for the safety of his children—especially his daughters—with a group of malcontents like this.

"Sergeant," Adamat whispered.

The hedgerow rustled, and Adamat caught a glimpse of Sergeant Oldrich's face. He had a sharp jawline, and the dim moonlight betrayed the bulge of tobacco in one cheek. "My men are in place," Oldrich responded. "Are they all in the dining room?"

"Yes." Adamat had observed the house for three days now. All that time he'd stood by and watched these men yell at his children and smoke cigars in his house, dropping ash and spilling beer on Faye's good tablecloth. He knew their habits.

He knew that the fat, bearded one stayed upstairs, keeping an eye on the children all day. He knew the two big thugs escorted the children to the outhouse while Roja the Fox kept watch. He knew the four of them wouldn't leave the children by themselves until after dark, when they'd set up their nightly card game on the dining room table.

He also knew that in three days, he'd seen no sign of his wife or his oldest son.

Sergeant Oldrich pressed a loaded pistol into Adamat's hand. "Are you sure you want to lead on this? My men are good. They'll get the children out unharmed."

"I'm sure," Adamat said. "They're my family. My responsibility."

"Don't hesitate to pull the trigger if they head toward the stairs," Oldrich said. "We don't want them to take hostages."

The children were already hostages, Adamat wanted to say. He bit back his words and smoothed the front of his shirt with one hand. The sky was cloudy, and now that the sun had set there would be no light to betray his presence to those inside. He stepped out of the hedgerow and was suddenly reminded of the night he'd been summoned to Skyline Palace. That was the night all this had begun: the coup, then the traitor, then Lord Vetas. Silently, he cursed Field Marshal Tamas for drawing him and his family into this.

Sergeant Oldrich's soldiers crept out across the worn dirt path with Adamat, heading toward the front of the house. Adamat knew there were another eight behind the house. Sixteen men in total. They had the numbers. They had the element of surprise.

Lord Vetas's goons had Adamat's children.

Adamat paused at the front door. Adran soldiers, their dark-blue uniforms almost impossible to see in the darkness, took up spots beneath the dining room windows, their muskets at the ready. Adamat looked down at the door. Faye had chosen this house, instead of one closer to town, in part because of the door. It was a sturdy oak door with iron hinges. She felt that a strong door made her family safer.

He'd never had the heart to tell her the door frame was riddled with termites. In fact, Adamat had always meant to have it replaced.

Adamat stepped back and kicked right next to the doorknob.

The rotten wood exploded with the impact. Adamat ducked into the front hall and brought his pistol up as he rounded the corner.

All four of the goons burst into action. One of the big men leapt toward the back doorway leading to the staircase. Adamat held his pistol steady and fired and the man dropped.

"Don't move," Adamat said. "You're surrounded!"

The remaining three goons stared back at him, frozen in place. He saw their eyes go to his spent pistol, and then they all went for him at once.

The volley of musket balls from the soldiers outside burst the window and glass showered the room like frost. The remaining goons went down, except for Roja the Fox. He stumbled toward Adamat with a knife drawn, blood soaking the sleeve of one arm.

Adamat reversed the grip on his pistol and brought the butt down on Roja's head.

Just like that, it was over.

Soldiers spilled into the dining room. Adamat pushed past them and bolted up the stairs. He checked the children's rooms first: all empty. Finally, the master bedroom. He flung the door open with such force it nearly flew off the hinges.

The children were huddled together in the narrow space between the bed and the wall. The older siblings embraced the younger ones, shielding them in their arms as best they could. Seven frightened faces stared up at Adamat. One of the twins was crying, no doubt from the crack of the muskets. Silent tears streamed down his chubby cheeks. The other poked his head out timidly from his hiding place beneath the bed.

Adamat breathed a sigh of relief and fell to his knees. They were alive. His children. He felt the tears come unbidden as he was mobbed by small bodies. Tiny hands reached out and touched his face. He threw his arms wide, grabbing as many of them as possible and pulling them closer.

Adamat wiped the tears from his cheeks. It wasn't seemly to cry in front of the children. He took a great breath to compose himself and said, "I'm here. You're safe. I've come with Field Marshal Tamas's men."

Another round of happy sobs and hugs followed before Adamat was able to restore order.

"Where is your mother? Where's Josep?"

Fanish, his second oldest, helped to shush the other children. "They took Astrit a few weeks ago," she said, pulling at her long black braid with shaking fingers. "Just last week they came and took Mama and Josep."

"Astrit is safe," Adamat said. "Don't worry. Did they say where they were taking Mama and Josep?"

Fanish shook her head.

Adamat felt his heart fall, but he didn't let it show on his face. "Did they hurt you? Any of you?" He was most concerned for Fanish. She was fourteen, practically a woman. Her shoulders were bare beneath her thin nightgown. Adamat searched for bruises and breathed a word of thanks there were none.

"No, Papa," Fanish said. "I heard the men talking. They wanted to, but..."

"But what?"

"A man came when they took away Mama and Josep. I didn't hear his name, but he was dressed as a gentleman and he spoke very quietly. He told them that if they touched us before he gave them permission, he'd..." She trailed off and her face went pale.

Adamat patted her on the cheek. "You've been very brave," he reassured her gently. Inside, Adamat fumed. Once Adamat was no longer any use to him, Vetas no doubt would have turned those goons loose on the children without a second thought.

"I'm going to find them," he said. He patted Fanish on the cheek again and stood up. One of the twins grabbed his hand.

"Don't go," he begged.

Adamat wiped the little one's tears. "I'll be right back. Stay with Fanish." Adamat wrenched himself away. There was still one more child and his wife to save—more battles to win before they were all safely reunited.

He found Sergeant Oldrich just outside the upstairs bedroom, waiting respectfully with his hat in his hands.

"They took Faye and my oldest son," Adamat said. "The rest of the children are safe. Are any of those animals alive?"

Oldrich kept his voice low so the children wouldn't overhear. "One of them took a bullet to the eye. Another, the heart. It was a lucky volley." He scratched the back of his head. Oldrich wasn't old by any means, but his hair was already graying just above his ears. His cheeks were flushed from the storm of violence. His voice, though, was even.

"Too lucky," Adamat said. "I needed one of them alive."

"One's alive," Oldrich said.

When Adamat reached the kitchen, he found Roja sitting in one of the chairs, his hands tied behind his back, bleeding from bullet wounds to the shoulder and hip.

Adamat retrieved a cane from the umbrella stand beside the front door. Roja stared balefully at the floor. He was a boxer, a fighter. He wouldn't go down easy.

"You're lucky, Roja," Adamat said, pointing to the bullet wounds with the tip of his cane. "You might survive these. If you receive medical attention quickly enough."

"I know you?" Roja said, snorting. Blood speckled his dirty linen shirt.

"No, you don't. But I know you. I've watched you fight. Where's Vetas?"

Roja turned his neck to the side and popped it. His eyes held a challenge. "Vetas? Don't know him."

Beneath the feigned ignorance, Adamat thought he caught a note of recognition in the boxer's voice.

Adamat placed the tip of his cane against Roja's shoulder, right next to the bullet wound. "Your employer."

"Eat shit," Roja said.

Adamat pressed on his cane. He could feel the ball still in there, up against the bone. Roja squirmed. To his credit, he didn't make a sound. A bareknuckle boxer, if he was any good, learned to embrace pain.

"Where's Vetas?"

Roja didn't respond. Adamat stepped closer. "You want to live through the night, don't you?"

"He'll do worse to me than you ever could," Roja said. "Besides, I don't know nothin'."

Adamat stepped away from Roja, turning his back. He heard Oldrich step forward, followed by the heavy thump of a musket butt slamming into Roja's gut. He let the beating continue for a few moments before turning back and waving Oldrich away.

Roja's face looked like he'd been through a few rounds with Sou-Smith. He doubled over, spitting blood.

"Where did they take Faye?" *Tell me*, Adamat begged silently. *For your sake, hers, and mine. Tell me where she is.* "The boy, Josep? Where is he?"

Roja spit on the floor. "You're him, aren't you? The father of these stupid brats?" He didn't wait for Adamat to answer. "We were gonna bugger all those kids. Startin' with the small ones first. Vetas wouldn't let us. But your wife..." Roja ran his tongue along his broken lips. "She was willing. Thought we'd go easy on the babies if she took us all."

Oldrich stepped forward and slammed the butt of his musket across Roja's face. Roja jerked to one side and let out a choked groan.

Adamat felt his whole body shaking with rage. Not Faye. Not his beautiful wife, his friend and partner, his confidante and the mother of his children. He held up his hand when Oldrich wound up to hit Roja again.

"No," Adamat said. "That's just an average day for this one. Get me a lantern."

He grabbed Roja by the back of the neck and dragged him out of the chair, pushing him outside through the back door. Roja stumbled into an overgrown rosebush in the garden. Adamat lifted him to his feet, sure to use his wounded shoulder, and shoved him along. Toward the outhouse.

"Keep the children inside," Adamat said to Oldrich, "and bring a few men."

The outhouse was wide enough for two seats, a necessity for a household with nine children. Adamat opened the door while two of Oldrich's soldiers held Roja up between them. He took a lantern from Oldrich and let it illuminate the inside of the outhouse for Roja to see.

Adamat grabbed the board that covered the outhouse hole and tossed it on the ground. The smell was putrid. Even after sundown the walls crawled with flies.

"I dug this hole myself," Adamat said. "It's eight feet deep. I should have cut a new one years ago, and the family has been using it a lot lately. They were here all summer." He shined the lantern into the hole and gave an exaggerated sniff. "Almost full," he said. "Where is Vetas? Where did they take Faye?"

Roja sneered at Adamat. "Go to the pit."

"We're already there," Adamat said. He grabbed Roja by the back of the neck and forced him into the outhouse. It was barely big enough for the two of them. Roja struggled, but Adamat's strength was fueled by his rage. He kicked Roja's knees out from under him and shoved the boxer's head into the hole.

"Tell me where he is," Adamat hissed.

No answer.

"Tell me!"

"No!" Roja's voice echoed in the box that formed the outhouse seat.

Adamat pushed on the back of Roja's head. A few more inches and Roja would get a face full of human waste. Adamat choked back his own disgust. This was cruel. Inhuman. Then again, so was taking a man's wife and children hostage.

Roja's forehead touched the top of the shit and he let out a sob.

"Where is Vetas? I won't ask again!"

"I don't know! He didn't tell me anything. Just paid me to keep the kids here."

"How were you paid?" Adamat heard Roja retch. The boxer's body shuddered.

"Krana notes."

"You're one of the Proprietor's boxers," Adamat said. "Does he know about any of this?"

"Vetas said we were recommended. No one hires us for the job unless the Proprietor gives the go-ahead."

Adamat gritted his teeth. The Proprietor. The head of the Adran criminal world, and a member of Tamas's council. He was one of the most powerful men in Adro. If he knew about Lord Vetas, it could mean he'd been a traitor all along.

"What else do you know?"

"I barely spoke twenty words with the guy," Roja said. His words were coming out in broken gasps as he sputtered through his tears. "Don't know anything else!"

Adamat struck Roja on the back of the head. He sagged, but he was not unconscious. Adamat lifted him by his belt and shoved his face down into the muck. He lifted him again and pushed. Roja flailed, his legs kicking hard as he tried to breathe through the piss and shit. Adamat grabbed the boxer by the ankles and pushed down, jamming Roja in the hole.

Adamat turned and walked out of the outhouse. He couldn't think through his fury. He was going to destroy Vetas for putting his wife and children through this.

Oldrich and his men stood by, watching Roja drown in filth. One of them looked ill in the dim lantern light. Another was nodding in approval. The night was quiet now, and Adamat could hear the steady chirp of crickets in the forest.

"Aren't you going to ask him more questions?" Oldrich said.

"He said himself, he doesn't know anything else." Adamat felt his stomach turn and he looked back at Roja's kicking legs. The mental image of Roja forcing himself on Faye almost stopped Adamat, and then he said to Oldrich, "Pull him out before he dies. Then ship him to the deepest coal mine you can find on the Mountainwatch."

Adamat swore to do worse to Vetas when he caught him.

CHAPTER

2

Field Marshal Tamas stood above Budwiel's southern gate and surveyed the Kez army. This wall marked the southernmost point of Adro. If he tossed a stone in front of him, it would land on Kez soil, perhaps rolling down the slope of the Great Northern Road until it reached the Kez pickets on the edge of their army.

The Gates of Wasal, a pair of five-hundred-foot-tall cliffs, rose to either side of him, divided by thousands of years of flowing water coming out of the Adsea, cutting through Surkov's Alley, and feeding the grain fields of the Amber Expanse in northern Kez.

The Kez army had left the smoldering ruins of South Pike Mountain only three weeks ago. Official reports estimated the number of men in the army that had besieged Shouldercrown as two hundred thousand soldiers, accompanied by camp followers that swelled that number to almost three-quarters of a million.

His scouts told him that the total number was over a million now.

A small part of Tamas cowered at such a number. The world had not seen an army of that size since the wars of the Bleakening over fourteen hundred years ago. And here it was at his doorstep, trying to take his country from him.

Tamas could recognize a new soldier on the walls by how loud they gasped upon seeing the Kez army. He could smell the fear of his own men. The anticipation. The dread. This was not Shouldercrown, a fortress easily held by a few companies of soldiers. This was Budwiel, a trading city of some hundred thousand people. The walls were in disrepair, the gates too numerous and too wide.

Tamas did not let that fear show on his own face. He didn't dare. He buried his tactical concerns; the terror he felt that his only son lay in Adopest deep in a coma; the pain that still ached in his leg despite the healing powers of a god. Nothing showed on his countenance but contempt for the audacity of the Kez commanders.

Steady footfalls sounded on the stone stairs behind him, and Tamas was joined by General Hilanska, the commander of Budwiel's artillery and the Second Brigade.

Hilanska was an extremely portly man of about forty years old, a widower of ten years, and a veteran of the Gurlish Campaigns. He was missing his left arm at the shoulder, taken clean off by a cannonball thirty years ago when Hilanska was not yet a captain. He had never let his arm nor his weight affect his performance on a battlefield, and for that alone he had Tamas's respect. Never mind that his gun crews could knock the head off a charging cavalryman at eight hundred yards.

Among Tamas's General Staff, most of whom had been chosen for their skill and not their personalities, Hilanska was the closest thing Tamas had to a friend.

"Been watching them gather there for weeks and it still doesn't cease to impress me," Hilanska said.

"Their numbers?" Tamas asked.

Hilanska leaned over the edge of the wall and spit. "Their discipline." He removed his looking glass from his belt and slid it open with a well-practiced jerk of his one hand, then held it up to his eye. "All those damned paper-white tents lined up as far as the eye can see. Looks like a model."

"Lining up a half-million tents doesn't make an army disciplined," Tamas said. "I've worked with Kez commanders before. In Gurla. They keep their men in line with fear. It makes for a clean and pretty camp, but when armies clash, there's no steel in their spine. They break by the third volley." *Not like my men*, he thought. *Not like the Adran brigades.*

"Hope you're right," Hilanska said.

Tamas watched the Kez sentries make their rounds a half mile away, well in range of Hilanska's guns, but not worth the ammunition. The main army camped almost two whole miles back; their officers feared Tamas's powder mages more than they did Hilanska's guns.

Tamas gripped the lip of the stone wall and opened his third eye. A wave of dizziness passed over him before he could see clearly into the Else. The world took on a pastel glow. In the distance there were lights, glimmering like the fires of an enemy patrol at night—the glow of Kez Privileged and Wardens. He closed his third eye and rubbed at his temple.

"You're still thinking about it, aren't you?" Hilanska asked.

"What?"

"Invading."

"Invade?" Tamas scoffed. "I'd have to be mad to launch an attack against an army ten times our size."

"You've got that look to you, Tamas," Hilanska said. "Like a dog pulling at its chain. I've known you too long. You've made no secret that you intend to invade Kez given the opportunity."

Tamas eyed those pickets. The Kez army was set so far back it would be almost impossible to catch them unawares. The terrain gave no good cover for a night attack.

"If I could get the Seventh and Ninth in there with the element of surprise, I could carve through the heart of their army and be back in Budwiel before they knew what hit them," Tamas said quietly. His heart quickened at the thought. The Kez were not to be underestimated. They had the numbers. They still had a few Privileged, even after the Battle of Shouldercrown.

But Tamas knew what his best brigades were capable of. He knew Kez strategies, and he knew their weaknesses. Kez soldiers were levies from their immense peasant population. Their officers were nobles who'd bought their commissions. Not like his men: patriots, men of steel and iron.

"A few of my boys did some exploring," Hilanska said.

"They did?" Tamas quelled the annoyance of having his thoughts interrupted.

"You know about Budwiel's catacombs?"

Tamas grunted in acknowledgment. The catacombs stretched under the West Pillar, one of the two mountains that made up the Gates of Wasal. They were a mixture of natural and man-made caverns used to house Budwiel's dead.

"They're off limits to soldiers," Tamas said, unable to keep the reproach from his voice.

"I'll deal with my boys, but you might want to hear what they have to say before we have them flogged."

"Unless they discovered a Kez spy ring, I doubt it's relevant."

"Better," Hilanska said. "They found a way for you to get your men into Kez."

Tamas felt his heart jump at the possibility. "Take me to them."

CHAPTER

3

Taniel stared at the ceiling only a foot above him, counting each time he swung, side to side, in the hemp-rope hammock, listening to the Gurlish pipes that filled the room with a soft, whistling music.

He hated that music. It seemed to echo in his ears, all at once too soft to hear well but loud enough to make him grind his molars together. He lost count of the hammock swings somewhere around ten and exhaled. Warm smoke curled out from between his lips and against the crumbling mortar in the ceiling. He watched the smoke escape the roof of his niche and swirl into the middle of the mala den.

There were a dozen such niches in the room. Two were occupied. In the two weeks he'd been there, Taniel had yet to see the occupants get up to piss or eat or do anything other than suck on the long-stemmed mala pipes and flag the den's owner over for a refill.

He leaned over, his hand reaching for a refill for his own mala pipe. The table next to his hammock held a plate with a few scraps of dark mala, an empty purse, and a pistol. He couldn't remember where the pistol came from.

Taniel gathered the bits of mala together into one small, sticky ball and pushed it into the end of his pipe. It lit instantly, and he took a long pull into his lungs.

"Want more?"

The den's owner sidled up to Taniel's hammock. He was Gurlish, his skin brown but not as dark as a Deliv's, with a lighter tone under his eyes and on his palms. He was tall, like most Gurlish, and skinny, his back bent from years of leaning into the niches of his mala den to clean them out or light an addict's pipe. His name was Kin.

Taniel reached for his purse, wiggled his fingers around inside before remembering that it was empty. "No money," he said, his own voice ragged in his ears.

How long had he been here? Two weeks, Taniel decided after putting his mind to the question. More importantly, how did he get here?

Not *here*, the mala den, but here in Adopest. Taniel remembered the fight on top of Kresimir's palace as Ka-poel destroyed the Kez Cabal, and he remembered pulling the trigger of his rifle and watching a bullet take the god Kresimir in the eye.

It was all darkness after that until he woke up, covered in sweat, Ka-poel straddling him with fresh blood on her hands. He remembered bodies in the hallway of the hotel—his father's soldiers with an unfamiliar insignia on their jackets. He'd left the hotel and stumbled here, where he'd hoped to forget.

Of course, if he still remembered all that, then the mala wasn't doing its job.

"Army jacket," Kin said, fingering his lapel. "Your buttons."

Taniel looked down at the jacket he wore. It was Adran-army

dark blue, with silver trim and buttons. He'd taken it from the hotel. It wasn't his—too big. There was a powder mage pin—a silver powder keg—pinned to the lapel. Maybe it *was* his. Had he lost weight?

The jacket had been clean two days ago. He remembered that much. Now it was stained with drool, bits of food, and small burns from mala embers. When the pit had he eaten?

Taniel pulled his belt knife and took one of the buttons in his fingers. He paused. Kin's daughter walked through the room. She wore a faded white dress, clean despite the squalor of the den. She must have been a few years older than Taniel, but no children clung to her skirts.

"Do you like my daughter?" Kin asked. "She will dance for you. Two buttons!" He held up two fingers for emphasis. "Much prettier than the Fatrastan witch."

Kin's wife, sitting in the corner and playing the Gurlish pipes, stopped the music long enough to say something to Kin. They exchanged a few words in Gurlish, then Kin turned back to Taniel. "Two buttons!" he reiterated.

Taniel cut a button loose and put it in Kin's hand. Dance, eh? Taniel wondered if Kin had a strong enough grasp of Adran for euphemism, or if dance was indeed all she'd do.

"Maybe later," Taniel said, settling back in the hammock with a fresh ball of mala the size of a child's fist. "Ka-poel isn't a witch. She's…" He paused, trying to figure out a way to describe her to a Gurlish. His thoughts moved slowly, sluggish from the mala. "All right," he conceded. "She's a witch."

Taniel topped off his mala pipe. Kin's daughter was watching him. He returned her open stare with a half-lidded gaze. She was pretty, by some standards. Too tall by far for Taniel, and much too gaunt—most Gurlish were. She stayed there, laundry balanced on her hip, until her father shooed her out.

How long had it been since he'd had a woman?

A woman? He laughed, smoke curling out his nose. The laugh ended in a cough and received no more than a curious glance from Kin. No, not *a* woman. *The* woman. Vlora. How long had it been? Two and a half years now? Three?

He sat back up and fished around in his pocket for a powder charge, wondering where Vlora was now. Probably still with Tamas and the rest of the powder cabal.

Tamas would want Taniel back on the front line.

To the pit with that. Let Tamas come to Adopest looking for Taniel. The last place he'd look was a mala den.

There wasn't a powder charge in Taniel's pocket. Ka-poel had cleaned him out. He'd not had a smidgen of powder since she brought him out of that goddamned coma. Not even his pistol was loaded. He could go out and get some. Find a barracks, show them his powder-mage pin.

The very idea of getting out of the hammock made his head spin.

Ka-poel came down the steps into the mala den just as Taniel was beginning to drift off. He kept his eyes mostly closed, the smoke curling from his lips. She stopped and examined him.

She was short, her features petite. Her skin was white, with ashen freckles and her red hair was no more than an inch long. He didn't like it so short, it made her look boyish. *No mistaking her for a boy*, Taniel thought as she shrugged out of her long black duster. Underneath she wore a white sleeveless shirt, scrounged from who-knew-where, and close-fitting black pants.

Ka-poel touched Taniel's shoulder. He ignored her. Let her think him asleep, or too deep in a mala haze to notice her. All the better.

She reached out and squeezed his nose shut with one hand, pushing his mouth closed with the other.

He jerked up, taking a breath when she let go. "What the pit, Pole? Trying to kill me?"

She smiled, and it wasn't the first time under the mala haze that he'd stared into those glass-green eyes with less than proper thoughts. He shook them away. She was his ward. He was her protector. Or was it the other way around? She was the one who'd done the protecting up on South Pike.

Taniel settled back into the hammock. "What do you want?"

She held up a thick pad of paper, bound in leather. A sketchbook. To replace the one lost on South Pike Mountain. He felt a pang at that. Sketches from eight years of his life. People he'd known, many of them long dead. Some friends, some enemies. Losing that sketchbook hurt almost as much as losing his genuine Hrusch rifle.

Almost as much as . . .

He pushed the stem of his mala pipe between his teeth and sucked in hard. He shivered as the smoke burned his throat and lungs and seeped into his body, deadening the memories.

When he reached out for the sketchbook, he saw that his hand was shaking. He snatched it back quickly.

Ka-poel's eyes narrowed. She set the sketchbook on his stomach, followed by a pack of charcoal pencils. Finer sketching tools than he'd ever had in Fatrasta. She pointed at them, and mimed him sketching.

Taniel made his right hand into a fist. He didn't want her to see him shaking. "I . . . not now, Pole."

She pointed again, more insistently.

Taniel took another deep breath of mala and closed his eyes. He felt tears roll down his cheeks.

He felt her take the book and pencils off his chest. Heard the table move. He expected a reproach. A punch. Something. When he opened his eyes again, he saw her bare feet disappearing up the stairs of the mala den and she was gone. He took another deep breath of mala and wiped the tears off his face.

The room began to fade into the mala haze along with his memories; all the people he'd killed, all the friends he'd seen die. The god he'd seen with his own eyes, and then put down with an ensorcelled bullet. He didn't want to remember any of that.

Just another few days in the mala den, then he'd be fine. Back to his old self. He'd report to Tamas and get back to what he was good at: killing Kez.

Tamas found himself a quarter mile under a thousand tons of rock just a few hours after leaving Budwiel's walls. His torch flickered in the darkness, casting light and shadows across the row after row of recessed graves carved into the walls of the caverns. Skulls hung from the ceilings by the hundred in a grisly tribute to the dead, and he wondered if this was what the pathway to the afterlife looked like.

More fire, he imagined.

He fought off his initial claustrophobia by reminding himself that these catacombs had been used for a thousand years. They weren't likely to collapse anytime soon.

The size of the passageway surprised him. At times the rooms were wide enough to hold hundreds of men. At their narrowest, even a carriage could pass through them without scraping the sides.

The two artillery men Hilanska had spoken of walked on ahead. They carried their own torches and they talked excitedly, their voices echoing as they passed through the varied chambers. Beside Tamas, his bodyguard Olem kept pace with a hand on his pistol and a suspicious eye on the two soldiers ahead of him. Bringing up the rear were two of Tamas's best powder mages: Vlora and Andriya.

"These caverns," Olem said, running his fingers along the stone walls, "were widened with tools. But look at the ceiling." He pointed upward. "No tool marks."

"They were carved out by water," Tamas said. "Probably thousands of years ago." He let his eyes run over the ceiling and then down to the floor. Their path sloped gently downward, punctuated from time to time by steps cut into the floor and worn by the passing of thousands of pilgrims, families, and priests every year. Despite these signs of use, these catacombs were empty of anything living—the priests had suspended burials during the siege, worried that artillery fire might collapse some of the caves.

Tamas used to play in caverns like these when his father, an apothecary, searched the mountains every summer for rare flowers, mushrooms, and fungus. Some cave systems went incredibly deep into the heart of the mountain. Others ended abruptly, just when things seemed to be getting interesting.

The passageway opened up into a wide cavern. The torchlight no longer danced on the ceiling and far walls, but disappeared into the darkness above. They stood on the edge of a pool of still water blacker than a moonless night. Their voices echoed in the great hollow space.

Tamas came to a stop beside the waiting artillery men. He cracked a powder charge in between his fingers and sprinkled it on his tongue. The trance swept through him, bringing dizziness and clarity all at once. The ache of his leg disappeared and the tendrils of light caused by the torches were suddenly more than enough for him to examine the cavern in its entirety.

The walls were lined with stone sarcophagi, stacked almost haphazardly upon one another thirty, maybe forty feet into the air. A dripping sound echoed through the chamber: the source of the underground lake. Tamas could see no exit but the one through which they'd come.

"Sir?" one of the artillerymen said. His name was Ludik, and he held his torch over the pool, trying to gauge the depths.

"We're thousands of feet beneath the West Pillar," Tamas said. "And no closer to Kez. I don't like being led into strange places."

The cock of Olem's pistol stirred the silence of the cave. Behind Tamas, Vlora and Andriya stood with their rifles at the ready. Ludik exchanged a nervous glance with his comrade and swallowed hard.

"It looks like the cave system ends," Ludik said, pointing with his torch across the pond. "But it doesn't. It keeps going, and goes straight toward Kez."

"How do you know?" Tamas asked.

Ludik hesitated, expecting reproach. "Because, sir, we followed it through."

"Show me."

They passed behind a pair of sarcophagi on the other side of the pond and ducked beneath a ledge that proved deeper than it looked. A moment later, and Tamas was standing on the other side. The cavern opened up again and led down into the dark.

Tamas turned to the bodyguard at his shoulder. "Try not to shoot anyone unless I say so."

Olem stroked his neatly trimmed beard, eyeing the artillerymen. "Of course, sir." His hand didn't leave the butt of his pistol. Olem wasn't the trusting sort these days.

An hour later, Tamas left the cavern and climbed up through brush and scree into daylight. The sun had passed over the mountains to the east and the valley was in shadow.

"All clear, sir," Olem said, helping him up to steady footing.

Tamas checked his pistol, then absently thumbed the contents of another powder charge onto his tongue. They stood in a steep valley on the southern slope of the Adran Mountains. By his guess, they were less than two miles from Budwiel. If that was correct, they now flanked the Kez army perfectly.

"An old riverbed, sir," Vlora said, picking her way among the small boulders. "It points to the west, then cuts south. The base of the valley is obscured by a hillock. We're not more than a half mile from the Kez right now, but there's no sign they've even bothered scouting this valley."

"Sir!" a voice called from within the cave.

Tamas whirled. Vlora, Olem, and Andriya all raised their rifles, pointing into the darkness.

An Adran soldier emerged. His shoulder sported a chevron with a powder horn beneath it. The man was a lance corporal, one of Olem's new company of elite soldiers, the Riflejacks.

"Quiet, fool," Olem hissed. "You want all of Kez to hear?"

The messenger wiped the sweat from his brow, blinking up at the brightness of day. "Sorry, sir," he said to Tamas. "I got lost in the mountain. General Hilanska sent me after you not more than a moment after you left."

"What is it, man?" Tamas demanded. Gasping messengers were never a good sign. They never hurried unless it was of utmost importance.

"The Kez, sir," the messenger said. "Our spies report they will attack en masse the day after tomorrow. General Hilanska requests you back at the wall immediately."

Tamas ran his eyes across the steep valley in which they stood. "How many men do you think we could bring through here in two days?"

"Thousands," Vlora said.

"Ten thousand," Olem added.

"A hammer of two brigades," Tamas said. "And Budwiel will be the anvil."

Vlora seemed doubtful. "That's a small hammer, sir, compared with that monstrous force out there."

"Then we'll have to strike hard and fast." Tamas examined the valley one more time. "Let's head back. Have the engineers start widening the tunnel. Get some men up here to shore up this scree so our passage won't cause a ruckus. When the Kez attack, we'll smash them against the gates of Budwiel."

CHAPTER

There were few things in the world more tedious, Nila reflected as she sat on the kitchen floor and watched flames curl around the base of the immense iron pot hanging over the fire, than waiting for water to boil.

Most manor houses would be silent at this hour. She'd always relished the quiet—the still night air that insulated her from the chaos of a servant's life when the master and mistress were at home and the house bustled with movement. There was a night not more than a few months past, though it felt like years, that Nila had known no life but the one in which she boiled water and did the laundry every week for Duke Eldaminse's family and the serving staff.

Lord Eldaminse was dead now, his servants scattered and his home burned. Everything Nila had ever known was gone.

Here in Lord Vetas's city manor on a side street in the middle of Adopest, the household never slept.

Somewhere in the enormous house a man was shouting. Nila couldn't make out the words, but they were spoken in anger. Probably Dourford, the Privileged. He was one of Lord Vetas's lieutenants, and he had a temper like Nila had never seen. He had a habit of beating the cooks. Everyone in the house feared him, even the hulking bodyguards who accompanied Lord Vetas on his errands.

Everyone feared Dourford except, of course, for Vetas.

As far as Nila could tell, Lord Vetas feared nothing.

"Jakob," Nila said, speaking to the six-year-old boy sitting beside her on the kitchen floor, "hand me the lye."

Jakob got to his feet and paused, frowning at her. "Where?" he asked.

"Under the washbasin," Nila said. "The glass jar."

Jakob rummaged around beneath the washbasin before finding the jar. He grabbed it by the lid and pulled.

"Careful!" Nila said. She was on her feet and beside him in a moment, and caught him by the shoulders as the jar came loose and he stumbled backward. She put a hand beneath the jar. "Got you," she said, and took the jar. It wasn't very heavy, but Jakob had never been the strongest child.

She unscrewed the lid and doled out a measure for the laundry with a spoon.

"No," she said when Jakob reached for the open jar. "You don't want to touch that. It's very poisonous. It'll eat right through your pink fingers." She snatched him by the hand and playfully bit at his fingers. "Like an angry dog!"

Jakob giggled and retreated across the room. Nila put the lye away on a high shelf. They shouldn't keep materials like this within reach of children. Even if Jakob *was* the only child in the house.

Nila wondered what life would be like if she was still in the Eldaminse manor. There would have been a party for Jakob's sixth birthday two weeks ago. The house staff would have been given a stipend and an extra afternoon off. Duke Eldaminse would have likely made another pass at Nila—or two, or three—and Lady Eldaminse would have considered putting her out on the street.

Nila missed the quiet of the nights doing laundry for the Eldaminse house. She didn't miss backbiting and jealousy among the serving staff, or Lord Eldaminse's groping hands. But she'd exchanged it for something worse.

Lord Vetas's manor.

There was a scream from somewhere in the basement, where Lord Vetas kept his . . . room.

"Pit," Nila said softly to herself, eyes back on the flame of the kitchen fire.

"A lady doesn't curse."

Nila felt her spine stiffen. The voice was quiet, calm. Deceptively placid, like the surface of the ocean undisturbed by the sharks circling beneath.

"Lord Vetas." She turned and curtsied to the man standing in the kitchen door.

Vetas was a Rosvelean with dusty-yellow skin. His back was straight, one hand tucked into his vest pocket and the other holding his evening glass of red wine with casual familiarity. Seen on the street, he might be mistaken for a well-dressed clerk or merchant with his white shirt, dark-blue vest, and black pants that she'd neatly pressed herself.

Nila knew that to assume anything about Vetas was a deadly mistake. He was a killer. She'd felt his hands on her throat. She'd looked into his eyes—eyes that seemed to see everything at once—and seen the dispassion with which he regarded living things.

"I'm not a lady, my lord," Nila said.

Vetas's eyes examined her clinically. Nila felt stripped beneath that gaze. She felt like a piece of meat on the butcher's block. It frightened her.

And it made her angry. She wondered for a moment if Lord Vetas would look that calm and collected in his casket.

"Do you know why you're here?" Vetas said.

"To watch over Jakob." She cast a glance at the boy. Jakob watched Vetas curiously.

"That's right." A smile suddenly split Vetas's face, warmth flooding his expression without touching his eyes. "Come here, boy," Vetas said, kneeling. "It's all right, Jakob. Don't be afraid."

Jakob's training as a noble's son left him no choice but to obey. He started toward Vetas, looking back to Nila for direction.

Nila felt her chest go cold. She wanted to throw herself between them, to take a hot iron from the fire and beat Vetas back. The false smile on his face was far more frightening to her than his customary stoic gaze.

"Go ahead," she heard herself say in a small voice.

"I brought you a candy." Vetas handed Jakob a treat wrapped in colored paper.

"Jakob, don't..." Nila started.

Vetas fixed her with his eyes. There was no threat behind them, no emotion. Just a cold glance.

"You can have it," Nila said, "but you should save it for tomorrow, after breakfast."

Vetas gave Jakob the candy and tousled his hair.

Don't touch him, Nila screamed inside. She forced herself to smile at Vetas.

"Why is Jakob here, my lord?" Nila said, pushing the question through her fear.

Vetas got to his feet. "That's no concern of yours. Do you know how to behave like a lady, Nila?" he asked.

"I...I suppose. I'm just a laundress."

"I think you're more than that," Vetas said. "Everyone has the ability to rise above their station. You survived the royalist barricades, then infiltrated Field Marshal Tamas's headquarters with the aim of rescuing young Jakob here. And you're pretty. No one ever looks past beauty, if it's dressed right."

Nila wondered how Vetas could possibly have known about the royalist barricades. She'd told him about Tamas's headquarters, but . . . what exactly did he mean about beauty?

"I may have further use for you than just"—he made a gesture toward Jakob and the laundry—"this."

Jakob was too busy trying to nibble at his candy as discreetly as possible to notice the disdain in Vetas's voice. Nila wasn't. And she feared what he meant by "further use."

"My lord." She curtsied again, and tried not to let her hatred show on her face. She might be able to kill him in the bath. Like she'd read in those mystery novels she'd borrowed from the butler's son at the Eldaminse house.

"In the meantime," Vetas said. He stepped into the hall outside the kitchen, keeping the door open with one foot. "Bring her in here," he called.

Someone cursed. A woman screamed in anger—an angry-wildcat yell. There was a struggle in the hall and two of Vetas's bodyguards dragged a woman into the kitchen. She was in her forties perhaps, her body sagging in all the wrong places from having had too many children, her skin wrinkled from work but unweathered by the sun. Her curly black hair was tucked back behind her head in a bun and the bags beneath her eyes spoke of little sleep.

The woman stopped when she caught sight of Nila and Jakob.

"Where is my son?" she spat at Vetas.

"In the basement," Vetas said, "and he won't be harmed as long as you cooperate."

"Liar!"

A patronizing smile touched Vetas's lips. "Nila, Jakob. This is Faye. She is unwell and must be watched at all times, lest she hurt herself. She's going to share your room, Jakob. Can you help watch her, my boy?"

Jakob nodded solemnly.

"Good lad."

"I'll kill you," Faye said to Vetas.

Vetas stepped to Faye and whispered something in her ear. She stiffened, the color draining from her face.

"Now," Vetas said, "Faye is going to take over your responsibilities, Nila. She'll do the laundry, and help with Jakob."

Nila exchanged a glance with the woman. She felt the knot of fear in her belly reflected on Faye's face.

"And me?" Nila knew what Vetas would do with someone who didn't have a use. She still remembered Jakob's dead nurse—the one who'd refused to go along with Vetas's schemes.

Vetas suddenly crossed the room. He took Nila by the chin, turning her face one way and then another. He forced his thumb into her mouth and she had to keep herself from biting down as he examined her teeth. He stepped away suddenly, and wiped his hands on a kitchen towel as if he'd just handled an animal.

"Your hands show very little wear from the laundering. Remarkably little, to be honest. I'll give you some lotion in the morning and you'll apply it every hour. We'll have those hands looking soft, like a noblewoman's, in no time." He patted her on the cheek.

Nila resisted the urge to spit in his eye.

Vetas leaned forward and spoke quietly so that Jakob could not hear. "This woman," Vetas said, pointing to Faye, "is your responsibility, Nila. If she displeases me, you'll suffer for it. Jakob will suffer for it. And believe me, I know how to make people suffer."

Vetas stepped away, throwing a smile toward Jakob. More loudly he said, "I think you need some new clothes, Jakob. Would you like that?"

"Very much, sir," Jakob said.

"We'll do that tomorrow. Some toys, too."

Vetas glanced at Nila, his eyes holding a silent warning, and he left the room with his bodyguards.

Faye adjusted her dress and took a deep breath. Her eyes traveled around the room. A mix of emotions ranged across her face: anger, panic, and fear. For a moment Nila thought she might snatch up a frying pan and attack her.

Nila wondered who she was. Why was she here? Obviously another prisoner. Another player in Vetas's schemes. Could Nila trust her?

"I'm Nila," she said. "And this is Jakob."

Faye's eyes settled on Nila and she nodded with a frown. "I'm Faye. And I'm going to kill that bastard."

CHAPTER

5

Adamat slipped through the side door of one of the dilapidated buildings in Adopest's dock district. He moved down hallways, brushing past secretaries and bookkeepers, always looking straight ahead. In his experience, no one questioned a man who knew where he was going.

Adamat knew that Lord Vetas was looking for him.

It wasn't hard to surmise. Vetas still had Faye. He still had leverage, and no doubt he wanted Adamat dead or under his thumb.

So Adamat stayed low. Field Marshal Tamas's soldiers were protecting his family—part of the bargain Adamat had struck with the field marshal in order to keep his neck from the guillotine. Adamat had to work from the shadows now, finding Lord Vetas and discovering his plans, and freeing Faye before any more harm could come to her. If she was even still alive.

He couldn't do it alone.

The headquarters for the Noble Warriors of Labor was a squat, ugly brick building not far from the Adopest docks. It didn't look like much, but it housed the offices of the biggest union in all the Nine. Every subdivision of the Warriors moved through this hub: bankers, steelworkers, miners, bakers, millers, and more.

But Adamat only needed to speak with one man, and he didn't want to be noticed on his way in. He went down a low-ceilinged hallway on the third floor and paused outside an office door. He could hear voices inside.

"I don't care what you think of the idea," came the voice of Ricard Tumblar, head of the entire union. "I'm going to find him and persuade him. He's the best man for the job."

"Man?" a woman's voice returned. "You don't think a *woman* can do it?"

"Don't start with me, Cheris," Ricard said. "It was a turn of phrase. And don't make this about men or women. You don't like it because he's a soldier."

"And you bloody well know why."

Ricard's retort was lost as Adamat heard the creak of the floorboards behind him. He turned to find a woman standing behind him.

She looked to be in her midthirties, with straight blond hair tied back in a ponytail behind her head. She wore a dress uniform with loose pants and a white frilled shirt of the type that might be worn by a footman. Her hands were clasped behind her back.

A secretary. The last thing Adamat needed.

"Can I help you, sir?" she said. Her tone was brusque, and her eyes never left Adamat's face.

"Oh, my," Adamat said. "This must look terrible. I didn't mean to eavesdrop, I just needed to speak with Ricard."

She didn't sound at all like she believed him. "The secretary should have kept you in the waiting room."

"I came in the side door," Adamat admitted. So she wasn't the secretary?

The woman said, "Come with me to the lobby and we'll make you an appointment. Mr. Tumblar is terribly busy."

Adamat gave a half bow at the waist. "I'd rather not make an appointment. I just need to speak with Ricard. It's a terribly urgent matter."

"Please, sir."

"I just need to speak with Ricard."

Her voice dropped slightly—instantly more threatening. "If you do not come with me, I will have you taken to the police for trespassing."

"Now look here!" Adamat raised his voice. The last thing he wanted to do was cause a commotion, but he desperately needed Ricard's attention.

"Fell!" Ricard's voice called from inside the office. "Fell! Damn it, Fell, what is that ruckus!"

Fell narrowed her eyes at Adamat. "What is your name?" she asked sternly.

"Inspector Adamat."

Fell's demeanor changed instantly. Gone was the severe gaze that brooked no argument. She let out a soft sigh. "Why didn't you say so to begin with? Ricard has us looking all over the city for you." She stepped past Adamat and opened the door. "It's Inspector Adamat here to see you, sir."

"Well, don't leave him in the hallway. Send him in!"

The room was cluttered but clean—for once. Bookshelves ran the length of each wall, and an ironwood desk framed the center of the room. Ricard was sitting behind his desk, facing a woman who looked to be about fifty. Adamat could immediately tell she was wealthy. Her rings were gold, set with precious gems, and her dress made from the finest cut of muslin. She fanned her face with a fine lace handkerchief and pointedly looked away from Adamat.

"You'll have to excuse me, Cheris," Ricard said. "This is very important."

The woman pushed past Adamat and left the room. Adamat

heard the door slam behind him and they were alone. Adamat thought briefly to ask what that had been about—then decided against it. Ricard was just as likely to spend an hour explaining as he was to tell Adamat it was private business. Adamat removed his hat and coat and returned Ricard's embrace.

Ricard sat back down behind his desk and gestured to the vacant chair. They spoke at the exact same moment:

"Adamat, I need your help."

"Ricard, I need your help."

They both fell silent, and then Ricard laughed and ran a hand across the bald spot on the front of his scalp. "You haven't needed my help for years," he said. He took a deep breath. "First, I want to tell you how sorry I am about the Barbers."

The Black Street Barbers. The street gang that supposedly reported to Ricard, but that had come after Adamat in his own home. Had that really been only a month ago? It seemed like years.

"Tamas wiped them out," Adamat said. "The survivors are rotting in Sablethorn."

"With my blessing."

Adamat nodded. He didn't trust himself to say more about the topic. He didn't precisely blame Ricard for the incident, but he now had far less faith in Ricard's people.

"Is Faye still out of the city?" Ricard said.

Something must have showed in Adamat's eyes. Ricard was a man who'd made his living reading facial tics and knowing what to say at the right moment. He stood up and opened the door a crack. "Fell," he said. "I don't want to be bothered. No people. No sound."

He closed the door and slid the latch, returning to his desk.

"Tell me everything," Ricard said.

Adamat paused. He'd fought with himself for days about whether to come to Ricard at all, and what exactly to say. It wasn't as if he didn't trust Ricard—it was that he didn't trust Ricard's people. Lord

Vetas had spies everywhere. But if he couldn't trust Ricard himself, then there was no one left in his life to turn to for help.

"Faye and the children were taken by a man named Lord Vetas," Adamat said. "They were held against their will to guarantee my cooperation. I gave Vetas information about my conversations with Tamas and my investigation."

Ricard tensed. Whatever he'd expected, this was not it. "You crossed Tamas?" *And you're still alive?* was the unspoken question.

"I've told Tamas all of it," Adamat said. "He has forgiven me—for now—and sent me on a hunt for Lord Vetas. I managed to rescue some of the children, but Vetas still has Faye and Josep."

"Can't you use Tamas's soldiers to go after Vetas?"

"I'd have to find him first. Once I do, I wish it were that simple. The moment Vetas finds out where I am, he will no doubt threaten me with Faye's life. I need to find him silently, track him, and get her out of his hands before I bring down Tamas's wrath upon him."

Ricard nodded slowly. "So you don't know where he is?"

"He's like a ghost. I looked into him when he first started blackmailing me. He doesn't even exist."

"If *you* can't find him, I doubt any of my people can."

"I don't need you to find him. I need information." Adamat reached into his pocket and removed the card Vetas had left him months ago. It had an address on it. "This is the only lead I have. It's an old warehouse not all that far from here. I need to know everything about it. Who owns it? Who owns the properties around it? When was it last sold? Everything. Your people have access to records I can't easily get my hands on."

Ricard nodded. "Of course. Anything." He reached to take the card.

Adamat stopped him, clutching Ricard's hand. "This is deadly serious. The lives of my wife and my son depend on it. If you don't think you can trust your people, just tell me now and I'll find him myself." *Remember what happened with the Barbers*, Adamat said silently.

Ricard seemed to get the message. "I have some people," Ricard said. "Don't worry. This will be safe."

"One more thing," Adamat said. "There are two people involved in this somehow that you might blanch at crossing."

Ricard smiled. "If it's not Tamas, I can't imagine who."

"Lord Claremonte and the Proprietor."

Ricard's smile disappeared. "Lord Claremonte doesn't surprise me," he said. "The Brudania-Gurla Trading Company has been trying to move in on the union since our inception. He's tricky, but he doesn't scare me."

"Don't be so quick to dismiss him. Lord Vetas works for him." And Vetas was holding Adamat's wife and son hostage. Claremonte, as far as Adamat was concerned, might as well have been holding Faye and Josep personally.

Ricard made a dismissive gesture. "You say that the Proprietor might be involved? I don't trust him, of course, but I thought you cleared him of treachery yourself."

"I never cleared him," Adamat said. "I just found out that Charlemund was the one trying to kill Tamas. One of the Proprietor's boxers was holding my family hostage. You know how he is about his boxers finding work elsewhere—no one works for someone else without the Proprietor's permission." Which meant that the Proprietor may be in league with Lord Claremonte.

"Tread carefully on this, my friend," Ricard warned. "Vetas may be trying to use you, but the Proprietor will cut and bury your entire family without so much as a thought." He glanced at the card Adamat had given him and put it in his vest pocket. "I'll look into this, don't worry. But I need a favor from you."

"Go on."

"Do you know Taniel Two-Shot?"

"I know *of* him," Adamat said. "Everyone in the Nine does. The newspapers were saying he was in a coma after a battle of sorcery on top of South Pike Mountain."

"He's not in a coma anymore," Ricard said. "He woke up a week ago, and he's disappeared."

Adamat's first thoughts went to Lord Vetas. The man was working actively against Tamas. He would leap at the chance to capture the field marshal's son. "Any sign of violence?"

Ricard shook his head. "Well, yes. But it's not like that. He left his guard duty of his own volition. Tamas had his own men guarding him, but my people were keeping an eye on him as well. That he slipped both our nets is rather embarrassing. I need him found quietly."

"Do you want him returned?" Adamat said. "I'm not about to make a powder mage do something he doesn't want to do."

"No, just find out where he is and let me know."

Adamat stood up. "I'll see what I can do."

"And I'll look into this Lord Vetas." Ricard held up a hand to forestall Adamat's protests. "Discreetly. I promise."

Tamas entered Budwiel's biggest mess hall and was nearly knocked over by the swirl of enticing smells wafting from inside.

He swept past the tables where hundreds of his men were having their evening repast and headed toward the kitchens, trying to ignore his hunger pangs.

The man he was looking for was hard to miss: big, fat, taller than most, with waist-length black hair tied behind his head and his olive skin showing just a touch of Rosvelean ancestry. He stood in one corner of the kitchens, on his toes to be able to see into the highest row of ovens.

Mihali was, officially, Tamas's chef. He and his cadre of assistants provided food of the highest caliber for Tamas's entire army, and even for the city of Budwiel. The people loved Mihali; the men worshipped him.

Well, perhaps they *should* worship him.

He was Adom reborn, patron saint of Adro, and brother to the god Kresimir. Which made him a god in his own right.

Mihali turned to Tamas and waved across the myriad of assistants, flour going up in a cloud around him.

"Field Marshal," the chef called. "Come over here."

Tamas stifled the annoyance at being summoned like a common soldier and made his way through the tables of bread.

"Mihali—"

The god-chef cut him off. "Field Marshal, I'm so glad you're here. I have a matter of great importance to discuss with you."

Great importance? Tamas had never seen Mihali so distressed. He leaned forward. What could possibly worry a god? "What is it?"

"I can't decide what to make for lunch tomorrow."

"You git!" Tamas exclaimed, taking a step back. His heart thundered in his ears, as if he'd expected Mihali to announce that the world would end on the morrow.

Mihali didn't seem to notice the insult. "I haven't not known what to cook for decades. I normally have it all planned out but... I'm sorry, are you mad about something?"

"I'm trying to fight a war here, Mihali! The Kez are knocking at Budwiel's front door."

"And hunger is knocking at mine!"

Mihali seemed so out of sorts that Tamas forced himself to calm down. He put a hand on Mihali's arm. "The men will love whatever you make."

"I'd planned poached eggs with asparagus tips, filet of salmon, lamb chops glazed with honey, and a selection of fruit."

"That's three meals you just named there," Tamas said.

"Three meals? *Three meals?* That's four courses, barely enough for a proper lunch, and I did the same thing five days ago. What kind of a chef serves the same meal more than once a week?" Mihali tapped flour-covered fingers against his chin. "How could I have messed up? Maybe it's a leap year."

Tamas counted to ten silently to keep his temper contained—something he'd not done since Taniel was a boy. "Mihali, we're going into battle the day after tomorrow. Will you help me?"

The god appeared nervous. "I'm not going to kill anyone, if that's what you're asking," Mihali said.

"Can you do anything for us? We're outnumbered ten to one out there."

"What is your plan?"

"I'm going to take the Seventh and the Ninth through the catacombs and flank the Kez position. When they try to attack Budwiel, we'll smash them against the gates and route them."

"That sounds very military."

"Mihali, please focus!"

Mihali finally stopped casting about the mess tent as if searching for tomorrow's menu and gave Tamas a level stare. "Kresimir was a commander. Brude was a commander. *I* am a chef. But since you ask: The strategy sounds very high-risk with an equally high payoff. It suits you perfectly."

"Can you do anything to help?" Tamas asked gently.

Mihali seemed to think on this. "I can make sure that your men remain unnoticed until the moment you charge."

Tamas felt a wave of relief. "That would be perfect." He waited for a few moments. "Mihali, you appear agitated."

Mihali took Tamas by the elbow and pulled him into one corner of the tent. In a low voice, he said, "Kresimir is gone."

"That's right," Tamas said. "Taniel killed him."

"No, no. Kresimir is *gone*, but I didn't feel him die."

"But the whole of the Nine felt it. Privileged Borbador told me that every Knacked and Privileged in the world felt it when he died."

"That wasn't him dying," Mihali said, waving the lump of bread dough still in one hand. "That was his counterstroke against Taniel for shooting him in the head."

Tamas's mouth was suddenly dry. "You mean Kresimir is still alive?" Privileged Borbador had warned Tamas that a god couldn't be killed. Tamas had hoped that Borbador was wrong.

"I don't know," Mihali said, "and that's what worries me. I've always been able to sense him, even when half the cosmos separated us."

"Is he with the Kez army?" Tamas would have to cancel all his plans. Rethink every strategy. If Kresimir was with the Kez army, they might all be swept away.

"No, he's not," Mihali said. "I would know."

"But you said that..."

"I assure you," Mihali said. "I would know if he was that close. Besides, he wouldn't risk an open confrontation between us."

Tamas balled his fists. The uncertainties were the worst part of planning for a battle. It always put him on edge, knowing he couldn't plan for everything, and this was a god-sized uncertainty. He'd have to go forward with his plans and hope that Mihali's help in concealing the troops would be enough.

"Now," Mihali said, "if we're quite through with that, I need help with tomorrow's menu."

Tamas poked the god in the chest. "*You* are the chef," he said. "*I* am the commander, and I have a battle to plan."

He left the mess hall and was halfway to his command tent when he cursed himself for not snagging a bowl of Mihali's squash soup.

Less than twenty-four hours after Ricard sent him looking for Taniel Two-Shot, Adamat found himself sitting back in Ricard's office near the docks.

Ricard chewed on the end of a rough-cut pencil and stared across at Adamat. What little hair he had left stuck up from the top of his head like a wind-blown haystack, and Adamat wondered if he'd slept at all in the time between their meetings. At least he was wearing a different shirt and jacket. The room smelled of incense, burned paper, and foul meat. Adamat wondered if there was an uneaten sandwich beneath one of the stacks of records.

"You didn't go home last night, did you?" Adamat asked.

"How could you tell?"

"Besides the fact that you look like the pit? You didn't change your boots. I haven't seen you wear the same pair of boots two days in a row since I met you."

Ricard looked down at his feet. "You would notice that, wouldn't you?" He wiped fatigue from his eyes. "Don't tell me you've already found Two-Shot?"

Adamat held up a piece of paper. On it, he'd written the address of the mala den where he'd found the hero of the Adran army wallowing in his own self-pity. He held the note out to Ricard. When Ricard reached for it, he pulled it back at the last second, as if suddenly changing his mind.

"I read something interesting in the newspaper this morning," Adamat said. When Ricard didn't respond, he took the newspaper in question from under his arm and threw it on the desk. "'Ricard Tumblar to Run for First Minister of the Republic of Adro,'" he said, reading the headline out loud.

"Oh," Ricard said blandly. "That."

"Why didn't you tell me?"

"You seemed to have a lot on your plate."

"And you're vying to become leader of our new government. What the pit are you doing business down at the docks for?"

Ricard perked up. "I've built a new place. Moving into it tomorrow, actually. Still in the factory district, but it'll be fantastic for entertaining dignitaries. Would you like to see it?"

"I'm a little busy now," Adamat said. When Ricard's face fell, he added, "Some other time, I'm sure."

"You'll like it. Gaudy. Grand. But stylish."

Adamat snorted. Knowing Ricard, "gaudy" only began to describe it. He tossed the paper on Ricard's desk. "Either you had less people looking for him than you made me believe, or your people are idiots."

"I don't recognize the address," Ricard said, grinning so hard it made his cheeks red.

Adamat wasn't in the mood for the enthusiasm. "After a battle, soldiers go straight for one of two things: either home or vice. Taniel Two-Shot is a career soldier, so I guessed vice. The quickest place to find that near the People's Court is to head northwest into the Gurlish Quarter. He was in the sixth mala den I checked."

"You got lucky," Ricard said. "Admit it. He could have gone anywhere. You just looked in the Gurlish Quarter first."

Adamat shrugged. Investigative work depended more on luck than he cared to admit, but he'd never tell that to a client. "Any chance you found the record for the address I gave you yesterday?"

Ricard sifted through the papers on his desk. A moment later he handed Adamat back Vetas's card. It had a name and address written on it in pencil.

"Fell checked herself," Ricard said. "The warehouse was bought by a tailor—of all things—two years ago. There are no records to indicate it had been sold after the tailor bought it, which means it didn't fall into the hands of the union. Must have been purchased privately. I'm sorry I couldn't do more to help."

"This is a start," Adamat said. He stood up and retrieved his hat and cane.

"You'll be taking SouSmith with you, won't you?" Ricard asked. "I don't want you going after this Vetas alone."

"SouSmith is still laid up," Adamat said. "He took some bloody damage from the Barbers."

Ricard grimaced. "He could go see Lady Parkeur."

Lady Parkeur was an eccentric middle-aged woman who lived with thousands of birds in an old church in High Talien. She always had feathers in her hair and smelled like a henhouse, but she was also the only Knacked in the city with the ability to heal wounds. She could knit together broken tissue and bone with the force of her will, and she cost more money than a Privileged healer.

"I spent every penny I had left to get myself healed by her after the beating I took from Charlemund," Adamat said. "I had to so I could go after my family."

"Fell!" Ricard yelled, making Adamat jump.

The woman appeared a moment later. "Mr. Tumblar?"

"Send a message to Lady Parkeur. Tell her I'm calling in that favor she owes me. There's a boxer, name of SouSmith, who needs mending. Tell her she needs to make a house call today."

"She doesn't do house calls," Fell said.

"She bloody well better for me. If she gives you any lip, remind her about that incident with the goat."

"Right away," Fell said.

"Incident with a goat?" Adamat said.

Ricard looked around. "Don't ask. I need a bloody drink."

"Ricard, you don't have to call in favors for me," Adamat said. He knew by experience how much Lady Parkeur cost for healing. The wait to see her was usually weeks. Adamat had only gotten in through a personal request from Field Marshal Tamas.

"Think nothing of it," Ricard said. "You've saved my ass more times than I can count." He recovered a bottle from behind a stack of books and drained the last finger of cloudy liquid from the bottle, then made a face. It was another moment before he ceased his search for more alcohol and dropped into his seat. "But don't think I won't ask you for more favors. This 'First Minister' business is going to be a rough time."

"I'll do what I can."

"Good. Now go find out about Lord Whatshisname. I've been thinking of a really big gift for you and Faye for your anniversary next year. I'd prefer that you're both around to give it to."

CHAPTER

6

Taniel cut the last silver button off his jacket and handed it to Kin. The stooped Gurlish examined the button closely in the light of a candle before sliding it into his pocket, just like he had all the others, and set a ball of mala on the table next to Taniel's hammock.

Despite the greed apparent on Kin's face, he had a worried look in his eyes.

"Don't go through it so fast. Savor. Taste. *Enjoy*," Kin said.

Taniel pushed a large piece of mala into his pipe. It lit instantly off the embers of the old mala, and he breathed in deep.

"You smoke more in a day than any man does in twenty," Kin said. He settled back on his haunches, watching Taniel smoke.

Taniel lifted his silver powder-mage button and rolled it between his fingers. "Must be the sorcery," he said. "Ever had a powder mage in here before?"

Kin shook his head.

"Never known a powder mage who smoked mala myself," Taniel said. "We all take the powder. Never need more to feel alive."

"Why the mala?" Kin busied himself sweeping the center of the den.

Taniel took a deep breath. "Powder doesn't make you forget."

"Ah. Forget. Every man takes mala to forget." Kin nodded knowingly.

Taniel stared at the ceiling of his niche, counting the hammock swings.

"Going to bed," Kin said, setting his broom in one corner.

"Wait," Taniel reached out with one hand, only to draw it back when he realized how pathetic he must look. "Give me enough to get through the night."

"Night?" Kin shook his head. "It's morning now. I work through the night. Most smokers come then."

"Give me enough for that, then."

Kin seemed to consider this, looking at the ball he just gave Taniel. From what he said, a ball like that should have lasted four or five days.

"Give me the powder keg, and I'll give you as much you can smoke for three weeks."

Taniel clenched the powder-keg pin in his fist. "No. What else?"

"I'll give you my daughter for the whole three weeks, too."

Taniel's stomach turned at the thought of the Gurlish mala man pimping his daughter to his customers.

"No."

"You like art?" Kin picked up the sketchbook and pencil Ka-poel had brought for Taniel.

"Put those down."

Kin dropped the sketchbook with a sigh. "You no have value. No money."

Taniel checked the pockets of his coat. Nothing. He ran his fingers over the silver embroidery.

"How much for my coat?"

Kin sniffed and touched the fabric. "Tiny bit."

"Give me that." Taniel set his mala pipe on the table and wriggled out of the coat, handing it over to Kin.

"You'll die of cold, and I won't pay for funeral."

"It's the middle of summer. Give me the damned mala."

Kin handed him a disappointingly small ball of the sticky black mala before disappearing up the stairs with Taniel's coat. Taniel heard the creak of feet on the floorboards above him, and Kin's voice speaking in Gurlish.

He settled back into his hammock and took a long draw at his mala pipe.

It was said that mala would make a man forget for hours at a time. Taniel tried to think back on the hours he'd lost. How long had he been down here? Days? Weeks? It didn't seem like a long time.

He took the pipe out of his mouth and examined it in the dim light of the den's candles. "Damned stuff doesn't work," he said to himself. He could still see Kresimir stepping out of that cloud after descending from the sky. A god! A real, live god. Taniel wondered what his childhood priest would have done had he known Taniel would one day grow up to shoot the god of the Nine.

Time hadn't stopped when the ensorcelled bullet went through Kresimir's eye, so it seemed the world could live without its god. But how many people had died trying to keep Kresimir from returning to the world? Hundreds of Adran. Friends. Allies. Thousands of Kez—hundreds by Taniel's own hand.

Every time he closed his eyes, he saw a new face. Sometimes it was a man or a woman he'd killed. Sometimes it was Tamas, or Vlora. And sometimes it was Ka-poel. Maybe it was the mala, but, by the pit, it made his heart beat faster when he saw the savage girl's face.

The steps creaked. Taniel looked up. Through the haze he could see Ka-poel come down the stairs. She crossed the room to his side, frowned at him.

"What?" he said.

She tugged on his shirt, then pinched her own long duster. *Jacket.* Damn. First thing she noticed.

He wrapped his hand around his ball of mala protectively.

Quicker than he could see, her hand darted forward and snatched the mala pipe from between his teeth.

"You little bitch," he hissed. "Give it back."

She danced away from his grasping hands to stand in the middle of the room, grinning.

"Ka-poel, bring me that pipe."

She shook her head.

His breathing came harder. He blinked against a sudden cloud in his vision, unable to tell if it was the mala or his own fury. After a moment of struggle, he sat up in the hammock.

"Give it back to me *now.*" He swung his legs over the edge of the hammock, but when he tried to stand up, a wave of nausea struck him harder than it ever had when he opened his third eye to see into the Else. He sank back into the hammock, his heart hammering in his ears.

"Pit," he whispered, clutching at his temples. "I'm all sorts of buggered."

Ka-poel set the mala pipe on a stool on the other side of the room.

"Don't put that there," Taniel said, his own voice now weak. "Bring it to me."

She just shook her head and shrugged out of her duster. Before he could protest, she crossed to him and swept it up over his hammock and up to his shoulders.

He pushed it away. "You'll get cold," he said.

She pointed at him.

"It's summer, damn it. I'm fine."

She drew the duster back up over his chest.

Again, he gave it back to her. "I'm not a child."

Something seemed to light in her eyes at that. She pulled the duster off him and threw it to the ground.

"Pole, what the..." His next words were lost in his own strangled cry as she lifted one leg over the hammock and straddled him, sitting directly on his lap. His heart beat a little faster as she wiggled her ass to get comfortable. In the closeness of the niche, their faces were almost touching. "Pole...," he said, suddenly breathless. The mala pipe, and even the little ball of mala in his hands, were suddenly forgotten.

Her tongue darted out and wet her lips. She seemed poised, watchful—like an animal.

Taniel almost didn't hear the sound of the door to the house upstairs being thrown open. Feet thumped on the floorboards. A woman began shouting in Gurlish.

Ka-poel lowered her head. Taniel's shoulders flexed, pushing him toward her.

"Captain Taniel Two-Shot!" The stairs rattled under a pair of determined boots. A woman in a dress suit, hat in hand, entered the room. "Captain!" she said. "Captain, I..."

She froze when she saw Taniel with Ka-poel in his lap. Taniel felt the color rise in his cheeks. A quick glance at Ka-poel. She gave him a small, knowing smile, but annoyance flashed in her eyes. She rolled off of him and swept her duster off the floor and over her shoulders in one quick movement.

The woman turned to one side, staring at the far wall. "Sir, I'm sorry, I didn't know you were indisposed."

"She's not undressed," Taniel retorted. His voice cracked and he cleared his throat. "Who the pit are you?"

The woman gave a slight bow. "I am Fell Baker, undersecretary for the Holy Warriors of Labor." Despite having found them in a compromising situation, she didn't seem the least bit embarrassed.

"The union? How the pit did you find me?" Taniel pulled himself to a sitting position in the hammock, though it made his stomach turn something fierce. He wondered how long it had been since he ate.

"I'm Ricard Tumblar's aide, sir. He sent me to find you. He would very much like to meet with you."

"Tumblar? Don't know the name." He settled back into the hammock and eyed Ka-poel. She'd sat on the stool on the far side of the mala den, tapping his pipe against her palm as she studied the undersecretary.

Fell raised an eyebrow. "He's the head of the union, sir."

"I don't care."

"He's asked me to extend to you an invitation to lunch."

"Go away."

"He says there's a great deal of money at stake."

"I don't care."

Fell examined him for a few moments before turning and heading up the creaking stairs just as abruptly as she'd arrived. The hushed sound of voices came down through the floor. They were speaking in Gurlish. Taniel glanced at Ka-poel. She returned his stare for a moment, then winked.

What the pit?

A few moments later the undersecretary came back downstairs.

"Sir, it appears you're out of money."

Taniel looked for his mala pipe. Oh. Ka-poel still had it. Right.

"Take that from her and give it to me, would you?" Taniel said to Fell.

Fell faced Ka-poel. The two women exchanged a glance that seemed full of meaning. Taniel didn't like that at all.

The undersecretary clasped her hands together. "I will not, sir." She crossed the room in two strides and grabbed Taniel by the chin, forcing his face toward her. Taniel grasped the woman's wrist, but Fell was stronger than she looked. She examined his eyes.

"Let go of me, or I will bloody well kill you," Taniel growled.

Fell took her hands away and stepped back. "How much have you smoked since you got here?"

"Don't know," Tamas grumbled. Ka-poel hadn't so much as moved when the undersecretary had rushed him. Some help she was.

"Eight pounds of the stuff in four days. That's what the owner told me."

Taniel shrugged.

"That's enough to kill a warhorse, sir."

Taniel sniffed. "Didn't seem to do much."

A perplexed look crossed Fell's face. She opened her mouth, shut it again, and then said, "Didn't do much? I . . ." She grasped her hat and went back upstairs, only to return again after a few minutes.

"The owner," Fell said, "insists he watched you smoke it himself. I examined your eyes. Not even a hint of mala poisoning. Pit, I've probably gotten mala poisoning just standing in the smoke and talking to you. You're god-touched."

Taniel surged to his feet. One moment he was in the hammock, and the next he had Fell by the lapels with both fists. His head spun, his vision warped, and his hands trembled with rage. "I am not god-touched," Taniel said. "I've not . . . I'm . . ."

"Kindly unhand me, sir," Fell said gently.

Taniel felt his hands drop to his sides. He took a step back and mumbled to himself.

"I'll give you a moment to clean up," Fell said. "We'll get you a new jacket on the way to see Ricard."

"I'm not going," Taniel said weakly. He stumbled to the corner, grateful for a wall to lean against. It might be that he *couldn't* go. He doubted he could walk more than twenty feet.

Fell sighed. "Mr. Tumblar offers the hospitality of his own mala den, sir. It is a much more comfortable location, and his den-keeper won't take your jacket. If you refuse that invitation, we are instructed to bring you there by force."

Taniel looked over to Ka-poel. She was cleaning her fingernails with what looked to be a sharpened knitting needle, almost as long as her forearm. She met his eyes briefly. Again that small, knowing smile. Again the annoyance in her eyes.

"Ricard's den has significantly more privacy than this, sir," Fell said, coughing once into her hand.

Taniel was not sure that whatever had just happened with Ka-poel was bound to repeat itself. "All right, Fell. But one thing."

"Sir?"

"I don't think I've eaten in two days. I could use some lunch."

Two hours later, Taniel was in the Adopest docks. The docks traditionally ran Adran commerce, governing the transport of cargo from the Ad River and its tributaries in the north all the way down through Surkov's Alley and across the Amber Expanse. With the war on, trade through Kez was at a standstill, and cargo that usually used the river was now sent over the mountains by mule and packhorse.

Despite the change in transportation, the docks were still the center of commerce in Adopest. Barges brought iron ore and raw lumber down the river to supply the Adran mills and gunsmiths, who turned out weapons and ammunition in the hundreds every day.

The docks stank of fish, sewage, and smoke, and Taniel was starting to miss the cool, sweet smell of mala in Kin's den. His escort consisted of Fell Baker the undersecretary and a pair of wide-shouldered steelworkers. Taniel wondered if the steelworkers were there to carry him to the meeting with Ricard if he decided not to go.

Ka-poel trailed along behind the group. The steelworkers ignored her; Fell kept a wary eye on her at all times. She seemed to suspect that Ka-poel was more than just a mute savage, while Taniel had a hunch that Fell might be more than an undersecretary.

Fell stopped in front of a dockside warehouse within spitting distance of the water. Taniel looked out from between the alleyways and across the Adsea. Even during the day he could see a glow on the horizon, and the conspicuous absence of South Pike Mountain. The view made him want to hide beneath a rock. The death throes of a god had leveled a mountain, and he'd gotten away with a month-long coma. He wasn't certain why he wasn't dead, but he suspected it had to do with Ka-poel.

He wondered if everyone else had been so lucky. Where was Bo? Where were the men and women of the Mountainwatch he'd befriended during the defense of Shouldercrown?

An image flashed through his mind of clutching Ka-poel to his chest as Kresimir's palace collapsed around him. Fire and stone, the burning heat of lava as the mountain collapsed.

"Hard to believe it's gone, isn't it," Fell said, nodding across the water as she opened the door to the warehouse and gestured for Taniel to go in.

Taniel gave one last glance to the east and jerked his head toward Fell. "You first."

"Fine," Fell said. She looked to the steelworkers, offering them cigars from a gunmetal case in her vest pocket. "Back to work for you, boys." The two men tipped their hats to Fell, took a light for their cigars and then headed back into the street. "Come on," Fell said. Once they were all in, she closed the door behind Ka-poel. "Welcome to Ricard's new offices."

Taniel had to keep himself from whistling. On the outside, the building looked like an old warehouse. The windows were shuttered, the brick long in need of refacing. The inside was another matter.

The floors were of black marble, and the walls were whitewashed behind crimson satin curtains. The building appeared to have but one main room, an echoing chamber two stories high and at least two hundred paces long, lit by a half-dozen crystal chandeliers. At the near end of the room there was a long bar, complete with uni-formed barman and well-endowed woman in nothing more than a petticoat.

"Your coat, sir," the woman said.

Taniel handed her his new dark-blue uniform jacket. He felt his gaze rest on her a little longer than was proper. Without looking at Ka-poel, he turned to examine the room. Artwork adorned the walls, sculptures were set at even intervals inside shallow recesses. This was the kind of wealth displayed by the highest echelons of nobility, even that of the king. Taniel thought that Tamas had stamped out this kind of wealth when he slaughtered the nobility. A thought occurred that perhaps Tamas had just changed the very rich and powerful for a new set of the same.

A man crossed the marble floor toward them. He wore a white smoking jacket, a cigar clenched between his teeth. He looked to be about forty years old, with a hairline receding well past the mid-dle of his head. He wore a long beard in the Fatrastan style, and the grin on his face reached his ears and even touched his eyes.

"Taniel Two-Shot," the man said, holding out his hand. "Ricard Tumblar. I'm a great admirer of yours."

Taniel took his hand with hesitation.

"Mr. Tumblar."

"Mister? Bah, call me Ricard. I'm at your service. And this must be your ever-present companion. The Dynize. My lady?" Ricard swept into a deep bow and took Ka-poel's hand in his, bending to kiss it gen-tly. Despite his forward nature, he eyed her as one might something pretty but far from tame, something that might bite at any moment.

Ka-poel didn't seem to know how to react to this.

"I'd heard you were a handsome woman," Ricard said, "but the stories didn't do you justice." He broke away from them and crossed to the bar. "Drink?"

"What do you have?" Taniel felt his mood brighten a little.

"Anything," Ricard said.

Taniel doubted that. "Fatrastan ale, then."

Ricard nodded to the barman. "Two, please. For the lady?"

Ka-poel flashed three fingers.

"Make that three," Ricard said to the barman. A moment later, he handed Taniel a mug.

"Son of a bitch," Taniel said after a sip. "You really do have Fatrastan ale."

"I did say anything. Can we take a seat?"

He led them toward the far end of the room. Taniel blamed his mala-addled mind for not noticing earlier that they weren't alone. A dozen men and half again as many women lounged on divans, drinking and smoking, talking quietly among themselves.

Ricard spoke as they approached the group. "Oh, I had a question for you, Taniel. How much black powder does the army use?"

Taniel rubbed his eyes. His head hurt, and he didn't come here to meet Ricard's cronies. "Quite a lot, I'd imagine. I'm not a quartermaster. Why do you ask?"

"Been getting more and more powder orders from the General Staff," Ricard said, waving his hand like it was a trifle. "I just thought it strange. It almost seems as if their requisitions double every week. Nothing to worry about, I'm sure."

The talking died down when Taniel reached the group at the end of the room, and he felt suddenly uncomfortable.

"I thought this was going to be a private meeting," Taniel said quietly, stopping Ricard with a hand to his arm.

Ricard didn't even glance down at the hand Taniel laid on him. "Give me a moment to make introductions and we'll get down to business."

He went around the room, giving names that Taniel immediately forgot, and titles that Taniel took no great note of. These men and women were the heads of the various factions within the unions: bakers, steelworkers, millers, ironsmiths, blacksmiths, and goldsmiths.

True to his word, when the introductions were finished, Ricard led them toward a quiet corner of the vast room, where they were joined by just one other woman. She was one of the first Ricard had introduced, and Taniel couldn't remember her name.

"Cigarette?" Ricard offered as they took their seats. A man in a jacket matching the barman's brought them a silver tray lined with cigarettes, cigars, and pipes. Taniel noticed a mala pipe among the recreation. His fingers twitched to take it, but he fought down the urge and waved away the servant.

"Your secretary said you wanted to meet with me," Taniel said, realizing with a start that Fell had disappeared. "She didn't say why. I'd like to know."

"I have a proposition."

Taniel looked at the woman again. She was older, with an air of disdain particular to the very wealthy. What was her name? And who did she represent? The bakers? No. Goldsmiths?

"I'm not interested," Taniel said.

"I haven't even told you what it is," Ricard said.

"Look," Taniel said. "I came because your undersecretary made it clear that she'd make me come even if I didn't want to. I've been polite. I've come. Now I'd like to go." He stood.

"Is this what you brought me here for, Ricard?" the woman said, looking down her nose at Taniel. "To see a mala-drunk soldier piss on your hospitality? I fear for this country, Ricard. We've handed it over to the uneducated soldiers. They don't know anything but vice and killing."

Taniel clenched his fists and felt his lip curl. "You don't know me, madam. You don't know who the pit I am or what I've seen. Don't pretend to understand soldiers when you've never looked into another man's eyes and seen that one of you would die."

Ricard leaned back on his divan and relit his cigar with a matchstick. He had the air of a man at the boxing ring. Had he expected this?

The woman fairly bristled. "I know soldiers," she said. "Sick, stupid brutes. You rape and steal, and you kill when you can't do that. I've known many soldiers and I don't have to kill a man to know you're nothing more than a churlish brigand in a uniform."

Ricard sighed. "Please, Cheris, not now."

"Not now?" Cheris asked. "If not now, then when? I've had enough of Tamas's iron grip on the city. I didn't want you to bring this so-called war hero here."

Taniel turned to go.

"Taniel," Ricard said. "Give me just a few more moments."

"Not with her here," Taniel said. He headed toward the door, only to find his way blocked by Ka-poel. "I'm leaving, Pole."

She returned his grimace with a cool-eyed shake of the head.

"Look at that!" Cheris said behind him. "The coward flees back to his mala den. He can't face truth. And you want this man at your side, Ricard? He's led around by a savage girl."

Taniel whirled. He'd had enough. His rage piqued, he advanced toward Cheris, one hand held in the air.

"Strike me!" she said, leaning forward to offer a cheek. "It'll show how much of a man you are."

Taniel froze. Had he just been ready to hit her? "I killed a god," he fumed. "I put a bullet through his eye and watched him die to save this country!"

"Lies," Cheris said. "You lie to me to my face? You think I believe this tripe about Kresimir returning?"

Taniel would have let his hand fly right then if Ka-poel hadn't slipped around him. She faced Cheris, eyes narrowed. Taniel suddenly felt fear. As much as he wanted to hurt this woman, he knew what Ka-poel was capable of.

"Pole," he said.

"Out of my face, you savage whore," Cheris said, getting to her feet.

Ka-poel's fist connected with her nose hard enough to send

Cheris tumbling over the back of the divan. Cheris screamed. Ricard shot to his feet. The group of union bosses still speaking quietly on the other side of the room fell silent, and stared, shocked, toward them.

Cheris climbed to her feet, pushing away Ricard's attempt to help. Without a look back, she fled the room, blood streaming from her nose.

Ricard turned to Taniel, his expression caught somewhere between horror and amusement.

"I won't apologize," Taniel said. "Neither for me nor for Pole." Ka-poel took a place at his side, arms crossed.

"She was my guest," Ricard said. He paused, examined his cigar. "More ale," he called to the barkeep. "But you are my guests as well. She's going to make me pay for that later. I'd hoped she would be an ally in the coming months, but it appears that is not the case."

Taniel looked to Ricard, then to the main door, where Cheris was demanding her coachman.

"I should go," Taniel said.

"No, no. Ale!" Ricard shouted again, though Taniel could see the barkeep heading toward them. "You're more important than she is."

Taniel slowly lowered himself back into his seat. "I killed Kresimir," he said. Part of him wanted to be proud of it, but saying it aloud made him feel ill.

"That's what Tamas told me," Ricard said.

"You don't believe me."

The barkeep arrived and changed Taniel's mug for another one, though he'd only finished half. New mugs all around and the man disappeared. Ricard drank deeply of his before he began to speak.

"I'm a practical man," Ricard said. "I know that sorcery exists, though I am not a Privileged or a Knacked or a Marked. Two months ago, if you'd told me that Kresimir would return, I would have wondered what asylum you'd escaped from.

"But I was there when the Barbers tried to kill Mihali. I saw your father—a man twice as pragmatic as I—go ghost white. He felt something from the chef and—"

"I'm sorry," Taniel interrupted. "Mihali?"

Ricard tapped the ash from the end of his cigar. "Oh. You're very much out of the loop, aren't you? Mihali is Adom reborn. Kresimir's brother, here in the flesh."

Taniel felt the hair on the back of his neck stand on end. Another god? Kresimir's own brother?

"What I'm trying to get at," Ricard went on, "is that your father believes that Mihali is Adom reborn. And if Adom has returned, why not Kresimir? So, yes. I believe you shot Kresimir. Is it possible to kill a god? I don't know."

He scowled into his mug. "As for the newspapers and the people, they are skeptical. Rumors fly. People are taking sides. Right now it all comes down to a matter of faith, and we have only your word and the word of a few Mountainwatchers that Kresimir returned and took a bullet in the eye."

Taniel felt his strength leave him. To be thought a fraud after all he went through? It was the final blow. He pointed to the door. "How do they explain South Pike? The entire mountain collapsed." He heard his voice rise with anger.

"You won't change anyone's mind by shouting," Ricard said. "Believe me. I'm the head of the union. I've tried."

"Then what can I do?"

"Convince them. Show them what kind of a man you are and then, only when they trust you, tell them the truth."

"That seems...dishonest."

Ricard spread his hands. "That's up to your own moral judgment. But me, I think a man who sees it like that is a fool."

Taniel clenched his fists. How could they not believe him? How could they not know what happened up there? Hadn't Tamas told the newspapers? Did even Tamas not believe what had happened?

Taniel didn't know where Tamas was. Budwiel, according to the soldiers who had been watching him when he awoke. Was Tamas even still there?

"Do you know where Bo is?" Taniel asked.

"Bo?"

"Privileged Borbador. Is he still alive?"

Ricard spread his hands. "I can't help you."

"You're not much good, Tumblar, are you?" Taniel wanted to punch something. He leapt to his feet and stalked back and forth the length of the room. No friends. No family. What could he do now? "Who was that woman?" he asked.

"Cheris? The head of the bankers' union."

"I thought you were the head of the union."

"The Noble Warriors of Labor has many subdivisions. I speak for the group as a whole, but each trade has their own union boss."

"You said I was more important than her."

Ricard nodded. "I did."

"How so?"

"How much do you know about politics in Adro?" Ricard countered with his own question.

"The power used to be with the king. Now?" Taniel shrugged. "No idea."

"No one knows where the power is now," Ricard said. "The people assume it's with Tamas. Tamas thinks it's with his council when in fact the council is all but fractured. Lady Winceslav is in seclusion after her scandal with a traitorous brigadier, the Arch Diocel has been arrested, and Prime Lektor is in the east, studying the remains of South Pike for some sign of the god Kresimir."

"So who is running Adro?"

Ricard chuckled. "That leaves myself, the Proprietor, and Ondraus the Reeve. Not exactly a noble group. The truth is, Adro is doing fine for now. Tamas and his men keep the peace. But that will only last so long. We need to continue with our plans. Since the beginning of all this, the council decided that as soon as Manhouch was out of the way, we'd set up a democracy: a system of government that was voted upon by the people. The country would be divided into principalities, each with its own elected governor, and those men would meet in Adro and vote upon policy for the country."

"Much like a ministry without the king at the head."

"Indeed," Ricard said. "Of course there must be someone to stand as the king."

Taniel narrowed his eyes. "I can't imagine Tamas taking that well."

"We won't call him a king, of course. And he would have little real power. He would serve as a figurehead. A single man the country can look to for leadership and guidance, even if the policy is determined by the governors—we are going to call him the First Minister of the People."

"I remember Tamas striking down an idea just like this that the royalists presented him with."

"Tamas approved this," Ricard said. "Believe me. None of us on the council has any interest in crossing him, especially not in such a public way. The key is that, like the governors, this new First Minister of the People will be replaced every three years. We've set the mechanism in place. It just needs to be carried out."

Taniel could easily tell where this was going. "And you intend to put yourself forward as a candidate."

"Of course."

"Why?"

Ricard sucked hard on his cigar and let the smoke curl out through his nostrils. It reminded Taniel of the smoke of his mala pipe. He could feel the lure of that blissful smoke pulling at him.

"The First Minister of the People will have little power of his own, but he'll have the eyes of all the Nine directed at him. His name will go down in the history books forever." Ricard sighed. "I don't have any children. I've been left by"—he stopped to count—"six wives, and deserved it every time. All I have left is my name. And I want it taught to every Adran schoolchild for the rest of time."

Taniel drained the last of his ale. The dregs of the hops at the bottom of the glass were bitter. It reminded him of Fatrasta, of hunting down Kez Privileged in the wilds. "Where do I fit into all of this? I'm just a soldier who killed a god that no one believes even returned."

"You?" Ricard threw his head back and laughed. Taniel didn't see what was so funny.

"I'm sorry," Ricard said as he wiped his eyes. "You're Taniel Two-Shot! You're the hero of two continents. A soldier who's killed more Privileged than any man in the history of the Nine. The way the newspapers tell it, you held Shouldercrown Fortress against half a million Kez all by yourself."

"Wasn't just me," Taniel muttered, thinking of the men and women he'd watched die on that mountain.

"But the common people think so. They adore you. They love you more than they love Tamas, and he's been the darling of Adro since he single-handedly saved the Gurlish Campaign decades ago."

"So what do you want from me? A sponsorship?"

"Pit, no," Ricard said, passing his empty ale mug to the barkeep. "I want you to be my Second Minister. You'll be one of the most famous men in the world."

CHAPTER
7

In northeastern Adopest there was a small section of the Samalian District that hadn't been burned when Field Marshal Tamas allowed the pillage of the nobility's property after Manhouch's execution. It was a commercial area, filled with goods and service shops that catered to the nobility. Rumor had it that during the riots the owners of these shops set up their own barricades and held off the rioters themselves.

Now, five months after the riots, the former emporium of the rich had been transformed into a marketplace for the middle class. Prices had been lowered, but not quality, and people traveled halfway across the city to wait in line for cobblers, tailors, bakers, and jewelers.

Adamat came early in the morning, before the larger crowds arrived, and found the tailor who had purchased Vetas's warehouse. Adamat sat down in a small café across the street from the tailor's and ordered breakfast, keeping an eye out for expected company. It wasn't long until he spotted it.

Adamat rose from his seat and crossed the street. He discreetly sidled up beside SouSmith and said, "Were you followed?"

To his credit, SouSmith barely started. "Bloody pit," SouSmith said. "Didn't recognize ya."

"That's the idea." Adamat had dyed his hair gray. A dry dusting of powder on his face made his skin appear cracked, making him look twenty years older, and he affected a limp. He leaned heavily on a new, silver-headed cane. His jacket and pants were the finest money could by—he'd had to call in favors just to procure them. But he needed to look the part of a wealthy gentleman.

SouSmith shook his head. "Wasn't followed," he said. "Been staying low."

"Good," Adamat said. "How do you feel?"

"Like pit. Bloody healing Knacked."

Despite what he said, SouSmith looked better. Just five weeks ago he'd been shot twice and stabbed, and had barely made it through alive. It would have been a long recovery without Ricard's largesse.

"Go to that café over there," Adamat said, "and get breakfast. Take a seat facing that store there." He indicated the tailor's shop. "I'm going in to make some inquiries."

As much as he wanted SouSmith to come inside the tailor shop with him in case it was merely a front for Vetas and Vetas had men stationed inside, SouSmith was too memorable of a man, and there was no disguising a boxer of his size. No sense in bringing him in until needed.

Adamat crossed the street and entered the shop. A quick perusal told him that this tailor specialized in high-end jackets. Mannequins were placed around the edges of the room, wearing everything from smoking and evening jackets to the kind a duke might wear to a ball. The shop smelled strongly of peppermint oil that the owner used to mask the scent of stored cloth.

"May I help you?"

The tailor came in from the back room. He was a dark-skinned Deliv; a small man with long, steady fingers. He wore a pair of thin-rimmed spectacles and a vest with protruding lapels stuck through with a variety of needles and pins.

"Haime?" Adamat said, affecting an accent common in Adopest's southern suburbs.

"I am he," the tailor said with a short bow. "Jackets and suits. May I take your measurements for a new jacket today?"

"I haven't come in search of clothing," Adamat said. He looked down the end of his nose and made a show of perusing the mannequins. "At least, not today."

Haime clasped his hands behind his back. "Some other business?"

Adamat pulled a piece of paper from his breast pocket and unfolded it. "My employers are looking to purchase a piece of property," he said. "Records show that you are the owner."

Haime seemed genuinely puzzled. "I don't own any property."

"You did not buy a warehouse on Donavi Street in the factory district two years ago?"

"No, I..." Haime suddenly stopped and tapped his chin with one finger. "I did. That's right. One of my clients asked me to make a purchase and then transfer the title into his name. He wanted to keep the affair quiet. Something about not wanting the newspapers getting wind of his employer's purchases."

Adamat felt his heart jump. There were very few organizations that could make the news with a simple purchase of property. One of them was the Brudania-Gurla Trading Company. And their head was Lord Claremonte, Vetas's employer.

"Could I get his name, please?" Adamat said. He pulled a fountain pen from his pocket and poised it above his piece of paper.

Haime gave him an apologetic look. "I'm very sorry, but my client requested I keep that information in confidence."

"My employer would very much like to purchase that building," Adamat said. "I'm sure that something could be arranged..." He removed a checkbook from his pocket.

"No, no," Haime said. "I'm sorry, it's not a matter of money. I'm a man of my word."

Adamat gave a long-suffering sigh. "I'm sure." He put away the checkbook and pen and gathered his hat and cane. He paused, making a show of looking around the mannequins once more with an admiring eye. His gaze stopped on one and he almost choked.

It was the same jacket Lord Vetas had been wearing the last time they spoke.

"I see you've a fine eye," Haime said, slipping over toward the mannequin. "This jacket is discerning and subtle. It would look fantastic on you."

Adamat felt his heart begin to beat faster. Vetas must have been the same client to purchase that warehouse and the jacket. If Haime knew that he knew, the tailor might become suspicious.

"No, I don't think it's my style."

"Nonsense," Haime said. "The jacket has a slimming effect and draws the eyes up to your face. I could make an entire suit to match."

Adamat pretended to think on this for several moments. The jacket was obviously tailored. He could see a slight discoloration at the waist, where a rip had been patched, and he realized that this might be the actual jacket Lord Vetas had been wearing. "This looks like the right size. Can you tailor it for me now?"

"Unfortunately, no. This particular jacket belongs to someone. He's picking it up in a few days. I could have a new one made up for you in..." He paused to think. "A week. Just let me take your measurements."

Adamat patted his pockets. "I seem to have left my own checks at home. I only have my employers'. I will not be able to make a payment today."

"You're obviously a gentleman, sir," Haime said. "You may just give me your address."

Adamat didn't have an address to give to him. He didn't want to risk any word of this reaching Vetas. That risk was already high, as Haime might mention the attempted purchase to Vetas just as a matter of course. Adamat withdrew his pocket watch. "I have an appointment in less than an hour," he said. "I must make it. Let me come back early next week for measurements."

Haime's face fell. A good salesman never let a mark go out the door without a commitment to buy. "If that works best for you."

"It does," Adamat said. "I'll be back, don't worry."

Adamat hurried across the street and found SouSmith waiting at the café.

"Any sign of Vetas or any of his eyes?"

SouSmith shook his head.

"Let's go," Adamat said.

"Breakfast still coming."

Adamat checked to make sure the tailor wasn't watching him through the window of his shop before taking a seat next to Sou-Smith. "The tailor isn't involved directly," Adamat said. "He bought and sold the property for one of his clients: I think it's Vetas. I saw the same jacket Vetas was wearing the last time I saw him, all the way down to the tailoring."

"You sure?"

"I don't forget, remember?" Adamat tapped the side of his head. "I could tell that the lines of that jacket matched perfectly. Unfortunately, the tailor wouldn't give me Vetas's name or address."

"Dead end."

"No. Vetas—or, more likely, one of his men—is coming to pick up that jacket in the next few days. It was being mended. I'm going to stake out the tailor and watch for who picks up the jacket. I'll follow them and find out where Vetas lives."

"Where you want me?" SouSmith's breakfast arrived: four

poached eggs with Novi goat cheese. He grinned as it was set in front of him and set about eating quickly.

"Nowhere," Adamat said. "I can't risk you being recognized. I can wear a disguise. You, however, can't."

SouSmith sniffed. Through a mouthful of egg, he said, "Can't leave you to follow him alone."

Adamat knew the risks. If Vetas or his man was good enough to mark Adamat, he could very well be a dead man. But SouSmith was a liability in this kind of work. He was easily recognized, and even if he wasn't, his size made him less than ideal for following someone.

"I'll do it alone," Adamat said.

Tamas lay in the tall grass of a knoll beneath the Adran Mountains and watched through his looking glass as the Kez army prepared to assault Budwiel.

Morning dew soaked his combat uniform. The cloud cover was low on this day and a rolling fog clung to plains outside of Budwiel. The air was heavy with moisture. He knew it would foul guns on both sides, but when Tamas looked toward Budwiel, he noted a ray of sunshine peeking through the clouds to bathe the city and clear the air.

No doubt Mihali's indirect participation in the battle.

And they would need every bit of his help. Tamas swung his looking glass back toward the Kez. His breath caught in his throat at the sight of their army. Rank upon rank of tan uniforms with green trim stretched for what seemed like forever. Long experience let him count their ranks with only a cursory glance.

One hundred and twenty thousand at least. And that was just their infantry.

They would send their recruits first to act as so much cannon fodder in order to test Budwiel's defenses. Five, maybe ten thousand of them would pour out across the fields, tramping down the wet grass and receiving the full brunt of grapeshot. They'd be followed quickly by the more experienced men, who'd form a strong backbone to the main assault and push the recruits on hard in front of them, even at the tip of their bayonets. Sorcery-warped Wardens would accompany the front of the second wave.

It was a foolish method of attack, in Tamas's opinion, but the Kez commanders had always favored a massed rush—no matter the cost in lives—above guile.

And it just might work. The key to throwing back the Kez assault would be to break the resolve of their second wave. To kill the Wardens and send the veterans running for cover. It would be hard to break such a sizable force.

But not impossible.

Which is where the Seventh and the Ninth came in. Once the Kez committed the main body, Tamas would order his men over the knoll at a dead charge into the Kez flank.

No matter the size of a crowd, they'd run if panic seized them.

The Kez cannon had been moved forward before dawn. They pounded away at Budwiel's fortifications, answered in turn by Hilanska's heavy artillery.

Tamas watched as the Kez infantry fell into rank a few hundred yards behind their artillery. He felt his stomach lurch.

"That's a lot of men, sir," Olem said from beside him.

"A great many," Tamas agreed. Was that unease in Olem's voice? Tamas couldn't blame him if it was. That many soldiers would make anyone nervous.

"Think we can break them?"

"We'd better. The cavalry will help."

"We've only two hundred, though," Olem said.

"All we need is the illusion of a brigade of cavalry. We're here to cause panic, and then slaughter. Not the other way around."

During the night, they'd had enough time to bring two hundred cavalry through the caverns. It was a testament to Tamas's engineers that they'd managed to get the caverns wide enough to accommodate the passage of ten thousand men plus a platoon of horse in just one night.

The real victory of the night, however, had been six field guns. Small, firing six-pound balls, and with five-foot wheels that would allow them to be moved easily, they were just enough to give the impression of an entire army on the Kez flank.

Tamas let his mind wander to the aftermath of the battle. They could rout the Kez, but they wouldn't be able to pursue for long. Tens of thousands would be dead, but to the Kez that was just another number. They would still have hundreds of thousands left. This battle would be to break the morale of their army. The Kez couldn't afford another loss on the psychological level of the Battle of Shouldercrown.

Tamas's spies already reported that there were grumblings in Ipille's ministry. Given enough of a spark, the army might even turn on Ipille, though that seemed too much to even hope.

"Sir," Olem said. "The columns are advancing."

Tamas pulled himself back to the present. It was bad luck to think of victory as the battle started. He had plans in place. If triumph came, then it would be time to implement them. Not now.

"Signal the men to get ready."

Vlora crawled onto the knoll next to Tamas as Olem hurried away.

"Are your men in place?" Tamas asked.

"You mean Andriya's men, sir?"

Tamas could hear the bitterness in her voice. He'd given Andriya command of the powder cabal for this battle, and it irked her. Tamas fought down his own annoyance. When would she learn that, skilled though she was, she did not have the experience to be in command?

"My powder mages," Tamas said sternly. "Are they in place?"

"Yes, sir."

"And you've sighted the last of the Kez Privileged?"

"They're hanging back," Vlora said. "They think we're on Bud-wiel's walls, waiting for them, so they're well behind the columns. Quite within range of us here. You signal the attack, sir, and we'll drop the Privileged."

"Excellent. Get to your position."

Vlora crawled off the knoll without another word. Tamas looked over his shoulder to watch her go.

"All ready, sir." Olem came jogging up the hill and threw him-self to the ground beside Tamas. "Time to hurry up and wait." He caught the way Tamas was looking.

"Still thinking of punching her, sir?"

Tamas gave Olem a wry look. Since when had his men gotten away with speaking that way to him? "No."

"You seem angry, sir."

"She has a lot of growing up to do still. I'm mostly sad. Had things gone differently, she might be my daughter-in-law by now." He sighed and brought the looking glass back to his eye. "Tan-iel might not have been on that damned mountain and lying in a coma under the House of Nobles."

Olem's voice was quiet. "He might not have been there to put a bullet in Kresimir's eye and save us all, sir."

Tamas drummed his fingers against his looking glass. Olem was right, of course. Change one event in history, and you might as well change everything that followed. What concerned him now was trying to find a way to bring Taniel out of his coma, and to keep his body safe until he did.

As if he could read Tamas's thoughts, Olem said, "He'll be all right, sir. I've got some of my best Riflejacks keeping an eye on him."

Tamas wanted to turn to Olem, to thank him for the reassur-ance. But now was not the time for worry or sentiment. "The lines are beginning to advance," Tamas said. "Make sure the men hold. I don't want the Kez to know we're coming until the right moment."

"They'll hold," Olem said with confidence.

"Make certain. Personally."

Olem moved off to check on the brigades, leaving Tamas alone on the knoll for a few precious moments. Soon, an unending stream of messengers would be requesting further orders as the battle began and raged throughout the day.

Tamas closed his eyes and envisioned the battlefield as a crow might.

Kez infantry formed a half circle facing Budwiel's walls. Their ranks would tighten as they advanced to account for the terrain, and fill in the gaps from casualties caused by Adran cannon. A single line of Kez cavalry, perhaps one thousand strong, waited on the Great Northern Road for the infantry to take the walls and throw open the gates, at which time they would charge into the city. The rest of their cavalry camped over two miles behind the battlefield. Most of them weren't even on their horses. They didn't think they'd be needed today.

The Kez reserves waited behind the rest of the army. Their numbers were a terrible sight, but Tamas's looking glass and his spies told another story: They were there for show only. Only one out of five had a musket. Their uniforms were mismatched and off-color. Tamas shook his head. The Kez had more men than they had guns. The reserves would break and run at the first sign of his troops.

The *rat-tat-tat-tat* of Kez drummers reverberated against the mountains, and Tamas felt the ground tremble as the mass of Kez infantry began their advance. He directed his glass toward the walls of Budwiel.

The heavy artillery, already firing on the Kez field guns, redoubled their efforts as the wall of infantry crept closer. Tamas could see soldiers of the Second on the walls, their Adran blues looking sharp, their discipline steady.

As the lines of Kez infantry reached the killing field, artillery blasted holes in their ranks. Those holes were quickly closed, and the tan-and-green uniforms marched onward, leaving a hundred dead for every dozen paces they gained. The smell of gunpowder reached Tamas on the wind and he took a deep breath, savoring the bitter sulfur.

He climbed to his feet and motioned over his signal-flag man. On the field below their vantage point, he watched as the mass of Kez reserves shifted forward to take places behind the infantry. Tamas scowled. If they were to take the city, it would be with the mass of infantry. Why would they even move the reserves into position...?

He felt a cold tingle down his spine. The Kez thought they'd be able to sack Budwiel today. They would secure the walls with their infantry and then signal the reserves into the city to burn, rape, and plunder. Tamas had seen them do the same in Gurla. If they breached the walls, it would be a horror beyond imagining.

To think they'd do it in a single day was beyond optimistic on the part of the Kez commanders.

He couldn't let that happen.

"Signal at the ready," Tamas said. The flagger beside him waved out the order. Tamas could see the eagerness in the man's face. The Seventh and Ninth were ready. They'd tear into the Kez flank with gusto. Tamas felt his blood begin to rise. "Wait...wait..."

Tamas blinked. What was that?

He put his looking glass to his eye. When he focused on the fields directly before Budwiel, he saw dozens of twisted men running toward the walls. They wore black coats and bowler caps. Wardens.

But these Wardens...Tamas swallowed. He'd never seen anyone run this fast, not even one of those sorcery-spawned killers. They covered the last few hundred yards to the wall with the speed of a racing Thoroughbred.

In his glass, Tamas could see the wall commanders bellowing. Muskets opened fire. Not a single Warden went down. They reached the base of the wall and leapt, clinging to its vertical face like insects and scurrying to the top. In a flash, they were among the gun crews, brandishing swords and pistols.

Wait, pistols? Wardens didn't carry pistols. Privileged had an aversion to gunpowder, and they were the ones who created the sorcery-spawned monsters.

Small explosions rocked the top of the walls. Bodies fell from the fortifications, and one by one, the cannons ceased firing.

Tamas rocked back on his heels. What was happening? How could those Wardens have gained the wall so easily? He smacked his looking glass in his hand. Without the cannons to keep them at bay, the Kez infantry would take the walls easily. They wouldn't have the threat of artillery at their backs to keep them from turning to face Tamas's brigades head-on.

"Sir," the flagger said, "should I signal the attack?"

"No," Tamas said. The word came out a strangled cry.

He continued to watch as the infantry reached the base of the wall. Ladders went up, and by the time the tan-and-green uniforms reached the top of the wall, Tamas could not see a single Adran soldier left standing. The Wardens had cut them all down.

"Sir." Olem appeared at Tamas's side. He drew his own looking glass to his eye. "What...what happened?" Tamas could hear his own disbelief reflected in Olem's voice.

"Wardens," Tamas choked out. He wanted to spit, but his mouth was too dry. They were soon joined by officers of the Seventh and Ninth. They all looked out at the battle together.

Kez infantry flooded the walls. Minutes later the front gates were thrown open. The Kez cavalry charged up the road toward the gates.

"We must attack, sir," said a major whose name Tamas couldn't recall.

Tamas whirled to his officers when he heard mutters of agreement.

"It's suicide," he said. His voice cracked. "Budwiel is lost."

"We could salvage the day," another voice said.

Tamas ground his teeth. He agreed with them. By god, he agreed with them. "Perhaps," he said. "Maybe we would be able to rout the tail end of the Kez army. We could destroy the reserves and set fire to the Kez camp. But then we'd be caught out on the empty plain, easily surrounded, and cut off from reinforcement."

Silence. These officers were brave, but they weren't fools. They could see he was right.

"Then what do we do?"

Tamas heard a boom echo out from Budwiel. Smoke and dust erupted from the base of the West Pillar. He yelled for a scout to check the tunnels, but already knew what had happened. The catacombs. Someone had set off an explosion inside of them, cutting off Tamas's entry back into Budwiel.

"I've been betrayed again," he whispered. More loudly, "We keep our backs to the mountain." He tried to think of the closest Mountainwatch pass into Adro. It would be a nightmare to move ten thousand men over any of the passes. "We march toward the pass at Alvation. Tell your men."

General Cethal of the Ninth Brigade caught Tamas's arm.

"Alvation?" he asked. "That will take over a month of hard marching."

"Maybe two," Tamas said. "And we'll be pursued." He eyed Budwiel. Smoke rose from the city. "We have no choice."

His stomach turned. Many of his men had family in the city, camp followers of the army. The Kez would put the city to the torch. The same fear techniques they'd used in Gurla. His men would hate him for marching away while the city burned, but it was their only hope for survival. He swore to get them back to Adro—to deliver them their vengeance.

CHAPTER

8

Adamat waited just a few shops down from the tailor's. He sat on a stoop, a newspaper in his hands. His disguise today was younger, with black hair neatly greased to one side of his head in the latest style of coffee shop owners. He wore pressed brown trousers and a dress shirt with cuffs rolled up to his elbows. A matching brown jacket lay across his knee. Before he'd left that morning a quick application of Dortmoth whale ointment had given his skin a youthful glow. A false black mustache and tinted spectacles hid his face.

Adamat watched over the top of his newspaper as traffic moved through the street between shops and cafés. For two days he'd watched Haime's shop. It was nearly three o'clock on the third day and he had yet to lay eyes on Lord Vetas.

His position gave him the perfect view of Haime's shop. He could see not only the exit and approach clearly but through the front window and nearly everything that went on inside as well. Men came and went from the shop. There were very few women. At around two thirty a trio of big, hard-looking men entered the shop. Adamat was sure they were Vetas's goons, but when they exited just a few minutes later, he could still see Vetas's jacket still hanging on the mannequin.

Adamat half read the articles in the newspaper. The standoff in Budwiel continued, though since the news was three or four days old, anything could have happened.

The paper reported that a sudden loss of income had caused Lady Winceslav to disband two of the eight brigades of the Wings of Adom. That could only bode ill for the war effort. Four more brigades held position north of Budwiel, while the last two stood guard at the smoldering remains of South Pike, should the Kez army try a crossing of the volcanic wasteland.

As Adamat began to read through a story on the effect of the war on Adran economics, the movement of Haime's door across the street caught his eye. He looked up in time to see a dress disappear through the door. A moment later a woman appeared in the window and began to speak with Haime.

She was a young woman with auburn curls. She couldn't have been more than eighteen or nineteen and, though young, she wouldn't be mistaken for a mere girl. She had a confident bearing with a straight back and raised chin, and the red evening dress she wore looked tailored for her figure.

Haime turned to Vetas's jacket and gestured. He waved his hand up and down the jacket and then motioned to the bottom corner, where Adamat had noticed the repaired rip. The woman nodded and Haime took the jacket down and wrapped it carefully in tissue paper.

The woman emerged a moment later with a brown box under her arm. She looked both ways, and Adamat resisted the urge to duck behind his newspaper. *Look casual*, he reminded himself. He didn't know her face. She most certainly did not know his.

She headed west down the street. Adamat climbed to his feet, folding the newspaper and tucking it under his arm, and picking up his cane.

He followed her at a respectable distance. The key to trailing someone was to stay far enough back not to be noticed but close enough that he wouldn't lose her if she deviated from her course suddenly. It helped to know whether she suspected that she was being followed. Adamat thought not, but one could never be too careful.

Adamat expected her to take a carriage within a block or two. She was dressed like a lady in that evening dress, and her heeled boots were not meant for long walks. But she stayed in the street and veered northwest, picking her way along slowly. She stopped by a street vendor's stall once to purchase a fruit tart, then continued on her way.

She turned down a quiet street in the Routs. It was a wealthy part of town, predominantly known for the banking district at its center. The street itself had less foot traffic, which worried Adamat. At some point he would become noticeable, and that would be the last thing he wanted.

He fell back another forty feet before turning onto the same street. He was just in time to see the woman disappear into a large three-story townhouse.

The house had a broad front that came all the way up to the street. The walls were white brick, and the shutters blue. It was quite large, of the type built to house several families of the growing middle class. If it involved anyone else but Vetas, Adamat would have passed the house by as being too out in the open and ordinary.

As it was, he wondered if perhaps he'd made a mistake. Maybe the jacket did not belong to Vetas. Maybe he'd been watching the wrong jacket through the window of Haime's shop. Perhaps the woman had noticed him following her and had come here to give him the slip.

Adamat cursed under his breath. There were too many variables.

He walked down the street at a slow pace, taking long, casual steps as if admiring the houses. He drew close to the house and made a mental note as to the number and street name, and let his eyes wander past each of the windows. Surely, Vetas would have a man keeping watch if this was his headquarters.

Nothing. Adamat tried not to dwell on disappointment, but there was absolutely nothing to mark this house as belonging to Vetas. He would have to check the property records.

Just as Adamat was passing by the last window, he caught sight of a face. It was a boy of six, watching as the traffic passed his home. He waved to Adamat.

Adamat waved back.

No. This couldn't be Lord Vetas's house. What use could he possibly have for a small boy?

Unless Lord Vetas had a son. That seemed unlikely. The boy shared nothing of Vetas's facial structure. A ward? No. Vetas was a spy for Lord Claremonte. He wouldn't keep a ward. Perhaps another hostage? That did seem a possibility.

Adamat continued down the street. He'd take the next carriage and come back and stake out the house. It was his only lead at this point.

He climbed into a carriage and took his seat, only to find someone else climb in behind him. It was a street sweeper, his face and clothes grimy from a long day at work in the sun.

"Pardon me," Adamat started to say, when he saw the pistol in the street sweeper's hand.

He felt a cold bead of sweat trickle down the small of his back.

"What's this all about?" Adamat said.

"Your pocketbook," the man said, his voice a growl.

Relief swept over Adamat. A mugging. That's all this was. Not one of Vetas's men, having recognized him going past. Adamat slowly removed his pocketbook from his vest and handed it to the thief. It wouldn't do the man much good. Only fifty krana in banknotes inside. No checks or identification.

The man flipped through the pocketbook with one hand, sure to keep the pistol on Adamat. A few moments and the man would exit the carriage and disappear into the afternoon crowds.

But then, this was the Routs. Who had the stones to pull a mugging on a residential street in the Routs in the middle of the afternoon? Adamat opened his mouth.

That's when he recognized the child in the window.

That boy was the son of Duke Eldaminse. The royalists had fought a small war with Tamas in the city center with the goal of putting him on the throne after Manhouch's execution. Adamat remembered the boy from a job he did for the Eldaminse family almost a year ago.

The thief looked up at Adamat. "Not good enough," he said.

"What?"

The thief flipped the pistol around in his hand, and the last thing Adamat saw was the butt of the weapon coming at his face.

When Taniel awoke, Fell was sitting next to his hammock.

They were back in Kin's mala den. Smoke curled through the air, but it wasn't mala. Cherry tobacco, by the smell. He could see Fell out of the corner of his eye, a short-stemmed pipe hanging from the corner of her mouth.

A woman smoking a pipe. Not something Taniel had seen often. Most of the women he knew preferred Fatrastan cigarettes.

The union undersecretary was a handsome woman. Far too severe for Taniel. With her hair back and thin face she reminded him of a governess he'd once had. He watched her for several moments through half-closed eyes, wondering what she was thinking. She didn't seem to notice that Taniel was awake. She was staring across the room. Taniel shifted in his hammock to see what Fell was looking at.

Ka-poel. Of course. She sat next to the stairs, forming a wax figurine with her fingers. Her satchel sat on her lap. She glanced up at the undersecretary every so often. She was making a doll. Of Fell.

Taniel wondered if the undersecretary seemed enough of a threat to her to warrant a doll, or if she had just started making one for every person they met. She was going to run out of room in her satchel if the latter proved to be the case.

The last four days were a blur. Taniel reached into his memory, but the only thing he found was mala smoke and the ceiling of Kin's mala den. Before that...

Ricard Tumblar wanted Taniel to run for the First Ministry with him.

That meant politics.

Taniel hated politics. He had witnessed firsthand the power grabs of the mercantile elite in Fatrasta as their war for independence marched toward success; the backstabbing, the conniving. Ricard claimed that none of that was to happen. Ricard claimed that these would be elections, open and fair to the public; that the government would be chosen by the people.

Ricard, like most politicians, couldn't be trusted.

But that didn't seem enough for a four-day mala binge. Why would Taniel come back to this hole and—

Oh yes. Ricard had mentioned something about informing Field Marshal Tamas that Taniel was awake and doing well. Ricard, no matter what Taniel had said, did not seem to understand that Tamas would demand Taniel's immediate presence on the front lines.

That was a good thing, Taniel tried to tell himself. He was useful. He could get back there and help defend his country.

By killing. The one thing Taniel seemed to be any good at. Pit, he'd even killed a god. Not that anyone believed it.

He shifted in his hammock, reaching for his mala pipe and the enormous ball of the sticky substance Kin had left him.

The mala was gone.

"Awake?" Fell said, her attention leaving Ka-poel.

Taniel pushed himself up. He checked his coat pocket—he still had a coat, that was good—then his trousers and the lip of the hammock.

"What are you looking for?" Fell asked. By her expression, she knew exactly what Taniel was looking for.

"Where's my mala?"

"From what Kin said, you smoked it all. You ran out sometime last night." Fell tossed something into her mouth and crunched. "Cashews?" she asked, holding out a paper bag made from an old newspaper toward Taniel.

Taniel shook his head. He checked the mala pipe. Nothing left. Then the floor. "That thieving Gurlish must have taken the rest of the ball. I got enough to last me weeks."

"I know the rate you were smoking that stuff," Fell said. "I don't think Kin gypped you. He knows where the money came from."

Taniel frowned. Where had the money come from? He looked up at Fell. Ah, that's right. Ricard.

"You know," Fell said, "Ricard's mala den has much better quality mala. The mats are silk, and the entertainment is better than Kin's daughter."

Taniel felt his stomach lurch. He fell back into his hammock. Kin's daughter. Taniel didn't remember anything. "Did I . . . ?"

Fell shrugged and looked to Ka-poel. Ka-poel gave a slight shake of her head.

Taniel let out a small sigh. The last thing he needed to do right now was bed a Gurlish mala-den owner's daughter.

"What do you want?" he asked Fell.

Fell tapped her pipe out on her shoe and put it in her pocket, then tossed more cashews into her mouth. "We got word from your father today."

Taniel sat up straight. "And?"

"A few things of note to report. The Kez were preparing to attack the next day. That would be three days ago. He was planning on leading a counteroffensive with his best men."

"How many Kez soldiers?"

"Rumors say a million. Tamas didn't say."

His best soldiers meant the Seventh and Ninth brigades. And rumors of a million? That was twice the size of the army at the Battle of Shouldercrown. Even if it were exaggerated ten times, Tamas was still leading ten thousand men against a hundred thousand. Bloody brash fool.

It somehow made it worse that Tamas would probably win.

"Oh," Fell added, as if as an afterthought. "He asked after you."

Taniel sniffed. "'Where's my damned useless son? I need him on the line.' Something like that?"

"He asked if you'd made any recovery and if the doctors thought his presence would help in any way."

"Now I know you're lying," Taniel said. "Tamas wouldn't leave a battlefield for anyone." *Not even me. Especially not me.*

"He's been very worried. We sent word that you seemed better, but who knows if it reached him before the battle." Fell reached into her paper bag for another cashew, a small smile on her lips.

"But you didn't tell him I'm awake?"

"No. Ricard thought that perhaps you'd like some time to recover."

So Taniel's entreaties to keep his father in the dark *had* done some good.

"More like he's worried that Tamas will send for me the minute he knows I'm not laid out."

"That too," Fell admitted.

"Of course." Taniel fell back into his hammock and sighed. He felt tired and used. What was he, other than a tool for others? "That old bastard Tamas—"

He was cut off by the sound of a door upstairs banging open.

The stairs into the den shook, and a young man burst into the room. Fell got to her feet.

"What is it?" she said.

The messenger looked around wildly at the den. His chest heaved from hard running. "Ricard wants you at the People's Court immediately."

Fell crumpled up the empty cashew bag and tossed it to the floor. "What has happened?"

The messenger looked at Taniel, then at Ka-poel, and back to Fell. He seemed on the verge of collapse.

"We've word from Budwiel. The city has fallen, put to the torch. Field Marshal Tamas is dead."

Nila sat beside the window, the curtains only slightly parted, and watched the world stroll by in top hats and coats, canes clicking on the cobbles, women tipping their bonnets back to enjoy the sun on their faces. The summer heat bore down on Adro, but no one seemed to notice. The weather was far too nice to care.

She wished she was out there enjoying it. Her room was too stuffy, and Vetas's men had nailed shut all the windows in the house. The air was thick and humid, stifling, and moment to moment she felt as if she was going to faint. Vetas had sent her on errands just yesterday, and the freedom of the sun on her face had felt so wonderful she'd almost left the city, forgetting Vetas and Jakob and all the terrible memories of the last few months.

Her heart leapt into her throat at the sound of the bedroom door opening, but she forced herself not to react outwardly. It wasn't Vetas. He came in from the hallway. Not from the door to the nursery, where Jakob played quietly with a small army of wooden horses and complained frequently about the warmth.

"Nila," a voice said. "You must get dressed."

Nila glanced at the dress laid out on her bed. One of Vetas's goons had brought it up for her an hour ago. It was a long chemise dress of white muslin with a high waistline. The trim was crimson, giving it a flair of color at the hem and the bust, and the ends of the short sleeves. It looked incredibly comfortable, and much cooler than the evening dress he'd told her to wear during her errands yesterday.

There was a silver chain on her bedside table with a single pearl the size of a musket ball, and in a box a pair of new black knee-high boots that she could tell with a glance would fit her perfectly. Three more outfits, each more expensive than the last, hung in the closet.

Presents from Lord Vetas. She'd never owned such fine clothing. The dress was plain enough, nothing gaudy, but the lines were absolutely perfect. A glance inside the hem had shown her the initials D.H.—Madame Dellehart, the finest seamstress in Adopest. The dress cost more than any regular laundress would earn in a year.

"Nila," the voice insisted. "Get dressed."

The expensive clothes and the jewelry made Nila sick to her stomach. She might as well accept presents from a demon as from Lord Vetas. She knew they came with a price.

"I'm not going to," Nila said.

Footsteps creaked across the floorboards. Faye knelt in front of Nila and took her hand.

They'd been cooped up in this manor together for six days and Nila still didn't know much about the woman. She knew that Faye's son was being held as a prisoner in the basement, and that she had other children elsewhere, also prisoners of Lord Vetas. She also knew that Faye would kill Vetas, given the opportunity.

At least, she'd try. Nila was beginning to wonder whether Vetas could be killed. He didn't seem human; he barely ate, he didn't sleep, and he didn't get drunk no matter how much wine he consumed.

Faye tugged at Nila's hand. "Up," she said. "Get dressed."

"You're not my mother," Nila said. The words came out as a snarl.

"She'd tell you the same thing if she were here."

Nila leaned forward. "She's dead. I never knew her, and neither did you. Maybe she'd tell me to break this window and cut my own wrists rather than give in to Vetas's demands."

Faye stood up. The kindly entreaty written across her face seemed to disappear and her expression hardened. "Maybe," she said. "If so, she was a fool." Faye began to pace the room.

Nila had guessed her to be a housewife of some middle-class merchant. She wondered what value Faye had to Lord Vetas. Faye hadn't spoken of it. And only a few words here and there about her children. In fact, the woman was far too calm. Ever since her initial outburst the night she'd been brought in, Faye had been meek as a dormouse. Nila imagined that if she had children, she'd not rest until they were out of danger. Faye was either very patient—and a stronger woman than Nila gave her credit for—or something else. Perhaps a ruse by Vetas? A spy?

That didn't make sense. Nila wasn't worth spying on. If Vetas wanted something from her, he was the type of man to torture it out.

Either way, Nila didn't trust Faye. She couldn't trust anyone here in the Vetas's lair.

"If you don't get dressed," Faye said, "Vetas will take out his anger on you or the boy. Maybe both."

"I'm not his whore," Nila said.

"He's not asked you to do anything degrading." The silent "yet" hung in the air for a moment. "Just to accompany him on his errands. It'll get you out of this damned house again. I'll keep an eye on Jakob while you're gone. Here," Faye said, "let me help you."

Nila let Faye pull her to her feet and strip off her old dress.

"There's new undergarments," Faye said, lifting a small box from the bed.

Nila snatched the box and threw it to the floor. "I've seen them, thank you," she snapped. "Only a whore wears a shift like that." She took a deep breath, realizing that her hands were shaking.

Faye let her arms drop to her side. She stepped to the nursery door, looking in on Jakob, and then closed it. She turned to Nila, hands on her hips.

"Have you seen the room in the basement?" Faye asked.

Nila stared back defiantly. Who was this old woman to demand things of her?

"Well?" Faye said.

Nila nodded sharply and tried not to think of the room with the long tables and blood stains and sharp knives on the bench.

"He showed them to me, too," Faye said. "When I first got here. I don't want to go to that room and I imagine you don't, either. So keep him happy."

"I'm..."

"I don't care who you are," Faye said, "or why you're here. But you seem to care for Jakob. Vetas is not the kind of man to hesitate in turning his insidious practices on children."

"He wouldn't."

Faye took a step closer to Nila. Nila made herself stand her ground, but a look in the woman's eye frightened her.

Faye said, "He cut off my boy's finger while I watched. While my children watched. We all screamed, and his goons held us back. Then he sent the finger to my husband, to ensure his cooperation in one of Vetas's plans." Faye spit on the floor.

"And what are you doing now?" Nila said.

"I'm waiting."

"For what?" Nila scoffed.

"My chance." The words were barely audible. Faye wiped a tear from the corner of her eye and took a deep breath. "There's time for fury. And there's time for patience. And Vetas's reckoning will come."

"What if I were to tell him what you said? How do you know you can trust me?"

Faye tilted her head to one side. "Go ahead and tell him if you want. You think he doesn't know that I'd pull his guts out through his ass if I got the chance?" Faye shook her head in disgust. "My husband is an inspector. He's a smart man, a principled man. He's always thought the nobility were a load of inbred fools. I once asked him how he could put up with a baron's mockery or the obtuse idiocy of a duchess long enough to finish a high-profile case."

Nila remained silent, watching the side of Faye's face while she talked.

"He said," Faye went on, "that swallowing his pride and being patient in the face of adversity had allowed him to feed and protect his family for years, whereas giving in to his instincts to fight back would only land him in prison, or worse. Waiting is all I can do right now. So I wait. And you should, too. Put on the damned dress."

Nila watched the woman for any sign of dishonesty. There was fire in her eyes. Fury. The kind only a mother is capable of.

"Give me some privacy," Nila said.

She was dressed by the time there was a knock on the door. Not from Jakob's nursery but from the hallway. Nila swallowed her fear as she heard the door open and was glad that she had put on the clothes.

"That's progress," Lord Vetas said. "Turn around."

She turned to face him, forcing herself to meet his eyes.

He looked her up and down and slowly swirled the wine in the glass in his right hand. "You'll do," he said.

"For what?" she asked.

If he heard the anger in her voice, he ignored it. "I've been trying to secure a luncheon with a woman named Lady Winceslav for some time. I have finally succeeded. You will accompany me to the luncheon as my niece. You are a shy girl, and will say nothing more than 'yes, ma'am' or 'no, ma'am.' I intend on courting her, and she'll be more amiable to the idea if I have a close female relative. I'll only need you for a few weeks, at most."

"Who is—"

"That is of no concern of yours. Play your part well and you'll find I allow you to keep the small measure of freedom I've permitted. Play it poorly and I will punish you. Understand?"

"Yes," Nila said.

"Good. Where's the boy?"

Nila wished there was some kind of lie she could tell him. But where else would Jakob be but in his nursery? "Jakob," she called, "come in here, please!"

The door to the nursery opened and Jakob skipped across the room. He looked up at Vetas with a smile on his face. "Hello!"

Vetas grinned at him. The expression reminded Nila of a polished skull she'd seen once in an apothecary's shop. "Hello, my boy," Vetas said. "How are you enjoying your new clothes?"

Jakob spun around, arms out, to show off a smart suit of a blue jacket, matching knee-length pants, and high socks. "They're very nice," Jakob said. "Thank you."

"My pleasure, child," Vetas said. "I brought you something." He stepped back into the hallway and came back with a box not much bigger than the one Nila's boots had arrived in. Setting the box on the floor, he flipped off the top to reveal a set of wooden soldiers and horses, twenty in all.

Jakob gasped with delight and set about pulling them from the box all at once, scattering them across the floor.

"Take them to your room," Nila said.

Jakob stopped unpacking and cast Nila a scowl. He put the toys back in and began to drag the box toward the nursery.

"Do you like them?" Vetas asked.

"Of course! Thank you, Uncle Vetas!"

"You're welcome, child."

Vetas's grin disappeared the moment Jakob was out of sight. He took a sip of his wine. "Be ready in half an hour," he said. He left the room, and Nila heard the door lock from the outside.

"*Uncle* Vetas," Jakob had said.

Nila wondered how Faye planned on killing Vetas, and if perhaps Nila would get her chance first.

CHAPTER
9

Taniel hurried through the streets of Adopest, blinded by disbelief. Tamas dead? It couldn't be. The old bastard was too stubborn to die. It was late morning and the traffic was thick, and he had to shoulder his way past pedestrians and dodge carriages and carts. He could hear Fell apologizing to the people Taniel bowled over.

Taniel paused momentarily to make sure Ka-poel was still with them. She was right beside him, faithful as his own shadow. Fell appeared out of the crowd. Of the messenger who'd found them in the mala den, there was no sign.

"Pole," he said. "Do you know if he's dead?"

Ka-poel seemed taken aback.

He took her by the shoulders and pulled her closer. "Did you ever make a doll of him? Do you have some kind of connection?"

Her frown cleared and she shook her head. Nothing.

"Pit." Taniel turned around.

"I'm sorry about your father," Fell said, coming up beside him.

"I'll believe the old bastard is dead when I see his body," Taniel said. He suddenly felt ill as a vision of Tamas lying cold and stiff in an open coffin filled his mind. He pushed the vision aside, but found himself leaning on Ka-poel for support.

She looked up at him with her glass-green eyes. They contained a mix of emotions: anger, confusion, sympathy, resolve. Her eyes hardened and he looked away.

"Where the pit are we, anyway?" he asked. "I don't recognize anything."

"Because you've been charging headlong through the crowds," Fell said. "This way to the People's Court." She pointed east. They'd been going north.

Taniel nodded. "Lead on," he said. He still had his hand on Ka-poel's shoulder. She hadn't moved it. "Pole," he said, "I..." He stopped. His mind was a haze, but the man coming toward him along the street looked familiar. Taniel could have sworn he'd seen him hanging around Kin's mala den. He was tall, with wide shoulders and a slight limp. Something was off about him.

The man looked up and into Taniel's eyes. It was all the warning Taniel got.

The man took two great strides toward Taniel. He shouldered Ka-poel out of the way and then Taniel felt the man's fist connect with his sternum. He was thrown up, above the heads of the crowd, and then tumbled to the ground, landing shoulder-first on the hard cobbles.

Taniel gasped in ragged breaths. Had his ribs been broken?

A small crowd gathered around Taniel. He heard voices asking if he was all right. A gentleman nudged Taniel's arm with his cane. A woman screamed.

Only one kind of creature could have hit Taniel that hard.

A Warden.

Taniel snatched the gentleman's cane, ignoring a shout of protest, and pushed himself to his feet in time to see a young woman thrown to the ground as the Warden pushed past her and grasped Taniel by the throat with both hands.

Steel jutted from the Warden's throat and stopped mere inches from Taniel's eyes. The Warden threw him to the ground and whirled, to reveal a stiletto jammed into the back of his neck right at the spine. The Warden gurgled, and attacked Fell, who danced out of the way quicker than Taniel would have given her credit for.

Taniel leapt to his feet and brought the cane down on the back of the Warden's head. The hardwood cane splintered from the force of the blow.

The Warden barely flinched. He turned toward Taniel, then back at Fell, as if trying to decide which threat to attack. While they watched, he pulled a handkerchief from his pocket and with the other hand reached back and slid the stiletto from his own spine. Vile, black blood spurted from the hole in his neck. Taniel heard someone be violently sick on the street.

The Warden pushed his handkerchief into his wound to stop the bleeding. The whole grisly procedure had taken less than five or six seconds. The Warden then turned on Fell, leaping quickly.

Taniel was ready. He jumped forward, holding the jagged end of the broken cane like a dagger in one hand. He drew back his arm to ram it into the Warden's back.

Something hit Taniel from the side. His teeth rattled. His vision went dark.

A second later and Taniel was staring up into the distorted face of another Warden. The Warden had his knee on Taniel's chest and his hands closed around Taniel's throat. Taniel squirmed, but he didn't have the strength to fight. He needed powder.

Taniel was able to bring his knee up between them, pushing the Warden's weight off his chest. He brought the broken cane around with his one free arm and stabbed it deep into the Warden's arm. The Warden laughed and put his knee back on Taniel's chest.

Taniel groaned as the knee was pushed into his sternum with additional weight. Ka-poel was on the Warden's back. She stabbed her long needle into the Warden's spine again and again. The Warden shook like a bull trying to throw off an unwanted rider. Taniel thought he felt something pop in his chest.

The Warden stood, unable to get Ka-poel off his back, and Taniel gasped, feeling the air rush back into his lungs with exhilaration. He needed to get out. To get away. He needed powder.

He rolled onto his belly and lurched up to his knees. The Warden lashed out with one boot, kicking Taniel back to the cobbles. Taniel struggled to his feet. Behind him, Ka-poel fought to stay on the Warden's back as he reached his over-long arms out behind him to try to peel her off.

People were calling for the city police now. The crowds had gathered, but kept their distance.

Ka-poel couldn't win this fight. But then, neither could Taniel. He reached out with his senses. There had to be powder around here somewhere. Someone had to have some.

He stumbled over to a young man in a bowler cap who was carrying a rifle over one shoulder. It was a Hrusch, and it looked freshly bought—it hadn't once been fired. Taniel grasped the young man by the front of his shirt. "Your powder horn! Give it to me!"

The young man tried to pull away. Taniel reached into his kit and felt his hand close around the smooth cylindrical shape of the powder horn. He wrenched it out of the bag triumphantly and spun back to see Ka-poel still on the Warden's back, if only barely.

"Pole, down!"

Ka-poel released her grip and was thrown to one side. Taniel held the powder horn like a grenade and threw it overhand. He reached out with his mind to ignite the powder and warp the blast to blow the creature to bits.

Nothing happened.

The Warden caught the powder horn in one hand. He stared

Taniel in the eye and flipped the horn around so the tapered end pointed toward himself, and *bit* through the horn. Powder spilled out from between his lips. His tongue lapped at the powder, grinding it between his teeth.

Taniel backed up until he thumped against the young man he'd stolen the powder horn from.

"Charges," he said. "I need powder charges!" A cold sweat broke out on Taniel's forehead. This Warden. This thing…

The young man turned and ran. Taniel heard screams and saw more people fleeing. He felt his boot hit something as he tried to step back again. The young man had dropped both his kit and his rifle.

Taniel rummaged inside the kit quickly, sure not to take his eyes off the Warden. There was a handful of powder charges. He crushed the end of one between his fingers and drew a line of the black powder on the back of his hand. The Warden was still eating the powder from the powder horn. *All of it.*

It didn't make sense, but somehow the Warden was a twisted reflection of Taniel himself. This Warden was a powder mage.

Taniel snorted the powder.

For a few moments, Taniel thought he might faint. At the edge of his vision the world went dark before suddenly becoming so stark it hurt his eyes. He flexed his hands, then felt his chest. No pain. He gritted his teeth and took the rifle in both hands.

The Warden charged him without warning. Taniel stepped to one side and gripped the barrel with both hands, bringing the stock back over his shoulder and whipping it out and around into the Warden's face.

The hickory stock shattered and the Warden went down with a satisfying thump. He flopped onto his stomach and pushed himself to his knees, then rammed himself into Taniel's chest.

Taniel backpedaled, trying to stay on his feet. He wouldn't be able to wrestle a Warden down on the ground—not if the Warden was in a powder trance. Taniel set one foot behind him to stop his backward movement and wrapped his arms around the Warden's middle. He jerked the Warden off balance and let go.

The Warden rolled away from Taniel and slowly got to his feet.

The creature's face was a mess of pulped flesh and slivers of wood. Blood streamed from his nose and mouth, and one of his eyes was swollen shut. He bared his teeth at Taniel. Half of them were missing.

"What the pit are you?" Taniel said.

The Warden cocked his head to one side. He lifted his brown hair, which was tied loosely over his right shoulder in a ponytail, to reveal the raised red welt of a brand. The image of a rifle about the length of a man's finger had been burned into his skin.

It was the brand that Kez Privileged gave to powder mages before their execution.

The Warden let his hair fall back into place. He watched Taniel for a moment, then looked to his side. Ka-poel was there, her long needle in hand, crouched low. She snarled at the Warden.

"Pole, get back..."

The Warden leapt toward Ka-poel. He moved with incredible speed, crossing the distance in the blink of an eye.

Taniel was faster now that he was in his powder trance. He shot toward the Warden, only to see the Warden twist at the last second. Taniel's fist soared past the Warden's face and he felt the Warden's fingers tighten around his neck once again.

The Warden wouldn't try to choke him this time. He'd wring Taniel's neck, snapping it like a child snaps a matchstick.

Taniel jabbed his hand at the Warden's chest. The Warden barely grunted. Taniel jabbed again and again, lightning fast. He felt the Warden's fingers lose their strength. Ka-poel threw herself at the Warden. He backhanded her, tossing her to the cobbles.

Taniel saw red in the corner of his vision. His mind's eye saw

Ka-poel's body in the street, her neck bent at the wrong angle, lifeless eyes staring into the sky.

The Warden suddenly sagged. Taniel made a fist with his hand, pulled it back...

And stopped in horror. His hand was covered in the Warden's black blood. Between his fingers, the flesh still clinging to it, he held one of the Warden's thick ribs. He looked down. The Warden, collapsed, stared back up at him. His coat was soaked through with blood.

Taniel saw the vision of Ka-poel's lifeless body again in his mind and rammed the Warden's own rib through its eye.

He stood for several moments, gasping in ragged breaths. Something touched him and he nearly screamed, his body was so tense. It was Ka-poel. She wasn't dead. She put one small hand on his, heedless of the Warden's blood.

"I've never seen a powder mage do that," Fell said, breathless, as she approached them through the empty street. The front of her secretary's smock was covered in black Warden's blood, as well as in some of her own. One cheek was red and swollen, but she didn't seem to notice.

"Where's the other Warden?" Taniel asked.

"He ran," Fell said.

"You're not just an undersecretary," Taniel said, remembering the long stiletto Fell had fearlessly jammed into a Warden's throat. "Wardens don't run."

"He did when he saw what you did to his friend," Fell said. "I kept him busy until then." She sniffed. "You're not an ordinary powder mage."

Taniel looked down at his hands. He'd punched through the Warden's skin and ripped out its rib. No one could do that. Not even he could, in the deepest powder trance. Then again, maybe a god killer could. Something had happened to him up on South Pike.

"I guess not." He looked around at the carnage. The closest people were over a hundred paces away, watching and pointing. He heard Adran police blowing their whistles as they grew close.

"This was a trap," Taniel said. "A Kez trap. How are they in the city? I thought Tamas rooted out the traitor Charlemund and his Kez accomplice."

"He did," Fell said. She seemed troubled.

Taniel fingered a powder charge and closed his eyes. Back in a powder trance. It felt incredible. His senses were alive. He could smell every scent on the air, hear every sound in the street.

His heart still thundered from the fight.

"I'm leaving," he said, taking Ka-poel by the hand.

"Ricard..." Fell began.

"Can go to the pit," Taniel said. "I'm going south. If Tamas is truly dead, and the Kez are making Wardens out of powder mages, then the army will need me."

Tamas rode beside Olem at the head of the Seventh Brigade. The column stretched out behind them, twisting along the Great Northern Highway as it rose and fell through the foothills of the Adran Mountains. His men were already dusty and tired, and the journey to get back into Adro had barely begun.

They marched northwest, unsheltered by Mihali's sorcerous fog that had allowed them to escape the Kez army four days before. To the east, the Adran Mountain Range cut into the sky with craggy, snow-topped peaks, while the sweltering summer heat beat down on Tamas's army. To the south and west, the Amber Expanse—the breadbasket of the Nine, and the source of the Kez's great wealth— spread out as far as the eye could see.

Tamas would have preferred to march on foot beside his men. But his leg still had a twinge to it, and he needed to be able to get up and down the column quickly. His orders had seen many officers' horses redistributed to the pickets, joining his two hundred cavalry in scouting.

"We're running out of food," Olem said from horseback beside Tamas.

It wasn't the first time Olem had mentioned rations, and it wouldn't be the last.

"I know," Tamas said. His men had their basic kit with a week's worth of road rations. No camp followers, no supply train. They'd marched double-time for four days now, and he had no doubt that some of his men had already finished their reserve against orders. "Give the order for half rations," Tamas said.

"We already did, sir." Olem chewed nervously on the butt of a cigarette.

"Halve it again."

Tamas looked west. It was infuriating. Millions of acres of farmland within sight, seemingly within a stone's throw. The reality was they couldn't be any farther away. The closest crops might be eight miles distant, without roads to reach them. No way to traverse the foothills and get down on the plain, forage with over ten thousand soldiers, and get back up to the road without losing a full two days' worth of marching.

It was their lead on the Kez armies that Tamas could not risk, even for food.

"Put together more foraging parties," Tamas said. "Twenty men each. Tell them not to range more than a single mile off the Northern Highway."

"We'll have to drop our pace," Olem said. He spit out his cigarette butt and reached in his pocket for another, only to examine it for a moment and slip it back in his jacket. He muttered something under his breath.

"What's that?" Tamas asked.

"I said I'm going to run out of cigarettes sooner or later."

Cigarettes were the least of Tamas's worries. "The men are exhausted." He turned in his saddle to look back along the column. "I can't push them double-time another day. The only way they've been able to go so fast for so long is thanks to the residuals of Mihali's food."

Olem saluted and headed down the column.

Tamas wished that the god had accompanied them on the ill-fated flanking maneuver. He ran his eyes over the faces of the men of the Seventh and Ninth. For the most part, his men met his gaze. These were hard men. His very best. They'd done twenty-five miles a day for four days. Kez infantry averaged twelve.

He caught sight of a rider coming up along the column. The figure looked huge, even on a cavalry charger.

Gavril.

Tamas tipped his hat to his brother-in-law as he came up alongside.

Gavril wiped the sweat from his face with one long sleeve and took a few gulps from his canteen. He'd discarded his grungy Mountainwatcher's furs on the heat of the high plains and wore only his faded Watchmaster's vest and a pair of dark-blue pants from an old cavalry uniform.

He grunted a hello. No salute from Gavril. Tamas would have been surprised to get one.

"What news?" Tamas asked.

"We've spotted the Kez," Gavril said. No "sir" either.

Tamas felt his heart leap into his throat. He knew the Kez were on his trail. It would be stupid not to realize that. But for four days they'd not seen any sign of the Kez armies.

"And?" Tamas lifted his own canteen to his lips.

"At least two brigades of Kez cavalry," Gavril said.

Tamas spit water all down the front of him. "Did you say *brigades*?"

"Brigades."

Tamas let out a shaky breath. "How far?"

"I'd guess fifty-five miles."

"Did you get close enough for an accurate count?"

"No."

"How hard are they pushing?"

"Can't be sure. Kez cavalry will make forty miles a day on the open plain if they push hard. An army of that size, and in the foothills—twenty-five, maybe thirty miles a day."

Which meant that if Tamas allowed his men rest and forage, the Kez would catch them in seven days. If Tamas was lucky.

"In six days," Gavril said, "you'll hit the edge of the Hune Dora Forest. The terrain will be too steep for cavalry to surround us. They'll be able to dog our heels, but nothing more. Not till we reach the Fingers of Kresimir."

Tamas closed his eyes, trying to remember the geography of northern Kez. This was Gavril's old haunt, back when he was Jakola of Pensbrook, the most famous womanizer in all of Kez.

"The Fingers of Kresimir," Tamas said. He knew the location, but it sounded familiar for more than just its mark on a map . . .

"Camenir," Gavril said quietly.

Tamas felt a sliver of ice creep down his spine despite the heat. A flash of memory, and once again he was standing beside a shallow grave, dug with bare hands in the cold of night beside the torrent of a raging river. The end of a daring—but ultimately failed—plan, and the most harrowing escape of Tamas's long career.

Gavril tugged at the front of his sweat-soaked vest. "We'll be going right by. I'm going to stop and pay my respects."

"I don't think I could find him," Tamas said, though he knew it was a lie. The location of the grave was burned into his memory.

"I can," Gavril said.

"It's quite a ways off the road. If I remember right."

"You'll stop too."

Tamas looked back at his column of soldiers again. They

marched on, the dust rising above them carried into the sky by a light breeze.

"I have men on the march, Jakola," he said. "I'm not stopping for anything."

Gavril sniffed. "It's 'Gavril' now, and yes, you will be stopping." He went on, not giving Tamas the chance to object. "You can lose the Kez entirely at the Fingers. We just have to reach the first bridge before them."

The Fingers of Kresimir were a series of deep, powerful snow-fed rivers off the Adran Mountains. They were impossible to ford, even on horseback. The Great Northern Road traversed them by a series of bridges built almost a hundred years ago.

"*If* we can reach the bridge before them," Tamas said, thankful to leave the topic of that lonely grave behind. "Even if we do, the cavalry can go west and around and be waiting for us when we come down onto the plains."

"You'll think of something."

Tamas ground his teeth together. He had eleven thousand infantry and two hundred cavalry, and just a four-day lead on a group of Kez cavalry that could very well equal his numbers. Dragoons and cuirassiers had more than just an edge on infantry in open battle.

"We need food," Tamas said.

Gavril looked toward the west and the tantalizing wheat fields of the Amber Expanse. "If we slow down too much to forage, the cavalry will reach us before Hune Dora Forest. Once we reach the forest, there are few farms. Foragers might bag deer and rabbits, but not enough to go around."

"And the city itself?"

Tamas remembered there was a settlement just south of Hune Dora Forest. Whether the forest took its name from the settlement, or the other way around, Tamas did not know.

"It's generous calling it a 'city.' It has walls, sure, but there can't be more than a few hundred people. We might be able to buy or steal enough food for a day or two." Gavril paused. "I hope you're not planning on stripping the countryside of everything. The people here have it hard enough. Ipille treats his serfs worse than Manhouch ever did."

"An army needs food, Jak... Gavril."

Tamas stared toward the mountains, barely noticing the white peaks. He had to balance this army perfectly. They needed food and safety. If they reached Hune Dora Forest without food, his men would begin to starve and desert. If they took too long to forage, the cavalry would reach them before the forest and have their way with the entire column.

Olem returned from his task, cantering up beside Tamas and Gavril.

"Olem," Tamas said. "Signal the column to stop." He paused to examine the countryside. To the left of the road an overgrown field sloped down toward a ravine a half mile off. "This here, it'll do."

"For what, sir?"

Tamas steeled himself. "It's time I talk to the men. Assemble them in ranks."

It took nearly an hour for the last of the columns to catch up. It was valuable time lost, but thus far Tamas had left the officers to tend to their men and keep them informed. If he was going to keep command of this lot—retain their discipline and loyalty over the next few weeks—he needed to speak to them himself.

He stood on the edge of the road and looked down the slope. The field had been trampled, the green replaced by Adran blue, standing at ease in ranks like so many blades of grass.

Tamas knew that many of these men would die without reaching their homes.

"'Tention!" Olem bellowed.

There was an audible shifting of legs and straightening of backs as eleven thousand soldiers snapped to attention.

The world was silent. A breeze picked up, blowing down from

the mountains and pushing gently on Tamas's back. To their credit, not a single soldier reached to steady his hat.

"Soldiers of the Seventh and Ninth," he began, shouting to be heard by all. "You know what's happened. You know that Budwiel has fallen and that the Kez push in to Adro, checked only by the Adran army.

"I grieve for Budwiel. I know that you grieve with me. Many of you question why we didn't stay and fight." Tamas paused. "We were outnumbered and outclassed. The fall of Budwiel's walls made our initial strategy obsolete and we could not have won that battle. As you all know, I do not fight battles that I will not win."

There was a murmur of agreement. The anger at abandoning Budwiel had dulled in the six days since. The men understood. There was no need to dwell on it further.

"Budwiel may have fallen, but Adro has not. I promise you—I *swear* to you—that Budwiel will be avenged. We will return to Adro and join our brothers and we will defend our country!"

A cheer went up among the men. To be honest, it was half-hearted, but at least it was something. He raised his arms for quiet.

"First," he said when the noise had died down, "we have a peril-ous journey ahead of us. I won't lie to you. We have little food, no baggage train or resupply. No reinforcements. Our ammunition will dwindle and our nights will be cold. We are utterly alone in a foreign land. Even now, the enemy has set their dogs on us.

"Kez cavalry are on our trail, my friends. Cuirassiers and dra-goons, at least our number's worth and maybe more. I'd wager my hat that they are led by Beon je Ipille, the king's favorite son. Beon is a brave man and he will not be beaten easily."

Tamas could see the fear in his men's eyes. Tamas let it stew for a moment, watched the growing sense of panic. And then he reached out his hand and pointed to his men.

"You are the Seventh and the Ninth. You are Adro's finest, and that makes you the greatest infantry the world has ever seen. It is my pleasure, and my honor, to command you on the field of battle, and if it comes to it, to die with you. But I say we will not die here—on Kez soil.

"Let the Kez come," Tamas roared. "Let them send their greatest generals after us. Let them stack the odds against us. Let them come upon us with all their fury, because these hounds at our heels will soon know we are lions!"

Tamas finished, his throat raw from shouting, his fist held over his head.

His men stared back at him. No one made a sound. He could hear his heart beating in his ears, and then somewhere near the back of the assembled troops someone shouted, "Huzzah!"

Another voice joined it. Then another. It turned into a cheer, then a chant, and eleven thousand men raised their rifles over their heads and bellowed their defiance back at him, buckles and swords rattling in a sound that could have drowned out cannon fire.

These were his men. His soldiers. His sons and daughters. They would stare into the eyes of the pit itself for him. He stepped back away from the road so that they would not see his tears.

"Good speech, sir," Olem said, sheltering a match from the wind as he lit the cigarette pinched between his lips.

Tamas cleared his throat. "Wipe that grin off your face, soldier."

"Right away, sir."

"Once this quiets down, get the head of the column moving. We need to make more headway before night comes."

Olem went off about his duties, and Tamas took another few moments to gather himself. He stared to the southeast. Was that his imagination, or could he see movement in the distant foothills? No. The Kez weren't that close. Not yet.

CHAPTER 10

Adamat had spent the night in darkness, tied to a chair. At some point he hadn't been able to hold back any longer and had soiled himself. The air smelled of piss and mold and dirt. He was in a basement of a heavily trafficked building and could hear the creak and moan of floorboards as feet moved across them.

He'd yelled out loud when he first awoke in utter darkness. Someone had come to tell him to shut up. He had recognized the grizzled voice of the thief and called him a bloody dog.

The thief had left, laughing to himself.

Morning had come hours ago. Adamat could tell by the light coming in through the cracks of the floor above him. He could hear his own stomach grumbling for food. His throat was parched, his tongue swollen. His neck, legs, and back were all sore from sitting tied to the chair for fourteen hours or more.

The whale ointment he'd used to smooth his wrinkles and hide his age was beginning to burn. The stuff was supposed to be wiped off in less than twelve hours.

He felt himself begin to drift and shook his head to keep himself awake. Sleeping in this situation was deadly. He needed to be awake. To be alert. He had a head injury. It would take more light to tell if his eyes were focusing properly.

It was difficult to tell where he was. Voices above him were muffled, and no particular smells—aside from those of his own piss and the cold damp of a basement—stood out.

Adamat heard the creak of a door, then saw a light off in the corner of his vision. He turned his head—a painful movement—to watch as a lamp bobbed down a flight of stairs. He could hear two voices. The thief was not one of them.

"He hasn't said much except call Toak a bloody dog," a man said. The voice was nasal and high. "Didn't have anything in his pocketbook but a fifty-krana note and a false mustache. No checkbook. No identification. He could be a copper."

A voice answered him, too low for Adamat to hear.

"Well, yeah," the first voice said. "Most coppers carry a city mark on 'em, even if they're trying for a bust. Could be one of those undercover-spy types. The field marshal has been using them to root out Kez spies."

Another murmured answer.

The first voice had an edge of panic when he resumed speaking. "We didn't know," he said. "Toak said to grab 'im, so we did. He followed the lady back to the house."

The speaker arrived in front of Adamat with the lamp. He held it to Adamat's face. Adamat couldn't help but shy away from the flickering candlelight. He blinked against the brightness and tried to see the speaker's face and that of the murmuring man. It could be Vetas. Vetas would recognize Adamat in a second, and then he'd be a dead man, or worse.

"My name is Tinny," the first voice said. "Look up at the gov'na."

Tinny grabbed Adamat's chin and turned it toward the light. Adamat hawked the phlegm from his throat into Tinny's eye. He was rewarded with a sharp crack across the face that knocked his chair over.

Adamat lay on his back, his hands crushed underneath him, stars floating across his vision. He couldn't help the moan of pain that escaped his lips. He wondered if his wrists were broken.

"Pick him up," the murmuring voice said.

Tinny hung the lamp from the ceiling and righted Adamat's chair. Adamat considered head-butting the man, but thought his head had taken enough damage lately.

"What do you want from me?" Adamat tried to growl the words, but they came out as a rasp from his dry throat.

"That depends," the murmured voice continued. "Why were you following the woman in the red dress?"

Why...? So it wasn't Vetas. Or Vetas hadn't recognized him yet.

"Wasn't following anyone," Adamat said. He tried to maintain a northwestern drawl. "Just shopping and going for a walk."

"Without any identification? And a false mustache? Put the light to his face."

Tinny grabbed Adamat's chin again and shoved the lantern up next to it.

The murmuring voice gave a soft chuckle. "Ah, you bloody fool."

"Fool for what? Going for a walk?" Adamat said.

"I wasn't talking to you."

The lantern pulled away from Adamat's face, and he could see Tinny clearly in the light. Tinny's eyes were wide, his complexion pale. "It was an honest mistake, gov'na. I swear."

"Leave," the voice murmured. "Wait. Tell the master we have Inspector Adamat."

Tinny hung the lamp back on the ceiling and left the room. Adamat couldn't help the cold fear that spidered up the back of his neck. He squinted in the poor light, trying to see the source of that murmured voice.

"Adamat," the murmuring voice said suddenly in his ear.

Adamat started. He hadn't heard the man move, and there wasn't another person in this dank basement. "Who, now?" Adamat said. Hold the pose. Play dumb. Don't let them break you.

A soft sigh in his ear. A sudden blade against his naked throat. He had the all-too-vivid recollection of a razor blade breezing past his throat not more than two months ago. He pulled back instinctively, a sharp breath escaping him. The knife did not follow. A sudden tug at his bound wrists and they were free.

He rubbed some feeling back into them and stared straight ahead. He didn't dare assume that he'd been released. He might take a knife in the ribs or across the throat at any time. No doubt the man behind him was ready for sudden moves, and even if Adamat overpowered him, Adamat was still in a basement beneath someone's headquarters.

Adamat still didn't know where he was. The murmuring voice belonged to someone who recognized him, even in such ill light. He cycled through the names of hundreds of men, trying to match a face to the voice, but to no avail.

He felt, more than heard, the presence move back in front of him. He could make out a heavyset shadow in a sleeveless shirt. A bald head shone in the candlelight. *Definitely* not Lord Vetas.

Adamat tried to blink the blurriness from his eyes and took in a deep breath. It caught in his throat at the slight scent of sweetbell and the recollection of a similar scent in his own home the same night that the Black Street Barbers had attacked him.

"Eunuch." The word came out of his throat with a strangled sigh of relief. He felt his body sag against the ropes still tying his ankles to the chair, only to stiffen again a moment later as the realization set in that the Proprietor's eunuch might very well be working with Lord Vetas.

The eunuch turned toward Adamat. "There," he said. "Pretense dropped. Now, what were you doing following the woman in the red dress?"

Adamat sniffed. The smell of his own piss was somehow less bearable now this his hands were untied.

"Working," he said.

"On?"

"I report to Field Marshal Tamas, and him only. You should know that."

The eunuch tapped the side of his jaw with one finger, considering Adamat through narrow, unfeeling eyes.

"We're on the same side, aren't we?" Adamat said. The question came out just a little too desperate for his liking.

"In a few minutes my master will have decided what to do with you. If he decides to let you live, I suggest that you keep this little run-in to yourself."

" 'If'?"

The eunuch shrugged. "I would like to know if we are working at cross-purposes. There are rumors about you, Adamat. Finding you where we did could mean one of two things."

Adamat waited for the eunuch to elaborate on what those two things were. He didn't. "That I'm with you, or against you?" Adamat hazarded a guess.

"These things are rarely so simple as 'with or against.' "

"I was following a hunch," Adamat said. "Trying to find someone."

"Lord Vetas?"

Adamat watched the eunuch for several long seconds. No tic. No hint. No giveaways. He was as unreadable as polished marble. Was the Proprietor working with Vetas, providing enforcement and tails, as Adamat feared?

"Yes."

"Why?"

Adamat looked at his hands. In the dim light he could see the dark welts where they'd been bound. His fingers all still worked. For that he should be grateful. He knew he wouldn't feel the real pain and ache until he tried to walk. He looked back up at the eunuch.

Still unreadable. The truth could get him killed in this situation. There were a hundred lies he could tell. Adamat considered himself a good liar. But he could get himself killed with the wrong lie, even one told well, or if the eunuch even suspected a lie.

The truth it was.

"He took my family," Adamat said. "Blackmailed me, and he still has my wife and oldest son. I want to get them back, and then kill him slowly."

"A lot of violence planned, for a family man," the eunuch said.

Adamat leaned forward. " 'Family,' " he said. "Remember that word. There is nothing that will make a man more desperate and more capable of violence than endangering his family."

"Interesting." The eunuch seemed unmoved.

A door opened. Light poured into the opposite side of the cellar, and footfalls thumped down the steps.

"The master says bring him up, gov'na," Tinny said.

The eunuch scowled. "Now?"

"Yeah. Wants to see him."

Adamat smoothed the front of his soiled jacket. He didn't think he could be more nervous than he'd been when sitting in a basement, tied to a chair, at the mercy of who-knew-who, but he was.

"I'm to meet the Proprietor?"

"It appears so." The eunuch extended a hand and helped Adamat to his feet. "Don't worry," he said. "There are three men who know his face in all the Nine. You won't be one of them."

Adamat wasn't reassured. He looked down at his pants, at the cold, wet stain sticking his trousers to his legs. "How will..."

"Ah." The eunuch gestured Tinny over. "Adamat is now a guest. Have a couple of the girls clean him up, and take him to the master in twenty minutes."

Tinny shifted from one foot to the other. "He seemed awfully insistent."

"Have you seen the master's new rug?"

Tinny nodded uncertainly.

"Do you want it to smell like this cellar?"

"No, gov'na."

"Clean him up, and *then* take him to the master."

Adamat's first order of business was to get a feel for his new location. He studied the decoration and architecture, but both were utterly useless to him. Polished wood floors creaked beneath his feet. The walls were plaster over wood, the candelabras of brass. It was a spacious affair, but demurely utilitarian.

Adamat was led into a bathing room with hot running water. His clothes were stripped from him without ceremony by a pair of handmaids, so quickly he couldn't protest the impropriety of it all. When the eunuch had instructed he be bathed by a couple of girls, Adamat had expected whores. These were sturdy washing women.

His back and hair were scrubbed quickly, cold water splashed over him to rinse off the soap, and a fresh pair of trousers presented to him. When Adamat emerged from the bathing room, the same two women combed his hair and straightened his collar.

Tinny was waiting beside the door. In better light, Adamat could see he was a sickly man of medium height. He wore a cut-across, double-breasted coat with squared tails and a starched cravat. The coat, along with the cream pants and knee-high boots, were so incredibly ordinary that Adamat doubted he could pick Tinny out in a line of men on the street, despite Adamat's having memorized his face.

It was Adamat's Knack, after all. He never forgot a face, and he wouldn't forget the Proprietor's either. Just one glance was all he needed.

Tinny handed Adamat his pocketbook.

Adamat flipped it open. The fifty-krana note was still inside. Along with Adamat's false mustache.

Adamat took a proffered coat from one of the women and stuffed the pocketbook inside. He did it all without looking away from Tinny. The man returned his gaze with a slight sneer and looked Adamat up and down.

"It'll be good enough," Tinny said. "At least you don't smell of piss no more." He gave Adamat a mean grin. "You've got a mark there on your face."

From where Tinny had struck him. Charming.

"I see you cleaned the spit from yours."

Tinny's grin turned down at the corners, and he gripped Adamat's coat. In a low voice he said, "Master gives the word and I'll carve you up. It'll take me three days to kill you. I know who you are. Copper. Don't like your kind."

This close Adamat could smell the wine on Tinny's breath. That hadn't been there before. Was Tinny so terrified of the eunuch he'd gone to get a drink? Interesting. Of more interest was the way Tinny stood; a slight lean to his left, caused either by his left leg being shorter than the right or by favoring an injury to his right.

Adamat jerked his coat from Tinny's grip.

"After you," Tinny said.

"I insist." Adamat waved his hand forward.

Tinny gave him a mocking bow and stepped into the hallway. Adamat watched his legs. A definite limp, favoring his right.

Adamat lashed out without warning, his boot connecting solidly with the side of Tinny's right leg. Tinny folded sideways, his yell of surprise muffled by Adamat's hand over his mouth. Adamat took most of his weight and lowered him to the floor, putting one hand firmly against his throat.

"Don't threaten to kill a man unless you know without a doubt you'll have the opportunity," Adamat whispered. "Now, I've spent the entire summer with the most powerful people in all the Nine breathing down my neck. Do you think I care about one limping henchman? Do you think I have the time for you?

"I'm going to go talk to your master. If it goes badly, he'll kill me, I have no doubt. But I promise, if they put me alone in a room with you, that it doesn't matter how securely they bind me—I'll get loose and I'll kill you."

Adamat released Tinny's neck and mouth.

Different kinds of men responded differently to those with power over them. Some got angry. Some took it silently. Some were so terrified they'd believe anything you said, no matter how outlandish.

From the look in Tinny's eyes, Adamat believed him to be the last of these.

Adamat made his way into the grand hall. His whole body ached from the night spent tied to a chair, and he worked to suppress his own limp. He passed a dozen men and women. Dressed unremarkably, just like Tinny. Probably messengers and the like.

Adamat had been in the lairs of perhaps half a dozen crime bosses in his life. Every one had either been an opulent palace or a scumridden den of iniquity. The Proprietor's headquarters was so ordinary that it almost shocked him. It might have been the offices of some powerful but money-conscious nobleman, for all he could tell.

In the grand hall there were enforcers. Big men, scowling at everyone, pistols in their belts. They flanked the front windows and door. Adamat saw a woman he recognized, a whorehouse madame from the east side of Adopest who'd once told Adamat where to find a killer. She was dressed in her very best, and she sat on a bench beside the front door. She looked like a girl waiting to see the headmaster.

Someone gripped Adamat's arm. He surprised himself by not leaping out of his skin, and turned to look up into the face of one of the big enforcers.

Before the man could speak, Adamat said, "I'm looking for the eunuch. He just sent me for a bath and I seem to have lost my handler. I'm to see the Proprietor now."

The enforcer opened his mouth, then closed it. He scowled. Obviously not what he'd been expecting.

"Adamat," a voice came.

The eunuch drifted across the grand hall and nodded to the enforcer. In the light of the day, Adamat could see that he was wearing a tailored brown suit with long coattails and an emerald cravat. The big man stepped away, and Adamat let himself be led down a side corridor by the eunuch.

"Where is Tinny?" the eunuch asked.

"He tripped. Fell down some stairs. I told him I'd find you myself."

"Ah." The eunuch didn't seem like he would dispute Adamat's story. "Well, if you'd step inside, the master will see you now."

They'd stopped in front of a door at the side of the corridor. Nondescript. Unadorned. Adamat looked up and down the hall.

"Here?"

"Yes."

"I see."

"You were expecting something else?" the eunuch asked. "Something more grand, perhaps?"

Adamat examined the plain trappings of the hall, caught sight of a woman with a bundle of papers in her arms, wearing a long, plain dress and looking so ordinary it hurt his brain.

"No, I suppose not."

The eunuch rapped on the door.

"Come," came the brisk order.

Adamat stepped into the room and closed the door behind him.

The room was very well lit, much to Adamat's surprise. It was a significantly sized office with fine wood paneling, high-arched windows, and a fireplace framed by ornate brickwork. Two well-worn chairs sat next to the fireplace, not far from the door. At the opposite end of the room was a wide desk, partially blocked by a screen. Adamat took note that, aside from the fine rug on the floor, there were no decorations.

Beside the desk sat a severe-looking woman with a sharp jawline and pronounced crow's-feet in the corners of her eyes. Her posture was immaculate, her dress smoothed over her legs. A half-knitted scarf sat in her lap.

"Inspector Adamat?" the woman asked.

Adamat nodded, looking curiously at the screen. He could hear pen scratches from behind it.

"My name is Amber," the woman said. She pronounced the word like "amba." "You must first know that if you see the master's face, even by accident, you will die."

Adamat found himself suddenly less curious as to what was behind the screen.

"Sit," the woman said, gesturing to one of the chairs beside the fire.

Adamat sat.

Amber went on. "I speak for the master. I am his mouthpiece, and you may address yourself to me as if I were he, and I will address myself to you also as if I were he. Now, I'd like to apologize for the evening you spent in our cellar. Most unfortunate."

The scratching of the pen had stopped. Adamat noticed that Amber was no longer looked at him, but behind the screen. Perhaps reading some kind of hand language from the master?

"It was wholly unpleasant, I assure you."

"To the matter at hand," the Proprietor said through Amber. "There is a man by the name of Lord Vetas that has been causing my organization no small amount of problems."

"I don't know the name," Adamat lied, wondering why he bothered. He'd already told the eunuch about Vetas and his family.

"Come now. He's kept it very quiet, but the name has been passed around the very top levels of Tamas's military cabinet. Along with yours. I'd find it a very large coincidence that my men stumbled across you following one of Lord Vetas's spies."

"Stranger things have happened," Adamat said.

"Such as Taniel Two-Shot," the Proprietor said, "a celebrated war hero, putting a bullet between the eyes of a god on top of South Pike Mountain? Or Field Marshal Tamas, one of the most reasonable men in Adro, declaring a chef the god of Adro?"

Adamat drummed his fingers on his pantleg and watched Amber as she watched behind the screen. It was disconcerting to carry on a conversation this way, but he seemed to have no alternative. "You don't believe that tripe, do you?"

"I didn't say I believed it," said the Proprietor through his interpreter. "I tend to only believe hard facts, but if I only *acted* on hard facts, I wouldn't be here. Half of my trade is whispers and rumors. Information."

"Information is power," Adamat agreed. "You've certainly made your living well enough."

"It's not just power, it's money. But I'll give you this for free: Field Marshal Tamas is dead."

Adamat clasped his hands together to hide the sudden shaking of his fingers. Was this true? Could the field marshal be dead? If that was the case, Adamat was suddenly without a sponsor. His campaign against Lord Vetas already had little enough backing for a man that dangerous, but sixteen soldiers and an open checkbook was nothing to scoff at. Adamat wasn't sure he was prepared to take on Vetas alone.

"How do you know?" Adamat said when he trusted himself to speak. His voice wavered.

"I received this missive from General Hilanska of the Second Brigade just this morning." A hand reached out from behind the screen and gave a note to Amber. She in turn gave it to Adamat. "I assume his other councillors—Lady Winceslav, Prime Lektor, Ondraus the Reeve, and Ricard Tumblar—all received the same note."

Adamat slipped the silk ribbon off the note and unrolled it. The letters were Adran, but the single paragraph gibberish.

"A cipher?" Adamat said.

"Indeed. It says—"

Adamat cut him off. "That Kresimir has returned and Field Marshal Tamas was cut off behind enemy lines with only two brigades. He's presumed dead."

Silence from the Proprietor. Amber stared behind the screen for several moments. Her eyes opened a little wider before she delivered the Proprietor's response. "That was . . . impressive."

Adamat gave the missive back to Amber. "A perfect memory makes ciphers very easy to decode. I spent two summers as a boy memorizing the keys to over four hundred different ciphers, both common and uncommon. That one is extremely rare, but I don't forget. Kresimir. I thought Taniel Two-Shot put a bullet through his eye?"

"Gods. Rumors. I've built this empire in Adro's underworld by making very good guesses, and my guess here is that General Hilanska wouldn't say such a thing unless he believes it fully."

Adamat leaned back. He stared at the screen, feeling less intimidated for some reason. What was behind that screen? What kind of a person? The hand Adamat had seen reach out was old, obviously male, with manicured nails. The Proprietor didn't spend his whole life behind a screen. Somewhere else he had an assumed identity. One that allowed him to move about in public.

"Only a handful of people in Adopest know this information," Adamat said. "Why tell me?"

The Proprietor seemed to hesitate. "Because it puts you to the wind. Tamas was your employer."

"And you want to employ me?" Adamat felt his hackles rise. In all his life he never thought he'd have a job offer from the Proprietor himself.

"Ricard Tumblar will ask you to help with his campaign for the new ministry. He'll offer to pay well. I can pay better. Other than that, what role could you possibly fill? A place back on the police force? I don't think you want to be walking the streets in uniform over the next few years."

"What would you hire me to do?"

"That brings me around to my first question. What interest do you have in Lord Vetas?"

Adamat tilted his head to the side. The Proprietor didn't know about Adamat's wife. Which meant the eunuch hadn't told him yet. It also meant either the Proprietor wasn't working for Lord Vetas or that he was not close enough that Vetas had told him about Adamat.

"He has my wife. I'm going to find him, rescue my wife, and kill Lord Vetas."

Adamat heard a low chuckle from behind the screen. He couldn't help but scowl.

"Perfect," the Proprietor said through Amber. "Just perfect."

"Why should you care about Lord Vetas?"

"As I said, he's been causing problems for my organization."

"What kind of problems?"

"Ones that I can't handle without things becoming very noisy. He has at least sixty enforcers, and one of them is a Privileged."

Adamat's heart jumped. A Privileged? Pit, how could he deal with something like that? "It might help if you were more specific about the problems."

"None that concern you."

Adamat smoothed the front of his shirt again. "A turf war, maybe? Vetas is moving in on your sources of revenue? Stirring up trouble in the underworld? Stealing your manpower, maybe?" That would explain why Roja the Fox was one of the guards holding Adamat's children hostage—but if Roja had gone over to Vetas *without* the Proprietor's blessing, it meant that Roja thought Vetas the stronger of the two.

A scary thought indeed.

"None," the Proprietor said, Amber's translation somewhat icy, "that concern you. This meeting is over. You may leave."

Adamat blinked at the abruptness of it. "You don't want to hire me?"

"Not anymore."

"And you're not going to kill me?"

"No. Out."

Adamat stood and examined the room once more, careful not to focus too much on the screen. Everything here was of a very fine quality, but not handcrafted. The paneling was milled, the candelabras secondhand. Even the desk looked like the kind that were made a dozen-a-day at a large carpenter's workshop. Nothing here that could be traced.

Except the rug. Gurlish, by the design, and even to an inexperienced eye the fibers were finely woven.

Adamat fished inside his jacket for a handkerchief. He blew his nose noisily and dropped it, then bent and snatched it from the floor, making sure to look away from the Proprietor's desk.

When he stood, Amber still had the expectant look on her face that told him he'd overstayed his welcome. She glanced toward the door and he nodded.

Outside, the eunuch stood by the door.

"Stay here," he said, going into the Proprietor's office.

Adamat took the moment alone to examine the fibers in between his fingers. There were only a few, all crinkled and dry. He couldn't tell them from the lint in his pocket. But he knew a woman who might be able to identify them.

The eunuch emerged from the office, pulling the door closed behind him with a click. He seemed troubled. "You're free to go," he said. "Of course, we can't just have you walk out the front door. Keep the clothes."

Adamat opened his mouth to respond, when someone grabbed him from behind. A rag was shoved over his mouth and nose, and the last thing he remembered was the overpowering smell of ether.

CHAPTER
11

Taniel was awakened from his half doze at the reins by the distant report of cannon fire.

Dark thoughts swirled in his mind, thick as the clouds of smoke in the mala den. He could still see the Warden eating black powder. He could still feel the powder-enhanced strength in the monster's twisted limbs. How could the Kez have made one of those creatures out of a powder mage? From what he knew of Wardens and Privileged, that seemed impossible.

Then again, so did stabbing a Warden with its own rib after ripping it from the creature's chest.

The sudden sensation of falling made him grip the saddle horn in a panic, startling the horse. The world seemed to spin around him. He took several deep, ragged breaths. Even once he knew that he wasn't actually falling, his heart still raced. Five days without mala. His hands shook, his mouth was dry, and his head pounded. The heat of the sun beating down didn't help any of it.

A cool hand suddenly touched his cheek. Ka-poel sat in the saddle behind him, arms wrapped around his waist for most of the journey, for she didn't know the first thing about riding a horse. It should have been terribly uncomfortable to have her clinging to him in this heat, but somehow it was the only thing that gave him relief.

Not that he'd admit it to her.

It was early afternoon and the mountains were closing in on either side as they traveled into Surkov's Alley. They'd spent the night in Fendale, a large city of some hundred thousand that was swelled to four times that number with army reserves and the refugees from Budwiel.

What little sleep Taniel had managed in Fendale was restless and plagued with nightmares. He'd read once that the only way to sleep well after forming a mala addiction was with more mala.

Ka-poel removed her hand from his cheek, to his decidedly uncomfortable regret. What would he do with this girl? She seemed to think he belonged to her in some way. He could sleep with her, he supposed, but the thought of it made him feel...conflicted. She was a savage, and his servant. A companion and nothing more. There wasn't a soul in polite Adran society who wouldn't think it most improper.

When had he ever cared about what society thought proper, he reminded himself. And a savage? Taniel had seen Ka-poel's sorcery. She'd saved his life on several occasions. She was anything but "just a savage girl."

Taniel tried to blink away the fog that permeated his mind, but with little success. Drifting off like that could be dangerous. They would reach the front by tomorrow evening, and from there he'd have to find out if there were any other powder mages left in the army, and news of his father. And of course, he'd have to report to...to who? Taniel had never reported to anyone but Field Marshal Tamas.

Could Tamas really be dead? Taniel was a little surprised to feel a lump in the back of his throat at the idea. He loved Tamas, admired him even, but he didn't like him, and they had never been especially close. After all, the old bastard had ordered him to kill his best friend. Taniel didn't even know where Bo was now. Maybe he'd died on the mountain, or been executed by Tamas weeks ago.

Taniel hoped they were both alive—Tamas and Bo. There were still things that needed to be said.

As for Ka-poel...Respect. That's all Taniel was feeling. And a feeling of hopelessness, for Tamas had been Adro's best chance at winning the war.

They stopped to rest in one of the many little towns in Surkov's Alley between Fendale and Budwiel. Normally a town like this would have a couple thousand residents. With the war on, it was overflowing. Supply trains flowed through the city, and infantry reserves walked the streets in their uniforms, enjoying a few days away from the front. Taniel watched as dozens of carts rolled by, carrying wounded and dead soldiers from the front. He'd seen hundreds of such carts since leaving Adopest. It didn't bode well for the war.

"Captain, if you ignore me for another moment, I'll have you flogged."

Ka-poel, seated next to him on a grassy bank while they ate their lunch, elbowed Taniel in the ribs. Taniel looked up, feeling genuine surprise that someone was talking to him.

A colonel sat on horseback, his narrow features twisted in a scowl. He pointed his riding crop at Taniel. "Captain, what brigade are you with?" He gave Taniel a moment to answer, and then, "Wipe that stupid look off your face. Is that such a hard question?"

"I don't have one," Taniel said.

"Don't have a...are you daft? Are you a captain in the Adran army or not? Be careful how you answer, son, or I'll have you brought up on charges of impersonating an officer!"

Taniel fingered the captain's stars on his lapel. They were gold, as he'd used his silver buttons to buy mala and these were the only replacements he could get on short notice. His powder-keg pin was in his pocket. Who the bloody pit was this man? Taniel had never answered to anyone other than the field marshal. He supposed that technically he was attached to a brigade. The Seventh, maybe?

Taniel shrugged.

The colonel's face turned red. "Major!"

A woman in her midthirties rode up beside the colonel. "Sir?" She had long brown hair tied back behind her head in a single braid, and a thin face with a beauty mark on her left cheek. She saluted the colonel and then looked down at Taniel.

"Have this man arrested," the colonel said.

"Charges, sir?"

"Disrespecting a superior officer. The man didn't salute me, or answer my questions, or stand in my presence."

The major climbed down from her horse and gestured to a pair of neatly dressed soldiers to join her.

Taniel watched the three of them approach. He took a bite of mutton and cheese, chewing slowly.

"Stand up, Captain," the major said. When Taniel didn't respond, she jerked her head to one of the soldiers. He bent to grab Taniel by the arm.

Taniel lifted the pistol from his lap and cocked back the hammer, pointing it at the soldier. "Bad idea, soldier." Taniel almost cracked a smile at the looks on the faces of the major and colonel, but he doubted that would help his position.

"Uh, sir," one of the soldiers said, "are you Taniel Two-Shot?"

"Yes," Taniel said, "I am."

"I used to be with the Seventh. It's a pleasure to meet you, sir, but it seems we're supposed to arrest you."

Taniel locked eyes with the major. "That's not going to happen today."

The major retreated for a moment and held a quiet conference with the colonel. A few moments later the colonel nodded and the major and the soldiers were dismissed.

Taniel returned to his lunch, only to find the colonel still sitting on his horse not ten feet away. The man rode a little closer. Taniel looked up. He wasn't in the mood for this.

The colonel's expression was still disapproving. "Captain, I'm sorry, I didn't recognize you. We've met before, but it was years ago. Your father was a great man."

Taniel swallowed a mouthful of food. How was he supposed to answer that? "Yes, he was."

"Captain, I should warn you. The field marshal was quite lenient with all his soldiers, especially his mages. With his death there's been a shift in policy in that regard. I doubt the General Staff will make an exception for you, even with your reputation. Point a pistol at a ranking officer again and you'll be—"

"Shot?" Taniel asked, not able to keep the smirk from his face.

The colonel scowled. "Hanged."

"Thank you for the warning. *Sir.*"

The colonel nodded. "I'm glad to hear you're on your feet again, Captain. We need you on the front." He paused for a moment, as if waiting for Taniel to stand and salute him. He could have waited all day for that, as far as Taniel was concerned. After nearly a minute he turned his horse and was off at a canter.

Taniel couldn't help but wonder why the colonel wasn't on the front with the rest of the army.

"Pole," he said. "I don't know if it's a good idea for you to come with me."

She rolled her eyes at him.

"I'm serious, Pole. It's a war zone. I know you've been in war before." Pit, she'd been with him facing down the same Kez Grand

Army just a couple months ago. He'd watched her butcher half the Kez royal cabal up on South Pike. "But I've felt...strange since you brought me back. I don't know what I'll do. I'd rather not get you killed."

Taniel again remembered the blood on her hands when he awoke from the coma. He had seen dead soldiers, and a man he felt he should recognize lying on the ground unconscious. Ka-poel had tried to explain it with hand gestures. Taniel had surmised that she'd traded a life for his. Whose, he didn't know, but the thought made him sick.

Ka-poel took the piece of cheese from his hand and tossed it in her mouth. That seemed like all the answer that Taniel was going to get.

"Oh well," he said. "I had to try. It'll be good to have you at my side."

Ka-poel pursed her lips in a sly smile.

"My *side*, Ka-poel. I don't—"

She put her finger to his lips, her smile widening.

"They won't like you being with me," Taniel said. "There are some women soldiers, and fraternization is strictly prohibited. It happens all the time, of course, but the officers like to keep up appearances. They might try to make you sleep in a different tent."

Ka-poel spread her hands, questioning.

"What? Fraternization? You know. Men and women being... together. Intimately."

She pointed between them, then made a flat, chopping motion with her hand. *But we aren't.* The grin on her face made the motion appear mocking, like a child denying that they'd done something wrong when they'd been caught doing it.

It made Taniel's heart beat faster, and he could feel his face go red. "All right, girl, we're going now. Just after I piss."

When he got back to the horse, he found her sitting in the saddle already, but toward the front, as if she expected him to sit behind her.

"Move back," he said.

She ignored him. He pulled himself up into the saddle behind her, and to take the reins, he had to wrap his arms around her waist. She snuggled up against his chest and he flicked the reins with a sigh.

The number of people along the road increased as they got closer and closer to the front. In the last ten miles there were so many tents that they filled the entire valley from one side to the other. It seemed like a sea of people—soldiers, smiths, whores, cooks, laundresses, and merchants. He saw soldiers with the stripes of just about every brigade in Adro, including all of the Wings of Adom, Lady Winceslav's mercenaries. By now she'd know that Tamas was dead. Taniel wondered if she'd pull her mercenaries out of the war.

The road seemed to disappear beneath the crowd, and Taniel knew they were just one good rainstorm away from it becoming a shit hole of mud. The Addown River cut through the whole thing, a dirty mess clogged with the waste of hundreds of thousands of people. There were barges moored here and there along the river— supply ships from Adopest, no doubt bringing food, weapons, and fresh recruits.

The tents gained some order as he finally reached the army proper. He didn't think he'd ever look forward to straight lines and discipline again, but after having to push his way through the final few miles he was glad to leave the reserves and hangers-on behind him.

For most of the trip down the Alley the cannon fire had rumbled together like thunder in the distance. Now he could pick out individual blasts. The artillery crew were working full-time, it seemed. That didn't surprise him; he'd seen the Kez Grand Army.

What did surprise him was the crack and spark of sorcery he noticed as he got closer. There were Privileged fighting on the front—on both sides. Most of the Kez Cabal had been wiped out at the Battle for South Pike or at Kresim Kurga by Ka-poel. And where had Adro gotten any Privileged?

It took some questioning, but Taniel was soon able to find the closest officers' mess. It was mostly full of officers from the Third Brigade. He tossed his powder-keg pin on the bar.

"I need a room," he said.

The barkeep eyed him suspiciously. "No rooms here, sir. All full up."

"Kick someone out," Taniel said. "I'm not sleeping in a tent in this mess." Pit. He'd skin a man who tried to do something like that to him. But Taniel wasn't about to leave Ka-poel anywhere in an army this size that didn't have a locking door.

"I'm sorry, sir. I can't do that."

Taniel looked down at his powder-keg pin. "You see that, right?"

The barkeep slid the powder-mage pin back across the bar toward Taniel. "Look, '*sir.*' There aren't any powder mages left in the army. They've all been wiped out. So don't try to pull one over on me."

Taniel rocked back on his barstool. All of them? Gone? "What do you mean 'wiped out'? How could they be wiped out?"

"They were with Field Marshal Tamas when he was lost behind the enemy lines."

"There's not a single Marked this side of Budwiel?"

"Not just this side of Budwiel. They're dead."

"Have you seen the bodies?" Taniel demanded. "Well, have you? Do you know anyone who has? Has there been recent news from Kez? I thought not. Now get me a drink, and have someone find out about getting me a room."

The barkeep folded his arms across his dirty apron and didn't move.

"Look," Taniel said, "if I'm the last living powder mage north of Budwiel, then I'm a damned celebrity. There are Privilegeds out there who need to be killed. I'll need a drink and eventually some sleep to be able to do that."

"Is this man bothering you, Frederik?"

A woman positioned herself at the bar and looked at Taniel, bemused. Taniel recognized her as the major with the beauty mark on her cheek. The one who'd tried to arrest him earlier that day. Had she followed him?

"Ma'am," Frederik said. "He claims he's a powder mage."

"He is. This is Taniel Two-Shot."

The barkeep ducked a quick bow. "Sorry, sir. What will you have?"

"Gin." Taniel cleared his throat. "No apology needed."

"And for the savage?"

Ka-poel was drumming her fingers on the bar, looking bored.

"Her name is Ka-poel, and she'll have water."

She smacked him in the shoulder.

"Wine," Taniel amended. "Something with a light taste."

The major regarded Taniel warily, sizing him up the way she might an enemy on the battlefield. "You let your servants treat you like that?" she asked.

"I'm sorry," Taniel said, trying not to let his irritation show. "I must have missed your name?"

"I'm Major Doravir, of the Third, adjutant to General Ket."

"My 'servant' is a Bone-eye, Major. A sorcerer more powerful than half the Kez Cabal put together."

Doravir seemed doubtful. "Is she your wife?"

"No."

"Your fiancée?"

Taniel glanced at Ka-poel. Had he given this major that impression? "No."

"Does she have a rank?"

"No."

"Then she doesn't belong in the officers' mess. She can wait for you outside."

"She's my guest, Major."

"With all the crowds, General Ket has declared that only spouses may stay with officers at the mess. Too many men bringing their whores back to sleep with them."

Taniel felt his fingers creeping toward the pistol at his belt, but remembered the advice the colonel had given him earlier in the day. No, he couldn't do that here. He turned to Ka-poel. "Pole, will you marry me?"

Ka-poel gave one serious nod.

Pit. Taniel hoped she saw what he was playing at. He turned back to Doravir. "She's my fiancée." He glanced at the barkeep. "Get me a room."

Doravir snorted out her nose. "You're funny, Two-Shot. You can stay with me in my room. Frederik, give him a key."

"And my fiancée here?"

"She can stay in the closet." Doravir gave Ka-poel a mocking smile. That did not bode well.

Taniel took the glass of gin from the bar and drained it in one swallow. It almost knocked him clean off his feet. How long had it been since he'd drunk hard liquor? He blinked a few times, hoping his eyes weren't visibly watering. "I'll stay somewhere else, thank you."

"Good luck." Doravir snorted. "There's not an empty room within five miles of the front, and with Tamas gone, no one will put up with a mere captain shoving them out. You'll have to push a private from his tent."

Taniel took some pleasure in the annoyance in Doravir's voice. "I think I'll do that, then. Come on, Ka-poel."

Adamat was slapped awake with rough hands. He jerked forward, reaching for a cane that wasn't there, and groggily took stock of his surroundings.

He was in the back of a carriage with one other man—the same pickpocket who'd pistol-whipped him before taking him to the

Proprietor's. The carriage wasn't moving. Outside, he could hear the general bustle of an evening crowd.

"Toak, was it?" Adamat asked.

The man nodded. He held a pistol in his right hand, hammer back, pointed at Adamat. "Get out."

"Where am I?"

"Quarter mile north of Elections Square," Toak said. "Get out."

Adamat climbed from the carriage and held his hand up to shade his eyes from the afternoon sun. As soon as he was off the running board, the carriage took off, disappearing down the street. Adamat rubbed his eyes and tried to get his mind working. He felt nauseous. What had they given him? Ah, yes. Ether. He'd be in a fog for hours yet.

He spent until just before dark at a nearby café, nursing a soda water to settle his stomach.

Why had the Proprietor offered him employment and then simply dumped him back on the street? A very strange way to act. The Proprietor was known for secrecy and efficiency. For keeping his promises and destroying his competition. He was not known for behaving strangely.

It had to be something Adamat had said.

Adamat blamed the ether when it took him well over an hour to realize the obvious.

The Proprietor had intended on paying him to go after Lord Vetas. But why pay a man to do something he already plans to do? Adamat shook his head. Stupid. On both his part and the Proprietor's. If Tamas was truly dead, Adamat would lose the few soldiers Tamas had granted him. Adamat couldn't take Lord Vetas alone.

Adamat knew where Lord Vetas was holing up. The house with the woman in the red dress. The house where he had seen the Eldaminse boy.

Now that he knew that, a frontal assault would be necessary. The same as they had done to rescue Adamat's family. Smash open the doors, take them by surprise. A man like Lord Vetas would have guards. What had the Proprietor said? At least sixty men and a Privileged.

Adamat needed manpower. He needed help. The Proprietor's help.

No doubt the Proprietor would have had him followed. The location of Adamat's safe house, and the errands he needed to run, were not things he wanted the Proprietor to know. Adamat climbed to his feet and called for a hackney cab.

He changed cabs three times and cut through half a dozen buildings before he felt confident no one was following him anymore.

It was well after dark when he arrived at the textile mill. The looms were still working despite the late hour. Adamat talked his way inside and climbed rickety wrought-iron stairs up to a room overlooking the mill's work floor. Inside he could see a woman leaning over a brass microscope. She was about forty, with hair dyed black to hide the gray roots. The walls of her office were lined with fabric samples of every kind—from cheap canvas to fine silks that cost a hundred krana for a yard.

He rapped on the door.

The woman waved him in without looking up from her microscope.

"Hello, Margy," Adamat said.

The woman finally looked up. "Adamat," she said in surprise. "What a pleasure."

"Good to see you." Adamat removed his hat.

"You as well."

Adamat took her hand a moment. Margy was one of Faye's oldest friends. Adamat considered telling her about the whole predicament before dismissing the thought. "I need some help," he said.

"Not a social visit, then?"

"Unfortunately."

Margy turned back to her microscope. "Don't you usually send Faye on these kinds of tasks? How is she, by the by? I haven't heard from her all summer."

Adamat cringed. "Not well. What with everything going on with the revolution and all that. It's played like the pit on her."

"Sorry to hear that." Margy suddenly spit on the floor, her face turning sour. "Damn that Tamas and his damned coup!"

"Margy?" Adamat couldn't keep the shock from his voice. Margy had always been outspoken, but he wouldn't have put her as a royalist by any means. She'd risen to be head foreman of the biggest textile mill in all of Adro by her own hand, not by any kind of appointment.

"He's gonna take us all to the pit," Margy said, wagging her finger at Adamat. "Just you wait. I hope you don't buy into all this nonsense about him trying to make a better world. It's just a power grab, that's all."

Adamat raised his hands. "I stay out of politics."

"We all have to choose sides one day, Adamat." She tucked a stray wisp of hair behind her ear and cleared her throat. Adamat could tell she was a little embarrassed by her outburst. "Now what did you need?"

Adamat removed the fibers from his pocket carefully, hoping he was giving her bits of the Proprietor's rug and not string from his borrowed jacket. "I need to find this rug," he said.

She took the fibers carefully. "This isn't pocket lint, is it? Faye brought me pocket lint more than once."

"I do hope not."

Margy put the fibers under her microscope and spent a moment adjusting knobs on the side. "Vanduvian wool," she said.

"High grade?"

"The finest. Whoever owns this rug is very, very rich."

"Any chance of tracing the rug?"

Margy stepped away from her microscope. "I'd say so. Only a few rug dealers sell Vanduvians. I'll ask around. Stop by in a couple weeks and maybe I'll have something for you."

"That long?" Adamat said.

"You need it sooner?"

"If at all possible. It's a rather urgent matter."

Margy sighed. "It'll cost you."

"I don't have much money on me."

"I don't want money," Margy said. "You tell Faye that she's taking me out for dinner at the Café Palms sometime before the leaves turn, and we'll call it square."

Adamat swallowed and forced a smile on his face. "I'll do that."

Margy turned back to her microscope. "Come by in a week and I'll know where the rug is from."

CHAPTER
12

As Taniel drew closer to the front, he realized that the Privileged sorcery he saw from afar was in fact coming from the Wings of Adom mercenaries.

The Wings of Adom held the western edge of the front, sandwiched between the rising mountains and the Adran army. They had four brigades on the front, their uniforms brilliant in red, gold, and white.

The Privileged sorcery from both sides was weak at best. Fire splashed against shields of hardened air, and lightning sprang from the sky to strike among the ranks, but the blasts of power seemed halfhearted. Even a mercenary army as prestigious as the Wings couldn't pay as well as a royal cabal, and it seemed the Kez were making use of the weakest and the youngest sorcerers. After the carnage at Kresim Kurga, who did they have left?

Taniel swung his kit over one shoulder and frowned at the west side of the Addown. The hillock on which he stood would make a good marksman's spot—high above and several hundred paces behind the fighting. But from what he could tell, the Kez had been pushing back the Adran army every day.

The front was about five miles north of Budwiel. The city smoked, flames visible over the poorest quarters of the city. Taniel wondered what the Kez had done with all those people. Many, certainly, had fled north when the city fell, but not all of them could have gotten out. Now they were slaves, or dead.

The Kez had a reputation for brutality toward the people they conquered.

Ka-poel sat down on the hillock and opened her satchel in her lap. She removed a stick of wax and began to shape it slowly with her fingers. Taniel wondered who she was making this time.

"Can you do sorcery without those?" Taniel lowered himself cross-legged beside her. "Without the dolls, I mean. And some bit of a person?"

She raised her chin and looked down her nose at him for a moment before returning to her work.

"And where the pit do you get the wax? I never see you buy anything. Do you even have any money?"

Ka-poel reached inside her shirt and withdrew a roll of banknotes. She shook it under Taniel's nose before putting it back.

"Where did you get that?"

She flicked him on the nose. Hard.

"Ow. Hey. Answer me, girl."

She raised her fingers, ready to flick again.

"OK, OK. Kresimir, I'm just asking a question." Taniel pulled his rifle into his lap and ran his fingers along the stock. No notches. A clean barrel. Brand-new, this was. Test-fired, according to the soldier who'd given it to him. *Never take a rifle you didn't fire yourself into battle.* It was Tamas who'd told him that. Tamas, who was most likely dead and buried in a mass grave along with the rest of the Seventh and Ninth.

Where did that leave the Adran army? Where did that leave Taniel? He wondered briefly if Tamas had left behind a will of some kind. Taniel had never thought about that before. Since he was a boy he'd always thought Tamas would live forever.

The fighting below consisted of nothing but an exchange of artillery. Some of the shells hit the soft ground, skipping through the Adran ranks, while others smacked into unseen sorcery and split apart, falling harmlessly to the ground.

The exchange seemed almost like a formality. Neither side was losing more than a few men, and none of the artillery pieces were being hit.

"Do you have any redstripes?" Taniel asked.

Ka-poel shook her head.

"Can you make me more?"

She scowled at him and pointed at the wax in her hand as if to say, *Can't you see I'm working on something?*

"I need my powder now," Taniel said.

Ka-poel stopped shaping the wax and looked at him for several moments, her green eyes unreadable. She nodded suddenly and pulled his powder horn from her pack.

Taniel's hands were shaking when he poured the first bit of powder into the paper to make a powder charge. The black grit between his fingers felt good. Almost too good. It felt like...power. He licked his lips and poured a line out on the back of his hand, lifting it to his face.

He stopped. Ka-poel was watching him.

One long snort, and it felt like his brain was on fire. Taniel rocked back, his body shuddering, shaking. He heard a whimper—pitiful and low. Did he make that noise? Taniel put his head in his hands and waited for what seemed like several minutes before the shaking finally stopped.

When he raised his head, the world glowed.

Taniel blinked. He hadn't opened his third eye. He wasn't looking into the Else. But everything seemed to glow regardless. No, he decided. Not glow. It was like the lines stood out sharper than they'd ever been. The world was clear in a way that a regular man could never understand. As if every moment out of a powder trance was spent under water and only now had he surfaced.

Was it like this when he took the powder to fight that Warden in Adopest? Had he just not noticed?

How had mala ever felt like a good alternative to this? How could any drug compare?

Taniel felt the grin on his face and didn't try to hide it. "Oh, pit. That's good." He finished loading a dozen powder charges before stowing them in his kit and hanging his powder horn from his shoulder. He got down on his chest and began to scan the enemy lines.

There were Privileged on the east side of the Addown. Most of them wore colorful uniforms and were surrounded by bannermen and bodyguards. A lot of Wardens, too. The Kez weren't scared of powder mages, not with Tamas gone. They'd relearn that fear in the coming days.

Primary targets.

There were officers. Practically anyone on a horse, it seemed. Where were all their cavalry? Strange that the Kez hadn't brought any of their cavalry north of Budwiel. Oh well. The officers would do.

Secondary targets.

There were artillerymen.

Tertiary targets.

Taniel felt the rumble in the ground before he heard the sound of hoofbeats. A few dozen yards to his left a group of some twenty Adran cavalry had gathered. Adran officers. A couple of generals. Taniel recognized a few of them.

General Ket was a handsome woman of about fifty—handsome, that is, if he didn't account for the ragged bit of skin where her right ear had been. Her broad face seemed somehow familiar, as if Taniel had seen her recently, when he knew for a fact it'd been years since their last meeting. She was the general of the Third Brigade.

Ket wasn't the only member of the group to have lost a bit of herself in battle. General Hilanska of the Second Brigade was morbidly obese and was missing his left arm at the shoulder.

None of them noticed Taniel.

They seemed agitated about something. Pointing and gesturing, all of them watching the battlefield through their looking glasses. Hilanska shouted for the artillery to be moved back.

Moved back? That was tantamount to conceding ground. Why would they...?

Taniel saw it now. Movement among the Kez lines. Whole companies coming up just behind their artillery. An assault. The Kez intended to push them back this day.

Taniel narrowed his eyes. There were huge men among those companies. Giant, twisted forms.

Taniel didn't know if these were regular Wardens, or the new kind made from powder mages, like the kind that had attacked him in Adopest.

Either way, this would go poorly for the Adran army.

Taniel noted that the Adran artillery was staggered every couple hundred feet. The artillery out front could be pulled back while those beside kept firing. This was planned. Perhaps this was what they'd been doing the last ten days. It made sense, if they knew they were going to lose the front line anyway.

Taniel didn't like it.

He left Ka-poel and headed down the hillock to join the officers, approaching General Hilanska.

"Sir, what's going on?"

The general gave Taniel a dismissive glance, then a second, longer stare. "We're pulling back, son."

"That's foolish, sir. We have the high ground. We can hold."

General Ket brought her horse around behind Taniel, looking

him up and down. He wondered if she remembered him. He must look different after four years.

"Are you questioning your betters, Captain?" General Ket asked.

"It's a stupid tactic, ma'am. It assumes loss."

"Captain, you'll earn yourself a demotion without an instant apology."

Another general, a blond man with a stiff bearing, added, "I'd imagine this is why he's still a captain."

General Hilanska held up his remaining arm. "Calm down, Ket. You don't recognize our boy here, do you? Taniel Two-Shot, hero of the Fatrastan War for Independence. I'm glad to see you among the living."

"General." Taniel dipped his head. Tamas had told him a tale or two when he was a boy about what kind of man Hilanska was— loyal, passionate. The best kind of companion to have with you on the line. He was fat and and old now, but Taniel imagined him to be the same kind of person.

"I don't care who he is," Ket said. "No one disregards rank in this army and gets away with it."

"Tamas—" Hilanska began.

"Tamas is dead," Ket said. "It's not his army anymore. If you'd—"

The argument was cut off by a messenger.

"Sirs, the enemy is advancing."

Ket spurred her mount down the embankment toward the front, shouting orders.

Hilanska's stallion pranced to one side as if in excitement. "Get my artillery out of there!" He looked down at Taniel. "I wouldn't go down there," he said. "They've got a new kind of Warden. Smaller. Smarter. Faster. Never seen anything like it. 'Black Wardens,' we've been calling them."

"They've been turning powder mages into Wardens," Taniel said. "They sent two to kill me in Adopest."

"Glad to see they failed. Powder-mage Wardens. How is that even possible?" Hilanska gave him a weighing gaze. "All right, Captain. Go down there and hold that line and I'll move my artillery back."

Taniel returned to Ka-poel at the top of the hillock. She was making progress on her doll.

"The Kez are attacking," Taniel said. "I'm going to fight." Why was he telling her? Was she going to stop him? Go with him?

She didn't answer him, so he grabbed his kit and headed down toward the front. Ka-poel would be safer back here out of the melee, he decided. But would he? Ever since Shouldercrown, he had wondered who was protecting who.

The Kez soldiers were already on their way, marching to the steady sound of the snare drums. Trumpets were sounding in the Adran camp, and more men rushed toward the front.

Taniel paused and scanned the approaching Kez. None of the Kez Privileged were advancing, but... there.

The Wardens in their black bowler caps and black jackets came through marching Kez infantry like dogs running out ahead of the pack. They practically flew across the empty field. Some carried small swords, others long pikes. They howled like animals, an eerie sound that lifted above the cannon fire and the snares and trumpets and made Taniel shudder.

Taniel dropped to one knee and sighted along his rifle. One breath. Two. Fire.

He willed the bullet on through the sky, burning the smallest bit of powder to keep it in the air. He focused on one of the Black Wardens. The bullet took only two or three seconds to bridge the space and...

He missed.

Taniel couldn't believe it. He was far behind the line, steady as a rock, with no distractions. How could he miss?

He reloaded his rifle. The Wardens were coming fast. Once they reached the Adran line they'd cause untold chaos. Taniel lined up another shot and squeezed the trigger.

The bullet tore through a Warden's eye, laying the creature out on the ground. None of the Warden's companions seemed to notice. One even snagged the small sword out of the still-twitching hand, barely slowing his charge.

There was no way Taniel was going to be able to stop any more. He had...what? Another two shots before the Wardens reached the earthworks that marked the Adran line?

Taniel drew the bayonet from his kit and unwrapped it, fitting the ring tightly around the end of his rifle. He stood, ready to charge, pausing only to scratch a mark in the butt of his rifle with an old nail he kept in his pocket. He thought suddenly of Ka-poel and wondered if he should have left her alone.

He joined the flood of Adran infantry heading to the front, elbowing and shoving his way through. They weren't moving fast enough.

A call went out to hold the line. Taniel wasn't going to be there in time for the initial shock. His legs pumped beneath him, covering ground three times faster than any of the others. He felt a snarl rise to his throat.

"Aim! Fire!" a nearby officer yelled.

A plume of smoke rose from the front of the Adran line. Many of the Wardens staggered. Some of them fell. Not nearly enough.

There was one section along the Adran earthworks that rose higher than the others. Taniel could see that several officers had taken the high ground. It was precisely where the Wardens would head. They'd leave the flat ground to the regular infantry and go straight for the strongest spots.

Even as the thought went through Taniel's head, he saw several of the Wardens change direction to run straight for the highest earthworks. One of the big brutes outstripped them all. He had several dark spots on his coat and his body twitched as more musket shots hit him, but nothing could take him down. He raised his sword and flew up the side of the earthworks, leaping over the top.

Taniel slammed into him in midair. The impact tore the air from his lungs, and they were both flung back over the earthworks, rolling down the side. He felt strong hands on his chest and was thrown off the Warden. He hit the ground and rolled to his feet to find the Warden already thrusting a small sword at his face.

Taniel parried with his bayonet and then thrust. The blade slid into the Warden almost up to the barrel, but seemed to have as much effect as the musket shots had.

The Warden threw itself backward, off of Taniel's bayonet and out of range of another stab.

Taniel whirled as another Warden came at him from the side. Taniel ducked and thrust, putting the tip of his bayonet into the tender spot below the creature's chin. He had to let go of his rifle and leap to one side to avoid the thrust of the first Warden's sword. Taniel drew his own short sword and waited for the attack.

The Warden paused to throw a whole powder charge into his mouth. He gnashed at the powder with blackened teeth and spit the paper on the ground.

Taniel had never been all that good with a short sword. He was fast and competent, but if this creature had any amount of training, he'd cut right through Taniel.

Taniel caught one thrust and pushed the Warden's sword to one side. The Warden bridged the gap with his other fist. Taniel was ready for it.

He caught the Warden's fist and slammed his forehead against the Warden's nose. He could feel the bone move back into the creature's brain. That alone should have killed it, but Taniel still felt struggle in the Warden's muscles. Taniel stepped back and slashed across the Warden's throat. It gurgled and collapsed, clinging to life, but it wouldn't be any more of a problem.

Taniel could feel the Warden's black, sticky blood all across his face.

"Oi!" Someone called from the earthworks above him. "They're coming!"

Taniel realized with a start that the rest of the Kez army was almost upon him. He snatched his rifle and scrambled up the earthworks, kicking dirt and swearing. The Warden had made it look easy. It most certainly wasn't.

Several hands helped pull Taniel to the relative safety of the earthworks, then thumped him on the back.

"Back to the line!" someone shouted.

Taniel shook his head, resting for a moment on the earthworks barricade. He clutched his rifle to his chest to keep his hands from shaking, and wondered if going over the earthworks like that had been a mistake.

Someone smacked him across the face. He half expected it to be Ka-poel, but when he lifted his eyes, he recognized Major Doravir. She looked furious.

"Do you have a death wish, Captain?" She grabbed him by the collar, shaking him like an errant schoolboy. "Well, do you? No one goes over that embankment without orders. No one!"

"Piss on your orders!"

Taniel shoved her away. He might have put his bayonet through her chest if he'd had any less control over himself.

She stared at him, a cold rage in her eyes. "I'll see you hanged, Captain."

"Try it."

"Load," came an officer's call. Taniel took a moment to orient himself. From the high earthworks he could see up and down the jagged line. Wardens were fighting behind the earthworks, clearing out whole groups of men, but the two he'd killed seemed to have tipped things in Adro's favor in the immediate vicinity. Soldiers bent to reload their rifles, readying for the Kez onslaught.

Taniel turned away from Doravir and stuffed a bullet down his rifle. Out of the corner of his eye he watched her storm away, yelling orders.

"Careful, Captain," a nearby soldier whispered. "If that one turns her eyes on you, she'll sleep with you or see you dead. Or both."

"She can go to the pit, for all I care."

"She's General Ket's sister," the soldier said. "She does what she wants. But she's a damned good officer. Don't let anyone tell you otherwise."

Ket's sister. That's why he thought he'd seen Ket more recently. The resemblance was strong, even if Doravir had a thinner build. "A damned good officer would let me do my job," Taniel said. He dropped a second bullet down his rifle and secured it with a scrap of cloth.

The soldier stared at him. "You feeling all right, Captain? You just loaded that twice, and without powder."

"Ask yourself," Taniel said with confidence he didn't feel, "what type of a man would leap the earthworks and go fight two Wardens by himself, then load his rifle without powder." He licked the powder off his fingers to keep the edge on his powder trance, and set the rifle against his shoulder. He sighted along the barrel. The Kez front line was still some two hundred yards distant. Well out of range of the muskets, while the Adran riflemen would open fire any moment.

Taniel found a pair of officers well back from the line and squeezed the trigger. He floated the two bullets simultaneously, pushing them toward their respective targets.

He caught one of the officers in the chest. The man clutched at the wound and slumped in his saddle, causing panic in his bodyguard. Taniel winced. The other bullet had missed the target. How could he be missing? Had the mala made him lose his edge?

"Kresimir be damned," the soldier beside him said. "You're

Taniel Two-Shot. Hey"—he tapped the man beside him on the shoulder—"This is Taniel Two-Shot."

"Yeah," the other soldier responded, "and I'm a general."

"He was just down in front of the barricade. Took on four Wardens all by himself."

"Nah."

"Saw it with my own eyes."

"Sure you did."

Taniel focused on the Kez lines. The *rat-tat-tatting* of their snares seemed to echo in his brain. He opened his third eye for a moment, watching as the earth was bathed in glowing pastels, splashes of sorcery covering every part of the battlefield.

"You ready to die with us, Two-Shot?" the second soldier asked, breaking Taniel's concentration. It wasn't phrased as a threat. Just a question.

"No, not particularly."

"We've been falling back every day. Sometimes twice. Every time the damned Kez advance like this. And each time, we lose three hundred men or more."

Taniel couldn't believe that. "Every time?"

The man nodded solemnly.

"Falling back..." Taniel craned his neck. The artillery had been wheeled away by now, back to the next row of trenches and earthen barricades. "Stupid bloody fools. We have to hold. We can't let them push us back like this. We're practically hemorrhaging troops."

"I don't know what an 'hemorg' is, but we're bleedin' men something fierce. We can't hold. We tried, but can't. Nothing stops those Black Wardens. No matter how many we kill, there seems to be more."

"You're awfully calm," Taniel said.

"Something peaceful about that, I think. Knowing you're going to die. That lad over on your other side—"

Taniel took a glance. The kid next to him didn't seem old

enough to shave. His hands shook so hard his musket was swaying from side to side.

"—that lad doesn't have the same opinion I do."

"It's just the jitters," Taniel said. "We all get them." Taniel glanced at the Kez. A hundred and fifty yards. He reloaded his rifle, lifted it to his shoulder, and fired.

"Not you," the first soldier said. "I heard you put a round in a Privileged's eye for your first kill."

"That I did. But I learned to shoot from Field Marshal Tamas himself." He paused. "They teach you to shoot at targets," he said to the young man beside him. "It's different when you realize there's a man on the other end, shooting back at you. I was sitting two miles away. I had surprise on my side. But, lad, you take a deep breath and pull that trigger. Fire straight and true, because you might not get another shot."

"Lad," Taniel had said. The boy was no more than five years his junior.

Taniel loaded his rifle while he spoke, set, and fired. Another officer dropped.

The boy looked at Taniel. His hands hadn't stopped shaking.

"I don't think your pep talk helped much," the first soldier said.

"Quiet down on the line!" That was Major Doravir. She had her sword raised above her head, a pistol in the other hand. "Aim!"

The Kez were almost in musket range. There were thousands of them. Rank upon rank upon rank. Taniel could see now why it was impossible to hold the line. He remembered the Battle of South Pike and how they'd almost lost the bastion a dozen times. They'd been guarding a pass from an enchanted bulwark only a hundred paces wide. Here, with nothing but earthworks between them and the Kez, it would be next to impossible to hold.

"Fire!"

The front line and much of the second of the Kez offensive fell beneath the volley. The Adran infantry began to reload.

Before a second volley could be fired, the Kez lines came to a stop. The new front line dropped to their knees and lined up their shots before firing.

Taniel threw himself behind the safety of the earthworks. He pulled the young soldier down with him and listened to the volley, and then the *thwap* of musket balls ricocheting off the dirt. The young soldier struggled to get back up. Taniel held him down.

"Line fire," Taniel said. "They'll fire that shot, then the next before they charge. You wait..."

The second volley sounded. Taniel counted to three before he let the boy back up and came up himself, ready to fire.

The Kez charged with a mighty roar, their bayonets leveled.

"Fire at will!" came the call.

Taniel took a deep breath of the smoke from the powder. It made his head buzz, his blood pump faster. His hands weren't shaking from mala withdrawal anymore. His body had found something so much better. He poured a bit of powder onto the back of his hand and snorted.

The Kez reached the bottom of the earthworks and began the steep climb. Taniel rose up high enough to fire down at them, when he spotted a Privileged about a hundred yards away with her hands twitching up sorcery. Taniel adjusted his aim and pulled the trigger.

The woman went down in a spray of blood, clutching at her throat.

Kez infantry poured over the earthworks like a flood breaching a levy. Taniel thrust his bayonet into a man's stomach, cracked another soldier across the face with the butt of his rifle. He leapt onto the rise to keep them from coming over, swinging and stabbing.

He barely heard the call for retreat.

"Hold!" he screamed, knocking a grenadier off the earthworks with his rifle stock. "We can hold!"

The young soldier who had been beside him went down with a bayonet through his chest. Taniel leapt off the bulwark to his aid, skewering the Kez infantryman like a side of beef.

The boy might die from a wound like that. It had gone straight between his ribs—likely through a lung. If so, he'd drown in his own blood.

But Taniel couldn't leave him there. The Adran soldiers were retreating.

"Hold! Hold, you bloody bastards!"

Taniel was almost alone on the earthworks. The boy lay at Taniel's feet. The first soldier he'd spoken to lay against the rear of the earthworks, dead eyes fixed blindly on the sky. Major Doravir was gone.

He reached out and felt the powder of the Kez infantry. A thought was all it took to light it. He used his mind to warp the blast away from him and away from the earthworks. The sound rang in his ears, sending him to his knees. Every ounce of powder within a dozen yards went up.

Powder smoke rose in the air, and charred corpses littered the earthworks. Groans and cries for mercy rose from the wounded. Men farther down the line had stopped their fighting to stare at Taniel. He took a step toward them, going to help hold the earthworks at the next spot, when he realized he couldn't see an infantryman in a blue jacket on his feet anywhere.

It was just a sea of sandy uniforms. The Kez had taken the earthworks.

The boy was still alive and coughing blood. Taniel slung his rifle over his shoulder and grasped the young soldier under the arms, pulling him backward toward the Adran camp.

It was a long haul, half carrying the boy over a hundred paces to the next set of earthworks. Most of the Kez ignored him. A few potshots skipped off the dirt nearby, but the Kez were too busy securing the new ground. They'd level the earthworks and move back to their own camp, where they'd push their artillery forward another hundred paces and prepare for tomorrow's charge.

Exhausted, his head still buzzing from the powder trance, Taniel reached the Adran army. "See to him," Taniel said when a surgeon came running. The surgeon balked and her eyes were wide.

"He's dead, sir."

"Just bloody see to him! Make him comfortable!"

"No, sir. He's not just dying. He's dead already."

Taniel dropped to his knee beside the young soldier and put his fingers on the lad's throat. No pulse. He used the same two fingers to close the young soldier's eyes.

"Damn it," he said.

The surgeon got on her knees next to him.

"I'm fine!" He pushed away her fingers.

"Your arm, sir."

Taniel looked down. His uniform had been torn through, leaving a bloody, jagged cut along his left arm. He'd not even felt it.

"Surgeon," a voice said, "tend to someone who's worth it." Major Doravir stalked toward them, her brown hair wild and her cheeks black with powder burns. Her jacket was gone, her white shirt stained with sweat and blood.

Taniel got to his feet. "Major Doravir," he said. "Didn't have the decency to die with your men, eh?"

Her backhand jerked his head to the side. He touched his cheek. That had been hard enough to rattle his teeth. "Do that again and I'll break your hand."

"I was the last one away from the front on the retreat," Major Doravir snarled.

"No," Taniel said. "I was. We could have held that bulwark. Instead we lost ground and who knows how many hundred men."

"I obey orders. You don't. No more warnings, Captain. I'll see you hanged." The major spun on her heel and marched off, shouting for the provosts.

Taniel rubbed at his chin and caught Ka-poel watching him from a distance. She headed toward the battlefield, where Kez soldiers were leveling the earthworks and civilians from both sides were already collecting the dead and wounded.

"Where the pit are you going?" Taniel shouted.

She pointed toward the battlefield and held up a doll. Damned girl. That wouldn't work like it did on Kresim Kurga. There were too many enemies here, and not enough dolls.

Taniel glanced toward Major Doravir. She was speaking to two soldiers with the insignia of Adran provosts on their shoulders. Military police. Doravir pointed to Taniel.

He decided it was a good time to make himself scarce.

CHAPTER
13

Tamas climbed out of his tent and finished buttoning up the front of his uniform. He adjusted the gold epaulets on his shoulders and he wondered if they'd have rain that day. The sky over the Adran Mountains to the east had just barely taken on a light halo, while the rest of the world slept on in darkness.

Tamas gazed at that slight brightening and wondered how things went on the other side of the mountains. Budwiel had fallen. The Kez were no doubt pushing their way up Surkov's Alley. Tamas hoped that his generals could handle the defense. He grimaced to himself. With Budwiel gone, the fight could only go in Kez's favor. His men needed him. His country needed him. His son needed him. He had to get across these damned mountains.

He could hear rustling in the camp, and the low whistles of sergeants as they kicked their men from their beds. The smell of smoke came from cookfires that no doubt had little over them.

Olem sat beside Tamas's tent. His forage cap was pulled over his eyes, his legs propped on a log in front of him, and his hands thrust deep in his pockets. The pose was an affected one. Olem's Knack eliminated the need for sleep.

"Quiet night?" Tamas asked, squatting beside the small, smoldering fire and rubbing his hands together. The heat of the summer didn't touch the early morning, not in foothills like this. He poked the coals with a twig, then tossed in the twig. No more than ash. There wasn't much to burn on the high steppe.

"Little bit of rustling, sir. Some grumbling, too." Olem sniffed as if the grumbling were no more than an annoyance.

His men were hungry. Tamas knew it, and it pained him.

"I put a stop to it, sir," Olem said.

"Good."

Tamas heard soft footfalls on the dirt. Olem shifted, and his hand emerged just a little from his coat. He had a pistol.

A carcass thumped to the ground beside Tamas. He started.

"Elk, sir," Vlora said as she squatted down next to him.

Tamas felt a little spell of relief. Meat.

"Any more?" he asked, his voice a little too hopeful.

"Andriya bagged one, too. He's portioning it out to the powder mages. This one's for the officers."

Tamas chewed on the inside of his lip. "Olem. Have it butchered and distributed to the men. A small, raw piece for each. Let them cook it themselves. We break camp in two hours."

Olem climbed to his feet and stretched. He returned his pistol to his belt and headed off, calling a few names.

"We'll reach Hune Dora tomorrow by midday, sir," Vlora said. Her shoulders were stained with blood from the elk. She had to have been burning a powder trance, otherwise there was no way a girl of her size could have carried an entire elk over her shoulders.

"How far?"

"About sixteen miles. Went up that way while hunting."

"And?"

"A small town, just like Gavril said."

"Walled?"

"The wall is an old ruin. Eight feet high, maybe. I wouldn't worry about it, though, sir. The city looks abandoned."

Abandoned? Tamas had hoped there would be some population, just so he could loot their stores of powder and food.

"Anything else up that direction?"

"The terrain turns steep. The road seems to follow the contours of the mountain ridges. Lots of bridges, from what I could see. Once we're in the forest, the dragoons will have a hard time encircling us."

"As I'd hoped."

"The bad news is, the road narrows considerably. We'll be able to march maybe just three or four men abreast."

That would require Tamas's column to extend to almost four miles long. Not conducive to an army being dogged by dragoons. Tamas swore under his breath.

He watched the sky for a moment. There wouldn't be rain today, he decided.

"I lied, before," Tamas said.

Vlora frowned at the embers of the fire. "Sir?"

"Back in Budwiel you asked me if there was any news about Taniel. I lied."

Vlora opened her mouth, but Tamas went on before she could say anything.

"A few days before we went through the caves, I received a message from Adopest. Taniel's savage was awake."

"And Taniel?"

"Nothing. But if one of them can come out of it, presumably the other. And I wouldn't think that little savage girl is stronger than my boy. He'll…" He heard his voice crack. "He'll make it."

He examined Vlora out of the corner of his eye. He thought he saw a tear on her face.

"How is your leg, sir?" she asked.

Tamas looked down at his leg. Mihali had healed it. He could walk. He could ride. Pit, he could dance if he wanted to. But deep inside the calf, it still hurt. The pain throbbed, right where they'd taken that blasted star of gold out of his flesh. Despite the healing powers of a god, there was still something wrong with it.

"It's fine," he said. "Good as new."

"You still walk with a limp," Vlora said.

"Do I? Just habit."

Vlora leaned back on her haunches. "I've heard that healed tissue has a problem readjusting itself. It needs help. Plenty of exercise and massage. If you'd like..."

"I don't think I need the gossip that would come out of you rubbing my leg," Tamas said. He chuckled, and was relieved when Vlora laughed as well.

"I was going to say have Olem do it, sir."

"I'm sure I'll be fine." Tamas watched Vlora a little longer. She glanced up at him, then back at the fire. She still wouldn't meet his eyes.

He found he missed their old familiarity. If things had gone better, she might be his daughter-in-law by now. Back before she went off to the university, she'd been the one soldier with the gall to call him Tamas. She'd hung on his arm, even hugged him in public.

Before she slept with that fop in Jileman and Taniel broke off their engagement.

Tamas climbed to his feet. "I want you and Andriya to keep on hunting. We need as much meat as we can get."

"We're going to run out of powder eventually, sir," she said.

"Get some from the Seventh's quartermaster."

"I meant the whole army."

Tamas drummed his fingers on his belt. An army on the march, without resupply or even wagons and camp followers. They would run out of everything. Sooner, rather than later. Their only advantage was a swift march, and that was lost with having to forage and the exhaustion brought on by hunger.

"I'll be sure the mages get what they need." His powder mages were still each worth more than a dozen men.

Vlora nodded. "I'll check with the quartermaster." She stood and abruptly headed off into the camp.

Tamas watched her go, and felt himself an old man, burdened with regret.

The camp grew louder over the next few minutes as the last of the soldiers were roused from their beds. A few cheers went up, and Tamas guessed Olem must have distributed the elk meat. It wasn't much, not when spread so thinly, but it was a bite more than they'd had.

Tamas broke down and stowed his own tent. He'd just finished tying his bedroll when Olem returned with a bundle of bloody canvas.

"I would have done that, sir," Olem said.

Tamas eyed the bloody canvas and felt his mouth watering. "I have you doing more important things. I was a soldier once, Olem. I can break camp as well as any man."

"If you insist, sir." Olem knelt beside the coals and produced a skewer, then unwrapped the bloody canvas to reveal a hunk of elk meat.

Tamas stood and looked to the south. Somewhere out there, the Kez cavalry were breaking their camp, probably hoping to overtake the Adran brigades before they were able to reach the relative safety of the forest.

Tamas heard, more than saw, a horse galloping through the camp. A few moments later and Gavril emerged from the still-dark morning on a shuddering charger.

Tamas grabbed the horse by the bridle as his brother-in-law swung down. The horse's sides were lathered, its eyes wild. Gavril had been riding hard.

"Sixteen thousand," Gavril said. "Ten and a half thousand dragoons and another five and a half of cuirassiers. Three full brigades of cavalry."

Kresimir. How could they possibly fight that many cavalry? "How far?"

"We can beat them to the forest if we leave now. I've not spoken with my northern outriders."

"Vlora just came from the north. We're sixteen miles from Hune Dora."

Gavril accepted an offered canteen from Olem and took a swig, then poured the rest over his head. His body steamed. "We won't have time to sack the city."

"She says it's abandoned. I'll have some men take a look, but we'll probably head right past it."

"Abandoned, eh?" Gavril scratched his bearded chin. "We could make a stand there."

Tamas cast an anxious glance to the south. He couldn't see the Kez cavalry, but it seemed to him he could *sense* them. "Maybe."

Olem stood and held out a pewter plate. On it was a steaming cut of elk.

"Burned on the edges and raw in the middle, but it's delicious," Olem said with a grin.

Tamas heard his stomach growl. There must have been two pounds of meat on that plate.

"Share it with Gavril," Tamas said. "I'm not hungry."

Olem cocked an eyebrow. "I can hear your stomach making bear calls from here, sir. You have to keep up your strength."

"Really, I'm fine."

Gavril grabbed the meat with his bare hands. "Suit yourself." He tore it in half and plopped one half back on the plate. He began to cram the rest into his mouth. Around bites, he yelled out to another rider who'd just come into camp.

"Sir," Olem said as Gavril strode off, "you need to eat."

"Get the men on their feet," Tamas said. A sudden urgency rose within him as a gust of wind nearly tore off his hat. "Have the advance column marching out of the camp in twenty minutes." He stared south until Olem was gone.

Sixteen thousand Kez cavalry. His two brigades of infantry would be ridden down. They'd die hungry, exhausted, and in a foreign land while the Kez burned their homes.

He couldn't let that happen.

He *wouldn't* let that happen.

Tamas strode toward the nearest tents. "Companies," he shouted. "Prepare for march!"

Sergeant Oldrich and his squad of Riflejacks were staying at a retired barracks on the southeast side of the Ad River, not far from the Lighthouse of Gostaun. The barracks was a big building, abandoned and empty but for the odd feral dog. The front doors were barred and chained, but one of the many side entries had been left unlocked.

Adamat entered the barracks through that door and crossed two empty parade grounds before he found the small mess hall where the captain and his squad were watching Adamat's four youngest children put on a play in the center of the mess.

Adamat stood in the door quietly, unable to keep the smile from his face as Astrit absently played with her black curls while she tried to remember the lines of the princess trapped in a tall tower by the evil Privileged who, judging by the costumes composed of robes and bedsheets, was being played by one of the twins.

"Daddy!" Astrit cried, catching sight of him.

He was mobbed by all the children crowding around him with hugs and kisses. He made sure to give each one a kiss, saying each of their names—except for the twins. He could never tell them apart, and he wasn't about to admit it.

Adamat wrestled on the floor with his children for several minutes before he was able to extract himself. He bid them return to their play, and joined Sergeant Oldrich at the table in the corner of the room.

"Coffee?" the sergeant offered, chewing absently at the tobacco tucked in his cheek.

"Tea, if you have it."

Oldrich called over to one of his men. "Tea!" He fixed Adamat with a frown. "You look awful. You got rolled, didn't you?"

"Yeah." Adamat found himself watching his children. They were beautiful kids. They really were. The thought of anything happening to them made his blood begin to boil and he forced himself to look away. "Got out of it fine, and I've found Vetas's headquarters."

"I didn't think you could." Oldrich lifted his coffee cup in a salute. "I figured the bastard would be in the wind after what you did to his boys in Offendale."

Adamat sniffed. "He's not afraid of me," Adamat said. "I don't think he's afraid of anything. You ever seen a machine powered by steam? They've got looms, hammers, printing presses..." Adamat was briefly reminded of his own failed foray into publishing but managed to push the thought away.

"Yeah," Oldrich said. "They have them in ships now, too."

"Exactly. He's like a steam engine. Just keeps going. No feeling, no thought. Just a task to do and he's going to do it."

Oldrich sipped his coffee. "Damn. Almost makes you feel bad for him."

"No," Adamat said. "I'll still rip his heart out when I find him."

"And I hope you get your chance. Shall we go get him?"

"How many men do you have again?" Adamat asked, though he knew well enough.

"Fifteen," Oldrich said. "Two to guard the children..."

"Five."

"Five to guard the children, that leaves us with twelve, counting you and me."

"Not enough."

"He's got enough goons to take on a squad of the field marshal's best?"

"He's got at least sixty enforcers and a Privileged."

Oldrich whistled. "Ah. I don't think there's anything we can do about that."

"Pit. Thank you," Adamat said as a cup of tea was set in front of him. He added two lumps of sugar and stirred it to cool. "Have you seen the morning paper?"

"No. You want one? Oi! Someone get the investigator a paper!"

Adamat cringed inwardly. He was hoping to find out that Oldrich *hadn't* seen a paper today. Not draw attention to one. Oh well. "Do you remember a Privileged by the name of Borbador?" Adamat changed the subject.

"I do," Oldrich said. His normally pleasant face was suddenly guarded.

"I think he'd do it for us. Borbador was one of the cabal's best and brightest. He held Shouldercrown against the Kez Cabal virtually by himself. I know Tamas left him alive and has him stashed in the city. If we could—"

"No," Oldrich said.

" 'No' what?"

"Privileged Borbador has a gaes to compel him to kill the field marshal."

"I know. I'm the one who told Tamas about the gaes."

"Then why would you ask me that? Releasing him would endanger Tamas and I won't do it."

Adamat held his head in his hands. He felt like he was doing that a lot lately. "It's our only chance against a Privileged under Lord Vetas."

"You could ask Taniel Two-Shot," Oldrich said. "He kills Privilegeds as a hobby, and rumor has it he's in the city."

"Newspaper said this morning he left for the front." Adamat realized his mistake as the words left his mouth.

"So you have seen a paper?" Oldrich nudged a spittoon from beneath the table with one toe, leaning over to spit into it. "Was there something in it you wanted me to see?"

"Sir," one of Oldrich's men called from the doorway. He was a young man, probably not much older than Adamat's son Josep. "Sir, you should see this." He rushed over to Oldrich and dropped a paper into his lap.

Oldrich lifted the paper. The headline read, "Budwiel Sacked, Field Marshal Tamas Dead." Oldrich was silent for several minutes as he read the article. The young soldier stayed by his side the whole time. When Oldrich finished, he handed the newspaper back to the soldier.

"You weren't going to tell me?"

Adamat felt like a child who'd been caught robbing the pantry. "I was," Adamat said. "After I figured out how to convince you to stay and help me." Adamat swallowed hard. He was about to lose the last bit of help he had to get Faye back. Once Oldrich was gone, it would be just Adamat with eight children to look after, and a wife and son still in his enemy's hands.

"There's no convincing," Oldrich said. "I was given an order. Tamas is my commanding officer and an old friend. He told me to see this thing through to the end regardless of whether he lived through the war."

"And you will?"

"Yes."

Adamat couldn't help but breathe a sigh of relief. He dabbed at his forehead with a handkerchief, realizing that he'd been sweating. "Thank you." He paused. "You seem to be taking this awfully well."

"The headline is sensational," Oldrich said, pointing to the paper. "It's actually 'presumed dead.' Tamas went behind enemy lines with the Seventh and Ninth and hasn't been seen since. Those are the two hard-as-nails brigades in the Adran army. Until I see a body, I'm going to believe that Tamas is in Kez, chewing up their army and spitting them out like toothpicks."

"So I won't be able to convince you to release Privileged Borbador with Tamas dead?"

"Sorry. You'll have to think of something else. And do it quick, because I can only help you take down Vetas until there's an army knocking on Adopest's front door."

Adamat stood. "I'll think of something."

"Also," Oldrich said, "with Tamas presumed dead, that means the clerks will tighten the noose on the checkbook he gave you. We'll need money for bribes or supplies sooner rather than later. If you've got some money stashed away..."

"I'll see what I can do," Adamat said. He reluctantly said goodbye to his children and headed for the door, only to have Oldrich join him in the hallway. "Sergeant?"

"I wanted to tell you something," Oldrich said in a hushed voice. He glanced into the mess. "If only to make you feel a little reassured. I don't want you to worry about your children. The boys have taken a real shine to them. Anyone finds us, comes in here looking for those kids, my boys'll scramble 'em good, and they won't be kind about it."

Adamat fought back the sudden tears in the corners of his eyes. "Thank you," he managed. "It does...it does mean a lot. Thank you."

Adamat got to his safe house by about one in the morning. He wearily climbed the stairs to the apartment above the landlady's, listening to the creak of his boots on the old wooden steps. Had it really been five days since he'd been here? He'd slept on a park bench, a hospice bunk, and a chair in a bar over the days since his meeting with the Proprietor as he planned his next move on Lord Vetas.

He needed a bath.

SouSmith sat next to a low-burning lamp on the sofa. The boxer looked up from a game of cards laid out in front of him, his brow furrowed.

"Bloody worried," SouSmith said.

Adamat closed the door with a sigh. He was hoping he'd have a good night's sleep before having to face SouSmith. He felt like the pit. His body hurt, he'd had little sleep in ten days, and he needed a good meal. He'd felt like this only once or twice before in his life, back when Manhouch succeeded his father and the commoners were restless and all police officers were working eighteen-hour days.

He never thought he'd feel like that again. He thought he'd left it all behind.

"Sorry," Adamat said.

SouSmith looked back at his game. He moved one card on top of another and pulled two off the table, setting them beside him on the sofa.

"Look like pit," SouSmith said.

"Feel like it, too."

"Where you been?" His beady eyes searched Adamat's face.

"The Proprietor reeled me in." Adamat limped over to a chair by the sofa and collapsed into it. "His boys worked me over all night before I got to see him. Turns out the whole thing was a big bloody mistake. Tossed me back out on the cobbles with 'sorry.'"

"You saw the Proprietor?"

Was that worry in SouSmith's voice?

"I came as close as one gets. Sat in the same room with him behind a black screen. Spoke to him through some knitting woman, like he's mute or something." Adamat frowned. Maybe the Proprietor *was* mute. Maybe the woman wasn't just a security measure but an interpreter. "Do we have any food?"

SouSmith jerked his thumb to a platter next to the sofa. Underneath the cover was a sandwich. The meat and cheese were warm, but it seemed like the best thing Adamat had ever tasted as he collected it and sank back into his chair.

Adamat felt a little strength return as he finished the meal. "He wants the same thing I want, it seems," Adamat said between the final few bites. "Lord Vetas has been causing him trouble. The Proprietor's boys only pulled me in because we were following the same woman." Adamat licked his fingers clean. "But now that the Proprietor knows we're after the same thing, it seems he's content to just step back and let me go at Vetas. Which is a bloody shame, because I need his help!" Adamat heard his own voice rise as he finished the sentence, and he grabbed the platter the sandwich was on and hurled it across the room. It clattered into one corner.

SouSmith leaned back on the sofa, his game forgotten, watching Adamat.

"I've never wanted to kill a man so badly as I do Lord Vetas," Adamat whispered. "I know where he is. I found his headquarters. I have a chance, and with the Proprietor's help I could do it, and he just pushed me back on the street." He took a shaky breath. "I'm going to do something very foolish, SouSmith, and I think you should walk away from me. Consider this the end of your employment."

SouSmith's eyebrows rose. "I'll decide that."

"I'm going to blackmail the Proprietor."

SouSmith began collecting his cards in one hand. A moment later he was done and he stood up. "For once," he said, "I agree with ya."

Adamat closed his eyes. He didn't blame SouSmith. Not one bit. But he'd been hoping against hope that SouSmith would once again refuse to leave. That he'd stay by Adamat's side and see this thing through.

SouSmith fetched his jacket from the rack by the door. "Sorry, friend," he said, "I'll die for ya, but the Proprietor won't stop with me."

Of course. SouSmith had his brother's family to worry about.

They shook hands, and Adamat heard SouSmith's heavy step down the stairs and out the front door.

Adamat fell back into his chair with his head in his hands.

SouSmith was big and powerful and he was worth five men in a fight, but he was also a friend. Adamat couldn't afford to have friends. Not with what he was about to do.

Adamat dragged himself to his feet just long enough to go find his bed. He didn't bother removing his clothes before he dropped into it.

CHAPTER

14

Taniel rubbed at his eyes and tried to remember what it felt like to sleep.

Five times in three days he'd fought in a bloody melee on the front lines. Five times he'd been the last one to leave the earthen defenses when the Kez proved too strong. Five times he'd been forced to make the long trek across the corpse-strewn fields dragging the wounded and dying, furious that they'd once again let the front fall beneath a Kez onslaught.

How many times could they retreat before the army was nothing but dead and wounded?

Taniel paused to look to the south. Budwiel was getting farther away every day. The front—or what had been the front until half an hour ago—was about a quarter mile away and obscured in powder smoke. The Kez soldiers were already leveling the earthworks and carting away their dead.

This last offensive had been a bad one. The infantry from the Seventeenth Brigade was mostly green and they'd broken and run before the retreat was even sounded. Taniel wondered if there was a single man unharmed after that mess. The groaning of the wounded in the surgeons' tents made his skin crawl.

He found Ka-poel sitting by the fire next to their tent. She stared at the coals, absently cleaning beneath her fingernails with the tip of one of her long needles. A pot of water boiled over the flames. She looked Taniel over once, then stared back at the fire.

Taniel dropped to the ground next to her. His whole body hurt. He was covered in countless cuts and bruises. A particularly nasty Warden had almost done him in, and he had a clean slice across the side of his stomach to show for it.

Ka-poel stood silently and moved around behind him, where she began to pull him out of the jacket. He didn't like when she undressed him—well, he *liked* it, but he'd heard officers muttering about the impropriety of their relationship already—but tonight he was far too tired to argue. She unbuttoned his shirt and cleaned his neck and torso with a hot, wet washcloth.

He lay on his side while she stitched the wound on his stomach, wincing every time the needle went in.

"Pole," he said while he lay there, "do you remember something being mentioned about Tamas putting together a school for powder mages in Adopest?"

She drummed two fingers on his arm. *Yes.*

"I think Sabon was in charge of it. I wonder if he's still up there. Pit, I could use his help." Taniel paused to think. Sabon's face floated in front of him, perfect teeth standing out against his black skin. Sabon was the only one Tamas ever listened to. He'd taught Taniel to shoot. A good soldier; a good man. "Damn it, I should have asked Ricard. Even if Sabon is with Tamas, there had to be a couple other powder mages left in Adopest. We need them on the front."

Ka-poel finished the stitching and Taniel climbed to his feet.

His shirt was nearly black, stiff with dried blood. He smelled like a slaughterhouse. He left it on the ground. Ka-poel would find someone to wash it for him. He fetched his one spare shirt from the tent and buttoned it up.

His tent was on the side of one of the mountain ridges that frames Surkov's Alley. It meant he had to sleep at an incline, but he also had a vantage over most of the valley, and right now he watched the Wings of Adom camp. The Wings' camp sat closer to the front than the Adran, and they held the east side of the valley with their flank against the river.

Reports were that the Wings were holding their front every day, but were forced to withdraw when the Adrans retreated so that the Kez couldn't flank them.

Tamas would have been furious had he been here to see it, that the mercenaries were putting forth a better defensive than the Adran army.

A pair of Wings brigadiers were making their way from their own camp toward the big, white-and-blue command tent at the rear of the Adran army. A few other officers seemed to be heading in the same direction. A meeting, it seemed. If Tamas were here, Taniel would be at that meeting.

A great many things were different with Tamas gone.

Not far from the command tent was the mess tent. In most armies the cooking was done by soldiers for their company, or sometimes even their squad. Here at the front, all the cooking was being done by one chef, or so the rumor went.

Mihali.

It wasn't hard to pick out the tall, fat figure making his way between the cookfires, checking on his small regiment of female assistants. Taniel frowned. Who was this man who claimed he was a god? Taniel had seen a god's face—Kresimir's—and put a bullet through his eye. Kresimir had looked like a god. Mihali did not.

Taniel took his jacket and headed down the mountainside toward the command tent.

Soldiers seemed to watch him everywhere he went. Some tipped their hats. Some saluted. Some just stared as he walked by, but Taniel didn't welcome the attention. Was he some kind of curiosity for them to gawk at? For years he'd always felt at home in the army, but now, with Tamas and the powder mages gone, Taniel felt alone, a foreigner.

He wondered what he looked like to them. He smelled like the alley behind a butcher, and he probably looked like one too. His body was covered in nicks and cuts, his black hair singed from a powder blast yesterday, his face dirty and bruised.

And he wondered what he was. He'd managed to escape serious injury in five hard, bloody fights. He'd been grazed by bullets seven times in the last two days. He'd been inches from being run through on half a dozen occasions. Was he just that fast? Or something else?

That kind of luck didn't happen. It was uncanny. Had it been like this in Fatrasta? No, he'd never been in an ongoing fight this bloody. He remembered ripping a rib from the Warden in Adopest and wondered if this luck was somehow connected to his newfound strength.

He reached the command tent, ignoring the guard who asked him to stop.

The tent was filled. There were perhaps twenty officers inside—what seemed like all the Wings brigadiers and Adran generals and colonels. Voices were raised, fists being shaken. Taniel slipped along the edge of the tent, trying to make some kind of sense of the argument.

He caught sight of a familiar face and moved up through the crowd.

Colonel Etan was ten years older than Taniel. He was a tall man with wide shoulders and brown hair cut short over a flat, ugly face. Not that anyone would tell him that he was ugly. The grenadiers of the Twelfth Brigade were the biggest, strongest men in the Adran army and one word against their colonel would find you at odds with all two thousand of them.

"What's going on?" Taniel whispered.

Colonel Etan gave him a quick glance. "Something about..." He paused to look again. "Taniel? Pit, Taniel, I heard you'd joined us at the front, but I didn't believe it. Where have you been?"

"Later," Taniel said. "What's the argument about?"

Etan's welcoming grin faded. "A messenger from the Kez. Demands that we surrender."

"So?" Taniel snorted. "There's nothing to argue about. No surrender."

"I agree, but some of the higher-ups don't. Something has them scared."

"Of course they're scared. They've been retreating from every fight! If they'd hold the line just once, we could break these Kez bastards."

"It's not that," Etan said. "The Kez are claiming they have Kresimir on their side. Not just in spirit, either, but that he's there in their camp!"

Taniel felt his whole body go cold. "Oh, pit."

"Are you all right? You don't look well."

"Kresimir can't be there. I killed him myself."

Etan's attention was now fully on Taniel. "You...killed him? I heard some wild rumors of a fight on South Pike before it collapsed, but you..."

"Yes," Taniel said. "I put a bullet in his eye and his heart. Watched him go down in a spray of godly blood."

"General Ket!" Etan shouted. "General Ket!" He grabbed Taniel's arm and shoved his way through the assembled officers. They all scrambled to get clear of him—no one stood their ground before a grenadier of his size.

"No, Etan..."

Etan pulled him out into the opening in the middle of the room, where the unfriendly faces of two dozen officers waited in tense expectation. "Tell them what you told me," Etan said to Taniel.

Taniel was once again terribly conscious of his frayed, bloody clothes and dirty face. The room seemed to spin slightly, the air hot and close.

He cleared his throat. "Kresimir is dead," Taniel said. "I killed him myself."

The clamor of voices made his head hurt worse than the sound of a musket volley. He looked around, trying to find an ally. He saw General Ket in the group, but she was no friend of his. Where was General Hilanska?

"Let him speak!" a woman shouted. Brigadier Abrax, of the Wings mercenaries. She was ten years younger than Taniel's father with a face twice as severe and short hair cropped above her ears. Her uniform was white, with red-and-gold trim.

General Ket took the sudden silence to sneer at Taniel. "You can't kill a god."

"I did," Taniel said. "I watched him die. I fired two ensorcelled bullets. I saw them hit. Saw him crumple. I was on that mountain when it began to collapse."

"Oh?" Ket demanded. "Then how'd you get down?"

Taniel opened his mouth, only to shut it again. How did he get down? The last thing he remembered was cradling Ka-poel's unconscious body as the building they were in began to buckle and fall.

"That's what I thought," Ket said. "The powder has gone to your head."

"He's a hero, sir!" Colonel Etan said.

"Even heroes can go mad! Provosts! Get him out of here! This meeting is no place for a captain."

Taniel was shoved to the side by someone, and he heard another voice say, "Kresimir isn't here! What kind of poppycock is that?"

"I've seen him."

Everything went still. Taniel recognized that voice. General Hilanska.

Hilanska was still seated while everyone else stood. He wore his dress uniform, decked out in dozens of medals, the collar freshly starched, his empty left sleeve pinned to his chest. The general looked tired, his immense weight sagging over the edge of the chair, his face pulled down from weariness.

Hilanska went on, his voice deep and level. "You've all seen him! At the parley this morning. He was there, you bloody fools, and you ignored him. The man at the back, who didn't speak. He wore a gold mask with only one eyehole. If any of you had bothered to listen, the Wings Privileged said he reeked of sorcery, more powerful than any they'd ever witnessed."

"That was only a Privileged," Ket said. "Not a god."

Hilanska struggled to his feet. "Call me mad, Ket. I dare you. Tamas believed Kresimir had returned. He believed Two-Shot here had shot him. But the bullets weren't fatal. Kresimir is, after all, a god."

Ket regarded Hilanska warily. "And yet Tamas still led the Seventh and Ninth behind the Kez lines to their deaths."

"He's not dead," Taniel said, feeling his blood rise.

Ket turned on him. "Says our dead field marshal's whelp."

"Whelp?" Taniel's vision went blurry. "I've killed hundreds of men. I've nearly held that damned line out there by myself the last two days. I feel like I'm the only one who wants to win this war, and you call me a whelp?"

Ket spat at his feet. "You'll take all the credit yourself? What an ego! Just because you sprang from Tamas's loins doesn't mean you have his skill, boy."

Taniel could barely think. He'd been on the front line every day fighting for this? Rage took control of him. "I'll kill you, you stupid bitch!"

Taniel felt his muscles tense to leap at General Ket, when something struck him in the side of the head. He staggered and tried to run at Ket. Hands grabbed him, arms pulled him away. He was hit again in the head. Thrashing and yelling, he was forced out of the command tent.

"Taniel," he heard Colonel Etan say in his ear, "calm down, Taniel, please!"

It took the sight of a half-dozen sharpened pikes leveled at his face to bring Taniel back from the brink of rage. The provosts—Adran military police—behind those pikes wore expressions that said they'd poke him full of holes in an instant.

"That's enough of that," Etan said, pushing away a pike. He was able to get the provosts to back off a few steps.

Now that the rage had passed, Taniel felt cold, weak. His whole body began to shake. Had he really just called Ket a bitch in front of the entire General Staff? What had come over him?

"Are you trying to get yourself killed?" Etan demanded. "I've heard rumors that there was a powder mage out on the front each of the last few days, throwing himself into the teeth of the enemy like he wanted to die. I'd never imagined it was you. You'll be lucky to get off with a flogging for this. Attacking General Ket! I can't believe it."

Taniel pulled his knees to his chest and tried to get his body to stop shaking. "Are you done?" Why was he shaking so much? It scared him worse than looking down the wrong end of a Warden's sword. Was it the mala withdrawal? His powder?

"Taniel..." Etan stared at him, and Taniel could tell there was genuine concern in his eyes. "Taniel, you dragged me five feet before I managed to clock you in the side of the head. I've dropped men twice your size with that punch, and I had to do it three times to even faze you. Pit, *I'm* twice your size! I know that powder mages are strong, but..."

"I'll take full responsibility," Taniel said. "Hopefully you'll not be reprimanded."

"I'm not worried about me."

"Captain?"

They both looked up. General Hilanska stood over them. The provosts were gone.

"Colonel, I'd like a word with the captain in private, please."

Etan left them, and Taniel slowly climbed to his feet, unsure as to whether he'd be able to stand but certain that General Hilanska might be his only ally left in this camp. "Sir?" He swayed to the side and stumbled. Hilanska caught him with his one good arm.

"Ket wants your head," Hilanska said.

"I'd imagine."

"You know," the old general said, "with Tamas gone, powder mages don't have any pull anymore. Some of the ranking officers seem to want to pretend you never existed."

Taniel leaned his head back and looked up at the darkening sky. Some stars were beginning to show, and the moon glowed bright on the eastern horizon. "Do you believe he's dead?"

Hilanska began to walk, forcing Taniel to follow him on wobbly legs. Taniel's hands were shaking a little less, now.

"I don't want to believe it," Hilanska said. "None of us do, despite how the others are acting. We all loved your father. He was a brilliant strategist. But all contact was lost. We haven't heard from any of our spies in the Kez army for three weeks now. We have to face the facts. Tamas is likely dead."

If Tamas was dead, so were Vlora and Sabon and the rest of the powder cabal and the Seventh and Ninth. Taniel felt his chest tighten. No tears. There wouldn't be any of those. Not for Tamas. But for him to be gone forever... "And Kresimir?"

"Whatever you did to him, he survived it."

"What of this Mihali? This god-chef?"

Hilanska shrugged. "Your father seemed to think he was Adom reborn."

"And you?"

"I don't have any evidence either way. His cooking is amazing. Supposedly, he and Kresimir have some kind of a truce. Something about letting the mortals fight it out." Hilanska spit out of the corner of his mouth. "I don't like the idea that we're being used in some kind of cosmic battle."

"No," Taniel said. "Neither do I." His head was starting to clear. Things weren't spinning anymore. "What can Ket do to me?"

"She's a general. You're a captain. A roomful of people just watched you try to kill her."

"I wouldn't have killed her. And I'm not just a captain. I'm a powder mage."

Hilanska said, "I know. Tamas kept you outside the rank system. If he was still here, you would have gotten away with it. Ket is a good general, but she has a narrow vision of things. Tamas knew that. You're just a captain now, though."

"Who has been ordering the retreats along the front?"

Hilanska stopped and turned toward Taniel. "I have."

"You?" Taniel had to keep himself from stepping back.

Hilanska set his hand on Taniel's shoulder, as a father might to his son. "We can't hold them," Hilanska said. "Up until you arrived, we had no answer to those Black Wardens. They just cut right through the infantry like nothing I've ever seen. They're faster and stronger than regular Wardens, and powder won't ignite near them. Even with you here, we can't hold the line."

"What about sorcery? The Wings have Privileged."

"Sorcery doesn't do a thing to the new Wardens. It's baffling, really. I can't imagine that the Kez Cabal would create something they might not be able to control."

Taniel mulled over that for a moment. His brain was starting to work again. That seemed a good sign. The rage was becoming a distant memory. "Maybe they didn't create them."

"What do you mean?"

"Well, we've never seen a Warden created out of a powder mage before. Maybe Kresimir did that. Maybe the remnants of the Kez Cabal have no say."

"It makes sense." Hilanska watched him for a few moments. "Where are you sleeping?"

Taniel looked up to the side of the mountain. "Have a tent set up there."

"I'll get you a real room," Hilanska said. "You need some sleep. Come find me in an hour, and I'll have something arranged. Now, though, I need to try to convince Ket not to have you hanged."

Taniel's heart had finally stopped pounding. He felt deflated, ill. "Thank you. General?"

Hilanska paused and looked back.

"I've been turned down for more powder by a dozen different quartermasters. They claim we don't have enough black powder and the General Staff is rationing it. Is there really a shortage?" Taniel thought back to Ricard Tumblar. The union boss had mentioned something about the supply demands from the front being unusually high.

"It's not as bad as all that," Hilanska said quietly. "I'll make sure you get what you need. Anything else?"

"Yes." Taniel hesitated, not sure if he wanted to know the answer to his next question. "Are there any powder mages left in Adopest? I know Tamas was training some new ones."

"They all went with him. Even the trainees."

"Pit. I'd hoped that Sabon was still here somewhere."

Hilanska's face fell and he let out a soft sigh. "You haven't heard?"

"Heard what?"

"Sabon's dead, my boy. Took a bullet from an air rifle to the side of the head over a month ago."

Hilanska patted Taniel on the shoulder and headed off into the night.

It was several moments before Taniel could manage to take another deep, shaky breath. He looked at the sky again. The daylight was only a sliver on the western mountains now; the sky above, a blanket of brilliant stars on dark blue.

Sabon, dead. His mentor. His teacher.

That had to have shaken Tamas. Perhaps enough that Tamas had made mistakes.

If Sabon was dead, then maybe Tamas was as well.

Was Taniel the last powder mage left in Adro? It seemed that way. The army retreated more every day. Kresimir was alive, and demanding their surrender. What could he do?

Fight.

The only answer.

CHAPTER
15

Tamas stood in the stirrups, watching through a looking glass as Kez scouts crested the last hilltop between the Kez cavalry and Tamas's two ragged brigades of infantry.

After a few more moments of examining the enemy scouts he sat down and handed the looking glass to Olem.

"We'll have about two-thirds of our men inside the forest by the time they reach us."

Behind him, the Hune Dora Forest rose above the plains. The prairie up to the forest had been logged to the twig a century ago, but Hune Dora itself was a barricade of trees, protected by royal decree and declared a national property of Kez. The terrain changed drastically here, as the rolling foothills of the prairie gave way to sharp mountain ridges that crept like mighty old roots toward the Amber Expanse.

Tamas suspected the difficulty in logging Hune Dora had as

much to do with the forest being protected as the king's hunting practices.

He spurred his mount around and rode to catch up with the rear of the column. The men marched at half-time as the elements of the column ahead of them adjusted from six abreast to four abreast in order to smoothly transition to the forest roadway.

"Colonel Arbor," Tamas said as he joined the rear guard.

Colonel Arbor was ancient as army standards went. He was ten years older than Tamas, and had long since lost most of his hearing and all of his teeth. Despite his age he could march, fight, and drink like a man of thirty, a fact he attributed to a glass of wine and fine cigar before bed every night. The colonel walked beside the very last men of the rear guard, rifle slung over his shoulder like a common soldier, cavalry saber at his side. The First Battalion of the Seventh Brigade was Tamas's very best. It was no accident they carried the rear.

"Eh?" the colonel said.

"I wish you'd ride." Tamas nearly had to shout, just to be sure the colonel would hear him.

The colonel flexed his jaw and popped out his false teeth into one hand. "Won't do it," he said. "My old bollocks hurt like the pit in a saddle. Besides, sir, we need horses for scouting." He eyed Tamas and Olem's mounts as if he thought they'd find better use with the rangers.

"We're going to have company in about fifteen minutes," Tamas said. "You've the rear guard. I want a walking retreat. Steady and brave."

Arbor cleared his throat and spit out a wad of phlegm. "Battalion!" he screamed. Farther up the line, a captain jumped half a foot in surprise. "Fix sword bayonets! Interlocking windmill. Livers in ten!"

The orders were passed up the column by sergeants, though half the brigade had probably already heard them. Arbor brushed his false teeth off on his uniform jacket and then slipped them into his back pocket. "Wouldn't want them to get damaged in the coming melee." He winked at Tamas.

"Right." Tamas urged his mount forward to join his powder mages farther up the column. Behind him, Arbor's battalion fanned out across the prairie, forming a half-moon shield around the rear of the column.

"Sir!" Andriya turned to Tamas with a salute as Tamas rode up to the group. Five powder mages gathered around Andriya. They'd all spent the night hunting and scouting, and looked like the pit, with bags beneath their eyes. Tamas could smell the black powder hanging around them like a cloud.

Tamas reined in. "The Kez van is just over that hill. About twelve hundred dragoons coming on hard."

"We going to stay and fight?" Andriya asked. He had the same hungry look he always did when it came time to shed Kez blood.

"No," Tamas said. "The van will be here about an hour before the rest. I want us to be well into the forest by that time. Don't worry," he added upon seeing the disappointment on Andriya's face. "We'll have plenty to kill."

He looked over the field of battle—for it was that. No doubt now that blood would be shed within the hour. He examined the tree line and the contour of the land, then the old stone walls of the abandoned city of Hune Dora. With more time to plan—a day, or even a few hours—he'd have been able to set up a trap and exterminate the Kez vanguard. As it was, he needed his men off the plains.

He pointed to where the forest rose sharply from the prairie. "Andriya, I want your team a few hundred yards out from the tree line. Vlora, put yours on those rocks over there." He pointed to the north. "As soon as they're within range, take horses off the front. Try to stumble the whole column. When they spread for a charge, kill their officers. Dismissed."

The powder mages scattered at a run. They'd be in place and

begin firing within a few minutes. It might buy his brigades a little extra time to get into the forest.

He'd placed his powder mages at high points to be able to make long shots, but the road itself fell into a wide, flat gully before rising once more into the trees. The Kez vanguard would have an easy charge.

Just inside the forest, the Seventh's Fourth Battalion had taken up firing positions. They'd give the First Battalion some cover if it came to a sprint into the woods.

Tamas whirled his horse to face northwest, toward the forest, then dismounted. He cracked a powder charge between his fingers and sprinkled some on his tongue. He felt the powder trance take hold.

"Carbine," he ordered.

Olem, who had been shadowing him silently this whole time, handed him a loaded carbine. Tamas lowered himself to one knee. The carbine was a shortened rifle, able to be fired and be reloaded on horseback easier than a long rifle, but it was still best to fire dismounted. Instead of an elongated stock to hold it steady, it had a steel handle attached to the barrel.

Tamas gripped the carbine tightly and lined up his shot on the horizon. He watched as the dragoon scouts drew closer.

A Kez dragoon was typically armed with a carbine, one pistol, and a straight sword. The older Kez commanders treated them as mounted infantry—that is, they rode horses but fought on foot. Younger commanders utilized them as light cavalry.

The current scenario would see them firing carbine, then pistol, and then making an open charge with the hope of breaking Tamas's rear guard. Tamas was willing to bet his horse on the tactic.

It wasn't long until the main company of the Kez vanguard breached the far hill. Tamas breathed out gently, sighting down his carbine. The dragoons were a little over a mile away and still in formation at four abreast. The horsehair on their spiked cavalry helmets waved in the wind, jostling as they rode.

Tamas heard the crack of a rifle come from his left and knew Andriya had taken the first shot. Several long seconds passed, filled with the reports of rifle fire.

The first dragoon stumbled. The horse fell, twisting as it went down. Another, then another fell. They slammed into the road in a cloud of dust. The horses immediately behind the front line became entangled and many of them went down, tumbling and thrashing beneath the hooves of their own allies.

Tamas didn't have to hear the screams of the horses for them to echo in his head.

They had to have known Tamas had his powder mages, yet they'd kept close formation. Tamas wanted to shake his head at the mistake. The dragoons should have been ready for it.

But then again, who is ready for a bullet to take them when the enemy is only a dot on the horizon?

He pulled his trigger.

A few seconds later his bullet entered a horse's eye. The beast jerked and fell. The rider went up and over his horse, hitting the ground hard enough to break his neck.

Tamas handed Olem his carbine and took a loaded one in its place.

The Kez column spread out from the road, widening their formation. More came over the hilltop. Tamas's initial elation at seeing a dozen brought down so quickly disappeared. He had twelve hundred more to deal with. Tripping up a few at the head of the column was hardly a victory.

He searched the breadth of the dragoons for an officer's epaulets. He found them quickly and rested his carbine against his shoulder. A deep breath. Let it out. Squeeze the trigger.

The bullet caught the young officer in the throat. He was thrown from the saddle, and Tamas was instantly on to the next target.

For the next couple of minutes, his powder mages fired at will, each bullet finding a deadly mark with few exceptions. The Kez vanguard drew closer.

"Better mount up, sir," Olem said, not a hint of nervousness in his voice.

Tamas could read the dragoon formation. They spread on the eastern side of the road in columns six deep. They would hit the First Battalion's flank, driving them away from the possible protection of the city of Hune Dora's walls. The dragoons would strike hard and fast, avoiding entanglement, and be back out of range of conventional musket fire within a few moments. They would be able to pull back around behind Hune Dora's walls, shielding them from powder mages, and then sweep an attack against the column's flank.

Tamas saw carbines lifted to shoulders. He swung up into his saddle and cleared the barrel of his carbine.

"Watch the wall," he said to Olem. "Let's go."

Arbor's First Battalion slowed to a crawl. Every other man suddenly stopped, whirled, and lowered to one knee. Tamas could hear Arbor scream the order to fire, and a cloud of powder smoke rose in the air. Fifty or more dragoons fell. The soldiers leapt to their feet, reloading as they resumed their march.

Tamas galloped toward the rear guard and drew his curved cavalry saber.

The dragoons let loose with their carbines, leaving their own clouds of powder smoke like a memory behind them.

The line of soldiers staggered. Some fell, some limped along, crying for help. None of them broke to tend to the wounded.

They'd been trained well.

The dragoons holstered their carbines in the saddle. Pistols were drawn, aim taken.

The second line of Adran soldiers turned, knelt, and fired.

A cloud of smoke went up from the dragoons as they returned shots with their pistols. They were out of the cloud only a moment later, swords drawn, as they came in for the charge.

Arbor's First Battalion turned to meet the charge. Their sword bayonets were fixed on the ends of their muskets, making the weapons long enough to act as pikes. Tamas cursed. Their formation was too loose...

The dragoons' thunderous charge was upon Tamas's soldiers.

Horses screamed as they were impaled upon sword bayonets. Men fell from their mounts. Adran soldiers were cut about the neck and face by straight-edged cavalry swords. The lines of infantry and cavalry met, disappearing in a bloody tangle.

Tamas leaned forward, urging more speed out of his charger, Olem right beside him. Across the field of battle, opposite him where the old walls of Hune Dora turned around a hill, another cavalry charge appeared.

Gavril was at the head of these cavalry. Two hundred cuirassiers in the dark-blue pants and crimson coats of the Adran heavy cavalry raced across the prairie just as the tattered remains of the Kez dragoons extracted themselves from the First Battalion.

Though still outnumbered three to one, Gavril's cuirassiers hit the dragoons with the force of an artillery shell. The collision was audible, the yells of the dragoons turning desperate at the sudden appearance of an enemy at their flank. Somewhere in the midst of the tangle a Kez trumpet belted out a desperate retreat.

A moment later and Tamas hit the fray himself. He swung his cavalry sword out and across, neatly severing the carotid artery of a Kez dragoon. He whirled in the saddle, barely catching the sword strike of another dragoon. He reached out with his senses and detonated a powder charge in the dragoon's breast pocket and immediately urged his charger forward, looking for the next target.

The last of the dragoon vanguard extracted themselves and fled back toward their brigades.

A cheer went up among Tamas's men. It carried from the First Battalion down the column and on to the Ninth Brigade, which was already safe inside the forest.

Tamas caught his breath as his charger picked its way through the bodies of men and horses to join Gavril. "Rein in your cuirassiers," Tamas shouted to Gavril. Gavril nodded and gave the orders.

"The main body of cavalry will be here in an hour," Tamas said, gasping, his heart still pounding, the powder smoke stinging his eyes and reminding him that he was an old man.

Gavril brought his mount close to Tamas and lowered his voice. "What will we do with the dead and wounded?"

Tamas examined the field of battle. There were at least a thousand dead and wounded, counting the Kez and Adrans together. The Kez couldn't have retreated with more than three hundred of their men. There was no way Tamas could march with his wounded.

"Arbor!" Tamas said, searching. "Olem, find Arbor."

A few moments later, the old colonel joined him on the field. He had a new cut on his cheek and powder burns on his sleeves. He'd seen action himself, it seemed.

"Sir?"

"Status of the First Battalion?"

"Fine and kicking, sir. We gave 'em pit. No exact count yet, but I lost no more than two hundred men."

Two hundred men from Tamas's best battalion. Almost a fourth of them. It was a staggering victory against almost twelve hundred dragoons, but Tamas couldn't afford to lose a single man, let alone two hundred of his very best.

"Pack up your wounded. Send them up the column. Strip the battlefield of everything useful."

"Permission to slaughter the horses, sir?" Arbor said. "We need the meat."

"Granted. Give your men a battlefield burial. I wish we had more time, but I mean to be off this prairie when the rest of the Kez get here."

Arbor gave a brisk nod and headed off, giving orders.

"A battlefield burial, sir?" Olem asked.

"Something we did on the march in Gurla. When another army pressed on us after a fight, we'd wrap our dead in their canvas tents with their names marked on the canvas and hope the enemy had the decency to give them a proper burial." Tamas sighed. He didn't like battlefield burials. The dead deserved more respect than that.

"Did they?"

"What?"

"Did they give them a proper burial, sir?"

"Four times out of five...no. They'd leave them to rot in the Gurlish sun."

Tamas swung out of his saddle and knelt down beside a wounded Adran soldier. The man stared into the sky, teeth clenched, his knee a bloody mess. A single glance told Tamas that the leg would most likely have to be amputated. Until then, how to move the man at all? Tamas drew his knife and held the handle to the wounded man.

"Bite down on this," he said. "It'll ease the pain a bit. Olem, have a few boys check the city. Maybe there are some abandoned wagons. Gavril, have your men catch any of the unwounded Kez horses. We might need them."

He looked toward the southern horizon. Soon enough, fifteen thousand cavalry would breach that hill.

It took four whole days of searching and over a thousand krana in bribes before Adamat found where Field Marshal Tamas had stashed Borbador, the last living Privileged from Manhouch's royal cabal.

It was funny, Adamat decided, that he was using the field marshal's own money to try to undo his orders.

Colonel Verundish stood beside him. She was a smart-looking Deliv woman in her fifties, her ebony skin a complement to the dark blue of her Adran uniform, with straight black hair tied back.

"He's here?" Adamat asked.

"He is," she confirmed.

They stood on a bluff at the very northernmost district of Adopest, where the rows of houses abruptly gave way to farmland. Here, the streets didn't smell so much like shit and soot. Here, there were fewer factories and people.

Not a bad place to live. If Adamat survived long enough to retire, maybe he could move his family out here.

Verundish nodded down to the manor below them. The grounds were overgrown, most of the windows broken, the walls vandalized. Like so many other manors belonging to the nobility, it had been gutted by Tamas's troops of anything of value and then opened to the public after the execution of its former owner.

Adamat followed Verundish down from the bluff and entered the manor grounds by a back gate. The sorry state of the place made Adamat sad. He had no love of the nobility, not by any stretch, but many of these manors had been architectural works of art. Some had been burned to the ground, some crushed to rubble for their stone. This one had got off lightly with mere vandalism.

They entered through the servants' quarters and made their way to the second floor. Adamat counted two dozen men and women, all soldiers by their look. They wore greatcoats over their uniforms, despite the summer heat, and each one gave Adamat a cursory glance as he went by.

A glimpse of a chevron over a powder horn told Adamat that these were Riflejacks—more of Tamas's best soldiers.

Verundish stopped outside the last room toward the rear of the servants' quarters. "You've got five minutes," she said.

"What will you do with him?" Adamat asked. "Now that Tamas is dead?"

The colonel's lips curled into a scowl. "*If* Tamas is dead—we'll wait for his generals to return to Adopest and hand him over to them. They'll decide his fate."

"Tamas isn't in danger from him anymore."

"I don't care what you think you know, Inspector," Verundish said. "The field marshal slaughtered the cabal for a reason, and this man is its last living member. Now go on." Verundish lifted a pocket watch in one hand and looked down at it. "Your five minutes is ticking."

Adamat opened the door and slipped inside.

Privileged Borbador sat tied to a chair in the corner of the room. His feet were bound tight against the posts of the chair, his hands locked in stiff iron gloves that would prevent his fingers from moving. He looked comfortable, for all the tightness of the ropes. He was thinner than the last time Adamat had seen him, and his chin sported a full-grown beard. In front of him was a stand, like the kind that musicians used to hold their music. Bo looked up from it.

"Bo," Adamat said, taking his hat in his hands.

Bo cleared his throat. "Yes?"

"My name is Adamat. We met a few months ago at Shoulder-crown."

"Inspector. Yes. I remember you. You're the one who brought my gaes to Tamas's attention."

Adamat grimaced. "I'm sorry. I was working for him."

"You're not anymore?"

"Well, the rumors are that he's dead."

Bo stretched his neck out and tilted his head from side to side. It was about the only part of him he could move. He didn't respond.

"Bo," Adamat said. "Has the necklace around your neck—the one supporting the gaes—loosened since his reported death?"

Bo's eyes narrowed. Not much, but just enough to give Adamat his answer. The gaes was still in place. Tamas was alive. And Bo hadn't told the soldiers guarding him.

"Interesting," Adamat said aloud.

"Think you could turn the page for me?" Bo nodded at the stand in front of him.

Adamat moved around to see a book propped on the stand. He

obliged by turning it to the next page and then smoothing the page out with one hand.

"Many thanks. I've been staring at that one page for about half an hour now."

Adamat asked, "How strong is the compulsion to kill Tamas?"

"Why do you ask?"

"Could you resist it? He's quite far from here. Could you resist the compulsion to go looking for him?"

"For a time," Bo said. "Yes. It's only six months since Manhouch's death. I think I have a year until the gaes kills me."

"Two minutes!" Verundish called from the hallway.

Adamat lowered his voice. "If I get you out, will you help me?"

"Help you do what?"

"I need to rescue my wife and kill a man who is a threat to this entire country." Adamat had no idea if Bo was a patriot of any kind, but the addendum sounded good.

"What is this, some kind of pulp novel?" Bo smirked at him.

"It's very serious, actually."

Bo's smirk dissolved. "Why do you need my help?"

"The man I need to kill has over sixty men guarding him—one of them is a Privileged."

"Really, now? You work for Field Marshal Tamas—who is reported as dead—and you're going after a man who's kidnapped your wife and has the kind of resources to have sixty enforcers and a Privileged at his disposal?" Adamat could practically sense Bo's desire to flex his fingers. "Have you ever thought of getting out of the investigating business?"

"You don't know the half of it," Adamat said.

"Get me out of here and I'll spend a week as a mime in the King's Garden," Bo said, "whatever you want."

Adamat regarded the Privileged for a moment. Was he in any shape to fight another sorcerer? Adamat knew a Privileged needed gloves to do his magic, to protect his hands from being burned by the Else, but there was no sign of Bo's. Could a Privileged even be trusted?

"All right," Adamat said. "I'll do what I can."

Verundish opened the door. "Time is up, Inspector."

Adamat followed Verundish back out of the servants' quarters. She stopped him once they'd reached the edge of the manor grounds. "You can find your own way back?" she asked.

"Yes." Adamat examined her for a long moment. She watched him, her brown eyes unreadable. He would have guessed her as the military type even without the uniform—her back was straight, her hands clasped behind her like a soldier at ease.

This was a great risk he was taking, but he had no other choice if he wanted to free Borbador—and then Faye.

"I need Privileged Borbador," Adamat said.

"Pardon?" Verundish was just turning to go. She stopped and looked back at him.

"I need you to free him."

Verundish cleared her throat. "That's not happening, Inspector."

"Name your price. Field Marshal Tamas is dead. Let Bo go and you and your men can join the defensive at Surkov's Alley. Or leave the country. That might be the best idea, with what I've heard from the front."

"That"—her words were angry, clipped—"is treason."

"Please," Adamat said. "Privileged Borbador is my only chance to save my wife—maybe even to save this country. Free, he's of value. Under guard, he just ties up you and your men."

"You should go now, Inspector," Verundish said.

Adamat let out a small sigh. He'd half expected her to arrest him right then and there. He should be glad she was letting him go.

"Inspector."

He paused. "Yes?"

"Seventy-five thousand krana. Banknotes. You have a week."

CHAPTER
16

Taniel walked among the corpses on the battlefield and wondered how many had died that day.

A few hundred? A few thousand?

Surgeons, thieves, the families of soldiers—they all picked their way among the bodies, finding the wounded first and getting them back to their respective armies before bothering to stack the dead into carts like so much firewood, then taking them to be buried in mass graves.

There were always far more wounded than dead. That's how it always was, even when sorcery was involved. At least, that's how it was immediately after a battle. Over the next week well over half of the wounded would die. Even more would end up crippled for life.

He'd picked a horrid profession, Taniel reflected.

Well. Not so much "picked." There's no picking your profession when Tamas is your father. Taniel couldn't think of a time when he didn't want to be a soldier. Vlora, the girl he'd thought was the love of his life, wanted to be a soldier, too. So Taniel had gone along with his father's wishes and trained to be a powder mage. It was the only life he'd ever known.

And now Tamas, Vlora, Sabon, and everyone else who'd ever influenced Taniel in his youth were all dead and gone.

Taniel tried to shake the weight of that thought from his shoulders and kept walking.

Soldiers weren't supposed to come onto the battlefield after a skirmish like this. The temporary truce after each battle that allowed either side to collect their own dead and wounded was tentative enough without armed, hot-tempered men taking to the field.

That didn't stop some of them from coming. Taniel watched a fistfight break out between a sobbing Kez soldier and a wounded Adran sergeant. It was put down quickly by both Kez and Adran provosts, and the offending parties hauled off.

"How long do you usually stay out here?" Taniel asked.

Ka-poel knelt beside the dead body of an Adran soldier. She looked up at him briefly before lifting the dead man's left hand and using her long needle to pick something out of the man's chewed fingernails. What was it? Hair from a Kez officer? Blood of someone still alive? Only she knew.

Taniel didn't really expect an answer. She'd been less than communicative lately, even for her.

She moved to the next body. Taniel followed, watching as she cut a bit of bloody shirt off a dead Kez officer.

Taniel had left his jacket and weapons back at camp. No need for anyone to know he was out here. Regardless, some of the Adran surgeons gave him respectful nods. Others a respectful distance.

He lifted his eyes to the Kez camp. Where was Kresimir? he wondered, a little thrill of fear working up his spine. The god was lying low. Unseen. Even when Taniel opened his third eye, there was no sign of the overwhelming glow of power that should surround a god.

At this point, Taniel worried more about being killed by the Kez than about falling into the god's hands.

The Kez marched forward every day. Sometimes only a few hundred feet. Other times as much as a quarter mile, but always a little closer to Adopest. Eventually the valley would open up into the Adran basin and the Kez would use their hugely superior numbers to surround the Adran army and strike at several cities at once. They'd ravage the countryside, and Adro would be forced to capitulate.

What would Tamas have done?

Bah. Tamas would have held the damned line. That's all the Adran army needed to do: keep from losing their front every damned day.

All Taniel could do was fight. He couldn't keep the generals from sounding a retreat, even when he felt the Kez about to break and run. He couldn't hold the whole thing by himself.

"That stuff you gather," Taniel asked as Ka-poel rose to her feet, "is it just from men who are alive?"

She nodded, depositing something into one of the tiny leather bags in her satchel.

Even the living left a bit of themselves behind on the battlefield. Blood, hair, nails. Sometimes a finger or bit of skin. Ka-poel gathered it all up and stored it for later.

Taniel jumped a little at the sudden crack of a musket, but it was just the sound of a provost shooting a looter. He licked his lips and looked at the Kez camp again. What if Kresimir was out here, walking among the dead? What if he saw Taniel? Knew who he was? What he'd done?

"I'm going back to camp," Taniel said. He looked over his shoulder several times on the long walk back, watching Ka-poel continue to pick her way among the bodies.

Dinner was being served as Taniel worked his way through the camp. Quartermasters were returning to their companies with rations of meat, kettles of soup, loaves of bread. Far better fare than soldiers usually saw on the battlefield. Taniel could smell the food, making his mouth water. This chef, Mihali, god or not, created incredible dishes. Taniel didn't know that bread could have the swirls of flavor and buttery softness that this stuff did.

Taniel stopped at his room. General Hilanska had found him a shed to bed down in. It wasn't much, but it was private. He snatched his jacket, slipping a few powder charges into his pocket, then hesitated at his belt. He should be able to wander his own camp without fear, but something told him to go armed. Perhaps just paranoia. Or maybe it was the idea that General Ket's provosts were still looking for him. Why they'd not found him yet was anyone's guess.

Taniel buckled the belt, with two pistols, around his waist.

He'd only taken a few steps from his tent when a soldier accosted him.

"Sir!"

Taniel paused. The soldier was a young man, maybe twenty-five. Still older than Taniel himself. A private in the Eleventh Brigade, by his insignia.

When Taniel didn't answer, the soldier went on hesitantly. "Sir, the fellows and I, we were wondering if you'd do us the honor of joining us for dinner. It's all the same food, sir, and the company is good." He held his flat-top forage cap in both hands, wringing it.

"Where?" Taniel asked.

"Just right over there, sir." The soldier perked up a little. "We've got a fifth of Doubin rum, and Finley plays the flute something fierce."

Taniel couldn't help but feel suspicious. He set a hand on one of his pistols. "Why are you so nervous, soldier?"

The soldier ducked his head. "Sorry, sir, I didn't mean to bother you." He turned to slink away, obviously distraught.

Taniel caught up to him in just a few quick steps. "Doubin rum, you say?"

"Aye, sir."

"Horrid shit. That's the stuff sailors drink."

The soldier's forehead wrinkled in a frown. "It's the best we can do, sir." There was a flash of anger in his eyes.

They both stopped in the middle of the path, the soldier still holding his hat. He glared at Taniel now. Taniel could imagine what was going through his head: *Damned officers. Think they're so high and mighty. Plenty of good stuff to drink at the officers' mess. Won't sit with a soldier, not for a moment.*

"What's your name, soldier?"

"Flint."

No "sir" on the end of that. Taniel nodded, as if he'd not noticed. "I got a taste for Doubin rum on the ship from Fatrasta. Haven't tasted it all summer. I'd be honored, if you'd have me."

"You mocking me?"

"No," Taniel said. "Not a bit. Lead on."

Flint's frown slowly began to slide. "This way, sir."

It wasn't more than twenty yards to Flint's fire. There were two men beside the fire, keeping Mihali's soup warm in an old iron pot. One had a large nose, crooked off to the side from not being set after breaking, while the other was a short, round man practically bursting from his uniform. The one with the nose froze at the sight of Taniel, a spoon lifted halfway to his mouth.

"Captain, sir," Flint said, gesturing to the two men by the fire. "The one with the nose there is Finley. Ugliest man in the Eleventh. And that round bit of meat there is Faint, on account that she fainted the first time she fired a musket. Finley, Flint, and Faint. We're the fellows of the Eleventh Brigade."

Taniel lifted his eyebrows. He'd not in a hundred years have guessed that Faint was a woman.

"Fellows, this is Captain Taniel Two-Shot, hero of the Fatrastan War and the Battle for South Pike."

Faint seemed skeptical. "You sure this is Taniel Two-Shot?"

"That's him, all right," Finley said. "I was with Captain Ajucare when we went after the Privileged at the university."

"I thought you looked familiar," Taniel said. "I never forget a nose."

Flint laughed and punched Finley in the arm. Finley fell off his chair, and Taniel heard himself chuckle. It was a raspy, nasty sound, like an instrument desperately in need of tuning. How long had it been since he'd laughed?

Flint fetched a folding cloth chair and brought it to Taniel. Finley poured them each a pewter tin of soup, and then bread and mutton was passed around.

They ate in quiet for several minutes. Taniel was the first one to break the silence. "I heard the Second took a beating a couple of weeks ago."

"Aye," Flint said. "That we did."

"We were on the wall," Faint said. "The wall in Budwiel when the Black Wardens came over."

Finley stared quietly into his soup.

"Faint here," Flint said. "She punched one of those Wardens in the nose with that ham fist of hers. Knocked him right off the bulwark."

"I'd imagine that gave him quite the shock. I heard it was bad," Taniel said. "I'm glad to see you got out."

"Most weren't so lucky," Finley said quietly. Flint and Faint's smiles disappeared.

Taniel cleared his throat, looking around. Usually a squad would eat together. "All that's left of your squad?" he asked as respectfully as he could.

Faint chuckled. Finley pushed her. "It's not funny," Finley said.

"It's a little funny," Faint said.

Taniel wondered whether to smile at the joke. "What?"

"Not our squad, sir," Flint spoke up. "This is all that's left of our company."

Taniel felt his mouth go dry. A company was usually about two hundred men. To lose all but three...

"No wounded?" he asked.

"Probably," Faint said. She ladled herself another tin of soup. "But not that we've seen. This deal with the Kez, where we clean up our own dead and wounded after each battle, only came about after Budwiel. We left Budwiel at a run. Left behind supplies, ammunition, weapons...loved ones. Everyone who couldn't run is now a slave, or worse."

"What's worse than being a slave?" Flint asked.

Finley looked up from rolling a cigarette. "Where do you think they keep getting those Wardens? Why torture and twist your own people if you've got prisoners?"

"It takes years to make and train a Warden," Taniel said.

"Does it?" Finley asked. He lit his cigarette with a burning stick from the fire. "Rumors are going around the men, rumors that they've got Kresimir himself in the camp."

Flint shook his head. "If they had Kresimir, we'd all be dead."

"We've got Adom reborn," Faint said. She held up her mutton and bread. "Mihali is keeping Kresimir from destroying us all."

Flint rolled his eyes. "Come on, now."

"There's another rumor," Finley said. He looked up, meeting Taniel's eyes across the fire. "There's a rumor Taniel Two-Shot put a bullet in Kresimir's eye, and now Kresimir wears a mask that covers half his face—and it don't have no eyehole in it." He leaned over, offering his smoking cigarette to Taniel.

Taniel took a long drag at the cigarette. Nasty things, he'd always thought, but he made exceptions for nights like this, when it was more about camaraderie than habit. "I heard a rumor," he said, coughing and turning his head toward Flint, "that there was Doubin rum at this fire."

"Now that"—Faint pointed at Taniel—"is fact." She retreated to her tent for a moment and came back with an earthen jug. "Get your flute, Finley," she said. "I've had enough of this dark talk."

Taniel was offered the jug first. He took a sip of the stuff and felt his whole body shudder. "Gah," he said, wiping his mouth on his sleeve.

"My da works for Doubin and Company," Faint said, taking the jug. "Tastes like a demon's own piss, don't it!" She threw back the jug, taking a long, hard drink.

Taniel leaned back, watching the fire, unable to keep from laughing when Flint spat a mouthful of the rum into the fire and the flames flared up momentarily.

"Don't waste it!" Faint shouted, nabbing the jug.

It didn't take more than a few more passes before Taniel could feel the stuff working through his system. His body loosened and his mind became bleary. He leaned back and watched the fire, and before long Finley began to play his flute.

It was a low, mournful sound. Not at all the kind of shrill dance Taniel had heard from that kind of instrument before. It didn't take long until Faint began to sing. Her voice, much to Taniel's surprise, was a clear tenor that cut through the night.

He found himself drifting in his own mind. The aches in his body dissolved and the front seemed a hundred miles away.

There was a rustle of sound, so very slight he could have imagined it, and then Ka-poel slid into his lap. Just like that. No asking or hesitation, but as quick as a long-familiar lover. Taniel would have been uncomfortable if he didn't already feel so warm. Content. Happy, even.

Taniel drifted for what seemed like hours, and woke with a shiver. He didn't know how long he'd been gone, but the sun had set and the starry sky spread out above them. Had he dreamed that moment of contentment?

No.

Flint stared into the red coals. Finley was putting away his flute, and Faint snored softly on the ground beside the fire. Ka-poel was nestled in the crook of Taniel's arm. Her eyes were closed, a small smile on her face.

Taniel lifted his free arm and brushed a bit of red hair from her forehead. It was growing back after the fight on the mountain, and it seemed a deeper, more vibrant red than before.

Taniel felt eyes upon him. Flint was watching.

"She's a pretty little thing," Flint said.

Taniel didn't answer. He didn't trust himself to. Words like *impropriety* and *savage* went through his head, but they didn't have the bite they usually did. What did those things matter? He might die tomorrow.

"Thank you," Taniel said to Flint, "for inviting me."

"It was our pleasure, sir. Not often soldiers get to dine with a hero like you."

"No hero. Not me. Just a man with nothing but rage in his heart."

"If you really had nothing but rage in your heart, that girl wouldn't be sleeping there sound as can be," Flint said. He winked at Taniel, and Taniel felt his cheeks grow warm.

"I should warn you, sir," Flint said.

"Yes?"

"The provosts are looking for you. Rumor is General Ket wants to hang you."

Taniel scoffed. "If they were looking for me, they could have found me. I'm on the front line every day."

"They don't want to arrest you in front of the men. You've saved a right large number of soldiers every day on the line. The men aren't sure whether you're a demon or an angel, but they think you're watching over them—fighting while the senior officers sit farther back and watch us die. There might be a riot if they arrest you on the line."

"It's not hard to find my room," Taniel said, glancing toward the little shed he and Ka-poel were staying in.

"The provosts are questioning around all quiet-like. They've asked us a couple times." Flint shook his head with a little smile. "Everyone tells them to look on the front."

Taniel picked at a bit of gristle stuck between his teeth. So, the infantry were watching his back. It made him feel sad, more than anything. He didn't deserve to be looked out for. He was only on the front because he knew nothing but killing. Not because he wanted to save the soldiers.

"Then I have something else to thank you for."

"Don't thank me, sir," Flint said. "Just keep looking out for us out there. No one else is."

"I'll try."

"Also, sir, avoid the Third. General Ket's brigade love her. Don't know why, but her men are loyal, and they might just turn you over to the provosts themselves."

Taniel shifted Ka-poel's weight on his shoulder and climbed to his feet, balancing her in his arms. She didn't respond to the jostling except to nuzzle her face closer to his neck. It was a feather's touch, soft and warm, and Taniel felt his body react to it.

"Good night, Flint," he said.

"Good night, sir."

Taniel carried Ka-poel back to their shed. He laid her down in his bed and covered her with a blanket before pulling a powder charge from his pocket.

He stared at the charge for several moments. A small hit of the powder and he'd see better in the dark. He wouldn't have to light a lamp. It wasn't like he was sleeping these days anyway. How long had it been? Two weeks since a proper night's sleep? Could humans exist like that? He felt wooden and sluggish, as if walking in a dream.

But when he had a bit of powder, he was as alive and awake as always.

Taniel took a pinch of the powder and raised it to his nose. He stopped. Lowered it and rewrapped the powder charge. He found a match and struck it, touching it to the lamp beside the bed. The shed was suddenly thrown into the light.

He got his rifle out from beneath the bed and began to clean it. The process calmed him, let him think. He pulled his mind away from Ka-poel, lying there in his bed, and away from the provosts and General Ket, and away from his father's death and the Kez army's inexorable push into Adro.

Taniel finished with the rifle and cleaned his pistols, then wrapped a few dozen powder charges. He looked at that powder. He needed it. Wanted it.

He didn't let himself take any.

His bayonet was last. He took it out of its leather wrappings and examined it in the light of the lamp. There was a bit of dried blood in one of the grooves. He picked it off, then polished the metal. He felt the bed move a little and looked up.

Ka-poel lay on her side, one hand resting on her hip, the other propped beneath her head. She watched him with those green eyes. Her shirt had ridden up a bit and he could see the ashen freckles at her waist and the sharp curve of her hips. He felt his heart beat faster.

"I have to kill Kresimir," Taniel said. "For good this time. But I don't know how to do it."

Ka-poel moved to the edge of the bed. She leaned over, reaching beneath the bed, and opened her satchel. She fished around a little bit before coming back up with a doll.

Taniel swallowed hard. The doll had been shaped from wax into the perfect resemblance of a person. Gold hair, a handsome face, stout shoulders, and almost feminine lips. Taniel knew that face. He'd seen it on the man who'd stepped out of a cloud after descending from the heavens.

Kresimir.

She'd never seen Kresimir. At least, so he thought. How could she know what he looks like?

"I don't think even *your* magic is strong enough to kill a god," Taniel said. "I shot him with two redstripes."

Ka-poel touched a finger to her chin thoughtfully. She slowly drew the finger down her throat and then over her shirt, between her breasts. It stopped, then back to her throat. She made a cutting motion, then spread her hand.

"Blood?" Taniel asked, his throat dry.

She nodded.

"Kresimir's blood?"

Another nod.

"I'll never get close enough."

She mouthed a word. *Try.*

"You want me to throw myself at a god, hoping I can draw his blood?"

Ka-poel swung her legs around to the edge of the bed. She took the bayonet out of his hands and set it on the bedside table. She lowered herself into his lap, legs straddling his own.

"Pole, I don't..."

She put a finger to his lips. He remembered the mala den back in Adopest. With her pressed firmly against him in the hammock, her face so close. He shuddered.

Ka-poel put two fingers to her lips, then pushed them against his forehead. She mouthed a word.

It wasn't spoken, but still seemed to echo in his mind.

Sleep.

Sleep.

He felt his back hit the bed and his eyelids shut, suddenly weighty as millstones.

Sleep.

"Why are you courting Lady Winceslav?" Nila asked.

The centerpiece of the dining room of Lord Vetas's city manor was a long ironwood table that could seat sixteen. Vetas sat at the head of the table, his plate empty, a glass of red wine in his right hand, his left lying flat on the table with fingers spread. Nila sat on his right. Jakob sat on his left, and Faye sat beside Nila.

When Nila was a girl, she used to dream of attending fine dinner parties, admiring her reflection in the polished silverware and drinking from a wineglass rimmed with gold. She never imagined that dream would turn into a nightmare.

For ten days now they'd been eating with Vetas every evening. Despite the normal bustle and the number of men around the house—upward of sixty some days—dinnertime was always quiet. He used the time to instruct Nila in proper dining etiquette, and to shower Jakob with compliments, praise, and gifts. Nila hated every minute of it. Vetas filled every moment with mundane chatter, going on with some instruction or asking them all questions about themselves.

Nila knew better than to take this as some kind of friendliness. Vetas was prying. Finding out new things about them and filing them away in that insidious mind of his.

He never let anything slip about himself, of course. He was a master at deflecting questions. Which was why Nila was surprised when he answered hers.

"Lady Winceslav," he said, "owns the Wings of Adom mercenary company. You've heard of them, I trust?"

"Everyone has," Nila said. She glanced at Faye. The housewife sat stiff in her chair, staring at the empty place setting beside Jakob. Each of the last ten nights, that place had been occupied by her son, Josep, a boy of fifteen or sixteen, who was missing the ring finger of his right hand. Tonight that chair was empty.

"Most everyone, yes," Vetas said. "Right now they are employed against the Kez army. I'd like to employ them elsewhere."

Nila moved the food around on her porcelain plate. She didn't want to be here. Didn't want to look at Vetas's soulless face anymore. "And that's it? They're mercenaries. Can't you just . . . hire them?"

"That's it," Vetas said. He gave her a tight smile.

That wasn't it, of course. There was some other reason why he was courting the Lady. Perhaps he wanted to hire the mercenaries as well, but his plans couldn't be that simple. Nila didn't care. She just wanted dinner to be over. It wouldn't be, though. Not until Vetas said it was.

"You want to use her," Nila said.

"Hmm?" Vetas lifted his wineglass to his lips.

"For whatever all this is about." Nila gestured down the table. Aside from the place settings here at one end, the table was covered with papers—correspondence, receipts, lists; everything involved with Lord Vetas's affairs. She'd read a few, when she'd gotten the chance. None of them seemed to mean anything.

Vetas smiled at Jakob. "The Lady Winceslav is an eligible widow and a very intelligent woman. She'd make a wonderful wife."

"A wife?" The word came out in a burst of laughter. Nila covered her mouth, petrified at the outburst.

"Yes," Vetas said, as if he'd not heard the disbelief in her voice. "A wife." He leaned toward Jakob. "You understand that every lord needs a good wife, and it's important to marry someone with connections."

"Yes, Uncle Vetas."

"Good child."

"Uncle Vetas, I thought that the nobility of Adro no longer existed."

Vetas gave the boy a nod. "The nobility of Adro is in hiding, my boy. Remember, you're heir to the crown. Someday the nobility will return, and when it does, you will be at their head."

Nila ceased moving the fork around her plate. This was the first she'd heard Vetas say anything about the nobility. She'd always assumed that Jakob, in his capacity as next in line for the crown, fit into Vetas's plans somehow, but he'd never spoken of it.

She waited for Vetas to go on. Instead, Vetas took a sip of his wine.

Faye was still staring at the empty place setting across from her. She'd begun to rock back and forth slightly, her mouth hanging open, her forehead wrinkled.

"You're just using everyone," Nila said. "Me. Jakob. Lady Winceslav." *What is your plan?* Nila wanted to shout. *Why are you in Adopest?*

Vetas looked slightly surprised. "Of course I am. That's what nobles do. But," he said, reaching over and patting Jakob affectionately on one hand, "it's all for your protection. The duty of the nobility is to protect the people, no matter what kind of distasteful things they have to do."

Nila slammed her hand down on the table, making Jakob jump. "Don't!" she said. She gripped the lip of the table to keep herself from shaking.

"Don't what?" Vetas asked innocently.

"Nila," Jakob said, "why are you shouting at Uncle Vetas?"

Vetas gave Nila that tight smile again.

She would have snatched up her knife and leapt at Vetas then and there if Faye hadn't spoken.

"Where is my son?"

Vetas's fingers drummed once on the table. His attention shifted from Nila to Faye. "Nila," he said without looking at her, "I think that you should take Jakob to his room, now."

"Isn't there dessert, Uncle Vetas?" Jakob asked.

"Of course, my child. I'll have some brought up to you. Run along."

Nila still wanted to grab that knife and leap at him. She waited, contemplating, wondering if she could move fast enough. "Jakob," she said, getting up from her chair and holding out her hand. "Come along."

She took Jakob upstairs and put him in his room, helping him get out a number of toys before going into her own room and rushing out into the hallway, stepping carefully to avoid the creakiest boards, until she reached the servants' stairs that descended into the kitchens. She descended halfway down the stairs and pressed her ear to the wall.

"... was burned down," Vetas was saying calmly, his voice muddled through the plaster. "There were eleven graves. Seems the fire took them all in their beds. The townspeople claimed there was nothing but bone and ash left."

A loud sob startled Nila. It was followed by the low sound of crying. Faye.

Vetas went on as if he hadn't noticed Faye's reaction. "I won't have time to go up and investigate it myself, but it seems as if your children are all dead."

"Where is my son?" Faye demanded. The crying dried up, followed by a few sniffs.

"I've also received reliable word that your husband has been imprisoned by Tamas. It seems that he confessed to being blackmailed, and the field marshal plans on having him executed for treason." Vetas's voice droned on, as if he were talking about the weather. "My contacts within Sablethorn are few enough, but I should have better information within a week or so."

"Where"—the table rattled as if someone had pounded it with a fist—"is my son?"

Vetas said, "With your husband arrested, you and your son are of no use to me anymore. I'll keep you around for another couple of weeks, but I've sold your son to the Kez. He'll be smuggled—"

There was a sudden scream and then a crash. The walls rattled once, and then there was silence. Nila held her breath. Had Faye attacked Vetas? Had she succeeded?

The silence dragged on. Nila thought she could hear the labored sound of heavy breathing coming from the dining room.

"That," Vetas said, "was not very smart." The dining room door opened, and Vetas spoke to one of his men. "Take her downstairs. I'll join you shortly."

Heavy footsteps entered the dining room. The sound of a struggle resumed.

"I'll kill you, bastard!" Faye said. "I'll take your eyes! I'll take your tongue! There won't be anything left when I'm done!" A slew of curses and screams followed Faye out of the dining room and soon became muffled as she was carried into the basement.

Nila listened for several minutes before hearing Vetas leave the dining room. His soft, measured footfalls traveled down the hall, and the basement door opened. Nila counted to one hundred before she descended the servants' stairs into the kitchen.

She looked around quickly. The kitchen had been rearranged since she was last here. She brought a stool over to the washbasin and got on it, rummaging around in the high cupboards. Nothing. She swore under her breath and got back down. There, under the sink. Back in reach of children.

She snatched the large jar of lye and set it on the kitchen table. It didn't take long to find an empty spice pot. She blew the leaves of spices out of the bottom and poured half a cup of lye into it.

"What are you doing?"

Nila nearly dropped the lye jar. She looked up.

Privileged Dourford stood in the doorway. His height and Privileged's gloves made him imposing, and all the house staff knew his temper.

"Just getting some lye, my lord," Nila said.

"For what?"

"Some of the sauce got on my sleeve from dinner." She pinched one sleeve of her dress, hoping he wouldn't actually look closely. "I want to wash it before it stains."

"I thought Lord Vetas made it clear you're not to be doing any of the laundry anymore."

"It's just a small stain, my lord." Nila smiled in a way she hoped would be shy and tucked her shoulders forward, squeezing her breasts together to accent her cleavage. "I didn't want to bother any of the house staff."

Dourford's eyes lingered on her bust. "All right. But make sure that boy is asleep. That damned harpy is going to get what's coming to her tonight, and it'll be hard to keep her quiet." Dourford rummaged in the cupboards until he found half a loaf of bread and left the room, chewing thoughtfully.

Nila put the large lye jar back and tucked the spice pot into her dress pocket. She returned to her room, wondering how hard it would be to poison both Vetas and Dourford at the same time.

CHAPTER
17

Adamat was wary as his hackney cab pulled onto the long suburban street that led to his house.

He hadn't been there for almost two months—not since the day he told Vetas that Field Marshal Tamas was on his way to arrest Arch-Diocel Charlemund. Adamat had been forced to trick Vetas and still almost gotten Tamas killed. Vetas would want Adamat back—either dead or alive.

Adamat was willing to bet that Vetas was having the house watched.

He kept an eye on the street on the approach to the house. No suspicious men, no figures lurking in windows with an undue interest in his home. Foot traffic was minimal in this part of town, just a family heading to the market and a single old man strolling briskly in the sun.

The carriage rolled to a stop three houses down from his own.

Adamat checked the snub-nosed pistol in his pocket. Loaded and primed.

He flipped the collar of his jacket up around his face, pulled his hat low, and stepped into the street. Handing a few krana to the driver, Adamat headed warily toward his house, his cane held firmly in one hand.

The shutters were closed, the blinds drawn as he'd left them. Adamat searched the front of the house for any sign that things had been touched or tampered with. Nothing.

Adamat opened the gate to the alleyway between houses and went back to his garden. Another short inspection showed him nothing out of order. He waited for several minutes, examining the house again and again. No new scratches on the lock, no footprints in the garden.

It slowly began to dawn on him that perhaps he wasn't as important to Vetas as he thought. Lord Vetas was playing some kind of larger game on behalf of his master, Lord Claremonte. Did Adamat matter anymore? After all, as far as Vetas knew, Tamas had had Adamat quietly executed for treason. What if Vetas had written Adamat off entirely? Maybe Faye and Josep were already dead, buried in a shallow grave somewhere.

Adamat clenched and unclenched his fists. No. He couldn't think like that. Faye was alive. Vetas still held her. And Adamat was going to get her back.

Adamat unlocked the back door and stepped into the house. He closed his eyes and took a deep breath. The rooms were warm and stuffy with the windows closed up, but it still smelled like old wood, books, dust, and a slight hint of lavender from the incense Faye used to burn. He drew his pistol and carefully searched each of the rooms.

Everything was just as it had been left: the bloodstains on the sofa and carpet from one of Lord Vetas's men, a bullet hole in the ceiling. Another in the hall and one in the floor, along with the rest of the unrepaired damage done in the fight with the Black Street Barbers.

Pistol in one hand, cane in the other, Adamat climbed the stairs to the second floor. Here was where the Barbers had attacked him. There was SouSmith's blood, almost black on the dark hickory stairs.

No one upstairs. No sign anyone had gone through his belongings or searched the house.

Adamat sighed and lowered the pistol. He was almost disappointed. It was as if Lord Vetas had forgotten him entirely.

He put his cane in the umbrella stand by the front door and headed to the kitchen. There might be some canned beans or something to eat in the pantry. Get some food, then find his shovel, and then...

Adamat was not nearly fast enough to react as something swung around the corner and took him full in the nose. Pain blossomed all over his face and he was suddenly blinking up at the ceiling through tears.

Someone towered over him. He was grasped by the lapels of his jacket and lifted off the ground and a moment later slammed into the wall. Adamat swallowed a mouthful of his own blood and tried to breathe through his nose, only to utter a whimper.

Adamat was held against the wall by two strong arms. He batted at them to no effect, then lifted his hand to wipe his eyes. He looked into the face of a man with coal stains on his cheeks and shirt. Adamat recognized this man—one of Lord Vetas's goons.

Adamat cleared his throat and tried to sound casual. "Kale, was it?"

"That's right." The coal shoveler's mouth twisted. "Been waiting for you for a long time."

Adamat's whole head hurt. His nose had to be broken. He probably looked an absolute mess. The second set of clothes ruined in a week.

"Lord Vetas wants a word with you," Kale said. "You come along quietly now, or I start breaking your teeth."

Where the pit had he come from? Adamat had checked the whole house. Man must have been hiding in the cellar. And what on earth had he hit Adamat with? A cudgel?

"Right," Adamat said.

Kale's grip loosened. Adamat felt himself slide down the wall until his feet were touching the ground. This man was fast. And strong. Pit, what Adamat would have given to have SouSmith here now.

"Clean yourself up," Kale said. He let go of Adamat's jacket.

Adamat felt his knees give out from beneath him and he collapsed to the floor. He'd landed on something. Just under his chest—his pistol. He wrapped his fingers around the butt blindly.

He felt a strong hand on his back. "I'm all right," Adamat said. "Just. Hurts. I'll get another shirt from my bedroom and then I'll come, no fight." His words were gurgled and nasal.

He pushed himself to his feet with some struggle. Pit, the pain in his face. It would take more than three fingers of whiskey to dull this. Adamat took three steps down the hall and turned, lifting the pistol, and pulled the trigger.

The sound of the gunshot made his head—somehow—hurt even more.

Kale regarded the pistol, then looked at Adamat.

Adamat looked at the pistol, then at Kale. Then at the floor.

The bullet was on the ground. It must have fallen out of the barrel when Adamat dropped the pistol.

Kale crossed the space between them in two long strides, knocking the pistol out of Adamat's hand and grabbing Adamat by the throat, lifting him into the air and slamming him against the front door. The walls rattled from the impact.

Adamat struggled to breathe. He kicked. He punched. Nothing he could do would loosen Kale's grip.

"That's going to cost you a thumb," Kale said.

Adamat flailed around with his right hand. He had to do something, he had to . . . he felt his hand touch the head of his cane where it sat in the umbrella stand. He gripped the cane as far down as he could, lifted it, and slammed it into Kale's temple.

Kale staggered to one side, letting up on his grip. Adamat shoved him away with one arm and brought the cane down as hard as he could.

The coal shoveler caught the blow with one hand even as he stumbled away from Adamat. He grabbed the end of the cane and jerked.

Adamat found himself in a sudden tug-of-war. Kale jerked again, almost pulling Adamat over. Adamat could see the coal shoveler's eyes tighten at the corners and knew he'd not keep ahold of the cane the next time.

So Adamat twisted the head of the cane. There was a quiet *click*.

Kale yanked hard on the cane. He tumbled to the ground and looked with some surprise at the end of the cane in his hand.

Adamat threw himself forward, cane-sword-first, ramming the short blade into Kale's stomach. He pulled back and rammed again, then again. Adamat stumbled to one side after the final thrust, staring at Kale.

The coal shoveler stared back. He held both arms across his stomach, whimpering from the pain.

"He'll know," Kale said. "Lord Vetas will know you're back, and he'll kill your wife."

Adamat stood up straight and leveled his cane sword at Kale. "She's still alive?"

Kale didn't respond.

"And Josep? My boy?"

"Get me a doctor," Kale said. "Do it now and I'll tell you about your boy."

"My next-door neighbor is a doctor. Tell me and I'll fetch him."

Kale let out a long, anguished sigh. "Your boy...your boy is gone. They took...I don't know where, but he's gone. Your wife is there...she..."

"She what?"

"Get me a doctor."

"Tell me." The pain in Adamat's head seemed to climb to a crescendo. It was agonizing, and by the look of his soaked shirt and jacket he must have lost a great deal of blood from his nose.

"Vetas...he'll know. He thought maybe Tamas took you in... that you were arrested, or shot...but now he'll know you're alive."

Adamat gritted his teeth. "Not if they don't find the body." He barely trusted himself to thrust straight and true, but his cane sword went into Kale's eye and only stopped when it hit the back of his skull. He pulled it out and waited until the body stopped twitching before he cleaned the blade on Kale's coat.

Adamat stripped to the waist and and tossed his bloody clothes onto Kale's body. He hunted about the house for any other sign that the coal shoveler had ever been here, then went and found his shaving mirror.

His bleary eyes and bloody face stared back at him. He barely recognized himself.

Adamat's nose was bent nearly perpendicular to his head. Every gentle touch as he probed his face forced him to choke down a scream.

He put one hand on either side of his nose and stared at himself in the eyes. It was now or never.

He grasped his nose and straightened it.

Adamat woke up on the floor of his kitchen to the sound of someone pounding on his front door. He slowly got to his feet and glanced in the mirror. Through all the blood and grime he could tell his nose was straight again. He wondered if it was worth the excruciating pain that even now made him want to collapse.

It took him a full minute with shaking hands to reload his pistol.

When it was primed, he went to the front door and peeked out the window.

It was one of his neighbors. An older woman, stooped from age and wearing a day dress with a shawl hastily thrown over her head. He didn't think he'd ever learned her name.

Adamat cracked the door.

The woman nearly screamed at the sight of him.

"Yes?" he asked.

"Are you...are you all right?" she asked in a trembling voice. "I thought I heard a gunshot, and then not five minutes ago came the most terrible scream."

"Gunshot? No, no gunshot. I'm terribly sorry at my appearance. I fell and broke my nose. I was just setting it. Probably the scream you heard."

She stared at him like he was some kind of specter. "Are you sure you're fine?"

"Just a broken nose," Adamat said, gesturing at his face. "An accident, I assure you."

"I'll run and fetch the doctor."

"No, please," Adamat said. "I'll go myself soon. No need to do that."

"Now, now, I must insist."

"Madame!" Adamat made his voice as firm as he could. It made his nasal passage vibrate, and the pain nearly dropped him to the floor again. "If you mind, I will attend to myself. Do not, under any circumstance, summon a doctor."

"If you are certain...?"

Damned busybodies. "Quite, thank you, madame." Adamat closed the door and surveyed the mess in his hallway. Blood everywhere. The rug, the floor, the walls. All over the door behind him.

It took Adamat several hours and quite a lot of Faye's spare linens to clean up all the blood. He worked urgently—no telling if another of Vetas's goons would arrive at any time. But he had to have the house cleaned out. There had to be no sign that he'd ever been here.

When it was done, Adamat finally cleaned himself. A full bottle of wine, and the pain in his head was a dull hum instead of a constant hammering. Night had fallen. He wrapped Kale's body in the soiled linens and dragged it out the back door, thinking how furious Faye would be once she found out what he'd used the linens for.

In the corner of Adamat's small garden was a toolshed, and under the toolshed an unused root cellar no larger than the inside of a small carriage. Adamat entered the root cellar and felt around in the dark for several minutes before he found what he was looking for: a rope on the cellar floor in a layer of loose dirt. He grabbed the rope and hauled, pulling free a stout wooden box.

He took the strongbox into the garden and returned to drop the body inside the root cellar. He rearranged the tools so it looked like no one had been in there for some time and closed the door behind him.

Inside the lockbox was every krana he'd saved since he first found out he owed Palagyi for the loan that had started Adamat and Friends Publishing. Adamat didn't trust bankers anymore. Not since his loan had been sold to Palagyi.

The sum came out to a little under twenty-five thousand. Not enough. Not nearly enough.

Adamat spent another several hours cleaning the house of all traces of blood and then gathered a travel case full of children's clothes, the strongbox, and his cane and pistol before he headed out into the street to look for a hackney cab.

Taniel lay against the earthen battlements and glanced up at the overcast sky.

Mountainous white clouds moved ponderously through the sky, rolling like foam on top of a wave as it crashed upon the beach. Bits of gray mixed into the clouds, here and there. Rain, maybe? He hoped not. The earthworks would turn to mud and the rain would foul powder on both sides.

Taniel could hear the distant drumming of the Kez. It seemed far away, from where he lay against the cool, hard earth. The shouts of the Adran commanders—those were closer. He wanted to tell them to stuff it. Every man on the line knew they'd likely die today. Every man on the line knew that the Kez would succeed in their attack, taking the earthworks again like they did yesterday, and the day before that.

Morale wasn't just dead; it had been hanged, shot, then drawn and quartered and buried in a rocky grave.

"Well?" Taniel said.

Colonel Etan stood a few feet back from the edge of the earthworks, waving his sword and lending his own reassurances to the meaningless chatter of the officers. He wore a bearskin hat with a purple plume, befitting an officer of the Twelfth Grenadiers. His eyes were fixed on the approaching Kez infantry, still well beyond the earthworks.

"Coming," Etan said.

Taniel scanned the clouds. "Wake me when they get here." He closed his eyes.

Some of Etan's grenadiers chuckled at that. Taniel opened his eyes to see who'd laughed, and flashed them a grin. He surprised himself at how easily he smiled. Just a few days ago the very act had seemed foreign. Now...

He caught sight of Ka-poel back behind Etan. She sat on the earthworks, her knee raised up, chin in her hand. She was watching the Kez advance. Even the grenadiers—the strongest, bravest men in the Adran army—had a wild, nervous look in their eyes. They knew what it meant to be on the front. But Ka-poel's eyes were thoughtful, piercing. Not a hint of fear. She looked as deadly as a Fatrastan wildcat.

Taniel wondered what she saw that the others didn't.

"Getting close," Etan said. His body was tense and he kept a white-knuckle grip on his sword.

Taniel wondered where Kresimir was. Why hadn't the god shown himself? Why hadn't he killed them all, scattering them with sorcery, instead of letting his army chip away slowly at the Adran defenses day after day?

"Here they come!"

Taniel gripped his rifle in both hands. The timing for this had to be perfect. No hesitation. He had to—

"Now!"

There was just a hint of a shadow in the corner of Taniel's eyes. Taniel thrust his rifle upward, ramming two and a half spans of steel straight up between the legs of a leaping Warden.

Taniel felt the rifle stock twist in his hands. He gave a shout and pushed up harder, lifting the Warden like some kind of macabre trophy and then slamming him onto the earthwork floor.

Even a Warden could be taken by surprise, it seemed. The creature lay still in utter shock for several moments, eyes wide, a look of panic on his face. Then it began to thrash, trying to pull off the bayonet that Taniel had rammed up its ass.

A dozen grenadiers fell on the Warden with bayonets and swords. It only took a few moments before all that remained of the Warden was a bloody mess of meat. Taniel pulled his bayonet out of the dead creature just as the Adran line opened fire.

"Get rid of it," Etan said. He and a pair of his men grabbed the dead Warden and hefted it over the earthworks, letting it roll down to the field below.

The advancing Kez wavered in the onslaught of musket fire. Hundreds dropped to the ground, but the Kez war machine marched right over them. They dropped their bayoneted muskets into a ready position and charged at a run.

Taniel got up on the earthworks and fired his rifle, dropping a Kez major from the back of his horse.

Etan stepped up beside Taniel. "It's been a pleasure knowing you, my friend," he said, eyes on the charging Kez.

"We're not losing today." Taniel rammed a cotton-wrapped bullet down his rifle, then cracked open a powder charge with his thumb. He snorted the charge in one long drag and rubbed his nose with the back of his hand. "Not today," he said. Then, louder, "We're not losing today."

Taniel felt a rising wave of anger. Why should they lose? Why should they turn and run? They were better than the Kez. The Adran army was feared all over the Nine.

He turned toward the grenadiers. "Are you Field Marshal Tamas's men? Are you?"

"The field marshal is dead," someone said.

Taniel felt the spittle fly out of his mouth. "Are you?"

"I'm the field marshal's man!" Etan lifted his sword. "Dead or alive, I'll always be!"

"Are you?" Taniel screamed at the grenadiers.

"Yes!" They answered with one voice, muskets raised.

"The Adran army—Tamas's army—doesn't lose. You can flee if you want"—Taniel pointed at the grenadiers—"when the trumpet sounds. Run back to those armchair generals, let the Kez shoot you in the back. But I'll be here until the Kez break."

"So will I," Etan said. He swung his saber.

"And I!" the grenadiers shouted in unison.

Taniel turned back to the Kez. "Send them to the pit!"

Taniel saw his father's face float before his vision like a tattered flag. He saw Vlora, and Sabon and Andriya, and all the rest of his fellow powder mages. He could see his friends in the Seventh and Ninth. Then they were gone, and the world was drenched in red as Taniel felt his legs carry him over the edge of the earthworks and straight into the teeth of the Kez infantry.

The crack of muskets and blasts of artillery were suddenly lost in the thunder of the charging infantry. Taniel gutted a Kez soldier with his bayonet, then locked the stock of his rifle with another. He shoved, sending the soldier reeling.

An officer's sword sliced neatly along his cheek, just beneath the eye. He felt the blade, but pain seemed a distant thing from within the powder trance, with so much adrenaline coursing through his body. He smacked the officer across the chin with his rifle then stabbed an infantryman.

The Kez were all around him and he felt a sudden panic. It didn't matter how quick or how powerful he was, he could be felled by sheer force of numbers, just like the Warden he and the grenadiers had hacked apart.

Taniel saw a bayonet aim at his heart. He dropped his shoulder and felt the point snag his jacket, ripping clean through, then slammed his fist into the soldier's face.

And suddenly Taniel was not alone. Adran grenadiers with their bearskin hats and crimson-cuffed jackets were beside him, muskets at the ready to push back the Kez assault.

"Shove!" Etan's voice rose above the din. "Step! Thrust! Shove! Step! Thrust!"

While the Kez infantry threw themselves forward with reckless abandon, the Twelfth Grenadiers moved in lockstep, every man chosen for his immense size and trained to meet the enemy unflinchingly. They'd come over the earthworks behind Taniel and now they pushed forward, bayonets working, chewing through the Kez infantry like so many farmers cutting hay.

Taniel forced himself into the line of grenadiers and joined their march. To his surprise, the Kez infantry seemed to melt before them. Taniel knew power. He knew speed. But the pure strength of these grenadiers working together shocked him. He felt the rhythm of their push deep down in his chest.

A Kez soldier threw himself over the line, crashing into Taniel and sending him back. The grenadiers closed up the empty spot, not missing a beat. Taniel wrestled with the soldier, throwing him to the ground and pressing his boot to the man's throat. A glance at the line, and then . . .

Out of the corner of his eye he saw a Warden tear through the grenadiers. The biggest and strongest that Adro had to offer were scattered like toys as the creature breached the line.

Another Warden crashed through. Colonel Etan staggered back, his brow bloodied. He recovered quickly, slashing with his heavy saber, taking the Warden's hand off at the wrist. The Warden threw himself forward and snatched Etan by the throat, picking up a man of fifteen stone and shaking him as a dog might a rat.

A trumpet sounded.

Retreat.

Fury tore through Taniel. No. He wouldn't fall back. He wasn't leaving this field without a victory.

Taniel snarled, the soldier beneath his boot forgotten. He could see Etan's eyes roll back as he went into shock. Taniel hefted his rifle, bayonet ready, and charged.

Something slammed into him from the side. He flew, a few moments of uncontrolled tumble sending his heart lurching before he hit the ground, bouncing off an infantryman's body. The jolt sent Taniel's rifle sliding from his hands, and when he came to his feet, he was unarmed.

There wasn't time to react. This new Warden was too fast. A heavy fist pummeled his face, sending him spinning.

Taniel righted himself, bracing for another blow. Mentally, he touched a bit of powder. There was no reaction. This was a Black Warden.

The next blow failed to land as the Warden thrashed about, Ka-poel on his back. She hung on by one of her long needles, which was buried deep into the meat of the creature's shoulder. She'd missed his spine by inches, and the needle could do nothing but infuriate him.

Taniel drew his boot knife. He squared his shoulders, ready to leap, when the Warden suddenly stiffened. He lurched forward, dropping to his knees. Ka-poel calmly withdrew her needle and stepped away from the Warden. She wore a vicious smile and in one hand held a half-formed wax doll. Her fingers worked furiously to finish the doll.

The Warden came to its feet, still wobbling, still lurching. It staggered to one side and then suddenly flew forward, charging the Kez.

Perhaps half the grenadiers still stood, their line ragged and broken, with more of them dropping beneath Kez infantry every second. The Warden cleared them with a single leap, landing among the Kez.

Most of the infantry ignored him. They were used to the Wardens, of course. It wasn't until this one took a discarded saber in his hand and began slicing up the Kez ranks that horror began to spread.

The panic was palpable. Taniel watched as the Kez began to scream and back away from the Warden. Some tried to stand and fight. Some even attacked him. A bayonet speared the Warden through the neck and the creature snapped the steel bayonet off the end of the musket and kept fighting. The Kez began to waver.

Taniel had killed Wardens in hand-to-hand combat, the same creatures that terrorized the Adran army, and now Ka-poel had turned one on the Kez. A thrill worked its way up from his toes until it reached his fingertips, and Taniel wondered just what he'd become that allowed him to fight a ferocious monster like that.

"To me!" He lifted his rifle over his head. "To me!" he shouted above the sound of the trumpets, blaring louder and louder for the grenadiers to retreat. "Bugger the trumpets, we fight!"

The Kez began to crumple. None of their snare drums were calling a retreat, but they fled all the same. The few Wardens left on the field were finally overpowered and mercilessly slaughtered. Some of the Kez threw down their weapons and fell to their knees in surrender.

The Warden that Ka-poel controlled chased the Kez almost the whole way back to their camp. A dozen other Wardens had congregated to try to put it down.

Ka-poel's eyes were alight with glee, and the wax figurine in her hands twitched and spun. Her lips opened in a silent laugh.

The Warden fought on. Stabbed, shot, sliced: it would not fall.

And then Ka-poel lifted the doll and pushed the head off with one thumb.

The Warden collapsed.

Taniel stared, openmouthed, at Ka-poel. How could this girl, the same woman who had pressed herself against him so intimately, fall asleep in his arms like a child one minute and then take to the battlefield with the power of a vengeful goddess the next?

She turned, as if feeling his gaze, and flashed him a shy smile. In an instant she was once again the girl he'd rescued from a dirty hut in the swamps of Fatrasta.

Taniel wanted to rush to her, to carry her away from this madness, to make sure that she was all right. But she wasn't his to protect, not anymore. Not since Kresim Kurga. He had a feeling that who—or what—Ka-poel really was had just begun to show itself.

Ignoring his own wounds, Taniel began to cast about for Colonel Etan. He found the grenadier beneath a dead Warden. Taniel rolled the corpse away. Etan was still breathing, much to Taniel's relief, but there was a profound look of panic in his eyes.

"I can't move my legs," Etan said.

Taniel dropped to his knees beside Etan and felt that same panic begin to rise within him. "It's all right," Taniel said. "We'll get you a surgeon."

"I can't feel my legs!" Etan gripped Taniel's arm. He gasped, and Taniel could see the strain on his face as he tried to move. "I can't feel them!"

Taniel felt his heart crack. Etan was one of the strongest men he knew. To die in battle was one thing, but to be broken...

"Get me a surgeon!" Taniel yelled. "And tell them to stop with the bloody trumpets. We won already, damn it!"

Etan seemed to sag. "We won?"

"We won." Taniel looked around the field. He could see soldiers running from the Adran side, coming to provide backup. If there wasn't a surgeon among them, he'd strangle someone.

"You held it," Etan said. "You held the line."

"No. You did. You and your grenadiers."

"Couldn't have done it without you." Etan was blinking rapidly now. Taniel searched him for a wound, trying to find something. Etan's fingers grasped the sleeve of Taniel's jacket, his knuckles bone white, his face drawn in pain. "I saw the way my boys looked at you. They would have followed you all the way to the pit just now. Just like Tamas. Just like your father."

"Don't say horrid shit like that," Taniel said. He felt hot tears on his cheeks. "I'm nothing like that old bastard."

"Taniel. Promise me you'll win this thing. Promise me you'll finish this. That this won't be the last victory Adro has."

"No need for promises," Taniel said. "You're not dying."

Etan pulled Taniel close. "I can't feel my bloody legs. I know what that means, you ass. I won't see a battlefield again. So you promise me now that you'll win this thing."

"I don't know if I can," Taniel said.

Etan slapped him. Taniel felt his cheek burn from the force of the blow. "Promise me." Another sharp blow nearly turned Taniel around. Even lying on the ground, unable to move his legs, Etan was strong. "Promise it!"

A woman, one of the surgeons, threw herself to the ground on Etan's opposite side. She looked him over, a frown on her face. "Where's the wound?"

"My back's broken," Etan said. His voice cracked. He looked Taniel in the eyes. "Promise me."

"No."

Etan's eyes were glassy with tears. "Coward. If I were dying, you'd promise me. Because you wouldn't have to answer to me then. But I'm not dying, and you won't promise it. Bloody coward."

Taniel turned his face away. He knew it was true.

They brought out a cart, one of the ambulances with a covered top and four cots to hold the wounded, to take Etan back to camp. Etan turned his head away from Taniel, and Taniel didn't walk beside him as they carted him away.

They had destroyed the Kez attack. Probably a thousand of the enemy soldiers dead. Twice that many wounded and another few hundred taken prisoner. It took Taniel a moment to realize he was surrounded by soldiers. The Twelfth Grenadiers. The smallest of them was a hand taller than Taniel. He wondered how many had died in the melee. Their losses had to be staggering.

One of them approached him. Taniel thought about turning away. He could push through them and head back to camp. Had they been listening? Did they hear their colonel tell Taniel he was a coward?

The stout man had his bearskin hat in one hand. His other hand was empty. Clenched in a fist. Taniel lifted his chin and waited to be punched.

"Sir," the grenadier said.

"Go ahead. I deserve it."

The grenadier seemed confused. He looked down at his fist, then flattened his hand. "Sir, you're not a coward. The colonel... no man wants to end up like that. The things he said... you're not a coward. We just watched you charge a brigade of Kez infantry *by yourself.* I want you to know: If you need something, anything, you just say so. I'll be there. I suspect most of these boys will say the same."

There was a round of nodding, and then the grenadiers began to trudge wearily back to camp.

Taniel stood alone in the field for several minutes, watching the surgeons cart off the dead and wounded. He felt someone behind him. He didn't have to turn around. Ka-poel.

He wiped the tears from his face with the sleeve of his jacket. "Don't you have bodies to examine, or some such thing?" he asked.

She took his hand. He wanted to pull away, but couldn't.

They stood together in silence as the blood of the living and the dead and the dying mingled together and made a red sea of Adran soil. Taniel lifted her hand in his. The movement was impulsive, sudden, and he wondered later what thought drove him, but he touched her hand to his lips firmly.

"I'm going to end this," he said. "I'm going to kill Kresimir. For good. You need his blood? I'll get it, even if I die doing it."

Out of the corner of his eye he saw her give a slight shake of her head.

Without warning she stepped in front of him and wrapped one hand around the back of his head and pulled him down to her, pressing her warm lips against his. It seemed as if fire raced through his veins at the touch, and when she finally stepped away, he was breathless. He fought the impulse to drop to his knees, telling himself it was just blood loss that left him so weak.

Then the moment was past, and silent as always, Ka-poel went about her business, leaning over the body of a dead Adran soldier.

Stunned, Taniel watched her for several minutes until something far behind the Kez line brought him out of his reverie. In an instant he was a soldier again: vigilant, watchful, ready to defend against new threats from the enemy.

The Kez soldiers were raising something into the sky above their camp, just north of Budwiel's city walls. It must have been eight stories high for him to be able to see it from this distance. He took a small hit of powder, sharpening his eyes.

It was an immense beam, hewn from what looked to be one giant tree. Soldiers and prisoners milled about the base and spread out in a fan behind it, pulling on long ropes tied to the top of the beam. It was lifted high and then suddenly it dropped ten or twenty feet—probably into a slot dug out of the ground—to stand straight in the air.

Taniel frowned. He could see something on the side of the beam. A person?

He focused his powder-heightened eyes. Yes. A woman, it seemed. Stripped naked, she was nailed to the beam by her wrists, and her hands were missing. A rope about her waist secured her to the beam.

Taniel was taken aback. Was she a traitor of some kind, put up there as a warning? The missing hands would indicate she'd been a Privileged. What could...

The body moved. Bloody pit, she was alive.

Her head lifted, and Taniel felt his blood go cold. He knew her. She'd fought him in Kresim Kurga, the holy city, when he tried to keep her from summoning Kresimir.

It was Julene.

CHAPTER
18

Tamas waited for the return of his night scouts and listened to the familiar sounds of his soldiers breaking camp.

There was a light chatter this morning—something missing over the last two weeks' worth of march since the fall of Budwiel. Someone laughed in the distance. Nothing like a full belly to bring a man's spirits up. Combine that with elation at the victory over the Kez vanguard, and Tamas could almost call his men happy.

Almost.

Tamas didn't like eating horse. It reminded him of hard times in Gurla, of starvation and disease and the desert heat, when they'd been forced to slaughter their own healthy horses to stay alive. The taste was slightly sweet, and gamier than beef. Meat that came from cavalry chargers tended to be tough.

Then again, at least his stomach didn't rumble.

"What is it, soldier?"

Vlora stood at attention on the other side of his cook fire. She snapped off a salute.

"Kez spotted, sir. Riding under a white flag."

Tamas flicked a bit of fat into the fire and watched it sizzle. He stood up, wiping his hands on an already soiled handkerchief. Another problem they faced—no camp followers meant no laundresses. Both his uniforms were dirty and stained, and he smelled like a cesspool.

Adom forbid you do your own laundry, a little voice in the back of his head said. Tamas chuckled.

"Sir?" Vlora asked.

"Nothing, soldier. I'll meet them on the edge of camp. Olem!"

"Coming, sir."

Tamas was joined by Olem and a small bodyguard of Olem's Riflejacks. Among the Ninth, stationed as the rear guard, the last tents were being rolled and stowed in packs and cook fires put out. They'd be on the march in twenty minutes. The advance elements of the Seventh were already half a mile down the road.

He passed a row of wagons. They'd been able to salvage them from the abandoned remains of Hune Dora. The bottoms were already stained from the blood of the wounded, and they smelled like death at ten paces. Today, they would carry the wounded that had survived the last two days.

"Have those washed out," Tamas said to Olem. "In fact, I want bathing mandatory. There's plenty of mountain streams in these woods. Organize it with the scouts. I want fifty men to stop and bathe in every mountain stream we pass. If we don't look to ourselves, we'll have disease rampant in the camp."

"Yes, sir." Olem rubbed at his dust-caked uniform. "I could use a little freshening up myself."

They left the edge of the Adran camp and passed the rear pickets. The forest beyond was still, the only sounds that of chattering squirrels and the call of birds. Tamas welcomed the birdsong.

It reminded him of peace, distracted him from the harsh call of the carrion crows and the memory of piled corpses that lingered behind his eyes.

Tamas saw the Kez riders before they saw him.

There were a dozen of them. They were still mounted upon their chargers in the middle of the road, watching the Adran pickets impassively. They wore the heavy breastplates of cuirassiers over tan uniforms with green trim. They dismounted as Tamas drew closer and one of them removed his helmet and approached.

"Field Marshal Tamas?"

"I am he," Tamas said.

"I am General Beon je Ipille," he said in Adran with a light accent. He extended his hand. "The pleasure is mine."

Tamas took the general's hand. Beon was a young man, perhaps in his late twenties. His face was boyish, touched by the same cabal sorceries that kept every king of the Nine looking young far beyond their years. That alone would have told Tamas that Beon was one of Ipille's sons, if not for the name and reputation.

"The king's favored son. Your reputation precedes you."

Beon tilted his head modestly. "And you, yours."

"To what do I owe the honor?" Tamas said. This was all a formality, of course. Tamas knew why Beon was here.

"I've come to inquire as to your intentions in my country."

"Only to return to my own, and defend it from the aggression of a tyrant."

Beon didn't even blink at the insult against his father. Tamas made a mental note of that. He was more levelheaded than his older brothers, it seemed. "I'm afraid I can't let you do that."

"So we are at an impasse."

"Not an impasse, I think," Beon said. "I've come to request your surrender."

"An impasse. I will not surrender," Tamas said flatly.

Beon nodded, as if to himself. "I was afraid you would say that."

"Afraid?" Tamas knew Beon's reputation. Fear didn't enter into it. Beon was almost recklessly brave. He seized opportunities a lesser commander might balk at. His courage had served him well.

"I do not relish chasing the great Field Marshal Tamas. You've already seen to my vanguard—how do you say, sending them back with their tails tucked between their legs?" He looked over his shoulder at one of the other riders. The rider was a dragoon, with a straight sword and lacking the breastplate of a cuirassier. "Their commanders barely escaped with their lives."

"You could just let me go on my way," Tamas said jovially. "I'll be out of your country in a few weeks."

Beon chuckled. "And my father would have my head. Your men are hungry, Tamas. You have no food, other than the horsemeat you salvaged from my vanguard. I'll be fair. I'll tell you what you face, and then you can decide whether to surrender. Yes?"

Tamas snorted. "That is more than fair."

"Good. I have ten thousand dragoons and fifty-five hundred cuirassiers under my command. My elder brother is about a week's march behind me with thirty thousand infantry. I know you have eleven thousand men. We outnumber you four to one. You have no hope of escaping this country. Surrender now, and your men will be treated with respect as prisoners of war." He paused and lifted his hand, as if swearing upon the Rope. "I've studied you, Tamas. You do not throw your men's lives away in needless causes."

"If you've studied me," Tamas said quietly, "you'll know that I do not lose."

Beon's expression was bemused. "You are a dead man, Tamas. Do you have any requests?"

"Yes. I have over a hundred wounded. If I hand them over to you, will they be treated with respect as prisoners of war?"

"So that you may travel faster? No. Any wounded that fall into our hands will be executed as criminals."

Beon was a gentleman through and through. It was entirely likely he was bluffing. Did Tamas dare risk it?

"Then, General, I have no more to say to you."

Beon gave a respectful nod. "I would wish you good luck, but..."

"I understand."

The Kez remounted and were off down the road within minutes. Tamas watched them go. That general would be trouble. Incompetence was practically bred into the Kez army, where nobles could purchase their commission or find themselves a general at the whim of the king.

Once in a while, though, talent rose above the chaff.

"Olem," Tamas said.

The bodyguard snapped to attention, but his eyes never left the direction the Kez had gone. Tamas knew he was itching for a fight.

"Sir?"

"Get me an ax and meet me at the head of the column."

The basic kits of all Adran infantry included a hand ax and a shovel. They were meant for cutting firewood and digging latrine pits.

A good commander utilized them for far more.

Tamas gathered his horse and rode to the front of the column. He found Colonel Arbor at the vanguard with his First Battalion. The colonel flexed his jaw, popping his false teeth out into one hand as Tamas fell in beside him.

"Nice day, sir. Trees keep the forest cool."

Tamas examined the road. It winded along a steep, heavily forested hillside. Enough light reached the ground for there to be a thick undergrowth; thorny and tangled. Without the road, the terrain would be nearly impossible to traverse.

"A word, Colonel," Tamas said. "Pick two platoons and bring them off to the side."

Arbor hollered for the Nineteenth and Thirty-Fourth Platoons. By the time they'd shuffled off the road and into the forest, Olem had joined them. He dismounted and handed Tamas an ax.

Tamas removed his jacket and his shirt and looked around at the men. "We have fifteen thousand cavalry dogging our tails," he said. "On horseback, they travel faster and easier than us. I mean to change that. Every time there's a narrowing in the terrain, like that one there"—he pointed to where the road cut into the hillside up ahead—"we're going to drop a few tons of rubble there. Gather rocks, fell trees. Any kind of debris. As soon as the column has passed, we're going to stop it up."

Tamas picked a nearby tree. It was wide enough that three men couldn't have reached around its base. It would do perfectly. He positioned himself on the side of the tree facing the road and began to chop.

The two platoons set about hacking at trees with axes and billhooks and gathering everything they could from the nearby forest. They stacked great piles beside the road. Tamas pulled two more platoons out of the column, and by the time the last of his men had passed, they had half a dozen immense trees ready to fall across the road.

Tamas turned his head at the sound of an approaching rider.

It was only Gavril. He reined in beside Tamas.

"You the last of our scouts back there?" Tamas asked.

"Aye," Gavril said. "The Kez are a mile behind me. They're not coming hard. I don't think they're in a hurry." He examined the work Tamas had been doing. "Cutting trees like a logger. I like this side of you. I hope all this work was worth it."

"It'll take them hours to clear this," Tamas said.

"Or they'll go around."

Tamas wiped the sweat from his brow. If they found a way through the forest, all of this was for naught. "Can they?"

"They'll have to scout it," Gavril said. "And they'll be cautious in case you've laid a trap. You might have bought us some time."

Tamas took his shirt from Olem, and a soldier brought him his charger. He climbed into the saddle. "Bring 'em down!" he shouted to the soldiers.

A few minutes later the trees crashed to the ground. They were felled so that they lay across each other, wedged to block the road. It wouldn't be as simple as throwing a rope around them and dragging them away with teams of horses.

The rest of the rubble was thrown to block the way, and Tamas ordered the platoons to march double-time to catch up with the rest of the column.

"Have your scouts find me good spots to block the road," Tamas said to Gavril.

"Consider it done."

"Olem, see that those two platoons are given a double ration of horsemeat tonight. They earned it."

"Yes, sir."

Tamas shrugged into his shirt. "Put your mind to anything else we can use to slow down the Kez. They might still dog us with a company or two, but I want to keep the bulk of their numbers as far behind us as possible."

"I heard you met with the Kez general," Gavril said.

"I did. It was Beon je Ipille. Ipille's youngest son."

Gavril grunted. "I've heard he's a decent sort—for Ipille's spawn, anyway."

"He is."

"How did it go?" Gavril asked.

"I have one regret and one hope."

Gavril seemed intrigued. "Your hope?"

"That I didn't make a grave mistake refusing to surrender."

"And your regret?"

"It's too bad Beon wasn't Ipille's first son. He'd have made a terrific king. I'm going to regret killing him."

"I came as quickly as I could," Adamat said.

"Have a seat."

Adamat took a chair opposite Ricard and leaned back. Ricard's face was grave. What hair remained on his balding head stuck out everywhere in unkempt wisps, and his eyes were tired, his beard uncombed, clothes rumpled. Very unlike Ricard.

Ricard stared at the floor. "You heard the news?" he asked, gesturing to the newspaper on his desk.

The paper proclaiming the death of Field Marshal Tamas was a week old now.

"All of Adro has heard it," Adamat said.

Ricard finally looked up. When he glimpsed Adamat's face, he nearly fell out of his chair. "What the pit happened to you?"

Adamat would have snorted if it didn't hurt so badly to do so. He imagined he looked far worse off than Ricard. Little sleep, his nose recently broken and reset, cuts and bruises all across his face. Adamat was a horror, and it was interfering with his work. No one liked being seen doing business with someone who'd had the piss beaten out of them.

"I've had a few run-ins lately," Adamat said.

Ricard waited for an explanation. Adamat wasn't about to give him one.

"Yes, well..." Ricard slowly tore his gaze from Adamat's face. "The country is in an uproar. The Kez are pushing the southern front, and with Tamas gone a few royalists have come out of the woodwork. He was the glue holding this whole nation together." Ricard ran his fingers through his hair. "Tamas's remaining councillors...we've already started bickering among ourselves. I don't know what we're going to do."

"Are you going ahead with the election?"

Ricard threw up his hands in exasperation. "We have no choice. We could declare martial law and delay the election, but the entire army is on the southern front trying to fight back the Kez." Ricard rubbed his eyes. "Which brings me to why I asked you to come in: Lord Claremonte is making his move."

Adamat sat up straighter. "And?"

Ricard spit on the floor, then seemed to immediately regret having done so. "He's declared his intention to run for prime minister of Adro."

"How could he?" Adamat breathed in disbelief. "He's not even Adran!"

"Ah, but he is. Or at least that's what the records he provided to the Ministerial Review Board says. Fell! Fell, get in here!"

The young woman Adamat had previously met slipped into the room. Her hair was done up in a braid that went over one shoulder, and she wore a frilled blouse loose about the neck. "Sir?"

"Fell, what have you got on Claremonte?"

"Nothing," Fell said. "If his birth records are forgeries, they're extremely good. We have people going over all the information we have on him. He's never actually claimed to be Brudanian, and the Brudania-Gurla Trading Company doesn't require Brudanian citizenship to become the head."

Adamat found himself watching Fell, suddenly suspicious, and he wasn't quite sure why. "Keep...keep talking," Adamat said.

"Sir?" Fell asked.

"Have you found a stronger connection to Lord Vetas?" Adamat's own knowledge about Vetas and Claremonte's relationship came through the Proprietor's eunuch, and through Vetas's own admission. If he'd been misled in some way, it could derail his entire line of inquiry.

"None that we can find."

"Why could he possibly want to be prime minister of Adro? Ricard, didn't you tell me yourself that the prime minister will be a figurehead?"

Ricard shifted uncomfortably in his chair. "That is *my* vision of the prime minster, yes."

"The truth is," Fell said, without waiting for Ricard's instruction, "the first prime minister will be the one to set the standard for every one to follow him. How much power the prime minister holds, and how he wields it, will depend entirely on how aggressive the first man to hold the office decides to be."

Adamat smoothed the front of his jacket. What was bothering him so much about this woman? There was something about her mannerisms that he'd not noticed before... something he couldn't quite put his finger on. "So if Claremonte is elected, there is the potential for him to wield as much power in Adro as a king?"

"Not as much as a king," Ricard said. "The design of the system has put parameters on that. However... quite a lot of power."

"Pit," Adamat said.

Fell crossed to Ricard's side. "Sir, if I may..."

"That's it!" Adamat stared at her.

"What?" Ricard asked.

Adamat reached in his pocket slowly, grasping the butt of his pistol. "You have the same way of speaking," he said to Fell. "Some of the same cadence as he does. It's not readily noticeable. Not like you're family or anything, but as if you've been trained at the same finishing school."

"As who?" Ricard asked.

"Lord Vetas."

Ricard and Fell exchanged a look.

"This is bad," Fell said.

Ricard agreed. "Very bad."

Adamat's gaze moved between the two. He found himself squeezing the butt of his pistol in one hand and the head of his cane with the other. He felt his jaw clench. What was going on here? What did they know that he didn't?

Ricard said to Fell, "I'm going to tell him."

"This isn't common knowledge," Fell said with a frown.

"What the pit are you two talking about?" Adamat asked.

Ricard leaned forward on his desk, leaning his chin on one hand. "Have you heard of the Fontain Academy in Starland?"

"No," Adamat said. Neither Ricard nor Fell seemed unduly ready to leap at him, so he loosened his grip on his pistol and cane. "A finishing school?" he guessed.

"Of a sort," Ricard said. "It's a very exclusive place. Of every thousand students they have, only one graduates."

"What makes it so difficult?" Adamat asked.

"The rigors," Fell spoke up. "Eighteen hours of work every day for twenty years. Training of every sort: martial, sexual, memory retention, etiquette, mathematics, science, politics, philosophy. Exposure to every school of thought in the known world. No contact with friends or family for the rest of your life. The willingness to become beholden to one man or organization against bribery or threat of pain or death."

"Sounds awful," Adamat said. "I would have heard of such a place."

"No," Ricard said. "You wouldn't have."

Fell was looking at her fingernails. "Only prospective clients know about the Fontain Academy. It costs as much as thirty million krana to purchase a graduate."

"Purchase? So it's slavery?" Adamat rocked back in his chair. Thirty million krana. That was a kingly sum. There were less than fifty people in all the Nine with access to that much money, and he didn't think Ricard was one of them.

Adamat wasn't sure if he believed this. How could an organization like that exist? Certainly slavery was still openly practiced in the world, but in the Nine? Not for hundreds of years. "Are you asking me to believe that you and Lord Vetas are graduates of the Fontain Academy?"

"It appears that way," Fell said. "I couldn't confirm it for certain, but for you to make the observation you did transcends coincidence."

"Then what can you tell me about him?"

"Every graduate has different specialties. But if he is a graduate, then he's dangerous. He'll be adept at blackmail and sabotage. He'll be smarter than most of the people in this city, including you. Proficient with all weapons, but likely favoring knives and pistols."

"What's your specialty?" Adamat asked.

Fell gave him a thin smile but didn't answer.

"Can we speak alone?" he asked Ricard.

Ricard nodded to Fell.

"Sir," Fell said. "The Fontain Academy is not a secret, strictly, but we do not advertise ourselves. This information is to be kept private."

"I'll respect that," Adamat said.

Fell left the room, leaving him alone with Ricard.

Adamat watched his friend for nearly a minute before he spoke. "You *purchased* a woman?"

"Adamat . . ."

"I didn't think even you would stoop to that."

"It's not like that, I—"

"It's not, is it?" Adamat raised his eyebrows.

"Well, maybe a little. But that's not why I did it."

"Then why?"

Ricard's face grew grim. "I love this country. I love my union. I will not see either torn apart by the machinations of a foreigner. I'll be the first prime minister if it kills me—or if I have to kill to do it."

"When?"

"When what?"

"When did you . . . purchase . . . her?"

"I finalized it over the summer. She arrived four weeks ago."

"And where the pit did you get thirty million krana?"

"She was ten million," Ricard said. "About half my fortune. She's only had ten years of schooling at the academy—it's normally twenty years."

Adamat shook his head. "Ten million for that girl. What were you thinking?"

"She runs my organization better than I can," Ricard said quietly. "In one month—just one—she's made me fifty thousand krana. She's straightened my ministerial campaign. Before her I had some good ideas, but now I have a serious chance at being the prime minister of Adro. She's worth every penny I spent on her."

"Can you trust her? What's to stop her from killing you and taking control of the union, if she's so smart."

Ricard said, "Loyalty. For the next thirty years of her life she belongs to me. It's the price of schooling at the Fontain Academy. And reputation. If she were to turn on me in some way, the academy would kill her themselves."

Adamat smoothed the front of his coat again. This was all too much. "That reminds me," Adamat said. "I need to borrow money."

"You still owe Palagyi money?" Ricard said, seemingly relieved to steer the conversation away from Fell. "I'm glad you finally got some sense into you. What the pit was that all about, refusing to let me pay him?"

"Palagyi is dead. And no, not that. I need fifty thousand krana. Now. In banknotes."

Ricard blinked at him. "Fifty? I can write a check for fifty. I'd do it in a heartbeat for you."

"It needs to be cash."

"Can't do it. No bank in Adro would let me take out fifty thousand all at once. I could have it for you in a couple of weeks."

"That's too long," Adamat said. He rubbed his eyes. Ricard was his only hope of getting the money to pay Colonel Verundish to release Bo. How could he himself possibly come up with that sum in a week?

Well, perhaps Ricard wasn't the only hope.

"You smell like the southbound end of a northbound ass," Gavril said.

Tamas sat and watched his charger nibble on a bit of dry grass beside the road. The column had stopped for a short rest, and he was up near the vanguard.

In the distance Tamas could hear the crack of rifles. Another Kez scouting party close enough to engage. The Kez had been dogging their heels ever since Tamas's meeting with General Beon. Their dragoons stayed close, traveling in groups of ten or twenty, flanking the rear guard and causing whatever mayhem they could.

Tamas was weary of it. He'd set a dozen traps, killed hundreds of Kez dragoons, but his men couldn't even stop to scavenge or they risked finding themselves flanked by more than just a few squads.

Gavril sniffed at the wind, as if to punctuate his previous statement.

Tamas looked down at his uniform. The dark blue didn't show stains badly, but the silver-and-gold trim had seen better days, and the linen shirt beneath the jacket was yellowed from sweat, the cuffs stained dark from powder burns and dirt. A thin crust of dirt covered his face and hands like a second skin, and he didn't dare imagine how his feet might smell once he peeled off his boots.

"I smell fine," he told his brother-in-law.

"First rule of bathing," Gavril said. "If you can't smell yourself anymore, it's time to wash. We're stopped for lunch. The last of the horsemeat is gone, so the least we can do is give the men an hour of rest. Follow that stream back there up a few hundred yards and there's a waterfall. Might give you some privacy."

"Are you going to give me your report?"

"After you bathe."

Tamas examined Gavril for a few moments. He was a different man from the one Tamas had met so many years ago. Jakola of Pensbrook had been a svelte, dashing character with a clean-shaven chin and broad shoulders. Gavril had gained a lot of weight during his time at the Mountainwatch. He carried it well, but Gavril would still be here long after the rest of them had starved to death.

The morbid thought gave Tamas a chuckle.

"I'm serious," Gavril said.

Tamas climbed to his feet. It couldn't be helped. A sudden boyish impulse struck him and he flipped Gavril a rude gesture before heading down the column. Men lay about the road, their uniforms soaked with sweat. No one saluted him. Tamas didn't make an issue of it. A ways down the resting column, two men broke out in a fistfight. Their sergeant broke it up quickly. People were growing hungry again, and tensions would only get higher.

He found the stream where a few dozen soldiers had stripped to nothing, washing themselves in the cold mountain water. Tamas passed them and headed upstream.

The stream cut through a gully, surrounded on either side by steep earthen walls. The trees rose even farther, towering hundreds of feet above him, giving Tamas the slight feeling of claustrophobia.

As the stream cut around a corner, Tamas could hear the rush of falling water. He stopped and examined the top of the gully. This was a horrible place to be. An army could come upon him, and he wouldn't hear it over the sound of the waterfall.

Every stop had pickets out a quarter of a mile. No one would come upon him without warning.

Tamas rounded the bend to find Olem was there already, stripped down to his trousers, standing with his face up against the shower of falling water.

Tamas stepped toward him, and a word of greeting died on his lips.

Vlora stood under the waterfall with Olem. She was completely nude, her uniform discarded with the rest of her gear on the bank of the stream. Olem had his hands in her dark hair, pulling them through the knots and tangles. She said something and Olem laughed, and then she turned toward him. She pushed her body up against Olem's. She opened her mouth, and Olem tilted his head down toward hers.

Her eyes flickered open. She stepped smoothly past Olem and turned her body away from Tamas. Olem said something, then stole a furtive glance at Tamas. He was suddenly washing his own hair vigorously.

"What's wrong?" A hand thumped Tamas's shoulder. "Haven't seen a naked woman before?" Gavril passed Tamas, heading toward the waterfall, already stripping off his shirt.

Tamas's heart leapt, and he said a silent prayer of thanks that he didn't jump two feet in the air. He quickly grew conscious of his voyeurism. He could feel his face growing red, so he strode to the waterfall, stripping off his uniform.

Vlora left the water and gathered her knapsack, dressing quickly. A minute later and Tamas was alone with Gavril and Olem.

"You know," Gavril said to Olem, tossing his uniform on the rocks beside the stream, "you're supposed to take your pants off when you shower."

Olem cleared his throat and gave an uncomfortable laugh. He glanced in the direction Vlora had gone.

Gavril gave a belly-shaking laugh. "That is a good-looking woman. I can see why you left 'em on." He elbowed Olem in the ribs, nearly knocking him over. Olem gave him a lopsided grin. A glance at Tamas and his grin disappeared.

"Vlora was engaged to Taniel," Tamas said. "Up until the beginning of this summer." He stared at Olem. What had he walked in upon? Had this been going on long, or was it a chance thing?

If Gavril noticed the tension, he ignored it. "Not engaged to him anymore, is she?" He shrugged his big shoulders. "Fine-looking woman is a fine-looking woman. Her being unpromised is only a bonus."

"I sometimes forget your.... habits... with women."

Gavril squared his body to Tamas, unashamed of his nudity. "You also forgot about that string of seventeen-year-old noble daughters trying to bag the most eligible bachelor in the Nine the year after Erika died... before we went to Kez. How many of those did you bed?"

Tamas had forgotten all about bathing. He clutched his jacket in one hand, jaw clenched. "Watch your mouth, Jakola."

At some point Olem had left the waterfall and gathered his shirt, jacket, and pistol from the ground. He began to slink downstream.

"We're going to have a talk, Olem," Tamas said.

Olem froze. Drops of water hung in his sandy beard.

Gavril's thick finger prodded Tamas in the chest. "You've had your share of women, Tamas. Including my sister. That means I can say what I want."

Tamas looked down at Gavril's finger, seriously considering snapping it off. Who the pit did he think he was, speaking to Tamas like that? If they'd been in public, Tamas would have had no choice but to call him out. As it were, he wanted to punch him in the nose. In a fight, Gavril had the strength and weight. Tamas had the speed, and if he had powder, it was no contest. He could...

He stopped himself. Here he was, deep in Kez territory, pursued by an army four times the size of his, and all he wanted was to feel clean again before the next battle. What was he doing? Gavril wasn't his enemy.

A glance over his shoulder told him Olem had gone.

"You're too much of a hard-ass, Tamas," Gavril said.

Tamas hung his uniform on the protruding root of a tree and stepped under the waterfall. The initial shock struck him to the core. The water was cold as ice, runoff from the mountain peaks towering over them to the east.

"Sweet Kresimir!" He felt his leg stiffen with the cold.

"I've taken colder baths at the Mountainwatch," Gavril said.

Tamas looked downstream, the way Olem had gone. "Vlora was engaged to my Taniel. He could be dead now, for all I know. I'll not have—"

"The engagement was broken off," Gavril cut him off. "You told me so yourself. Let it go. How many times did you fool around behind Erika's back?"

"None," Tamas said. His voice came out colder than the stream.

Gavril made a face like he didn't believe a word of it. He opened his mouth, but Tamas spoke first.

"Question my honor," Tamas said. "Just try it."

"Won't say another word about it."

"Good. Now give me your damned report."

"The Kez have fallen back almost eight miles. Some of your road-blocks have worked, some haven't. The cavalry can't be more than two abreast on these roads, so their own column is miles long. They've got scouts ranging everywhere they can through the woods to try to find shortcuts. I have my rangers keeping an eye out for small companies that try to flank us, but so far our worst enemy is the lack of food."

"How long until we reach the Fingers of Kresimir?" Tamas scrubbed his fingers through his mustache. He needed a shave, badly.

"Six days."

"Good."

"About that, I have bad news."

Tamas sighed. "Just what I was hoping to hear."

"The Kez have sent their cuirassiers around to the west to cut across the plains. That's fifty-five hundred heavy cavalry. What they lose in going around Hune Dora they'll gain by having flat ground. If my guess is right, they'll reach the Fingers right about the time we do.

"Last time I went through the Fingers," Gavril continued, "the forest ended about a mile from the first river. Open, flat plain all the way to the water, then a narrow wooden bridge."

"A perfect place for the Kez to trap us."

"Exactly."

Tamas closed his eyes, trying to see the space in his mind. It had been thirteen years since he last passed through the area. "I need to break the Kez."

"What?"

"Break them. I can't have the cavalry dogging us all the way to Deliv. Even if we lose them for a time crossing the Fingers, they'll be there waiting for us in the Northern Expanse, and on the open plateau we won't stand a chance against three brigades of cavalry."

"How are you going to break that many cavalry? You've only got eleven thousand men, Tamas. I've seen you work miracles before, but this is out of your league."

Tamas stepped out from under the cold water and snatched his uniform from the roots. He pulled his pants on over his wet body.

"We're going to march double-time. We can make it in four days. That'll give us preparation time."

"You can't march double for four days on empty stomachs."

Tamas ignored him. "Take twenty of your fastest riders. Take extra horses—some of those we captured from the Kez. Go ahead to the Fingers."

"I thought we were going to slaughter the horses so the men could eat."

"Slaughter them when you get there. I want you to destroy the bridge."

Gavril stepped out of the water and shook his great head, spraying water everywhere. It reminded Tamas of watching a bear fishing in a river. "Are you mad?" Gavril asked.

"Do you trust me?"

Gavril hesitated a few seconds too long. "Yes?"

"Destroy the bridge, slaughter the horses, and start making rafts. Swear your men to silence about the bridge. Once we catch up to you, the story is that the bridge was washed out and you were sent on ahead to build rafts."

"You better have a damned good reason for destroying that bridge before we cross it," Gavril said. "Otherwise my men will string me up for trying to get our whole army killed."

Tamas pulled his jacket on. "Do it. Only take men you trust."

He began walking down the stream as Gavril began to dress. He paused when Gavril called out behind him.

"Tamas," his brother-in-law said. "Try not to get us all slaughtered."

CHAPTER
19

"Have you wondered," Taniel said, "why they always sound the retreat?"

He sat at Colonel Etan's bedside in a small inn off the main road in the town of Rue, about two miles behind the front line. It was a quiet town, though the echo of distant artillery still reminded Taniel that there was a war carrying on without them.

Etan was propped up in his bed by a pile of feather pillows. A nurse was stationed just outside the door to see to his needs, while a steady stream of Etan's grenadiers had been coming and going all day, wishing him well and taking orders to the front.

Only a wounded colonel would get this kind of treatment, Taniel knew. He'd heard of a few infantrymen who'd broken their backs. Most died from neglect within a few months.

Taniel watched his friend out of the corner of his eye and made a few marks in his sketchbook, outlining Etan's strong jaw in charcoal.

Etan had refused the offer to step down from his post. Said he could—and would—still command the Twelfth Grenadiers, even if he had to do it from a chair. Rumors were that General Hilanska was going to force Etan's resignation.

Taniel hoped not. Retaining command of his grenadiers was the only thing keeping Etan from surrendering to despair.

"We retreat," Etan said, "because we're always overwhelmed." He dipped a feather pen in an inkwell and finished a sentence on the paper in his lap. He'd cursed and shouted when Taniel had first pulled out his sketchbook. Now he seemed to be doing his best to ignore the fact that Taniel was sketching him.

Taniel studied Etan's face, his mind elsewhere. Something seemed wrong about the trumpets. The retreats. Every damned time. "You know Tamas's campaign history as well as any historian. How many times has he sounded a retreat?"

"Seven, if memory serves."

"Out of how many battles?"

"Hundreds."

"And the last few weeks how many times have we fallen back before the Kez?"

Etan sighed, setting down his feather pen and rubbing his eyes. "Taniel, what does it matter? The generals don't have a choice. It's either fall back with heavy losses or suffer the deaths of every man on the front."

"What if one of the generals is in league with the Kez?" Taniel mused aloud. "Ordering the retreat early each time?"

"Those are dangerous accusations."

"Tamas believed there was a traitor—"

Etan cut him off. "And he was right. He caught the bastard. Charlemund won't see the light of day again, no matter what threats the Church makes."

"Tamas might not have caught all the traitors," Taniel said quietly.

"These generals were handpicked by Tamas. Every one of them has supported him for years, even through the coup—where the risks of failure were high, and they'd all be labeled traitors. They are capable and loyal."

Taniel took a small pinch of powder and snorted it off the back of his hand. He fought to clear his mind. There was a time when the tiniest bit of powder would allow him to focus and think, but it seemed harder and harder to do so.

Powder. That was the other thing bothering him.

"Do you have access to quartermaster reports?" Taniel asked.

Etan finished writing another missive and set it on the table beside his bed. "For my regiment, certainly."

"I don't need them for your regiment. I need them for the entire army. Can you get them?"

"I'd need to pull some strings..."

"Do it."

Etan's mouth hardened into a flat line. "Because I'm so disposed to doing you favors right now."

"Please?" Taniel said, sketching Etan's shoulders.

"Why?"

"Something that's been niggling in the back of my mind. I just want to see how much black powder the army has been using."

"All right," Etan agreed with a sigh. "I'll see what I can do." He fell silent and for several minutes there was nothing but the sound of Etan's feather pen scratching away at the paper. Etan seemed enthralled by his work. Since his paralysis, Etan had rushed head-long into the administrative duties of his rank. He'd spent the last three days checking on supply reports, reading recruitment numbers, and leafing through dossiers of men who might be considered for rank advancement.

Taniel was glad Etan had something to do to keep his mind off his injury.

The sound of Etan's pen suddenly stopped. "How do the Kez

have so many bloody Black Wardens?" he asked. "Didn't—doesn't—your father have a hard time finding them as it is?"

"Can't say for sure," Taniel said as he gave a little more shape to Etan's chin in his drawing. He'd wondered the same thing himself. "The Kez purge their countryside of powder mages every two years and make regular sweeps in the meantime. Tamas always assumed the mages they rounded up were executed. His spies never reported anything else."

Etan tapped the feather pen on the paper. "You think that maybe the Kez have been imprisoning them?"

"That's my thought," Taniel said. "Kez has a much greater population than Adro, which could partly account for their numbers. And I think Kresimir is the one turning them into Powder Wardens. It can't be coincidence that these new bastards appeared at the same time as Kresimir."

Etan began to write again, only to stop a moment later. "Oh," he said. "I got something for you."

"Eh?"

Etan produced a silver snuffbox and handed it to Taniel. "I heard you lost your old one on South Pike. Thought you'd like it."

Taniel flipped open the lid. Inside, it was engraved with the words "Taniel Two-Shot, the Unkillable."

"The Unkillable?" Taniel scoffed.

"That's what the boys have taken to calling you."

"That's absurd. Anyone can be killed." He held out the snuffbox. "I can't take this."

Etan began to cough. He fell back with a grimace, clutching his side. "Take it, you stubborn bastard, or I'll start screaming at you for being a coward again. You and that girl of yours saved our asses out there."

"She's not my girl."

Etan snorted. "Oh, really? Rumors are getting around, Taniel." Etan looked down at his hands. "I shouldn't tell you this, but the

General Staff wants you two separated. Says it's bad for morale, having a war hero gallivanting around with a savage."

"You believe all that? Agree with it?" Taniel stiffened. He didn't have to sit here and listen to this drivel.

Etan made a calming motion. "I see your face when you look at her. Same way you used to look at Vlora." Etan shrugged. "I won't judge. Just warning you about the rumors."

Taniel forced himself to relax. The way he used to look at Vlora? This was almost as preposterous as the grenadiers calling Taniel "unkillable." "What should I do? I'm not going to send her away."

"Marry her?"

Taniel laughed, shaking his head at the absurdity of the statement.

"I'm not joking," Etan said. "The General Staff can say anything they want about propriety, but if she's your wife, they have to stuff it." He began to cough again, harder this time.

"You need rest," Taniel said. Etan's face had turned as pale as Taniel's sketch paper. In the hours of the afternoon Taniel had almost forgotten the severity of Etan's injury. His sudden frailty brought it all back.

"I need to write out more orders."

"Rest." Taniel took the paper and quill from Etan and set them beside the bed. He put the snuffbox there with them and headed for the door.

"Taniel."

"Yes?"

Etan plucked the snuffbox off his bedside table and tossed it to Taniel, who caught it in one hand.

"Take it," Etan said. "Or I'll have you shot."

"All right, all right. I'll take it." He closed the door behind him.

Ka-poel was waiting in the hallway, sitting on the ground just outside the door with her legs crossed, one of her wax dolls in hand.

She stowed it and stood up. If she'd heard what Etan had to say about her, she gave no indication.

"Can you do anything for him?" Taniel asked.

A slight shake of her head.

"Damn it, Pole. You practically brought me back from the dead, and you can't..."

She held up a finger, her forehead wrinkling in a frown. Taniel thought she might go on, but instead she turned and walked away.

He followed her down and through the common room of the inn, where wounded soldiers talked and drank while they waited to be sent home or back to the front. There was a somber air to the room. A woman sat in one corner, alone, her leg amputated at the knee. She moaned to herself, a lonely keening sound that everyone tried to ignore.

The weather outside didn't improve Taniel's mood. The sky had threatened rain for a week now, every day a little cloudier. Yesterday there'd been a misting drizzle in the evening—just enough to make the grass slick and the fighting all the more treacherous.

Taniel stopped just outside the inn and wondered if he should have gotten a drink before heading back to the front.

A pair of provosts approached from the street. Both carried heavy steel pikes and wore Adran blues with green trim and the insignia of mountains crossed by cudgels.

Coincidence, Taniel wondered, or were they waiting for him?

"Captain Taniel Two-Shot?"

"What?"

"You're to come with us, sir."

Definitely waiting for him. "On whose authority?"

"General Ket's."

"I don't think I'll do that." Taniel touched the butt of his pistol.

"We're placing you under arrest, sir."

Arrest? This had gone too far. "On what charge?"

"That's for General Ket to say."

One stepped forward, taking Taniel by the arm.

Taniel jerked away. "Get your hands off me. I know my rights as a soldier of the Adran army. You'll tell me the charges or you'll go to the pit." Taniel's senses told him that they didn't have an ounce of powder. They'd come ready. For him.

Or had they? The provost jerked hard on Taniel's arm, like he was some kind of unruly child. "Come quiet-like now. We're to bring the girl as well. Where is she?"

Where had Ka-poel gone? Taniel looked around, pulling his arm away from the provost.

"Now, sir! Don't make us—"

Taniel's fist connected with the provost's chin, sending the man to the ground. The other provost lowered his pike and stepped forward threateningly. Taniel shifted to one side, grabbed the pike by the shaft, and jerked the man off balance. The provost stumbled forward, and Taniel planted a fist into the side of his head.

The first provost came to his feet, already swinging. His ears were red, his face twisted in an angry grimace at having been sucker punched to the ground. The provost was easily a head taller than Taniel and weighed four stone more.

Taniel caught the provost's fist and slammed his opposite hand into the man's elbow. He heard the snap, saw the blood and the white bone sticking out of the flesh.

The provost's scream drew more attention than Taniel wanted. He let the man fall to the ground and then started walking briskly toward the front.

Arrest him? General Ket had the gall to arrest him? It seemed like Taniel was the only thing left between the Kez and Adopest. He'd killed half of their remaining Privileged, giving the Wings a clear advantage on the field, and he'd run out of room for notches on his rifle, he'd killed so many infantry.

Ka-poel joined him a few moments later. One minute he was walking alone, trying to ignore the stares of anyone who'd seen him break a provost's arm, and the next she was beside him, strolling along as if nothing had happened.

"Where the pit were you?"

Ka-poel didn't respond.

"Well…" Taniel gritted his teeth. Pit. A general had an arrest warrant out for him. They'd come sooner or later, in force. What could he do? Break the arms of every provost in the army? "If they come again, disappear just like that. I don't want them getting their damned hands on you."

She nodded.

Taniel felt his steps grow in purpose as he headed back toward the front. He changed his course a little and went toward the cooking tents.

Taniel found his goal in the third mess tent he looked inside.

The master chef, Mihali, was alone inventorying barrels. He held a piece of charcoal in one hand and paper in the other. His long black hair was tied behind his head in a ponytail.

"Good afternoon, Taniel," Mihali said without turning around.

Taniel came up short as the tent flap fell closed behind him. "Have we met?"

"No. But I'm friends with your father. Please, come in."

Taniel stayed warily near the tent flap. Ka-poel had come inside behind him, and she seemed to have no reservations about plopping down on a barrel in one corner.

"Tamas is dead," Taniel said.

"Oh, don't be silly. You don't believe that."

"I've come to accept it."

Mihali still hadn't turned around. Even with his back toward Taniel, he had a kind of presence that made Taniel second-guess his decision to come there. There was something about him. A smell, maybe? No. Something more subtle. Just the slightest sense of familiarity.

"Tamas is very much alive," Mihali said. His lips moved silently, finger wagging as he counted barrels in one corner of the tent. "Along with most of the Seventh and the Ninth. They're being pursued heavily right now by three full brigades of cavalry and six brigades of infantry."

Taniel snorted. "How can you know all that?"

"I *am* Adom reborn."

"So. You *do* claim to be a god?"

Mihali finally turned around with a sigh, making marks on his paper. He had a pudgy, elongated face that spoke of a mix of Adran and Rosvelean ancestry. His white apron was stained with flour and blood, and there was a piece of potato peel stuck to the side of his clean-shaven chin. "Is it that hard to believe? You've attempted to kill one god."

"I saw Kresimir descend from the clouds. I saw his face. I looked upon Kresimir and I knew with every bit of me that he was a god. You..." Taniel trailed off, watching the master chef for the anger that was sure to come.

"Not so much?" Instead of taking offense, Mihali laughed. "Kresimir was always so much better at appearing effortlessly grand. Your father needed to come to believe on his own. You, I think, need a more direct approach." Mihali approached him and held a hand out toward his head. He stopped suddenly, recoiling. Taniel noticed that Mihali's hand was trembling.

"May I?" Mihali asked Ka-poel.

Ka-poel returned his stare, her eyes daring him to try.

Mihali extended his hand once more toward Taniel. As it drew closer, it trembled harder and harder, as if affected by some unseen force. Finally, the chef's fingers brushed Taniel's skin.

Taniel felt a spark.

Then it seemed as if the universe flashed before his eyes. Countless years zoomed by, filling Taniel's memories like they were his own. He saw Kresimir's original descent from the heavens, and then felt Kresimir call to his brothers and sisters to aid him in rebuilding the Nine. He witnessed the chaos of the Bleakening, and the relentless march of the centuries. Lifetimes rushed past in a blink of an eye.

And then it was all gone.

Taniel staggered backward, gasping.

Ka-poel had done something similar to him once, several months ago. It had left him breathless in its emotion and magnitude, though it had only been a few moments' worth of memories.

This was two thousand years' worth.

It took him some time to recover. When he did, he said, "You are a god." Not a question this time.

" 'God' is a funny word," Mihali said, turning back to his inventory. He made a mark on his paper and silently counted sacks of onions. "It implies omnipotence and omniscience. Let me assure you, I am neither."

"Then what are you?" Bo had once said that the gods were nothing more than powerful Privileged. With memories like that, how could Mihali be anything but a god?

"Semantics, semantics!" Mihali threw up his hands. "For the sake of argument, let's say yes, I am a god. I don't think either of us has the time for a theo-philosophical argument right now. Please, have a seat." Mihali picked up a wine barrel like it weighed no more than a couple pounds and set it beside Taniel, then went to get another.

Taniel tried to nudge the barrel over a few inches. He couldn't. He frowned, then looked at Mihali as the chef fetched a barrel for himself and one for Ka-poel.

Ka-poel's hand casually brushed Mihali's arm.

"Now, girl," Mihali said as a man might gently reprimand a daughter, "none of that." He gently touched her fingers.

There was a flare of fire, and Ka-poel danced away, blowing on her fingertips and scowling at Mihali. Had she been trying to collect a hair from the chef?

Mihali deposited himself on his wine barrel. "Unlike my brothers and sisters, I decided to stay on in this world after organizing the Nine. Hidden, of course. But learning." There was a far-off look in Mihali's eye as he stared at something Taniel could not see. "Distant stars are beautiful and curious, but I found the people here so varied and enchanting I couldn't leave."

Mihali glanced at Ka-poel. "I've studied the Bone-eyes. Not in depth. Being in Dynize and Fatrasta, so far away from Adro, taxes my strength. I never knew how Kresimir and the rest left the planet. They always called me a homebody for not wanting to explore the cosmos. Anyway, the Bone-eyes have incredible magic. So very different from anything Kresimir or the others could imagine. You, my dear, are truly terrifying. So much potential."

Mihali didn't look terrified. If anything, he seemed intrigued.

The chef turned to Taniel. "And powder mages! Kresimir wouldn't have expected that. After all, gunpowder wasn't invented until hundreds of years after he left." Mihali drummed a pudgy finger on his chin. "He's going mad, you know. That Bone-eye bullet you put in his eye was never removed. It's in his brain, causing him incredible pain every day."

Taniel tried to work moisture into his mouth. Kresimir, a god, was going mad. All because of him. "Does he know who shot him?"

"I believe he knows. What you did on South Pike is barely a rumor in the Adran army, and the only two to survive that battle on the Kez side were Julene and Kresimir." Mihali paused. "Of course, he has Julene. Then he must know."

"He nailed Julene to a beam. Cut off her hands. Why would he do that?"

Mihali frowned. "Julene. Misguided child. She may or may not have deserved that, but I don't think torture does anyone any good."

Taniel noticed that Mihali had sidestepped the question about Julene. He decided not to press it.

"How can I kill him?"

"Kresimir? Hmm. What makes you think I'd tell you?"

Taniel rocked back. "But . . . you're on our side. Aren't you?" He felt his muscles tense, a bit of fear touching his heart.

"I defend Adro. It's my country, after all. However, Kresimir is still my brother. I love him. I will not see him dead. I would, however, like to stop him. Help him. If I can get that bullet out of his brain, I might even be able to reason with him and end this whole thing."

Taniel's fingers curled into fists. "I'm going to kill him."

"That may be your path." Mihali examined his inventory paper. Once again, he seemed to be counting.

It was several moments before Taniel spoke again. "The generals. Do they know . . . ?"

"Oh, Tamas told them. Most of them don't believe it."

"But they know you're a powerful Privileged?"

Mihali nodded. "An uncomfortable truth. They asked me to participate in the fighting and I refused. After all, the Privileged with the Wings of Adom are doing a fine job keeping the remainder of the Kez Cabal in check."

"Did you tell them that Tamas was alive?"

"Of course."

Taniel blinked at this. "Then why haven't they told me? Hilanska . . . surely he would have said something if there were hope."

"Not even a god sees everything," Mihali said. "I do not know. But I don't trust the generals. I'm sure that most of them have Adro's best interests at heart. But a few . . ."

"General Ket."

Mihali shrugged. "The provosts are here, by the way."

Taniel stepped to the tent flap and took a peek. Dozens of them had gathered outside.

"Pit. Can I get out the back way?"

"They've surrounded the tent. It's probably best that you go with them."

"I won't let them arrest me. The bastards. I—"

Mihali cleared his throat. "As I said. It's probably for the best. For now, anyway."

Taniel's mind raced. What to do? Run for it? Go out, dignified, and let them take him away? "Answer me this, first: What has happened to me? I'm stronger and faster than before. I've never felt this kind of power. It took enough mala to kill a horse just to get me buzzed. I know it's more than just being a powder mage. Is it because of her?" He flung his finger toward Ka-poel, who raised an eyebrow in response.

Mihali hesitated for several moments. "You've been tempered," he said. "This girl here has you wrapped in protective sorceries. Kresimir's returning strike after you shot him was enough to bring down South Pike Mountain. It should have shattered your mortal body. That blow he gave you could very well have killed me, for all my knowledge of sorcery. But you..." Mihali chuckled, as if something was funny. "You, it just made stronger."

"That doesn't make any sense, it—"

"It's time to go," Mihali said.

Taniel took a deep breath. "All right. Ka-poel, stay here. I don't want them touching you." Without waiting for an answer, he stepped out of the tent and into daylight.

The provosts surrounded him quickly, their pikes leveled.

"All right, you bastards. Take me to General Ket, I—"

Someone brought a truncheon down on his head, hard. Taniel staggered forward, spitting blood from the blow. Another hit his stomach, then his knee. He collapsed to the ground. He was cursed and kicked and beaten, and when he thought he could take no more, he was pulled to his feet and struck about the face and head until he lost consciousness.

CHAPTER 20

Tamas listened to his stomach growl as his charger trotted along the road at the rear of the column. Ahead of him, the men of the Ninth Brigade shuffled to the crack of a single drummer boy's snare. The air was hot and oppressive, even with the cover of tall pine trees. The summer humidity soaked through Tamas's soiled jacket and made every breath a labor.

He watched one of the infantry in the column ahead of him. The man was tall, with dirty-blond hair pulled back in a ponytail over one shoulder. About twenty minutes ago his shoulders had started to sway dangerously as he marched. He'd be the next to faint. Tamas would have put money on it.

Every so often the soldiers would glance back at Tamas's charger with hungry eyes. They watched with the same looks every scout and officer who was still riding. It was unsettling.

They'd slaughtered the last of the Kez horses two days ago and distributed the meat. Tamas heard rumor that some of the company quartermasters were holding back and selling the last precious pounds. He'd tried to get to the bottom of it, but no one would confess. Every stream they passed saw a dozen men leave the line, throwing themselves into the mud in search of tiny fish and crawdads. Their sergeants had to beat them back into the column.

"They think they're going to get a meal soon," Olem said.

Tamas shook himself from his reverie. He felt light-headed, weak. He'd not eaten in four days. The men on their feet needed it more than he did. At least there was some periodic grazing for the horses.

Olem pointed up to a pair of buzzards circling high above the treetops.

"Ah," Tamas said.

"They've been following us for fifty miles," Olem said.

"You can't be sure it's the same vultures."

"One of 'em has red on the tips of his feathers."

Tamas grunted. Words were coming slow out of his mouth. The heat didn't make him feel much like talking.

"That red-tipped buzzard kept on when most of the others stayed behind at the camp two mornings ago, when we slaughtered the horses." Olem pursed his lips. "I think he's hoping for the big payday."

Tamas looked up at the buzzards. He didn't want to talk about them. He'd seen far too many on far too many battlefields. "I haven't seen you smoke for a week," he said.

"Too bloody hot, pardon the language, sir." Olem patted his breast pocket. "Besides. I'm saving my last one."

"A special occasion of some kind?"

Olem continued to watch the buzzards. "Gavril told me we might be making a stand at the Fingers. I figure it'll be nice to die with a cigarette between my lips."

Tamas couldn't help but scowl. "Have you told anyone? About the stand, I mean."

"No, sir."

"Damned Gavril. Needs to keep his mouth shut."

"So it's true, then?"

"I don't intend to make a last stand, Olem. I intend to break the Kez. Last stands are for men who plan on losing."

"Quite right, sir."

Tamas sighed inwardly. Soldiers had a strange sense of fatalism. Most of them didn't realize that any odds could be beaten with the right maneuvering.

"Olem…" Tamas began.

"Sir?"

"About what I saw the other day…"

A muscle jumped in Olem's jaw. "What do you mean, sir?"

"I think you know what I mean. *Vlora*. If I'd come a few minutes later, I think I would have found the two of you in a much more compromising position."

"That was the hope, sir."

Tamas blinked. He'd not expected that kind of bluntness. "Can't hold your tongue to save face, can you?"

"Not to save my life, sir."

"I won't have that kind of fraternization, Olem."

"What kind, sir?" The corners of Olem's eyes tightened.

"You and Vlora. She is a captain, you are—"

"A captain," Olem said. "You made me one yourself." He touched the gold pins on his lapels helpfully.

Tamas cleared his throat and looked up. Those damned buzzards were still there. "I mean that she is a powder mage. You know my mages are a different contingent of the army. I won't have you crossing that line."

Olem looked like he wanted to say something. He worked his jaw around, chewing on a phantom cigarette. "Yes, sir. Whatever you say, sir."

The sarcasm in Olem's tone leaked through like water through paper. It nearly shocked Tamas. Olem was normally so loyal, so quick to obey. He opened his mouth, a rebuke on his tongue.

The soldier with a ponytail staggered and fell out of line, hitting the ground hard. Two of his companions stopped to help him.

"Head up the line," Tamas said. "Call for rest. The men need a sit-down."

Only too grateful to get away, Olem spurred his mount on, calling out, "Field Marshal orders the column to halt! Fall out!"

Tamas could hear the order repeated farther up the column. Slowly, the line of soldiers came to a stop. Some men went looking for the closest stream, some men relieved themselves in the woods, and others slumped to the ground where they were, too exhausted to move.

Tamas opened his canteen and drained the last few drops. The water was hot and tasted of the metal. "Soldier," Tamas said, pointing to a man who looked the least worse for the wear. "Find me some clean, cold water and fill this, then tell your sergeant you're off latrine duty tonight."

The soldier took the canteen. "Aye, sir."

Tamas climbed down from his charger and hung the reins from a tree limb. He paced the width of the road, trying to work some feeling back into his legs after riding half the day. He stopped once and looked south. No sign of the Kez. The woods were too thick. According to the latest reports, the head of the Kez column was ten miles back. They had dragoons ranging in the area in between, trying to catch Adran stragglers and harass the end of the Adran column, but what mattered to Tamas was where the bulk of the cavalry were.

He was going to need that heavy lead.

"Sir."

Tamas turned to find Vlora standing next to his charger. Her uniform was dirty, jacket loosened at the neck, her black hair tied back behind her head. He had the brief image of her naked beneath the waterfall, leaning in to kiss Olem. He willed the image away, trying not to let his embarrassment show on his face.

"Captain."

"How is the leg, sir?"

Tamas flexed the muscles in his leg, felt them twinge. Riding hadn't helped it loosen at all, but the pain wasn't too bad. "It's fine, thank you. Any luck hunting?"

"The deer are keeping well away from the column. If we range more than a mile or two from the road, we won't be able to carry our prey back. A few squirrels and rabbits. Enough to keep the powder mages fed."

At least his mages were keeping up their strength. He felt his stomach twist at the mention of rabbit.

"If we camped for more than one night, or even slowed down a bit, we might be able to bag some deer."

"Sorry, Captain. I can't allow that. We have to reach the Fingers well ahead of the Kez."

"The scouts say we'll be there in two days, sir."

"That's right," Tamas said. "Once we cross the first river, we'll burn the bridge and take it easy for a couple of days. Rest and restock."

"I certainly hope so, sir. The men are looking poor."

Tamas turned his attention to the soldier who had fainted. He was sitting up now, drinking out of a canteen, talking to one of his fellows. Tamas clasped his hands behind his back and faced Vlora.

"Captain, you and I both know that what happened the other day was completely out of order."

Vlora didn't even blink. "You mean, when you watched me bathe?"

Tamas could have slapped her for that. Damned girl. She knew what he wanted to say, and she wasn't going to make it easy.

"You and Olem..."

"Sir, I don't think that's any of your business. With all due respect."

"I am your commanding officer—"

"Yes, sir. And you've always made it very clear that what two soldiers want to do in their spare time is up to them, as long as it doesn't break convention between the ranks."

"This is different." This *was* different, Tamas told himself. "I won't have one of my Marked gallivanting around with my bodyguard, do you understand? I won't have my bodyguard going around with...with..."

"A whore?"

She had spoken quietly, but Tamas felt the breath taken from him.

"That's what you want to say, isn't it, sir? You want to call me a whore for what I did to Taniel? A slut? I can hear the words on the tip of your tongue, even if you don't speak them."

"Watch your tone, soldier," Tamas warned.

"Permission to speak freely, sir?"

"Permission denied."

Vlora ignored him. "You don't think I know what I did to Taniel? You don't think it kills me inside knowing that I threw away everything we had for a few months of passion with some idiot?"

"Permission denied, Captain."

"You don't hear the men talk." Vlora's voice rose. "You don't hear what everyone says about me behind my back—even to my face. You don't see the sneers. 'Vlora, she'll spread her legs for anyone now.' You don't hear them whisper that outside your tent at night, placing bets on who can be the first to get me on my back."

"Permission denied!" Tamas stepped forward. Any other soldier would have shrunk beneath the red fury in Tamas's eyes, but Vlora refused to back down.

"I spent eighteen months alone while Taniel was in Fatrasta because *you* sent him there. Taniel, the war hero. People talked about how every woman in Fatrasta was ready to throw themselves on him. And then to hear he had a little savage girl, following him everywhere. What was I supposed to think of that? No man would look twice at me at the university. They knew who I was. They were too afraid of Taniel to say any nice thing to me."

Vlora spat the words in Tamas's face, her voice dripping with bitterness, her whole body trembling with rage. "Then a man appears who doesn't care whose fiancée I am. He charms me, loves me, and assures me there's not another in the world that can make him so happy. I trusted him." Vlora's face twisted in disgust. "Then I find out he was bedding me just to *make you look bad.*"

The pain in Vlora's eyes and the malice in her voice was more than Tamas could bear. Once, he had been her father, her friend, her mentor. But now he had become nothing more to her than an object of hatred, an enemy to despise.

"Get out of my sight, Captain. If we weren't at war, I'd have you court-martialed."

Vlora leaned forward, closer than anyone who didn't know Tamas as well as she did would have dared. Close enough to embrace him. Close enough to stick a knife in his ribs if she wanted. "Kill me yourself, if you want it done so badly," she said. "Don't hand the job over to lesser men."

She whirled on her heel and strode down the column. Soldiers stared openmouthed at her as she went past, then turned to look toward Tamas, waiting for his wrath to follow like thunder after lightning.

Tamas watched Vlora almost disappear around a bend in the road. She made an abrupt stop as Olem rode into view. The bodyguard leaned over his horse, said something to her. She put her hand on his thigh. He pushed it away gently and gave a meaningful glance at Tamas.

Vlora grabbed Olem by the belt and pulled him off his horse, pushing him into the woods off the trail. Tamas swore under his breath and took two steps down the column.

Someone cleared their throat. Tamas looked around.

It was the soldier he'd sent for water. "Your canteen, sir."

Tamas snatched the canteen. When he looked again, Olem and Vlora were gone.

He took several deep breaths and went back to his horse.

"Sir, you mind if I ask how long until we march again?" the soldier asked.

Tamas took a long draw of water. It was so frigid it seemed to burn his throat going down. It made his teeth hurt.

"Thirty minutes, damn it. Get some rest."

Adamat rapped on the door of the foreman's office in the textile mill. Below him, dozens of steam-powered looms thundered at full tilt throughout the day, creating a racket that drowned out all but the loudest shouts. Hundreds of workers tended the millworks, moving about the floor like so many insects.

Adamat let himself into the foreman's office. Inside, the sound was greatly reduced.

"Margy," he called.

The woman emerged from the back of the room and smiled when she saw Adamat. He leaned in and kissed her on the cheek.

She stepped back from him in shock. "What in all the Nine have you done to yourself?"

"Fell down the stairs," Adamat said. His voice whined nasally, and his face still hurt as if the broken nose had happened only an hour ago.

Margy harrumphed. "Looks more like you got it punched in," she said. "I alway told you putting your nose in other people's business was going to get it broken."

Adamat threw his hands up in mock surrender. "I've only got a moment, Margy. I just dropped by to see if you had a lead on that rug."

"Fine, fine." Margy moved over to the desk beside her microscope and began leafing through papers. "I sent Faye a letter last week," she said.

"I'll ask if she got it." Adamat leaned against the doorpost and closed his eyes. His face hurt. His back hurt. His hands and his head hurt. Everything hurt, and he wasn't getting enough sleep. He couldn't recall the last time he'd eaten more than toast and tea. He opened his eyes again when Margy pushed a piece of paper into his hand.

"That's the buyer," she said. "I couldn't get a name, just the address from a check receipt."

"Thanks, Margy."

"Tell Faye to come visit soon, will you?"

"Of course."

Adamat left the textile mill and didn't look at the paper until he was outside. With no name, it would be more work for him to find out the owner of the address, and knowing the Proprietor, Adamat would have to go through several layers of fake names *and* addresses before he found the Proprietor's identity.

He hailed a hackney cab and looked at the address.

He had to look again, blinking to be sure his eyes weren't playing tricks on him.

This was an address he knew.

The weather had grown overcast as the morning progressed, and Adamat stopped by his safe house in western Adopest to get an umbrella. He paused in the hallway. The door to the flat was open.

Part of him screamed to just turn and walk away. He might not survive the next run-in with Vetas's goons.

He drew his pistol and checked to see if it was loaded before pushing gently on the door.

SouSmith sat on the sofa. His arms were folded over his stomach, his chin resting on his chest as he dozed. His shirt was covered in blood.

"SouSmith?"

The big boxer jerked awake. "Ah."

"What happened?"

SouSmith cocked an eyebrow at him, as if it were strange of Adamat to ask after his bloody shirt. "What happened yourself? Someone break your nose?"

Adamat called for the landlady to put a kettle on, and closed the door behind him. "You're soaked with blood."

"None of it's mine," SouSmith said. "Least, not much. Nose?"

"One of Vetas's goons was waiting at my old house. Hit me in the face with a cudgel. Now what's this? You can't be sitting in a man's living room covered in someone else's blood without an explanation."

"Four o' Vetas's men came by my brother's place," SouSmith said. "Shot one of my nephews. Me and Daviel . . . we killed all four."

"Pit, SouSmith. I'm sorry. Is your nephew . . . ?"

"Kid was twelve. Daviel had just got it together to send 'im to school." SouSmith stood up and stretched. The blood on his shirt was black and dry, probably hours old. His piggish eyes glinted with anger. "I'm in," he said. "Proprietor or no, I'm 'a see Vetas burn. Then I've got to see to my family."

Adamat was about to ask what they did with the bodies when he remembered SouSmith's brother was a butcher. He probably did not want to know. He gave a wary nod.

Could he trust SouSmith? What if Vetas's goons had turned him? What if, like Adamat, SouSmith's family was being held by Vetas?

Could he even afford to ask these questions? Adamat needed every man he could get on his side.

"Get cleaned up," Adamat said. "You left some clothes here."

"We going somewhere?"

"I have to see a man about fifty thousand krana."

Adamat stepped out of the carriage in the Routs—the very best part of town, filled with large brick bankers' houses. The streets were wide, paved with flat cobbles, and lined with towering elms. Adamat tilted his hat up and looked for the house he wanted.

There—in between two of the immense city townhouses owned by the wealthy bankers sat a small, austere house with a well-kept garden. Adamat headed up the walk to the house, followed closely by SouSmith.

"The Reeve, right?" SouSmith asked.

"Yes." Ondraus the Reeve. One of Tamas's councillors, and an architect of the coup that overthrew Manhouch. He was a sour, unfriendly old man. Adamat did not relish a second meeting. He pounded on the door.

He pounded for ten minutes before he finally heard the latch inside move, and the door opened a crack.

"For a wealthy man," Adamat said, "I'm surprised you answer the door yourself."

Ondraus the Reeve glared at Adamat through narrowed eyes. "Get off my front step, or I'll have you jailed for harassment." Ondraus was wearing a robe and slippers. His hair was unkempt.

"I need money," Adamat said. "Your accountants told me I've been cut off."

Ondraus sneered at him. "Tamas is dead. Whatever access to funds he promised you is gone. I'd suggest you find employment elsewhere."

"See, that's a problem. May I come in?"

"No."

Adamat leaned on the door. Ondraus started, reeling back into his tiny foyer.

"Wait out here, please," Adamat said to SouSmith. The boxer nodded.

Ondraus stormed toward his office. Adamat drew the pistol from his pocket and cleared his throat.

The Reeve froze when he saw the pistol. "What is the meaning of this?" he demanded.

Adamat drew his eyes across the room. It had changed little in the months since Adamat's last visit. The mantel had been dusted, the fireplace cleaned, but the carpet showed no more wear and the smells were exactly the same. The house seemed almost unused.

"I can see through the open door to your office there," Adamat said, "a bell cord. Hardly worth noticing on my last visit, but I find myself wondering, in a house with three rooms and no servants, why you have a bell cord." Adamat motioned toward the only chair beside the fireplace. Ondraus took a seat.

"Are you here to rob me?" Ondraus said. "All my money is in investments. As you can see, there's nothing of worth here. I don't even keep a checkbook in my home."

"See," Adamat continued without acknowledging the interruption, "my guess is that bell cord leads to a system of rooms beneath your house, and in one of those rooms you have a permanent staff of four large, dangerous men ready to come to your defense if you need it. And off of those rooms leads a tunnel, likely going to one of these nearby manors that you own under a false name. You don't live in it, of course. You just use it to conceal your comings and goings under your other name."

Ondraus watched Adamat from the chair, saying nothing. His glare was less angry now and more . . . calculating. For some reason the change made him far more frightening.

"You haven't yet told me that I'm a dead man," Adamat said. He considered Ondraus for a moment. "I suppose you're not the type."

"What is your insurance?" Ondraus asked.

"Letters. Sent to certain friends I have in the police force."

"Telling them that I am the Proprietor?"

It was a thrill to hear Ondraus say it out loud. No denial. No admission. A simple statement, and it made the hair on the back of Adamat's neck stand up. "No, of course not. Telling them that if I disappear, my body can be found beneath your house. No one wants to investigate the Proprietor. But my friends on the force will have no problem combing through the affairs of one accountant. You're known as a shut-in. Shut-ins are always interesting. My friends might even find it fun. And when they find out about the rooms beneath your house, and the bodyguards, and the manor and the huge amounts of money in your portfolio, they will become extremely interested indeed."

Ondraus scoffed. "You think that will save you?"

"Yes, I do." Adamat felt a crack in his confidence. What if Ondraus just didn't care? A man with his connections could just disappear if an investigation started on him. "I think that my life is a trivial thing to spare, if it will save you even a few months' worth of scrutiny and trouble.

"If that is not the case," Adamat added, "I have sent another letter to a friend in the publishing business, telling him I know who the Proprietor is. If I wind up dead, and he hears of an investigation of my death involving you, he'll draw conclusions and, let me say, he's not a very smart man. He values headlines far more than his own life."

Ondraus began to chuckle. It was a dry sound, and for a moment Adamat thought he was coughing. "Very clever," he said.

"If you'd given me help, instead of deciding to let me take Vetas on my own, I wouldn't have even wondered about your identity."

"You'd have still wondered," Ondraus said, waving one hand dismissively. "What do you want?"

"Fifty—no, seventy-five thousand krana in cash, and your help killing Lord Vetas and rescuing my wife."

Ondraus steepled his fingers and leaned back. "You need to learn to get more out of your blackmail. I'm one of the richest men in the Nine."

"I'm not interested in your money. I just want to get Faye back."

"Vetas still has a Privileged."

"That's what the money is for. If I have the money, I'll have my own Privileged."

Ondraus mulled this over. "Resourceful. And if I decide to let you live once Vetas is dead?"

"I'll forget you exist."

"You surprise me, Adamat," Ondraus said. His body was no longer tensed and angry. He lounged back in the chair, steepling his fingers. "The lengths you're going to. I was warned years ago that you were the most principled, tenacious man on the Adopest police force. I actually have gone to a few small lengths to avoid you."

"Believe me," Adamat said. "If this didn't involve my family, I wouldn't be here."

"Well, in that case, I have a stipulation. After this is over, you promise to work for me when I have need of you."

"No."

Ondraus held up his hand to forestall the protest. "I'll pay you, if it happens. The work will likely be dangerous. But agree to this, or I'll kill you and SouSmith, and see what happens."

Adamat searched Ondraus's eyes. There was an iron resolve there that told him Ondraus would do just that. And maybe...a hint of humor? A touch of a smile on his lips? Was Ondraus enjoying this?

"Agreed," Adamat said.

"Wonderful." Ondraus paused. "Does SouSmith know?"

"He thinks I'm here to ask for money," Adamat said. He left out that he'd told SouSmith he planned on blackmailing the Proprietor. SouSmith might make his own deductions, or he might not. If he did, he was smart enough to keep quiet. No need telling Ondraus any of that.

"You'll have it tomorrow," Ondraus said. "I'll have it delivered to...?"

"I'll meet your man in Elections Square. By the stains."

"You're not to come here ever again," Ondraus said. "Our contact will be through my eunuch. You may go now."

Adamat slid his pistol into his pocket with the sudden realization that he was no longer in control.

"And Adamat," Ondraus said, "if I ever have need to regret this, everyone you've ever loved will regret it too."

CHAPTER
21

At some point during the beating they'd put a black hood over Taniel's head and now he tripped and struggled as he was shoved through the camp by the provosts. He could hear their warning to those who passed to stay clear, and their quiet curses when he stumbled. Disoriented, he would have fallen but for the strong arms beneath his armpits. His head pounded, his body a knot of pain.

They forced him up a set of stairs and dragged him inside a building. An inn? Officers' mess? He didn't know. He was thrown into a chair, then tied down. He tried to struggle. The effort earned him a cuff on the back of the head.

Taniel slumped against his bonds and strained to hear some sound that would tell him his location. Nothing but the chatter of soldiers outside the building, too low to hear the voices. He might have been anywhere in the Adran camp.

How much time passed, he couldn't be sure. The air grew cooler, so it must have been night. His face was completely numb. They had to have beaten it into a mess. He felt along his teeth. All there. His shirt was soaked—probably his own blood, and as he sat there, it grew cold.

The numbness in his body began to fade, along with his last powder trance, leaving him to feel the full pain of the beating, when he finally heard the door open. Multiple sets of heavy footsteps. Then another set. Lighter, but no less military.

His hood was pulled off. A match was struck and the lanterns on the wall lit. The room was no bigger than three yards square and was bare but for two chairs and the lanterns on the wall.

General Ket stood above him, arms crossed, her face impassive. She was flanked by two of her provosts. The men glared at him, cudgels held in such a way as if they were daring him to move.

"You'll need more men," Taniel said.

She seemed taken off guard that he spoke first. "What?"

"If you're going to beat me into submission, or whatever it is you're here to do."

"Shut up, Two-Shot." Ket scratched at the stub of her missing ear and then began to pace. "I should have you shot."

"You'll have to hang me," Taniel said. He couldn't help but chuckle. Shot. These officers all acted like they knew everything, but you can't put a powder mage in front of a firing squad. Not one armed with conventional rifles, anyway.

One of the provosts put his full weight behind his fist and slammed it into Taniel's jaw. Taniel's head snapped to the side and his vision spun. The provost became a fuzzy blur. Taniel hawked a wad of bloody phlegm at the provost, and the man drew back for another punch.

Ket held up a hand. "That's not necessary, provost." She rounded on Taniel. "Is this a joke to you? You're looking at being executed!"

"For what?" Taniel scoffed. "Holding the line?"

"For what?" she echoed incredulously. Ket stopped her pacing to face him. "Insubordination, conduct unfitting an officer, disobeying direct orders. Physically assaulting an officer. The way you act verges on treason."

"Go to the pit," Taniel said. He was proud when he didn't flinch at the provost coming toward him.

Ket stopped the man again.

"Keep it up," Taniel said. "I can do this all night. Treason? Is it treason to be the only officer in this bloody army that seems to care about winning a battle? Is it treason to rally the men? Give them something to stand up for? You talk to me about treason, when the trumpets sound a retreat every time we're about to win a battle."

"That's a lie!" Ket stepped forward, and for a moment Taniel thought she'd hit him herself. "We sound the alarm when the battle goes against us. You're down on the lines. You don't see the desperation of the fight where you are."

Taniel leaned forward, straining at his bonds. "I don't see it because I'm winning." He leaned back. "You're scared of me. Have you gone over to the Kez? Is that why? You're scared I'll—"

Ket didn't stop the provost this time. Taniel's words were cut off by the blow, and he was genuinely surprised to find his teeth still there when his head stopped ringing.

Taniel tasted blood. He swallowed. "Is that why you arrested me in secret?" Taniel spoke around a swollen tongue. "Had me dragged through the camp in a hood? So no one could see me?" Taniel snorted and looked the provost in the eye, daring him to hit again.

General Ket scratched at her ear. "You are very popular," she admitted as she began to pace again. "But even the popular— someone like you, who the common soldiers call a hero—need to be disciplined. Otherwise the army falls apart. It's unfortunate, but that's the way it is. I'd make you a public display, but the other generals don't agree with me. They think if the men see you flogged, it'll hurt morale and, Kresimir knows, it's already low enough."

"So you're not going to kill me."

"No. At least, not yet. This is your one and only warning."

"And you expect an apology?"

"Indeed. Several, in fact. Starting with Major Doravir, and ending with me."

Taniel shrugged. "Not going to happen."

"Excuse me?" Ket's eyebrows rose in genuine surprise.

"I nearly killed a god. I've slaughtered dozens of Privileged. Maybe over a hundred. I've lost count. In the absence of Field Marshal Tamas—by the way, why was I told he was dead? I have it from the mouth of a god that he's not. Ah, yes. The god we have in our own camp. The god that the high command are pretending doesn't exist.

"Where was I? In the absence of Tamas, I'm your best tool against the Kez. I'm rallying the men and killing the remaining Kez Privileged and Wardens. So no. I won't bloody well apologize to anyone. My father didn't abide fools. I may not like my father much, but we share that in common."

General Ket remained silent through the whole speech. Taniel was surprised by that. He expected to be cut off by a provost's fist halfway in. He was ready to spit the words through his broken jaw if he had to.

"Tamas is lost to us," Ket said. "There's no way he'll survive in Kez. It's better to assume he's dead. And as for Mihali...if he wasn't so popular among the men, we'd have him removed. He's a very persuasive madman, nothing more."

"Then why are we fighting this war at all?" Taniel asked. "If Kresimir is on the Kez side, we can't win. Unless. Ah. Unless you don't think Kresimir is there at all. You don't think any of this supernatural stuff is real."

"I believe what I see with my own eyes," Ket said. "I see two opposing armies. If there was a god present, we'd all be dead. Now." She paused to drag a chair over in front of Taniel and sat down, crossing her legs. "The threat of physical pain obviously means nothing to you. Death?" She examined him for a moment. "No, not that either."

She continued. "This is what's going to happen: Your records will be transferred to the Third Brigade. You'll keep your rank—but commanding a company of picked riflemen who will take on the tasks I assign. No more of this mucking about on the front line. You're not an infantryman."

"You want your own pet powder mage, eh?"

Ket went on as if she hadn't noticed him speak. "You'll apologize to Major Doravir. In public. After which you will read a prepared note—again, in public—that apologizes for your misconduct and swear on your father's grave that you will keep the regulations of the Adran army."

"I'll do no such thing."

"The savage girl is no longer to share your room. I don't approve of such illicit relationships among my officers. Especially not with a savage."

Taniel sneered. "There's nothing illicit going on."

"I wasn't finished! The girl will be placed with the laundresses of the Third. You'll be allowed to speak with her ten minutes each day. No more."

"That's preposterous!" Taniel leaned forward. "She's not Adran army, she's—"

He was silenced by the provost's fist. The blow nearly knocked him over, but the other provost stepped up and held the chair steady.

"Do not interrupt me again," Ket said coldly. "I've put up with your insubordination long enough. Rumors are the girl is some kind of sorcerer. I'll have her watched. If she attempts to leave the camp, she'll be beaten. If she attempts to find you, she'll be beaten. Understand? Oh, and before you say anything—yes, I can keep her here. This is a time of war. Conscription is a reality."

Taniel waited for a few moments before speaking. "I'll kill any man who lays a hand on her."

"You make any threat you want, but you can't protect her all the time. You'll do all these things for me, or I'll hand your girl over to the Dredgers. You've heard of them, haven't you? The scum of the

Third. Men so low that the Mountainwatch wouldn't take them. I reform such men, and if I don't succeed, I execute them." General Ket stood up and walked over until she was right next to Taniel. She whispered, "I don't approve of rape, nor encourage it. But I understand it's a powerful psychological tool, and don't think I won't give your little savage girl to the Dredgers to do with what they will."

Taniel wondered if he could kill her right then. He'd have to use his teeth to do it. Tear out her throat. The provosts could be fast enough to stop him. But it might be worth a try.

"I'm not a monster, Captain. I'm not doing this on a whim. It is my duty to impose order upon this camp and I will do it even if it costs your little savage her innocence. Do you understand?"

Taniel felt the fury leave him. He wouldn't—he couldn't subject Ka-poel to that.

"Yes," he said.

General Ket headed toward the door. "Untie him. Clean him up. He's confined to quarters until he apologizes to Major Doravir."

Tamas watched the slow march of his column as they emerged from the trees of Hune Dora Forest and onto the floodplain of the river known locally as the Big Finger.

The plain was perhaps a half mile across, from the forest to the edge of the river. The ground was rocky, but not overly so, and filled with rich, sandy silt. During a wet summer it might have been impassable by large numbers of cavalry and so given them a greater advantage, but as it was, the plain was dry and hard.

The Big Finger was the first in a succession of mountain-fed rivers collectively known as the Fingers of Kresimir. It was deep and fast-flowing and impossible to cross without sturdy rafts that could be pushed across and land on the other side farther downstream. Or by way of the bridge.

The bridge was nowhere to be seen.

Tamas heard the cries of dismay as the news was passed on down the column. He felt a twinge of pain for his men. They were starving, tired, beaten by the heat, and they'd just arrived at their one hope of delivery and found it gone.

They didn't know that Tamas had ordered the bridge destroyed.

Across the floodplain, near the river, Tamas could see smoldering bonfires. Flanks of meat roasted above them, the last of the horses taken from the Kez a week ago. Enough for a meal for ten thousand men.

Gavril rode across the floodplain, and Tamas noted he'd kept his own horse alive. He gave Tamas a salute, then said loudly, "Damned bridge washed away."

"Bloody pit!" Tamas slapped a fist into the palm of one hand.

Gavril went on. "We slaughtered the rest of the horses and scouted for wood for rafts. I'll need men to build them."

"All right. We've got half a day until the Kez reach us. Olem!"

The bodyguard nearly jumped out of his saddle. He brought his horse up alongside Tamas. He'd been hanging back ever since the incident with Vlora.

"Sir?"

"Organize getting the men fed. Gather the officers so I can brief them."

"Yes, sir." Olem flicked his reins and headed down the column, slumped in his saddle like a boy whose dog had just died.

Gavril brought his horse up closer to Tamas. "What the pit did you say to that man? I've not seen someone look that guilty since the Lady Femore's face when her husband caught me in bed with her and his sister."

"I told him I didn't want him continuing relations with Vlora."

Tamas watched Olem as he shouted for men to help him distribute food. He'd have to keep it organized. Eleven thousand hungry men were liable to start a riot. "I ordered Vlora to stop as well. She... vehemently... disobeyed." Tamas couldn't tolerate that kind of insubordination, not in a time of war. He didn't know what he was going to do about that. He'd been avoiding it for two days.

Gavril let out a loud guffaw and slapped his knee. Tamas thought about reaching across and punching him off his horse, but decided against it. Wouldn't want to risk breaking his neck, even if it would have done him good.

"Did everything go smoothly?" Tamas asked in a low voice, jerking his head toward the river.

"It did," Gavril said. "Knocked out the bridge yesterday, though the boys weren't happy about it. I can't promise they won't say anything."

"Last thing I need is rumors going around that I gave the order."

"I'll do my best to keep them quiet," Gavril said, "but if this turns into a death trap, I'm going to curse your name with my dying breath." The expression he wore told Tamas he was only partially joking.

"That seems fair. How close are the cuirassiers?"

"My outriders say a day." Gavril scratched his beard. "I hope you're certain about this. We could have gotten the army across the river and been safe for another two weeks, foraging and resting, and then faced them on the north side of the Fingers in better shape."

"I am certain," Tamas said. He looked to the west. The Big Finger meandered out of sight behind Hune Dora Forest about a mile downriver. Tomorrow he'd have a whole brigade of heavy cavalry riding upstream on that floodplain. He'd be boxed in and outnumbered. "I won't face three brigades of cavalry under Beon je Ipille on the open plains of the Northern Expanse. It would be suicide, even for me. Are you coming to my meeting?"

Gavril looked toward the bonfires. "I'll give Olem a hand organizing lunch."

"Good. The men will need their strength. I'm putting them to work next. It's going to be a long night."

Tamas rode toward the gathering of his officers, only a stone's throw from the river. Some of them were still on horseback. The rest were on foot, having given their mounts over to Gavril's rangers two weeks ago.

He ran his eyes over the assembled men. Every one of his generals, colonels, and majors were present. He dismounted.

"Gentlemen," he said. "Gather round. Forgive me for not providing refreshment. I left my god-chef back in Budwiel."

The comment received a few forced chuckles. Tamas felt his heart fall a little and made himself reevaluate his officers. They were a sorry lot. They were gaunt and unshaven, their uniforms dirty. Several wore the fresh scars of their skirmishes with Kez dragoons. Those still in possession of their horses had followed his example and given the better portion of their rations to the marching soldiers. They were tired, hungry, and he could see the fear in their eyes. Fear that hadn't been so stark before finding out the bridge was gone.

"As you can see, the bridge we'd hoped to cross to escape our pursuers is washed away. This has forced me to make a change in our plans. The Kez dragoons will be here in full force by the end of the day. The cuirassiers will be here tomorrow."

"That's not enough time to get everyone across the river," someone said.

Tamas searched for the source of the voice. It was a major, commandant of the quartermasters of the Ninth Brigade. He was missing his epaulets, and he bore a two-day-old gash across the bridge of his nose, the congealed blood almost black.

"No, it's not," Tamas admitted.

A clamor of voices went up. Tamas sighed. On a normal day these were his best officers. Not one of them would have interrupted him. Today was not a normal day.

He raised his hand. A few moments passed, but the hubbub died down.

"A panicked crossing of the river on hastily made rafts will leave our army fractured and in disarray. Beon's dragoon commanders would not hesitate to attack en masse the moment they arrived. So we're going to wait, and make a panicked crossing of the river tomorrow afternoon."

His officers stared back at him, uncomprehending. No one said a word until Colonel Arbor flexed his jaw and popped his false teeth into one hand.

"You're setting a trap," Arbor said.

"Precisely."

"How can we set a trap for half again our number of cavalry?" protested General Cethal of the Ninth Brigade. He was a stout man of medium height. He had a particular wariness for cavalry, since a flanking maneuver by Gurlish cavalry had cost him two regiments and his left eye ten years ago.

"By making ourselves a ripe target." Tamas picked up a straight stick and cleared away some of the tall grass so he could draw in the sandy dirt of the floodplain.

"But we *are* a ripe target," General Cethal said.

Tamas ignored him. "Here is our position." He drew a line to represent the river, and then chevrons for the mountains. "The smaller division of heavy cavalry will come from the west. The larger number of dragoons, from the south. General Cethal, what is the first thing we teach prospective officers at the academy?"

"Terrain is key."

"Indeed."

"But sir," General Cethal insisted, "you've put us on a flat floodplain with almost seventeen thousand cavalry bearing down on us. I can't think of many worse situations."

"We have our backs to the river," Tamas said. "And we have significant manpower. The terrain will be very different tomorrow."

"You mean to shape the terrain to your needs?" General Cethal shook his head. "It can't be done. We'd need a week to prepare."

Tamas stared hard at General Cethal. "Expecting defeat will surely bring it," he said quietly.

"I'm sorry, sir," Cethal said.

Tamas took a moment to look each officer in the eye before going on. "The ancient Deliv, back before the Time of Kresimir, were foreigners to the Nine. Our own ancestors were just some of the barbarians the Deliv faced. The Deliv had barely a fraction of the fighting men, but they were better organized. A Deliv legion could march thirty miles and create an entire fortification to camp all in one day. They survived because they had the discipline and the will. We shall do the same."

As he spoke, Tamas had been drawing lines in the dirt with his stick. He pointed at one line. "The soil is somewhat rocky, but the dirt is loose and easy to dig." He pointed to a series of Xs. "Hune Dora Forest has an abundance of wood."

Colonel Arbor squatted beside the crude drawing and examined it for a moment. He suddenly laughed. "It might work. Should I get my boys digging?"

"Your battalion has the first rest. We'll be working all night, so it'll be done in shifts. Then you'll chop trees. General Cethal, your men will be digging."

"My men? The Ninth?"

"Yes. All of them."

"Do you intend to create a palisade?" General Cethal asked.

"Not quite," Tamas said. "Get digging. I'll come around in an hour and give each company specific instructions." He made a shooing gesture with his stick. "Get to work."

Tamas watched his officers head off toward their men. It was going to be a long night. He hoped that when morning came, and battle was joined, his efforts would be worth it. Otherwise he would have exhausted all of his men for nothing.

"Mihali," he whispered to himself, "if you're still with us...I need some help."

It was the closest thing to a prayer he'd ever spoken.

*   *   *

Adamat and SouSmith watched the abandoned manor where Privileged Borbador was being kept. The street was empty, the air silent. Dark clouds threatened on the southern horizon, and the wind was beginning to pick up. They were in for a stormy night.

There were no signs of Verundish's soldiers in the manor. Adamat wasn't sure whether that was a good thing or not. He'd left the money yesterday at an address the Deliv colonel had given him. He couldn't help but think of all the things that could go wrong, or wonder whether she had taken the money and simply changed where they were hiding Bo.

Adamat headed down the hill and navigated the ruin until he found the servants' quarters. Bedding was gone, debris picked up. The only sign soldiers had ever been there was warm ashes in one of the fireplaces. Adamat grew more nervous with each step. Was it all for naught, blackmailing the Proprietor and gathering the money?

The door to the room where they'd kept Bo was closed. He turned the knob and stepped inside.

Privileged Borbador was gone. The chair, the bed, even the stand and the book were still there, but Bo was gone.

"Bloody pit!" Adamat kicked over the book stand. "That bloody..." He dropped into the chair, head in his hands. She'd just taken the money and left, just like that. And with her, Privileged Borbador, and any hope Adamat had of getting his wife back.

SouSmith leaned in the doorway, watching Adamat with a frown. "What'll you do?" he asked.

Adamat wanted to gouge his own eyes out. What could he do? He thought he'd known despair, but this...

The hall floorboards creaked. SouSmith turned. Adamat pulled the pistol from his pocket. If that was Verundish, he'd shoot her without a second thought.

Bo stepped past SouSmith and into the room. His hair was brushed back, his lapels straightened, and his beard shaved and styled into thick muttonchops.

Adamat felt the strength go from his limbs. He slumped back in the chair and stared at the Privileged.

"I thought you looked beat up the last time we spoke," Bo said. "What happened to your nose?"

"I'm going to hit the next person who asks me that." As long as they weren't a Privileged, Adamat added silently.

Bo gave a thin smile. "Thank you," he said, "for getting me released. They treated me well enough, but no one likes being tied up like that, not even able to move my hands." He flexed his fingers. "So stiff."

"You're welcome," Adamat said. "Now you'll hold up your part of the bargain?"

"I have some things to do." Bo stepped to the window and looked out.

Adamat felt his chest tighten. Things to do? "I need you now."

"You'll have me tomorrow."

"You're not going anywhere without me," Adamat said. "I need to make sure I have your help."

"You don't trust me?"

"I can't afford to," Adamat said.

"If I decide to ignore our deal, you wouldn't be able to stop me." It wasn't a question, but a statement.

"Probably not," Adamat agreed.

They locked gaze for a few moments, and Adamat had to remind himself how young Bo really was. Twenty? Maybe twenty-two? His eyes were so much older, like a man who'd seen more than his share of suffering and lived to talk about it.

"Suit yourself," Bo said.

"You'll only need one night?"

"Yes."

"SouSmith," Adamat said, "go to Sergeant Oldrich, and then the eunuch. Tell them I plan on acting tomorrow, then meet me at the safe house."

The big boxer nodded and left.

Adamat followed Bo out into the street. The Privileged walked with a purpose, like he had things to do, his head held high and his eyes alert. They had to walk for half an hour before they found a carriage. Bo gave the driver directions and they got inside.

"The eunuch," Bo said, taking his hands out of his pockets. Adamat realized he wasn't wearing Privileged's gloves. "As in 'the Proprietor's eunuch'?"

Adamat smoothed the front of his coat. "Indeed."

"That's a dangerous friend you have. The cabal tried to kill him a couple times. Failed, obviously."

"The Proprietor or the eunuch?"

"The eunuch," Bo said. "The Proprietor had an uneasy truce with the cabal, but Zakary never liked the eunuch. Didn't try to kill him again after a Privileged he sent after the eunuch wound up dead."

"The eunuch killed a Privileged?"

"It's not common knowledge," Bo said, "but yes." The Privileged fell silent for the rest of their trip, looking out the window and fingering something beneath his jacket.

The demon's carbuncle, Adamat guessed. The jewel around his neck that would eventually kill him if he didn't avenge the death of Manhouch.

"We're here," Bo suddenly said.

They climbed out of the carriage in the middle of Bakerstown. The air smelled of hot bread and meat pies, making Adamat's mouth water. "I'm going to get something to eat," he said, stopping beside a pie vendor.

"Get me one too," Bo replied, "then come upstairs." He disappeared inside a squat brick building sandwiched between two bakeries.

Adamat paid for two meat pies and followed Bo inside. When he reached the top of the stairs, he found himself in a one-room flat. There was a table and a bed, with an old mattress stuffed with straw, and one window looking out into an alley behind the bakery.

Bo stood on a chair in the middle of the room, pressing his fingers gently against the ceiling.

"What are you doing?"

Bo didn't answer him, but hit the ceiling once, hard. The plaster gave way and a box suddenly dropped into the room, hitting the floor with a crash.

Adamat waved plaster dust away from his face as Bo opened the box. Inside was a pair of Privileged's gloves and what appeared to be thousands of crisp banknotes, bundled together by silk ribbon.

"I would have expected something a little more...magical," Adamat said.

Bo pulled on the Privileged's gloves and flexed his fingers, then began setting stacks of banknotes on the floor next to the box. "I wasn't raised as a Privileged," Bo said. "Not like most of the others. I came off the streets originally."

"So...a box in the ceiling?"

"I'm not stupid. The wards on this box will blow anyone that's not me halfway across the room if they touch it."

"Ah."

"How much did you pay Verundish to let me go?"

"Why?"

"How much?"

"Seventy-five thousand," Adamat said.

Bo handed him two stacks of banknotes. "Here's a hundred."

"I can't take these," Adamat said, trying to give them back. "I still need your help, I..."

Bo rolled his eyes. "Take them. I'll still help you. I don't care how you got the money, but it couldn't have been easy. I pay my debts back double, when I can."

Adamat only put the banknotes in his pockets when he realized Bo wasn't going to take no for an answer. At a quick guess, Bo had over a million krana in that box. It was a mind-boggling number for a man like Adamat. But to a man like Bo, who'd been a member of the royal cabal, it was probably a trifle.

The Privileged bundled it all up in brown paper and wrapped it with a bow like it was one big package he'd just acquired at the store, keeping back four stacks of krana and secreting them about his person. When he was finished, he stood and nodded to Adamat. "Let's go."

Bo wouldn't let Adamat come with him inside the next time they stopped, nor the time after that. It was the fourth stop, well after dark, when Adamat finally got curious enough to follow him.

They were in one of the more pleasant parts of town, where the growing middle class lived in smart, two-story houses and walked the line between the nobility and the poor. It was not unlike where Adamat himself lived, if a little more crowded.

Bo left the carriage and headed down a long alley between two tenement buildings of spacious flats. Adamat waited for a moment before slipping out after him.

He paused by the edge of the alley, watching around the corner, as Bo knocked on a door. A moment later he was admitted inside.

Adamat inched his way down the alley until he reached a window looking into the flat.

Inside, he could see a pair of children playing next to a large fireplace. A boy and a girl, maybe eight and ten years of age. The window was open to take advantage of the stiff evening winds. Adamat moved to the next window that looked into a kitchen.

A man with a long mustache and burly shoulders stood next to the kitchen table, frowning at Bo. The woman sat at the table, busy with her knitting.

"Just ten minutes of your time," Bo was saying. He drew a stack of banknotes from his pocket and tossed it on the table.

The woman dropped her knitting needles and held a hand to her mouth. The man sputtered over the amount. Bo drew another stack and added it to the first.

"Whatever you say," the man said. "Just let me get my coat."

The door opened, and Adamat was forced to press himself against the wall, hoping the darkness would conceal him from Bo's eyes.

Bo followed the man out into the alleyway and gestured for him to come down farther. They weren't ten feet from Adamat when they stopped.

"Now what's this all about?" the man asked.

Bo lifted his gloved fingers in the air and snapped them.

The man's head twisted around a hundred and eighty degrees. Bo deftly stepped out of the way as the body staggered and fell. He seemed to regard the dead man for a few moments before he turned and headed back toward the carriage.

Adamat couldn't help himself. He'd seen gruesome murders in his time, and bad men do terrible things, but the abruptness...He stepped from the darkness. "What the pit is the meaning of this?" he hissed.

"Keep walking." Bo grabbed him by the arm in a surprisingly firm grip and spun him about, pushing him toward the carriage.

Adamat had no choice but to allow himself to be dragged along. The carriage was soon heading down the street, and Adamat struggled to find a voice to express what he'd just seen. The murder had been quick and cold. A trained assassin couldn't have done it better.

"Here," Bo said. He grasped something beneath his shirt and yanked, then tossed it into Adamat's lap. "Take this. I don't want the bloody thing anymore."

Adamat stared down at the ruby-red jewel sitting in his lap. "Is that the demon's carbuncle?" He wasn't sure if he wanted to touch it.

"It is," Bo said.

"I thought you had to kill Tamas," Adamat said. "How did...?"

Bo looked rather pleased with himself. Not at all like someone who'd just snapped a man's neck not two dozen paces from his wife and children. "I had to avenge the king. That man there was the headsman who loaded Manhouch into the guillotine."

Adamat finally drew a handkerchief from his pocket and lifted the jewel to see it better by the light of the streetlamps outside the carriage. It was warm—no, hot—to the touch and seemed to throb with its own inner light. He wondered how much a jeweler would pay for a sorcerous piece of art like this.

"Gorgeous, isn't it?" Bo said.

"It can't have been that simple. A god made the precedence for the gaes. You can't just kill the executioner and have it be all. Can you?"

"Kresimir was just a man," Bo said. His eyes narrowed as if at something that made him angry. "Just a damned man with a bloody huge amount of power. He may be smarter than most, and have more time to think and plan, but even the so-called gods make mistakes."

"Is this thing . . . safe?" Adamat asked.

"Quite."

Adamat wrapped it in his handkerchief and put it in his pocket. "Why didn't you just tell Tamas?"

"I wasn't sure," Bo said. "I only had the thought recently, and I would have looked a damn fool if his soldiers had killed an innocent man only for the carbuncle not to come off."

"You weren't sure? What the bloody pit kind of man—?"

Bo held up his hand and gave Adamat a cold, long stare. "At what point have you ever gotten the impression that there are good people in the royal cabal?"

"You've given me that impression," Adamat said. He swallowed hard. "Yes. You have."

"Well, get past it." Bo turned toward the carriage window. "Because I'm not a good man. Not in the slightest. I just pay my debts."

Adamat watched the Privileged for several minutes. Was that regret in his voice? A frown at the edges of his mouth? It was impossible to tell. Members of the royal cabal were dangerous men, he reminded himself, and were not to be trusted.

He just hoped that Bo really was on his side.

CHAPTER
22

Tamas judged he had two hours before night fell and the Kez dragoons would be close enough to scout his position.

The sound of his soldiers chopping great trees on the edge of the Hune Dora Forest echoed across the floodplains, and teams of men dragged the trees by hand across the dusty grassland to where Tamas had decided to make his stand. Closer, the scrape of a thousand shovels on sandy dirt made Tamas's skin crawl. He hated that sound. It felt like someone scraping a nail across his molars.

He found Andriya cleaning his rifle down near the river. The Marked's belt had become decorated with squirrel tails over the last few days. He didn't have the same look as the rest of the soldiers. His cheeks were slightly rounded from eating well and his face lacked the lines of exhaustion.

His eyes, though, betrayed him. They were wide and bright, shifting constantly. Like the rest of Tamas's mages, Andriya had been floating in a powder trance for weeks running. It was a terribly dangerous thing to do. Going powder blind could see any of the mages dizzy, disoriented, unconscious, or even dead.

"I'd back off on the powder, soldier," Tamas said gently.

Andriya looked him up and down. His lips twisted, and for a moment Tamas thought Andriya would snap at him.

"Right, sir," Andriya said. "Probably should."

"Where is Vlora?"

Andriya shrugged. Tamas couldn't help but wonder where the discipline was going in his army.

"What was that?"

"Don't know, sir."

"Find her."

"She won't talk to you, sir."

"Come again, soldier?"

"She said—and of course, I'm only quoting—that you could go to the pit."

Tamas inhaled sharply. This wouldn't do. This wouldn't do at all. He quickly thought over his options. He could have her flogged. Had a regular soldier said something like that to him, he wouldn't have hesitated. Vlora was...was what? Another time, he might have thought she was kin. But she'd made it clear that was no longer the case.

Besides, a public flogging on the eve of a major battle? He rolled his eyes to himself. *That* would help morale.

He could give her a public reprimand. What if she defied him? He'd have no choice but to impose more severe punishment. With her temper, he might have to have her hanged.

"Get the powder cabal together," Tamas said. "I've got assignments for you. Tell Vlora to be there."

Andriya saluted and went about cleaning his rifle. Tamas headed toward the bonfires to find something to eat.

The soldiers had been organized into lines. Olem stood at the head of the lines along with the better part of his Riflejacks—all trusted men that could keep the infantry in line. The last of the horsemeat was distributed quickly as soldiers approached with their pewter dishes.

The camp was coming together even as work continued on Tamas's preparations. Tents were pitched, small fires made. Parties were sent out to forage the woods or fish the river. Fights broke out and were quickly put down, only to start up again somewhere else. Food seemed to be the main instigator as soldiers tried to get in line for seconds. The meat might keep them going through the night, but morale was low, and the food wouldn't last through tomorrow.

"Sir."

Andriya's voice broke through Tamas's thoughts. Nineteen men and women stood assembled before him: the entirety of his powder cabal, including the recruits Sabon had managed to gather before his death.

"We're running low on powder and bullets," Tamas said without preamble. He caught sight of Vlora at the back of the group, but did not wait to hold her eye. "Tomorrow we'll be fighting almost sixteen thousand cavalry. I'm setting a trap that should even the odds, but it's going to be a brutal battle."

Tamas looked around, suddenly feeling weary. His leg ached. He thought to take some powder, but stopped himself. Save it for the soldiers. He walked to a large rock and sat down, gesturing for the powder mages to be at ease. Most of them sat on the sandy ground. Vlora remained standing, her arms crossed. Tamas ignored her.

"I'm going to redistribute bullets and powder among the men so that you have enough for the next twenty-four hours. Your first job: Do not let Kez scouts get within a half mile of us. Do not let them take the high ground along the mountain." He pointed east to the slope of the Adran Mountains. "Do not let them see what we're up to. The life of every soldier depends on this.

"However," he went on, "I want them to see we're doing *some-*

thing. A little digging. Preparations and rafts. Perhaps trying to rebuild the bridge. Every so often, let one of their scouts get closer, and then let him get away with a bullet in the arm, or something equally convincing."

"Tomorrow should be much of the same. I expect Beon to attack as soon as his cuirassiers arrive. He knows an opportunity when he sees one, and he never hesitates to take it."

"And if he senses the trap?" Andriya asked.

"Then we cross the river tomorrow night, and deal with Beon on the other side of the Fingers." Tamas had a very good feeling that would not be the case. Beon needed to stop them now. The farther north they got, the better chance they had of finding succor in Deliv and crossing back into Adro. Tamas prayed that would spur on Beon. He dreaded the idea of facing the Kez on the open plains of the Northern Expanse.

"We'll have teams," Tamas said. "Nine and three. Nine on watch, killing Kez scouts, and three resting."

"We don't need rest," Andriya said. He grinned at Tamas. His crooked teeth were stained yellow. "We just need powder."

Tamas held his hand up toward Andriya. "You'll have your time to kill Kez," he said. "You all need some rest tonight."

It was perhaps six o'clock, and the hot sun burned red over the Amber Expanse to the west. Tamas wondered if the coming night would be his last in this world.

The Kez outnumbered him. He was growing old. Not as fast or as sharp as he'd once been. Beon might see through the trap and outmaneuver him, or circle at a distance, content to pick off Tamas's troops until Tamas made it across the river, then head west around the Fingers and wait for Tamas on the Northern Expanse.

Had it been a mistake to order Gavril to destroy the bridge?

"Sir?"

Tamas jolted out of his reverie. The powder mages were gone, all but Vlora. For a moment he imagined she was a little girl again—ten years old—seeking his approval. The sun had sunk in the western sky and the camp was completely pitched. The bonfires had burned low, all sign of the horse carcasses gone. Thousands of men worked on the floodplain while thousands more chopped trees on the edge of the Hune Dora Forest.

"Where are they?"

"Sir?"

"The powder mages."

Vlora had a hint of worry in her eyes. "You dismissed them over an hour ago. Told me to stay."

"And you've been waiting this whole time?"

"You seemed preoccupied."

Tamas took a shaky breath. He suddenly remembered dismissing Andriya and the rest of the mages, but it was like looking back in time through a thick fog.

Getting old indeed.

"Have you been eating, sir?"

Tamas's stomach growled. "I had some horsemeat earlier."

"I was watching you, sir. You didn't take anything when you went to check on the bonfires."

"I'm sure I did."

Vlora dug in her belt, then handed him a white tuber. "Found these truffles in the forest yesterday. You should eat. Take them, Tamas."

Tamas put out a hand reluctantly and she dropped them there.

He hesitated, staring at the truffles. Truffles grown in forests of the Adran Mountains were delicacies in most of the Nine. They were small and pale-cream colored. He'd never much liked truffles.

"Thank you," he said.

Vlora leaned on her rifle, staring over toward the forest. He gazed at the side of her face. He'd watched her grow from a fledgling powder mage into a capable soldier, one of his best. She was strong, with a beauty that the years would dim but never fully diminish. He felt a pang of loss, once again, that this girl would never bear him a grandson. He looked again at the truffles in his hand.

"What I said, Tamas—sir, I shouldn't have spoken to you that way. Not in front of the men."

"No, you shouldn't have."

Vlora stiffened. "I'll accept whatever reprimand you see fit."

Tamas didn't know his heart was capable of breaking. Not after all these years. He took a deep breath. "You're a grown woman. Olem is a good man. He'll make you happy."

She seemed surprised by this. But not in the way Tamas expected. "He's just another man," she said. "Someone to warm the nights." She closed her eyes. "We're soldiers. Tomorrow, one of us might be dead. Even if we both survive the battle, we'll move on and find others. It's the life we've chosen." Her eyes opened again and she looked across the camp. "All of us."

Ah. What every soldier knew so well. Lovers were brief, passion burning like a candle—hot at the center and easily doused. It was too hard to keep the flame kindled longer than a season or a campaign. "It can be a lonely life," Tamas agreed.

"You think we can win tomorrow?" Vlora asked.

Tamas looked toward the forest. At his soldiers going about their tasks. They were dragging trees across the floodplains now, toward the camp. The sound of billhooks hitting wood carried in the night. A rifle fired somewhere. Soldiers foraging, or powder mages scaring off Kez scouts?

"I think we can win every battle," Tamas said. "This...this will be difficult. The whole fulcrum of my plan could topple if the Kez catch too good a look at my preparations. We are low on powder and bullets, and the men are half-starved. We have to win tomorrow, or we'll die here."

He felt cold suddenly, despite the heat, and very old.

"I don't want to die here, sir," Vlora said. She hugged her rifle.

"Neither do I."

"Sir."

"Yes?"

"Gavril...he said you buried someone beside the Little Finger, long ago. Who was it?"

Tamas felt himself whisked away. Felt the spray of the raging river on his face, the mud and blood caked on his fingers from digging a grave by hand.

He forced himself to stand, trying not to favor his bad leg. It needed the exercise. "I've buried countless friends. More enemies. Kin, and those close enough they might as well be. I want to see Adro again. I want to know if my son survived his ordeals. But before then, there is a lot of work to do. That is all, Captain. Dismissed."

Taniel sat brooding in his quarters, watching out the window as a line of wagons carried wounded soldiers away from the front. He thought about opening the window and asking how the battle was going. But he already had a guess: badly. This lot had probably taken a mortar round—their wounds were bloody and varied, and by their uniforms they were all from the same company.

General Ket had sent him to an inn about five miles behind the line, under guard twenty-four hours a day. It seemed like weeks since Ket had given Taniel her ultimatum. He knew it had been a single night.

The provosts had demanded to know where Ka-poel was. Taniel had shrugged and told them to stuff it, but inside he'd worried about what they'd do when they caught her. Had they been given orders to give her a beating like the one they'd given Taniel? Or worse? Without dolls of them, would Ka-poel be able to fend off the provosts?

General Ket had come by his quarters early this morning to tell him that every day he refused to apologize to Major Doravir was another day that men died on the line.

Taniel would be up there now if it weren't for General Ket. He wouldn't let her convince him it was his fault that the line was being pushed back again.

Outside his window, Taniel caught sight of a young man. It was a boy, really. Couldn't have been more than fifteen. His leg had been taken off at the knee. Whether by a cannonball or a surgeon, Taniel didn't know, but he was struck by the calm on the boy's face. While men three times his age wailed over any number of flesh wounds, the boy sat stoically in the back of a wagon, his stump hanging off the edge, watching serenely while a fresh group of conscripts were sent to the front.

Taniel lifted his sketchbook and began to outline the boy's face.

A knock sounded at the door. Taniel ignored it, wanting to give the boy's portrait some shape so that he could finish it later.

He'd almost forgotten there even had been a knock, when it sounded again. The wagon outside was moving on, and the wounded boy with it. Taniel dropped his sketchbook on the table and went to the door.

He was surprised to find Mihali there. The big chef held a silver platter aloft in one hand, a towel over the opposite arm. His apron was dirty with flour and what looked like smudges of chocolate.

"Sorry to bother you," Mihali said, sweeping past Taniel. Two provosts followed the chef inside. One held a folding table, the other a bottle of wine. "Right there," Mihali told them. "Next to the window. Now some privacy, please."

The provosts grumbled, setting up the table and then retreating into the hallway.

"Sit," Mihali instructed, pointing at the only chair in the room. He deposited himself on the edge of the bed.

"What's this?" Taniel asked.

"Dinner." Mihali swept the lid off the silver tray. "Braised side of beef with quail's egg quiche and sweet goat cheese, and served with a red wine. Nothing fancy, I'm afraid, but the wine is a lovely 'forty-seven and has been chilled."

Nothing fancy? The smell rising from the platter made Taniel shudder with pleasure. His mouth watered immediately, and he found himself at the table unable to remember sitting down, with a piece of beef already on his fork. He paused. "May I?"

"Please, please," Mihali encouraged. He popped the wine cork and poured two glasses.

It was a little unnerving that Mihali watched him while he ate, but Taniel quickly learned to ignore the chef's presence and was soon reaching for seconds.

"What," Taniel asked, eyeing Mihali, who was on his third glass of wine, "is the occasion?"

Mihali poured Taniel another glass. "Occasion? Does there need to be an occasion to eat well?"

"I thought so."

Mihali shook his head. "I heard they'd relegated you to quarters and were feeding you soldier's rations. That qualifies as a war crime in my book."

"Ah." Taniel smiled, but couldn't be sure that Mihali was actually joking. He leaned forward, taking his wineglass, and noted that the wine bottle was still full after, what, five glasses between the two of them? Perhaps Mihali had a second bottle hidden somewhere.

"I have a letter for you," Mihali said, removing an envelope from his apron.

Taniel paused, a fork halfway to his mouth. "From?" he mumbled around a mouthful of quail's egg.

"Colonel Etan."

Taniel tossed his fork down and snatched the letter. He tore it open and ran his eyes over the contents. When he was finished, he pushed his chair back and took a deep breath. He wasn't hungry anymore, not even for Mihali's food.

"What is it?" Mihali asked.

"None of your..." Taniel swallowed his retort. Mihali had come all this way from the front with a full meal, and delivered a letter that would likely not have reached Taniel otherwise. The chef deserved his thanks, not his anger. "I asked Colonel Etan to pull the quartermaster records regarding black-powder use in the army."

"Oh?"

"He also pulled requisition orders. They don't match up. The army has requisitioned three times as much powder as they've used, and nearly twice what has actually reached the front line."

"It's getting lost somewhere?" Mihali asked.

"More likely stolen. Corruption's not unheard of in any army, even ours, but Tamas cracks down on it hard during wartime. These records"—he tossed the envelope on his bed—"mean that the quartermasters are in on it. And at least one member of the General Staff. Someone is making millions off this war."

"As you said," Mihali responded, "it's not unheard of."

"But powder...we'll run out quickly at this rate. The whole country, and then it doesn't matter how much better our troops are, we'll be ground beneath Kez's heel. Damn it!" Taniel drummed his fingers on the silver platter in front of him. He wanted to throw it across the room, but there was still a bit of beef left. "Can you get me out of here?"

"I'm sorry, but I don't think so," Mihali said with a sigh. "As I told you before, the General Staff doesn't listen to a word I say." Mihali patted his belly. "Tamas—now he has an ear for good sense, even if he is mistrustful of the person giving it. These generals can't see past the ends of their noses."

Taniel leaned back and sipped his wine. Something about Mihali's steady tone and unruffled attitude helped calm his nerves. "They're some of the best in the Nine, believe it or not." To his surprise, there was no grudge in his tone. "Though I can't say that speaks well for Adro, or against the rest of the Nine."

Mihali chuckled. "That certainly explains why we haven't lost yet. Despite being so heavily outnumbered."

"How is it going on the front?" Taniel asked. "I mean, I can see..." He gestured out the window, the memory of the wagons full of dead and wounded still fresh. "But I've had no real news for two days."

"Not well. We lost almost a mile yesterday." Mihali's face grew serious. "You were about to change things, you know. Stopping that advance last week gave the men their first victory in months. They had heart. I could sense it. They would have charged after you, right down Kresimir's throat."

"Pit. I have to get out of here. Back on the front. And I need to find out who's profiteering off our black powder."

"How?"

"I'll strangle every quartermaster in the army until one tells me. You're sure you can't get me released?"

"Most of the General Staff doesn't even believe I'm a god. To them, I'm a mad chef. The only way you'll get out of here, Taniel, is if you apologize to Major Doravir."

Taniel stood up and went to the window. "Absolutely not."

"Don't pit your pride against General Ket's," Mihali said. "That woman makes Brude look humble."

Brude. One of the saints—er, gods. Taniel watched Mihali down a fourth glass of wine out of the corner of his eye. It was easy to forget what Mihali was. After all, one would expect a god to look, and act, as grand as any king. Not dribble wine out of the corner of his mouth and then clean it up with a shirtsleeve.

"What can I do?" Taniel asked. He wondered if Mihali had given advice to his father. He couldn't imagine Tamas soliciting advice from a chef, even if he did believe that Mihali was a god.

"Apologize to Doravir."

Taniel blew air out through his nose.

"I can't see much," Mihali said quietly, looking into his wine-glass. "The future is always moving, always blurry, even to those with the vision to see it. What I can see is that if you stay in this room, we'll continue to lose ground every day. The Kez will push us out of the valley and surround us, eventually forcing a surrender. Or we'll run out of powder, and the same will happen."

Taniel scoffed. "I'm just one man. I can't make that much of a difference."

"One man always makes a difference. Sometimes it's a small one. Other times, he tips a war. And you . . . you're not human. Not anymore."

"Oh? Then what am I?" Taniel asked. Mihali made less and less sense as he continued to speak.

"Hmm," Mihali said. "I don't think there's a word for it. After all, you're the first of your kind. You've become like Julene."

Taniel heard his own sharp intake of breath. "I'm not a Predeii."

"No. Not precisely. You're not immortal, after all. Then again, neither is Julene. She's just ageless. I don't think your sorcery would ever let you become ageless. Even with Ka-poel's help. But you're the powder-mage equivalent of a Predeii."

"This is ridiculous. Where *is* Ka-poel?"

"Hiding. I offered her my protection—with some reservations, of course. That girl makes my skin crawl. She didn't accept it. I might need her help at some point, though."

Taniel rubbed his temples.

"Another glass of wine?"

"I think I've had enough."

"Suit yourself." Mihali poured himself another one. His cheeks were flushed, but other than that there was no sign he'd drunk seven glasses. The wine bottle, Taniel noted, was still full.

"You said that you can see a little of the future," Taniel said. "If I apologize to Major Doravir, what then?"

Mihali stared into his wineglass. "Motion. That's what I see. It's a small event, but it stirs things up. It makes the certain uncertain. And right now, the certain does not bode well for us."

Taniel snatched a quill pen and took the back of Etan's letter. Quickly, ink smudging the page, he scrawled out a note. "Can you get this to Ricard Tumblar?" he asked. "I can't send it regular post. If someone on the General Staff is profiteering, they'll have eyes everywhere."

"I can send one of my girls," Mihali said, taking the letter.

"Thank you. Do you know where can I find Major Doravir?"

"As it happens . . . yes."

CHAPTER

23

Tamas watched the sunrise over the Adran Mountains to the east and wondered if it would be the last he would ever see.

The Kez dragoons had caught up with them late the day before. They made camp over a mile into Hune Dora Forest. He'd spent half the night watching their campfires flicker in the night and listening to them sing cavalry battle hymns. Every so often a gunshot would punctuate the distant sound as one of their scouts got too close and met a powder mage's bullet.

Now, the world was quiet but for the sound of the swift river on the rocks behind him. Tamas lay on the ground, leaning against his saddle about a hundred paces from the river. He held a powder charge in his hand, kneading the paper between his fingers.

In his mind he could see the dragoons climbing from their tents, stretching in the crisp morning air and preparing Fatrastan coffee over their cookfires. They'd be unhurried. Restful. They knew that their heavy cavalry wouldn't be here for some time yet, and that Beon wouldn't attack before he had his full force.

"Where are the cuirassiers?" Tamas asked. His breath fogged as he spoke. Despite the heat of the summer days, the mornings were still chill this close to the mountains.

Gavril stared sullenly toward the tree line as if he expected the dragoons to appear any moment. "Not more than a few hours away. I'd expect them here by noon."

"They'll be in formation by two o'clock. One, if Beon's generals are organized."

"Not long to get ready."

"Long enough. Olem."

The bodyguard stirred from his lookout position a few paces from Tamas's side. "Sir?"

"Pull our pickets back from the forest. Are the rafts done?"

"Aye, sir. Three big ones."

"Begin ferrying troops across the river. Start with the wounded, then the greenest troops. Take your time at it. I expect the Kez to attack between one and two o'clock. I want about a thousand of our men across the river by then. Enough to be convincing, but not enough to destroy our ability to fight."

"Very good, sir. Anything else?" Olem's tone was crisp. Ready for battle.

"Does everyone know where they are meant to be when the fighting starts?"

"Yes, sir. We drilled them half the night."

"Make things chaotic. I want lots of milling about. Fistfights. If you have to 'lose' one of the rafts in the river, so be it. This has to be convincing."

"I spoke to Colonel Arbor last night, sir. His men are going to hide their kits and rifles. Make like they've abandoned them."

"Good. Dismissed. Wait. Find me Andriya and Vlora."

Olem flinched at the mention of Vlora's name. He saluted and was off.

The wind was blowing westerly, and Tamas could see a low cloud cover inching its way off the Adran Mountains. If rain was coming, it would make this a miserable fight. Beon might even delay his attack, making all of Tamas's preparations be for nothing.

He wondered idly if Mihali had heard his prayer last night.

"What are you up to, Tamas?" Gavril asked.

"Kind of obvious from this end, isn't it?"

"I've been ranging since you arrived yesterday. To me, it looks like a half-finished defense."

"Perfect." Tamas climbed to his feet. The camp was shaped in a square. To the north, the Big Finger raged along its banks. To the east, a scree slope leading up to the mountain prevented a flanking maneuver by Kez cavalry. To the west and south, a mound of earth about three feet tall had been piled all around the camp. It was a standard short defense, from behind which infantry could take easy cover.

It would barely slow a cavalry charge.

To the west, the mound had been topped with tree trunks, propped together to form giant Xs. Between them, sharpened stakes had been driven into the ground. It was a thick, deadly defense against cavalry. A few hundred men worked hard at adding to those stakes as the mound of dirt swung around to defend the south. It wasn't nearly enough men. There would be a gap in their defenses about an eighth of a mile long. A gap through which ten thousand dragoons would charge.

"Sir."

Tamas broke away from his examination of the camp. Andriya and Vlora stood at attention. Neither looked like they'd slept all night. Damned fools.

"Gather the powder mages," Tamas said. "I'm sending you across the river."

They stared back at him blankly. "Sir?" Andriya said. His hands twitched on his rifle. "You promised we'd be killing Kez."

"You can do that from the other side of the river. I'm not risking any of my mages in the melee. I want you where you can shoot without being shot—or stabbed."

"You want us to cross in shifts to keep the Kez scouts at bay?" Vlora asked.

Tamas hesitated. A chill wind cut through the camp and he noticed a low fog creeping its way down from the mountains and across the floodplain.

"No. I want the Kez scouts getting a good look at the camp now. They're welcome to get as close as they dare."

"Sir, I'd rather be on this side of the river," Andriya said.

Tamas sighed. "Not today, Andriya."

Andriya gripped his rifle. "Please, sir." He bared his teeth. "You promised I would get to kill Kez."

"From a distance." Tamas clipped the words off firmly. "Besides, they'll be watching for the Marked. They'll feel more confident with you on the other side of the river."

"You're coming with us, then?" Vlora said.

Tamas frowned. "No. Why would I?"

"You're one of the powder mages, sir."

"No. I have to remain in close in order to command."

"That's not fair." Andriya was livid. He stared toward the forest, straining like a hound that could smell its quarry. "I've got every right to put my bayonet through a Kez noble's eye. I want blood on my hands."

" 'Blood on my hands, *sir*,' " Tamas corrected. He didn't need this. He had fifteen thousand cavalry about to rain down on him, and just when he thought he might have sorted things out with Vlora, Andriya was becoming insubordinate. "Cross the river. That's an order, soldier."

He turned away from Andriya to make it clear that the conversation was over. The two powder mages left him alone with Gavril. Tamas and Gavril remained silent for a few minutes, watching the organized chaos evolve in the camp. Men shouted. Tamas thought he saw a punch thrown. A little while later, the first raft was launched. It got away from the handlers and was pulled downstream with no one on it. A cry of dismay went up from the brigades, and Tamas didn't think it was feigned.

"Where do you want me?" Gavril asked.

"On your horse," Tamas said. "You and your rangers should take the eastern flank, in case some of Beon's dragoons attempt the scree."

"All right," Gavril said.

"Here." Tamas unhooked the cavalry saber from his belt and handed it to Gavril. "Better to swing from horseback."

"You're not going to be mounted?"

Tamas smiled, though he didn't feel any mirth behind it. "I'm taking the center. If I'm not mounted, the men won't see when I fall."

Gavril seemed to think on the gravity behind those words before accepting the cavalry saber.

Tamas took the small sword from his saddle and hooked it to his belt.

"I'll see you after the battle," Gavril said.

Tamas clasped hands, then was surprised when Gavril pulled him into an embrace. Gavril held him for a moment, then headed off to join his rangers.

Olem returned an hour later.

"Any of the men eat this morning?" Tamas asked.

"Caught a lot of fish in the river, actually. Andriya bagged a pair of goats on the mountainside. There was a little leftover horse. Every man had a bite of something."

"Let's hope it's enough," Tamas said.

Olem looked up. "At least the buzzards will eat well."

Tamas watched as the fog he'd seen earlier moving in slowly enveloped the entire camp. It wasn't thick—barely two feet deep. Enough to obscure the ground but not the camp itself. The clouds had moved in from above. They threatened rain, but Tamas had seen this kind of weather before. There'd be nothing more than a light mist.

Strange weather for a summer day.

At eleven thirty, Tamas caught sight of a pair of horsemen to the west, nearly a mile away at the bend in the river. He sprinkled some black powder on his tongue, and the men came into sharp relief. Tan-and-green uniforms under shining breastplates, and wearing plumed helmets.

The cuirassiers had arrived.

Adamat stood on the sixth floor of the Dwightwich bell tower with a looking glass at his eye. He was examining a fellow with shifty eyes who was wearing a faded red waistcoat and knee-length trousers and sitting on the stoop about a hundred paces from Lord Vetas's headquarters.

"They have another lookout on the corner of Seventh and Mayflew Avenue," Adamat said. He could hear the scratching of a pen behind him. He scanned the streets once more with the looking glass and then handed it to a young woman by the name of Riplas—the eunuch's second-in-command. She took his spot at the window while he turned to the assembled group in the cramped bell tower room.

"You're sure you have everyone?" the eunuch asked Adamat.

Adamat looked at the eunuch out of the corner of his eye. If he had any idea Adamat was blackmailing his master, he'd given no indication when he showed up the day before with forty of the meanest street scum Adamat had ever seen: boxers, gang members, dockworkers, pimps, and bodyguards.

"I've been watching them on and off for almost two weeks," Adamat said. "They change their posts, but between your reports and mine I think we have everyone."

He guessed that Vetas was employing over a hundred heads, based on the comings and goings from his headquarters. That was no small operation, and any thirty of them could be in the headquarters at any given time. The Proprietor had said Vetas had sixty enforcers.

Adamat looked over at Bo. The Privileged was down on his haunches in one corner of the room, his eyes closed, hands folded inside the sleeves of his jacket. He opened his eyes, as if he'd felt Adamat's gaze upon him. Adamat shuddered. He was still unnerved by the casual murder of Manhouch's headsman the day before.

"Vetas's pet Privileged is there," Bo said. "Right now. She's not some hired fool, either. She's got cabal-level stuff at her beck and call."

A bird burst from the bells above their heads, causing Adamat to jump. He noticed that he was the only one to do so and smoothed the front of his coat. A powerful Privileged? That wasn't good. Not at all. He was depending on Bo to be able to neutralize Vetas's Privileged even as Adamat's men seized the place.

Bo must have sensed the unasked question. "I'll kill her. Don't worry about that."

"If it turns into any kind of a fight between you two, we're all dead men," the eunuch said.

"Well, you're not exactly a man," Bo said with a smirk. He nodded to Riplas. "And she's not." His smirk suddenly turned to a frown. "And she's *definitely* not."

Adamat turned to see Fell standing on the bell tower stairs. The Fontain Academy graduate wore a fitted waistcoat, sans tails, and a pair of tight men's pants tucked into her boots.

"Ricard can't spare any men right now," Fell said, "but he sent me."

The eunuch turned toward her with a look of disgust. "Does he know the resources the Proprietor is shifting for this operation?" he asked.

"As a matter of fact," Fell said, cocking her eyebrow, "he doesn't. I'm sure he'll be interested to know."

Adamat stepped between them. "It's more help than you realize," he said to the eunuch. For Ricard to send his ten-million-krana servant into harm's way meant a great deal.

"Bah," the eunuch sneered. His fingers tapped rapidly against the side of his leg. He seemed on edge—not the quiet, thoughtful killer Adamat had met months ago.

Adamat stepped back to the window and took the looking glass from Riplas. "Any more lookouts?" he asked.

"None."

"Then take the final assignments down."

Riplas left the room. She had the positions and descriptions of all of Lord Vetas's lookouts. She'd hand them over to the eunuch's goons, and they'd do the rest.

Everything was in place. Now Adamat just had to wait.

He lifted the looking glass to his eye and returned his gaze to Vetas's headquarters. Over an hour passed, and he watched from his vantage point as the eunuch's goons took care of Vetas's lookouts. He felt the sweat roll down the back of his neck as he waited. So much could go wrong. The slightest slip, and Faye was dead.

"What if he doesn't come outside today?" Bo asked.

The front door to Vetas's headquarters opened, and a familiar figure stepped outside. He wore his sharp black coat, top hat, and carried a cane in one hand. Adamat felt his heart jump at the sight.

"That's not going to be a problem," Adamat said. "He's leaving now."

Lord Vetas checked the street with the smallest twitches of his head. Probably receiving signals from his lookouts—the closest of whom Adamat had left undisturbed.

Vetas gave an almost imperceptible nod. A woman came through the door—the same one he'd seen in the red dress weeks ago, with the auburn curls—and together they headed south down the avenue. They were followed two steps back by a pair of well-dressed and well-muscled men. A few seconds later a third came out the door, waited for a moment, then followed.

"I'll keep on his trail," Fell said, disappearing down the stairs.

"Take his tail," Adamat said to the eunuch, "and then meet us at the house. Bo?"

Bo stood up, stretching his gloved fingers. "I'll get a little closer and unravel the Privileged's wards. It'll take me some time, but I'll be ready when you get back."

Sergeant Oldrich was waiting for Adamat in the chapel beneath the bell tower. He sat in a pew, legs up, a wad of tobacco in one cheek. He tipped his hat back, watching as Bo slid out one exit.

"So," Oldrich said, turning to Adamat, "you got yourself a Privileged."

Adamat steeled himself. He couldn't be sure how Oldrich would react after having specifically stated he wouldn't help Adamat rescue Bo. "I did."

"I heard Verundish dismissed her men and left town yesterday. I thought that might have been the cause."

"I did what I needed to. He's freed of his gaes, if that makes a difference."

"Oh?"

"He killed the guillotine operator who took off Manhouch's head."

"Huh," Oldrich said. "Well, I'm sure the field marshal will be delighted. You ready?"

"Let's go."

Oldrich's soldiers fell in with them as they left the chapel, and Adamat told them to stay back a hundred paces.

Adamat, in turn, trailed Fell. He saw her weaving in and out of foot traffic as they headed farther into the city. The streets were crowded just after lunch—that would make it harder for Vetas's men to spot Adamat, but just as hard for Adamat to keep track of them.

It was a little over thirty minutes before Fell stopped and waved Adamat forward. They stood at a busy intersection, just around the corner from a flower market. Fell had her back against the wall, her shoulders slumped as if she didn't have a care in the world. Adamat came up beside her and mimicked her body language.

"His tail is over there," she said, slowly tilting her chin upward in one direction.

Adamat saw the man right away. He was eating a meat pie and scanning the crowd with a mistrusting leer. Not subtle, but an effective lookout. Not far behind him, Adamat spotted the eunuch.

"Vetas is inside the flower stall around the corner," Fell said. "Leave him to me. Have your soldiers take his goons."

"I want him alive."

"So do I," Fell said.

Adamat needed him alive so Vetas could tell him where Josep was. He wondered why Fell would want him breathing.

"I'm going," Fell said. She disappeared around the corner, casual and graceful as a cat.

Adamat gave the signal to Oldrich, then tilted his hat forward to hide his face and followed Fell.

He made his way to the middle of the street and was soon joined by Oldrich and six of his men. They each examined bouquets or pretended to talk, but he couldn't help but think they looked far too obvious.

Vetas's two goons were standing outside of the Parkside Flower Boutique, watching the crowd, their arms crossed, not the least bit subtle. Adamat glanced toward the tail. The man was gone. Adamat hoped that meant the eunuch had taken care of him.

Adamat could feel every muscle tighten as he watched the flower shop entrance out of the corner of his eye. Maybe Vetas had already spotted them and disappeared out the side. What if his goons warned him, or Vetas was able to slip into the crowd?

His hands were beginning to shake from nervousness when Lord Vetas finally emerged from the flower shop with the woman in the red dress. She carried a bouquet of flowers. He handed a package to one of his goons and scanned the flower market.

His eyes locked onto Adamat's. Adamat felt a cold sweat break at the corner of his brow. He tensed, ready to chase Vetas through the streets.

Fell emerged from the flower shop, strolling out like a paying customer. A stiletto dropped from her sleeve and she gracefully swung it around over Vetas's shoulder and pressed it to his throat.

The two goons stepped back, shouting. Both drew pistols. The crowd split apart.

Adamat felt like he was in a dream. He watched himself draw his own pistol and fire it. One of the goons went down. The other took a cudgel to the back of the head from one of Oldrich's soldiers, and the rest of the soldiers quickly fell in around Vetas, obscuring him from the crowd.

Adamat shouldered his way through the soldiers until he reached Vetas.

Lord Vetas was on his knees in front of Fell, a stiletto still to his throat. She'd relieved him of two very similar-looking daggers and a small pistol, both of which were lying on the ground behind her.

Adamat took great pleasure in the mild look of surprise on Vetas's face. It died quickly when Vetas saw Adamat.

Vetas smiled. "Adamat! I suspected you might still be alive."

"Is she still alive?" Adamat pressed the hot barrel of his pistol against Vetas's face.

"Every pain you do to me," Vetas said, not flinching at the heat of the pistol barrel, "I will return to you and your wife tenfold. I want you to remember that, Adamat."

"So she is alive?"

"Quite," Vetas said. "Though she won't be in an hour and forty-two minutes if I haven't returned." He paused, looking around at the soldiers. "I suspect you know where my headquarters is. You've probably been watching me very closely. Bravo. But do you have enough men to get in there?"

"You mean past your Privileged?" Adamat asked. "Yes. Yes, I think I do. Where is my boy?"

Vetas gave a sickeningly self-satisfied smile. "An hour and forty-one minutes. Are you sure you have time for this?"

Adamat looked at the woman in the red dress. Oldrich held her tightly by the arm. She glared at him through narrowed eyes, but he could see that her hands trembled. "Who are you?" he demanded.

"Nila," she said.

"What do you do for him?" He pointed at Vetas.

"Nothing! I . . . nothing. I don't work for him. I'm just there to watch Jakob. He's only a boy!"

"What was Vetas buying in there?"

"Flowers!"

"For who?"

"Lady Windeldwas, or something like that." Nila brushed the hair out of her face.

"Lady Winceslav?"

"Yes, that was it."

"Why?"

"I don't know." For all her fright, she was remarkably calm beneath the torrent of questions.

Adamat turned back to Vetas. "Why?"

"An hour and forty minutes, Adamat," he said.

Adamat brought his pistol back and slammed the butt across Vetas's face. "Secure them," he said to Fell. To Oldrich, "Sergeant, give her four of your men. We need to get off the street before the police get here."

Fell dragged Vetas to his feet, still holding the stiletto to his throat. Oldrich sent four of the men with her, along with Nila and the two wounded goons, and the rest of the soldiers followed Adamat.

They met up with the eunuch three blocks down from Vetas's headquarters.

"My men are in position," the eunuch said.

"Where's Bo?" Adamat asked, wheezing from the effort of the run.

He found the Privileged around the corner, standing in the middle of the street. Bo wore black gloves over his Privileged gloves to conceal them. He was muttering to himself, his gloved fingers working silently in the air in front of him, as if he was playing an invisible piano with one hand and plucking a harp with the other. There were three or four people watching him as if he was some kind of madman. He certainly looked the part.

"We have to go in now," Adamat said. He hunched over his pistol, trying to conceal it from view while he reloaded it.

Bo's fingers continued to work the air. "I said I'd need time."

"We don't have much time," Adamat said. "His men have orders to kill Faye if he doesn't return at a prescribed time."

"Unfortunate," Bo said with a scowl. "Tell the eunuch to get his men in place."

The order was given, and five minutes later the eunuch joined Adamat and Bo.

"We're ready," the eunuch said.

Bo looked him up and down, eyes lingering on the tailored suit and the bald head. "You make my skin crawl."

"I'll take that as a compliment."

Adamat smoothed the front of his jacket. "Sergeant?"

Oldrich's remaining soldiers had fetched their rifles. They were beginning to get looks from the passersby. "We're ready," Oldrich said.

"Let's make it a parade, then." Bo turned on his heel and marched down the middle of the street, heading toward Lord Vetas's headquarters. His fingers twitched, making music that only he could hear. Adamat exchanged a look with Captain Oldrich. This was not how they'd taken the house in Offendale.

Bo didn't slow as he rounded the corner and stepped his way toward Vetas's house. When he reached the middle of the street directly in front of the house, he turned and faced it. He raised his hands above his head. In one of the windows, a lookout shouted a warning.

Even though Adamat couldn't open his third eye, he could still feel it when a Privileged standing at his elbow reached into the Else. Sorcery flowed into the world, and Bo threw his arms wide, and the entire face of the building collapsed like a piece of cake sliced by a giant knife.

Adamat stared at the dust rising from the rubble. Men inside the house stared back, coughing and waving away plaster dust. The shock was plain on their faces.

Sergeant Oldrich drew his sword. "Charge!" he screamed.

All pit broke loose.

CHAPTER

A column of heavy cavalry appeared on the floodplain down-river, west of Tamas. The plumes on their helmets waved gently in the breeze, their mounts stepping with confidence despite the low cover of fog.

Tamas lifted his looking glass and examined the enemy.

The officers were out front with their red epaulets, shouting orders, sabers raised.

Fools.

A rifle cracked from somewhere across the river. A few moments later a Kez officer tumbled from his horse.

They advanced at a leisurely pace, as if it were nothing more than a parade drill. More rifle shots rang out from Tamas's powder mages, and cuirassiers began to fall. The column continued to advance.

"This weather might foul our powder, sir," Olem said, looking up at the clouds.

Tamas said, "It won't rain."

"It's awfully damp, sir. Strange, this fog. Never seen it sweep down off the mountains so quickly."

"That's because this is an answer to a prayer."

Tamas heard a trumpet echo through Hune Dora Forest and looked to the south. There was movement among the trees half a mile away across the floodplain where only hours ago Tamas's infantry had been cutting trees and dragging them to camp.

The dragoons emerged from the forest.

Tamas felt his breath catch in his throat. So many cavalry in one place.

He'd seen a force like this perhaps three times in his life. Each time, he'd been numbered among those cavalry, and the enemy had been swept before them. The horses stepped in line, well trained and fearless. Unlike the cuirassiers, someone among the dragoons had the foresight to remove the officer's epaulets, so they would be harder to pick out for Tamas's powder mages.

Behind him, the panic among the Seventh and Ninth Brigades seemed to rise in pitch, and Tamas worried that the act had outgrown itself. He'd witnessed hard infantry of the line break at the sight of a magnificent cavalry formation before.

And the Kez cavalry *were* magnificent. The armored breasts of the cuirassier warhorses seemed to form a wall of moving steel. Their plumes quivered with the movement, and the immaculate uniforms of their riders only added to their majesty.

Tamas searched the line of cuirassiers. In a powder trance, he could see the faces of each man, even at this distance. But picking out one face among so many was nearly impossible. "I wonder where Beon will position himself," Tamas said. He pointed with his small sword to the southwest. "There, likely, so that he can sweep with his cuirassiers around the barriers we've set up and join his dragoons in the slaughter." Tamas turned to his bodyguard. "Tell me we're going to win, Olem."

" 'We're going to win, Olem,' " Olem said, putting his last cigarette in his mouth.

Tamas stepped onto a rocky outcropping to give himself a better view of the battlefield.

"Men," he shouted, "take the line!"

Nila was pushed into a doorway by one of the soldiers.

She squeezed her eyes closed, fighting tears she knew so desperately wanted to come. To have escaped soldiers so many times and then fall into Lord Vetas's clutches, and now this? Who were these people? What did they want?

A man grabbed her by the arm and shoved her up a narrow flight of stairs. They went up two floors, shouting and cursing the whole way. Nila fought them out of instinct more than anything else. She clawed at a soldier's face, only for her arm to be bent around behind her and her face shoved up against the wall.

"Pit, this girl is a hellion," the man said. She tried to twist in his grip. He put pressure on her arm and she gasped from the sudden pain. It felt as if it would snap at any moment.

She was thrown into the corner of a small, windowless room. The plaster was yellow and bare, the only furniture a squat table with a stub of candle.

They hadn't gone far before finding this building, not more than a couple of blocks. Nila had no idea if this was planned, but there seemed some confusion among the soldiers.

Lord Vetas was pushed to the ground beside her. She stared at him—the only familiar face in this chaos. He was calm, collected. Completely unperturbed. Nila hated that she looked to him for some kind of reassurance. She knew none would come.

"Watch him," the woman said. She was young, and could not

have been more than ten years older than Nila, but her eyes were as cold as Vetas's. Nila had heard someone call her Fell. The soldiers seemed hesitant to follow her orders, but after Fell gave them a long stare, they turned to watch Vetas.

Fell had drawn a pair of wrist irons from beneath her coat. They weren't typical irons, even Nila could see that. Instead of a horseshoe-looking metal with a crosspiece, they were thick bands with only a single loop of chain between them. The two soldiers turned Vetas roughly onto his stomach, and the irons were snapped around his wrists. He rolled over, examining Fell.

"Drovian irons," he said. "Very professional."

"Turn around," Fell said to Nila.

"No," Nila said.

Fell grasped her by the arm and jerked her forward onto her knees. Fell stepped behind her, and Nila felt the cold metal of the wrist irons close on her skin.

There was a shout from downstairs. Fell turned to one of the soldiers. "Do not take your eyes off of him," she said, and disappeared down the stairs.

Despite Fell's instructions, the two soldiers retreated to the hallway, where they stood near the door, leaning on their rifles.

"What is happening?" Nila asked Vetas.

Vetas's face was impassive, unmoving as always. He didn't so much as glance at her.

He watched the two soldiers for a moment before rocking back on his hips and deftly sliding his shackled wrists beneath his legs and out in front of him, like a contortionist performing a trick. Nila felt her eyes widen a bit. The wrist irons hurt like all pit, and even if they hadn't been so tight, she couldn't have done that—and Vetas was a man well over forty.

Nila glanced nervously between Vetas and the soldiers. How could they not see him? Did they just not care?

Vetas pulled something off the bottom of his shoe: a wooden

knob. It looked like the handle of an ice pick Nila had seen men use to move blocks of ice in the winter, but it had no pick attached to it.

Another handle came off the bottom of his other shoe, and Vetas searched through his slicked hair with his fingers, drawing out a long wire after only a moment of searching. He wrapped the wire around one handle and then the other.

Nila had been with Lord Vetas long enough to know what it was: a garrote.

Vetas got to his feet in one smooth motion, like a snake rising from the grass. He crossed the room in a few silent steps.

One of the soldiers must have seen him coming out of the corner of his eye. The soldier whirled, raising his rifle. Vetas slammed an elbow into the soldier's throat. The soldier staggered to one side, gurgling painfully for air. The other soldier had his rifle up in time, but the long bayonet was impossible to use in such close quarters. Vetas grabbed the stock of the rifle and smacked the soldier in the nose with it. When the man reeled back, Vetas slid around him, dropping the garrote into place.

Nila's mind whirled. She eyed the soldier's fallen rifle—she could have used it on Vetas if not for the irons locking her hands behind her back. The two soldiers soon lay dead in the hall. Blood trickled across the floorboards, flowing to fill the grooves.

Vetas, his face still and unmoving as stone, searched the soldier for keys.

The creaking of the floorboards was the only warning. Vetas looked up and suddenly fell back into the hallway, out of Nila's line of sight. Fell soared past, knife at the ready.

Nila could hear the dull thumps of flesh on flesh. Grunts, a few quiet curses—those came from the woman.

The pair tumbled back into the room. Nila screamed as both of them tumbled over her outstretched feet.

They struggled on the floor, legs intertwined, the knife pressed flat between them. Nila kicked indiscriminately. She wanted them away from her. The knives, the anger—one slip, and Nila could be dead.

Fell rolled off of Vetas and sprang to her feet.

She struck at him, fast as a viper. Vetas, still on his knees, caught the knife on the metal of his wrist irons. She struck again, and again, and each time Vetas moved impossibly fast to block her. Between the strikes he managed to regain his footing.

They circled warily, and Nila pulled herself into the corner as much as possible.

She hoped they'd kill each other. But what then? She had no way of getting the irons off her hands.

Fell and Vetas seemed at an impasse. Their circling stopped. Fell changed hands with her dagger, then changed back.

Nila didn't hesitate. Months of anger and fear came to a head, and with a shriek of rage she kicked Vetas in the back of the leg.

Fell struck out at Lord Vetas at the same time. The blow to Vetas's leg sent him leaning backward. The knife slid past his eye, cutting one cheek badly. He caught Fell's hand, deftly sliding the garrote around her wrist, and swung about.

Fell had no choice but to follow his swing, or risk losing her hand. Vetas stepped close to her, and she tried to step away. It was like some kind of grisly dance.

Vetas slammed his head forward into Fell's cheek. The woman staggered backward, hitting the window.

Vetas had let go of his garrote. Dazed, Fell couldn't have seen the kick coming. She took a boot square to the chest, and tumbled out the window.

Vetas turned to Nila. There was a quiet click, and his wrist irons fell off. He held the key up in one hand.

Nila shrank away from the darkness in his eyes.

"You bet the wrong way, laundress," he said. He tossed the key on the floor. "You'll pay for that tonight. I promise. If not you, then the boy will."

He left the room, leaving Nila to let the sobs wrench themselves from her throat. Her whole body shook. She crawled over to the key. It took a few minutes with her trembling hands to get it into the lock and free herself.

She stared at the destruction. Two dead soldiers, a broken window, and Lord Vetas was gone. She took the time to collect herself. Deep breaths stopped the sobs, and she dried her tears. This wasn't the time to give in to emotion.

She could run. She knew that.

But if she ran, Vetas would do unspeakable things to Jakob. It was no empty threat. He wouldn't hesitate.

Nila crept down the stairs, only to find the other two soldiers dead in the hallway on the first floor. One's head was twisted at an impossible angle. The other had been bayoneted with his own rifle.

There was a crowd gathering in the street looking at the bodies through the open door. A woman was screaming for the police. Someone pointed at Nila.

It only took a moment to find a back door to the building. Nila took it, slipping down an alleyway and into the crowd.

She had to make her way back to Vetas's house and try to get Jakob away.

Adamat put his head down and charged into the gaping hole left in Vetas's headquarters by Bo's sorcery.

He shot the first man to raise a weapon, and then tossed aside his spent pistol and drew his cane sword.

Oldrich's soldiers were the first to follow Adamat into the fray, their bayonets making short work of Vetas's goons. The eunuch's men followed them in, and Adamat could hear pistol shots and the sounds of fighting from the other side of the buildings. They'd formed a cordon around Vetas's headquarters. Now they just had to tighten it.

A horizontal pillar of flame shot through the wall of one of the rooms inside, missing Adamat by not more than a few feet, the heat of it sending him reeling to one side.

The flame splashed over one of the eunuch's men, sending him screaming, running into the street. The pillar grew longer by the second, extending into the street and completely enveloping Privileged Borbador.

Adamat felt his heart leap into his throat. If Bo died, Vetas's Privileged would kill them all...

The flames abated, leaving Bo standing unhurt, like a rock that had been pounded by the surf. Bo advanced, his hands held out in front of him, fingers plucking at invisible strings.

Wind tore at Adamat's coat and buffeted through the innards of the building, knocking men from both sides off their feet before slamming through the wall and pushing back the pillar of flame. Bo raised his hands above his head and was suddenly running forward, his jaw locked and determined.

Lightning shot at Bo. He batted it aside with one hand as he scaled the rubble into the building, then leapt through the inner wall with a roar.

The house shuddered and shook as the two Privileged locked in battle. Adamat stopped in his tracks as he realized they could all be killed by the slightest mistake by either of the Privileged. One finger twitched the wrong way, one hand pushed aside accidentally, and every one of them would be dead.

The Privileged's flames had lit curtains on one side of the house. The fire spread to the table, quickly, and black smoke filled the ruined building.

He had to find Faye.

A man with a scar cutting across his lips stumbled toward Adamat, half blinded by the smoke. He swung a small sword wildly, crashing into a chair. Adamat leapt back, blocking a second swing with his cane sword, then a third. He felt the handle of his cane shift beneath his fingers—it was not meant to block the flailing sword of a man this big, and would splinter from the shock.

He leapt inside the scarred man's guard and drove the cane sword between his ribs. The man lurched back, bellowing in pain, and Adamat let him go.

"Faye!" he yelled. "Faye!"

The smoke was getting thicker. Where would Vetas have kept her? The basement? Did he have other prisoners here? The boy had been on the second floor when Adamat saw him in the window weeks ago, but the boy was not his concern.

Adamat heard a woman's scream. It was coming from upstairs.

The building was being quickly abandoned. Men ran past Adamat, some of them fighting the flames, some of them fighting each other. Adamat blinked through the tears brought on by the smoke. There, the staircase.

He made his way to the stairs. The house creaked. The flames were moving quickly now, spreading across the furniture at alarming speeds. There was paper everywhere, even in the foyer. Parchments and books, tables against all the walls. It looked more like a clerk's office than a place where Lord Vetas planned whatever campaign he was waging.

What if he wasn't keeping Faye here? What if she was somewhere else and the scream Adamat had heard was another?

Smoke filled the staircase as Adamat made his way up it. He pulled a handkerchief from his pocket, pressing it over his face. He stood dismayed at the top of the stairs, staring down a long hallway and a row of at least a dozen doors. The heat from downstairs was growing. It would spread up the stairs at any moment—if the smoke didn't kill him, the flames would. It would take too long to search the place. How could he find Faye in time?

"Faye! Faye!"

Adamat tried the first door. Locked. He kicked it open. A small room with two soiled beds and a nightstand. Empty.

He drew his foot back to kick open the next door when a scream came from farther down the hall. He rushed toward the source of the sound. One of the doors was open. He swung around the corner, cane sword raised.

Faye stood over the body of a man, a bloody candlestick in one hand. On her face she wore a look so vicious that Adamat scarcely recognized her. Adamat saw the face of a small boy peeking out from behind a curtain on the other side of the room.

"Faye!"

She looked up and nearly collapsed when she saw him. She dropped the candlestick and might have fallen had Adamat not caught her.

They stared at each other for one long moment, and Adamat wondered if it was perhaps she who was supporting him and not the other way around, as his knees felt like so much jelly.

"Where's Josep?" Adamat asked.

"Gone. They took him."

"I'll get him back," Adamat said. He looked at the boy. "That's the Eldaminse child, isn't it?"

"It is," Faye said. "Come on." She held out a hand to the boy. "Don't be afraid, this is my husband."

Adamat stared at his wife. "I..." he said.

"Shh." She pressed a finger to his lips. There were tears in her eyes. "We have to go."

Adamat nodded. "Quickly, let's—" He stopped in the hallway. The smoke was too thick, and there were flames leaping from the staircase. He tore off his jacket. "Press this to your face," he said to Faye, and gave his handkerchief to the boy. He led them away from the stairs, down the hallway and toward the front of the building. They might have to jump to the rubble below, but a broken leg was much preferable to being roasted alive.

Adamat froze as a great groaning noise rose above the sound of the flames. Was it the house creaking under the strain of the battle or some kind of sorcery?

"This way," Faye said, pulling him back into action. She led him around the corner, where another staircase went down to the first floor. There were no flames shooting up this one, but he took it cautiously.

Something slammed through the staircase wall and tumbled down the stairs into a pile of smoldering clothes. Adamat thrust Faye behind him, pointing at the pile with his sword.

Coughing, sputtering, it stood up.

It was Bo. Flames still licked at his clothes, and his muttonchops were singed. He beat at the flames for a moment, and then scowled through the smoking ruins of the stairwell wall.

Bo held a hand over his head. A *whump* split the air, making Adamat's ears pop. The flames died instantly. Bo's fingers jerked to one side, and wind whipped through the house, sucking smoke away like a giant bellows inhaling above a fire.

The staircase was suddenly full of cool, clean air. Adamat gasped in a great breath of it, holding Faye tightly. She clutched the Eldaminse boy to her skirts.

Fire whipped past Bo, over his shoulder. The Privileged turned his head, as if mildly perturbed. Slivers of ice the size of daggers shot from above his head and *thwapped* into something out of Adamat's sight. Bo nodded to himself.

"You can come down now," Bo said. "I think it's safe."

"You think?" Adamat crept slowly down the stairs until he reached the base.

They passed the kitchen and entered the sitting room at the back of the house. On the near wall, impaled to the masonry by icicles dripping blood, was the other Privileged. It was a woman, Deliv by her dark skin. Bo didn't spare her a second glance. Faye shielded the Eldaminse boy's eyes.

"Faye," Adamat said, "this is Privileged Borbador, the last remaining member of the Adran royal cabal."

"Forgive me if I don't shake your hand," Faye said. "I don't think I want to touch your hands."

Bo's black gloves had been burned off by the flames, but his rune-covered Privileged's gloves were white and pristine, as if brand-new. He clasped his hands and rocked back on his heels. "Understandable. Where's Vetas?" he asked.

"Fell has him," Adamat said.

"That woman, I'd very much like to meet her. Properly, that is."

Adamat couldn't help but wonder what that meant. "I don't think you do," he said.

"I think I'll be—"

A scream from outside cut off Bo's sentence. He cocked his head, like a dog listening for a whistle. "Oh, pit," he said. "You didn't tell me there were two."

"What, another Privileged?" Adamat began casting around for somewhere to hide. But what could protect them? There was no hiding from a Privileged.

Bo sneered, rolling up his sleeves. "Yes," he said. "Get down!"

The world exploded in a blast of plaster and wood. Adamat was thrown from his feet and knocked about, buffeted by forces beyond his control. He tried to grab for Faye—for anything, but found himself on the ground a moment later.

Everything was silent. Had the attack killed Faye? Or Bo, for that matter? Adamat moved cautiously, not sure whether all the parts of him were intact. A beam had fallen across his chest, the air swirling with smoke and dust. It felt like the whole house had landed on him.

He didn't feel anything broken, and he was able to move the beam just enough to wriggle out from beneath the rubble. He used his fingers to gingerly feel across the whole surface of his chest. Not much pain.

Adamat climbed to his feet. The Eldaminse boy was nearby, apparently unhurt. Adamat wasn't sure whether to be relieved or worried that through all the excitement the boy had hardly made a noise.

"Go on," Adamat said to him, "hide in the kitchen!" The Privileged might still be here. The boy rushed past, and Adamat shook his head to clear it. Where was Faye?

Panic rose inside of him. Faye. She was gone. Separated from him by the blast. The roof had caved in, and he'd avoided most of it . . . sweet Kresimir, was she beneath the rubble?

"Faye! Faye!"

"She's right here," a voice said.

Adamat turned to find the eunuch standing in the doorway. He was holding Faye up beneath one arm. It looked like she'd injured her ankle. They were both covered in plaster dust.

Adamat eyed the eunuch. They'd done it. Taken Vetas. Saved Faye. Would the eunuch turn on him now for blackmailing the Proprietor? Bo wasn't here. Adamat didn't even know if the Privileged was alive. Adamat didn't know where Sergeant Oldrich was. No one would ask questions if the eunuch quietly killed them both and disappeared.

"She's safe," the eunuch said.

"Thank you."

The eunuch was surprisingly gentle as he helped Faye into the room. Adamat stepped toward them, arms out.

The stiletto handle seemed to materialize in the side of the eunuch's neck. When he opened his mouth, blood poured out, and he dropped to his knees. Faye, suddenly unsupported, toppled to the side, only to be caught by Lord Vetas.

CHAPTER

25

No one moved at Tamas's shouted order. The thick chaos of soldiers milling against the edge of the river did not change.

Tamas felt his heart begin to beat faster.

"Men of the Seventh! Take the line!"

Nothing. His hands shook. He'd overplayed himself. This false panic he'd meant to create had become real. He'd defeated himself before the battle even began.

"First Battalion!" a voice cut through the crowd. Someone shoved their way out of the press. It was old Colonel Arbor. He held his rifle in one hand, his teeth in the other. "To the line, First Battalion!"

Tamas swung around. The Kez cavalry continued to advance slowly. They were a half a mile out on the western front. The dragoons to the south began to move forward. Vlora and the rest of the powder mages continued to fire from across the river, whittling away at their numbers.

Adran infantry began to peel away from the mob by the river and get to their positions. Too few of them. Too slowly.

Then more. And more. Soldiers left the riverside and raced across the camp to the mound of dirt separating them from the Kez cavalry. They threw themselves to the safe side of the mound and readied their rifles, loading bullets and fixing bayonets. Tamas took a deep breath. He felt his heart soar. If he could have kissed every one of his men then and there, he would have.

He turned back to the Kez advance and his heart stopped.

The advance had ceased less than a quarter of a mile from Tamas's position.

Fifteen thousand Kez cavalry wedged Tamas's army completely against the river and the mountains.

He saw a man ride to the front of the cuirassiers. Had Beon figured out Tamas's game? Did he sense a trap?

The man, Tamas recognized, was Beon je Ipille himself. Brave, to come out to the front of his heavy cavalry, when he knew a powder mage's bullet might end him any second.

Beon seemed to cock his head at Tamas's position. His lips moved briefly, then he kissed his sword and raised it.

A salute. Beon was saluting Tamas. The motion stunned him. *You stand and fight*, the salute seemed to say, *when you could have run*.

Beon's sword fell and the earth trembled as fifteen thousand sets of hooves thundered toward Tamas.

"Hold!" Tamas yelled, gripping his rifle. He turned away from the cuirassiers. Their charge would be stopped by the sharpened stakes and crosses. They'd pull up hard and exchange fire with the Ninth, or advance slowly to try to navigate the defenses.

Between Tamas and the dragoons, however, there were no such

apparent obstacles—only a thin layer of white fog over the ground and then the raised earthworks behind which his men crouched.

Three hundred yards. The dragoons leaned over their mounts, urging them faster. A bullet whistled over Tamas's head and took a dragoon between the eyes. Tamas raised his rifle, lined up a shot, and fired. He lowered, reloaded, and repeated.

Two hundred yards. Dragoons raised their carbines and twisted their faces in wordless cries.

One hundred yards. Tamas's lines opened fire. Hundreds of dragoons fell from the first volley alone. The rest charged on, heedless of their comrades' fall.

Seventy yards. The dragoons opened fire with their carbines. Tamas's soldiers crouched behind their earthen wall, reloading.

Fifty yards. Dragoons let their carbines drop and raised their pistols.

Thirty yards. The line of dragoons aimed pistols.

Twenty yards.

Ten yards.

The front line of dragoons disappeared.

Tamas closed his eyes for a brief moment as the screams reached him.

The momentum of the cavalry unit at full gallop had carried them headfirst into a concealed trench. Almost twenty feet wide and just as deep, it stretched the entire length of the "opening" Tamas had left in his defenses. The trench was topped with stakes covered in grass and other debris. A poor disguise in the light of the day, but the fog had covered them completely. They cracked under the weight of the warhorses.

Tamas had once seen a row of carriages go straight into the Adsea. The first carriage had plunged around a steep corner and off the end of a pier. The second had followed, the driver seeing the drop only at the last second, while the third driver's attempts to slow his horses had failed.

This was much like that, but instead of three carriages, it was thousands and thousands of dragoons heading straight into his trench.

By the time the dragoons had managed to arrest their charge, the trench was nearly filled with screaming, thrashing horses and writhing men trying to escape the press. The line of Kez dragoons stared in horror at their fallen comrades.

Tamas shuddered at the thought of being at the bottom of that trench.

"Fire!" Tamas yelled.

The Seventh Brigade opened fire at the Kez dragoons. Their horses milled in panic at the edge of the trench, officers shouting and waving their swords, trying to get the horses at the rear of the column to back up so they could organize a withdrawal.

Tamas reloaded and fired again. The dragoons began to organize. If they were given a chance to disengage, they still had thousands left. They could reorganize and hound Tamas's flank when he turned to deal with the cuirassiers.

"Bayonets!" Tamas ordered, lifting his rifle in the air.

Every forty paces of the trench, they'd left a ten-foot-wide path of solid ground. They were unmarked, and the way would be unsure in the fog, but Tamas had to counterattack.

Tamas headed across the closest of these paths, straight into the flank of the withdrawing Kez dragoons.

He reached out with his senses, taking in the closest powder charges and igniting them with his mind. The small explosions killed men and horse alike, rattling Tamas's teeth from their proximity. His soldiers flooded around him, howling as they set upon the dragoons with their long-sword bayonets.

The melee erupted along the whole line as the five thousand men of the Seventh Brigade slammed into the Kez dragoons. Without the impact of their charge, and against the long reach of sword bayonets, the dragoons lost their advantage.

Tamas ran toward the closest dragoon. He thrust his bayonet up and into the man's exposed side, then jerked his rifle savagely to tear open the wound. The man fell from his horse, and Tamas danced back out of the way as the animal panicked and bolted.

Something hit him hard from the side, knocking him off his feet. He landed on the ground, the breath knocked from him, and was immediately pushing himself back up.

"Sir!" Olem had lost his rifle and drawn his sword. He rammed it into the thigh of a dragoon and made a dash for Tamas.

Tamas got to his feet, only to have Olem hit him full on in the chest. They both went down as a straight cavalry sword whooshed through the air where Tamas's head had been.

Olem rolled off of Tamas and helped him to his feet.

Tamas's own rifle had disappeared in the melee. He drew his sword.

"Time to back off, sir," Olem shouted over the din of gunfire.

"We're not done here yet. Seventh!" Tamas slid his sword into its scabbard and pulled a rifle out of the mud. It still had its bayonet fixed. He pointed it at the closest dragoon and ran, hoping Olem was behind him.

He reached out, detonating more powder as he drew closer to the dragoons once more. On either side of him, his infantry pressed the attack.

Tamas felt a stinging breeze along the right side of his head, just above his ear. He felt suddenly dizzy, but charged on. Each step, however, the dragoons seemed to get farther away.

It took Olem yelling into his ear to bring him back to reality. "They've retreated, sir!"

Tamas stopped and looked about him, taking in the carnage. Thousands had died in that charge, and thousands more were stuck in that trench—broken men and horses dying a slow death. The screams rang in his ears. "Right. Back to the line." He grabbed Olem's arm to steady himself.

They took a safe path across the trench. The rest of the Seventh had turned away from the retreating dragoons and were making sure none of the rest would get out of the trench alive. Tamas saw one dragoon grab an Adran soldier's foot and beg for mercy. The soldier put his bayonet through the dragoon's eye.

Tamas felt Olem's hand on his shoulder.

"You've taken a bullet along the side of your head, sir," Olem said.

Tamas touched his head and his fingers came back crimson.

"A straight crease," Olem said. "Bloody, but doesn't look deep."

Olem's left arm hung at his side. His sleeve was in bloody tatters, nearly cut from him. He noted Tamas's questioning gaze. "Just a flesh wound, sir."

"Tamas, you bloody dog!" a voice bellowed. "The Ninth has crumbled! Our flank is lost!"

The words brought Tamas's head up and around. Gavril rode by at full tilt, followed by the rest of his rangers heading to the west.

"Colonel Arbor!" Tamas cast about for the colonel, finding him near the edge of the trench, taking a pair of wounded Kez officers prisoner.

"Sir!"

"Hold this position." Tamas waved his sword over his head. "Men of the Seventh, to me!"

Tamas began to sprint to the west, fueled by adrenaline and the powder of the battle. Already, he could see the damage. There were countless cuirassiers inside the line of defenses. Some of the Ninth had already begun to flee, running deeper into the camp or throwing themselves into the river.

The cuirassiers pressed hard on the southwestern corner. The defenses had all but collapsed, except for a small knot of men. Tamas recognized General Cethal on horseback. Even as he caught sight of the general, Cethal's horse was pulled down.

Tamas came up short. He stamped the butt of his rifle on the ground and shouted to be heard.

"Line, form!"

Olem fell in beside him. To his left and right, soldiers of the Seventh stood shoulder to shoulder.

"Load!"

Rifles and muskets were quickly loaded.

"Aim!"

His men brought their weapons to their shoulders.

"Fire!"

The Seventh fired above the heads of the milling members of the Ninth. A slew of cuirassiers fell from their horses.

"Bayonets, forward!"

The "aim and fire" had given the rest of the Seventh time to fall in behind him. Tamas now had an infantry wall six lines deep, bayonets bristling. They marched forward, lockstep. Soldiers of the Ninth fell in or were pushed aside. He aimed his line directly toward where he'd seen General Cethal fall.

They encountered the heavy cavalry thirty paces later.

Cuirassiers locked in combat had lost their greatest weapon—the charge—but they had some advantages over dragoons. They were armored, providing protection against bayonets, and their heavy sabers were more effective against armed infantry.

"Hold the line!" Tamas ordered as his men began to bring down cuirassiers. They stabbed and slashed, putting the men and horses down before stepping past them and continuing the push.

Tamas spotted General Cethal through a break in the fighting. Cethal was on the ground, twenty paces away. His face and hands were bloody, his saber raised above him. A dismounted cuirassier knocked Cethal's sword to one side and thrust with his own.

Tamas broke his formation, charging between two men on horseback. The cuirassier above Cethal drew his sword back and thrust again. Cethal's body twitched.

The cuirassier didn't even see Tamas.

Tamas's bayonet entered the spot beneath his arm where the

straps of his breastplate met. Tamas rammed the bayonet in deeper, pushing it until the barrel of his rifle was soaked in blood. He pushed a final time and let go of the rifle, throwing himself to his knees at Cethal's side.

Cethal stared back up at him in horror, his hands crimson with his own blood.

Tamas heard the clash of swords and Olem's challenging yell, but they all seemed distant to him.

Cethal had been stabbed at least four times through the chest and stomach. His hands were covered with countless cuts, and his face was a mess. He blinked at Tamas through the blood.

"My boys," he gasped, "they broke."

Tamas took Cethal's hand in his and squeezed.

The ultimate betrayal. Your men breaking and running, fleeing around you.

"You didn't," Tamas said. "You stood."

"I'm not a coward," Cethal said. "Bloody Beon. Never seen cuirassiers so nimble. They danced between the trench and our . . . our fortifications." Cethal rammed his empty hand into one of the wounds in a futile attempt to staunch the bleeding. "You stop the dragoons?"

"We did."

Cethal drew in a sharp breath. "Don't be hard on my boys. I wanted to . . . to run, myself. Damned cuirassiers." He blinked again. "You find Beon and . . ." He coughed, and cleared his throat. ". . . give him my regards. That was a bloody fine bit of horsemanship." He pulled his hand out of Tamas's and used it to try and staunch another wound. "Go on. Men need you. I'll be . . . fine."

Tamas stripped off his coat and put it beneath Cethal's head. He stood up. His line of infantry had passed him and pushed on. He wrenched his bayonet out of the cuirassier's body and ran to catch up.

The heavy cavalry had fallen back. All but a handful had been unhorsed, and those had turned tail to flee. One by one, pockets of Kez cuirassiers surrendered.

He caught sight of the last of the fighting. His soldiers pressed in, presenting a wall of bristling bayonets to the remaining Kez. Tamas shouldered his way into the melee, and was not the least bit surprised to find Beon at the center of it.

Beon's helmet was gone. His breastplate hung off him by one strap, and the side of his cheek had been laid open. He favored one arm. Beside him the last of his bodyguards was run through and thrown to the ground. Beon stepped back, hair soaked with blood and sweat, and threw down his sword.

"I surrender," he said loudly. "We surrender."

One of the Adran soldiers stepped forward. He cocked his rifle back and aimed his bayonet at Beon's neck.

Tamas could stand it no more. The blood. The neglect of mercy. He dashed forward and grabbed the soldier's rifle by the hot muzzle and thrust it aside.

"He said," Tamas proclaimed loudly, "that he surrenders."

Adamat lurched forward, a curse on his lips, only to stop when Vetas pressed the stiletto against Faye's neck.

"I promised you pain tenfold," Vetas said. "I want you to remember that." His forearm flexed, and Adamat closed his eyes, unwilling to watch Faye's life blood spill from her throat.

"Step away from him."

Adamat opened his eyes. Vetas looked slightly confused. His forearm strained, but the stiletto got no closer to Faye's throat.

"Please," Bo said, coming around the corner, "just step off to one side."

Adamat snatched Faye, pulling her away from Vetas. Lord Vetas's nostrils flared, eyes flashing anger, but it was clear he couldn't move.

Bo's fingers twitched. Invisible sorcery tossed Vetas across the room, slamming him into the wall beside the impaled Privileged. Bo walked up beside Vetas and took the man's chin in hand roughly, turning his head to see the dead Privileged.

"She was good," Bo said. "Real worthy of cabal membership. That's what I did to her. The other one—your backup—he wasn't that skilled. It only took a moment. And you." Bo tapped a gloved finger beneath Vetas's chin. "I don't like you. I saw that room you keep in the cellar. I've known men like that in the cabal. I was over-joyed to hear that Tamas had slaughtered them."

Bo stepped back and looked at Vetas thoughtfully. Vetas was still pinned to the wall by Bo's sorcery. Bo said, "I bet you were the type of child who tortured animals for fun. Tell me, did you ever pull the wings off of insects?"

Vetas didn't respond.

"Answer me!" Bo bellowed.

Vetas flinched. "Yes."

"That's what I thought. How does it feel?"

A single twitch of Bo's finger. That's all it took and Vetas's right arm was ripped off by invisible forces. Adamat didn't know who screamed louder: Vetas, from the pain, or Faye from the shock. Adamat clutched Faye to his chest, worried he'd fall at any moment, and his stomach felt like it might turn inside out.

Bo's finger twitched again. Vetas's other arm dropped to the ground beside him. There was a flare of fire at his shoulders.

"We'll cauterize those wounds," Bo said. "Wouldn't want you to die too quickly. That's the point among you types, isn't it? To keep them alive as long as possible?" Bo smacked Vetas once, then again. "Isn't it? Tell me! Isn't it?"

Adamat lurched forward and grabbed Bo's arm. Bo whirled on him, hands raised, fire in his eyes. Adamat did his best not to shy away. "That's enough, man! Enough!" He couldn't believe himself. Dashing forward to spare Vetas. An hour ago, Adamat was ready to do every pain in the world to Vetas. Now, he just felt ill.

Bo lowered his hands, nodding, muttering to himself. "Take them," he said, pointing to Faye and the boy. "Vetas isn't going anywhere. Get them out of here."

Adamat put an arm around Faye's waist, letting her take the weight off her ankle as he led her out of the smoldering ruin of a building.

The street was filled with people. Onlookers stood well back, a hundred paces at least, their curiosity warring with their fear of the sorcery. Immediately in front of the building, the eunuch's men had gathered with their wounded and prisoners, and some were heading inside now that the fire and smoke were gone. Adamat saw Sergeant Oldrich and Riplas, moving among them, giving orders.

Adamat gestured Riplas over. "The eunuch is dead," he said quietly.

The eunuch's second-in-command rocked back a step, eyes wide. "What? How?"

"It was Lord Vetas. He must have gotten away from Fell. Speaking of which..."

Fell emerged from the groups of onlookers. She held her arm carefully to one side, her body covered in cuts. She limped over to him.

"Vetas, he..."

"He's inside," Adamat said, choking back anger. Fell had told him she could hold Vetas. She had obviously been overpowered. Oldrich's soldiers had probably been killed as well. He didn't trust himself to say more.

When Fell returned, her cold demeanor was somewhat sobered.

"What are you going to do with him?"

"I want to know what he did with my boy...other than that, I don't care."

Fell and Riplas seemed to size each other up for a moment. "You're the eunuch's second in command?" Fell asked.

"Yes."

"Let's talk." Fell jerked her head, and the two women moved aside for a private conference.

Adamat squeezed Faye, as if to reassure himself that she was still there. She nestled against his chest, her eyes closed, her face wet with tears.

"The children?" she asked suddenly.

"Safe," Adamat said. "I'm sorry I couldn't come sooner."

"You came. That's all that matters."

Adamat fell to his knees beside her, pressing her hand to his lips. "I could die now. I have you back."

"Please," Faye said. "Not yet. My ankle hurts quite a lot."

CHAPTER
26

Taniel found Major Doravir in the Wine's End, an upper-class gentleman's club that had been appropriated for use by the army as an officers' mess hall. The room was lined with rich crimson damask and smelled heavily of cigar smoke. The armchairs scattered throughout the club had been upholstered with the furs of big cats from the Gurlish continent. In one corner, a sergeant was playing a grand piano. The conversation was somber and muted, though a few officers seemed to note Taniel's entrance.

Taniel paused in the doorway and adjusted the collar of his dress uniform—a gift from Mihali. Most of his possessions had been lost when South Pike collapsed, including his various uniforms. Somehow the fat chef had gotten Taniel's measurements and had had a new one made for him. It even had the proper silver buttons with powder kegs on them.

He examined the room slowly, hat tucked under his arm, and tried not to think about the provosts waiting outside for him. If he failed to apologize, he imagined they'd take him straight back to his quarters.

Taniel spotted Major Doravir near the bar, playing cards with an older officer of about fifty and two other majors. He took a deep breath and crossed the room, weaving his way through the chairs, giving a small nod to the few men who called out to him.

Major Doravir, her back to the wall, couldn't possibly have missed his presence, but she didn't bother to look up when Taniel stopped beside her table.

The older officer—a colonel by his uniform, though Taniel couldn't place the face—was speaking.

"And I said to them, it's the lack of noble blood. I understand Tamas's cull was a political thing, but there's no arguing that the lack of nobility among his officers has cheapened the whole army. By Kresimir, if he couldn't..." The old officer paused, frowning at Taniel. "Ah, Captain. Fetch me another beer. Now, where was I? If he couldn't... get to it, Captain, I'm thirsty."

Taniel ignored the colonel. "Major Doravir," Taniel said.

Doravir glanced up from her cards. "You're being rude to Colonel Bertthur."

Bertthur? Where did he know that name from? "My apologies, Colonel"—Taniel didn't look at the man—"but I must speak with Major Doravir."

"It's 'Colonel' now," Doravir said, touching the bars at her collar. "And whatever you have to say to me"—she set her cards facedown on the table and leaned back in her chair—"can be said in public."

Taniel swallowed a mouthful of bile. "Congratulations on your promotion, Colonel."

"I say," Bertthur stood up.

"Sit down, sir," Taniel snapped. "This has nothing to do with you. Colonel Doravir, I'd like to offer my deepest apologies for any"—Taniel rolled the sentence around in his head, trying not to spit it out—"insult I may have given you with my recent conduct."

Taniel couldn't help but notice that the murmur of conversation had completely disappeared. It felt as if a hundred sets of eyes were staring at him. They probably were.

"Colonel Bertthur is my husband," Doravir said. "Apologize to him."

Husband? The man must have been twenty years her senior.

"I did," Taniel said. "And I apologized to you. Now if you'll excuse me." Taniel turned on his heel.

He paused when Bertthur cleared his throat. "Was that Taniel? Tamas's brat?"

Keep walking, Taniel told himself.

"Two-Shot," Bertthur said. "Come back here this instant. Colonel Etan!"

Taniel froze. Etan was here?

"Colonel, isn't this the man who got you crippled?"

"He's the man who saved my life," Etan's voice returned.

"He saved my life, too!" someone shouted.

"And mine!"

"Bah. I remember you now, Two-Shot," Bertthur said. "It must have been five, six years ago. A whiny little bastard. A piss-poor soldier. You'd rather run off with that dark-haired whore of yours, neglecting your training. I never saw anything in you. Huh. Looks like she didn't either."

A whore? Vlora? He might have wanted to call her that and worse when he'd caught her with that fop at the university, but Taniel would be damned if he'd let some fool officer go on about his love life. He balled his hands into fists and slowly took a breath to calm himself. He didn't have to listen to this. He could just walk away.

"Bertthur, I think you've had enough," Etan's voice said. "Perhaps it's time to retire for the evening."

"Go to the pit, Etan," Bertthur went on. "Taniel, I can see that things haven't changed. No respect for authority. No military decorum. You've just traded one whore for another."

"Bertthur!" Etan's voice held some warning.

"But now it's a savage whore! What will he think of next? I bet your father is rolling over in his grave every time you bed that bitch."

Taniel's whole body shook. The fury threatened to overwhelm him. He forced himself to remain calm. Slowly, he turned around.

"Bertthur," Taniel said. "I don't remember a Colonel Bertthur. I remember a *Captain* Bertthur. An ass of a man who held his rank only because he was the bastard son of a duke. Field Marshal Tamas swore that man would never hold a higher rank as long as he was left alive."

Bertthur turned red. "That's a week in the stocks for you, Two-Shot."

"You're a braggart and a fool, Bertthur. You're a disgrace to the uniform."

"Two weeks!"

Taniel charged toward Bertthur and the officer shrank back, as if expecting to be punched. Taniel gripped the colonel's bars on his collar and ripped them off, tossing them to the side.

"A month!" Bertthur roared.

Something soared through the air and struck Bertthur in the side of the face. It looked like mashed potatoes.

"Who did that?" Doravir demanded.

A dinner roll hit Bertthur on the nose. He reeled back, suddenly under assault from every manner of dinner food. Someone flung a whole dish of sauce on him, staining his uniform.

"You're not a free man anymore, Two-Shot!" Bertthur fumed. "Your father is dead. You'll see two months in the stocks, and I'll hand your little savage whore over to my men!"

Taniel took a step forward and plowed his fist into Bertthur's chin, sending the older man to the ground. He could hear the crack of the bastard's jaw breaking.

"Provosts!" Doravir shouted.

Damn this. Damn them all. Taniel righted Berrthur's chair with his foot and leapt up on it.

"Friends," he shouted, raising his arms for quiet. The officers' mess suddenly calmed, and to Taniel's surprise, he had silence within moments. "The General Staff has deceived us all," Taniel said. "Field Marshal Tamas is not dead. He hasn't even been captured. He's leading the Seventh and Ninth through Kez as we speak."

"A lie!" Doravir shouted.

Tamas raised his voice to drown her out. "Haven't you wondered where the Kez cavalry are? They're chasing Tamas!"

Taniel was shoved off the chair by a provost. The man had no sooner laid his hands on Taniel than a major tackled him to the floor. Taniel got to his feet. "We only have to hold these Kez bastards for a few more months! Fall will be here soon and then winter, and Field Marshal Tamas with it!"

A musket butt slammed Taniel in the stomach. He doubled over in pain, but forced himself up. "No retreat! No surrender!"

The officers' mess erupted in a roar of cheering. Food was flying everywhere. Taniel was forced to the floor by the back of his neck, his face ground into the carpet.

"You're finished, Two-Shot," Doravir hissed. "You're a dead man!"

Taniel didn't care. The officers would all tell their men, and their men would hold the line. They'd do it for Taniel. They'd do it for Tamas.

Nila felt a sense of dread grow in the pit of her stomach as she neared Vetas's manor. Black smoke billowed above the street, and men's screams carried on the wind. The sound of fighting grew more distinct as she drew closer, and above it all a sound that she'd only heard once or twice in her life but was unmistakable—the thump of sorcery.

It had to be Privileged Dourford. She could see the tall Privileged in her mind's eye, laughing gleefully as he slung sorcery at unknown attackers, burning men to a crisp with the flick of his fingers.

The sorcery seemed to have an echo. There'd be a thump, and then another one just as loud if not louder almost immediately after. The combat was still going on as she rounded the corner of the next street over and approached the manor from the rear. Smoke poured from the windows on all three stories of the manor. Flames licked the smoke, curling like fingers around the window frames. A crash, and then another.

No, this wasn't any echo.

Sorcery fought sorcery inside the building.

Nila ran toward the manor, her dress gathered in both hands. She remembered hearing the kitchen staff say that Lord Vetas had called a second Privileged from somewhere down south. She was supposed to have arrived this morning. Was that woman fighting Dourford?

There was a great *whump* and Nila felt her ears pop. She staggered to one side of the street, trying to keep her feet. The flames had disappeared from the manor. Another *whump*, and the smoke burst from the windows as if propelled by a giant bellows, and no more followed it out.

Nila froze in her tracks, more frightened by the sudden silence than she had been by the sorcery. Who had won? Who had even been fighting? Was Vetas in there? Was he still alive? Could Jakob have survived all of that?

She didn't know if she could make herself go inside. She took several deep breaths, gathering her courage.

A crack split the air, throwing Nila off her feet. She landed on the street hard enough to scrape the skin off her palm.

One side of the house collapsed, crashing in on itself. She stared, openmouthed, as the walls crumpled and part of the roof slid off one side, clay shingles falling into the alley with a sound like a thousand wind chimes in a hurricane.

Nila climbed to her feet and was running toward the house before she could think. Her palm throbbed, her dress bloody, but she didn't care about that. Jakob was still inside, up on the second floor. His nursery faced the other street, and even at this angle she could tell that if he was inside, he'd been crushed. But maybe he was lucky. Maybe he'd been under the bed, or protected by the door frame, or . . .

The back wall of the manor suddenly blew outward, sending plaster, furniture, and bits of what looked to have once been a human out into the street.

A man stood in the wreckage. He was of medium height, with ruddy muttonchops on an otherwise clean-shaven face and loose pants and matching jacket that wouldn't have looked out of place on a street in the bankers' quarter. He wasn't particularly handsome, nor was he ugly, but Nila felt a jolt when she first saw him.

He held his hands high, fingers poised in white Privileged's gloves as he looked down on the mess he'd just made all over the thoroughfare. The gathering crowd pulled back in fear. A woman fainted when she realized what the juicy red meat scattered in the street was. A man vomited.

The Privileged surveyed the gathered crowd and lowered his hands. He turned and disappeared inside the wreckage of the house. Before he did, however, Nila caught sight of something on his gloves: the symbol of the Adran Mountains with the teardrop of the Adsea beneath them.

This wasn't just any Privileged. This was a member of the Adran royal cabal.

Something told Nila that Dourford hadn't stood a chance.

Nila picked her way through the wreckage and ducked beneath a beam, entering the house as close as she could get to the servants' stairs.

The sitting room was completely crushed. She could hear a man calling for help, and another moaning. A body lay in the mangled timber, covered in plaster dust, unmoving. She heard someone speaking from the other room. It sounded like Lord Vetas.

Nila moved slowly into the kitchen. It remained almost completely untouched by the collapse, but it seemed that the servants' stairs had taken the worst of it. She wouldn't be climbing up to the second floor that way.

She stepped over to the door to the dining room and listened. Silence, but she could hear someone moving. She looked through a crack in the door. She heard herself gasp at the sight of a woman, body hanging limply from dripping shards of ice, nailed to the back wall of the dining room. She wore Privileged's gloves. Vetas's other Privileged?

Someone spoke. A man's voice. He was saying...

Lord Vetas slammed into the back wall of the dining room hard enough to rattle the remains of the house. Something shifted in the wreckage, and Nila heard someone scream. Lord Vetas, though, didn't make a sound. The Adran Privileged stepped into view. He spoke quietly, his face angry. He grabbed Lord Vetas by the chin and forced him to look at the dead Privileged.

The Adran Privileged stepped back suddenly. His voice was suddenly calm and collected. Nila heard him say, "I bet you were the type of child who tortured animals for fun. Tell me, did you ever pull the wings off of insects? Answer me!"

Nila had some satisfaction in seeing Vetas pull back in fear. His mouth moved, the word too low to hear.

"That's what I thought. How does it feel?"

Nila pulled away from the door. Vetas's scream drowned out the calls of the wounded and dying in the rest of the house. She turned toward the kitchen, looking for another way to get through the wreckage. Panic set in. She had to find Jakob. She had to get away from the house. Even as she began to breathe harder, the adrenaline setting in, a wave of relief swept over her. Vetas was gone. If he wasn't dead yet, he would be. That bastard had finally found someone stronger and crueler.

She put him from her mind. He wasn't worth another thought. Jakob, though . . .

"Nila?"

Nila's gaze darted around the kitchen. A child's voice. Where had it come from?

"Nila, quick, hide in here."

She found Jakob in the bottom of the pantry, tucked behind a sack of flour. She glanced at the door to the dining room. "There's no room for me in there," she said, helping him out of the pantry.

"What about Faye?" Jakob asked. "And Uncle Vetas."

A moan emanated from the dining room. Nila took Jakob by the shoulder and pushed him out through the broken wall the same way she'd come in.

The crowd outside had retreated to what they deemed a safe distance from the house, seemingly content to wait for the police and fire brigades to arrive. Someone grabbed Nila by the arm as she pushed her way through the throng. She shoved them off without a comment, not bothering to look back, and kept her grip on Jakob's shoulder.

Her mind was already racing. She still had her buried silver outside the city. She had no money, no clothes but the ones on her back. They'd have to walk all the way to the city limits, find the silver, and then tomorrow they could come back into the city and find a place to sell it.

A night or two spent sleeping in the street wouldn't kill them.

They were four blocks away, when Nila noticed that everyone she passed was staring at her. It was another block before Jakob pointed at her dress and she realized that the blood from her palm was everywhere. It looked like she'd been rolling in it. Two more streets down and they reached a string of shops.

"Do you need help, ma'am?" a passing gentleman asked, pressing a handkerchief to his mouth. He looked queasy at the sight of her.

She showed him her palm. "Just skinned it, is all," she said, trying to keep her tone level. "Looks worse than it is."

The gentleman seemed relieved. "There's a doctor right over there," he said, pointing two shops down. "She accepts walk-ins."

"Thank you so much," Nila said.

She waited for a moment until the gentleman continued on his way. She had no way to pay for a doctor. She'd have to deal with the pain until…

Nila remembered the silver necklace with the large pearl hanging about her neck. A "gift" from Vetas.

The doctor was an older woman in a white dress and sharp eyeglasses perched on her nose. She was seeing a patient, but one look at Nila's bloody dress and she rushed to see what was the matter.

Nila did her best to make small talk as the doctor cleaned and then wrapped her wound. She had fallen, Nila told the doctor. A nasty fall, but nothing was sprained. Payment? "Oh, my. I seem to have left my pocketbook at home. Can you keep this necklace until I return to pay you?"

The arrangement was struck, and Nila even borrowed a fifty-krana note against the necklace. She pulled Jakob out the door, relieved that he'd stayed quiet through the entire exchange.

Nila had only gone another half a block before a thought struck her.

The Privileged. The one who'd come out victorious and then torn Vetas's arms off—he was a member of the Adran royal cabal.

"Jakob," Nila said, directing him over to a street side café, "can you wait here for a few minutes?"

Jakob's eyes grew wide. "Don't leave me alone."

"Just for a few minutes. Here, let me buy you glass of milk. Sit right here, inside, and wait for me to come back." She paused, thinking. "If I don't come back, I want you to ask directions to the nearest barracks. Tell the commanding officer that you're looking for Captain Olem. He'll be away, fighting on the front, but the officer will help you find someplace to stay."

"You're not coming back for me?"

"I am," Nila said, "but just in case I don't, that's what you're to do."

The boy seemed to take stock of her confidence and straightened his back. "Yes, Nila."

She bought him a glass of milk and put him on a chair just inside the café, asking the waiter to keep an eye on him for half an hour. Ten krana bought her an old apron from the café, and she wrapped it around her middle. It concealed the blood on her dress nicely.

Then Nila backtracked her way to Lord Vetas's manor.

The police had arrived, and the fire brigades were crawling all over the manor. A white sheet had been laid over the remains of Dourford, and the fire brigades pulled a twisted body from the wreckage. All of Lord Vetas's men had disappeared, along with whomever they were fighting. The number of police kept her from wanting to get any closer to the building.

She began to make a circuit of the area, checking each of the nearby streets. Surely there were lookouts, or . . . or . . . someone!

Nila found nothing. Lord Vetas's men, the Adran soldiers, the cabal Privileged; they'd scattered to the wind.

She widened her search.

It wasn't until five streets over that she caught sight of a man with ruddy muttonchops and a pressed suit of clothes walking along the thoroughfare with a wide rug, rolled thick enough that it might have a body inside, over his shoulder. He wasn't wearing any Privileged's gloves, but Nila knew it was the same man—the cabal Privileged.

She ran to catch up with him. He walked slowly under the weight of the rug and he was whistling loudly to himself. Surely this couldn't be the same man?

He turned a corner.

Slowly, Nila crept up to the edge of the building. Maybe it wasn't him. Privileged didn't carry things themselves. They had servants for that.

She rounded the corner and nearly screamed.

About ten feet down the alley, the man was sitting on his rolled rug. He had his feet up on an old wine barrel as if he'd been there all day.

"Can I help you?" he asked.

Nila glanced into the street. Surely he wouldn't harm her. Not on a busy street in broad daylight.

"Sir," she said. How to talk to a Privileged? She'd spent some time with Rozalia when she was with the royalists months ago, but that had made her just as uncomfortable. Privileged were not to be trusted. "My lord?"

His eyes narrowed, but he didn't correct her. This was the same man, all right. And he didn't like someone noticing that he was a Privileged. She braced herself, ready to run.

"Yes?" he asked, his voice amiable.

"You're a Privileged," she said. "From the Adran Cabal."

The man raised an eyebrow. "What makes you think that?"

"I saw you splatter Lord Dourford across the cobbles about an hour ago."

"That was his name?" the Privileged said. "I thought he looked familiar. That pompous prick was a member of the Kez Cabal. Bah, I'm surprised they let him in. Less talent than a Knacked." He looked her up and down. "Now what can I do for you? Make it good, because I'll have to kill you after."

Kill her? Nila had no doubt he would, given the need. Members of the royal cabals were notoriously cruel. She cleared her throat and straightened her back. "Due to your duty as a member of the royal cabal, I will give into your protection Jakob Eldaminse, next in line for the crown of Adro." She let out a sharp breath, only now realizing that she'd been holding it.

The Privileged's eyebrow remained cocked. Slowly, as if realizing that she was serious, the eyebrow lowered. He threw his head back and laughed.

Nila felt a nervous smile dance upon her lips. Had she said something funny? "You'll do it, then?"

"What? Oh, pit no. You think I want some noble brat hanging on my hip? That kid is, what, four?"

"Six."

"Six. Right." The Privileged stood up. "The Adran nobility is dead. They're not coming back." He paused and looked around. "Where is the boy, anyway?"

"Hiding."

"Smart."

"Sir," Nila said. "My lord, you have to. He has no one else to protect him."

"He seems to have you."

"I'm just a laundress."

"You dress like a waiter."

"The apron? No, I'm a laundress."

"I'm pretty sure that you're a waiter," the Privileged said.

It took her several moments to realize that she was being teased.

"My lord!" she said in a voice that she hoped was commanding, "you have to protect Jakob Eldaminse."

"No, I don't." The Privileged sighed as if suddenly tired, and though he'd looked to be in his midtwenties just a moment ago, he suddenly seemed elderly. "I'm done with the Adran nobility." He blinked and then seemed to look more closely at her. "Have we met before?"

She shook her head.

"Oh well. I should be off. This rug won't keep all day."

Nila felt a rising panic inside her. It hadn't worked. The Privileged wouldn't protect Jakob. It wasn't as if she were trying to hand the boy off, she told herself. It was that he needed better protectors than she. "You're not going to . . ."

"Kill you? No. You're trying to hide one of the last living members of Manhouch's extended family. You're not going to tell anyone about me anytime soon."

"I will," Nila said.

"Excuse me?"

"I will tell them. Unless you swear to protect Jakob."

"You're adorable."

"I'm serious."

"I'm sure you are." The Privileged bent and lifted one edge of the rug, tipping it upward against the wall and examining it for a moment as if figuring out the best way to get it back on his shoulders.

Nila felt numb. What would she do now? Sure, she could get ahold of some money, but what then? "Your rug is bleeding."

"So it is," the Privileged said, glancing at the dark stain soaking through the fabric. "I thought I cauterized those wounds."

A cold finger crept its way up Nila's spine. "Who is that?" she asked.

"Him? Some idiot named Vetal or something."

"Vetas?"

"Yeah. Him."

Nila stormed over to the rug and kicked it. Then again, then again.

The Privileged grabbed her by the arm, pulling her away. "He's unconscious," he said, "and I want him alive so that I can torture him some more. For information," he added.

Nila stumbled away from the rug and leaned up against the wall of the alley. She felt like she was going to be ill. Everything had been so clear in her mind as she'd escaped Vetas's grasp. Now it was full of questions. Part of her wanted to cry. She quelled the feeling and stared at the wall, trying to come up with some kind of plan.

She was surprised to find the Privileged still standing there a few moments later.

"Don't you have something to do with *that*?" she said, jerking her chin at the rug.

The Privileged stepped closer. Nila refused to step back.

"My name's Bo," he said.

Nila sniffed.

"Look, I won't keep the boy," Bo said. "I'm not in any position to protect him. I'm a hunted man myself. But I can give you two a few days of safety while you figure out what to do."

"Why?"

Bo chuckled. "Because you're brave enough to demand things of a Privileged on your own, and from what I gather, you know this fellow"—he tapped the rug with his toe—"and because you're rather attractive. A few days is all, though." He pulled a pencil and paper from his breast pocket and scribbled something on it. "I have to go put my rug into storage. Gather the boy and meet me at this address. For Kresimir's sake, make sure you're not followed."

CHAPTER
27

You have to hold still, sir."

Tamas resisted the urge to twitch away from Olem's needle. Olem had shaved the side of Tamas's head and cleaned the bullet gash with frigid mountain water and now he made tight stitches with catgut. The wound ran almost the entire length of the side of Tamas's head. It was an eerie feeling, knowing that had the path of the bullet been an inch to one side, it would have turned Tamas's head into a canoe.

"Sorry," Tamas muttered.

The air reeked of death as the corpses of thousands of men and horses stank in the midmorning sun. His soldiers had labored the entire rest of the day after the battle and all this morning in an effort to dig all the bodies from the trench. The men had been laid out, their kits and supplies stripped from them, while the horses were prepared for eating.

War may need decorum, but his army needed food and supplies.

The moans and cries of the wounded reached him. Both Kez and Adran were being treated to field surgery in an impromptu hospital. Neither army had a proper team of doctors beyond the rudimentary skills of soldiers who'd seen countless wounds.

Tamas watched as Gavril picked his way through the camp toward him.

All signs of the chaos and disorganization they'd used to lure in the Kez cavalry were gone. A team of engineers was hard at work making a proper bridge over the Big Finger. Cook fires everywhere smoked with horsemeat. Quartermasters took stock of supplies they'd stripped from both Kez and Adran dead. There were piles of boots, kits, blankets, and tents, along with rifles, ammunition, even powder horns and charges.

Gavril reached Tamas and sat down on the ground beside him. "General Cethal is dead."

Tamas bowed his head for a moment of silence, further frustrating Olem's attempts at stitching.

"I'm surprised he lasted this long," Tamas said. "Tough old dog. What reports?"

"Based on the bodies so far, we're guessing about two thousand dead on our side. Another three thousand wounded. About a quarter of those will join the dead within a week. Half our wounded are incapacitated."

Thirty-five hundred casualties to this battle. Over a fourth of Tamas's fighting force. It was a heavy blow.

"And the Kez?"

"Based on bodies alone, we can guess that only twenty-five hundred of them got away. The rest are either dead or captured."

Tamas let out a long breath. A decisive victory in anyone's book. Most of the enemy, including all of their high officers, either killed or captured.

"Give our boys a rest," Tamas said. "Any Kez who can stand, put him to work burying the bodies."

"What are we going to do with all these captives?" Gavril asked. "We can't take them with us. Pit, we can't even carry our own wounded—don't forget that Beon's brother is still coming on hard with thirty thousand infantry."

"When will he reach us?"

"Our prisoners are being sketchy about time frames, but piecing things together, I'd guess they are about a week behind us."

Close enough that if Tamas allowed himself to be slowed by wounded and prisoners, the Kez infantry would catch him before he could get to Deliv.

"How is Beon?"

"Asked to see you," Gavril said.

"Right. Olem?"

Olem wiped the needle off on his jacket. "All done, sir. Doesn't look pretty, but the stitches are tight. Try not to do any strenuous thinking in the near future."

Tamas held up a field mirror. "I look like a bloody invalid. Bring me my hat."

"It'll rub against the stitches."

"Wrap it in a handkerchief. I'm not going to parley with the enemy looking like this."

Olem wrapped Tamas's head, and Tamas gingerly sat his bicorne hat on top of it.

"How does it feel, sir?"

"Hurts like the bloody pit. Let's go see Beon."

Tamas let Gavril and Olem walk out in front of him as they crossed the camp. Gavril had come through the battle with little more than a black eye, while Olem had a tendency to ignore his own wounds. His left hand was wrapped tightly, and fresh blood soaked through his white shirt at the shoulder. "Olem, see to yourself," Tamas said as they neared the prisoners.

"I'm all right, sir," Olem said.

"That's an order."

Olem relented and limped back to camp. Tamas was sorry to see him go, but Olem needed rest and medical attention.

The prisoners had been put in a makeshift stockade overnight. They were bound hand and foot and watched over by the Seventh Brigade. The Ninth couldn't be trusted with prisoners right now— they'd taken the worst of it in the cuirassier charge, and most of them still wanted blood.

"Field Marshal to see General Beon," Gavril said to one of the guards. The man headed into the stockade. He emerged a few minutes later with Beon in tow.

The Kez general didn't look so well. His left arm was in a sling. Stitches on his forehead and the back of his right hand looked crooked and painful. He walked with a pronounced limp.

"General," Tamas said.

Beon gave him a weary nod. "Field Marshal. I should thank you for saving my life from your men yesterday."

"You are most welcome."

"Ah," Beon said. "I *should* thank you. But I won't." He let his head sag. "I don't know if I can live with the shame of such a defeat."

Gavril leaned against one of the wooden stakes that made the stockade. "Don't be so hard on yourself," Gavril said. "It's Tamas, after all."

Tamas suppressed his annoyance to keep it from reaching his face. "Deceit may not be a gentleman's tool, but in the end, victory is all that matters on the field of battle."

"Too true," Beon said. "The trench. It was well done. Dug and concealed, all in one afternoon. My scouts kept at bay, and that bit of fog concealed it completely. You played me, Field Marshal. You knew I'd order the charge when I saw you trying to cross the river."

Tamas allowed himself a small nod.

"Bravo," Beon said with a sigh. "What now? As you can see,

you've taken thousands of us hostage. We're hundreds of miles from the nearest city that might afford ransom. Thousands of both sides will die of improper treatment and disease within the next couple of weeks."

"I've sent a man to your camp and called for a parley," Tamas said. "I intend to ransom all of your soldiers and and most of your officers in exchange for food, supplies, and a promise of parole."

"Parole?" Beon seemed surprised. "As a man of honor, I must tell you that a great number of my officers will not adhere to the conditions of parole. The moment your prisoners are free of your hands, they will be set back to fighting you."

"As a man of honor, I expect you to tell me which of your highest officers are, in fact, men of honor."

Beon chuckled. "Ah. And those are the ones you will ransom back to the remnants of my army? I see. You realize, of course, that the honor will only stand until my brother catches up with his infantry, and relieves me and my officers of our command?"

"I do. And I never said I would ransom *you*."

Beon tilted his head to one side. "I can't imagine any use you would have for me. My presence will not prevent my brother from launching an attack when he catches you."

"Still. I'd rather you not be on the other side for the time being."

"You don't trust me not to break my parole?"

"It's not that, either. By the way, General Cethal sends his regards."

"He mounted a valiant defense. I've broken greater numbers of infantry with fewer cuirassiers. Tell him it was a fine stand."

"He's dead," Tamas said.

Beon lowered his head.

Someone cleared his throat. Tamas turned to find a messenger at his shoulder.

"Sir, the Kez are here for the parley."

"Of course. General Beon, if you will?"

The Kez had sent what remained of their officer corps. A colonel, five majors, and six captains. Tamas ran his eyes over them. The Kez retreat had been last-minute. Only two of the majors had wounds on them. That meant the rest had fled before even entering the melee.

The parley proceeded much as he expected. The Kez rattled their sabers and made demands, but in the end, they knew they were beaten. They traded powder and ammunition in exchange for having their surviving officers returned to them—with a few notable exceptions. Food, and information regarding how things went back in Adro, were exchanged in return for their soldiers.

"You cannot possibly think we will allow you to keep Beon je Ipille," the Kez colonel said. "He is third in line for the crown!"

"'Allow' me?" Tamas said. "It is I who am allowing you to leave with your lives. Almost four thousand men in exchange for road rations, information, and a shaky promise of parole? I'm the one being robbed. I'll keep General Beon until his father offers to trade safe passage back to Adro for his son's life. We will make the exchange of prisoners at first light tomorrow."

They exchanged information about the landscape in northern Kez and the position of the infantry brigades under Beon's brother. The Kez returned to their camp, noses raised, proud even in defeat.

"My father hates you," Beon said as they walked back to the Adran camp. "There isn't a chance in the pit he'd trade my life for those of your army. Especially after my failure here."

"I know." Tamas stopped and turned to Beon. "You will be accorded every respect due to a prisoner of your status. I expect your word of honor that you will not attempt to escape my camp and that you will not attempt to transfer information about the disposition of my army to your own. In exchange, you will be given a tent, full freedom of the camp, and the choice of any two menservants from your own army."

"I give my word of honor," Beon said.

"Very good."

Beon was escorted to the stockade to select his menservants, leaving Tamas alone with Gavril.

"You really trust him?" Gavril asked.

"Yes."

"Then why are you keeping him here?"

Tamas removed his hat and gingerly touched at the fresh stitches on his scalp. It would be months before the hair grew back properly to conceal the wound. In the meantime, he would look like some half-mad fool.

"He's the only one of Ipille's sons worth anything as a human being. I intend to return to Adro and throw back Ipille's army. According to them"—he jerked his head in the direction of the retreating Kez officers—"Ipille is personally in Adro. If I can manage to kill him and his two oldest sons, Beon will be king of Kez and he might actually listen to reason and help me end this war."

"Ah." Gavril scratched at his beard. "What else did you find out about Adro?"

"Last the Kez cavalry heard, Ipille had burned Budwiel and was slowly but steadily advancing up Surkov's Alley. Hilanska and the rest of the generals are holding fast with the help of the Wings of Adom. Supposedly, Kresimir himself is there, but he's not using his powers to aid the Kez army."

"I thought Kresimir was dead."

"That's not what the Kez think. After South Pike collapsed, Privileged Borbador told me that you can't kill a god."

"If he's alive," Gavril reasoned, "he probably wants whoever shot him in the face."

"I know," Tamas said. "We march tomorrow afternoon. I need to get back to Adro and put myself between the Kez army and my son. If Kresimir is alive, I'll make him wish he had been destroyed at South Pike."

*   *   *

Adamat stopped with his hand on the door to a decommissioned grain mill in the factory district of Adopest. He looked over his shoulder and tried to tell himself he was no longer at risk of being followed. Lord Vetas was captured, his men taken or scattered, Adamat's family now safe. He was being paranoid, he reasoned, and pushed the door in.

Or was he? He made his way past a secretary's desk, long empty and half-rotted, and past the millworkers' bunk rooms, which smelled like an animal had made a nest in them and then died.

Adamat had successfully blackmailed the Proprietor. Lord Vetas's master, Lord Claremonte, might have other spies in the city. And there was still the Kez army pushing its way north through Surkov's Alley.

Would Adamat and his family ever really be safe again?

He went through another door that led to the mill's main workroom. The room was several hundred feet long with over a dozen millstones placed at intervals along one wall. Most of them were either broken or missing completely, the machinery left to rot when the mill was abandoned. The sound of the river, over which this portion of the mill was suspended, filled the room.

Bo sat with his chair tilted back on two legs, leaning against the wall next to the door. Beside him, Fell held a pipe between her lips and stared at something in the distance. Her shirtsleeves were rolled up, and there were flecks of blood on her arms.

"You missed the morning's festivities," Bo said to Adamat.

"You call torturing a man 'festivities'?" Adamat asked.

"I'm not a good person," Bo said.

Adamat cast a glance over Bo's clothes. "You've blood on your shoes."

Bo swore, then licked his thumb and ran it over the top of one of his shoes.

"How is your wife?" Fell asked, taking the pipe from her mouth.

Adamat hesitated. "She has...had a rough time of things." That was as much of an understatement as Adamat had ever made. Faye had been beaten and abused. She'd cried for two days straight and wouldn't allow any of the children out of her sight for more than a few minutes. She grew from melancholy to cheerful and back again in seconds, but Adamat wouldn't expect anything different from someone who'd been through what she had. "She's strong," Adamat said. "She'll be fine."

Bo let his chair thump down onto four legs and stood up, stretching. "I'm happy to hear that."

Strangely enough, Bo sounded sincere. Privilegeds weren't known for their empathy.

"Hit me," Bo said to Fell.

A smile flickered across Fell's face. She reached into her pocket and withdrew a cashew, then tossed it in the air. Bo caught it in his mouth.

"I need to get back to Ricard," Fell said, gathering her bag of cashews and a leather satchel at her feet.

"Go on," Bo said. "We'll take it from here. It was good working with you this morning."

Adamat held up a hand. "A question."

"Yes?" Fell asked.

"Did either of you see a young woman or a boy after we vacated Vetas's manor?"

"The girl in the red dress?" Fell asked.

The one she'd let escape, along with Vetas, very nearly getting Faye killed? "Yes. Her."

Fell shook her head.

Bo hesitated a moment. "Maybe...no. No, I don't think I saw them."

"Pity," Adamat said. "Faye asked me to look for her. She was another prisoner of Vetas, and the boy may be a royal heir."

"I'll put my ear to the ground," Fell said. She gave them each a nod, her glance lingering on Bo, and then made her exit.

"How was the 'work' this morning?" Adamat asked after Fell had left.

"She's very good at putting a man to the question," Bo said, either missing or ignoring the innuendo in Adamat's tone. He cracked his knuckles and headed down the long line of millstones. "Not as good as I am, but then, I am a cabal Privileged." Bo glanced over his shoulder as if to be sure Fell was gone, then said, "Don't trust that woman."

"I wasn't planning on it."

"Good. She's loyal to Ricard and to her precious Academy. Nothing else. And I'm not even sure if she's more loyal to Ricard than she is to the Academy."

"I imagine she'd say the same thing to me about you," Adamat said.

"Oh," Bo said, "I don't think you should trust me, either. But you only have to deal with me for another couple of days. As soon as this Vetas business is cleaned up and I think your family is safe, I'm in the wind."

Bo led Adamat down the stairs at the end of the room and into the wheel room beneath the mill. For each of the millstones above them, there was a wheel down here with one end dipped in the water. Or at least, there used to be. Most of them were missing, leaving an empty channel of water flowing through one side of the floor.

Lord Vetas was strapped to an upright gurney in one corner. His arms were missing—of course, Bo had taken those off two days ago. A bloody blanket covered his body; likely more for Adamat's sake than for Vetas's. His eyes were closed, his breathing shallow.

Bo kicked the gurney and Vetas's eyes shot open. He immediately tried to recoil from Bo, but his bonds kept that from happening.

"You remember our friend Adamat?" Bo asked.

"Yes," Vetas whispered, not taking his eyes from Bo.

"He has a few questions. Answer them."

Adamat centered himself before his former tormentor and tried to force himself to remember what Vetas had done to his family. This pitiful creature before him didn't deserve pity or compassion.

"Where is my son?" Adamat asked.

"I don't know."

"What happened to him?"

"Sold him."

Adamat rocked back on his heels. "Sold him? What do you mean?"

"Slavers."

"There are no slavers in Adopest!"

A hideous giggle wormed its way up through Vetas's throat, only for him to swallow it when Bo took a step forward. "Kez smugglers," Vetas said, his voice still quiet. "Used to take powder mages out from under Tamas's nose and send them in to Kez."

"My boy is not a powder mage," Adamat said.

Vetas blinked back at him. His eyes, once serpentine and unfeeling, were now just...dead, was the only way to describe them. They showed fear when they glanced toward Bo, but other than that, nothing.

"Why would you sell him to the Kez?"

"My Privileged said he was a powder mage."

Adamat began to pace. Josep, a Marked? That seemed impossible. "How long ago?"

"A week."

"Have they taken him from the country?" Adamat felt his chest tighten as he began to panic. Smugglers dealing in human beings—especially powder mages—wouldn't wait to get their cargo out of the country. In all likelihood, Josep was gone already, far beyond Adamat's reach.

"I'd imagine," Vetas said.

"What do they want them for?" Adamat said. "The Kez don't want powder mages alive. They've no need for smugglers. They use assassins."

"Experimentation," Vetas said.

"What do you mean?"

"I don't know. Just a guess."

"Where can I find them?"

Vetas looked away for a moment. Adamat stepped forward menacingly. There was no fear in Vetas's eyes. Not until Bo began to rub his thumb and forefinger together.

"A pub near the waterfront," Vetas said, his eyes twitching toward the water flowing through the mill trough.

A pub, eh? Probably not more than half a mile from this very place. "Tell me everything," Adamat said.

He questioned Vetas for half an hour, getting the names of contacts, locations, and passwords. He had to be thorough. Slavers in a place as civilized as Adopest tended to operate in utmost secrecy, and would have taken dozens of precautions.

Adamat finished his questions and headed immediately toward the door. He couldn't get away from Vetas fast enough. The man revolted him. He'd taken Adamat's wife and children and put them through unspeakable trials. He'd plotted against Adro, and he'd dealt with the lowliest of scum.

Bo jogged to catch up with Adamat as he climbed the stairs back to the mill's main floor.

"You didn't ask him anything else," Bo said.

"I don't need to know anything else."

"Claremonte's plans? His designs on Adro? You don't want to know all that?"

Adamat stopped and turned to the Privileged. "Later. I have to get my son back."

"It's too late. If slavers have him, he'll be out of the country by now."

"How would you know?" Adamat demanded.

"Common sense," Bo said. "And remember. The royal cabal was a dark place. Dealing with slaves was one of many things they did."

"Bah!" Adamat strode toward the front of the mill.

Bo kept up, much to his annoyance. "We've been questioning Vetas for two days. Claremonte is planning something big. Not even Vetas knows it all, but Claremonte might even have plans of invasion!"

"And I suppose you're going to help stop him?"

Bo's silence made Adamat sigh. The Privileged had no interest in helping. He'd probably leave the country now that his debt to Adamat was paid. It seemed that Bo had just enough civic sense of duty to try to convince Adamat to help stop Claremonte.

"Even Vetas said that your son would be gone by now," Bo said.

"And you trust him? That's awfully naïve for a cabal Privileged."

Bo leaned in toward Adamat. "I *broke* him," he said in words that were nearly a growl. "He wouldn't dare lie to me."

"It was too easy," Adamat said. "I know what type of man Vetas is. He's keeping something back."

Doubt flickered across Bo's face, then resolved itself in a scowl. "No. He won't. He can't. Like I said, I broke him."

"You should keep at it." Adamat's stomach twisted at the words. This kind of torture made him sick. Even when applied to Lord Vetas. "There's no telling what else he has in that head of his."

"He'll be dead within hours," Bo said.

"Ricard's orders?" Perhaps Ricard thought Vetas was too much of a liability to keep alive for long. If Claremonte managed to find and rescue him, the following wrath would be terrible indeed.

"I don't take orders from Ricard. No, nature will finish what I started. It's taken what little knowledge I have of healing to keep him alive. I tore his arms off, and then spent the last two days questioning him. You think he'll live long? No. By nightfall I'm throwing his corpse into the Adsea and getting the pit out of this country."

"Well, then." Adamat took a deep breath and smoothed the front of his coat. Here he was, back to square one. All his allies were gone. The Proprietor had cut off contact. Ricard was busy dealing with the fallout of Vetas's capture, and Bo was leaving the country. Adamat was alone again. "I guess this is good-bye."

Bo tugged at the fingers of his right glove and pulled it off. He extended his hand. "Thank you."

"No," Adamat said, clasping the hand. He felt his heart skip a beat. Privileged did not shake hands with anyone. Not ever. "Thank you."

Bo headed back toward the mill basement. Adamat watched him go, hoping that perhaps he'd change his mind and stay in the country. Maybe he'd even help Adamat rescue Josep. But after a moment Bo disappeared downstairs.

Adamat headed into the street. This would be difficult. Maybe, just maybe, he had one friend left in Adopest.

Adamat paused on his doorstep and looked through the front window.

The blinds were drawn, but through the cracks he could see the twins playing on the rug in the living room. One of them had a wooden boat. The other one wanted it, and pushed the first over, snatching for the toy.

Adamat felt a smile tug at the corner of his mouth. They'd been through so much, but they still played and argued like regular children. He'd expected them to be worse for the wear after their ordeals. Fanish, his oldest daughter, shouted from the back room, and a moment later she entered and separated the two, then berated them soundly.

He pushed the door open and stepped inside. It didn't take long for all the children to mob him as they all sought for a hug or a kiss. He knelt and let them fawn over him. Felt the relief to have them back home. He never would have thought he'd welcome the shouting and shoving after a long day of walking the street... but he finally had his family back.

The smile slid from his face. No sign of Faye.

"Where's your mother?" Adamat asked Fanish, gently prying Astrit off his leg.

"She's in bed, Papa."

"Has she been down today?" Fanish looked at the younger children and shook her head. She was old enough to know her mother had been through a lot, and to notice readily that she was acting strange. She was also smart enough to want to keep the other children from worrying.

Adamat took his daughter aside. "Has she eaten?"

"No."

"What did you have for dinner?"

"Soup. It's still over the fire."

"Where'd it come from?"

"Ricard's assistant brought it by. Enough for three days for the whole family."

"Fell?"

"Her. Yes."

Adamat's fists tightened. The woman who almost cost Adamat his wife by letting Vetas escape. He'd never forget that. He stopped himself from getting worked up. This was no time to hold a grudge. "Get me a bowl of soup."

He set his cane next to the front door and hung up his hat, then took the soup from his daughter and headed upstairs. In their bedroom, Faye was lying with her back to the door, blankets pulled up around her shoulders even though it was summer and the house was quite warm.

"Faye," he said gently.

No response.

He went around to her side of the bed and sat gently on the edge. He could see the rise and fall of her shoulders as she breathed softly. Her eyes were closed, but long intimacy told him she was still awake.

"Love," he said, "you need to eat something."

Again, no response.

"Sit up," he said. "You need to eat."

"You didn't take your boots off." Her voice was quiet and timid. Not at all the scolding brashness that he was used to, and that worried him.

"I'm sorry, I'll sweep up. You need to eat now."

"I'm not hungry."

"You haven't eaten all day."

"I did."

"I talked to Fanish."

She was lying to him, and now she knew that he knew. "Oh."

"You have to keep up your strength."

"Why?" She pulled the blanket tighter around her shoulders.

"For the children. For me. For yourself."

Faye didn't say anything. Adamat could see tears rolling down her cheeks, her eyes squeezed closed. He put a hand gently on her arm. Didn't she know she was safe now? Couldn't she tell that the children needed her more than ever? That *he* needed her?

"I'm going to find Josep," he said.

Her eyes opened. "You know where he is?"

"I have a lead."

"What is it?"

Adamat patted her arm and stood. "Nothing to worry about. I'll be back late tonight, though."

There was a knock on the door downstairs, and Faye shifted around in the bed, her movements jerking, her eyes wide and wild.

"It's just SouSmith," Adamat said, trying to calm her. "He's going with me."

"What is this lead? Where is my boy?" Faye demanded.

"It's nothing to—"

She grabbed him by the arm, her grip vice-like. "Tell me."

Adamat sank back onto the bed. He didn't want to worry her, but it seemed it couldn't be helped. "Vetas sold him to Kez slavers. Supposedly, Josep is a powder mage. I'm going to go meet with the slavers and try to get him back."

"No," Faye said, surprising Adamat with the force of the word. "You'll do no such thing. You've already scraped through so much danger. I'll not wait here for word of your death."

"I've dealt with worse than slavers," Adamat said.

"I know the type of men Vetas did... *business* with." Faye spat the word. There was panic in her eyes. Adamat could see that her desire to get her son back was warring with the need to protect her husband and her remaining children.

"I have to get Josep back. I won't leave him to the Kez."

Faye squeezed his arm tighter. "Be careful."

"I will." Adamat extricated himself from Faye's grip as gently as he could. Tears were streaming down her face as he left the room and headed down the stairs. SouSmith stood in the front hall, coat buttoned tight, smiling at the children playing in the living room.

The boxer nodded to Adamat. "Ready?"

"Yes." Adamat glanced up the stairs to his bedroom and took his cane from beside the door. "Fanish, check on your mother in a half hour or so."

"Yes, Papa."

"Good girl. SouSmith, let's go."

CHAPTER

28

"Everything OK?" SouSmith asked as they took a hackney cab away from Adamat's home. The evening air was warm and windy. Adamat decided there would be a storm tomorrow.

"Fine," Adamat said.

SouSmith didn't seem to believe him, cocking an eyebrow.

"Fine!" Adamat said, louder.

SouSmith nodded to himself and settled against the side of the hackney cab.

Adamat looked out the window and watched the people going about their nightly errands. There was a small boy on the corner, trying to sell the last of his newspapers, and an older couple out for a stroll before it turned dark. Adamat wondered if they had any inkling of what was going on in their city. The chaos. The war.

He wondered if they cared.

Night was falling when the hackney cab dropped Adamat and

SouSmith off two blocks from the dockside pub called The Salty Maiden. Adamat could see the beaten sign, rocking in the wind from its post. What a stupid name. The Adsea wasn't salt water.

He checked the snub-nosed pistols in his pocket while SouSmith did the same. The boxer frowned during their preperations, not looking at Adamat.

"Sorry," Adamat said when he was ready to go.

"Eh?"

"I didn't mean to snap at you," Adamat said. "You're a good man. A good friend, for coming with me to do this. It could be very dangerous."

SouSmith grunted. "You still paying me, ain't you?"

"Yes."

The boxer nodded, as if it were a matter of course that he'd come with, but his frown dissolved.

They headed toward the pub, and Adamat listened to the click of his cane on the cobbles, then on the wood as they entered the boardwalk. This pub was out on the pier—a bad location. Only one exit, though no doubt smugglers had a boat hidden underneath for a quick getaway.

Not the ideal place to confront slavers.

Adamat pushed the door open and was met with silence.

A half-dozen sailors lounged around the dimly lit, one-room building. Not a mean-looking lot. Most of them were young men in their prime wearing white cotton shirts, open at the chest, and knee-length trousers. They all blinked at Adamat as if he were a three-eyed fish.

Acting inconspicuous was out of the question.

Adamat sidled up to the bar, while SouSmith leaned up against the door frame, taking in the sailors with his piggish eyes. Adamat slid a fifty-krana note across the bar. "I'm looking for Doles," he said.

The barkeep's expression didn't change. "I'm Doles. What'll you have?"

"Brudanian whiskey, if you have it," he said.

Doles, who was dressed like an ordinary sailor—and probably was—took the banknote and stuffed it in his pocket. He reached beneath the bar, not taking his eyes off Adamat, and brought up a decanter of dark liquid. He slammed it on the bar with enough force to make Adamat jump, then poured a shot into a small, dirty cup.

"Bad season for it," Doles said.

The script was just as Vetas had said. Adamat's mouth was dry, and he had to concentrate to keep his hand from shaking as he reached out and took the glass of whiskey in one hand. "Never a bad season for Brudanian whiskey," he replied.

Adamat had had a cudgel pulled on him enough times to know the signs. Dole's wrist twitched behind the bar. A moment later his hand came up, cocked back and swinging a piece of polished wood the length of a man's forearm.

Adamat drew his pistol with his left hand and raised his right to grab Doles's wrist, arresting the swing of the cudgel.

"I think we should settle down," Adamat said, his pistol aimed at the barkeep's nose.

Doles didn't even blink. "Yes. We should."

Adamat blanched. He felt the cold barrel of a pistol touch the back of his neck, and his hackles went up.

"Drop it," Doles said.

Adamat rolled his tongue around his parched gums. His heart hammered in his ears. "I die, you die," he said.

"I'll take the risk." Doles didn't seem concerned.

The pistol barrel pressed harder against the back of his neck. Adamat slowly lowered his own pistol and set it on the bar. Doles picked it up and unloaded it. "Kill them, dump the bodies out beyond the breakers."

Adamat felt rough hands grab him by the arms. He was pulled around to see SouSmith receiving similar treatment. Three of the sailors held him, knives drawn to his throat, while two others man-handled Adamat down to his knees.

"Don't do it here," Doles said with some annoyance, gesturing to the sailors. "I don't want blood on me floorboards. Do it downstairs."

"I'm here about a boy," Adamat said as he was shoved toward one corner of the room.

Doles didn't answer him.

"Someone you smuggled into Kez," Adamat said.

A rug was pulled back to reveal a trapdoor. SouSmith began to struggle violently, and one of the men holding Adamat joined the other three to wrestle SouSmith toward the corner.

"Vetas is dead!" Adamat said.

The sailor stopped pushing him toward the trapdoor. Adamat jerked away from his grip and faced Doles, who was holding up one hand.

"Dead? Really?"

"Yes," Adamat said. "We took him and his men, and Vetas is dead."

Doles sighed. "Damn it. We'll have to move again." He twitched his head, and Adamat was grabbed and pushed. Adamat tried to struggle, but the sailor was far stronger than he. His cane had been lost by the bar, and his hat knocked off. He snagged a handful of the sailor's hair and fought back.

Doles walked around the bar and watched the struggle impassively. "Either up here or down there," Doles said. "Don't make no difference to me. 'Cept I'll have to clean the blood up if you die here." He paused. "Well, we're moving anyway. Guess it doesn't matter."

"He's my son!" Adamat said. "Please, I just want him back. Don't you have children?"

"Nope," Doles said, leaning against the bar. He seemed amused by the struggle between SouSmith and his sailors.

"A father? You had a father! Please!"

"I did," Doles said. "Bastard and a drunk. Woulda killed him myself had he not fallen off a dock and drowned."

Adamat stepped back, and his foot touched air as he fell into the trapdoor. He snagged one arm on the ladder leading down beneath the pier, and the other on the floor. A sailor stomped on his hand, and Adamat let out a yell.

"I'll pay you!" Adamat said. "For my boy, I'll pay to get him back."

Doles chuckled. "You can't afford it."

"A hundred thousand krana. In cash!"

Doles's eyebrows climbed his forehead. "Well. Let up, boys." He stepped forward and kicked the sailor still grinding his heel into Adamat's fingers. "I said, let up!"

The sailor stepped away from Adamat, and the others ceased wrestling with SouSmith. The moment they'd loosened their hold, SouSmith grabbed one by the face and picked him off the floor, tossing him through the window. There was a strangled scream and a splash.

"Let up!" Doles bellowed.

SouSmith froze, a snarl on his face, the arm of a sailor grasped between two hands as if he was ready to snap a twig.

Doles glanced out the broken window, then frowned at Sou-Smith. "A strong bugger," he muttered. Louder, "Three hundred thousand," Doles said. "That's the price for your boy."

"Three hundred...?"

"Take it or leave it," Doles said. "And by 'leave it' I mean we'll kill you now."

Adamat felt his mouth work soundlessly. Even with the money Bo had given him, he didn't have three hundred thousand krana. He'd have to borrow from Ricard.

"I'll do it."

Doles seemed skeptical, but he spit in his hand and reached down. Adamat took the offered handshake and choked down a scream when Doles gripped his freshly crushed hand and squeezed. Doles lifted him out of the hole, stronger than Adamat would have expected.

"What's his name?" Doles asked.

"Josep."

"Ah, I remember him. Stubborn lad." Doles's face soured. "He's already in Norpoint."

Norpoint was the only Kez harbor on the Adsea, far to the south. Adamat felt his heart skip a beat. If Josep was already in Norpoint...

Doles said, "It'll take me about six days to go down and get him back. I'll have to grease some palms. The Kez never like losing a powder mage they thought they had under wraps," Doles mused out loud, speaking for all the world as if this was a business meeting, and he hadn't just been about to have Adamat killed.

"Fifty thousand tomorrow," Doles said. "Here, before sunup. Then two hundred and fifty when I get back from Norpoint."

"And then?"

"We'll meet at The Flaming Cuttlefish," Doles said. "It's a pub close by."

"I know it."

"Good."

Adamat nursed his crushed hand and hoped that none of the fingers were broken. It would certainly be stiff in the morning.

"How can I trust you?" he asked.

Doles made an openhanded gesture. "You can't. Want your boy back?"

"Yes."

"Then this is your only chance."

Adamat examined the man. A slaver. Nothing respectable or trustworthy about him. He had an honest face, though Adamat found that honest faces were almost always deceptive. "I'll be back here in a few hours with the money."

"I'll see you then," Doles said. He gestured to the door. They were dismissed.

The sailor SouSmith had thrown through the window suddenly stuck his head up through the trapdoor. His face was bloody from the glass, his clothes and hair soaked, silt on one shoulder. "I'll kill you!" he screamed at SouSmith, hefting himself up through the trapdoor.

Doles tripped the man on his mad dash toward SouSmith, then set a boot on the sailor's backside. He waved good-bye to Adamat, then said to his man, "Stay down, or I'll let the big one tear you apart."

Outside, SouSmith turned a sneer toward the pub.

"That could have gone better," Adamat said. "Then again...it could have gone worse."

SouSmith's sneer slowly left his face. "Yeah. You need me to come back with ya?"

"Yes. Yes, I think that would be a good idea."

"I'll be ready for 'em next time," SouSmith said, and for a moment he looked as if he considered going back in and killing the lot.

Adamat looked the big man over. He didn't seem worse for the wear. His shirt had ripped. Not many people get the drop on SouSmith.

"I'm sure," Adamat said. "Let's go get the money."

Taniel sat in a chair in the middle of the tent, his hands clasped in irons and his legs shackled. There wasn't an ounce of powder anywhere within fifty feet of the command tent, and above all the cautions that the General Staff had taken with his arrest, that concerned him the most. They were being careful with him. Too damned careful.

He was flanked by a pair of provosts. Two more stood behind

him, and another four were at the back of the command tent. Each man held a truncheon at the ready and was eyeing him like he was some kind of dangerous degenerate.

The tent was barren, austere. There were a dozen chairs in the back, most of them empty, and at the front a table with five places—one for each of the senior General Staff of the Adran army.

Taniel inspected the tent with a quick glance. Colonels Doravir and Bertthur were seated just behind him. Bertthur's broken jaw was held in place by a linen tied around his head. To Taniel's surprise, Brigadier Abrax, the senior commander of the Wings of Adom, sat near the tent flap. What interest could she have in these proceedings?

In the back corner, Colonel Etan sat in his wheeled chair, nodding encouragement. Taniel forced a confident smile he didn't feel. No one else had come to support him.

Then again, perhaps they wouldn't let anyone else in the tent.

This was, after all, a court-martial.

Cloth whispered as the front of the tent parted and the generals filed in. Everyone stood. The provosts grasped Taniel roughly beneath the arms and pulled him to his feet, the chains on his ankles nearly making him trip and fall.

Generals Ket and Hilanska were the only two Taniel recognized. He should know more of the senior staff than this, shouldn't he? Or had Ket stacked the cards against him by selecting new generals to serve on the jury? Taniel tried to meet Hilanska's eye, but the one-armed general kept his gaze on the floor, a scowl on his face. This didn't bode well.

The generals sat, and Taniel was allowed back in his chair. General Ket took the middle seat, scratching furiously at the stub of her missing ear. Her eyes traveled about the tent for a moment and then came to rest on Taniel. She gave a slight shake of her head, like a prison warden denying parole.

"This court-martial is in session," Ket said. "I will be presiding.

As you all know, this is a time of war. In such cases, Adran military law allows us to proceed with a drumhead court-martial. No prosecutor or defensive council was consulted. An investigation was carried out swiftly and privately over the course of the last seven days, and now, according to Adran military law, we will determine guilt and sentencing."

Taniel heard the tent flap at the back of the room part, and the sounds of the camp outside grew momentarily louder before the flap was closed again.

A frown passed over Ket's face at what she saw. Taniel thought about turning around, but Ket was still speaking.

"We've lost eight miles of ground and over three thousand men over the last seven days due directly to the chaos caused by Captain Taniel and his proclamation that Field Marshal Tamas is still alive, and that the General Staff is in league with the enemy. Captain Taniel is accused of fomenting rebellion among the ranks. The charge: treason. Does the accused enter a plea?"

"Not guilty," Taniel said. He knew the customs of the court. This was standard procedure—or at least, that's what Colonel Etan had told him, and Etan had studied military law at the university. Taniel couldn't help the feeling, however, that everything was going to go against him.

General Ket went on to read another dozen charges, including insubordination and assaulting a superior officer. Taniel responded with "not guilty" to every charge.

There was a clink of silverware behind him, and General Ket scowled. Taniel turned around to find Mihali passing out small plates to everyone sitting in the back—even to the provosts. Mihali came to the front with a stack of plates balanced on his arm and began to set them on the general's table.

"Provosts," Ket said, "remove this man."

"Oh, it's just refreshments," Mihali scolded, bringing a plate to Taniel. "Wine cake sprinkled with chocolate shavings and a touch of pepper powder. There will be hot coffee outside after the court-martial." His back to the generals, Mihali winked at Taniel.

None of the provosts had responded to Ket's command. They were too busy eating.

Taniel couldn't quite muster the strength to smile. He took a proffered slice of cake and tasted a bite, his chains clinking, and found it absolutely perfect. When everyone had finished, Mihali gathered the plates and retreated to the back of the tent.

Ket's cake remained untouched. "The investigation has concluded and the evidence has been presented to the judges, each of whom has made his or her own private determination. On the charge of treason, how do we find?"

"Guilty."

"Not guilty," General Hilanska said.

Ket stared into Taniel's eyes. "Guilty."

"Guilty."

"Guilty."

Taniel felt as if the bottom of his stomach had dropped out.

Ket went on. "By a majority, the defendant is found guilty of treason. The court-martial has reached its verdict. The penalty for treason is death by firing squad."

"That won't work on a powder mage," Mihali said helpfully from somewhere in the back.

"Silence in the court!" Ket pounded her gavel on the table.

"I'm not allowed to speak for myself?" Taniel demanded. "To address these idiotic charges?"

Ket sneered. "Were you or were you not given a full briefing by Colonel Etan on how a wartime court-martial is carried out?"

"I was."

"Then you'll know that you are not permitted to speak. Another outburst like that and I'll have you removed."

Taniel bit his tongue. Removed from his own trial? This was a load of buggery!

"In the case of a powder mage," Ket said, "the execution will be carried out by hanging."

General Hilanska leaned over to Ket and whispered something in her ear. She nodded slowly. Ket took a deep breath, as if collecting herself.

"I've been remiss by jumping to the inevitable conclusion of this court. The judges will now retire in order to discuss the sentencing of the guilty party. Court is in recess for one hour." The generals stood.

"May I speak to the court?"

General Ket paused, about to exit the back, and frowned past Taniel's shoulder. "This is a military court. I do not know who you are, ma'am, but civilians are not permitted."

"It will just take a moment. My name is Fell, undersecretary of the Noble Warriors of Labor and personal assistant to Ricard Tumblar. I am here to speak on behalf of Mr. Tumblar."

Taniel turned in his seat. Fell stood at the back of the room. She wore a tan suit jacket and sharply pressed shirt and trousers, her hands tucked casually into the pockets of her vest.

"Absolutely not," Ket said. "Provosts, remove this woman."

The gendarmes had no qualms about heading toward Fell.

"General Ket!" Fell said loudly. "This man who you seem so eager to sentence to death for the love of his country is in the running for second chair to the first prime minister of Adro!"

"Politics has no place in the Adran military," Ket said. The provosts paused, unsure as to whether to remove Fell now that Ket was facing her directly.

"Captain Taniel Two-Shot is a military hero on two continents," Fell said. "You might eschew politics, but you will destroy popular opinion of this war and of your command if the captain is executed."

"I don't care for public opinion. Leave this court."

"General Ket," Fell said emphatically, "if Taniel Two-Shot is executed, the factories will shut down in protest. Replacement boots, uniforms, buttons, musket kits, shirts, and hats will stop coming to the front. Hrusch Avenue will cease to produce rifles and muskets. The newspapers will make sure every single soul in Adopest knows that Taniel Two-Shot, hero of Adro, son of the supposedly late, and most definitely great Field Marshal Tamas, has been executed on trumped-up charges."

"Are you threatening me, Miss...?"

"Fell."

"Fell." Ket rounded the table and crossed the room, gesturing to the provosts. "Are you threatening this war effort?"

Fell put a hand to her chest in shock. "Me? Threaten you? By Kresimir, General Ket, I would never think to threaten you. After all, I can see Taniel's face right there, tenderized like a side of beef by your provosts. I wouldn't want to end up like that. No, I am merely providing context for the consequences of the decision of this court."

"Your master controls the unions. Therefore, you're threatening me."

"No." Fell waggled her finger like a parent scolding a child. "My master heads the unions. The unions have the power to strike, and Mr. Tumblar cannot stop them if they so desire. Do you want that to happen?"

Ket leaned in toward Fell. To her credit, the undersecretary did not so much as flinch.

"This court is in recess for one hour!" Ket whirled and stormed out of the tent, followed by the other generals.

Fell dragged a chair up to the middle of the room. She waved her hand at the provosts flanking Taniel, and they hesitantly took a step back. Fell deposited the chair beside Taniel and sat down.

Taniel studied Fell for a moment. She was dressed sharply, looking far more a businesswoman than an undersecretary or personal assistant. Her eyes, though, were tired, and Taniel could see a recent scar on her cheek covered by a layer of face powder. She reached into her pocket and removed a brown bag. "Cashew?"

Taniel didn't know what to make of the woman. She, and her master, could have very well just saved Taniel's life...but a man like Ricard always had his price.

"You're going to owe Ricard a great deal if you live through this," Fell said in a low voice.

And there it was. "I didn't ask for his help."

"No, but he gave it. You're an honorable man, aren't you, Taniel?"

The idea of owing Ricard Tumblar anything made Taniel's stomach turn.

"What's Ricard's price?"

"Three years," Fell said. "As a politician. You'll be expected to attend galas and address the public. Everything will be scheduled for you. When you're not in the public eye, you can do anything you want—bed whomever, smoke all the mala in the world. Not a hard life at all." Fell shrugged. "But if Ricard happens to die or be killed, you'll have to step up as prime minister of Adro."

"I don't want that."

Fell gave him a tight smile. "Then you're more qualified for the job than Ricard is."

Taniel wondered if that was something that Ricard himself would have said, or if the undersecretary had just made a jab at her master.

"I thought that Hrusch Avenue hadn't unionized." Taniel glanced meaningfully toward the tent flap where the generals had exited.

"*They* don't know that."

"Is Ricard serious about those threats?"

"I'd rather not find out."

A bluff, then. Taniel had to give credit to Ricard. Bluffing the senior staff of the Adran army took courage. "Has Ricard ever tried blackmailing Tamas?"

"Oh, pit no. Tamas would have strung Ricard up like a marionette."

"I'm glad to hear he has limits."

The hour-long recess for the court stretched into two hours, and then into three. Mihali served coffee and another round of cake.

Taniel couldn't help wondering where the pit the generals had gotten to. What could be taking them so long?

"This is a good thing, you know," Fell said between bites of cake.

Colonel Etan, his chair wheeled up beside Taniel, agreed. "At this point, the sentencing requires a four-out-of-five vote. If they'd returned at the hour, or earlier, it would not have looked good for you. They've been arguing this whole time, which means that more generals than just General Hilanska are trying to save your skin."

The tent flap was swept aside, and the generals reentered the room. Fell and Etan both retreated to the back, and the generals took their chairs.

Ket examined Taniel for several moments before speaking. The anger had left her eyes. Steely determination replaced it. "This court," she said, "has found the defendant guilty of treason. We have decided to drop the remainder of the charges and commute upon the guilty one sentence, to be carried out immediately:

"Captain Taniel is hereby stripped of his rank in the Adran army and dishonorably discharged. As this is a closed court, the verdict is private—however much I'd like to announce to the world that Taniel is no longer one of us, he will be allowed twelve hours to gather his things and quietly leave the camp. Any failure to do so will be met with swift reprisal. Court is adjourned."

Taniel could hear Doravir protesting from the back that the sentence was too light. Etan loudly argued that the sentence was too harsh. The provosts released Taniel from the irons and stripped him out of his uniform jacket.

He didn't argue. He couldn't argue. He barely noticed when the generals had left.

How could they do this to him? After all he'd done? All he'd given?

"Taniel."

He looked up. Etan sat in front of him, an orderly waiting to wheel him off.

"Taniel, you know I don't believe any of this treason garbage. None of them do either. If they did, they'd have executed you, regardless of Tumblar's threats. They just wanted you out of the way. If there's anything you need, just let me know. I have a house in North Umpshire if you need someplace quiet to recover. Bring the girl if you'd like."

Ka-poel. Taniel let out a shaky sigh. What should he do with Ka-poel? Send her back to Fatrasta? Would she even go?

"Thanks," Taniel said.

It was some time before he realized that the tent was empty. Fell was gone. It occurred to him that he should have asked her if Ricard received his letter regarding the missing gunpowder.

Taniel managed to climb to his feet. His legs shook, and he wondered where he could get some mala. No. Not mala. He needed powder. That would be easier to find anyway. He had to gather his things. What did he even have? His sketchbook and charcoals. The rifle wasn't even his—army issued, though he might be able to slip off with it anyway. He could sell the buttons off his army jacket.

Taniel cursed. The provosts had taken his jacket.

He cursed again when he noticed the tent was not, in fact, empty.

Mihali sat at the back, sipping a cup of coffee. He met Taniel's glance with the slight rise of his eyebrows.

Taniel wondered what it would be like to punch a god. "Did you see that, you bastard?" Taniel said. "'Apologize to Doravir.' That's what you told me. 'Save the war.' How the pit does this save anything? Stripped of everything I know?"

"The future is always changing," Mihali said. "Coffee?"

"Go to the pit."

Taniel left the command tent and headed toward his quarters. He wasn't two dozen steps outside when he was joined by Brigadier Abrax. It only took him a few moments to realize why she was there.

"Do the Wings of Adom usually perch at a court-martial, waiting to recruit new mercenaries?"

Brigadier Abrax was a serious woman in her forties, with short blond hair and a sharp white-and-red uniform. "Awfully full of yourself, Two-Shot. I can see why Ket wanted to be rid of you. What makes you think I've come along recruiting?"

"Nothing. Sorry, ma'am." Taniel reminded himself that he was not in a position to insult the senior commander of the best mercenary army in the world.

"I have, of course," Abrax said. "Come recruiting, that is. I want to offer you a spot in the Wings of Adom."

Taniel had never thought highly of mercenaries. At best, they took your money and did everything they could to avoid actually fighting. However, he had to grudgingly admit that the Wings had a reputation for slogging into the melee along with the ordinary infantry. He'd seen them do it himself during this war.

Taniel stopped and turned to the brigadier. "The General Staff would be furious."

"What do I care?" Abrax said. "I don't report to anyone but Lady Winceslav and Tamas. Not to the General Staff. Besides, I just watched them court-martial their best soldier. I don't have a lot of faith in their ability to do anything right. Even if you are a pompous ass with no respect for authority, you're worth fifty men, and I mean to see you in my army."

"That was an incredibly backhanded compliment," Taniel said.

Abrax gave him a shallow smile. "I meant every word."

"Ricard Tumblar seems to think he's bought me."

"If you feel as if you must repay him," Abrax said with a shrug, "feel free to do so. But after this war is over. I have the feeling you would much rather be on the front than in Adopest trying to win over the snakes in politics. At least here you're allowed to shoot your enemies."

Taniel looked around the camp. It was muddy and chaotic, the moans of the wounded rising from the field hospitals and the crack of gunfire drifting back from the front. Still, he couldn't imagine leaving it for a desk or a podium in Adopest.

"What do you propose?" he asked.

"You'll be a major in the Wings of Adom with full pay and benefits. I'll place you outside the chain of command and you'll only report to me. Your sole mission will be to kill enemy Privileged and Wardens. I don't like to complicate things further than that."

"And the other brigadiers will agree to this?"

"They love the idea," Abrax said. She leaned toward him. "Tamas recently stole one of our very best. He did it fairly, I think, but it still stung. The brigadiers consider this revenge."

Taniel examined Abrax. She seemed sincere. Tamas had had nothing but good things to say about the Wings, and being in a mercenary company was certainly preferable to having to sit out the rest of the war.

"Who did Tamas steal?"

"A young brigadier by the name of Sabastenien," Abrax said.

The name rang a bell, but Taniel could not give it a face.

"How long do you want me in the Wings?"

"Until the end of the war. We disband between assignments. You'll be paid in full and disbanded, with the option to muster for our next assignment."

"Ka-poel?"

Abrax frowned. "Your savage?"

"Yes."

"Bring her with if you want. I don't care who you're bedding. I put on a good front, but I'm not a prude."

"I'm not sleeping with her. She accompanies me on the battle-field as my spotter."

Abrax seemed to mull this over for a few moments. "I can't promise any more than a private's wages for her."

"Oh, ah..." Taniel almost stepped back. No one had even considered actually *paying* Ka-poel in the Adran army. "That sounds fair."

"We have a deal?"

"I think so."

"Report to our camp in two hours," she said. "We'll get you bedded down in temporary quarters and then outfit you in the morning. I want you on the field killing Kez by noon tomorrow."

CHAPTER
29

Tamas climbed from his bedroll. He paused once, taking a deep breath.

"Getting old," he muttered.

Every morning his limbs ached a little more, especially his leg. Every day it took him just another couple of seconds to climb from the bed. Worse now, sleeping on the hard ground. Every night for the last five weeks.

Five weeks. Hard to believe it had only been that long since he'd faced the Kez Grand Army, planning how he'd take them from the side and smash them against the gates of Budwiel. Bloody stupid, now that he looked back on it, thinking he could take the entire Grand Army with two brigades.

His arrogance got him into this. Had he been there, manning the walls beside Hilanska and the rest, they would have fought off those Wardens and sent the Kez army to the pit.

Tamas got to his feet. He pulled on his shirt, long since yellowed and stained with blood—his own blood, and that of others—then on came his uniform pants and boots. Olem had polished the boots during the night, like he did every night. He understood that a field marshal needed to keep up appearances. Finally, Tamas put on his jacket, and he stepped out into the morning air with his bicorne tucked under one arm.

Gavril stared down at him from on horseback. Somehow, he kept that Watchmaster's vest of his immaculate. His pants were ripped and stained, his arms and shoulders covered with powder burns, nicks, and cuts, but the faded colors of the Watchmaster's vest showed no wear but that of time and washing.

Gavril had Tamas's charger saddled and ready, and held the reins out to Tamas.

"I'm not going on some bloody jaunt with you," Tamas said.

"Then why are you dressed?" Gavril looked around the camp. No one had stirred yet. Tamas let them off easy the last couple of days, sleeping until past eight in the morning. They'd earned their rest, and with the Kez cavalry broken, their remnants sworn to leave Tamas be, and the infantry still a week off, Tamas could afford to give his men some slack.

"The army is marching today," Tamas said.

"We'll catch up."

Stubborn bastard. Why did Gavril need this? Why did he need to drag Tamas along with him? The dead were best left buried, undisturbed. They cared not for the sentiments of the living.

Tamas would rather have tipped his hat to the west and bowed his head in respect for a few minutes. It would have been more practical.

"Get on your damn horse," Gavril said.

Tamas climbed onto his mount.

They rode west in silence along one of the many rivers that made up the Fingers of Kresimir. Tamas didn't know if this one had a name. The locals probably called it something—not that there were many locals in this part of Kez.

Northern Kez, with its countless farms and ranches, had once been filled with people. The alternating droughts and floods of the last ten years that had caused Adro so many problems had also affected Kez, and huge portions of the Kez population had gone to the eastern cities in search of work. He imagined those cities even more crowded and dirty than Adopest.

Tamas wondered how Adopest had fared in the war. The canal over the mountains should be finished by this time, alleviating some of the strain off the Mountainwatch for trade. With war with the Kez, food would have to come from Novi and Deliv.

Tamas and Gavril came down out of the highest foothills to where Kresimir's Fingers began to meet. The Fingers didn't all converge, not all at once. It was several days' ride to the place where they did, and their destination was not that far out onto the plains.

The ground turned rocky—great boulders and sudden ravines that made Tamas wonder if the mountains had once come out this far, and if so, what god or force of nature had knocked them down.

The terrain had provided a good place to hide from Ipille's Wardens, long ago.

They crossed a rocky bluff and then descended into a gully where two of Kresimir's Fingers met. Tamas rubbed at his shoulders, suddenly cold despite the summer sun beating down upon them.

He saw it then. A cairn, not more than fifty paces from where the two rivers met. It was about four feet high and six feet across, sandstone rocks gathered from the area and stacked.

It had changed little in the last thirteen years. The bloody fingerprints both Tamas and Gavril had left, their hands raw from digging the stony earth, had been washed away. A necklace—a treasured possession of the dead that Tamas had left on the highest stone—was gone, but the rest of the cairn remained undisturbed.

Tamas climbed down from his horse and tied the reins to a

stunted tree. He approached the cairn slowly. Thoughtfully. Now that he was here, the dread he'd felt in coming seemed silly.

He turned to Gavril.

The big man, with all his stubbornness in making Tamas accompany him on this pilgrimage, seemed reluctant to get any closer.

Tamas took a shaky breath. He reached out and touched the top stone of the cairn.

"Camenir," he said, and found it felt good to say it aloud.

A crunch of footsteps sounded on the rocky soil as Gavril finally joined him.

"I doubt anyone but you or me remember the name." In his head, it had been a musing thought. Aloud, it sounded callous, and Tamas instantly regretted saying it. Gavril was the last of Camenir's kin. His relatives on the Kez side, dead by Ipille's orders. The ones on the Adran side not numerous, and those alive having long disowned him.

Tamas tried to picture Camenir in his mind, and found he could not. He looked a lot like Gavril, he thought. Not as big. Quite a bit younger. A sloppy, casual manner and a genuine smile that most found endearing.

"How did you do it?" Gavril stood beside the cairn, head bowed. "Do what?"

"How did you go on? After what happened?"

Tamas was surprised to hear accusation in Gavril's voice.

"What choice did I have?"

What did Gavril want him to say? Did Gavril want him to admit he'd slept his way through half the eligible ladies in Adopest, and quite a few ineligible ones? Did Gavril want him to point out that he'd killed more men in duels in the short time following Erika's death than he had in all his angry youth?

"I saw grief in you," Gavril said. "I saw it eating through you after Erika's murder. After Manhouch denied your demands that we go to war. When you came and said you wanted to kill Ipille, I knew it had to be done. But... but after we failed, after Camenir died, you changed. All those signs of grief I'd seen in you were gone. You went back to society. Smiled at all those fools who'd laughed behind their hands at the box containing Erika's head. You entertained guests and walked the streets laughing."

"What choice did I have?" Tamas repeated.

Gavril gripped his shoulder and turned him around to look him in the eye. "You never grieved for Camenir. You never cared that my little brother died." Tears sprang up in Gavril's eyes, his face red.

"What did you want?" Tamas was suddenly angry. Had Gavril held this against him all these years? Did Gavril think that Camenir meant nothing to him? "Did you want me to turn to the bottle, like you did?"

"I wanted you to show some decorum!" Gavril's voice rose sharply. "Show some regret. Any sign of emotion for my brother! A man who died for you!"

This close, Gavril towered over him, but Tamas felt no fear. Only rage and regret. "That's rich, coming from you," Tamas spat. "Do you think climbing into an ale cask showed decorum?"

Tamas barely saw the fist coming. One moment it loomed, big as a ham, and the next his ears rang as he stared at the ground from his knees. He blinked away a sudden haze. Blood leaked from his mouth and nose, spattering on the dusty ground. Not the first blood he'd left on this spot.

He climbed to his feet, wobbling on his knees. Gavril glared at him, daring him to hit back.

So he did.

The look of surprise on Gavril's face as Tamas's fist connected with his stomach gave Tamas a jolt of satisfaction. He followed it up with another punch, doubling Gavril over.

"I lost my wife, you bastard," he growled.

Gavril wrapped his arms around Tamas and lifted him with a

bellow. Tamas felt a thrill of fear as his feet left the ground. To a man with Gavril's strength, he might as well have been a child.

He brought his elbow down on Gavril's back, eliciting a yell from the big man.

Gavril lifted him high, then pounded him into the ground. Tamas felt the air leave his lungs, the feeling leave his legs, and his vision blurred. He hacked out a cough and dug one hand into the fat of Gavril's stomach.

They rolled in the dirt for what felt like hours. Swearing, kicking, punching. It didn't matter how hard Tamas hit Gavril, nothing seemed to stop him. Even without a powder trance, Tamas still considered himself a pit of a fighter. Gavril broke his holds. Absorbed his punches. And he gave as good—or better—than he got.

Tamas climbed to his feet and kicked Gavril. His brother-in-law shoved him backward, and Tamas felt his back hit the rocks of the cairn.

"Stop!" he said.

Gavril looked up, his face bruised, one eye blackened and his nose bloody. He saw the cairn behind Tamas and lowered his fist.

Tamas limped away from the cairn and lowered himself against an old fallen log.

He felt along his ribs. One of them might have gotten cracked. His face felt like a rug after the housekeeper had beat it for an hour. The back of his jacket had ripped—he could tell just by moving his shoulders. One of his boots was on the other side of the cairn, and Tamas didn't even remember it coming off.

"You want to know what happened to me?" Tamas said.

Gavril grunted. He lay on the ground across from Tamas, legs splayed.

"That night we buried Camenir is the night I decided to kill Manhouch." Tamas gathered up a wad of spit and hawked it into the dirt. It was red. "I decided to start a war. Not for the people's rights or because Manhouch was evil or any of the other drivel I tell my supporters. I started a war to avenge my wife and my brother."

Tamas took a deep breath and stared at his stockinged foot. His sock had ripped a week ago and his big toe stuck through it. "I couldn't do it in a world of grief. I had to feel out my friends. Charm my enemies. That was the first step: to convince them I was still Adro's favored son. Manhouch's protector. The next step was putting Manhouch's head in a basket.

"Then, of course, the war. Which"—Tamas held up one finger—"I almost didn't go through with. The earthquake and the royalists nearly knocked me off my course. My heart bled when I saw the shambles in which Adopest had been left. But Ipille sent Nikslaus and put me back on my path to vengeance."

Tamas let his finger drop. "The path will end when I cut out Ipille's heart for taking my family."

The air was still. The only sound that of the water where the two rivers met.

"That was a nice speech," Gavril said.

"I thought so."

"Had that memorized long?"

"Most of it for years," Tamas said. "Had to do a little improvising. Never thought I'd be giving it to you."

"Who, then?"

Tamas shrugged. "My grandchildren? My executioner? Taniel's the only one who knew the real reasons I planned the things I did."

The sound of a horse whinnying brought Tamas's head around. Up on the bluff, perhaps a hundred feet away, were two riders. He squinted into the afternoon sun as his fingers looked for his pistol. It had come out of his belt and lay a dozen paces to his left.

The riders began to head down the bluff toward him. The glare of the sun lessened, and he recognized two familiar faces: Olem and Beon je Ipille.

"Company," Tamas said.

Gavril craned his neck and looked toward the bluff. "Is that Beon and Olem?"

"Yes."

"I could break Beon's neck. Bury him next to Camenir. Would be poetic justice in that."

"My—our—quarrel isn't with Beon. It's with his father."

"I've heard Beon is Ipille's favorite."

"Ipille's 'favorite' son changes every six months or so. Beon just lost a major battle with me. I think if we killed him now, Ipille would say he deserved it."

"Not a loving father."

"No."

Olem and Beon came to a halt some dozen paces off. Olem looked down at Tamas's dislodged boot, then around the gully. "Seems there was a fight," he said.

"Ambushed. We dumped the bodies in the river," Tamas said.

"Of course," Olem said. He didn't sound convinced.

"I thought that you were given orders to stay in the camp?" Tamas said to Olem.

"Sorry, sir," Olem said. "The general here asked me to accompany him as his chaperone so that he did not break his word of honor in leaving the camp."

"And why did you feel the need to follow me?" Tamas turned to Beon.

Beon frowned toward the cairn. "I have heard a story," he said. "Regarding a powder mage, and two huge brothers with great strength." His eyes flicked to Gavril. "An old story, passed around in my father's court. One that my father has taken great pains to stamp out."

"So?" Gavril said, his tone petulant.

Beon seemed unperturbed. "The story caught my childhood imagination. It comes to an end when an entire company of my father's Elite disappeared in the Fingers of Kresimir. Some of their bodies were found. Some weren't. I always wondered if that was really the end of the story."

Tamas and Gavril looked at each other.

Tamas asked, "And you thought you might find the end of the story by following us out here?"

Beon was looking at the cairn again. "I thought, perhaps. I see a powder mage, a widower by my father's orders, and one very large man with great strength. I predict that the story I heard has a sadder ending than my childhood imagination would have hoped." He bowed his head toward them and turned his horse around. "I'm sorry to have disturbed you."

"It did," Gavril called out.

Beon stopped and looked back. "Did what?"

"The story. It had a sad ending."

"No," Beon said. "The story is not over yet. But the ending will be very sad regardless."

CHAPTER
30

The Flaming Cuttlefish was a fisherman's pub. Like The Salty Maiden, it was located out at the end of a pier, suspended about ten feet above the water. Unlike The Salty Maiden, it was packed with all kinds. There were factory workers, seamstresses, millers, and even a few gunsmiths. The pub was known throughout the city for cheap, delicious freshwater oysters. In one corner of the room a fiddler was sawing away a seaman's tune, and the whole pier swayed with the stamp of a hundred feet.

The barmaid had assured Adamat that that was normal.

Adamat nursed his beer and let his eyes wander around the room again. He sat with his back to the wall, watching the exits. No signs of the slaver, Doles, or any of his men. No sign of Adamat's son.

It was near midnight. Doles was supposed to meet him here yesterday, but had never come. Riding out his optimism, Adamat had come back and waited all day, a case filled with two hundred fifty thousand krana in cash sitting on his knee. He was tired and nervous, and every minute that passed he grew angrier.

SouSmith, sitting beside him, stifled a yawn. He was drumming his fingers to the tune of the fiddler, his eyes wandering. Adamat could tell he was losing focus.

"Pit!" Adamat swore, getting to his feet.

SouSmith started. "Huh?" He came alert, looking around for signs of danger.

"He's not coming," Adamat shouted above the music and stamping. "We're done here."

SouSmith followed him out into the night, and for the second time in a week Adamat found himself standing in the dark, on a pier, with nothing to show for himself. He kicked a pier piling and swore when it bruised his toe. He nearly threw his case into the water, but SouSmith grabbed his arm.

"You'll be sorry 'bout that."

Adamat looked down at the case. All of his money; his savings, the money Bo had given him, plus another fifty thousand from Ricard. Yes. He *would* have been sorry.

"I'll have to go to Norport now," Adamat said. He was already doing the math in his head. He'd have to charter a boat—and not just any boat, but a smuggler to get him into the Kez-held town— then he'd need to locate Josep and free him from the Kez. There might be Privileged involved, though rumor had it Taniel Two-Shot had killed most of the Kez Cabal on South Pike. Then he'd . . .

SouSmith shook him by the arm.

"What is it?" Adamat asked, annoyed that his thoughts had been interrupted.

"Norport? You mad?"

"No. I have to get my son back."

SouSmith sighed. He pulled a pipe from his pocket and set it between his teeth, then packed it with tobacco. "Have to let it go," he grunted.

"He's my boy," Adamat said. "How can I let him go?" He slumped against the same pier piling that he'd just kicked.

"He's outta reach," SouSmith said gently.

"No. He can't be." Adamat tried to resume his previous train of thought. So much he'd have to do. "Will you come with me?"

SouSmith puffed on his pipe for a moment. "Yeah."

"Thank you," Adamat said, relief washing over him. Norport would be dangerous, but going alone into Kez territory might be suicide.

"One condition."

"What's that?"

"Sleep on it."

Adamat hesitated for a moment. He should prepare tonight. Get his supplies together, find a smuggler... then again, finding a smuggler *would* be far easier in the morning. Most of Adamat's contacts were asleep by this hour. "Fine," he said. "I'll sleep on it."

SouSmith accompanied Adamat home before taking his own leave. Adamat watched SouSmith's hackney cab clatter down the street, then headed inside.

The house was quiet but for the soft sound of one of the children crying. Adamat removed his boots and hat, and hung his jacket by the door. He passed the children's rooms, pausing briefly beside Astrit's. She was the one crying. Fanish sung softly to her, holding her tight and rocking her back and forth. Neither of them saw Adamat.

He crept into his own room. The lamp was burning low, like it always was when Adamat was still out late.

Faye sat up in bed. Her eyes were red, her long, bedraggled curls framing her haggard face. The faint light of hope in her eyes died when she saw him, and Adamat felt his shoulders slump in defeat. He sat down on the bed beside her and buried his face in his hands.

"You tried," Faye said. She was better, he thought. Despite her appearance, she'd been growing stronger over the last week, spending time with the children. She still stayed away from the windows and avoided going outside, though Adamat couldn't determine the reason. Perhaps she feared being seen by one of her former captors?

"I'm going to Norport," Adamat said when he'd regained his composure.

Faye's hand, gently stroking his arm, froze. "Why?"

"To get Josep back. I can find him there, and if I can't find him, I can pick up his trail."

"No."

"What do you mean?"

"I mean no." Faye's tone was firm. "I'll not have you risking your life over this. Not anymore. I've lost Josep, but I have eight more children, and I can't provide for them and protect them without you."

"You won't—"

"I said no."

Adamat could tell by her tone there'd be no argument. No hope at all. She'd do everything in her power to keep him from going. "But—"

"No."

He tried to find the courage to tell her off. To tell her that he had a duty to his son, that he could still get his boy back.

The courage never came.

In the morning, Adamat went to return the money he'd borrowed from Ricard.

A secretary met him in the lobby of Ricard's new headquarters. She opened her mouth with a word of greeting, but something on his face must have stilled her tongue, and she led him back to the room off the side of the building that was Ricard's office.

The room was much larger than his old office, but no cleaner.

The whole room reeked. There were oysters on one shelf, probably from the same pub that Adamat had been to last night, and from the smell of them they were three days old. The scent was made worse by some kind of incense burning on Ricard's desk.

He ignored Ricard's greeting and threw himself into the chair across from him.

Ricard frowned and leaned back in his seat, and the two of them regarded each other for a few moments. Ricard's eyes went to the case on Adamat's lap.

"They never showed," Adamat said, tossing the case on the ground. "They took my fifty-thousand-krana deposit and disappeared. Now my boy is gone forever, along with any hope I have of getting him back. I should never have trusted them." Adamat could hear the disgust in his own voice.

Ricard got that look on his face when he was about to say "I told you so," but instead quietly said, "We all make mistakes."

Adamat wanted to break things. He wanted to go on a violent rampage, destroying Ricard's expensive furniture and chandeliers and crystal decanters, then throw himself on the ground in the middle of the mess and sob.

"I don't know what to do now," he said.

Ricard said, "I have something I could have you look into."

Adamat fixed Ricard with a long look. How could Ricard think he'd want to take a case right now?

"It would keep your mind off things," Ricard went on. "There are accusations of profiteering within the ranks of the Adran army. I need to follow up on those accusations and find some evidence."

"That's a job for the provosts," Adamat said.

"Not when the corruption runs all the way up to the General Staff."

"No," Adamat said. "I'm done with military dealings. Find someone braver and stupider."

Ricard stifled a smile. "You're the bravest and stupidest man I know."

"I can attest to that," a voice said from the back of the room.

Privileged Borbador stood in the doorway. He wore a slimming day jacket, his face pink from a morning shave, a cane in one hand. His Privileged's gloves were nowhere to be seen.

"Who the pit are you?" Ricard asked.

"Privileged Borbador, at your service." Bo bowed his head slightly. "I understand you have a letter for me."

"Oh," Ricard said in surprise. A confused look crossed his face. "How could you possibly know that I have a letter for you?"

Bo smiled.

"Right. From Taniel Two-Shot," Ricard said. He searched through his papers until he discovered the letter, then brought it to Bo.

Bo leaned up against the doorway as he read the note. He turned it around, looking at some kind of report that had been written on the back. His eyes narrowed, and he glanced at Adamat. "Did you tell him that Tamas is still alive?"

"I did," Adamat said.

"We have no evidence of that." Ricard spread his hands.

"He is," Bo said. "And when he gets back, he's going to gut his General Staff."

"If the army runs out of powder, Adro will have been conquered long before Tamas returns."

Bo chewed on his lip. "Any word from Taniel Two-Shot? Other than this letter, I mean."

"He is being court-martialed as we speak. I sent my undersecretary down to intervene on my behalf, but I won't know the results for days."

"Court-martialed? For what?" Bo's tone was flat. Adamat thought it his imagination, but the temperature of the room seemed to have dropped.

"Mostly trumped-up charges," Ricard said. "Disobeying orders, attacking one of the General Staff. But Taniel suspects that some of the General Staff are war-profiteering, and may even be in league with the Kez, which would explain why they're court-martialing their only powder mage."

Bo waved the letter. "Yes, I read that. Pit. Pit, pit, pit. I suppose I could go kill them all, if they haven't hanged him by the time I get there."

"That wouldn't be very good for the war effort," Adamat pointed out. "And we don't know which of the generals are profiteering."

"You think I give a damn about who it is?" Bo snapped. Bo raised his hand, and even though he wasn't wearing his Privileged's gloves, Adamat felt himself shrink into his chair. Bo took a deep breath and closed his eyes for a few minutes before speaking again. "I'll take care of this," he said. To Ricard, "I may need your help."

"My organization is at your disposal."

"Good."

Bo left as quickly as he'd arrived, and Adamat found himself alone with Ricard once again.

"Well, that's interesting. You've made yourself some rather fascinating friends." Ricard plucked a half-smoked cigar from an ashtray and examined it, as if deciding whether to finish it off. He tossed it into the rubbish bin at his feet.

"I'd rather not have had to," Adamat murmured.

"You need a break. Not more work. I see that now. You should come on a trip with me," Ricard said.

"What? Where?"

"The grand opening of the Pan-Deliv Canal!" Ricard stood up and threw back the curtains on his window to reveal the ugliness of the factory dock-fronts with the backdrop of a rainstorm raging across the Adsea. He cocked an eyebrow at the weather and closed the curtains.

"I thought it was called the King Manhouch Canal?"

"No king, no King Manhouch Canal." Ricard opened his cigar box and offered one to Adamat, which he refused.

"I will not let you cheer me up," Adamat said.

Ricard waved his hand in front of him as if envisioning a sign hanging from the wall. "I wanted to call it the Tumblar Crossing, but my Ministerial Election Committee seems to think that humility looks better to the voting public, while the council wanted something to strengthen ties with Deliv." Ricard struck a match and lit his cigar. "I give up so much for the greater good."

"You poor man," Adamat said.

"You'll come to the grand opening?"

"No." What could possibly make Ricard think that Adamat would want to travel, after all his ordeals? He closed his eyes, trying to escape the stink of those oysters. "What about Privileged Borbador?"

"I'll leave word for my people to help him. Come with me. I insist," Ricard said.

"Absolutely not. My wife is in no shape to travel. My children—"

"Your children can come. I'll hire the nannies, and you and Faye can ride in my carriage. We leave this afternoon."

"Faye will not go!"

"She's already agreed."

Adamat narrowed his eyes. "Liar."

"Cross my heart," Ricard said. "I visited her yesterday."

"She would have said something."

"She didn't, apparently. Go home and ask her. My bet is that she's already packed. It'll do you both good to get out of the city."

"If you planned this all out, why that rubbish about the profiteering generals?"

"I wanted to get your thoughts on it. You weren't very helpful."

"I couldn't possibly—"

"All expenses are on me," Ricard said. He leaned over his desk, his nose wrinkling as incense wafted in his face. "Go home and get ready. My carriage will pick you up in three hours. No more arguments."

"I won't be bullied." Adamat tried to get angry. He wanted to lean across the desk and smack Ricard, but the fury just wasn't there. Ricard was right. He needed to get out of the city and have some fresh air. If the children could come, and Faye had already agreed, perhaps it would do them all some good.

"Three hours," Ricard said.

Adamat kicked the travel case, sending stacks of banknotes across the floor. "All right, damn it! Just throw out those damned oysters!"

Ricard stood up straight and nodded, pinching his nose at the pungent odor. "Agreed."

Taniel didn't know whether to curse his luck or to praise it.

General Ket could very well have sent him to the noose. She had the backing of the rest of the senior staff—all but General Hilanska, it seemed. Fell's arrival couldn't have been more timely, and Abrax's offer of employment with the Wings would let him stay on the front.

But to be thrown out of the Adran army? The thought still made him stumble. He'd been raised in the army. He'd marched and killed and bled for them for nearly half his life and now they tossed him aside like unwanted trash, all because he accused the General Staff of helping Kez.

And perhaps they were. Their retreat orders were suspiciously well timed, and their refusal to hold the line even when the Kez were beaten was baffling.

Nothing Taniel could do about it now except join the Wings of Adom. He'd have a chance to finally finish off the Kez Privileged, and maybe once all those damned sorcerers were dead, they'd stop making Wardens of any kind. Of course, Taniel also needed a way to get Kresimir's blood so that Ka-poel could kill him.

That seemed like the easy part.

An explosion sent Taniel reeling. He regained his feet a moment later. Where had it come from?

There was confusion in the Adran camp, but it seemed the explosion had come from the south. Taniel rushed to a hillock and looked south to the Kez camp.

In the far distance, miles away, beyond the Kez camp and the immense beam where Julene hung in the sun, he could see the city of Budwiel. The walls of the city smoldered. Low clouds hung above it—or was that smoke? A gunpowder explosion? Possible.

The Kez camp was a flurry of activity, all of it directed back toward Budwiel. Was that Tamas, finally returning? No, it couldn't be. Tamas wouldn't attack the Kez rear unless he was damned certain that the Adran brigades would attack from the front.

It *would* have been an opportune moment to strike. Taniel cocked his head, listening for the trumpets to call the men to arms.

His gaze drifted to the beam erected in the middle of the Kez camp and Julene's body hanging from it and he wondered again how she'd ended up there. She had been so willful, so powerful. Had Kresimir done it? Taniel couldn't imagine anyone else having the power to subdue her like that.

Taniel waited. Silence. There wasn't even an alarm in case the Kez attempted a surprise attack.

The sun was just setting when Taniel reached his quarters in a small shed. He had a couple hours to find Ka-poel and gather his things. Should he say good-bye to anyone? Etan would remain in contact. Was there anyone else?

Taniel leaned against the door to the shed he'd been using as quarters. No. There wasn't anyone else. For all his time in the Adran army, Taniel had few friends. That should have made it easier to leave.

It should have . . .

Taniel opened the door. The waning sunlight slashed across the inside of the room.

Ka-poel lay naked on the cot, her hands stretched above her head, her face hidden in the shadows. Taniel felt his face turn red. He averted his eyes.

"Pole, what are you doing?"

A fist connected with his stomach, doubling him over. A pair of hands shoved him inside. He fell to the floor, trying to gather his wits as the door closed behind him.

Taniel scrambled to get to his feet. Something hard slammed into his back and he felt a blade against his throat. His mouth went dry.

"Don't move, powder mage."

A match was struck and the lantern beside the bed lit. There were five men crowded into the small room. They leered down at Taniel. Each one carried a truncheon or a knife. The lot of them reeked of whiskey. They wore Adran military jackets with a patch on the shoulder that showed the emblem of a shovel.

Dredgers. Third Brigade. The lowest of the low in the entire Adran military.

General Ket's men.

One of the soldiers took a swig from a bottle in his hand and punched Taniel in the face. The blow was hard and well placed, forcing Taniel down farther. By the soldier's stripes on his shoulder, he was a captain.

Taniel stared at the floor, watching long tendrils of bloody saliva drop on the wood. "Who the pit are you?" he spat.

The captain sniffed. "General Ket told us we'd get this little piece here. We thought we'd start early." He set the bottle on the nightstand and began to loosen his trousers. "And you're going to watch."

Taniel looked at Ka-poel out of the corner of his eye, trying to ignore her nudity. Her face was bruised and black, her lip split and bloody. She'd been beaten badly.

He surged to his feet. Someone was quick enough with a truncheon to bash him across the shoulders. Taniel didn't even feel it. His right hand grasped the captain's chin, fingers in the man's mouth. His left hand grabbed the captain by the forehead.

Taniel felt the pop and tear of muscles, bone, and tendon as he tore the captain's jaw off. Deep inside, the sound frightened him, but all objections were silenced by his rage.

He took a truncheon blow across the side of the face and turned on the wielder. His fist hit the soldier's nose hard enough to kill him instantly. Red filled Taniel's vision like a thick fog, and his body moved as if on its own accord.

Taniel couldn't remember killing the last three, but he was soon surrounded by five corpses, their blood still warm on his hands and shirt. He dropped to his knees beside Ka-poel. She was breathing lightly. Her eyes fluttered open.

"Shh," Taniel said when her mouth opened. He covered her with a blanket and then snatched his only other jacket from the bedpost, throwing it on over his blood-soaked shirt. He grabbed his sketch-book and his kit and threw them in his bag, then lifted Ka-poel in his arms. There was nothing else in this room that mattered.

He spotted her satchel, discarded in the corner, and grabbed it as he left.

Taniel sprinted the entire way to the Wings camp. As soon as he reached the pickets, he began to call for a doctor. Confused infantrymen regarded him from their posts as he raced by.

The brigadiers' tents were not hard to find in the center of the camp.

"Is this Abrax's tent?" Taniel demanded.

The two sentries exchanged a glance.

"Brigadier Abrax! I must see her now!"

"Two-Shot?"

Taniel whirled to see Abrax approaching from the way he'd come. She was probably just returning from the Adran camp, and he realized they'd spoken less than twenty minutes ago.

"What the pit are you..." Her eyes took in his bloody shirt and Ka-poel's bruised body. "What happened?"

"I need a doctor for her. Now!"

"Get a doctor," Abrax barked at the sentries. "Bring her into my tent. There, set her on the cot. What happened to her? Holy saints, what happened to you? You're covered in blood. Did you do this to her?"

"No!" Taniel roared the word before he was able to control himself. "No. I didn't. She's all that matters. See to her, please."

"It'll be done," Abrax said.

"I've just killed five men," Taniel said. "Soldiers in the Third Brigade. It was in self-defense, but they'll be coming for me shortly."

Abrax blinked at the news. She opened her mouth, then shut it. "You were attacked?" she finally managed.

"Yes."

"Details, man. *Now!*"

"Five men jumped me in my quarters. They had Ka-poel like this...they were going to...while I watched." Taniel heard his words flow out in broken, rushed sentences.

"You were unarmed?"

Taniel nodded.

Abrax put her hand to her mouth and studied Taniel. "You're in shock. Sit down. Were you in a powder trance?"

"No."

"Five men," she breathed, almost too low for Taniel to hear. "With his bare hands." She glanced at Ka-poel. "The doctors will be here soon. Stay here."

Abrax crossed to the head of the tent. "Stewart!" she bellowed as she went. Abrax stepped outside, but she spoke loudly enough that Taniel could hear her clearly. "Ah, there you are. Get our best internal investigators. Send them to the Adran camp immediately. There has been a quintuple murder and I want to know the exact circumstances leading up to it."

"We going after someone? Or trying to determine how the victims arrived at their deaths?" a male voice asked. Stewart, Taniel assumed.

"We're not going after anything but the truth. And they're not victims, they're potential rapists. Dig up everything you can on them. I want to know exactly what type of people they were and what they were doing before their deaths."

"Yes, ma'am."

"And close the camp to the Adran provosts and stifle any rumors going around."

"Of course. Anything else?"

"Stay close. I'm sure I'll need something."

Abrax returned to the tent a moment later. Taniel thought to stand, and realized that he'd taken Ka-poel's hand at some point. He decided to stay by her side.

"Thank you," he said.

"Believe me this," Abrax said, her face flushed, her brow furrowed. "If you've lied to me, I'll put the noose around your neck myself. But I won't see a man lose his life because he defended himself and his loved one."

The doctor came moments later. Taniel refused to leave the tent, but did avert his eyes as the doctor examined Ka-poel. She struggled a little—he hoped that was a good sign.

"I've given her something to help her sleep," the doctor said after her examination. She glared at Taniel. "She's suffered a brutal assault."

"It wasn't him," Abrax snapped.

The doctor's glare lost its bite. "She wasn't raped, and she had blood beneath her nails, and her knuckles are bruised. She gave them a good fight. That might help you catch them."

"They're dead already," Taniel said flatly.

"Good. Her languid state is from exhaustion. She might have

fought them for hours. Her left arm is broken, and she might lose an ear. No concussion, though, and that's remarkable."

Taniel returned to Ka-poel's side, barely noticing that Abrax lowered herself into a chair nearby to watch them.

Taniel wasn't sure how late it was when he heard angry shouting outside the tent. Abrax lifted herself warily from her chair and went outside.

"What did I say about a closed camp?" Abrax demanded.

"Brigadier Abrax," a sharp voice said.

Taniel put his head in his hands. Doravir.

"You're harboring a man wanted for the murder of four infantrymen and a captain of the Third Brigade. Release him to our custody now."

CHAPTER
31

Nila felt her fingers shaking as she tried to position the needle beside her target.

"Don't be nervous," Bo said. His voice was soft and soothing. He sat cross-legged on a faded pillow in one corner of the room beside the only window, a musty old tome of a book cradled in his lap while he watched her. "If you mess up, it's all right. I'll only be burned from the inside out by otherworldly fire, consumed like a bale of hay soaked in lantern oil."

"You're not making this any easier," Nila said. She took a deep breath and stabbed the needle into one of his Privileged's gloves. The positioning looked right. It had to be perfect for the gloves to work properly.

"I know," Bo said. She could hear his grin in his tone.

"Why can't you do this yourself?"

"Because I hate sewing. And you're a laundress. You're probably far better at it than I am anyway."

And Nila owed him. Even if he didn't say it, Nila was certain it had crossed his mind.

She was painfully aware that Bo had offered to shelter her and Jakob for three days. That had been nine days ago, and she wasn't entirely certain why he hadn't forced them out into the street. A Privileged seemed the last type of person to whom she would want to owe a favor, so when he mentioned that he had several pairs of ripped gloves that needed mending, she volunteered.

That was before she knew that the stitching on Privileged's gloves had to be perfect. Absolutely perfect.

She wondered why else he'd let them stay. Perhaps he expected to bed her. Out of the corner of her eye, she could see that he was watching her. He seemed to do that a lot, but only when he thought she wouldn't notice. It made her nervous.

But he'd given her and Jakob food, shelter, and the first pleasant company she'd had in a long time. He was calm, quiet, and hadn't tried to force himself on her. Yet.

Every time she started to wonder what it would be like to let herself sleep with him, she had to remind herself of Dourford, splattered across the street. Bo wasn't just a man. He was a Privileged. Privileged were dangerous people.

"This requires a skilled seamstress," Nila said. "I can sew, but this is—"

"You're doing fine."

She returned to her task. She'd managed to finish three of the twelve gloves he'd stashed away for repair. Whether any of them could be used...

"Will you really burn from the inside out if I do these wrong?" Nila asked.

"No."

"You git!"

"They won't work, though. Which is just as likely to get me killed." Bo set his book to one side and climbed to his feet, joining her at the table. He put on one of the finished gloves and snapped his fingers. "Nothing. This one won't do." He tried on another glove. "Nor this." He tossed the two useless gloves in their own pile and put on the third. Again, he snapped his fingers.

A small flame appeared at the tips of his fingers. The flame went out and he removed the glove, putting it in his pocket. "This will. Excellent."

"Do you want me to . . ." Nila reached for the two useless gloves.

"Don't worry about it. I'll dispose of those ones."

For a moment she thought he was going to return to his pillow and his book. Instead, he pulled out a chair and sat down. He kicked out another chair with his feet and put them up, leaning back with his hands folded behind his head. "Where's the boy? I haven't heard a peep out of him all day."

"He's playing in his room. I told him to keep quiet so that you could read."

"Very considerate of you."

Nila made a mistake in her stitching. She cursed under her breath and pulled the needle back out to try again. Why was he watching her? What did he want?

"You're a very good-looking girl. Did you know that?"

Oh. That was why. Nila felt her heart skip a beat. She'd heard rumors that Privilegeds had a powerful sex drive. That cabal Privileged each had several concubines, and that few women could resist them.

"I've been told that before," Nila said.

"You should wear your hair back more often. It helps display those cheekbones."

Nila didn't trust herself to speak. Had he asked about Jakob because he was hoping to get her alone? Would he give her an ultimatum: Either get out or come to my bed? Nila resolved not to do it. She still had her silver hidden outside the city. She'd been thinking about this ever since Bo first took them in. She'd get the silver and take Jakob northeast into Novi. They would head to the capital and get a small house there, and she'd take up as a laundress.

Bo opened his mouth.

Here it comes, Nila thought.

"Do your parents live in the city?"

"I won't...! What?"

"Your parents," Bo said. "Do they live in the city?"

Nila was taken aback by the question. "My parents are dead," she answered curtly. This wasn't what she'd expected him to say. "I'm an orphan."

"Oh," Bo said. "Sorry to hear that."

"I never knew them."

Bo was staring at the ceiling. His tone was wistful. "I knew my father a little before he died. I spent some time in an orphanage, too. Then out on the streets for me."

Nila almost laughed. Was this how he'd try to get her to bed? Make them feel some kind of kinship? "And then the royal cabal?"

"No. First Taniel Two-Shot. And then his father, Tamas, took me in. That's where the dowsers found me. Did you ever get tested as a child?"

Bo knew Field Marshal Tamas? He'd been adopted by him? That seemed far-fetched. "Tested?"

"By the cabal dowsers. For ability."

Nila saw another mistake she'd made. She pulled out the needle and used the tip to pick out the thread. "Of course. They came to the orphanage every year."

"You should try again," Bo said. He removed a pair of gloves from his pockets and tossed them on the table. "Sometimes the dowsers miss someone."

Nila wanted to roll her eyes. He was still flirting with her. She could tell by the tiny smile at the corners of his mouth, and by the playful tone of his voice. "I don't think so."

"Suit yourself." Bo put the gloves back in his pocket.

There were several blissful minutes of silence while Nila sewed and Bo sat in his chair, rocking back on two legs and staring at the ceiling. Nila's mind began to wander. Maybe she shouldn't go to Novi. Perhaps she should head across the ocean to faraway Fatrasta. Less likely she or Jakob would ever be found or recognized.

"Jakob," Bo suddenly said. "His last name was Eldaminse, right?"

"Yes."

"And you worked for his family?"

Nila nodded. The Eldaminse house. That seemed like so long ago. Had it really only been four months? Memories of that place felt like visions of a world from a dream.

"Did you know anything about his father's business?"

"I was a laundress."

"Servants hear everything. That's why so many of them spy for the cabals."

Nila blinked. "They do?"

"Well. Indirectly. They don't know *who* they're spying for, they just know they're being paid for information."

"I never did. I was taught never to snoop."

"Pity." Bo rocked his chair down onto all four legs and stood up. "Jakob," he called, heading down a short hall toward the room Nila and Jakob were sharing.

Nila paused in her sewing and cocked her head to one side.

"Jakob," Bo said, his voice muffled, "do you remember if your father was ever visited by any military men?"

Nila couldn't hear Jakob's answer.

"Really? Interesting. How long ago was that?" There was a pause, and then, "Thank you, Jakob. You were very helpful."

Bo returned to the room. He grabbed his jacket off the hook.

"Where are you going?" Nila said.

"For someone taught never to snoop, you sure look like you were listening hard."

Nila felt her cheeks redden.

Bo smiled. "I'm heading to the Public Archives. I'll likely not be back until tomorrow. There's a small stack of banknotes hidden under the windowsill. Feel free to get you and the boy some food." He stopped in the door, his gloves in one hand. He seemed preoccupied. "Are you sure you don't want to try on my gloves?"

Nila pushed her chair back and stood up.

"I've had enough of this," she said.

Bo's eyebrows rose. He seemed genuinely surprised. "Of...?"

"Your flirting. I'll leave if you want us to, but I'm not going to bed with you."

Bo took several quick steps across the room, coming to a stop with less than a handbreadth between them. He leaned forward, and Nila could hear her heart thumping in her ears. She became acutely aware that if Bo did try to force himself on her, or to hurt her or Jakob, she couldn't do a thing about it.

"I flirt with everyone," Bo whispered in her ear. "And if you wanted to go to bed with me, I wouldn't say no. But I've never raped a woman and never will. So stop cringing every time you catch me looking at you. I like looking at people. I find them fascinating."

Nila's throat was dry. A glance down showed her that Bo still wasn't wearing his gloves. "If you don't expect me to go to bed with you, why haven't you made us leave?"

"Because I like you," Bo said. "And I like the kid. But I'm leaving the city soon and you should figure out your plans. I won't be here longer than a week." He stepped away. "See you tomorrow?"

Nila swallowed. "Yes."

"Glad to hear it."

Tamas's army crossed the last of Kresimir's Fingers and ascended the wide plateau of the Northern Expanse almost seven weeks after they'd left Budwiel.

The Northern Expanse, like the Amber Expanse to the south, was a breadbasket of the Nine. Unlike the Amber Expanse, it was not home to cattle farms or wheat fields but to immense bean fields, which could survive better with little water.

Tamas ordered forage teams to spread out across the plateau, under the command of the most levelheaded sergeants in the army. He needed to strip the land of its resources while making this as painless to the native population as possible.

He rode at the head of the column, eyes on the northern horizon. It would be several days before they crossed the Deliv border and could see the city of Alvation, but he couldn't help that his heart beat faster with every step. Soon, they'd find relief. Soon, they'd cross the Charwood Pile Mountains and descend into Adro, taking the fight back to the Kez.

Gavril rode up beside Tamas. He and his horse were coated in dust from coming up behind the column. Not far behind him, an old man rode a pack mule. He had a hard time keeping up with Gavril's charger. Tamas reined in his mount. Olem stopped too, his eyes vigilant despite the plateau being empty but for their army.

"Who is this?" Tamas said, nodding at the old man, who was still fifty paces off.

"A Kez bean farmer."

"Why is he here?"

"Wanted to talk to you."

Tamas cocked an eyebrow at Gavril. This was the last thing he needed. Why on earth would Gavril bring him here? "Does he know who I am?"

"Yes, and he has some interesting things to say."

What could an old bean farmer on the Northern Expanse have to say of interest?

The old man brought his burro up beside their horses.

"Are you the field marshal?" the old man said in Adran. The Kez accent was so thick that the words were barely distinguishable. His face was wrinkled, his skin brown from the hot sun of the plateau and perhaps a mix of Deliv blood. Labor and trade went on freely between the Deliv to the north and Kez farmers on the plateau.

The old bean farmer was emaciated. He might have been plump at one point, but the skin now sagged from his cheeks and sickly splotches on his face spoke to malnutrition.

The man's eyes held a smoldering anger that surprised Tamas.

"I speak Kez," Tamas said in Kez.

"Are you the field marshal?" the bean farmer said again in Kez.

"I am. Good afternoon."

The bean farmer spit at the feet of Tamas's charger. He bared his teeth and glared, as if daring Tamas to do anything about it.

Tamas looked at Gavril. His brother-in-law, still bruised from their fight last week, just shrugged his shoulders.

"Something wrong?" Tamas asked.

"You tell me."

Tamas shot another glance at Gavril. What was this all about?

"I can't imagine."

"You took my crop," the old man said. "It was a good one this year, considering the drought. You took my wife and daughters. Your blasted men broke my son's legs when he refused to serve them!"

Tamas scowled. Damned infantry. Even the best couldn't keep themselves under control. He'd ordered that women be left alone under penalty of death. The food, they needed, but Tamas didn't need his soldiers raping and killing their way across the Kez countryside.

"What company did this?" he asked Gavril.

"None of ours. The man and his son were alone in his hut when the forage teams found him. The place had been stripped bare, all the furniture broken. The boy's legs were broken, like he says. The lad will be a cripple for life. Looks like it happened weeks ago."

"I'm sorry about your wife and daughters," Tamas said, "but it wasn't my men."

"Are you calling me a liar?" The bean farmer edged his mule closer to Tamas.

Tamas took a deep breath and reminded himself that striking an old man wasn't the best way to end a conversation. "When did this happen?"

"Eighteen days ago," the bean farmer said.

"It couldn't have been us. We just arrived."

"Then who was it? I know Adran troops when I see them." The bean farmer leaned over to pluck at Tamas's jacket. "Adran blues, with silver trim. I'm not a fool!"

"How many men?"

"Thousands of ya!" The bean farmer spit again.

"Gavril, any sign an army came through here recently?"

Gavril rode off a few feet to confer with one of his scouts. He came back a moment later. "Foraging teams are all reporting the same thing—the land's been stripped clean. All the crops were harvested early, or burned, and the men have come across dozens of empty farmsteads."

Tamas drummed his fingers on his saddle horn. The forage he'd been expecting on the Northern Expanse—gone. All of it. Nothing for his men to eat on the way to Alvation.

"Well?" the bean farmer demanded. "What do you have to say for yourself?"

"Which way were they headed?" Tamas asked.

The bean farmer seemed taken aback. "North."

"Olem, give this man enough food for him and his son and send him back to his home. Let him keep the mule." Tamas flicked the reins. "Gavril."

Tamas left the cursing old bean farmer in Olem's hands and rode back to the head of the column. Gavril came up beside him, letting his charger keep pace with Tamas's.

"This doesn't make sense," Tamas said. "We don't have any troops in northern Kez."

"I'd say the old man isn't right in the head, but the place has been swept clean. It would have taken a great number of men to come through and strip the plateau like this."

Tamas gripped his saddle horn. How was he going to feed his men with no forage?

"How many?" Tamas asked.

Gavril scratched the stubble on his chin. "At least a brigade or two."

"Wearing Adran blue, but not Adran." Tamas mused it over in his head. "Shit! They're trying to slip into Adro."

"The Kez?"

"It must be. They come through here, acting like an invading army—bluff their way through Alvation and then take an unsuspecting Mountainwatch. They might be in Adro already."

"What should we do?" Gavril asked.

Tamas let his fingers play upon the butt of one of the saw-handled dueling pistols stuck in his belt. A gift from his son. "We keep going. We catch up to them and take them from behind."

CHAPTER
32

Ricard Tumblar's carriage jolted along the winding highway at the base of the Charwood Pile Mountain Range, headed north toward the Pan-Deliv Canal. Mountains rose above them immediately to the west, and there were more in the distance to the north, their white tops looking like frosting on peaked cakes. The carriage thumped, then clattered over a stone bridge crossing a tributary of the Ad River and then it was back to the pitted dirt road.

Adamat stared out the window and tried not to think of the jarring of the ground. The last thing he needed was to throw up all over the velvet interior.

Five days in a carriage was no pleasant prospect, even one as fancy as Ricard's. The undercarriage employed the very newest leaf-spring suspension and the thick, padded seats helped absorb some rocking of the road, but nothing prevented Adamat's head from hitting the roof when they hit a particularly deep hole in the road.

Damn these northern roads.

At least Faye seemed to be enjoying herself, as much as she could under the circumstance. She had become even more withdrawn after her decision not to go after Josep. Her weeping had stopped, though, and she seemed more resolved to put on a good face for the other children.

"We'll have these roads fixed up better once the canal comes into more use," Ricard was saying, his head craned out the window. "I'd like to see the whole thing cobbled, with a full-time union crew to tend to maintenance year-round."

Adamat longed to reach their destination. Just a couple hours away, or so Ricard had said. They'd be staying at the finest hotel in northern Adro. Room service, massages, hot running water. The hotel was brand-new, built to accommodate dignitaries and businessmen taking the canal over the Charwood Pile.

"Couldn't you just leave it to the Mountainwatch?" Adamat asked. "The maintenance, I mean. We're in the foothills. That counts as their territory."

Ricard wagged a finger under his nose. "No! No, no, no. I fought tooth and nail for the canal to be a union project. The Mountainwatch wanted in on it. Claimed it was their jurisdiction, or some such tripe, but this is a union job! The union employs good, hardworking Adrans. Not the convicts and malcontents of forced labor like the Mountainwatch."

"Surely they're guarding the pass," Adamat said.

"No," Ricard said proudly. "Purely union, even down to the lock guards."

That surprised Adamat. The Mountainwatch was more than just a forced-labor institution. It had a long tradition of guarding the high places—they were the gatekeepers of Adro, and they'd proved that again in the recent defense of Shouldercrown Fortress.

Adamat understood that Ricard was proud of his unions, but unionizing the defense of the country seemed strange.

They stopped for a midday meal several miles south of the canal. Adamat and Faye dined with their children and their hired nannies while Ricard met with Fell about plans for the mountain. When lunch was over, Adamat wandered outside to stretch his legs.

The inn sat next to a small stream—runoff from the mountains. Adamat listened to the bubbling sound it made as it meandered under the road and down toward the river, then looked north.

Adamat could see the locks of the canal from where he stood. They worked their way up the side of the mountain like steps, the road zigzagging its way up beside them. The whole setup looked like a model at this distance, and even seeing it with his own eyes, he scarcely believed it to be real. A canal going over an entire mountain range!

The locks themselves were a feat of engineering never before seen in this world. They were built purely by the labor of men, no sorcery at all, unless you count the few Knacked that the union no doubt employed for their various skills. Despite the rigors of the journey, Adamat knew that touring the locks prior to the grand opening was going to be worth the whole trip.

Josep would have loved to have seen the canal.

Ricard and Fell came outside, studying a map together and pointing at the road. He could hear them discussing the benefits of cobbles versus brick or poured concrete.

Something on the mountainside caught Adamat's eye. At this distance, he couldn't be sure, but . . .

"Ricard," he said, interrupting the two, "do you have a looking glass?"

Fell said, "I do." She went back to the carriage and returned a moment later, handing Adamat a looking glass.

"I thought you said that the grand opening wasn't until tomorrow," Adamat said to Ricard.

Ricard squinted toward the canal. "It's not."

"You're not supposed to have any traffic on the canal?"

"Not yet. I mean, they've been tested, but no commercial traffic until after the grand opening. Why, what do you see?"

Adamat put the looking glass to his eye and found the locks. They came into focus, and then he saw what had caught his eye.

Each of those locks held a ship—and not just any ships, but oceangoing merchantmen with rows of cannon and tall masts. There had to be dozens of them, and he could see the tiny figures of men working the locks as the entire row of ships slowly descended the side of the mountain.

The ships bore green-and-white-striped flags, marked in the center with a laurel wreath. Adamat felt his legs grow weak and a growing dread in the pit of his stomach.

He thrust the looking glass into Fell's hands. "Get the children back in the carriages. We're going back to Adopest. Now!"

"What?" Ricard demanded, snatching the looking glass. "What is wrong with you? The grand opening is tomorrow, we're..." He fell silent as he put the looking glass to his eye.

"It's a good thing you didn't let the Mountainwatch guard your canal," Adamat shouted over his shoulder as he ran toward the inn. "Otherwise it would have been harder for the Brudania-Gurla Trading Company to bring their whole damn fleet across it."

"They're going to send me to Adopest," Taniel said.

One of Ka-poel's eyes opened. The one that wasn't swollen shut.

Taniel went on. "General Ket says this is a civil matter because I'm no longer in the Adran army and I'm not officially in the Wings of Adom yet. I'm to be sent back to Adopest under house arrest to await trial." Taniel paced the short length of the tent. He held in his hand a note from Brigadier Abrax telling him the conditions of his house arrest. "That could take months. The war might be over by then, and we'll have lost."

Taniel stopped pacing and dropped onto his cot. What could

he do? He'd spent the last hour arguing with Abrax. The brigadier claimed her hands were tied, that she could do nothing but provide Taniel with a small house in Adopest. The Wings of Adom's charter did not allow them to admit anyone awaiting trial.

"I'm going to kill her," Taniel said.

Ka-poel struggled to sit up in her cot. They'd been given a tent in the corner of the Wings' camp at the farthest point from the Adran army. Her green eyes were wet. Taniel suspected she'd cried during the night.

He thought that perhaps his rage would fade as the days passed and Ka-poel was sitting up and able to move. If anything, seeing her wounds heal slowly made him even angrier. Her lips were swollen and cracked, her face still bruised.

She spread her hands, awkwardly because her arm was in a sling. *Who?*

"General Ket. She must have ordered what they . . . what they did to you. She must have known she wouldn't be able to send me to the noose so easily. Those men had you for hours."

Ka-poel shook her head.

"No? 'No' what? The doctor said you fought back. That you . . ."

Another emphatic shake of her head. She motioned with her thumb over her shoulder and then made a snatching motion. She pointed to herself.

"They caught you?"

She thought for a moment, and then made a walking motion with her fingers.

"Followed you?"

A nod.

She reached for her satchel and winced. Taniel lifted it for her. She took it from him and began to rummage around inside.

Ka-poel began to lay out dolls on the cot. They were instantly recognizable: General Hilanska, General Ket; the entire General Staff of the Adran army.

Taniel stared at the dolls. Each time he saw one, he was amazed by the detail she put into the wax, but here it was something more. He *knew* all of these people. Some of them, like Hilanska, he'd known since childhood. Bits of real hair protruded from the wax in places. A drop of blood was rubbed on one of them. It made his skin crawl.

"Why were you making dolls for them?" Taniel asked.

Ka-poel tilted her head to the side as if to tell him it was a stupid question.

"Just in case, right?"

A nod.

"And the Dredgers caught you while you were getting something of Ket's to use in her doll?"

Another nod.

If she wasn't already bruised, Taniel would have smacked her. What she'd done was incredibly dangerous. If people suspected the nature of her sorcery and saw her skulking about the general's quarters, she could have been beaten *and* locked up.

"Still," he went on, "they said that she'd told them they could have you." The anger ebbed. Only a little, but it was enough to make his muscles relax. He leaned back in his chair, putting his hands over his face. "I should still kill her."

Ka-poel thrust her thumb at herself. *I will.* A flat hand, as if to stop, and she mouthed the words "*If I need to.*"

"Pit, Pole, I—"

"Knock, knock!" The voice came from outside the front of the tent. "May I come in?"

Mihali. The damned chef. If it weren't for him, none of this would have ever happened. Taniel would still be in the Adran army and Ka-poel would never have been beaten by Ket's thugs.

"Go to—!" Taniel started, when Ka-poel lay a soft hand on his arm.

She nodded. Taniel took a deep, calming breath. It didn't help.

"Yes," he called.

The flap was swept back and Mihali ducked into the tent, carrying a wide platter. Steam rose from beneath the platter cover with the smell of warm bread and, what was that? Eggs.

Taniel looked away. He wouldn't give Mihali the satisfaction of eating his food.

Mihali set the platter on Taniel's cot and removed the lid. He leaned over it, wafting the smell of it toward him. "Warm cornmeal cake with a sweet crust drizzled in maple honey with poached eggs on the side."

Ka-poel's face lit up. Cornmeal cake was a Fatrastan staple, uncommon in the Nine. She snatched one up immediately, tossing it between her hands until it cooled enough to hold.

Taniel smiled, though he tried to cover it with a cough. He wasn't about to let Mihali see him pleased.

"What do you want, Adom?"

"Oh, please," Mihali said. "Call me Mihali. 'Adom' has such a high-and-mighty connotation."

"Well"—Taniel's mouth watered at the smell of the cornbread— "what do you want?"

"I've come to apologize," Mihali said.

Ka-poel patted the cot beside her.

"Thank you!" Mihali took a seat, and Taniel felt a stab of jealousy.

"Apologize? For telling me to make amends with Doravir and getting me kicked out of the Adran army?"

Mihali's eyebrows rose. "Heavens, no. That needed to happen."

"It *what*?" Taniel sputtered.

Mihali waved a hand as if it were of little consequence.

"I came to apologize because I told you that I would not help you kill Kresimir and that I did not think he needed to die."

Taniel couldn't help it any longer. His hand reached out, as if it had a mind of its own, and took a piece of cornbread. He bit in and was instantly glad. The cornbread was soft and moist, seemingly melting in his mouth, and the honey tasted as if it were straight from the comb.

"You changed your mind?" Taniel asked around bites.

"I wish," Mihali said, plucking a piece of cornbread from the platter and smearing it with fruit spread, "that this could be solved amicably. Or even at all. A couple of months ago I made a deal with Kresimir that neither of us would contribute to the war directly. Since then it's gone badly for the Adran side—as you can tell—but things are not well in the Kez camp either." Mihali paused to lick honey and crumbs off his fingertips. "Kresimir has taken to killing his own people at an alarming rate."

"Good," Taniel snorted.

"No," Mihali said. "Not good. I speak with Kresimir often. We can bridge space for that purpose, and when we do, I can see a bit into his mind. He's going mad." Mihali swallowed and looked down at his cornbread sadly. "Quite thoroughly mad."

"I don't care."

"Taniel, how long do you think a mad god would stick to killing his own people? He might very well try to destroy the Nine. Perhaps even the whole world. I don't think he could—not even Kresimir is that powerful—but if he tried, it would probably kill every living thing in this part of the world."

"I already stopped him once," Taniel said.

"Which makes you particularly suited to the task."

"Couldn't you stop him?"

"Sorcery is predictable in some ways," Mihali said. "There are patterns that all Privileged use, from the lowliest sorcerer all the way up to Kresimir. I can predict those patterns and counter them. However, if Kresimir lashes out in his madness, it will be completely random. I could protect myself, but no one else."

Taniel thought on this for a few moments. Could a god actually go mad?

"It's from the bullet, isn't it?"

Mihali seemed to think on this for a moment. "I have heard reports—when I lurk about the generals' staff meetings—from their spies. There is a rumor in the Kez camp that Kresimir coughs blood into his pillow. That he wanders the halls of his compound at night and accosts his own guards, demanding to know whether they are the eye behind the flintlock."

Taniel's mouth went dry. The eye behind the flintlock. Who else could it possibly be but him? Kresimir was looking for him in his madness. The words felt like bile coming out, but Taniel asked, "Can he be healed? At least enough to see reason?"

"I don't know," Mihali said. "I broached the subject with him last night. He was furious. The explosion over in Budwiel? You must have heard it. That was him. It killed thousands of Kez camp followers."

"No great loss."

Mihali scowled. Taniel felt a flicker at the edge of his senses, like sorcery was being used. He suddenly wondered whether he should be this close to Mihali.

"Those people," Mihali said, visibly restraining himself, "were not soldiers. They were laundresses and bakers and boot makers. Their lives were snuffed out in an instant because I asked Kresimir the wrong question and he grew angry." Mihali shook his head. "I understand that killing is your profession, but every loss of life is great. Especially so many, and all on the..."

Mihali fell silent. He helped himself to another piece of corn-bread and chewed thoughtfully. His eyes fell on the dolls laid out opposite him by Ka-poel, and his fingers twitched as if he were nervous.

"He's coherent enough to create these Powder Wardens," Taniel said.

Mihali said, "It's the only thing that gives me hope for his recovery. He's not all gone. I might be able to heal him. I would need to restrain Kresimir, though, and I can't do that on my own."

Mihali was looking at Ka-poel when he said that. Taniel didn't like it one bit.

"How?"

"She can do it," Mihali said, nodding at Ka-poel. "I think I mentioned that in my varied lives I have had some contact with Bone-eyes. Their magic is uniquely suited to fighting, harming, protecting, and even controlling individuals. I've never known one with even a fraction of Ka-poel's power. And to think, she taught herself to do all this..." Mihali trailed off. He was breathless, his face flushed.

Controlling individuals, Mihali had said. Did Ka-poel control Taniel? He knew that she had protected him before, and he'd seen what she could do with those dolls of hers.

"And if he's healed?" Taniel asked. "Will he end this war? Leave Adro alone?"

"I believe so. He's not been well."

"You *believe* so? Or you *know* so? He made a promise to destroy Adro."

"A promise that will not be kept. I'll see to it." Mihali spread his pudgy hands, looking from Ka-poel to Taniel. "Please. Help me. Help my brother."

Ka-poel pointed to her broken arm, and then to Mihali.

Mihali's eyebrows went up. "Of course. I've been remiss." He closed his eyes, and Ka-poel suddenly gasped.

Taniel lurched forward, putting his arm behind her back so that she wouldn't fall. "What did you do to her?"

Ka-poel shrugged Taniel away from her and undid the sling around her arm. She flexed and moved it, nodding to herself. He looked at her face. The bruises were gone.

"I can heal your wounds as well," Mihali said.

Taniel flinched away. "I'll keep them, thank you." Silently, Taniel called himself a fool. Why refuse the healing powers of a god? Was he afraid of Mihali's sorcery? Or perhaps afraid of owing someone else? Abrax and Ricard has already done Taniel favors that would require years to pay off.

Taniel touched his fingers to the tender swelling on his face from the beatings given to him by Ket's gendarmes. "I'll keep it as a reminder."

"I ask," Mihali said, standing up, "that you consider my request. In exchange, I have a gift—freely given."

Taniel was wary of any gift given by a god. After all, nothing was free. "What?"

Mihali removed a handkerchief and a knife from his pocket. He pressed one thumb against his knife, then into the handkerchief for a moment, and then handed it to Ka-poel.

His blood. The blood of a god. Taniel felt his heart beat a little faster. What could Ka-poel do with this? Could she control Mihali? Kill him?

Ka-poel tucked the handkerchief silently into her satchel, her face unreadable.

Mihali stepped away from them both and busied himself putting the remaining cornbread and eggs on a tin plate, which he handed to Ka-poel. He lifted his empty platter and gave a bow. "Please," he said, "consider my request—my plea—for help." He bowed low and then left.

Taniel took a shaky breath and looked down, only just realizing that he still held the letter regarding his house arrest. He was to be escorted to Adopest early in the morning. They'd assigned him eight provosts—four from the Wings of Adom, four from the Adran army.

There would be no fighting the Kez or killing their gods for Taniel.

Ka-poel reached out and touched Taniel's chest. She thumped him several times above the heart.

"What?"

She pointed to him and then spread her hands, questioning. Then back at him.

"I don't know what you're getting at, girl," he said, trying to quell his frustration.

She indicated his heart again and pointed emphatically.

"What do I want?"

A nod.

Taniel took a deep breath. "I want to kill something right now. I'm furious. I should be out there fighting. I was born to fight—born to protect Adro."

She pointed at him again, then at the floor. *What do you want now?*

"I want to protect you."

Ka-poel smiled then, and Taniel felt his heart jump. She leaned toward him and pressed her lips to his.

"I'm going after Kresimir's blood," Taniel said.

Mihali paused over an immense pot of soup, the ladle halfway to his lips.

"I see."

"Ka-poel has agreed to subdue him, but she needs his blood. I'll need help getting into the Kez camp."

Mihali considered this for a few moments before taking a sip of his soup. "Mmm. That's good. Needs a little more pepper, though." He brought a jar of whole peppercorns from his apron and poured a measure into the palm of his hand. He ground his hands together, watching the pepper fall into the pot. He stirred the soup, then took another sip. "Perfect."

"It can be hard to take you seriously sometimes," Taniel said. "No. I misspoke. All of the time."

Mihali chuckled, but Taniel hadn't been making a joke.

"The Kez camp," Taniel urged.

"I can conceal you so that you walk right through the Kez sentries,"

Mihali said, moving to a wide iron grill in the middle of the cooking yard. He began flipping turkey legs with practiced speed.

Taniel ducked as he heard the sound of a shout behind him. A glance over his shoulder told him it wasn't directed at him. Walking through the Adran camp was dangerous, even in civilian clothes with a tricorn hat pulled down to conceal his face. He was supposed to be under guard by the provosts right now.

"They won't notice you here, either. Have a turkey leg." Mihali picked up a leg with his tongs and handed it to Taniel.

"That looks hot."

"Nonsense. A chef would never give a guest something that would burn them."

Taniel took the turkey leg with some trepidation. The bone was only warm, despite having just come off the flames, and when he bit into it, juice ran down his unshaved chin. He didn't speak until he was done eating. "How can you make me unseen?" Taniel asked. "Before, you had to ask Ka-poel's permission to touch my mind."

"I just did," Mihali said.

Taniel froze in the midst of picking the last bits of flavor off the turkey leg. He looked around. "I don't feel unseen." He glanced down at the turkey bone. "Did you..."

"Yes," Mihali said. "Doing any kind of constructive sorcery directly to the human body is one of the most difficult things a Privileged can accomplish. That's why healers are so rare. I figured out about a thousand years ago that the easiest way to get a spell into a person was through their stomach." Mihali picked up a turkey leg and took a bite. A sudden look of worry crossed his face. "Let's have that be our secret, hmm?"

Taniel snorted. "I won't tell on you."

"Oh, thank you." Mihali finished his turkey leg noisily and then lifted another off the grill. "Care to take one to Ka-poel?"

"Will it make her unseen? And if I'm unseen now, how will she see me? Or how are you seeing me?"

"I can see you because I'm a god. Ka-poel will be able to sense where you are, and the spell doesn't muffle your voice."

"If I sneeze?"

"Uh"—Mihali tapped the tongs against his apron, leaving a greasy stain—"Don't. The spell does have its drawbacks. For instance, it is designed to drop as soon as you get close to Kresimir's sphere of influence. It would backfire to have Kresimir sense my intrusion."

Taniel looked at his hand. He certainly didn't feel unseen. "How long did it take you to come up with this?"

"A few moments."

"Really?"

Mihali raised an eyebrow. "We're not called gods necessarily because we're the most powerful Privileged—though that is an interpretation. We're called gods because the things that regular mortals struggle for days, weeks, or months to accomplish take us only the effort of a thought."

"Ah. Well, I'm going now."

"Wait." Mihali produced a deep pewter mug seemingly out of nowhere and crossed to his pot of soup. He ladled the mug full and set a lid on it. "Take this to Ka-poel. It'll help her sleep while you're gone."

Taniel turned to go, when he thought better of it. "Adom—Mihali?"

"Hmm?"

"Will you protect her?"

"I feel after giving her my blood, that it is I who need protection," Mihali said. He winked. "That girl is like a glass teapot filled with gunpowder. So fragile, but with such a power for destruction." He straightened up and swung the ladle into a salute. Soup spattered on his apron. "No harm will come to her."

"Thank you," Taniel said. "Now I'm going to get some of your brother's blood."

CHAPTER
33

Tamas watched Olem rub down his horse as the camp settled in for the night. A low fire of brush and prairie twigs crackled in a stone ring in front of him. The sun still shone in the western sky, lighting the plateau with a brilliant hue of reds, oranges, and pinks.

Their second day on the plateau, and their supplies were already running low. They'd slaughtered thousands of Kez horses after the battle fourteen days before, but only been able to carry a limited amount. What little food they had needed to be rationed. A pound of meat per man per day was not much.

Tamas lifted his head at a sound carried on the wind. He waited a few seconds, then returned to gazing at the flames. Beside him, Olem was snapping twigs and feeding them into the fire.

His rangers still hadn't found this mysterious Adran army, but there were plenty of signs of their passing. Stripped bean fields, burned farms. The dead and the dying, the old and the infirm of what was left of the farmers of the Northern Expanse. The plateau was already a dry, exhausted land. Whatever army had come through two weeks ago had killed everything living.

Per his orders, the army had dug a six-foot trench around the entire camp. It was backbreaking work, but he'd be damned if he'd be caught at night by an army he didn't see coming. Some of his soldiers were still digging. The sound of shovels scraping rocks and dirt, the curses of infantry working after a long day's march.

Tamas lifted his head again. That sound. What was it? He cocked his head to one side, trying to find a location.

Nothing.

Had the Deliv turned on him? The king of Deliv had been firm in his response earlier this summer when Tamas had asked for allies against the Kez. They'd promised to stay out of the war entirely.

"May I join you, Field Marshal?"

Tamas looked up. The lengthening shadows tricked his eyes for a moment before he made out Beon je Ipille. Tamas gestured to the bare ground on the other side of the fire. Beon lowered himself gingerly to the ground, crossing his legs beneath him. The Kez general's eyes were sunken, his face pale. He was one of the few Kez officers that Tamas had kept with him as prisoners—the rest were paroled to the Kez army.

"How is your arm?" Tamas asked.

Beon looked down at his left arm where it hung in a sling. "It is well, thank you. My physician says that the arm is not broken, but I lost quite a lot of blood in the melee. I should recover in time. Your injuries?"

"Fine." Tamas ran a couple of fingers over his ribs, wincing at the tenderness. He didn't think they'd cracked from his fight with Gavril, but his body felt like one big bruise. "I'm wishing I'd brought Dr. Petrik along when I left Budwiel. But then again, my plans at the time were greatly different from how things ended up."

Beon nodded, staring into the fire. He took a deep breath and opened his mouth, only to close it again. It was several minutes before he finally spoke.

"I remember riding through the Northern Expanse once," Beon said. "It must have been six or seven years ago. I went along with some of my father's Privileged on a delegation to Deliv. This land was greener, more full." Beon smiled sadly. "Towns threw festivals in our honor. There were thousands of people—proud, happy farmers.

"Now I can't help but wonder: what has happened to my country?" Beon looked around. "The last two days, I've seen countless abandoned farms. The bean fields are all gone. The land is brown and dry. I've heard reports of the droughts, both here and in the rest of the Nine, but I didn't imagine it to be so bad.

"What's more, where are all my people? We passed a farm this morning. The crop—and there had been a crop, I'm not so removed that I can't see that—was trampled, and the farm buildings burned remnants. I must ask you, Field Marshal. Have you sent men on ahead? Are you destroying these lands?"

"The desolation you see," Tamas said, his pride pricked at the accusation, "was not caused by my men. I swear it."

"It must have been bandits, then."

Tamas wondered how much he should tell Beon of his suspicions. "I don't think so."

Beon didn't seem to hear him. "Two days ago," Beon said, "I rode past an old man on a pack mule. He begged me to right the wrongs and expel the Adran foreigners that were ravishing our lands." Beon spoke carefully, as if testing the waters before a swim.

"My scouts tell me another army has come through this way," Tamas said. "And reports from what serfs remain in the area say that they wear Adran blues. This makes me wonder, as I know for a fact that I have no men in northern Kez."

Beon gazed at Tamas, brow furrowed, as if trying to decide whether Tamas was speaking the truth.

Tamas asked, "Do you know whether your father sent legions north, disguised as Adrans, in order to sneak through Deliv and over the mountains?"

"I don't. Besides, our soldiers wouldn't do this to their own land."

Tamas wondered where Beon got such a high regard for the morals of infantry.

Olem suddenly grabbed his rifle and surged to his feet. "Sir," he said, "did you hear that?"

Tamas paused and listened. Nothing.

Wait. There. It sounded like a shout. Very distant. He climbed to his feet. Nearby, a slight rise in the terrain gave him a better vantage point. He scanned the horizon, listening for the shout again.

"There," Olem said, pointing north.

Dust rose off the plateau, a billowing trail of the kind made when multiple riders were coming hard. "Saddle my mount," Tamas said to Olem. "Quickly!"

Tamas ran through the camp. A few hundred yards from his own tent, the powder mages were camped together. Most of them were there, their legs splayed, boots off, talking as they passed around a bottle they'd got from who knew where. Vlora stood when she saw Tamas.

"Andriya, Vlora," Tamas barked. "With me! The rest of you, raise the general alarm. Riders on the northern horizon."

"How many, sir?" Vlora asked as they headed back to the north end of the camp.

"That's what we're going to find out," Tamas said. "Do you know where Gavril is?"

"Ranging," Andriya answered.

"Where?"

"North, I think."

"Pit. You two, get horses."

Olem brought Tamas his horse and rifle. He threw himself into the saddle and headed north, not waiting for anyone else. Olem caught up to him quickly enough—he'd not yet unsaddled his own mount from the day.

"What's happening, sir?" Olem shouted over the sound of hooves thundering on the dusty soil.

"Riders," Tamas said. "A lot of them."

"Could it just be Gavril's rangers?"

Tamas wanted to say yes, but he fixed his eyes on the cloud of dust rising in the distance. It was getting larger. Too big to be less than twenty horses, and Gavril's rangers worked in pairs.

They left camp behind and headed north along the main road. A glance over his shoulder told Tamas that more riders were following him out of the camp, a few hundred yards behind him.

Tamas fumbled in his pocket for a powder charge as his body rocked up and down with the motion of the stallion beneath him. He put it straight in his mouth and bit down, tasting the bitter sulfur and the grit between his teeth. He spit the soggy charge paper out as the powder trance coursed through his veins.

The ground rushed by beneath his charger's hooves and the horizon came into stark relief. He found the cloud of dust and traced it to the source. There, miles away, a single horseman.

Tamas frowned. Just one? The horseman lay low on his mount, clinging to the horse's neck. Tamas thought he recognized him as one of Gavril's rangers.

A few moments later, breasting a rise in terrain behind the ranger, came more riders.

Their uniforms were blue with silver trim, and they wore the conical, horsehair helmets of Adran dragoons.

Tamas swore. Adran dragoons? It couldn't be. If they were, the ranger wouldn't be fleeing before them. Tamas looked over at Olem, but the bodyguard couldn't see that far.

"Dragoons," Tamas shouted at him. "Chasing one of our rangers! They're wearing Adran blues, but they're not friendly."

Olem responded by urging his mount harder.

Tamas put his head down and counted the beats of the hooves as they closed the distance between themselves and the ranger. As he drew closer, he was able to tell that the dragoons were perhaps a half mile behind the ranger. The ranger's horse frothed at the mouth, shaking its head hard. It wouldn't last much longer.

Tamas waved his pistol at the ranger, motioning for him to stop. The ranger's horse shuddered and swayed, eyes rolling as the ranger reined in beside Tamas. The ranger's face and front were covered in dust, smeared and muddy from his sweat.

"Where's Gavril?" Tamas demanded.

The ranger gasped for breath, trying to speak, before he threw his hand out behind him. "Far...back...fought so I could... escape."

"Who are they?"

"Kez! We thought they were friendlies, but they fell on us the moment Gavril spoke in Adran."

Tamas whirled toward the dragoons and quickly counted. Sixteen. They waved their carbines and hollered, showing no sign of slowing at the sight of Tamas and Olem. They'd be upon him in minutes. He raised his off hand to steady his pistol and closed one eye. He squeezed the trigger.

In his head, he counted seconds, concentrating on the powder, keeping the bullet flying far beyond when it should have fallen. At the same time, his hands worked to holster one pistol and draw the other.

One. Two. Thr...

A dragoon near the rear of the group fell, the bullet taking him neatly in the eye.

Tamas steadied his second pistol and fired. Another dragoon fell. Again, at the rear of the group. Tamas didn't want to scare off the dragoons, and it didn't seem like they noticed their comrades' fall.

"Olem! With me!"

Tamas dug his heels in and spurred his horse forward. He holstered his second pistol and drew his heavy cavalry saber. It felt good in his grip, the old leather handle worn and strong.

The dragoons aimed their carbines at seventy yards. They fired, and Tamas heard one bullet whistle past his ear.

Hitting a single riding target from horseback was difficult at best, if you weren't a powder mage.

He cocked his saber back and eyed the lead dragoon. The man was missing an ear. Earless stowed his carbine and drew his straight cavalry sword in one quick motion.

Hand still on the reins, Tamas dug into his front uniform pocket for a small handful of bullets.

Tamas studied the position of Earless's sword, then ran his eyes over the next few dragoons, all in a pair of seconds. Tamas leaned to his right, bringing his saber up high.

Then they were upon each other.

Tamas slid to his left in the saddle, narrowly avoiding the stroke of Earless's sword. His cavalry saber bit through soft flesh, the top three inches cleaving through Earless's neck. Tamas worked a bullet up to the top of his fist and flicked it in the air with his thumb, burning powder from a spare charge to send it into the heart of the next dragoon. He followed through with his saber cut, bringing it over his horse's head and deflecting the stab from a dragoon on his left.

He flicked another bullet into the air and burned powder, sending it backward and into Earless's spine.

Back over his mount's head with his saber, Tamas sawed on the reins. A dragoon at the rear of the group leaned toward him with a savage slice.

Parry. Parry again.

The dragoon was fast, and skilled. Tamas flicked a bullet into the air, sending it into the dragoon's shoulder. The dragoon dropped his sword, clutching at his arm, and Tamas rammed his saber into the man's chest.

Tamas spun around, looking for the next enemy, only to see two of the dragoons surrender to Olem. In the distance to the south, puffs of powder smoke rose from a pair of figures—Vlora and Andriya. Tamas rode to one of the surrendered dragoons.

"Where is Gavril?" he said in Kez.

The dragoon stared back at him.

"Where is Gavril? A big man! Where is he?"

The dragoon shook his head.

"Pit." Tamas cleaned and sheathed his sword. "Olem, with me!"

"Sir, my horse is lame." Olem was already dismounting. His horse was in a panic, blood streaming from a wound beneath its neck.

"Then take one of theirs!"

"The prisoners..."

"Leave them! I'll not lose another brother in this forsaken country!"

Tamas pushed on without waiting for an answer. A while later, he looked over his shoulder to see Olem and the powder mages struggling to keep up.

The sun set on the western horizon, bathing Tamas in twilight. He kept on, the hot night air whipping his hair and jacket, drying the blood on his cheeks. His charger began to struggle, breathing hard, slowing despite his continued urging.

Olem was lost to him as darkness spread on the plateau. The eerie sound of howling brush wolves reached his ears above the whistling of the wind. His powder trance wore off, and he chewed another powder charge to bring it back again. The road passed in a blur and the pounding of hooves.

He did not know how far or how long he'd ridden when his charger stumbled. He jolted from the saddle, thrown for several feet, and landed hard on his shoulder.

Tamas staggered to his feet. Silence. Nothing in the night. No sound of hooves from his soldiers following. No sign or sound of dragoons. Just the desperate gasping of his charger.

Where was Gavril? What had happened to him? Tamas ran a hand through his sweaty, dirty hair. His hat was gone, blown off he knew not when. He stumbled over to examine the horse, his legs wobbly from riding too long and too hard.

The charger lay on its side. It rolled its eyes at him, foam and blood at its nose and the corner of its mouth. Tamas blinked away tears and tried to calm the beast with a hand on its flank. It twitched and tried to stand up, only to let out a shuddering scream. The sound shook Tamas's soul.

The horse's leg had shattered, bone sticking out from the side. It must have stepped in a hole and stumbled from exhaustion.

Tamas drew his pistol. He loaded it slowly, carefully.

The shot rang out across the plateau.

Tamas gathered his saddlebags, ammunition, pistols, and rifle. He began to walk north.

He didn't know when he'd stopped. Only that he was suddenly on his knees, staring at his hands. They were raw from the reins. Where had his riding gloves gone? He shook his head and thought to stand and keep going.

Instead, he dropped his head into his hands. Another brother. All that remained of his family gone except, perhaps, his son. Tamas had failed again.

He should have stopped. Interrogated those Kez dragoons. Found out if Gavril was even alive, and where they'd taken him. How many dragoons in their company.

Tamas knew he'd been a fool, riding on like that. A desperate fool, trying to save his brother. Alone.

Tamas wept.

The tears were dry when Tamas heard hoofbeats on the road. They came on at a steady canter from the south. One set, from the sound of things.

"Tamas?" a female voice called.

Vlora.

She shouted his name again. The hoofbeats grew closer, then stopped. The crunch of gravel as she leapt from her horse. Then hands on his shoulders, shaking him.

"Sir, please. Answer me. Tamas!"

Tamas took a long breath, holding it for several beats before letting it out.

"I'm here." His voice surprised him, coming out a whispered croak.

He felt something forced into his hands. He looked down. A canteen. He took a sip.

"Your horse..."

"Broke its leg," Tamas said. "I had to put it down."

"I know. I saw it. Almost two miles back. You kept walking, all this way?"

"Poor creature. Died because I wouldn't stop."

Vlora put her cool hand on the back of his neck. "Drink more."

"Couldn't find Gavril," Tamas said. "Tried. Couldn't. Failed again. Another brother, gone. My last. I..." He felt the tears coming again and stopped to take several deep breaths. "Where's Olem?"

"His horse threw a shoe nearly fifteen miles ago."

"Fifteen miles..."

Vlora took his face in her hands, forcing him to look up at her. He wondered what she saw then, in his eyes. A broken old man, dirty from the road?

"Tamas," Vlora said, "you rode nearly forty miles. It will be dawn in an hour."

Tamas blinked the tears out of his eyes and looked up. It felt like he was looking at a different world. The moon was high overhead, the stars bright.

She examined him for several moments. He knew she could see that he was low on powder and ammunition. He'd dropped his rifle at some point. But not the pistols. Not the ones Taniel had given him. No, he wouldn't leave those behind for the world. Taniel—his boy—had given them to him.

Tamas struggled to his feet, letting Vlora take some of his weight. He looked north. Forty miles. He was in Deliv now. Closer to Alvation than he was to his own army.

Foolish. Bloody foolish of him.

Vlora went to her horse and began unloading her saddle.

"What are you doing?"

"We're camping here," Vlora said.

"I've got to return..."

"Don't be stupid, Tamas. The army will catch up in two days. If you keep going tonight, you'll be utterly useless when we reach Alvation."

She was right, of course. Not that he liked it.

He drew himself up. "I'm your—"

"My commanding officer. I know. Here's a bedroll. I'll take first watch."

Tamas looked down at the bedroll thrust into his hands, then up at the moon, and finally to the north, where Alvation sat somewhere in the darkness, just off the edge of the plateau.

"Another brother," he heard himself say again. "Another."

CHAPTER
34

Tamas didn't wake until the heat of the noonday sun finally drove him out of a restless sleep. He sat up suddenly, looking down stupidly at the hat in his lap. He lifted it, turned it around. It wasn't his. Far too small.

Vlora. She was gone, and Tamas wondered if her coming to find him the night before had been just a fevered dream.

"She went looking for water for the horses, sir."

Tamas looked behind him. Olem sat on a rock, carefully cleaning his carbine. He had saddlebags and canteens. Tamas rolled his tongue around inside his mouth. It felt dry and hot, his tongue two sizes too big.

"Canteen," Tamas said.

Olem tossed him a canteen and Tamas drank hungrily.

"When did you catch up?"

"Just after dawn," Olem said. He was looking at Tamas strangely. "You don't look so well, sir."

Tamas ran his hand through what was left of his hair and gingerly felt along the stitches in his scalp. "Lost my hat last night."

"Ah." Olem's gaze seemed to say, *What, we're not going to mention you rode off like a madman last night? What the pit is wrong with you?*

Tamas looked away. "There's not much water on this damned plateau."

"We passed an old river bed in the night," Olem said. "I couldn't tell if there was anything in the bottom. Vlora has gone to check."

Tamas got to his feet and walked a few circles around the camp. He felt awful. His legs were sore and cramped—especially his bad one—his crotch chafed, his face wind-burned and hands raw. He had a pounding headache, from too little water and too little rest. Every time he stopped his circuit, he couldn't help but look north, toward Alvation, then again to the south.

Vlora returned an hour later with the horses and full waterskins.

Late in the afternoon, they were joined by the rest of the powder mages and ten of Olem's Riflejacks. Not long after that, several of the rangers caught up with them. Tamas immediately sent them out scouting to the north.

Late in the day, Tamas saw riders on the northern horizon, miles off. They never came closer, but Tamas could see they were wearing blue uniforms with silver trim. Who were these impostors? Were they Kez, as he suspected?

The army reached Tamas by late the next day. They pitched camp there, and Tamas's first order of business was to find the Kez dragoons he'd fought two days earlier.

There were three of them. They were a ragged lot, their horses, weapons, supplies, and helmets confiscated. Their faces were burned from the sun. One of them walked with a heavy limp, and dried blood on his trousers said the wound was recent. Another was missing two front teeth.

The third was missing his boots. He'd wrapped the bloody remnants of his jacket around his feet.

One of their guards pointed at the man with his jacket wrapped around his feet. His white undershirt was stained brown and yellow from sweat and blood. He had short brown hair and large muttonchops. "That's their lieutenant," the guard said. "That's what his jacket said, before he tore it."

"Where are his boots?" Tamas asked.

"Took them away," the guard said. "To try to get him to talk."

Tamas sighed. "Go find them. No way to treat an officer, even a prisoner of war." He turned to the lieutenant and spoke to him in his own language: "What is your name?"

The man stared past Tamas.

"Tell me your name, and I'll give you your boots back."

"What?" the man said with a thick Adran accent. "I don't speak Kez."

Tamas rolled his eyes. "I know you're a Kez officer. Keep pretending to be Adran and I'll have you shot for desertion." He leaned forward. "I can do things to my own men that I can't do to a prisoner of war."

The man's eyes flicked to Tamas. He flinched. "Lieutenant Mernoble," he said. "The King's Thirty-Fourth Dragoons."

"What are you doing here, Mernoble?" Tamas asked. "We are in Deliv."

"Weren't in Deliv when you caught us," Mernoble said.

"You came from the north. The only thing north at the time was Deliv."

Mernoble returned his gaze to the spot over Tamas's shoulder and didn't speak. A few moments later, the guard returned with Mernoble's boots. Tamas took them and handed them over to Mernoble.

Mernoble took the boots. "With your leave?"

Tamas nodded.

Mernoble sat on the ground and gingerly unwrapped his feet. Tamas winced at the sight. The lieutenant's socks were torn and soaked with blood, his feet raw. It looked like he'd been walking without boots for miles. He slipped the boots on carefully, unable to suppress a groan when he returned to his feet.

"Have they been given water?" Tamas asked. When the guard didn't answer, Tamas turned to him. "Well? Water, or food?"

The guard shook his head.

"Damn it, man, go get them food. They're soldiers, just like you."

The guard scurried off.

"He's getting you some food," Tamas said in Kez.

Mernoble nodded gratefully.

"Why were you in Deliv?" Tamas asked again.

Mernoble took a deep breath and returned to staring past Tamas.

Tamas scowled. "Do you know who I am?"

The man shook his head.

"I am Field Marshal Tamas."

Mernoble swallowed. Hard.

"Come with me," Tamas said. To one of the other guards, "Where is General Beon's tent?"

"Are you sure that's wise, sir?" The guard seemed confused.

"What do you mean, man? Where is the general's tent?"

"Just over there."

Tamas walked through the camp until he found Beon sitting beside a low fire of twigs and old horse dung. The general struggled to stand when he saw Tamas. At the sight of the prisoner, his eyes narrowed.

"General Beon," Tamas said, "I have gathered by your demeanor that you would be greatly interested in knowing who has been burning, raping, and robbing their way through the bean farms on the plateau."

"I would," Beon said. His tone was icy. "I discovered it last night, in fact. These men are Kez officers, pretending to be Adran." He looked down at Mernoble's feet. "Who gave him back his boots?"

Tamas looked from Beon to Mernoble. The lieutenant's eyes were wide with fear, and suddenly Tamas understood. It had been Beon who ordered Mernoble's boots taken away. Likely, he'd ordered the lieutenant be left unfed as well. Tamas's own men would have been more than happy to go along with it. "I did."

"I demand that this man's boots be removed, and that you organize a firing squad. I want these men executed tomorrow morning for crimes against the people of Kez."

Tamas bit back a reply. He'd not be ordered around by a prisoner, even if he did respect Beon. Instead, he turned to Mernoble. "It seems time to explain yourself, Lieutenant."

Mernoble's hands were shaking. "What would you like to know?"

"Everything," Beon said. For his youth, his demeanor was commanding.

Tamas put a hand on Mernoble's shoulder. "First, tell me where Gavril is. He was a big man. Captured by your unit two days ago, before you chased my ranger back to my camp."

"They took him back to Alvation," Mernoble said.

"Alive?"

"Yes."

Tamas let out a small sigh. That was the first thing he needed to know. Now to find out the rest.

"Is that all, sir?"

"No. Start with your brigade," Tamas said.

"I am with the Thirty-Fourth Dragoons, attached to the Nineteenth Brigade of His Majesty's Grand Army," Mernoble said. "We were sent north..."

"Who?" Tamas asked. "How many?"

"Two brigades. The Nineteenth and the Twenty-Fourth. We

were sent north seven weeks ago with the aim of capturing the Deliv city of Alvation."

"For what purpose?" Tamas asked. Now was his chance to ask questions. This man might clam up once he realized how his answers benefited the enemy.

"So that we could besiege the Mountainwatch above Alvation. We were to take Alvation, then the Mountainwatch, then come over the Charwood Pile and down into Adro."

"And the uniforms?" Tamas asked.

"A ruse. To make the Deliv think that an Adran army had sacked Alvation."

Tamas's breath caught in his throat. If the Kez attacked Deliv while masquerading as Adran, it might force Deliv into the war on the Kez side.

"Have you succeeded?"

Mernoble looked at Beon, but only got an icy stare for the effort. "We took Alvation," he said. "About a week and a half ago. The Mountainwatch commander saw through our disguise, so we haven't entered Adro yet. The Mountainwatch is under siege."

"How do you explain this treatment of my people, Lieutenant?" Beon asked. "Of *our* people?"

"I'm not proud of it, sir," Mernoble said, casting his eyes downward. "When we left the Grand Army, we were ordered to travel lightly and quickly. Live off the land with a limited supply caravan. Conscript as needed. The order came from His Majesty himself. When we found the Adran rangers, we were on a scouting mission, looking for more food and conscripts."

"My father sanctioned this treatment?" Beon growled the question.

Mernoble nodded.

"Who is the general in charge of the Nineteenth?"

"It was Field Marshal—I mean, General Tine," Mernoble said. General, after being demoted because of his failure to take the

South Pike Mountainwatch. "Was?" Tamas asked. Tine was a capable commander, but pragmatic and often cavalier with his men's lives. Tamas would not have been surprised to see him act in this manner.

"He was hanged, sir. For treason."

"Hanged?" Beon said.

"That's what I heard, sir. And I saw the body. Last week."

"He was a general," Tamas said. "The orders would have had to come straight from Ipille." He stepped away, taking a deep breath of the evening air. This was strange. Very strange. Ipille was a tyrant, but he was no idiot. He wouldn't have wanted to provoke war with Deliv.

Tamas returned to the pair. "Who the pit would convince Ipille it's a good idea to attack Alvation?"

"I don't know sir, I..."

"Yes?"

"Well, I'm not privy to that information, but I had heard rumors."

"Go on."

"It was the Privileged."

"What Privileged?" Tamas felt his hackles rise. Most of the Kez Cabal had died on South Pike, or so he'd been told.

"Rumors were he came out of Adro. His Majesty's own envoy. Only took him two days to convince His Majesty to attack Deliv."

Tamas put his hands on Mernoble's shoulders, feeling suddenly desperate. "His name, damn it. What was it?"

"He's the same that hanged Field Marshal Tine. The same in Alvation right now."

"Tell me his bloody name."

"Duke Nikslaus, sir."

Adamat paced his living room and tried to decide what to do with his family.

It had taken them four days' hard travel to return to Adopest. He'd not seen Ricard since that afternoon when Adamat had spotted Brudania-Gurla Trading Company ships coming down the canal lock system. Ricard had insisted on going to find out what the devil was going on, while Adamat had taken his family back to Adopest right away.

He feared that Ricard had been captured.

Adamat tried to remind himself that he had far too little information with which to make informed decisions. Perhaps there was another explanation for the Trading Company ships. But his mind kept going back to one thing: Adro had been invaded by Brudania.

It was as if all of Adamat's nightmares were coming true. Claremonte was bringing the might of the Trading Company fleet down on Adopest. With the entire army tied up against the Kez in southern Adro, the capital city was completely defenseless. The Mountainwatch had been muscled out of defending the canal by Ricard himself. There was absolutely nothing to stop Claremonte from sailing down the Ad River and taking the city.

How long had Claremonte been planning this? He must have quietly captured the lock system weeks ago, and bribed the Deliv navy to let him sail his fleet up the canal from the ocean.

What did Claremonte want with Adro? To conquer it? Did he want their resources? Was the Brudania-Gurla Trading Company in the employ of the Kez? Or were they operating on their own? Adamat found the latter thought somehow more terrifying than the former. If both Brudania and Kez wanted Adro, Adopest would be torn apart between them.

He had to get his family out of the city. Who knew what an occupying army would do?

But where to go?

They were trapped. One army to the south, one to the north.

He could send them to Novi. Adamat didn't know anyone in Novi. Perhaps he could...

There was a knock on the door. Adamat snatched the pistol from his desk and took a sip of wine before heading to the front hallway.

"Stay upstairs," he said when he saw Astrit looking curiously down from the landing.

He opened the door to find a servant there. Adamat recognized him, though he'd never heard the man's name. One of Ricard's.

"Inspector Adamat?" the servant said.

"Yes?" Adamat said cautiously.

"Mr. Tumblar requests you at the Warriors' headquarters, sir. There's a carriage waiting."

"He's back?"

"Arrived less than an hour ago, sir," the servant said.

Could this be a trap? Were agents of Lord Claremonte there now, waiting to kill Adamat when he showed his face? Or was Adamat just being paranoid? "Did he say anything else?"

"No, sir. Just requested your presence."

"I'll be a moment."

Adamat went out to the garden behind the house where Faye was sitting alone with a book. The sun shone down between the rooftops, and Faye had her head tilted back, face to the light, her book sitting in her lap.

"Love," Adamat said gently.

Faye jumped. The book slid from her grasp, and she put a hand to her chest.

"Don't sneak up on me like that," she said. "Was someone at the door?"

Adamat fetched the book and gave it back to her. "Yes. A messenger from Ricard. He's asked to see me."

"Well?"

"I want you to go to Novi," he said.

"I will not."

"Please, no more arguing." They'd fought the entire trip back from the north over what she and the children should do. She wanted to stay in the city. He wanted her to get out. "You'll be safer in Novi."

"Just like I was safer in Nafolk?" she asked, bristling.

"Faye..."

"Don't 'Faye' me," she said. "We'll stay together. No more sending us off for our own good. Me. The children. We're not going anywhere."

Adamat opened his mouth to protest, but couldn't think of what to say. He wasn't going to win, he knew that, but he still wanted to fight. Couldn't she see it was better for her to be somewhere safe?

Adamat leaned forward to kiss the top of her head. "I'm going to see what Ricard has to say," he said.

CHAPTER
35

Taniel crossed the no-man's-land between the Adran and Kez armies under the cover of dark.

He supposed he could have done it during the day. He'd walked unseen through the Adran camp just to try out Mihali's spell. It worked. But some deep reservation kept him from trusting Mihali completely.

He arrived just after midnight. There were sentries stationed a half mile out from the Kez camp. If the Kez operated anything like the Adran army, many of the sentries would be Knacked—men who could see in the dark or hear quiet noises and had the third eye. Taniel had forgotten to ask if the spell worked against the third eye.

Or if he made sounds when he walked.

He stopped a few dozen yards from the closest sentry and poured a measure of black powder across the back of his hand. A single, long snort and the powder was gone.

Taniel dusted off his nose and crouched in a shallow streambed. There wasn't much cover to speak of in the valley. What little brush there was had been stripped by the Adran camp for burning or to make space for tents or just because soldiers got bored. Taniel could smell that a latrine had been dug nearby.

He measured the space between the two closest sentries. Fifty paces, give or take. He headed for the gap.

A twig snapped beneath his foot, and one of the sentries turned toward Taniel.

"Password!" the sentry demanded in Kez.

The sentry waited for a few moments. The barrel of his musket wavered, and he squinted into the dark.

"Powell?" the sentry called. "Powell!"

"Heh?"

The reply came from less than ten feet away. Taniel could feel his heart beating in his throat.

"You see anyone out there?"

"What kind of fool question is that? I'd a-raised the alarm if I did."

"I thought I heard something. Coulda been a spy."

"Idiot. If it was a spy, he knows I'm here now."

"Oh." The first sentry seemed pleased with himself. "Then we scared him off, did we?"

"By Kresimir, you're daft. Just watch the night."

Taniel skirted the spot he'd heard the voice come from. Even with his Marked eyesight he couldn't make out a figure in the darkness. The sentry must have been damned good at hiding.

Taniel passed a few dozen more sentries without incident and then he was in the heart of the Kez camp. He wasn't sure when Mihali's sorcerous invisibility would cease, so he did his best to keep low as he crept through the camp.

It was desolate. In the Adran camp there was always someone awake. Men telling stories or women doing laundry, no matter the hour. The fires were kept going most of the night, and there was always the hum of quiet voices. The Kez camp, however...

The tents were in perfectly straight lines, giving Taniel good vision down the aisles. He didn't spot a soul for five minutes, when he finally caught sight of a squad of Kez guards. They marched double-time through the center of the camp, eyes straight ahead, muskets held over their heads. It looked more like they were being punished than that they were on guard duty.

Taniel avoided the few patrols and made his way toward the rear of the camp. It wasn't hard to find his objective.

The command tent was as big as a city administration building and was made up of a dozen smaller tents. Guards were posted at even intervals around the entire tent complex. Light shone through the walls, and Taniel's Marked hearing could make out the sound—if not the words themselves—of heated argument.

Someone was still up. That suited Taniel fine.

He hunkered down behind a soldier's tent and watched the main entrance. He didn't need anything fancy. Just someone who'd know their way around the Kez camp. A high-ranking officer would be the best.

It didn't take long before whatever argument had been taking place died down. Five minutes later, officers began exiting the tent.

Taniel watched them go, noting what direction they went.

A major. Another major. A colonel—good. A general. Even better.

He shifted in his hiding spot, ready to follow the general at a distance, when someone else caught his eye.

Taniel recognized the man. Field Marshal Goutlit—Tine's replacement. Tamas had always referred to Goutlit as a competent bureaucrat, a man who thought of losses as nothing more than numbers on paper and had no qualms about sending ten thousand men to their deaths if it would win him even a trivial victory.

Goutlit immediately headed south, toward the rear of the Kez camp. One of the guards broke off from the command tent and followed.

So did Taniel.

Goutlit's sleeping quarters was a farmhouse only a few hundred yards from the command tent. The field marshal went inside while the guard took up a station beside the front door.

Taniel rounded the farmhouse once. Two windows, both with shutters fastened tight. No other door but the front.

He pressed himself up against the wall of the farmhouse and crept back around to the front. A hand over the guard's mouth and a knife between the ribs and into the man's left lung was enough to keep him from making noise. Taniel removed the knife and rammed it into the guard's heart, then slowly lowered the body to the ground.

"Pouli," Goutlit called from inside. "Get in here."

The door creaked when it opened. The farmhouse was dark but for a light coming from the only other room.

"Pouli," Goutlit said from the other room. "They didn't bring the girl I asked for. Damned quartermasters can't do a thing right. Go and fetch her this instant. It's late enough as it is, I want to be asleep in half an hour."

Taniel grabbed the dead guard by the belt and dragged him inside, then closed the door.

"I said this instant, man. If I have to—"

Goutlit came out of his room carrying a lantern. He was a balding man of medium height and square shoulders and a strong gaze. He'd removed his jacket and was shaking his head, obviously in a bout of anger. He froze when he saw the body of his guard.

Taniel was on him in a moment, bloody knife in one hand, the other pressing over Goutlit's mouth to cut off a strangled cry.

"Shh," Taniel said. "Quiet now, or I cut out your heart." He waved the knife in front of Goutlit's eyes. "This is how it works: If you call out, I kill you. If you try to run, I kill you. I'm faster and stronger than you and I won't hesitate. Do you understand?"

Behind Taniel's hand, Goutlit whispered, "I only speak Kez."

"Don't lie to me. I met you years ago at a ball thrown by Manhouch and you spoke Adran fine. Now tell me, do you understand?"

Goutlit inhaled sharply. "Yes."

Taniel stepped away from Goutlit, but watched him carefully out of the corner of his eye. He checked outside the door. No alarm. No one suspicious that the guard was not at his post.

"Can you see me?"

"What?" Goutlit said. "Of course."

So Mihali's invisibility was gone for certain.

Goutlit slowly sagged into a chair. "Who are you?" he asked in Adran. "Are you here to kill me? I have money. I can make you a rich man."

"I don't care about your money," Taniel said. "I won't kill you if you cooperate."

Goutlit, Taniel remembered his father saying, was not a brave man. His strength was arithmetic. He stayed as far from the fighting as possible and only engaged the enemy when he had overwhelming force.

"I will not betray my country," Goutlit said, chin up.

Taniel left the dead guard and pounced on Goutlit. The man let out a high whimper and tried to press himself into his chair. "If you don't help me, I won't think any more about snuffing out your life than you would of killing a mouse in your pantry."

Another whimper.

"No need to betray anything," Taniel said. "No one will ever question your loyalty. Though you may want to come up with some reason as to why Pouli here wound up dead." Taniel left

Goutlit, smelling mildly like piss, in his chair and finished getting Pouli's boots off and then took the man's pants and jacket. They'd be a bit too big, but they'd have to do.

"Tell me about Kresimir," Taniel said.

Goutlit remained silent.

"The god," Taniel said roughly, "living in your camp. Where is he?"

"He's living in the old keep. About a mile south of here. He was in Budwiel, living in the mayor's mansion, but two days ago it was destroyed by Adran sorcery."

Taniel chuckled. "Adran sorcery, huh? Does the General Staff believe that?"

Goutlit licked his lips. Enough of an answer.

"So he's in Midway Keep?"

Goutlit said, "That's it."

"Guards?"

"Prielights."

Elite guards of the Kresim Church. As far as Taniel knew, the Church had made no public proclamation about the war. It seemed like they were ready to defend their god, though. "How many?"

"I don't know."

"Inside or out?"

"Both."

"Does Kresimir ever come into the camp?"

Goutlit shook his head. "Never. We always go to him."

"Is it true he wears a mask with no right eyehole?"

"Yes."

Taniel tongued his teeth. Interesting.

"Who are you?" Goutlit asked as Taniel put on the dead guard's pants.

Taniel tightened his belt. "Change your pants. You smell like piss. And get your jacket."

Goutlit's hands shook as he changed his clothes. Taniel watched, just to be sure the man wouldn't try to slip out a window.

Taniel spotted the liquor cabinet in the corner. He crossed to it and found a bottle of Starlish whiskey, pouring out half a measure. He held the glass out to Goutlit.

The Kez field marshal drank it hungrily in two great gulps, then doubled over coughing. Taniel cringed and listened for any voices outside the farmhouse. Nothing.

"You're him, aren't you?" Goutlit asked.

"Who?"

"The eye behind the flintlock. Taniel Two-Shot."

Taniel felt his chest grow cold. So. The rumors Mihali had heard were true. Kresimir was looking for him. "Let's go," Taniel said, shouldering the guard's musket. "Remember—any false word or movement and you are a dead man."

Goutlet straightened his jacket. The whiskey seemed to have given him courage. "What do you want of me?"

Taniel opened the front door. The god was coughing blood at night, Mihali had said.

"You're going to help me steal Kresimir's bedsheets."

CHAPTER

36

Are you sure this is wise, sir?" Olem asked. "We're awfully close to the city."

Tamas gazed through his looking glass at the city of Alvation. It was an unwalled city, spilling along the north side of a shallow river that flowed from the northeast and wound along the Northern Expanse. Most of the buildings were two or three stories, smoke rising from their chimneys, with stone-shingled roofs. It was a major intersection of the Great Northern Highway and the Charwood Pass—a Mountainwatch toll road that took trade up over the Charwood Pile and into Adro.

He guessed Alvation to number around a hundred thousand souls. Not as large a city as those in the south of Kez or on the coast of Deliv, but not a small one, by any means.

"No, not entirely," Tamas answered.

Olem lay at Tamas's side. Vlora on his left. Behind him, the rest of his powder mages made camp in an abandoned farmhouse while Tamas, Olem, and Vlora crouched in a dry irrigation ditch and observed the city from three miles out.

An abandoned farmhouse. This close to the city. Something was surely wrong here.

"I don't see any sign of the Kez army," Olem said.

"There." Vlora pointed. "Do you see where the Charwood Pass first enters the city from the west? A little way east of that. Blue-and-silver uniforms. The Kez impostors." Vlora was in a powder trance, like Tamas himself. They'd both be able to see farther and clearer than Olem.

Tamas searched until he found the spot she'd indicated. A group of some fifty soldiers moved through the stalls of an open market, pointing and shouting. They had several large carts and were filling them from the vendors' stalls.

"Nikslaus is bleeding the city for all they've got," Tamas said. "Sending his men out to collect a tax."

Tamas traced the outside of the city with his looking glass, then to where the city met the Charwood Pass. He squinted to see into the long shadows cast by the late-day sun. Figures milled about. More soldiers. Tamas spotted barrels, carts, horses.

"I sense a lot of powder in the city," Vlora said.

"There's an army camped there."

"More than usual."

Tamas didn't know what that could mean. Perhaps the Deliv had been stockpiling powder here in preparation for a war with Kez or Adro. "Interesting."

Vlora said, "At the base of the mountain. Looks like their head-quarters for besieging the Mountainwatch."

"I see it," Tamas said.

"Where the pit is the Deliv army?" Olem asked.

Tamas continued to examine the city. It was a question he'd asked himself a few times. "King Sulam might be gathering an army even now. Or Nikslaus took the city fast enough that word hasn't yet reached Sulam." It was a possibility he didn't want to consider. The Deliv had a proud history of having a swift, efficient army—even if their current one was rather outdated. "Likely, Nikslaus plans on being over the mountains before Sulam responds. Then he can pin it on the Adran army and bring Deliv into the war."

Olem said, "They're occupying the city, sir. The people *have* to know that it's Kez soldiers in disguise." He chewed on his fingernails—he'd been doing that ever since smoking his last cigarette.

"I don't know," Tamas said. "Nikslaus isn't an idiot. He'll think of something."

"Should we bring the army forward? Call for an attack?" Olem asked. "If we position at night, we may be able to blindside them."

"If they don't already know we're here." Tamas cursed quietly under his breath. "They've got Gavril, remember?" The city had no walls, which made it easier to take without artillery, but the Kez were entrenched. They had all the supplies, and knew the lay of the land. Urban warfare would be chaos.

"Sir," Vlora said. "Look at the church steeple near the center of the city."

Tamas scanned along until he found the church.

"Above the bell tower," Vlora said.

Tamas took a sharp breath. Above the bell tower of an old stone Kresim church hung dozens of bodies. Men, women, white Kez, and black Deliv. Children. He felt his stomach turn, and for a moment Sabon's dead face flashed before him.

"Bloody Nikslaus," Tamas said.

"Should we go back, sir?"

"Back?"

"To the army. We'll have to come up with something to take the Kez by surprise."

Tamas examined the bell tower again, then the city as a whole. He ran his gaze along the tops of the buildings, considering angles of attack. He would have to get his men close to the city under cover of night, then cross the shallow river and catch as many of the Kez out in the open as they could.

The best he could hope for in that situation, even if the Deliv rose up and sided with Tamas, would be a weeks-long urban melee with the Kez. And he couldn't afford that, not with thirty thousand Kez infantry still coming on from the south.

"Congratulations, Olem. You've just been promoted to colonel."

"Sir?" Olem's mouth hung open.

"I need someone to head back and give commands to the Seventh and Ninth, and they're not going to take it from a captain."

"But sir, the ranks?"

"I think we can skip 'major' and all that."

"Thank you, sir, but I think—"

Tamas held up a hand to forestall any protestations.

"I have things to do, Olem. First"—Tamas collapsed his looking glass—"I'm going in to find Gavril and get him out. I have an old friend in the city who might help me. Then I'll kill Nikslaus. Then, and only then, we'll go to battle."

Nila sat beside Jakob's bed and listened to the soft sound of his snores. The boy's chest rose and fell slowly, his face peaceful. It reminded her of the cherubs she'd once seen painted on the ceiling of a church. Outside the open window she could hear the sound of a carriage clattering by on the cobbles.

They'd moved from Bo's apartment in the factory district to a small house in one of the few fashionable areas of High Talien, in Adopest's northwest side. From what Bo had said, he had several such "safe houses" scattered around the city. She had wondered at one point where he had gotten the money for all this before remembering that he was a member of the Adran royal cabal.

It was easy to forget, sometimes. Cabal Privileged were known for their cruelty and power. Not for their quiet humor, flirting smiles, and silent generosity.

But he was leaving tomorrow. Heading south, he'd said, to rescue Taniel Two-Shot.

Nila would find herself alone once again, sole guardian to the little boy sleeping before her. What was she going to do with him? Go to Fatrasta? To Novi? Live out the quiet life of a single laundress and tell everyone that Jakob was her little brother?

Would Jakob be able to live with that as he grew older? After all, he'd been a duke's son. Not more than a couple of months ago there had been the very real possibility of him becoming king. She would have been his caretaker and surrogate mother, maybe even a noblewoman by decree of the new king. She would have had wealthy suitors and servants and actual power.

How life would have been different.

But it wasn't.

Now she had to figure out where they would go when Bo left the city. It occurred to her that the silver she'd buried in a graveyard outside the city might not even still be there. Someone might have found it and taken it, and then where would she be? She didn't want to think about it.

She heard the front door of the house open and shut, and her heart beat faster until she reminded herself that they were under Bo's protection—at least for another day—and that Lord Vetas could no longer harm them.

Bo stepped into the room, treading quietly. He knew that Jakob went to bed by eight in the evening. He gestured for her to join him in the kitchen.

"Can the boy watch himself for a few hours?" Bo asked after she'd closed the door to Jakob's room. The words were rushed, and his eyes were alight. He was excited about something.

He wanted to take her somewhere. Where could it be? She felt her cheeks grow a little warm. "Well, he's sleeping. He might get scared if he wakes up and no one's in the house with him."

"Can he read?"

"A little."

"Good. Write him a note. I need your help. We'll be back in just a few hours."

"I could wake him and take him with us."

"You won't want him with us," Bo said.

Nila felt her cheeks flush.

"Not for that," Bo said, giving her a lopsided smile.

Nila's cheeks felt on fire. Was that disappointment in the pit of her stomach?

She suddenly wondered how young Bo really was. He seemed so confident, and his status as an Adran Cabal member made her think of him as quite a bit older, but there were times he looked barely twenty.

"Come on," Bo said.

She wrote a note for Jakob and left it on the kitchen table beside a glass of water, then joined Bo in the carriage. He pounded on the roof, and they were off.

"Do you know what you're going to do when I leave?" Bo asked as the carriage jostled along through the streets.

Nila looked down. She had hoped that, perhaps, he would stay a little longer. "I haven't decided yet."

"I can't imagine you have much money," Bo said.

"A little. I have some silver buried outside of the city that I took the night Tamas's soldiers came to the Eldaminse house. I hope it's still there."

"And if it's not?"

Nila swallowed. "I don't know."

They rode along for several moments in silence, and then, "I'll leave a couple hundred for you when I go," Bo said.

A couple hundred could buy her and Jakob passage to Novi, or pay for a week in an inn.

"Thank you," Nila said, not sure what else to say. "That will go a long way toward helping us start a new life."

"A long way? It should go the whole way."

Nila frowned at Bo.

"A couple hundred thousand krana?"

"Hundred thousand..." Nila sputtered. She and Jakob could live the rest of their lives comfortably off a couple hundred thousand krana. "What, why would you...?"

Bo waved a hand as if it were nothing. Nila turned to stare out the window, partially so that Bo could not see the tears forming in her eyes.

"The house, too," Bo said. "The one we're in now. If you decide to stay in Adro, the house is yours. I've already put the title in your name."

She couldn't help but stare at Bo. Who was this man? Why was he doing this? He was a Privileged of a royal cabal—some of the most powerful men in all the Nine. People like that didn't take notice of orphan boys or lonely laundresses.

"Why?" she asked.

Bo shrugged. Several moments passed before Nila realized that she wasn't going to get a real answer. She dried the tears in the corners of her eyes and took a deep breath, letting it out slowly.

"Thank you," she said.

Bo was looking at his feet. He seemed uncomfortable with the thanks, as if he didn't feel he deserved it. Another shrug.

"Where are we going?" Nila asked.

"When I was a boy," Bo said, apparently happy to change the subject—he lifted his finger to the carriage curtain to look at the darkening sky outside—"Field Marshal Tamas took me in off the streets. He didn't want Taniel playing with an uneducated ruffian. He gave me a place to sleep and hired tutors for me and Taniel."

Nila remembered watching Field Marshal Tamas sleep, her knife ready to kill the man who'd brought so much suffering to Adro and killed the king, before she'd been distracted by Captain Olem. "That seems very kind of him," she said.

"I hated those damn tutors. I abhorred reading and writing, but Tamas told me I had to practice my letters. So I did. By copying all of his correspondence while he slept. His old ones, his new ones. Tamas kept all his letters in a strongbox, the lock of which I picked easily."

Nila couldn't help but give a shocked laugh at that.

Bo smiled too. "I kept all the copies I made. Just in case. I've always been good at planning ahead. Part of being a successful street rat, I suppose. Anyway, in one of those letters, from when he was a young man, Tamas talked about forcing the nobility out of the army in order to combat corruption. It seems that many of the nobles were purchasing supplies with government money and then selling them elsewhere in order to line their own pockets."

"And what does this have to do with me?" Nila asked. Bo had spoken at length over the last week about his quest to find evidence of profiteering among the General Staff in order to exonerate Taniel Two-Shot after his court-martial. Nila was willing to help if she could, but it worried her to leave Jakob by himself.

"Tamas's letter mentioned one name in particular. Duke Eldaminse."

Nila breathed in sharply.

"We're going to Duke Eldaminse's manor," Bo said. "Or what's left of it, anyway."

Nila hadn't been back to the Eldaminse manor since the night the soldiers had come and taken away Lord and Lady Eldaminse. Nila had barely escaped being raped before taking Jakob and fleeing into the darkness of the early morning. "I...don't know how I can help you."

"Well, I hope you can," Bo said. "I've not heard word from the south since finding out that Taniel was being court-martialed. At best he's in prison. At worst, he's already dead. I need evidence to condemn the General Staff that court-martialed him, or I'm going to have to go down there and kill a lot of soldiers to get him out." Bo scowled at his ungloved hands. "I'd rather not do that. So inconvenient."

They arrived at the manor an hour later. The sun had set and the streets were dark. Rows of city manor houses rose like ghosts of ages past out of the shadows. Less than six months ago this street had been well lit and home to dozens of noble families and hundreds of servants. Now the windows were dark, the yards silent. A chill went up Nila's spine at the sight of the Eldaminse manor. Even in the darkness she could tell that fire had destroyed part of the roof, and one of the chimneys had collapsed.

"Are you all right," Bo asked. She felt his hand touch her shoulder. He was wearing his Privileged's gloves.

Nila cleared her throat. "Yes."

He handed her a lantern and then lifted his own, lighting it with the snap of his fingers.

"Thank you," Nila said. The light illuminated the drive and threw the yard into deeper shadows. Somehow, it reassured her. "This way."

She led him up the front drive and in through the main door. The grand hall had been ransacked. The paintings and sculptures were gone or defaced, and the chandelier had been cut down and stripped of semiprecious stones. Someone had written illegible words on the wall with what might have been feces. The house smelled like a farmyard.

"What are we looking for?" she asked.

"A safe," Bo said. "Somewhere Eldaminse would have kept his correspondence and books."

Nila lifted her lantern high and headed toward the stairs. "It'll be gone already. Everything of value has been looted."

"I have to try."

The rest of the house looked much like the grand hall. The furniture was smashed or missing, everything of value removed, the walls covered in graffiti. Nila couldn't help but feel sorrow at that. The house had once been a happy place, full of life and riches. Jakob had once run down these halls, chasing the servants with a wooden musket. She was glad Bo had left the boy in his bed.

The duke's office was on the second floor in the southeastern corner of the house. The moment she entered the room, she knew they weren't going to find anything. The room was covered in scorch marks, and part of the floor and outer wall were missing. Someone had tried blowing open the safe with gunpowder. They'd used a lot, by the looks of it. The duke's desk had been reduced to splinters by the explosion.

She pointed to the mangled lump of metal over a dozen paces from where the safe had once sat.

"That's it," she said. "The duke's safe."

Bo stooped to examine the safe. Anything that had been inside it would have been destroyed by the explosion, or stolen after. He kicked the metal, then swore, hopping around the room on one foot while he held his toe. "Pit, pit, pit!" Bo stumbled toward the hole in the floor and Nila found herself grabbing him by the back of his jacket, pulling him back before he could fall.

He let out an exasperated sigh. "Ten days of work and this was my best lead." He dropped onto the floor, cross-legged. "Are you sure there's nothing else?"

"I was just a laundress," Nila said. "I've only been in this office a couple of times, and I was always trying to think of a way to keep Eldaminse from taking me to his bed."

Bo pounded a fist on the floor. "Damn!"

"Can't you just go down south and..." She made a gesture with her hands.

"And what? Magic Taniel out of whatever cell they've locked him in? It's a bit more involved than that."

Nila sat on the floor next to Bo.

"If I don't have the evidence to convict the General Staff, I'll have to use sorcery," Bo said. "Well, I'll start with bribes. Bribes might work, but they're notoriously unreliable. Someone is just as likely to take your money and then turn you in as they are to help you. If bribes don't work, I'll have to kill people. I don't *actually* enjoy killing people, despite what some might think of royal cabalists. And I certainly don't want to kill Adran soldiers. Taniel wouldn't ever forgive me."

Bo stared at the floor, looking angry and sad all at the same time.

"Wait!" Nila got to her feet.

"What...?"

"I came in here once and Lord Eldaminse was kneeling by the fire."

"Most people do," Bo said, his tone a little annoyed.

"No. Eldaminse always sat by the fire. He had this great big chair." Nila skirted the hole in the floor and approached the fireplace. "Right here. And he never put the wood in himself. Always summoned a servant to do it. So when I saw him kneeling there, I thought it was strange."

Bo was on his feet now, too. "A lockbox, you think? Hidden under the flagstones?"

"Maybe," Nila said. It had to be. It was all Bo had left, and Nila suddenly found herself wanting him to find the answers he needed. She dropped to her knees beside the fireplace and began trying to squeeze her fingers between the cracks. She searched for a hidden switch or a recess she could grab to move the stone. Nothing.

"Move," Bo said. He tugged on his Privileged's gloves and raised his hands. Nila scrambled out of the way. The flagstone suddenly cracked, and the pieces—each far bigger than Nila could have lifted herself—flew to the side. Bo grinned down at the floor. Beneath the flagstone, untouched by the explosion that had destroyed the safe, was a small lockbox. She grabbed it by the straps on the sides and lifted it out.

Bo destroyed the lock with a flick of his gloved fingers and the lid sprang open. Inside were several leather-bound books, each about the size of a pocket ledger, and Nila realized that could very well be what they were.

Bo opened one of the books and flipped through it. The grin on his face grew wider. "Yes," he said. "This is exactly what I needed." He dropped the book back into the lockbox. Then he closed his eyes, hands flat on the lid of the lockbox. He almost looked like he was praying.

A thought occurred to Nila. "Bo," she said.

"Yes?" He didn't open his eyes.

"Won't they arrest you when they find out who you are?"

"More than likely."

"And won't they kill you if you try to rescue Taniel with sorcery?"

Bo's eyes opened. "Almost certainly. I'll be right back." He left the room, hurrying like a man who had just realized he'd left the kettle on in the kitchen.

Nila listened to his footfalls down the hallway and then down the stairs. She could hear the sound of his boots crunching on the gravel drive outside.

She was alone now, in this great manor that had once been her home. She lifted her lantern and did a slow circuit of the duke's office. Several minutes passed, and Nila began to wonder where Bo had gone. Had he abandoned her?

No. She realized that the lockbox was still sitting on the floor, and beside it a pair of Bo's Privileged's gloves.

She sat down next to the lockbox and flipped open the lid. Taking a book in one hand, she began to leaf through it slowly. She recognized the duke's penmanship on each page. There were what appeared to be diary entries and then, later on, columns and figures.

Once in a while there would be a name, underlined. None of it made any sense to her.

She put the book back. The next one was much the same, and again with the third. Bo would have to sort these out and find what he was looking for, but he seemed happy to have these. She picked up his gloves. Strange that he would leave them here.

Nila listened for the sound of his footfalls in the house or on the drive. Nothing.

She stared at the gloves by the light of the candle. This was one of the pairs she'd mended. She could tell by the coffee stain next to one of the runes. On an impulse, she slid the glove over her hand.

She'd expected a shock. Perhaps something that would hurt her. There were stories about Privilegeds who warded everything they owned so that other people couldn't use them. But nothing happened when she put the glove on. She slid the other over her left hand.

They were too big for her by quite a bit. Why had Bo been so eager for her to put them on? She didn't remember ever having to put on gloves when the Privileged dowsers had visited her orphanage when she was young.

Nila held her hand away from her face and shied away, closing her eyes. She snapped her fingers.

Again, nothing.

"I really thought that would work."

Nila nearly leapt out of her skin. She tore the gloves off her hands and threw them on the floor.

Bo stood in the doorway, watching her.

"What?" Nila said, getting to her feet. "You thought what would work?"

Bo strolled into the room. How had he gotten back upstairs without making any sound? "You don't have the glow in the Else," Bo said, "but people who haven't before tapped their potential rarely do. I thought there was something about you. Perhaps a Knack, or maybe even sorcery. I've been waiting almost two weeks for you to finally try on a pair of Privileged's gloves."

Nila smoothed the front of her dress and turned up her nose. Trickery! "Well, I'm not a Privileged," she said. "Get that out of your head."

Bo crossed the room quickly. She took a half step back, and suddenly she felt the sting of his palm across her cheek.

Fury rose up inside her. He had slapped her! Unprovoked. She drew back her fist.

"Wait!" Bo said.

Nila wasn't sure why she'd stopped.

"Look."

Nila looked at her hand, the one cocked back in a fist, ready to beat Bo to a pulp. It was wreathed in blue flame. She could feel the heat of the flame on her face but not on her hand. She gave a shout and leapt back, shaking the hand until the flame went out. What had happened? How had she done that?

"Sorry about the slap," Bo said, his eyes both gleeful and wary at the same time. "I needed to elicit an emotional reaction from you."

"You could have just kissed me," Nila snapped.

"Oh? I'll keep that in mind next time." Bo rubbed his chin. "It appears, young lady, that you are a Privileged. You can tap into the Else. What's more—and this is really interesting—you weren't wearing gloves just then."

CHAPTER
37

Tamas and Vlora slipped into Alvation under the cover of night.

The river was easy enough to cross—slippery and treacherous, and cold as Novi's frosted toes, being runoff from the mountains— but no more than thigh-deep.

As they made their way past the mills and into the tenement district, Tamas realized he'd never heard streets so quiet in the middle of the night. If he closed his eyes, he might imagine himself out on the plateau but for the infrequent step of boots on cobbles from patrolling Kez and the occasional bark of a dog. There was no one about but the patrols. He didn't even hear the familiar slosh of chamber pots being emptied out of windows.

Nikslaus had the city under martial law, and from the look of the bodies hanging from the bell tower in the city center, he was serious about punishing infractions.

Tamas took note of the powder that Vlora had sensed. There

did seem to be quite a lot of it scattered throughout the city, and not just in munition caches. They had enough to supply twenty brigades—which seemed strange, because there weren't any Deliv soldiers around and it was far more than the Kez could carry.

As they passed through the market district, there was a sudden shout nearby. Tamas stopped to listen, and a moment later the crack of muskets filled the air.

Tamas motioned for Vlora to follow and sprinted toward the sound. It couldn't have been more than two or three streets over. He climbed a nearby market building and headed quietly toward the edge.

The street below was a war zone.

Bodies littered the cobbles, no more than lumps in the darkness, lying in pools of their own blood.

An experienced eye told Tamas that the Deliv had sprung a trap on a Kez patrol. The initial volley had done its work, cutting down half the patrol, but the rest had taken the fight to the Deliv partisans and were making short work with their bayoneted muskets.

Tamas drew his pistols.

"Not our fight," Vlora whispered urgently in his ear.

He hesitated a few moments, and that was long enough for the Kez patrol to finish cleaning up the partisans. What remained of the Deliv fled into the night. The patrol regrouped to tend to their dead and make prisoners of the wounded partisans.

Tamas descended from the rooftop and headed back down the street. When they'd gone far enough, he said, "An organized resistance. They're trying to take back the city."

Vlora had her nose to the wind, her ear cocked. She nodded slowly as her eyes searched the night. Like him, she was in a powder trance, listening, smelling—trying to get a bearing on the state of the city.

"But how organized?" she asked. "We're trying to liberate the city in one day. Not help a small group of partisans."

484   *Brian McClellan*

Of course she was right. Tamas needed to keep perspective. He had a goal for the night, and needed to reach it.

They passed out of the market district, then a small suburb of close-packed houses, before they reached a wealthier part of town. Along the way they passed two more fights between Deliv and false Adran soldiers. The houses became farther apart, most of them surrounded by gardens with high walls, and the street was wide enough for six carriages. Tamas felt like he finally knew where he was.

Hailona's home was one of these manors.

Tamas heard the sudden sound of a man shouting. Another voice joined the first and then a musket blast. The racket grew louder— it was coming up the street behind them. Tamas cast about for someplace to hide but saw only the empty, wide street and walled yards.

"Quick," Tamas said. He dropped to one knee, making a hammock of his fingers, and jerked his head at the wall beside them. Vlora put her foot in his hands, and he pushed her up and over the brick wall. She put her hand back down, but even when he jumped, it was well out of reach. Tamas looked back down the street.

A small group of Deliv appeared around the bend. There were eight—no, nine—of them. Most limped desperately as they fled from an unseen foe. They wore greatcoats and wide-brimmed hats, concealing their features. One stopped and fired a pistol around the corner of the walled yard they'd just rounded. He leapt back from returning fire.

Tamas dropped to the ground, pulling his legs up and covering his face with his coat and hat. The only place to hide was in plain sight. At best, they'd think him a drunk or vagrant.

He watched beneath the brim of his hat as the Deliv worked their way along the other side of the street, looking over their shoulders continuously.

The source of their fear revealed itself a few moments later. A man ducked around the corner behind them, aimed his musket, and fired. He wore the Adran blues—but he was no Adran. He was followed by more of the same. They ran across the street, taking cover behind the thick-grown trees beside the street, firing haphazardly at the Deliv as they retreated.

One Deliv staggered and fell. He waved on the rest of them, cursing loudly when others stopped to help.

Tamas felt his fingers close around the hilt of his small sword. His heart began to beat harder. Could he just watch this slaughter and stand idly by?

The Deliv were outnumbered two to one, and most of them were wounded. Wherever they were retreating to, they wouldn't make it.

A Kez soldier dashed behind one of the decorative oaks that lined the street. He was less than a dozen feet away and hadn't seemed to notice Tamas's huddled form. He stopped to reload his musket, clearing his barrel and priming the powder. Tamas felt his knuckles so tight on his sword they chafed. His trance-attuned hearing picked up Vlora's whisper from on top of the wall: "Not our fight."

Tamas's sword entered the Kez soldier's throat from the side, right between his esophagus and his spine. The man dropped without even a gurgling protest. Tamas felt his legs pump hard, the pain to his right barely registering as he crossed the street in a dozen long strides.

One of the soldiers turned toward him. Tamas slashed his sword upward, cutting through the front of the man's face, then followed through by plunging his sword into the ribs of the next soldier.

They all knew he was here now. Panicked shouting rose in the street.

The world seemed to move at a snail's pace. Tamas sensed a spark hit the powder pan of a pistol, traveling toward the barrel. In the instant before the weapon fired, Tamas reached out and absorbed the energy of the blast, throwing it behind the swipe of his sword as it took a man's head clear off.

A soldier—a woman—drew her sword, only to fall from a bullet in the eye. Tamas's mind barely registered Vlora's help as he switched to the next target. A man with a captain's silver collar dashed up the street toward Tamas, his small sword at the ready.

Tamas threw himself forward, breaking inside the man's guard in two quick strokes and disemboweling him. Tamas spun for the next Kez soldier and...

None were left. The street was clear. The only sounds were the moaning of the wounded and dying, and Tamas's own panting. He felt his heart hammer at the inside of his chest. He cracked a powder charge and sprinkled it on his tongue. The hammering began to subside.

The Deliv were still retreating up the street. One even turned toward Tamas, pistol raised, and fired. Tamas felt his heart skip a beat as the bullet ricocheted off the street not far from his feet. The Deliv swore loudly enough to be heard across fifty paces and dropped his pistol. He grabbed one of the other Deliv by the shoulder and pointed toward Tamas.

The small group came to a stop. They all stared toward Tamas as he stood among the Kez bodies.

Tamas looked over the group. How well could they see him in the dark?

Regardless, he didn't have time for this. He had a mission to finish. Halley's manor was just down the street. Unfortunately, the Deliv group was in between him and Hailona's manor.

He looked across the street. The shadow of Vlora's head was just visible at the top of the wall. He reassessed the height.

Tamas broke out in a run across the street. One of the Deliv shouted for him to stop.

His foot hit the wall about two feet up. His boot caught just enough friction to send him up, and he pushed off with all his strength. He grabbed the top of the wall, felt Vlora's hand grasp his arm, and then he pulled himself up and rolled over, falling with a thump to the garden below.

Tamas rolled over onto his back, hoping he hadn't just cracked a rib in his fall. He took a deep breath. He felt some pain, but not too much.

"You all right?" Vlora asked, crouching beside him.

"Getting too damn old for fights like that." He climbed to his feet and ran his fingers along the hilt of his small sword. "But that felt good. Very good. I needed a fight like that." He paused, saw that Vlora was looking at him strangely. "What?"

"Now I know where Taniel gets it," she said. After a few seconds, she added, "You're the only other one I've seen move as fast as him. None of the other powder mages can do it. We're all stronger and faster than regular men, but you and Taniel... damn."

Tamas's heart hammered in his chest, too hard. He wasn't just *getting* old. He *was* old.

They headed across the garden and crossed the wall again a hundred yards later. The group of Deliv was still in the street, now behind Tamas, and were checking the dead and finishing off the wounded Kez soldiers. Tamas and Vlora crossed the street farther down, unnoticed.

They kept on down the same street and turned two corners before they reached Hailona's city manor.

It was a grand affair with a short gravel drive, manicured lawn, and a brick façade with evenly spaced windows. The roof was tall and steeply slanted and must have had over a dozen chimneys.

The windows of the manor were dark, the driveway lanterns unlit. Tamas ran across the lawn and around the back of the house. He passed by the servants' quarters, where there would likely be someone still up, and found the observatory porch.

The observatory had belonged to Hailona's husband before he died twenty years ago. The last time Tamas had been here it was

Hailona's study. He paused at the glass door to the observatory as a thought occurred to him.

He didn't even know if she still lived here.

Tamas sought to recall if Sabon had ever mentioned Hailona selling her city manor. Not likely. He was usually taciturn when it came to the subject of his sister.

It was better that way.

Tamas forced the door with his shoulder, wincing when it made a loud noise. He paused, listening for the sound of footsteps or of a servant sounding the alarm.

Nothing.

He stepped inside. Vlora followed after him a moment later.

The study was different from the last time he'd been here. No telescope. A different desk. Where it had been, a large globe of the world rested on a stand in the corner.

Tamas felt the creeping fingers of panic in his bowels. What if she wasn't here? She was his only link in this city. How would he find Gavril?

"This," Tamas whispered, "might not be her home."

Vlora touched his arm. "Is that her?"

There was a portrait above the mantel. It was a Deliv man that Tamas didn't recognize. He wore a military uniform, and his head was shaved bald. Behind him stood Hailona.

Tamas let out a soft sigh of relief. This was the right place after all.

"I'll have to go wake her up," Tamas said. He wasn't looking forward to this part. A gross invasion, entering her bedchamber at this time of night was not the best way to reignite a long-forgotten acquaintance.

Especially if she'd remarried.

Vlora hissed at him. She stood beside the window, her fingers on the curtain.

He went to her side. There were people outside, coming straight for the observatory portico. Tamas blinked. It was the same group he'd saved from the Kez soldiers. Was her husband among them?

"Hide!"

Tamas made for the closest door, sliding inside and closing it all the way but for the slightest crack. He checked his surroundings. A closet, albeit a big one. Vlora barely moved, electing to slide behind a thick curtain. Tamas swore quietly. Neither of them could extricate themselves without alerting the occupants of the room.

Tamas watched the room through a crack in the door. He could hear hushed voices outside, but not make out what they were saying. The glass door opened and the group filed in.

Most seemed wounded in some way. Two of them had to be carried. Tamas could smell the gunpowder and blood—but then again, that may have just been him.

"Get us some lights," a woman's voice said. "Ruper, take them to the sitting room. Fetch towels. Get a fire going. We need hot water."

Tamas recognized that voice. Even after fifteen years he recognized the voice, and it surprised him.

Hailona.

Doors opened and shut, feet pounded frantically into the rest of the manor house. There was grunting and cursing as the wounded were carried to another room.

A male voice spoke up as someone fumbled around in the dark. "They'll come for us."

"I know," Hailona said. She sounded miserable.

A lantern was lit, casting the room into light and shadow. Tamas blinked his eyes to let them adjust. Through the crack in the door he could see a Deliv with a black braided ponytail over one shoulder. The man suddenly swept his arm across a desk, throwing parchments, weights, and a small stack of coins to the floor.

"Someone must have sold us out!" he said. "I'll find them, I'll kill them with my bare hands."

"Calm down, Demasolin," Hailona said.

"I will not! All is lost. They were ready for us. You saw it as well as I. The bloody Adrans! Indier took a bullet through the eye the moment she stepped into that room! A dozen musket men, all concealed in the shadows. Someone had betrayed us."

"They're not bloody Adrans," Hailona said. She sounded uncertain. "You heard them speak in Kez."

"A ruse! Two brigades in Adran blues! You think we wouldn't have heard about two brigades of the Grand Army splitting off from Budwiel to come up here? Our spies are better than that."

"And our spies in Adro?"

"We have few spies in Adro! They're supposed to be allies."

"Tamas would never—"

Demasolin whirled on Hailona. "Don't you defend him! That damned butcher would do anything, and you know it."

"And Sabon?" There was steel in Hailona's voice. "You think Sabon would let him attack Deliv?"

Tamas felt his breath seize in his chest. Oh, pit. She didn't know Sabon was dead. He'd sent her a message, but it must not have reached her. He squeezed his eyes closed, trying to control his breathing.

"There's a reason your parents disowned him," Demasolin said.

Tamas heard a loud crack. Demasolin reeled back into view, clutching his cheek. Hailona stormed after him. It was the first time Tamas had gotten a good look at her.

She had not aged well. Her features were wrinkled, her hair gone gray. There were well-defined crow's-feet in the corners of eyes red from unshed tears. Her jaw was set, her hand raised to strike again.

"Speak ill of my brother again," she said quietly, her voice a challenge.

Demasolin squared his shoulders. "You dare strike a duke of the king?"

A duke. No wonder he thought Tamas a butcher. The nobility of all the Nine feared and hated Tamas, even his supposed allies. Just what Tamas needed.

Hailona was about to speak when Demasolin held up one hand. He sniffed the air. His eyes suddenly darted around the room.

"There's someone here," he whispered.

Tamas could see Vlora's hiding spot from his own. The curtains shifted slightly. Tamas laid his hand on the hilt of his sword and took a long, quiet breath. He put his other hand on the closet door, ready to push it open at any moment.

Demasolin drew his sword and began to make a long circuit of the room, sniffing and casting about. Tamas let himself relax and opened his third eye. Demasolin glowed faintly in the Else.

He had a Knack.

Demasolin had just passed Vlora's hiding spot when he suddenly whirled and thrust his sword into the curtains with a shout.

Tamas choked down a startled cry.

Nothing had happened. Demasolin pulled back the curtains.

"An open window," Hailona said. "Really?"

"There!" Demasolin said, gazing out into the night. "Someone flees!" He dashed out the door, sword at the ready, and into the night.

The room was empty but for Hailona. He could see her rush to the door, watching Demasolin disappear. A moment later she came back into the room, her shoulders slumped, and dropped into a divan.

Tamas felt a great dread in the pit of his stomach. His heart thundered in his ears, and he paused for a moment to gather his nerve. Charging into a brigade of Kez was easier than this.

He took his hand off his sword and pushed the closet door open. "Hello, Halley," he said.

When Adamat arrived at the headquarters of the Noble Warriors of Labor, Ricard wasn't there. In fact, no one was there but the porter and the bartender, and the latter poured Adamat a glass of Gurlish beer from a chilled cask and directed him to wait in the foyer.

Adamat elected to let himself into Ricard's study.

He waited for almost three hours, growing more and more nervous as he watched the light begin to wane and darkness fall over the Adsea, before the sound of the doors in the foyer bursting open brought him to his feet.

Adamat went to the door of Ricard's office and nudged it open with his toe. Through the crack, he could see Ricard striding through the foyer, tossing his coat angrily on the floor. The union boss's thinning hair was standing straight off his head, and his white shirt was wet with sweat. "Get me a drink!" he yelled. Fell trailed behind him, along with a half-dozen other assistants.

No sign of Lord Claremonte's men. Adamat stepped out of Ricard's office, feeling a little sheepish about his suspicions.

Ricard strode past him into the office and threw himself into his desk chair.

"We're buggered, Adamat," he said.

Instead of asking why he'd been left waiting for three hours, Adamat said, "Why?"

"The Brudania-Gurla Trading Company has invaded our country."

"What did you find out?" Adamat asked.

The porter brought Ricard a bottle of dark whiskey and a glass. Ricard threw the glass in the fireplace, where it exploded in a tinkle of shiny shards, then grabbed the bottle and pulled out the stopper, downing a quarter of the bottle in several long swallows.

Adamat yanked it from his fingers. "You getting shit-faced isn't going to help anyone."

"You don't understand," Ricard said. "Claremonte's coming, and he's bringing everything he has with him." Adamat could see in Ricard's eyes that he wasn't just angry or flustered; he was scared. Adamat had never seen his old friend like this. There was real fear in his eyes.

"Has Brudania invaded?" Adamat asked.

"Pit if I know. Not a damn shot was fired. No one even tried to stop me when I went up to the locks to ask questions. Claremonte just bribed every union member on the canal and brought his fleet over. Simple as that. They'll be here tomorrow."

"Tomorrow?" Adamat blanched. "How could they possibly be here that quickly?"

Ricard pointed out the window, though it didn't even face the direction of the canal. "We built the canal to bring goods over the mountains quickly. It can support the draft of Claremonte's merchantmen, and the Ad River has been deepened the entire way down. The union has spent the last five years replacing every bridge on the Ad just so that we can do exactly what Claremonte is doing now. Nothing can stop him."

"Surely there's something."

"I've spent every minute since I returned trying to come up with an option. I wasted an hour talking to blacksmiths to see if we could build an immense chain fast enough to stop him, but it can't be done."

Ricard looked like a drowning man who couldn't quite reach the rope being lowered to him. His face was flushed, and Adamat now noticed that his pants were torn up one leg at the calf.

"You're bleeding," Adamat said.

Ricard looked at his leg and gave a sigh. He made no motion to staunch the wound.

Fell came into the room. Her hair was back, her uniform tidy. Not an eyelash out of place.

"He's bleeding," Adamat told her.

She knelt by Ricard's side and exposed the wound, tying it up.

"Anything?" Ricard asked her.

"We're still working on it."

"We have to organize a defense," Adamat said.

Ricard hiccuped. He reached toward the whiskey bottle. "There's no time."

"There's police," Adamat said, pulling the bottle out of Ricard's reach. "Some soldiers. Call on the people. You have the newspapers. Use them."

"A militia," Ricard said, sitting up, his ears perking like a dog's.

"Yes." Adamat felt his heart begin to race. "This city is not indefensible. There's a million people here. Use the newspapers. You remember the crowd at Elections Square when Tamas put Manhouch's head in a basket. There's the will. The manpower. People will rise up to defend their homes."

Ricard leapt to his feet, knocking Fell back on her ass. "Fell," he said, helping her up. "Draft a letter. Inform the newspapers. I want the front page first thing in the morning. Tell them every home in Adopest is to have a newspaper by sunup. I want the presses working all night! Get me the union bosses. I want everyone involved. We'll do it. We'll defend this city!"

Adamat felt a smile spread over his face. This was the Ricard he knew.

Ricard snatched him by the hand. "Adamat, thank you. I knew you had it in you. Whatever I'm paying you, double it."

"You aren't..." Adamat said, but Ricard was already racing out of his office. Adamat stood there for a moment, dumbfounded. Ricard shouted to his footmen and assistants, giving orders like a line commander. He was in full swing now, and he wouldn't stop until he'd organized a defense of the city.

The office was suddenly quiet and cold, and Adamat looked around for a glass to pour himself some whiskey. Finding none, he took a sip from the bottle.

"Sir," Fell said, breaking the silence.

"Hmm?"

She stood with her hands behind her back, chin up. "I never apologized, sir. I want to do that now."

"For what?" Adamat felt his anger stir. He knew for what: for almost getting his wife killed. For not containing Lord Vetas like she said she would.

"Lord Vetas," she said. "He got the best of me. I should have taken more men."

Adamat fought down his anger, forced himself to remain calm. Another swig of whiskey helped. "He was good at what he did. He got the best of me far too many times." As he said the words, he felt something shift in the back of his mind. He frowned.

"Sir?" Fell asked when he'd been silent for several moments.

He held up a hand for quiet. He needed to think. Vetas had gotten the better of him on many occasions. All evidence said that he was a genius planner with no heart for remorse and no hesitation considering lives lost.

"Is he dead?" Adamat asked.

"Vetas? Yes. He died two weeks ago. Bo got rid of the body."

"And where is Bo?"

"He's disappeared," Fell said. "Ricard even offered him a job, but he wouldn't take it."

Adamat smoothed the front of his jacket. He'd told Bo about his reservations over Vetas. That perhaps Vetas hadn't told them the entire truth, or even led them astray. He even...

"Damn!" Adamat said. "Vetas. He knew everything. He got the better of us one last time. Not even Bo could get it out of him."

"How do you know?" Fell asked.

"The pier." Adamat shook his head. She wouldn't know what he was talking about. "I asked Vetas for a way to track down my boy, and he sent me to the slavers that Josep was sold to. He told me who to ask for, and the passwords to use. But he gave me the wrong password! The slavers attacked me. I barely got out with my life, and I was so intent on getting Josep back that it didn't occur to me until now."

Adamat slumped against the wall. There was nothing he could

do about it now. Vetas was dead. There'd be no reckoning, no confrontation. What little advantage Adamat thought they may have gained over Claremonte was gone—if that wasn't made apparent enough by Claremonte's sailing his fleet over the Charwood Pile Mountains.

"What information did you get from Vetas?" Adamat asked.

Fell frowned. "Reports. His master's plans."

"What plans?"

"Campaign plans for the ministerial election. His platform for reformation within the city."

"They're all trash," Adamat said.

"But there was good information there. We found other hide-outs. More of his men in the city."

"He wants us to think we have some kind of advantage. We don't. Everything we learned from Vetas is suspect."

Adamat took his hat from the peg beside the door and gathered his cane. He felt so very tired.

"What are you doing?" Fell asked.

Their only hope was Ricard's ability to rouse the city. Otherwise it would be in Claremonte's hands by tomorrow night.

"Going home. I'm going home to my wife. I'll see you at the north gate of the city tomorrow morning."

CHAPTER
38

Midway Keep was a historical monument, a castle of vanity built not for comfort or even defense but to look imposing. Its walls were tall but easily scaled, the indefensible number of entrances brimming with fortifications. The keep towered over the Addown River and menaced the main highway. To the peasants it may have been breathtaking.

To anyone skilled in warfare it was a joke.

It had been built some three hundred years ago by a juvenile king who considered himself an architect. To Taniel, it seemed the perfect place to house a mad god.

Taniel watched the keep from the shadow of a sprawling oak standing solitary in the middle of the Kez army. He could hear the soft sounds of a snoring infantryman nearby. Otherwise, the night was still.

He checked that last thought when he realized he could also

hear Field Marshal Goutlit's unsteady, terrified breaths. The Kez officer crouched beside him, still smelling faintly of piss, and fidgeted with the collar of his jacket. Taniel watched him out of the corner of his eye. A wrong move here, a suspicious noise, and Taniel was a dead man.

Of course, he'd be sure to take Goutlit with him.

"Where's the servants' entrance?" Taniel whispered.

"I don't know."

Taniel drew his belt knife.

"I, uh, think it's over there. To the right."

Taniel pushed the knife back in its sheath. "Is it guarded?"

Goutlit swallowed hard and eyed Taniel, as if afraid to say he didn't know.

A light caught Taniel's eye, just in the corner of his vision. He crouched a little farther down and watched the keep for several moments. There. He saw a light moving in a high-arched window.

Goutlit saw it too. He scooted back, pressing himself up against the big oak behind him. Taniel grabbed a handful of Goutlit's jacket to keep him from moving farther.

"Where's Kresimir's room?" Taniel asked.

"There," Goutlit's voice came out dry and raspy. He lifted a finger. "That tower there, just above the light."

A sudden whine cut through the night. It was a low keening that rose sharply into a wail. A low thump accompanied it, and then a human scream that grew louder and louder until Taniel was sure that a banshee was going to come out of the tree above them.

Just as quickly as it began, the sound was over. Distantly, from the keep, he heard a sound like crashing furniture.

"What the pit?"

"Kresimir," Goutlit said, his voice barely a whisper. "Every night." Goutlit turned to stare at Taniel. "Every night he's looking for the eye behind the flintlock."

Taniel shivered involuntarily.

"Every morning they find bodies," Goutlit said. "Usually just a few, but sometimes as many as a dozen. Prielight Guards, servants. Kresimir's concubines. Some of them are strangled while others have been burned through by sorcery."

"Shut up," Taniel said. His skin was beginning to crawl. He set his musket against the tree and watched while the light in the keep moved farther and farther away from Kresimir's tower.

"You can't kill him," Goutlit said.

"What?" Taniel snapped.

"That stuff about Kresimir's bedsheets. Do you think I'm a fool? You're going to try to finish the job you started on South Pike, aren't you?"

Taniel remained silent. There was fear in Goutlit's voice.

Goutlit went on, "He can't be killed. About twenty have tried so far. Assassins from your own army. From the Church, and even one of Ipille's—though Kresimir doesn't know that."

The Church had tried to have Kresimir killed? Even while their Prielights guarded him? Now, that was interesting. There must be a division within the Kresim Church.

"No one's gotten close enough, I'd imagine," Taniel said.

"Oh, they have." Goutlit swallowed hard. "I saw one assassin with my own eyes. A woman. She tried to open his throat. Her knife bent on his skin."

Taniel remembered shooting at Julene once, in her cave-lion form. The bullet had simply skimmed off her skin like a smooth stone off of water. And now Taniel was trying to steal from the god who'd managed to nail her to a beam.

"Not enough force."

"He was hit by a cannonball, walking the front. It shattered on him! Killed half a nearby gun crew and a colonel."

Goutlit had begun to talk louder. His voice was high-pitched, and he breathed heavily. His whole body began to tremble. Taniel shook him by the front of his jacket. It didn't seem to help.

Taniel realized he had a problem. He would need to scale the walls of the keep. Easy enough by himself, but impossible for Goutlit.

The simplest thing would be to just kill the man. He was an enemy, after all. A Kez. Their field marshal.

Taniel lay a hand on his knife. Goutlit didn't seem to notice. A quick stroke, silent as can be. It wouldn't be the first man Taniel had killed, nor the last.

Then again, this was butchery. Goutlit was his prisoner.

"Take off your clothes," Taniel said.

Goutlit seemed to snap out of whatever fear had been racing through his mind. "I beg your pardon?"

"Clothes. Off."

"I refuse."

"This is me saving your life," Taniel said. "I can either tie you up, to be found in the morning, or I can kill you. Tell me now, but decide quickly."

Taniel thought for a moment that Goutlit would cry out. Was this the indignity to break him? Goutlit watched Taniel in silence and then removed his jacket.

"You can keep your underclothes on," Taniel said, "but make it quick." When the field marshal had stripped to his underwear, Taniel motioned with his knife at the tree. "Climb."

Goutlit's eyes widened. "I can't possibly..."

Taniel grabbed Goutlit by the back of his neck and shoved him at the trunk of the giant oak. Goutlit scrambled up to the lowest branch awkwardly. Taniel gathered Goutlit's clothes and followed him up.

"Keep going."

Goutlit was about thirty feet in the air before he clutched a thick branch and absolutely refused to climb farther. His eyes rolled wildly, and Taniel could hear his teeth chatter.

"I won't go higher. Kill me now."

"This will do." Taniel fastened Goutlit to the tree branch tightly, using Goutlit's own belt and pants as restraints. "It's not comfortable, but you'll live."

Taniel stuffed one of Goutlit's socks into the field marshal's mouth.

He ignored Goutlit's squeals of protest and began to descend. By the time he reached the ground, he couldn't even hear the man, and once he'd taken a few dozen steps, Goutlit was all but forgotten.

Taniel timed the Prielight patrols around the base of the keep and slipped up to the wall after the last patrol had passed. The keep had once had a moat, but that had long ago filled in, leaving only a swampy lowland and a few ponds behind.

The walls of the keep were easily sixty feet high, and the one leading up to the tower that was Taniel's target couldn't have been less than a hundred. No small climb.

He left the musket in some weeds and secured his pistols and dagger before beginning the climb. Immense blocks of granite, half Taniel's height, were stacked at a slight incline, each one with a lip that gave his fingers a couple inches of room to hold on to. Taniel tested his grip with both hands, then hauled himself up.

He was halfway up the wall when a Prielight patrol passed under where he'd been. He hung off the wall, breathing quietly and praying they'd not stumble across his musket. A raised voice, even a suspicious glance upward, and he'd be finished. He silently cursed himself for taking the dead guard's uniform. The Kez military tan stood out against the dark granite of the keep like a beacon.

The patrol kept moving, and Taniel resumed his climb.

He reached the top of the wall, just under the parapets. He could hear the steady tread of a patrolling guard just above him, and then another sound. It seemed quiet and distant at first, and then grew louder.

Taniel pressed himself against the stone, his fingers and arms aching from the climb. What was that sound? He looked down.

Far below, another Prielight patrol. Was someone sounding an alarm?

He let go of the wall with one hand and carefully dipped into his pocket, taking a powder charge between his fingers. He'd make noise if he snorted it, so he crushed the end of the charge and sprinkled it in his mouth.

That infernal sound would not go away.

His powder trance intensified and he clung to the wall for a moment of dizziness.

Taniel almost began to laugh.

The guard above him was whistling.

A scream shattered the quiet of the night, nearly making Taniel lose his grip in surprise. It came from one of the windows below him.

His heart hammering in his ears, Taniel heard the guard on the parapet curse softly to himself, and then the sound of running footsteps as the man went to see what was wrong.

There was no time to waste. Taniel couldn't be sure if the scream had been Kresimir, or one of the god's victims, or even someone raising the alarm on Taniel. He pulled himself up to the parapet and peeked over. No one.

On the parapet, Taniel padded quietly toward Kresimir's tower. He could make out other guards on the opposite walls of the keep, all of them looking down toward the source of the scream. None of them seemed to have noticed him.

He reached the tower and swore. No door on this level. He looked up. Another fifty feet of climbing, in full view of the guards on the parapet. Wait. A window, not fifteen feet above him.

Taniel threw himself up the stone wall, climbing as quickly as he dared, and in only a few moments he was through the window.

He found himself in the spiral staircase of the tower. He glanced back the way he'd come and had to stop to blink away a dizzy spell.

It was a long way to fall.

Taniel climbed the tower stairs until the stairs ended in a thick iron-bound door. He paused there and wondered what kind of a ward a god would put on his bedroom. He looked down and was grateful that his hands were not shaking. No sound of footsteps below him. No breathing from inside the room. Kresimir must be out.

Taniel pressed gently on the door. It opened with a single long creak that made him cringe.

He paused at the sight of the room.

Taniel had expected something like he'd seen in Kresimir's palace on South Pike: a fine bed with expensive silk and lush carpeting and wall hangings, preserved against nature and time. But this... this was not the opulent quarters of a god.

The rug was nothing more than a soiled sheet. The curtains— perhaps once fine—were now torn and bedraggled. There was a full body mirror, shattered. A four-poster bed lay slanted against one wall, two of the posts destroyed.

Was this really Kresimir's room? It showed signs of habitation. There was a table by one window, set with a meal. Taniel crossed to that and glanced out. He was just above the Addown. On the table was a tankard, half full of beer. A mouse, unafraid of Taniel, nibbled on the bread.

This had to be a mistake. Taniel had seen Kresimir's palace. He'd seen Kresimir's city. The god who created those things would not live in a tower like this.

What could he do? Goutlit must have lied to him. Taniel gritted his teeth. He'd climb back down and go skin that worm. Half the night, wasted, just because...

His eyes fell on the bed. The sheets were covered in blood; spattered rust-colored stains.

Taniel opened his third eye.

He dropped to his knees, staggered by the kaleidoscope of colors within the Else. Thousands of pastels swirled and moved, as if sorcery itself was born in this room. Taniel had to breathe deeply, suppressing the urge to vomit. The whole mountainside of South Pike hadn't looked like this after months of Kez Privileged slinging their strongest sorcery at Shouldercrown Fortress.

Taniel forced his third eye to close and slowly got back to his feet. He drew his dagger and staggered to the bed.

He grabbed the sheet and tore it off the bed. One or two long strips would do it. He could wrap them around his waist, beneath his jacket, and be out the window in less than a minute.

Taniel stopped. He'd heard something. Just the wind, or...

Footsteps on the stairs.

He finished his cuts and grabbed a handful of bloody linens. He made a dash for the window.

The door opened.

A Prielight Guard stood in the door, a platter with fresh bread and cheese and a bottle of wine. He stopped, mouth open in surprise, at the sight of Taniel.

The silence was broken as the guard threw the platter to the floor and drew his sword, running forward with a shout.

CHAPTER
39

Tamas wasn't sure which bothered him more: the look of sudden fear in Hailona's eyes, or what she said immediately afterward.

"It's true. Adro has invaded Deliv!" The words came out as a gasp. Hailona put one hand to her mouth. "You're here, so it must be true." She rocked back in her seat, and for a moment Tamas thought she might fall.

He rushed to her side and tried to take her hand, but she pulled back as if it were a serpent.

"Get back," she said breathlessly.

"It's not true," he said. "None of that."

"How can I be sure? Where is Sabon?"

The question Tamas dreaded the most. He evaded it. "Look at me. Am I in uniform? Have you seen me in public since this army took Alvation? They're not my men!"

Hailona stared at him as if in shock.

Tamas went on. "Do you think I'd be stupid enough to attack Deliv? To risk them joining the war when Kez has sacked Budwiel and threatens the very heart of Adro? No, Hailona, this is a plot by the Kez to turn our nations against each other."

Hailona visibly steeled herself. She stood, taking a deep breath and squaring her shoulders. Some of her old regality returned then and she seemed younger.

"Explain yourself," she said. Her gaze was hard, accusing.

Tamas felt himself flinch. Fifteen years since they'd last spoken. How could he convince her?

"I have two brigades of men camped a day outside the city. We were trapped in Kez after the battle of Budwiel. My men are bloodied, tired, and starving. We came north for succor in Alvation. Imagine my surprise to see soldiers in Adran blue holding the city."

"Can you prove it?"

"Prove it? Those soldiers out there—I'd bet half of them only speak Kez. The ones who speak Adran do it with an accent thicker than my Deliv. I don't know what's happening here any more than you do, but I have my suspicions."

"You'll have to do better than 'suspicions,'" Hailona said. "Demasolin will be back any moment. He won't believe you." She said the words as if she didn't believe him either.

"Who is he?" Tamas glanced toward the door Demasolin had taken to chase Vlora.

"My brother-in-law. The duke of Vindren."

"You remarried? I didn't know."

"Ten years ago. I asked Sabon not to tell you. Where is he? Demasolin will not trust him either, but a countryman is more believable than an Adran."

Tamas pulled back. He felt like he'd been slapped in the face. She'd asked Sabon not to tell him that she'd gotten remarried? Sabon was like a brother to Tamas. At one point, he'd been close to marrying Hailona and now she glossed past it like it wasn't any kind of issue.

He mentally checked himself. He had more important things to worry about.

He heard steps coming down the hallway. The door opened, and an older Deliv gentleman in a servant's evening jacket stood in the doorway. He seemed startled to find Tamas there and glanced between Hailona and Tamas quickly. He tensed, as if ready to spring between them.

"It's all right, Ruper," Hailona said. "How is everyone?"

"Ferhulia will die before the night is over," Ruper said. His voice had the educated politeness of a butler. "Inel might make it, but we have to move him. We can't stay here. They'll come for us."

"Who?" Tamas demanded. "Who is coming for you?"

"The general in command of the . . ." She hesitated just a moment before saying, "Adran army. His name is Saulkin. We tried to kill him tonight but it was a trap. He saw me clearly when we retreated and he knows who I am."

"We could have barely minutes, ma'am," Ruper said.

The glass door to the observatory portico opened. Demasolin strode through the door. He removed black gloves and threw them to the table, only to freeze in place when he saw Tamas.

"Who is this?" His gaze cut through Tamas, his eyes narrowed. Tamas was able to see him better now. Demasolin was in his thirties, perhaps, with a clean-shaven face and strong jawline. He had the bearing of a duke, Tamas decided.

"An old . . . friend," Hailona said. "Did you catch the intruder?"

Demasolin continued to stare at Tamas. "Apparently not." His nose twitched as he sniffed. "She got away," he said. "Leapt the garden wall like it was nothing. A powder mage. I'd bet my life on it." Another sniff. "As is this one."

In one quick motion Demasolin discarded his pistol and a belt of powder charges, throwing them away from Tamas. He drew his sword. "Powder mage or not, I will gut you. Remove your weapons."

"You think you can?" Tamas asked quietly.

Tamas was tired. He'd made this entire trek north just to reach Alvation, where he thought he'd find succor, only to find the city held by the enemy and the very people that he'd looked to for help now suspicious of him.

He knew he should disarm. Let them see he wasn't a threat. Take the time to explain himself.

But if what Ruper said was true, more soldiers would arrive any minute. Tamas would not disarm for one man with a sword.

Tamas laid a hand gently on the hilt of his sword.

Demasolin darted forward.

Tamas drew his sword and set his back foot in less time than it took to blink. Demasolin came on quickly.

"Stop! He'll kill you!"

Demasolin slowed. Tamas relaxed, suddenly wary. Was Hailona talking to him? She knew who he was. What he was capable of.

"Demasolin," Hailona said. "Please, wait. He'll kill you."

"I've killed powder mages before," Demasolin said between gritted teeth. "I've killed a Privileged. I am the duke of Vindren!" He said it like the name would mean something to Tamas.

It did, finally. A tickle in the back of his memory. Vindren. A man with a Knack for smells. Nose like a bloodhound. Quick as a powder mage in full trance.

Tamas lowered his sword.

"You surrender?" Demasolin said.

"No."

Demasolin took another step forward.

"I feel like this is a waste of our time," Tamas said.

"It was you, wasn't it?" Hailona suddenly said. "Outside in the street. Who killed all of those soldiers. I told you it was a powder mage," she said to her brother-in-law.

"I only saw a shadow," Demasolin said. The tip of his sword wavered.

"It was I," Tamas said. "Do you want a demonstration?"

"I don't take well to threats, old man."

Tamas examined Demasolin. Muscles taut, ready to lunge. His bearing, confidence, and stance all said that he was a gifted swordsman.

A young woman suddenly burst through the door. She wore her hair up, a greatcoat over her shoulders, and Tamas could sense two pistols under the coat. "Ma'am," she said, with only one quick glance at the two men pointing their swords at each other, "there are soldiers in the street."

"Put your swords up!" Hailona hissed at Tamas and Demasolin. To the young woman, she said, "How many?"

"Eight, ma'am, but..."

"What is it?"

"They're all dead, ma'am. Freshly dead."

Hailona looked at Tamas.

Tamas shrugged. "I only killed the ones chasing you."

There was a low knock on the glass door to the portico. Everyone looked that way. From Tamas's position he could see Vlora. She was carrying something large. He gestured her in.

She kicked the door open and swung through, tossing a body to the observatory floor with a thump. "This might answer your questions," she said.

"One of my captains," Tamas said by way of introduction. "Vlora, meet Lady Hailona, former governor of Alvation."

Vlora spared Hailona a look. "Taniel told me about her. One of your past lovers. She was pretty back then, wasn't she?"

Hailona gasped. Tamas groaned. Demasolin spun toward Tamas.

"Field Marshal Tamas," Demasolin roared. "On guard, you dog!"

He leapt at Tamas with startling speed. Tamas was barely able to bring the point of his sword up in time. Immediately on the retreat, he parried twice and danced backward. He could feel his leg protest in sudden agony when he twisted away from a particularly savage thrust.

Tamas was suddenly falling. He landed on his ass, crashing into a potted plant and knocking it over. He kept his sword up in a defensive position as Demasolin pressed forward.

A pistol fired, bringing Demasolin up short. Tamas stared at the tip of Demasolin's sword, barely able to register how fast the man moved. It was like fighting a Warden, with all their speed and none of their clumsiness.

Vlora held a smoking pistol pointed at the ceiling in one hand. In the other, a loaded pistol aimed at Demasolin. Plaster drifted down from the ceiling. "Stop," she said. "Drop the sword. I won't miss."

Demasolin looked once at Vlora, then once at Tamas, lying as he was at a disadvantage on the ground. Tamas tried not to let his pain reach his eyes.

Show no weakness.

Demasolin threw his sword to the floor with a snort of disgust.

Tamas heard several sets of footsteps in the hallway outside. Faces appeared at the door. Swords and pistols were drawn. Vlora kept her pistol trained on Demasolin.

Hailona made a calming gesture with both hands. To the people at the door, she said, "Everything is fine here. Prepare to leave. We have to get out of the manor."

Vlora nudged the body at her feet with one toe. It was a man in an Adran coat, with brown hair and a mustache. He was alive, his eyes wide, looking at Vlora in fear. "This one can answer some questions," Vlora said.

Demasolin crossed the room and grabbed the front of the man's coat with both hands, pulling him into a sitting position on the floor. The soldier's hands had been tied with his own belt.

"Why are his boots missing?" Demasolin said.

Vlora lowered her pistol. "Less willing to run if he doesn't have boots."

Tamas slowly climbed to his feet while the attention was away from him. He couldn't tell which hurt more—his leg or his pride. *Too old for this.* He tested the leg gently. It seemed to take weight. A momentary bout of weakness? He better not risk it.

He sheathed his sword and limped to the large desk in the middle of the room so he'd have something to lean on. Hailona watching him. Her eyes held something between suspicion and fear.

"Who," Demasolin demanded of the prisoner, "are you?"

The man's eyes remained wide as they flitted between the unfriendly faces in the room. He remained silent.

Demasolin shook him by the front of his coat and switched from Deliv to Adran. "Who are you? Speak, now!"

Nothing.

Demasolin slapped the soldier, openhanded. The soldier suddenly struggled, grappling with Demasolin, trying to throw him off, only to stop immediately when Vlora set the barrel of her pistol against his neck.

Vlora leaned over the soldier. In Kez, she said, "Do you understand me?" It was a soft tone, almost seductive, and Tamas wouldn't have heard it if he wasn't in a powder trance still.

The soldier nodded.

"Do you value your life?"

He nodded emphatically.

"Darling, if you want to live through the night, you'll answer the good man's questions. If not..." She gently rubbed the end of the pistol barrel against the soldier's neck.

Again with the tone, almost seductive. It was a side of Vlora Tamas had not seen before.

"I...I am Galhof of Adopest. Adran soldier," the man said in Adran. His accent was thick, the words broken.

"Try again," Vlora said in Kez. She hadn't stopped caressing the soldier's neck with her pistol. "You'll either have to get a better Adran accent or develop a sudden immunity to bullets."

The soldier's eyes almost seemed to bulge out of his head as he tried to look at the pistol touching his neck without turning his head. He cleared his throat. "My name *is* Galhof," he said in Kez, "but...I am a Kez soldier."

"What are you doing in Alvation?" Demasolin asked. "What are your orders?"

"We're to take the Mountainwatch above the city."

"Why the ruse, then? Why the Adran coats?"

"Don't know, sir," Galhof said. "I'm just a soldier."

Tamas didn't have time for this. "Guess," he growled.

"So that Deliv blames Adro for the attack."

"But," Hailona spoke up suddenly, "how did they expect the ruse to hold? There are already suspicions." She shot a glance at Demasolin. "I've been saying for a week I thought you were Kez."

The soldier looked around the room again as if seeking allies. He said nothing.

Tamas felt a sudden dread in the pit of his stomach. It grew heavier as certainty within him grew. When he spoke, it came out a croak. "They plan on putting Alvation to the torch. Oh, pit. All of it. They're going to burn it all, kill every man, woman, and child. They'll leave behind just enough evidence to condemn Adro. By the time anyone has stopped to think about it, Deliv will already be at war with Adro."

"Not even the Kez would stoop to that," Demasolin said.

Tamas was certain now. "The man in command of this army is a monster."

"Who?"

"Duke Nikslaus. The king's favorite Privileged. He'll stop at nothing to win this war."

"I know that name," Hailona said softly.

Tamas shot her a warning glance. Now was not the time to bring up his history with Nikslaus.

Ruper suddenly appeared in the doorway again. "Ma'am," he said, "we have to go. The lookout has spotted soldiers coming down the main street. Over a hundred of them. We have to go now."

"The wounded?" Hailona asked.

"We'll have to carry them, or leave them for the Adrans."

"They're not Adrans," Hailona said. "They are Kez. Quickly now. Get everyone to the cellar. We'll take the old passage across the street to Wyn Manor and go to Millertown."

The butler didn't even blink at the correction. "Very good, ma'am." Ruper disappeared again.

Demasolin retrieved his sword from the floor and stopped beside Tamas. "We're not done, old man," he said, sliding it into its sheath with a click. "They call you a savior in the Adran papers. I name you a butcher and a traitor to your own crown."

"I'm all of them," Tamas said with a shrug.

Demasolin seemed taken aback by that. He strode from the room.

Tamas looked over at the Kez soldier. "He knows where we're going," he said.

"Right," Vlora said. She grabbed the soldier by the back of the neck and forced him outside.

Haliona put a hand to her mouth. "That man . . ."

A shot rang out on the porch.

"A soldier's lot in life is to die for his country," Tamas said.

"He was our prisoner."

"He's spent the last couple of weeks terrorizing your city, along with his countrymen. Justice must fall swiftly, or it might not fall at all."

"Is that what you said about the Adran nobility when you sent them to the guillotine?"

"Yes."

"You always said you were a soldier," Hailona said. Her voice was accusing. "Do you accept your own death as inevitable?"

Tamas leaned over to rub his leg. "Death is always inevitable. I

gave up on the idea I'd die surrounded by my grandchildren earlier this year." He couldn't help but look toward the door Vlora
had just left by. His thoughts leapt to Taniel. Was he alive? Had
he come out of the coma? So far away. Nothing Tamas could do.
"One day," he said, "I'll die for my country. I'd rather it be on the
battlefield than at the hands of a Kez headsman."

"You really believe it, don't you?"

"What?" Tamas asked.

"That you are in the right."

"Of course."

"Could there have been a better way than killing all those
people?"

"Likely," Tamas said. "But I didn't take it."

Tell her, something said inside of him. *Tell her about Sabon's
death. It has to happen sooner or later.* Better she find out from him
than from someone else.

"I need your help," Hailona said.

"I was about to say the same thing."

Hailona frowned. "My husband—Demasolin's brother—was
taken by the Ad...the Kez. He's being held in the city's main
prison. Tonight we tried to rescue him and free all the prisoners
there. It was one of over twenty attacks all across the city we've
been planning for over a week. We failed, and if our failure was any
indication, so did the other attacks."

"The prison—are they holding all of their prisoners there?"
Tamas asked. "They captured one of my outriders on the edge of
the plateau a few days ago. That's why I came here with just Vlora.
To try to rescue him."

"I don't know. Demasolin has eyes all around the city. You may
ask him."

But whether he'd answer a question from Tamas was another
thing.

Tamas found Demasolin watching out the front door for any

sign of the Kez. Tamas could hear the sound of soldiers in the street, beyond the manor walls. They were moving quietly, probably too low for Demasolin to hear.

The Deliv gave Tamas a glance filled with disdain.

Tamas ignored it.

"Four days ago," Tamas said, "the Kez took one of my outriders as we crossed the plateau coming north. I came to the city to get him back. I understand your brother is a prisoner as well. I think we could help each other."

Demasolin didn't so much as look toward him. "I don't think I want your help," he said coldly.

Tamas bit back a retort, gritting his teeth. Shortsighted bastard. Typical nobleman.

"My son," Tamas said quietly, "lies half-dead because he chose to save Adro instead of himself. He is in Adopest, and I don't know whether he still lives. The man the Kez hold prisoner is my late wife's brother. He may be the last kin I have left alive."

Tamas went on. "You think me a beast. You might be right. But the Kez hold your brother, and they hold mine. I think if we work together we can get them both back."

Demasolin didn't reply. Tamas waited for a few heartbeats before turning away.

Nothing else he could say would sway the man.

"Wait," Demasolin said suddenly. "Three days ago they brought in a prisoner by the south gate. A giant of a man, wearing a Mountainwatch Watchmaster's vest."

"That was him."

"My contacts say he's in the same prison. I'll help you."

"Thank you," Tamas said.

"I'll help you, but I will not hesitate to kill you if I need to."

CHAPTER
40

Taniel drew his knife and threw himself forward.

He grasped the Prielight Guard by the chest and pushed both himself and the guard backward through the door. They tumbled down the stairs, a jumble of limbs and grunts and curses. Taniel was able to arrest his own fall by grabbing onto the walls of the spiral staircase.

The Prielight went down a few more steps and landed with his back against the wall, dagger drawn. He wiped blood from the corner of his mouth.

"Guards!" the Prielight yelled.

The Prielight sprang upward, swinging his knife. Taniel dodged one blow and then another. Despite being at a disadvantage in the tower stairs, the Prielight was incredibly fast, forcing Taniel to dance away from quick jabs at his feet.

Taniel swung down for the Prielight's head, only to have the guard move out of the way. The counterstrike sparked against the stone steps beside Taniel's foot.

Taniel stomped on the Prielight's wrist to trap his hand, and leaned over, stabbing quickly at the neck.

He felt the Prielight's fist slam into his groin. Nausea swept through him as he fell with his back to the stairs. His stomach felt like it had flipped. The Prielight Guard scrambled up the stairs and raised his knife.

Taniel planted both feet on the Prielight's chest and shoved.

The guard cried out in dismay as he tumbled back down the stairs.

Taniel turned to run back up to the tower when something caught his eye. There was a figure on the stairs, just down from where he and the Prielight were fighting. In the darkness it seemed no more than a shadow, and Taniel felt cold fingers creep up his spine.

The specter wore a mask with a single eyehole, and long white robes.

Kresimir.

Taniel flew up the stairs, propelled by fear. He slammed the tower door behind him and checked the far window. A straight drop into the Addown. No telling how deep the river was there. The fall could still kill him, and even if he survived it, he'd be swept down the river into Budwiel.

But better to take his chances than face certain death at Kresimir's sorcery.

Taniel felt his pockets. The bloody sheet was gone. If he left without it, all this was for nothing.

There, in the middle of the floor. He must have dropped it when he attacked the Prielight. Taniel snatched up the strip of linen and stuffed it into his belt.

The tower door opened.

The Prielight charged him without hesitation. Taniel grappled with the guard, shoving them both toward the far window.

Over the Prielight's shoulder he caught a glimpse of Kresimir.

"Stop," the god said.

The voice was like the toll of a bell echoing in Taniel's head.

The Prielight staggered away from Taniel, clutching at his ears. Taniel grabbed the Prielight by the shoulders and shoved him toward Kresimir, then sprinted for the window.

Just a few steps and he lunged, throwing himself as far from the keep walls as possible. The wind whistled by his ears as he fell, his heart in his throat, the dark water of the Addown rushing up to meet him.

Taniel plunged into the inky depths, the force of the impact pushing the breath from his body. His feet sank into the silt at the bottom of the river and he could feel himself torn by the current as his fingers desperately groped for the surface. His lungs burned. His jaw ached from trying to force himself to keep it closed.

A moment later and he breached the surface, gasping for air.

The keep was already behind him and pulling away quickly as he was swept along by the river. It didn't take long to realize that he was being dragged toward the banks. He felt his leg slam into a rock and then he was again plunged beneath the water for a moment. He sputtered back to the surface.

People in the keep were shouting and pointing after him. He'd have to strike for the opposite bank of the river and float it all the way down to Budwiel. The current was fast enough to keep him ahead of any pursuing Prielight Guards, and he might be able to disappear in the ruins of the city until the next night. He set his eye on the other bank.

Taniel blinked. Something was wrong.

The river bank no longer slid by. The water was moving—Taniel could feel the current pull at him—but he wasn't.

Taniel's stomach lurched as he was suddenly viewing the bank from above it. How could that be? He was still in the water.

Confusion, then realization set in.

He—and a whole lake's worth of water—had been scooped out of the river by sorcery. It was as if a giant had fetched a drink with a cupped hand and Taniel was in that hand. His stomach lurched as he was lifted higher and then began moving back toward the keep.

Taniel swam to the edge. There was nothing there but a long drop to the hard ground. He reached out probing fingers. They bumped against a wall of hardened air.

A few moments later and Taniel—along with thousands of gallons of water—was dropped unceremoniously in the courtyard of the keep.

Muddy water from the Addown cascaded across the limestone cobbles. Taniel got to his feet, ankle-deep in water, and looked around wildly.

"On your knees!"

Prielight Guards poured into the courtyard, shouting in Kez. There were dozens, and when Taniel reached out with his senses, he was dismayed to find they were carrying air rifles—no powder on any of them.

He reached for his knife, only to find it gone, lost in the river. One of his pistols was missing as well, and the other one soaked through. The powder would be useless. He drew it from his belt anyhow and flipped it over. On the walls above, Prielight Guards aimed their air rifles.

"Down!" The first guard to reach Taniel menaced him with a long pike. "On your knees, swine."

He seemed surprised when Taniel darted forward, past the head of the pike, and cracked his pistol butt across the man's face. Taniel discarded the pistol and plucked the pike from the Prielight's fingers. He braced himself. This, he realized, was a fight he could not win.

An air rifle popped, and then another. Bullets ricocheted off the courtyard cobbles. Taniel sprinted toward the closest Prielight. *Keep moving,* he told himself. *Make a harder target. And get among the guards so that, at the very least, some might get hit by friendly fire in the confusion.*

"Stop."

Taniel staggered, almost dropping the pike. He suddenly felt woozy and out of breath. Again, the word tolled like a giant bell.

Prielight Guards threw down their weapons and shrank to their knees, clutching at their ears.

Taniel forced himself to keep going. Every step was like slogging through a bog.

"I said stop." Kresimir appeared at one of the courtyard doors. The water of the Addown he'd dumped in the courtyard seemed to shrink beneath his feet and dry up, so that when he stepped it was on parched cobbles.

Taniel kept moving. His body wanted to stop, but he knew he couldn't. He had to press on. To get away from the god.

"Why do you not obey my orders?" Kresimir's voice was the deepest bass Taniel had ever heard. It rang within his ears. The god tilted his head to one side, as if curious. He pointed at the cobbles. "Kneel."

"Go to the pit," Taniel spat. His whole body shook from the effort of moving.

"Kneel!"

The keep quaked. One of the Prielight Guards screamed. Taniel could feel Kresimir's confusion behind the mask.

"Take him," Kresimir whispered.

Prielight Guards surged to their feet. It was a struggle for Taniel just to move as he tried to react to their advance.

Fighting was out of the question.

Taniel's pike was taken from him. Someone slammed the butt of an air rifle into his back, dropping him to his knees.

"A spy, my lord," the guard captain said. "Another assassin."

"From who?"

Fingers curled into Taniel's hair and his head was wrenched back so that he looked up at Kresimir. "Answer your god, cur," the guard captain said.

Taniel cleared his throat and spit the contents at Kresimir's feet.

The butt of a rifle smacked across his face.

"Amateurs," Taniel said. General Ket's provosts had hit him harder than that.

"Adran, my lord," the guard captain said.

Kresimir took a small step back. "Who ordered you here?" He paused a moment, and then, "Why does he not answer? His god *compels* him."

The next blow was a pike handle to Taniel's chin that he feared had dislocated his jaw. Something hit him in the stomach. He was dragged up by the hair and hit again, then again. Amateurs these were not. Compared with these, the first blow had been gentle.

"Answer your god," the guard captain said.

Taniel remained silent.

"Break his arm."

One Prielight took ahold of Taniel's wrist, bending it painfully back, and then brought a knee up against his elbow as one might break a branch for the fire. Taniel gritted his teeth, trying not to scream. Once. Twice. Three times.

"Break it," the guard captain said again.

"I can't. It's like trying to break a cannon barrel." The Prielight rubbed at his knee.

"Get a hammer."

"Fools." Kresimir's voice made the Prielights cower. He stepped up and looked down on Taniel.

Taniel felt the warmth of sorcery like the slow approach of a flame.

"Beg," Kresimir said.

Taniel shook his head.

"Beg!" Kresimir's jaw twisted with sudden strain, and Taniel felt the heat come on quickly. He drew back involuntarily, ready for the worst kind of pain.

Kresimir suddenly threw himself backward, a wail escaping his lips. It grew louder and louder, and might have shattered the stones of the keep had it been longer. As it was, Taniel thought that for a moment it would drive him mad. The god fell to the ground, swatting at invisible flames, whimpering.

Taniel felt the chuckle rise within him. It burst forth from his mouth like a funny thought at an inopportune moment.

Ka-poel's wards. It had to be.

Kresimir couldn't break them.

Kresimir cowered on the cobbles. His mask had fallen off. He stared at Taniel through one eye of fear. The other eye was pus-filled, oozing black liquid over a swollen, purple cheek. "What did you do to me?" Kresimir asked.

Taniel couldn't stop laughing. "Oh," he said. "That wasn't me. You met Pole."

Taniel tried to move. He still couldn't.

Kresimir groped blindly for his mask. He returned it to his face and climbed to his feet, but did not approach Taniel again.

"Fetch the Adran traitor," Kresimir said. There was fear in his voice. "Have him identify this spy."

Taniel waited on his hands and knees, head sagged from exhaustion. Kresimir had sent his men out just thirty minutes ago.

"A traitor," Kresimir had said. Who was it? Taniel had suspected all along that it might be Ket. She'd been too enthusiastic about ordering the retreats. Maybe Doravir.

Of course, it might be someone lower. A general's aid, or even courier. Plenty of people had access to the kind of sensitive information that would give the Kez the edge.

Taniel had a feeling it wasn't a lower-ranking officer, though. He suspected a colonel, or maybe even a general.

Kresimir paced slowly in one corner of the keep courtyard. Every few minutes he'd turn his one good eye toward Taniel.

Taniel stared back in defiance. He'd brought down this god. He'd put a bullet in Kresimir's eye. He'd proved a god could feel pain.

He wouldn't give Kresimir the satisfaction of watching him grovel.

Of course, Taniel knew he might think otherwise after a few days of torture. He had to be realistic. Ka-poel's wards seemed to protect him from sorcery. Perhaps even from permanent physical damage. But he knew from experience that he could still feel pain.

Funny, that. Her protection might just be his undoing. The Kez could torture him indefinitely.

Footsteps approached from a hallway adjoining the courtyard. Taniel rocked back on his knees. He'd see this traitor and spit in his eye before he died.

"My lord, you summoned me?"

Taniel's head jerked around.

The traitor was an older, heavyset man. He wore the epaulets of a general, and the left sleeve of his blue Adran uniform was pinned across the shoulder to make up for the missing arm.

General Hilanska.

"Who is this assassin?" Kresimir gestured toward Taniel.

"My lord?" Hilanska turned. His eyes grew wide at the sight of Taniel, and his mouth worked silently for a moment.

"You know him?"

"I do indeed, my lord. He is the very man you seek: the eye behind the flintlock. Taniel Two-Shot."

"I feared..." The words came from Kresimir's mouth as a whisper.

Taniel got to his feet. It was like trying to stand beneath the weight of the entire keep, his knees buckling beneath him, legs shaking from the effort.

"I'll kill you," he said to Hilanska.

"Was he sent here?" Kresimir asked.

The general seemed troubled. "No, my lord. He should be under arrest in the Wings of Adom camp right now."

"Why?" Taniel demanded. "My father trusted you!" Everything that had happened: the arrest, the court-martial, the attack on Ka-poel. Had that all been Hilanska?

"He mentioned someone named Pole," Kresimir said.

Hilanska frowned. "I don't know anyone...ah. There is a girl named Ka-poel."

"Is she a great sorcerer? Why did I not know of her?"

Taniel surged forward. The guards clustered around, menacing him with pikes and air rifles. "Not another word, Hilanska!"

"She's just a child, practically. Two-Shot's companion. A savage."

"And a sorcerer?"

"A Bone-eye. A savage magician of some kind. Negligible powers."

"Kill her."

Taniel snarled wordlessly. He felt a pike blade catch his shoulder, tearing through his skin and flesh as he forced his way through the circle of Prielight Guards. One of the guards threw himself in front of Taniel. Barely even slowing down, Taniel snatched the guard by the throat and crushed his windpipe.

Hilanska turned to run, but he was too slow. Taniel leapt after him, fingers grasping, ready to crush the traitor's skull between his palms.

And he would have, had Kresimir not stepped between them.

The god raised a hand, and Taniel felt that same sluggish weight fall upon him.

He tore through it, batting away Kresimir's hand. His body didn't feel like it was his own, and he gave in to the rage flowing through him.

Taniel expected his fists to strike steel when he touched the flesh of the god. Instead, Kresimir crumpled before him, crying out. Taniel's knuckles cracked hard against Kresimir's jaw, then his face. Kresimir's mask clattered to the ground, and Taniel found himself straddling the god, pounding away.

Kresimir's nose was a fountain of blood, and his teeth gave way to the beating.

Taniel's fingers curled around the god's throat when the Prielights pulled him away. He flailed about with his fists, sending several of the Prielights to the floor before he himself was beaten down.

"Don't kill him!" Kresimir shrieked, scrambling to get to his feet. His face was crimson, his white robes soaked with blood. "Don't kill him," he said again. Kresimir returned the mask to his face and backed slowly away from Taniel. "Hang him high. I want the world to see what becomes of a man who thought he could kill God."

The Prielights dragged Taniel across the hall. He kicked and screamed, throwing what punches he could. As he was pulled out of the hall, he could hear Kresimir speaking once again to Hilanska:

"Tomorrow I burn the Adran army."

"Are you sure, my lord? What about Adom?"

"He will burn with the rest."

Adamat spent the night in the arms of his wife and rose early to make his way to the riverfront.

It was only about seven o'clock, but a thin crowd had already turned out. By the blaze of the sun rising in the east over the abandoned Skyline Palace, Adamat could tell it would be a beautiful day. Few clouds hung above him. The sky was blue and gold.

He found a spot where the crumbling wall of the old city overlooked the Ad River as it came into Adopest but before it hooked around the bend and met up with the Adsea. Adamat sat on the wall and dangled his feet over the edge, eating a meat pie he'd bought from a vendor in the street. He still felt burdened by the loss of Josep. Perhaps Faye was right—the other children needed him now. He had to somehow protect them from this new threat.

He hoped that Josep would forgive him.

No sign of ships on the river to the north. Perhaps Ricard had oversold it. Surely the Trading Company merchantmen couldn't sail all the way down the Ad River so quickly?

Yet still he waited. Ricard had not given an estimate of when Lord Claremonte's ships would arrive, and Adamat did not want to miss it. He had no plans, no grand schemes to throw Lord Claremonte from his goals. Adamat could only watch. Something told him that this day would be one to live in his mind forever.

By eleven o'clock, the crowd had thickened to the point that carriages could no longer navigate the streets. Noise filled the air as people shouted among themselves. No one really seemed to know what was going on. Their only information came from the newspaper article that Ricard had run the night before.

There was certainly excitement in the streets, and the police were out in full force. More than one old veteran wore faded Adran blues and sported a fifty-year-old musket on his shoulder. Other men had brought their whole families out and were picnicking on the old city wall. Pastry bakers and meat pie vendors were hawking their snacks to the crowd.

Adamat bought a newspaper from a newsie lad and perused Ricard's front-page article. It was a rousing speech that called the people out to defend their city against the oppressions of foreign invasion and tyranny. Adamat lowered the newspaper to watch a pair of children splashing in the muddy water of the Ad like it was a carnival day.

He flipped through the newspaper while he waited for Claremonte's ships. Unsubstantiated rumors out of Kez that Field Marshal Tamas was still alive. Fresh news from Deliv that an Adran army was besieging one of their cities—preposterous.

The slow rise of shouts throughout the throng brought Adamat's nose out of his newspaper.

Ships on the horizon.

They began as white dots slowly creeping down the river and steadily drew closer as the afternoon went on. They were moving at an almost reckless pace, especially for merchantmen navigating a freshwater river. They came on at full sail with the current, the wind at their backs.

It was two o'clock before the ships finally reached Adopest. Adamat had never sailed on an oceangoing vessel and had only been to ocean port cities a handful of times in his life. Most of his knowledge of them came from books, but he could tell the lead vessel was a fourth-rate ship of the line, and he counted twenty-three gun ports on just one side. It seemed to be the biggest of the ships, and it waved the green-and-white-striped flag, in the center of which was a laurel wreath, that was the emblem of the Brudania-Gurla Trading Company.

The ships furled their sails and drifted downriver. Adamat could see sailors rushing about the deck, and Brudanian infantry staring passively back at the crowd awaiting them in Adopest. The gun ports were open.

If Claremonte was invading, his ships could destroy most of the city without even disembarking crews and soldiers.

There was no motion among the longboats. The infantry seemed content to stand on the ships and do nothing, and the sailors were...

Adamat watched them carefully. What was going on? He cursed his limited knowledge of seafaring. Crossbeams were lowered, sails unhooked and stowed, and very soon it dawned on Adamat that they were taking down the mast.

He didn't even know that ships could *do* that. It made sense, though. While the bridges along the northern Ad had been replaced for the passage of masted ships, the ones in downtown Adopest had not. If Claremonte wanted to get his fleet onto the Adsea, where it would be most effective, he'd have to drop the masts completely, float down the river, and reinstall them on the open water.

Adamat desperately wanted to do something. This immense crowd of people seemed to have no direction. Like him, they simply watched while the masts were lowered. What more could they do? The ships sat at anchor out in the river, and they were heavily armed. It would have taken the Adran army to stop them.

He was surprised at how quickly the masts were removed, and Adamat gave up his seat on the edge of the wall to walk with the ships as the anchors were raised and they headed downriver.

He was even more surprised when the ships weighed anchor once more between the bridges, coming to stop just a half mile from the outlet to the Adsea.

They'd stopped, he noted, next to the towering Kresim Cathedral in the new city.

Adamat descended the old city wall and fought his way through the throng to cross the bridge and head toward the Kresim Cathedral. He cast his gaze toward the ships every so often, but nothing had changed. Still a flurry of activity on board. Still no sign of lowering the longboats or firing the cannons.

Between the Kresim Cathedral and the Ad River was an amphitheater where the Diocels of the Church could address significant crowds. By the time Adamat reached it, the amphitheater was overflowing with people trying to get a better look at the tall ships.

It was a death trap. Adamat cursed everyone inside that amphitheater for their stupidity. Hundreds would die if Claremonte opened up with a single salvo.

Adamat thought he spied a familiar face nearby, and muscled his way toward the river. There was Ricard, surrounded by his assistants and the other union bosses, Fell at his side.

"Ricard, what the pit is going on?" Adamat demanded.

"No idea," Ricard said. He seemed just as confused as the rest of the crowd, and regarded the ship with caution. "I've got my boys out in force, armed to the teeth with whatever they could find, but if Claremonte opens fire, there's not a damn thing we can do about it. We can only stop him if he tries to come ashore."

"And who would be stupid enough to do that?" Adamat asked.

"Look," one of the union bosses said, "they're lowering a longboat."

Adamat peered toward the ship. Sailors scurried about the deck, and suddenly a longboat swung out and was lowered into the river. A rope ladder was dropped, and men began to descend onto it.

"Give me a looking glass," Adamat said. Fell handed him hers.

He found the longboat and examined it for a few moments. There were a half-dozen Brudanian soldiers. Some rowers. A few men in top hats.

Adamat stopped and focused on one face in particular.

"He's here," Adamat said. "In the longboat."

"Who?"

"Claremonte."

"How the pit would you know?"

"I saw his likeness once. A small portrait at a Trading Company stock house, back before he rose to be head of the company."

"Let him come, the bastard," Ricard said. "We'll be ready for him."

Claremonte looked anything but worried. He laughed at something one of the rowers said, then clapped a soldier on the back. He was a striking man, with high cheekbones that contrasted with a body grown soft with age and wealth. His eyes were alive and happy, nothing like his late lackey, Lord Vetas.

The longboat rowed away from the ship, Lord Claremonte standing in the bow like a commander leading the invasion of a foreign land.

Which, unless Adamat was completely wrong, was what he was.

But where were his men? Why would he come to land practically alone, into the teeth of a waiting mob who'd been told he was coming to take their homes from them?

The longboat stopped about some distance from the shore and threw down an anchor. Lord Claremonte stood up straight, facing the amphitheater, and spread his hands.

"Citizens of Adopest," he began, a smile on his face, the words booming inhumanly across the river.

CHAPTER

41

Tamas watched from the vantage of an old church tower as rain fell in thick sheets across Alvation.

The early morning was dim and cloudy, and Tamas didn't think that it would get much lighter outside as the day went on. Tamas couldn't even see the Charwood Mountains, though they rose less than a mile from his current position.

An excellent day for his army to sneak up on the city.

A terrible day for a battle.

Powder would be wet, the ground muddy, and with the Kez wearing Adran uniforms, neither side would be able to tell friend from foe.

The street below was full of Kez soldiers moving supplies.

He watched them work with no small amount of trepidation. If he was right, and he feared he was, Nikslaus's last act when he pulled out of the city would be to put it to the torch, slaughtering civilians and leaving enough chaos behind that no one would bother to question who was behind the attack.

The Mountainwatch above Alvation was about twenty-five miles away. Early this morning, Tamas had heard the faint report of cannon fire from that direction. Nikslaus had the Mountainwatch under siege.

It wasn't a strong Mountainwatch. Not a bastion like South Pike; more of a fortified toll road. It wouldn't hold long against two brigades of Kez soldiers.

Tamas had sent Vlora back to the Seventh and Ninth hours ago.

He missed her now. No one to watch his back. The Deliv partisans didn't trust him, so he spent most of his time watching the Kez soldiers—watching for patterns, waiting for Nikslaus to make his move. One eye always on the road, on the chance Tamas would see Gavril among the prisoners being forced to do hard labor for the Kez.

Tamas heard a noise in the chapel beneath the tower. The large main door opened and closed again. A moment later, a set of footsteps rang on the stone stairs. Tamas brushed his fingers along the grip of one pistol and then took a powder charge between his fingers. He opened it carefully, only taking the tiniest pinch, and sprinkled the black powder on his tongue.

Just enough to keep him going. To fend off exhaustion and sharpen his eyes. Not enough for him to risk going powder blind.

He hoped.

Hailona ascended the belfry steps and joined Tamas at the top, where he stood beside the enormous bronze bell. He tipped his hat to her.

"Halley," he said.

"Tamas."

They stood in silence for several minutes.

Tamas stole a glance at her once or twice. He'd been unfair in his first assessment last night. She was still a regal woman. Stately, her back straight, arms held just so in a way that said she was equally comfortable in a silk gown worth more than a soldier makes in a year and in the plain brown wool that she wore now.

It wasn't that she had aged *poorly*. She had just aged.

They all had, he reflected. He himself, Hailona, Gavril. She'd been the governor of Alvation for almost three decades. She'd ruled beside her first husband for twenty years, then alone at the king's bequest for another ten. That was more than enough to age a woman beyond her years.

"You never came back," she said suddenly.

"Halley…"

She spoke over him. "I never really expected you to. I don't blame you. Not terribly, anyway. I see now what your goals were, what has driven you the last fifteen years. I can't say I agree with them, but I understand, at least."

Tamas had had dozens of lovers over the few years immediately after Erika died.

He only regretted one of them.

"You caused me a lot of pain after you left," Hailona went on, "when I still thought you might come back for me. You came and stayed for a few months, and then disappeared. But… I want you to know something. I want you to know that you made me feel amazing in those few weeks. Like a woman who could stand up against the world. That in my long life, only two men made me feel that way: you and my first husband."

"Your second husband…"

Hailona gave a choked laugh. Tamas glanced out of the corner of his eye to find that her face was red and she held a handkerchief to her mouth. "My husband is a coward. Pit, I can't even say his name." She sighed, leaning against a column beside the bell. "I respect him. He's one of the finest merchants in southern Deliv, but he's also one of the biggest cowards in southern Deliv. I do not love him."

Tamas stared out into the pouring rain and pondered the unsaid words. She didn't love her husband—but she loved Tamas. He swallowed a lump in his throat.

He cleared his throat. "I'm sorry, Halley. For what it's worth. I'm sorry."

"You're sorry..." She laughed again. It came out a half sob.

Tamas felt his heart being torn in two. This woman beside him was a powerful creature. She could stand up beside Lady Winceslav among the best women to seek his hand in marriage, before the world found out just how bitter of an old widower he really was.

Hailona smoothed the front of her dress and visibly calmed herself. "I met the general of the Kez army when they first arrived," she said, her tone suddenly businesslike.

"They took us by surprise. Marched in, pretending to be Adrans. He gathered all the nobility together at the governor's mansion that first night. Told us we were prisoners in the city. He had an impeccable Adran accent. Spoke Deliv equally well. Not a trace of Kez. I was convinced, at first.

"Then I started thinking. I knew you. From Sabon's letters I guessed he had great influence in your decision making. Neither of you would ever attack Deliv. Then I thought maybe one of your generals had gone mad. Gone rogue. This general—he seems a madman. Dangerous and deadly."

"Did you see his hands?" Tamas interrupted softly.

Hailona frowned. "No. He kept them tucked away beneath his coat. I thought it strange, now that you mention it, but didn't give it a second glance."

"He doesn't have any," Tamas said.

"No hands?" Hailona seemed taken aback. "I feel like I would have heard of a Kez general with no hands."

"It was a...recent development," Tamas said. "And he's not a general. He's a Privileged."

"How could a Privileged have no...oh." She stared at him in

silence for several moments. "You took them, didn't you?" Another long pause. "You hate Privileged so much?"

"I hate *him* so much." Tamas tried to keep the emotion out of his voice. He wasn't successful. "Duke Nikslaus was the one who arrested and beheaded Erika, and then brought me her...her..."

He felt her hand touch his shoulder gently. He squeezed his eyes shut. Felt the tears swelling within them. He would never forgive himself for failing Erika.

"Tamas," Hailona said.

He cleared his throat. "Was Sabon really disowned?"

She removed her hand from his shoulder and returned to lean against the column. "Being a powder mage was never illegal here in Deliv. Nor was it ever state-sponsored, like in Adro. Our parents thought he should have joined the Deliv army. But if he had, they would ignore his gifts. As if he wasn't a powder mage at all. When you came along and asked him to join you and be in the first powder cabal in the world, he was ecstatic. I've never seen him so happy. My parents didn't understand."

"He never told me," Tamas said.

"He wouldn't," Hailona said. She smiled at Tamas, and he remembered how beautiful she had been all those years ago. "You're his best friend."

"And he was mine."

The smile disappeared. "Was?"

"He's dead, Halley."

She took a quick step back, then another. "What? No. Not Sabon."

"Shot. By a Kez Warden. One of Duke Nikslaus's men."

"You...you let him die?"

"I didn't. It was an ambush, I..."

The softness in her eyes a moment ago was gone. Any love, any feeling, also gone. She breathed heavily, clutching at her dress, her eyes filled with horror. She turned and fled down the belfry stairs.

"Halley!"

Tamas heard the door to the chapel slam below. He fell back against the bell, felt it rock slightly from his weight without making a sound. He shook his head and stared out into the rain sightlessly.

Was all he left behind misery and death? Sorrow, widows, and grieving families? He made his hands into fists. How dare she blame him? Sabon was his best friend. His closest confidant for the last fifteen years.

No, she was right to blame him. He was a harbinger of death, it seemed. Not to be trusted with the lives of anyone dear.

It was perhaps an hour before Tamas heard the chapel door open below. A slow, measured step lit upon the stairs. Tamas frowned, wondering who it was for only a moment before the mint-tinged smell of cigarette smoke wafted up the stairwell.

"Sir," Olem said as he joined Tamas. He wore a greatcoat and forage cap pulled down over his eyes, soaked from the rain. Beneath the coat, his Adran blues. He wore the colonel's pins Tamas had given him last night. That seemed like an eternity ago.

"I thought you ran out of those." Tamas looked at the cigarette between Olem's lips.

Olem drew it from his mouth, turned it sideways as if it were a peculiar thing, and blew smoke out his nose slowly before returning the cigarette to its place. "Stopped at a tobacconist on the way through town."

"I see you have your priorities straight."

"Of course. You don't look so well, sir."

Tamas looked back out across the city. "Sometimes I feel like a pestilence."

"That argument," Olem said after a moment's consideration, "could be made."

"You make me feel so much better."

"I try, sir."

"What are you doing here? I told Vlora to give the signal, not order you here. And how the bloody pit did you get past the river in broad daylight?"

"I pretended I was a Kez colonel pretending to be an Adran colonel," Olem said. "It was disturbingly easy."

"They didn't ask for papers or proof?"

"In this rain?" Olem gestured at the downpour. "You don't understand an enlisted man, sir. Nobody asks for bloody papers in this kind of weather."

"Sloppy."

"I call it lucky. I also have news."

Tamas straightened up. "What kind of news?"

"A Deliv army is about a day and a half outside the city. Coming from the west. Our outriders spotted them just a few hours ago."

"How big?"

"Several brigades, at least."

"Pit."

"That's not a good thing, sir?"

"Maybe. We need to launch an attack soon."

"We won't be ready, sir."

"We have to. Something to tell the Deliv that there is more going on here than meets the eye. Otherwise their brigades will fall on us, thinking we are the ones holding the city.

"Come with me," he said, heading for the belfry stairs. "And keep a hand on your pistol. I might be starting a fight I can't win."

Vlora was waiting at the bottom of the stairs.

"My powder mages?" he asked.

"Waiting in an abandoned factory a quarter mile from here."

Tamas gestured for her to join him. He checked the street outside the chapel before crossing over to Millertown. The ground was muddy from the rain, a frothy slurry of refuse and garbage. They cut through several alleyways to avoid Kez patrols and then entered one of the larger mills.

A pair of Deliv partisans guarded the door. They let Tamas pass through, eyeing Vlora and Olem suspiciously. Tamas climbed the stairs to the second floor.

Demasolin was examining a report while a few of his captains and spies looked on. He glanced up when Tamas entered, but did not greet him.

Tamas counted the men in the room. Six of them, if it came to a fight.

Tamas removed his gloves and threw them on the table for emphasis. "Why didn't you tell me about the army?" he demanded.

Demasolin glanced up again. "What army?"

"Don't be bloody coy with me. You've got the entire city running with your spies. I know you can get people in and out. There's a Deliv army just over a day's march from here."

"You didn't need to know." Demasolin returned to reading his report.

Tamas planted both hands on the table in front of Demasolin and leaned over it until his face was only a few inches from Demasolin's. "You want to go another round? You willing to bet my leg will go again? Because you're putting my whole army in danger."

He heard the creak of movement behind him as Demasolin's underlings shifted uncomfortably. Tamas would leave them to Olem and Vlora if it came to blows.

Demasolin set the report facedown on the table. He leaned back in his chair, and his fingers crept slowly toward the sword at his hip.

"If the Kez know," Tamas said, "which they undoubtedly do, they'll torch the city tonight and be gone by morning."

"They won't torch anything in this weather."

"Nikslaus will find a way. That leaves you all dead, and my army sitting there looking guilty while whoever survives the Kez slaughter will say Adro did it. No one wins if your king attacks my army. Would you risk the lives of everyone in this city, and the lives of Deliv soldiers, because you think I'm a butcher?"

Demasolin's fingers stopped their movement toward his sword. "We'll have to act tonight. Just after dark."

"Have you found where they moved the prisoners?"

"We have."

Tamas bit his tongue. How long had Demasolin been sitting on that information, too?

"Can you provide a distraction?" Tamas asked.

"No," Demasolin said. "You have one man in there," he said. "I have dozens. Including my brother. I'll be going after them, and it'll be you who provides a distraction."

"Where are they being held?"

"I don't think you need to know that."

Tamas wanted to reach across the table and strangle Demasolin. Even so, he wasn't sure if that was a fight he wanted to start, and he wasn't keen on risking his leg going out again. He had better people to strangle.

Demasolin produced a map of the city and spread it out across the table. "The main city barracks is here. There are about two hundred men stationed there. Get close enough to detonate their powder reserves and it'll bring every soldier within a half mile running."

Tamas spun the map around so the south end was facing him. He ran his eyes around the marks, then spaced his fingers and did some math.

"No," Tamas said. "You've tried this already. Your failed attack last night. Someone is feeding the Kez information. They'll be ready for your attack on the prison and for mine on the barracks."

"What else can we do?" Demasolin said. "I don't know who the damned traitor is."

"You want a distraction? I'll give you a distraction. This General Saulkin. He's staying at the governor's manor, correct?"

Demasolin answered hesitantly. "Yes."

"Is he still there?"

"As of an hour ago, yes."

"Tell your spies that Field Marshal Tamas is going to kill Saulkin."

"And how will that help?"

"Because Saulkin is Duke Nikslaus, and I cut his bloody hands off. If he knows I'm in the city, he'll forget about everything else."

"Then you'll walk into a trap." Demasolin held up one hand. "Don't get me wrong. The world will be a better place if you die today. But if he kills you right away, this city may die with you."

Tamas ran his fingers along the map, memorizing the streets of the city. "I walked into one of his traps twice now. I don't intend to do it again. Do me a favor, though . . . don't give this information to your men until about six o'clock."

"Are you going to tell me how you plan on avoiding a trap?" Demasolin asked.

Tamas tapped the map absently. "I don't think you need to know that. Remember. Six o'clock. I'm going to kill this bastard once and for all."

CHAPTER
42

The beatings lasted through the night.

They pummeled Taniel with cudgels and fists. He faded in and out of consciousness but was, mercifully, out for most of it. He could feel the cold air on his skin when they finally took him outside. Through bloody eyes he could tell that the sun barely touched the tips of the eastern mountains.

Dawn was here.

Ka-poel might already be dead.

Taniel's feet dragged behind him as the Prielight Guards carried him through the Kez camp. A thousand voices reached his ears along with the sounds of an army preparing breakfast. Taniel wondered if any of them knew—or cared—who he was.

He was dropped unceremoniously on the ground. Taniel lay facedown, groaning into the dirt. His whole body felt numb and destroyed, smashed to a pulp by Prielight Guards. His body would be one giant bruise in a day or two. If he lived that long.

He felt along the inside of his mouth and wondered at the resiliency of his teeth. Was that Ka-poel's sorcery at work? Keeping him from breaking bones? His ribs *felt* broken, though Taniel didn't think he had the strength in him to check.

Did he?

Taniel opened his eyes. Men moved and worked all around him. A sea of legs and feet.

"One, two, pull! One, two, pull!"

The mantra was repeated again and again. What could they be doing?

He dragged his hand along through the dirt until he could see it. Moved a finger, then another. They were all still working. That was something, wasn't it? Those cuts on his knuckles. Where had they come from?

Oh. Right.

Those were from Kresimir's teeth.

Strong hands lifted Taniel to his feet. He swayed back, nearly falling. His arms were lifted, wrists bound together by strong cord.

"Make it tight," someone said. "He'll be up there a while."

Up where?

Taniel's arms were lifted above his head. He felt the rope between his wrists snag on something and the guards stepped away. Taniel's legs gave out beneath him, but he didn't fall.

"One, two, pull!"

Taniel's whole body jerked as he was lifted from the ground by his wrists.

"One, two, pull!"

Panic caused Taniel to flail about with his legs, but there was nothing beneath him but air. He looked up.

He hung from a hook fastened to an immense beam being lifted perpendicular to the ground. Teams of men pulled on ropes to raise the beam until it pointed at the sky.

The vision of Julene, nailed to a beam in the middle of the Kez camp, her hands gone at the wrists, haunted his memory.

He vomited down the front of himself.

"One, two, pull!"

It took the workers some time to get the beam in place. Taniel's back finally hit the wood and his feet scrambled for purchase on the beam. There was none to be had.

He was facing the Adran camp. In the early dawn light he could see soldiers gathering on the front lines, pointing and talking. A few officers were examining him through looking glasses. He closed his eyes, unable to bear looking back. Those men he'd thought to lead to victory would see him here now.

He had to warn them. What had Kresimir said last night? He planned to burn the army, and Mihali with it.

A rasping noise reached him. It was guttural and base, but it had a pattern to it. Slowly, Taniel realized someone was laughing.

"Two-Shot," the voice said.

Taniel craned his neck.

There, not much farther than spitting distance to his left, was another immense beam. They must have moved it up closer to the lines during the night. And still hanging there, the seared stumps of her wrists crossed in some kind of sick entreaty, was Julene.

"Didn't think I'd see you here, Two-Shot," she said.

Taniel looked away from the Predeii.

"Sorry, is it my voice? They haven't given me water in two months." She stopped and cleared her throat. Another long, raspy laugh. "The problem with not being able to die is just that." A cough, and then another laugh.

Taniel closed his eyes, hoping she would stop talking.

"You look good, Two-Shot," Julene said. "I mean it. Look at me.

Kresimir tortured me for weeks before he hung me up here. I'm curious why he didn't do the same to you. Don't worry. A couple of weeks and you'll be good as new. Me, though. I'll never heal. Kresimir made sure of that. I haven't seen a mirror lately, but tell me, can you still see that charming scar on my face?"

Had she gone mad from hanging from the beam for so long, unable to die? Taniel's arms were beginning to ache from the strain of holding his weight. They could only get worse as long as he was up here. He finally turned to look at Julene.

She was hideous. Most of her hair was gone. Her skin, which once looked young and supple, was now cracked like old leather. Her face had been particularly savaged—the tip of her nose cut off, most of her teeth gone. She grinned at Taniel, as if she knew what must be going through his mind.

There was madness in her eyes.

"Charming as always," he said. He looked up at his hands, tied about the wrist. They were starting to hurt more now. He tried lifting his legs but gave up after several moments with a groan—half pain, half anger.

"The pain doesn't go away," Julene said. "Even after months. Even after your arms are numb it will still throb deep down in your shoulders. I find"—she moved her head slowly to one side, a look of agony moving across her face—"that switching the arm that holds all the weight gives you some relief."

Taniel closed his eyes. Would he last that long? Would he still be alive in months, watching his country burn, unable to do a thing?

From the Adran army he saw a rider heading toward the Kez lines with a white flag billowing above him.

A call for truce? Or had that traitor Hilanska finally convinced the General Staff to surrender?

Taniel began to struggle harder. He had to get off this rope.

*   *   *

Tamas found Hailona in the mill's basement, an old granary. It was the only private room in the place. It smelled of dry old wheat, the scent dusty in Tamas's nostrils.

Hailona looked up when he knocked on the door frame of the open door. Ruper, the butler, was just inside. He stood when he saw Tamas.

"You killed my little brother," Hailona said.

Tamas knew that wasn't fair. Knew he wasn't in the wrong. Sabon had known the risks of being one of Tamas's soldiers. But Tamas also knew that convincing Hailona of that would be next to impossible.

"I need your help."

"Go to the pit. Get out of my sight."

"Hailona..." Tamas took a step forward.

Ruper got between them, blocking the path to his mistress with his body.

Tamas narrowed his eyes at the butler. "Hailona, I need a way into the governor's mansion. I'm going to kill the man who killed my wife *and* your brother."

Ruper moved forward until his chest touched Tamas's. "My lady has said for you to leave, sir."

Hailona held up a hand. "Ruper, it's all right." She dried her eyes with a handkerchief. Her hand remained up, as if asking for time to think. After a few moments, she let it drop. "Ruper, I want you to show Tamas the secret passage into the mansion."

"Are you sure, ma'am?"

"Yes."

Tamas stepped back from the butler. "Thank you, Halley."

"Kill the bastard, Tamas," Hailona said. "Make him suffer." She took a shaky breath. "Then I don't ever want to see you again."

"I understand."

Tamas left the mill. Vlora was waiting for him out in the rain. She wore a tricorn hat and a greatcoat. She tipped the hat toward Tamas, water pouring off the front. She leaned against a rifle, and he could see her blue uniform beneath the greatcoat and a pistol at her hip.

"Did Olem head back to the army?"

She nodded.

"Where are the others?"

"Waiting."

Tamas nodded. A few minutes later Ruper joined them in the street and they made their way out of Millertown. At the edge of the mill district, lounging around the outdoor seating of an otherwise abandoned streetside café, was Tamas's powder cabal.

He'd only brought the best. The ones that Sabon had been training during the summer in Adopest were still in the city. They didn't have the experience or training for a mission like this.

His powder cabal was outfitted much the same as Vlora, in greatcoats and tricorn hats. Every one of them had as much weaponry and powder at they could carry, from pistols to swords and daggers. Tamas felt a smile touch his lips. Eight men and women, every one of them a talented powder mage. As good as an army, as far as he was concerned. Tamas checked the streets quickly for any sign of Kez patrols, then turned to his mages.

"We're going to provide a distraction so that the Deliv can rescue the political prisoners being held by the Kez," Tamas said. "Gavril is among those prisoners. I'd like to be there to get our man out, but we have a more important task.

"Ours is to cut the head off this Kez abomination of an occupying army. We're going straight for the throat. You all know my history with Duke Nikslaus, so you all know that I choose to do this with some...relish."

There was a low chuckle among the powder mages.

"But as I said, we're to provide a distraction. I intend on luring in as many soldiers as possible. There will be Wardens, no doubt. Perhaps several dozen. The odds, despite our skills and talents, will be very heavily against us. This mission smacks of revenge for me. I won't ask you to throw your lives away for my vengeance."

One of his mages, a girl not much older than Vlora by the name of Leone, spoke up. "You expect to die here, sir?"

"I never expect to die in battle. An expectation like that has a habit of coming true. However... there are times, more than others, when the chances I'll lose are much greater."

"That's a fancy way of saying he expects to die," Vlora said.

Tamas shot her a look.

"Sir." Andriya raised his hand.

"Yes?"

"I signed on to kill Kez. I've got fifty-seven notches on my rifle from the last two months. I wanted a hundred by the end of the campaign. Will there be forty-seven Kez there?"

"I'd expect."

"Very good, sir. I'm coming."

"The rest of us are, too," Vlora said quietly.

"Thank you."

"Not doing it for you, sir," Andriya said. "Doing it to kill Kez."

"I appreciate it all the same. Ruper. If you please?"

They followed the butler through the streets, dodging Kez patrols as they went. Tamas watched the patrols from the shadows. There was an urgency in their step, and an extra vigilance. Tamas recognized the look. He'd seen it before in the eyes of comrades in Gurla, patrolling an unfriendly city on the last day before a withdrawal with the expectation—and fear—that anything could happen.

The governor's mansion was back in the same wealthy part of town as Hailona's manor. Their small group dashed from walled garden to walled garden until they reached a small wooded park well off the main street. Ruper led them into the woods to a groundskeeper's shack.

It was a small building, barely large enough for all of them standing. Ruper moved a table, then pulled up an old rug and tossed it aside to reveal a trapdoor. He lit a lantern, and they descended into a cellar.

The cellar was rough-cut, descending past topsoil and into the clay earth. From a quick glance, it could have been any root cellar, about four feet wide and a dozen long, with a small room at the far end. When they reached the room and turned the corner, a sharply angled tunnel led off into the darkness.

Tamas counted nearly four hundred paces, sloshing through mud, trying to keep his greatcoat from scraping the damp sides of the tunnel, before they ascended a set of stone steps and came out in a somewhat more spacious basement. It was a stone room, with a dust-covered wardrobe in one corner, a double bed, and an empty musket rack. At the opposite side of the room a spiral staircase led upward.

"This room and passage," Ruper said, his first words since joining them, "were made as an escape route long ago, when unrest was common in this part of Deliv." Ruper gestured toward the staircase. "That will take you up to the second floor. It comes out from behind a false bookshelf into the main office of the governor. I'll return to my mistress now."

Tamas caught Ruper by the shoulder before he could go back down into the passage. "Tell Halley that...tell her I'm truly sorry I never came back."

Ruper pulled himself from Tamas's grip and headed down into the passage with the only lantern, leaving Tamas and his mages in darkness.

Tamas took a small touch of powder to his tongue, letting him see ever so slightly in the utter blackness. He headed up the staircase slowly, as quietly as he could. It creaked beneath him as the wrought iron ground together beneath his weight.

At the top of the staircase there was light. It came in through a pair of holes just a couple inches too short for Tamas to look through comfortably. He set his face against the wall, gazing through the looking-holes.

He could see very little. A double door on the opposite side of the room. A candelabra. The top of a sofa. He opened his third eye.

There were blots of color in the Else. Just bright enough to be Wardens, but too far away from him to be inside the governor's office. No sign of a Privileged.

Tamas pushed gently on the door.

It rolled forward silently, then slid to the side with nothing more than a touch of a finger. Tamas stepped out into the governor's office. It was a large room, with dozens of gilded candelabras, shelves full of books, two magnificent fireplaces, and a grand window that looked out over the courtyard in front of the manor.

The room was empty.

Tamas let out a sigh of relief and called softly for his Marked to come up. They filed into the room, tracking mud on the pristine red carpets. He directed them with hand signals to cover the doors and windows.

They checked the adjoining rooms and the hallway immediately outside.

Vlora joined him by the bay window a few minutes later. "No one in these office suites, sir," she said. "A couple of Wardens downstairs by the front door. Andriya says he can hear soldiers talking in the servants' quarters on the first floor."

"Good work."

"What now?"

"We wait."

"Are you sure Nikslaus will come back here, sir?"

"I have a good guess."

Andriya returned to the room at that moment. "Sir, luggage in the master bedroom."

Tamas checked his pocket watch. It was just after six o'clock. "Timing will be everything."

Tamas watched out the bay window. There were a dozen or so soldiers in the yard. They stood at attention, facing the gate, muskets on their shoulders. Tamas spotted a Warden in one corner of the yard, barely visible from his vantage point.

He checked his watch every few minutes. Would Nikslaus come back here? Had the news already reached him that Tamas was coming for him? Maybe he'd read Nikslaus wrong. Maybe Nikslaus would rather flee than attempt to catch Tamas.

Tamas brought his attention back to the courtyard outside as several horsemen came through the front gate. They were followed closely by a carriage decked out with lace curtains and fine gilding. It pulled around the turnabout and came to a stop. Tamas was so close he could have tossed a rock through the window and hit the top of the carriage.

The door opened and a Deliv woman stepped out. She looked about sixteen. She wore a fine gown that displayed her ample bosom. Tamas felt a wave of disappointment as she got her feet on the gravel drive and looked around regally.

Not Nikslaus.

Tamas stepped away from the window.

"Sir!" Vlora motioned him back over. Someone else was getting out of the carriage. It seemed a struggle for him, leaning his forearms against the door frame. It was a man. He wore white Privileged's gloves. A Warden appeared from the mansion, grasping one of the arms and helping the man down. His face was partially concealed by a tricorne hat.

Tamas prayed the Privileged would turn his head just a little bit so Tamas could get a look at his identity.

The Privileged stopped to talk to one of the soldiers. The voices were too low for Tamas to make out. The soldier gave the Privileged a brisk nod, then turned to the others. "We leave in two hours!" he said loudly. "Anyone who's not ready to move out by dark will be shot."

Tamas's gaze was still locked on the Privileged in the tricorne. It had to be Nikslaus! But Tamas still couldn't see his face. Whoever he was, he chatted amiably with the young lady beside him.

They had just mounted the steps to the mansion when a messenger came galloping hard into the courtyard and came to a stop in a spray of gravel. The messenger leapt from his horse and ran to the Privileged.

Tamas felt his heart begin to beat faster.

The messenger saluted and breathlessly gave his report. The Privileged pushed him away with an elbow and spun toward the mansion.

Tamas heard the doors below burst open. The Privileged's voice echoed through the building.

"Get everyone!" he screamed. "All my Wardens, to me! I want five hundred soldiers here in twenty minutes. Give the order! We leave within the hour!"

"But, sir," Tamas heard someone say, "the city!"

"I don't give a pit about the city. Deliv can enter the war with Adro for all I care. He's here, you fool! He's here!"

"Nikslaus," Tamas whispered.

Tamas watched as messengers scrambled out the front mansion drive, going out to give Nikslaus's orders.

"Well, Demasolin," Tamas muttered, "you have your distraction."

Urgent steps sounded on the staircase in the foyer accompanied by Nikslaus's frantic orders.

Tamas looked down to find one hand already on the grip of a pistol, the other on the hilt of his sword. His fingers itched.

"He's coming," Andriya hissed from his station by the door.

"Do we wait for him here?" Vlora said.

Tamas blinked and saw the bodies of Deliv politicians hanging from the steeple of the Alvation cathedral. He saw Sabon's dead eyes gazing up at him from Charlemund's gravel drive, and the countless soldiers Tamas had lost trying to catch Nikslaus.

He saw Erika's head floating before him. Her face, frozen in horror, blond hair caked with blood, skin severed neatly at the neck. He saw Nikslaus's grin as he presented Tamas with the head of his dead wife.

Tamas poured an entire powder charge into his mouth. His body felt like it was on fire as energy coursed through him. Vlora must have seen something on his face.

"Pit," Vlora swore. "Andriya, get out of the way."

Tamas burst through the double doors of the office, drawing his pistol in one hand.

"Nikslaus!" he bellowed.

CHAPTER
43

"Citizens of Adopest," Lord Claremonte's voice boomed.

The shock of the amplified sound made Adamat's knees grow weak. "Pit," he hissed, "he has Privileged with him!" It was the only way he could be heard above the roar of the crowd like this.

"My friends," Lord Claremonte continued, "my brothers and sisters. My countrymen! I bring you greetings from the farthest corners of the world. I have come today to meet you, my fellow Adrans, and to lower myself humbly before you on gracious knee to offer myself as candidate for the post of First Minister of our fair country." At this, Claremonte lowered himself down on one knee and bowed his head. A moment passed and he rose back up, spreading his arms as if to embrace every man, woman, and child on the riverbank.

"This is a great nation! We have so much. We have the unions, the army, the Wings of Adom, the banks, and the Mountainwatch.

We have industry unparalleled in the modern world. We have the mightiest heroes that any country could hope for in the likes of Taniel Two-Shot and the late Field Marshal Tamas."

Lord Claremonte sighed and bowed his head, as if overcome with emotion. "Field Marshal Tamas died for you, my friends. He died for me. For all of us to be free of the Kez tyranny. He had such incredible vision and stride, and I will not let it die with him!"

The crowd was utterly silent now. Adamat heard someone drop a coin, and he cursed himself for waiting with bated breath for Claremonte's next words.

"For what this country needs now is hope. And for that, I have brought with me nine thousand of Brudania's finest soldiers to throw in with the Adran army and push back the Kez aggressors." He threw his hand back toward the line of Trading Company ships waiting in the river. "I have brought cannon, and rifles, and supplies. I have brought food, and money. I bring treasures from the four corners of the world, all of which will be put toward the war effort against the Kez."

"I do this freely. I ask no thanks, nor hold back any of my wealth on reservation. I only ask that you consider me a worthy candidate for the coming election."

Adamat noticed that other longboats were being lowered now. These ones were filled with Brudanian soldiers, and they were free once they hit the water and began rowing toward the riverbank. Claremonte's own longboat had drawn anchor and was slowly drifting closer to the amphitheater.

"My countrymen," Claremonte continued in the silence that followed, "this country needs change. This is a forward-thinking nation! A place of intellectual and industrial prowess. In my ministerial duties, I will continue to support that change and push us forward into the coming century. We will forget the old ways. The superstitions. The foolishness.

"Gods—what have they done for you?" He shook his head.

"Nothing. These rumors you've heard about Kresimir and Adom returning? They are true! But know this; we will not tolerate them. They have no place in this world of ours, and I mean to show them that.

"We may be mortal, but we are fierce and we are proud, and even the gods will tremble at this mighty nation of Adro.

"It starts today, my friends. Our new world."

The final word seemed barely a whisper, but Adamat felt his heart hammering in his chest. Something was happening. What was Claremonte about to do? What could he possibly be...? Adamat brought the looking glass in his hands, hitherto forgotten, back to his eye and focused on Claremonte.

Claremonte turned to a woman at his shoulder. The woman raised her hands to reveal white gloves covered in crimson runes—a Privileged.

Adamat read the inaudible words on Claremonte's lips: "Bring it down."

Sorcery cut through the clear sky, eliciting a gasp of terror from the assembled crowds. White lightning, like knives flashing, cut through the air above the amphitheater and smashed into the Kresim Cathedral. Dust billowed in great clouds above the immense building as invisible blades sliced clean through the stone façade.

An invisible fist smashed into the dome of the cathedral, and all at once the building collapsed in on itself. People ran from the falling stonework, screaming in terror, but the destruction was contained by sorcery, and to Adamat's eyes it looked as if no one was harmed.

When the dust had settled, Adamat turned his eyes back on Claremonte. Once again the man stepped to the prow of the boat to address the crowd. He raised his arms.

"This is only the beginning, my brothers and sisters. This world. We will take it back!"

*   *   *

Tamas's first bullet would have taken Nikslaus through the eye if a Warden hadn't flung the Privileged aside. The bullet slammed into the Warden's shoulder, making him jerk. The twisted creature drew his sword and bounded up the stairs toward Tamas.

Tamas drew his sword and charged the Warden. The creature bellowed a challenge, and Tamas answered with a silent snarl. Their swords clashed loudly once, twice, and then Tamas was inside the Warden's guard. He grabbed the Warden by the neck, feeling the strength of the powder coursing through him, and tossed it off the hallway balcony to the foyer below.

Nikslaus had rolled down the stairs and picked himself off the marble floors. One of his gloves had come off—Tamas paused at that. No, the whole hand had come off.

He had been wearing false hands. A ruse to fool his own soldiers into thinking he could still do sorcery? Perhaps. Tamas didn't care as he flew down the stairs three at a time.

Nikslaus fled toward the front door, gesturing wildly at Tamas and screaming at his men, "Kill him!"

The air was already bitter with the scent of black powder. Tamas felt a surge of energy, and an explosion tore through the Kez soldiers as Vlora ignited their powder.

Soldiers came at him with swords drawn. Nikslaus was smart enough to keep some of his soldiers without powder, it seemed. Tamas caught a thrust with the tip of his sword, flipping it to the side and ramming his own sword into the soldier's chest. He kept moving forward. Nikslaus backed away from him, face painted with terror.

A knife spun past Tamas's face and clattered against the marble banister behind him. He spun toward its owner, a Warden, and grunted as the creature hit him with the force of a charging bull.

Tamas felt himself lifted into the air and then slammed into the banister. It cracked from the force of the blow, sending him and the Warden tumbling over the edge of the stairs and a short drop to the floor.

He felt the creature's fingers close on his throat. Tamas grasped it by the wrist and slammed his other palm into the Warden's elbow. The creature's arm snapped, bending ninety degrees the wrong way. Tamas grabbed the Warden by the lapels and kicked, flipping it off of him.

By the time Tamas had gotten back to his feet, the room was filled with soldiers. Most of them were dead or dying, shot by a mage or blown to bits by their own powder horns, but there were still enough of the Kez to get in the way.

Tamas spotted Nikslaus as he fled down a side hallway.

"Pit!" Tamas swore. He lurched to his feet only to fall again. The Warden with the broken arm had grabbed Tamas's leg. It swung a knife at Tamas.

Tamas jerked his leg out of the Warden's grip, and its knife slammed into the marble floor. The beast surged forward, and Tamas deflected the knife with the guard of his sword. He pummeled the Warden's face with his hilt, then danced back out of range of another knife thrust.

The creature got to its feet.

And came crashing down again as Andriya leapt from the upstairs hallway and landed behind it, bayonet ramming through its skull and brain.

"Well," Andriya said, running toward the Kez infantry, "go kill the duke!"

Tamas dashed toward the hallway where Nikslaus had disappeared. It was a long hall, perhaps a hundred yards into another wing of the manor. Tamas opened his third eye, fighting off the dizziness, and searched for signs of Wardens or the Privileged.

A soldier leapt out of a side room with a shout. Tamas closed his third eye, reeling back as he felt a sword slice cleanly along the side of his stomach. He fended off another thrust and drew his second pistol, firing from the hip. The shot took the Kez soldier in the chest. The man lurched forward, then tried to step back. A look of surprise crossed his face as he fell to the ground.

Tamas left him where he was and sprinted along the hallway. The pain of his bad leg throbbed like the beat of a drum and the cut along his side stung in the open air. He slowed as he rounded the corner at the end of the hallway, only to find another hall leading off a hundred paces long.

No sign of Nikslaus.

"Sir!" Vlora came up beside him, breathing hard.

"He came this way," he said.

She nodded and trotted out ahead of him.

Vlora was about fifteen paces ahead of him when a Warden burst out of the cover of a doorway and slammed into her. His momentum took them both across the hallway and out of sight, into another room.

"Vlora!" Tamas ran forward, only to stop when a voice called out.

"No closer." Nikslaus. The voice came from just inside the doorway where Vlora and the Warden had disappeared.

"I'm coming to kill you," Tamas said.

"Not if you want this one alive."

Tamas looked down. Both pistols were spent. He might be able to angle a bullet around the corner. No. He *knew* he could.

"Vlora?" Tamas called out.

No answer.

"If she's dead," Tamas said, "I've no reason to stop myself from coming around this corner."

Tamas heard a deep, angry grunt, and then Vlora's voice. "I'm all right, sir."

"For now," Nikslaus said, "but if she bites my Warden again, I'll let him snap her neck. I'm using her as a shield, Tamas. If you angle a bullet around that wall, it'll hit her."

Tamas sheathed his sword and drew a pistol. He reloaded quickly, steadily, and then shoved it in his belt so he could reload the other.

"How is your leg?" Nikslaus called. "I'm surprised you can put that much weight on it."

"It was healed by a god. It feels fantastic. How are your hands? Did Kresimir grow them back for you?"

Tamas was satisfied to hear a low curse.

"Surrender, Tamas, or I kill the girl."

"Kill her," Tamas said. "I don't care."

"I think you do. I recognize this one. Vlora. I never told you that was one of my little schemes, did I? Having her seduced." Tamas heard another low grunt—the Warden—and then Nikslaus's laugh. "You probably thought it was the nobility. Well, that's what the fop thought, too."

"She betrayed Taniel," Tamas said. "Like I said: kill her."

Nikslaus clicked his tongue disapprovingly. "Oh, Tamas. I know everything about you. I know your hopes and your fears. I know your favorites. She's always been one of your favorites. Did you think about bedding her after Taniel canceled the wedding? I know you did. So suddenly available. How that must have tempted you."

Tamas opened his third eye and stepped away from the wall. He could see Nikslaus's bright glow in the Else through the wall. It was several dozen paces back from the corner. Closer, he could see the dull glow of the Warden and the barely perceptible glow that Vlora gave off in the Else. The Warden was using Vlora as a shield. Tamas would likely hit Vlora if he tried to angle a bullet around the corner.

"Throw your pistol down, Tamas, and I'll let her live," Nikslaus said.

"Why should I trust you?"

"You've no choice. The courtyard is filling up with soldiers. I don't care how many mages you brought, you're outnumbered and outmatched. You throw down your weapons and come out, and I give my word that this girl lives."

"Why so magnanimous?" Tamas said. He drew his second pistol. He aimed one at the glow of the Privileged and one at that of the Warden.

"Not sure what's come over me," Nikslaus said. "Maybe it's the prospect of your head on a pike!" His voice rose to a shout. "Think of it, Tamas. Only a couple months ago, it was me trapped inside a manor, while your soldiers filed into the courtyard. What a reversal of fortunes! Maybe I'll cut off your hands before I kill you."

Tamas examined the walls. Marble over limestone, most likely. To pierce it, he'd have to put half a horn's worth of powder behind a bullet, and concentrate energy around the bullet to keep it from fragmenting. One, he could do. Not two.

"I wouldn't take the time," Tamas said. He lowered the pistol aimed at Nikslaus and uncocked the hammer. He set it on the floor and slid it out into the middle of the hall where the Warden could see it.

"I'm unarmed. Now let her go," Tamas said.

"When I see you on your knees!" Nikslaus screamed.

Tamas focused on the smudge of color in the Else that was the Warden. He concentrated on his bullet, and set the barrel of his other pistol against the wall and pulled the trigger.

He dropped the pistol as soon as he'd pulled the trigger and leapt and rolled into the hallway, snatching up the other pistol and coming up into a crouch. The pistol kicked back in his hand as he touched the powder with his mind.

Both shots had hit the Warden. The first, through the wall, had gone low, cutting through the creature's neck. The second took it between the eyes, just over Vlora's shoulder. The Warden collapsed backward, Vlora still in its grip.

Tamas caught sight of Nikslaus running across the room behind the Warden.

Tamas gently wrested Vlora from the dead Warden's grip. The

creature had been holding a knife to her throat. She had a cut there, leaking crimson, but Tamas could not tell how deep.

"Vlora. Vlora!"

Her eyes were slightly glazed, her face panicked. There was a shard of marble embedded in her cheek. Tamas pulled it out, brushing her hair out of the way with one hand.

She shook her head suddenly, as if coming out of a dream. "I'm alive," she said. "I'm alive. I'm fine." She seemed to be speaking more to herself than him.

Tamas removed a handkerchief from his pocket and pressed it to her throat. She could still speak, so the cut wasn't too deep. "Keep pressure on it."

"Go," Vlora said. "Go after him."

Tamas took off his greatcoat and wadded it into a ball. He lifted Vlora's head and put it underneath. "Andriya! Pit, where is he? Andriya!"

Leone appeared suddenly, her bayoneted rifle held at the ready. She set her rifle on the ground and squatted beside Vlora.

"Stay with her," Tamas said. "Vidalslav makes the cleanest stitches. When the fighting dies down, make sure she sees Vlora first."

Tamas retrieved his other pistol and checked the room. Nikslaus had fled through a side door. He caught sight of the Privileged running across the lawn, heading for the front gate.

"Sir," Leone said, "we've taken the house, but the courtyard is filled with soldiers."

Tamas dropped a bullet down the barrel of one of his pistols and rammed cotton batting down to keep it stable. "I don't care," he said. "I have a man to kill."

Taniel sagged against the rough-hewn wood of the beam from which he hung, what little strength he had sapped from his struggles.

He'd tried to loosen his bonds. No amount of wiggling would get him out of them. What else could he do? He looked down. No use anyway, he supposed. Kez guards stood at the foot of the beam at the bottom of a fifty-foot drop. Could he survive that far of a fall? Would he land, only to have the Kez finish off his broken body?

How would Tamas have gotten out of this? The old bastard may have been mean, but he was clever, too.

Julene had watched him struggle for all of an hour. She seemed amused by it, if anything, and the madness in her eyes seemed to come and go.

"Why did he do this to you?" Taniel asked.

Julene gave that choking laugh again. "I ask myself that every day."

There'd be no help from her, Taniel decided. She was clearly as mad as the god who put her there. He looked up at the hook from which he hung, and then toward the Adran camp. Even at this distance, without a powder trance, he could tell that the General Staff was gathering. Equal commotion was going through the Kez camp. Both sides were preparing for a parlay.

Was that when Kresimir planned to kill them all?

"Kresimir didn't want to come back," Julene said.

Taniel turned his head sharply toward her. The madness was gone from her, and her eyes were suddenly lucid.

"He wouldn't have, if I hadn't summoned him like I did," she went on. "He doesn't care that Tamas killed Manhouch. The fate of the mortals of this world don't concern him. I was so wrong." Julene coughed, then swallowed hard, her broken face somehow twisting to look more bitter. "If I live another twenty thousand years, I could not possibly make a mistake again like I did by summoning Kresimir." Her whole body shuddered, and she threw back her head, moaning in agony.

Taniel turned away. He couldn't look at that. Cruelty for the sake of cruelty. Gods, it seemed, were capable of pettiness just as much as the next man.

Taniel scanned the Adran camp, looking for familiar faces. It was too far to make out individuals.

By now Ka-poel would know what had happened to him.

If she was still alive.

Taniel flexed his arms and pulled against his rope. He lifted a few inches, and then fell back. His struggling all morning had exhausted him.

"What are you doing, powder mage?" Julene said.

"Trying to get away." He pulled himself up again. He gained an inch. Maybe two.

"You can't. You fall from here and you'll break your legs."

"Maybe I can shimmy down."

Julene rasped out a laugh. "They'll just put you back up."

Taniel spotted a movement in the Kez camp. It wasn't significant, and he knew not what drew his eye in that direction. He willed himself to see farther.

A small figure was winding its way through the soldiers. A hooded shape—it could have been a child. But Taniel knew that build. He knew how to read the sway of the walk, from long familiarity.

Ka-poel. What was she doing here? She had to get out, to leave the camp before she was caught!

No one paid her any mind. The soldiers were preparing for something big. She was a few hundred yards away, just working her way through the camp in no particular hurry.

Taniel flexed again. He lifted himself up until his face nearly touched the hook. Every fiber of his body trembled from the effort, his bruised flesh crying out in pain.

"What do you plan to do, powder mage?" Julene's voice was steady. The rasp was gone. A glance in her direction showed her staring intently at him.

Taniel let himself drop, gasping at the effort. "I'm going to kill Kresimir."

Ka-poel was getting closer. What did she plan on doing when she got to him? Her sorcery couldn't get him off this beam.

In the distance, in the no-man's-land between the armies, Taniel saw a lone figure head out from the Adran camp. Tall and fat, wearing a white apron. Mihali.

It only took a moment of searching before Taniel found Kresimir standing at the head of the Kez lines. The god had changed his bloody clothes for clean ones and still wore his mask. He, too, began heading toward the middle of the field.

Taniel lifted himself up until he reached the hook. Inch by inch, he felt with his fingers. His struggles *had* loosened his bonds. Perhaps not enough to slip out of them, but...

Taniel grasped the hook with both hands and placed his feet flat against the beam. He pressed with his legs, working his toes against the wood like the feet of a clamp. Firmly braced on the beam, he pushed up, willing even more strength from his already burning thighs. Just a couple inches was all he needed...

And he was there! He worked his bonds along the curve of the hook until suddenly the rope was free. A wave of giddiness swept over him, nearly making him fall. He was free of the hook! He could drop from this height anytime he wanted.

He looked down and his stomach lurched. That didn't seem like such a good idea.

Grasping the hook, he turned himself around so that he was facing the beam.

"You're a stubborn bastard," Julene said.

Taniel didn't answer her. Slowly, he began working his way down the rough-hewn beam. He dug his fingernails and the toes of his boots into the wood as if he were scaling a cliff face. Every muscle protested in agony. There was no way he could scrape his fingernails the entire way down.

He worked down the first few feet and stopped, gasping for breath.

"Can you really do it?" Julene asked. "Kill Kresimir?"

Taniel worked his way down another foot.

"It's the savage, isn't it? By pit, her sorcery is potent. She might be able to kill him."

Taniel remained silent. Another foot. He could do it.

He looked down. There were four guards stationed around the base of the beam. None of them noticed his descent. He'd have to get near enough to the ground to drop on one of them, and then fight the other three—his hands still bound. Ka-poel would be there by now. She could...

She entered his line of vision suddenly, approaching one of the guards at a quick pace. The guard straightened and said something, holding out a hand. Her small fist darted out, slamming into his throat. The guard fell to his knees, gurgling blood.

Another foot. Taniel's heart thundered in his ears. He had to keep moving.

"Make me a promise," Julene said.

"Faster, faster, I have to go faster," Taniel whispered to himself.

"Promise you'll kill me. Shoot me in the head with one of those bullets you used to blind Kresimir. I won't survive that. Not in my weakened state. Consider it an act of vengeance, if you like."

Taniel looked down. Ka-poel was grappling with another guard. A third grabbed her by the shoulders.

"Promise me, Taniel."

Taniel was struck by the pleading in her voice. He stopped just long enough to look at her. "I promise," he said.

Julene gave a shrill laugh.

Below, the three guards had forced Ka-poel to the ground. Taniel took a deep breath and closed his eyes.

Then he let himself fall.

CHAPTER
44

Tamas followed Nikslaus through a side door of the mansion and out onto the lawn. The ground was soaked, rain coming down in thick sheets. Even though it was only half past six in the afternoon, the sky was darkening. A grandfather of a storm was blowing in.

The Privileged was just rounding the corner to the front of the mansion as Tamas came out the door. He set off in pursuit.

He reached the corner of the building and stopped. A quick glance showed fifty, maybe sixty soldiers in the courtyard. They hid behind carriages and sculptures, exchanging fire with the powder mages inside.

Nikslaus leapt onto the running board of a carriage, hooking one arm through a handstrap. Tamas could hear him yelling between the volleys of musket fire:

"Go!" Nikslaus pounded on the roof of the carriage with one

stub and ducked inside. The carriage took off down the short drive and turned into the street.

A bullet took a chip out of the masonry just above Tamas's head. He flinched away. They'd spotted him.

Tamas examined the soldiers. Too many. Even at his best. Most of his powder was gone, used in that shot through the limestone. He checked the garden wall about fifty paces away. Too tall.

Tamas heard a commotion around the corner and risked a glance.

The powder horn of a Kez soldier suddenly exploded, ripping the man in half. Another followed, and then another. Men began to throw their muskets, horns, and charges away to avoid being killed. It had to be Vlora. Only she had the range igniting powder to kill men all the way by the gates. She must have gotten to a window, or had someone directing her. It was dangerously stupid to ignite powder blind, both for yourself and for your allies.

The front doors of the manor suddenly burst open. Andriya flew through them. He held a bayoneted rifle in both hands and was screaming at the top of his lungs. His eyes were wild, his hat gone, his greatcoat billowing around him. He leapt on the closest Kez soldier, skewering the man mercilessly.

It was the best Tamas was going to get for cover.

He set off at a sprint across the lawn, cutting behind the Kez soldiers. Most ignored him, their eyes all on Andriya.

Tamas neared the gate. A soldier turned toward Tamas, desperately trying to fix the bayonet to the end of his musket. Tamas sprinted toward the soldier, put his foot on a rock near the driveway, and launched himself in the air. He cracked the man in the chin with one boot and was past him and through the gate.

There were more soldiers in the street. Tamas realized he was alone in the midst of twenty or more Kez infantry.

He ignited all the powder nearby. He used his mind to warp the blast away from him, but he'd never been as good at that as some, and the shock wave knocked him off his feet.

Tamas crawled to his knees, then to his feet. He tried to shake the dizziness. The ache of his leg suddenly pushed through his powder trance, making him stumble as he searched for Nikslaus's carriage.

The ground was littered with bodies. Nearly every one of the soldiers had been killed outright. Only a few moaned in agony, clutching at missing limbs. Gore and blood filled the street. The sight of it—the smell of powder and blood—made him retch.

There, at the end of the street. Nikslaus's carriage was heading down the main thoroughfare of the city toward the mountains, disappearing into the deluge. Tamas could see the driver frantically whipping his horses. Civilians leapt out of the way as the carriage surged forward.

Tamas tried to run. He lurched sideways, catching himself with one hand on the lip of an overflowing rain barrel. He pushed back to standing and kept on, moving slower, trying to get his head to stop pounding. He felt something dribble down his cheek and touched his face. There was blood there. It felt like it was coming from his ears.

He couldn't stop now. The carriage was getting farther and farther away. Before too long it would break out of the city and head up into the mountains. Nikslaus would get away again.

Tamas crunched one of his few remaining powder charges between his teeth and forced himself to run.

The street cobbles pounded away beneath his feet. He let the powder trance take him over completely, feeling the burn of powder through his veins. Shops and houses flew by him. Tears formed in the corners of his eyes as he ran faster than a horse, his heart thumping in his ears. His hat came off, whipped away by the wind, and rain pelted his face.

The carriage reached the eastern edge of the city well ahead of him. Tamas could see the land in his mind's eye. A few hundred yards of sloped parade grounds, filled with Nikslaus's soldiers and their ill-gotten gains from looting the city, before the mountains rose steeply and the road entered a valley, where it crept gradually higher into the Charwood Pile.

There'd be thousands of Kez soldiers in that parade ground. Tamas had to kill Nikslaus before he reached the mountain. He stopped to catch his breath, and leveled his pistol at the back of the carriage. No. Not now. Too many Deliv in the streets. He needed a clean shot.

Tamas neared the edge of the city. The downpour had become a deluge. The carriage was lost to him, but he had no doubt of Nikslaus's destination. No doubt, also, that the powder in his pistol pan was wet.

A crowd began to emerge out of the rain, and the sound of shouting suddenly rose above the thrum of rain against the ground. There were men everywhere, choking the street.

It took Tamas a few moments to realize they were fighting. A brawl? No. A battle, a bloody melee. Every one of them wore the dark-blue coats of Adran infantry, but he was able to make out two sides. It appeared that every man on one side had torn off their white shirtsleeves and wrapped them around their right arms.

Tamas grabbed a man without a white band on his arm. "Kez?" he asked in Kez.

The man seemed taken off guard. "Yes," he answered in Kez.

Tamas ran the man through and shoved him off the end of his sword with one boot. He turned just in time to parry the thrust of a bayonet. It came from a soldier with a white band. The soldier was about to lunge again when he came up short. "Field Marshal!"

"Where's Colonel Olem?" Tamas asked, saying a silent prayer of thanks that his men recognized him.

"No idea, sir. He led the charge."

"The bands?" Tamas gestured to the shirtsleeve tied around the soldier's arm.

"Colonel Olem's idea, sir. Keep us all straight."

"Good."

The soldier suddenly stripped off his jacket and tore the other arm off his undershirt. "Here, sir."

Tamas let him wrap his arm. "Thank you. What are your orders?"

"Slaughter the Kez," the soldier said. He lifted his rifle and charged off with a yell.

Tamas stood, still in a little bit of shock at the melee. He'd not heard horns or drums or seen any kind of panic in the Kez soldiers that said that the Seventh and Ninth had arrived. Didn't Nikslaus have scouts? Then again, who could see anything in this rain?

Despite the ferocity of the battle, not a shot was being fired. It was too wet for that. Olem must have convinced the other generals and colonels of the need to charge straight in.

It was a commander's nightmare. Already the parade grounds had been turned into a muddy quagmire. The downpour was so thick Tamas could barely see twenty feet in front of him.

Nikslaus's carriage must have been slowed by the rain. It had to have followed the road, otherwise it would get bogged down in the mud.

Tamas set off at a trot along the cobbles.

The fighting raged all around him. The sound of screams and yells, the ring of sword on sword, rose intermittently above the pounding rain. The cobbles were slick with rain and blood.

He fought his way through, sword out in front of him, right arm raised so that his soldiers could see the dirty white band tied just below his shoulder. He shoved and stabbed, paused for only a moment to urge on infantry from the Seventh, and then moved on down the road, searching for Nikslaus.

How had the duke's carriage gotten through this melee? Had his driver shoved forward, trampling soldiers on both sides, desperate to escape Tamas's wrath? Or had the duke given him the slip, and somehow concealed the carriage from Tamas in order to escape back into the city?

Tamas caught sight of Colonel Arbor, his uniform soaked through, holding his false teeth in one hand while he used his cavalry saber to give a pit of a fight to a Kez captain. A particularly thick sheet of rain came down, concealing the colonel. Both men were gone the next time Tamas looked.

Tamas fended off a bayonet thrust and opened his third eye, fighting the dizziness that came with it. Specks of color rose out of the storm, dancing like candles in a drafty room—Knacked soldiers on both sides of the fighting.

He swept his gaze back toward the city. Nothing that way but Knacked. No Privileged. A few Wardens.

The rain fell harder. Lightning lit the darkening sky, giving Tamas a brief glimpse through the deluge and across the entire battlefield.

Men struggled in the mire of the parade field, boots sliding and squelching. They were a sea of blue uniforms, drenched and muddy. Tamas wondered if the strips of white were even helping them tell friend from foe. He guessed that thousands would die this night to the swords of their own comrades.

Lightning flashed again, and Tamas saw something forty or fifty paces ahead, just off the road. A crash of thunder followed immediately. He felt his whole chest shake from the sound. His third eye had shown him a fire among the wreckage—not of flame but of light in the Else that betrayed the presence of a Privileged.

What he'd seen a moment before resolved itself into the wreckage of a carriage as Tamas drew closer.

It looked like the driver had swerved, one wheel going off the cobbles and into the soft, wet mud. The carriage had tipped over and slid down an embankment, ending top-down in two feet of water at the bottom of a ditch, wheels still spinning.

Infantry fought around the carriage as if they didn't notice it was there, despite the fresh skid marks in the mud and the driver frantically trying to cut loose six crazed horses.

Tamas slid down the embankment some fifteen paces away,

watching the carriage warily. No sign of Nikslaus. Tamas's third eye told him the Privileged was still within. No Wardens, either. Was this an accident? Or a trap?

Tamas approached, one hand on the muddy bank to keep his balance, the other holding one of his pistols. The powder in the pan might be wet, but the residue in the muzzle would still be dry and he could light it with a thought. One shot. That's all he had.

That's all he needed.

Tamas wrenched the door off the carriage and stooped to look inside. Nikslaus lay in the rising water of the ditch, his back against one side of the carriage. Tamas snagged the Privileged's coat with one hand and pulled him through the door, out of the water, and up onto the bank.

"I'm going to watch you die," Tamas shouted above the rain. He rammed his pistol into his belt and grasped Nikslaus's coat by the collar. He'd do it with his own hands. For Erika. For Sabon. For all the powder mages who'd died in the duke's grasp.

Tamas blinked the rain out of his eyes as he lifted Nikslaus up in front of him. Once more, to look his enemy in the eye.

Something was wrong.

Nikslaus's head lolled at an impossible angle, eyes staring blankly toward the sky. Muddy water poured from his mouth.

The man who'd haunted Tamas's dreams for well over a decade—who'd killed his wife and his best friend and caused a war that threatened to destroy his country—had broken his neck and drowned in a ditch.

Tamas dropped the body. He opened his third eye, just to be sure. The light of the Else was gone from Nikslaus.

He took a few steps back, stumbling in the water, and fell against the opposite bank. Nikslaus had died, from an accident no less, just moments before Tamas reached him.

Tamas hammered his fists into the mud. He kicked a carriage wheel hard enough to break several spokes and bend the iron strake that held the wheel together. He slipped in the mud, falling to his knees.

He slumped forward in the same water that had just drowned Nikslaus, rain falling in his eyes. He still had his shot—for a moment, he considered putting it in his own brain. He'd lost Erika, he'd lost Sabon, he'd lost Gavril. And now he would never avenge them. He gripped his pistol, Taniel's gift. No. Not everything. He still had his son.

"Please! Please, help me!"

The call brought Tamas back. He looked down to see that Nikslaus's body was being carried away down the ditch with the force of the storm waters. A fitting end, even if Tamas hadn't brought it about himself.

He climbed the embankment in time to hear the voice again.

"Please! I've lost my knife!"

The carriage driver was struggling in the mud, kicked and shoved by frightened horses as he tried to cut them loose. It looked like he'd managed to free all but two of the panicked beasts.

The fighting continued around them. Tamas knew he needed to get back to level ground and find his officers, to bring some kind of cohesion into the melee. With Nikslaus gone, the Kez might very well break and run.

A horse screamed, and Tamas again heard the sound of the pleading driver.

Tamas climbed the wreckage of the carriage and lowered himself down just behind the driver. The man was on his knees, trying to dodge thrashing hooves as he cast about in the water for his knife.

"Here," Tamas said. He pushed the man aside and drew his sword, and with two quick strokes, the horses were free. They rolled to their feet and were off, splashing upstream through the ditch, away from the carriage. They would be impossible to catch until they calmed down, and one of them might very well break a leg in these conditions, but at least they were free.

Tamas turned to the driver. The man cowered before him, blinking in fear at the epaulets on Tamas's uniform.

"Thank you, sir," the driver said.

"Find the closest Adran officer," Tamas plucked at the white sleeve tied around his arm, "and surrender yourself. That's the only way you'll survive the night."

The driver ducked his head, the water dripping off the brim of his forage cap. "Sir, thank you, sir. The duke, is he...?"

"He's dead."

It may have been the darkness and the rain, but it seemed that relief washed across the driver's face. "What about the powder, sir?"

"Powder?" Tamas asked. "What powder?"

The color drained from the driver's face. "The whole city. It's filled with it. The duke was going to kill all those people!"

Tamas turned toward Alvation. Black powder! That's why he sensed so much. Nikslaus must have strung it through every building, ready to be touched off at his command. That's the only way he could have leveled the city in one night.

Tamas struggled up the embankment and began to run back the way he'd come. The Wardens would probably set it off, even if it meant dying themselves. No hope that a conscientious officer would countermand Nikslaus's orders.

There'd have to be tens of thousands of pounds of powder throughout Alvation to destroy the whole city. They could have set it off and then swept through the wreckage, slaughtering the survivors. What better way to frame Adro for the attack? No one would suspect a Privileged like Nikslaus of using black powder.

Tamas would never make it in time.

The first blast was so large it shook the ground. A cloud of fire rose up over the market district as high as a four-story building and the shock wave knocked hundreds of fighting soldiers off their feet.

Tamas tripped and fell, bashing one knee on the cobbles. He was back running with a limp a moment later, eyes on the city, waiting for the next blast. The fire was gone almost as quickly as it had risen, but Tamas could see the outline of a plume of smoke and steam rising into the evening sky.

That wouldn't be all of it. He had to get back into the city and...

And what? Stop the Wardens from lighting the powder? He didn't know where they were, and the city was quite large. He could try to find the powder caches, but no doubt the Wardens would have blown them up already.

Another blast rocked the city, this time on its far side. Tamas was ready for it, and managed to keep his footing despite the rumbling of the ground.

Each one of the blasts was no doubt killing hundreds. He could suppress the blasts, or redirect the energy, but trying to contain that much powder would be like boiling water in a sealed teakettle—it would rip him apart.

Tamas entered the city, shoving his way through the melee, and spread his senses outward. There was a munitions dump on the next street, he could feel it. Enough powder to level ten city blocks.

Tamas sensed the match being touched to powder somewhere inside the munitions dump, and already it was too late to suppress the explosion. The pressure built in Tamas's mind, the explosion rocketing outward from the gunpowder.

Tamas grasped the energy, ready to redirect it. His mind reached out for the rest of the powder to see how much he'd have to stop.

A scattering of powder charges was easy. A powder horn was no problem. Even a barrel of powder, Tamas could redirect.

Fifty barrels of powder went at once.

Tamas grasped the energy and pushed it straight down beneath him. It felt like he'd attached a hundred cannons to his boots and fired them all at once. The energy coursed out, throwing up dirt, rock, and cobbles, and Tamas could see the shocked faces of the soldiers closest to him just before they were vaporized in an instant.

It was too much. He couldn't contain so much powder. His body groaned and twisted, and his skin felt ready to split.

All of this took less than a heartbeat. Tamas could feel consciousness slipping, and with it the will to control the force of the explosion.

He'd failed his wife. He'd failed his soldiers, his son, the people of Alvation and Adro.

He'd failed them all.

The world went black.

Taniel landed square on the shoulders of one of his guards. The man crumpled beneath him, absorbing some of the impact, but Taniel's legs still buckled beneath him and he rolled, howling in pain, up against the base of the beam.

The two remaining guards froze, their eyes wide, in the midst of trying to bring Ka-poel under control.

Taniel forced himself to his feet and caught the swing of a musket butt on the rope binding his hands. He lashed out with one boot, kicking in the side of a guard's knee, and then slammed his tied hands across the face of the other.

Ka-poel's hood had fallen back in the struggle. Her eyes were wide, her short red hair wild. She lifted her chin under Taniel's brief scrutiny. The moment was over, and she wicked a drop of blood off the end of her long needle and darted forward, drawing her belt knife to saw through Taniel's bonds.

"You shouldn't have come," Taniel said.

She finished cutting his bonds and thrust a powder horn into his hands. He tore the plug out with his teeth. The powder poured into his mouth, tasting sulfuric on his tongue, crunching between his teeth. He sputtered and choked, but forced himself to swallow a mouthful of black powder.

The powder trance raced through him, warming his body,

tightening his muscles. The pain of his wounds and bruises faded to the back of his mind.

Ka-poel finished dispatching the four guards with her belt knife. She stood up and sniffed, wiping the blood off.

Taniel looked around. Despite the activity in the camp, plenty of soldiers had begun to notice their fight. An officer was running toward them at the head of a squad, pointing and shouting for others.

Taniel rubbed at his wrists. He and Ka-poel were in the center of the Kez army, completely cut off and with no hope of rescue. He'd have to kill a hundred thousand men to escape this.

"Pole." He bent at the knee, fetching one of the guard's muskets, and winced. Not enough powder in the world to completely drown out the pain. "I don't think we're going to get through this."

Ka-poel surveyed the Kez army, like a general surveying her troops.

Taniel hefted the musket. It was a cheap make, nothing like the Hrusch rifle he was used to. He retrieved the bayonet from the guard's kit and fitted it into place. It would have to do. The Kez were coming—fifty, maybe more now. And any fighting would bring the notice of the rest of the army.

"Pole," he said, "I love you."

Ka-poel touched one finger to her heart, then pointed at him. She tossed her satchel on the ground in front of her. It landed with the top open, and she lifted her hand.

Her dolls began to rise out of the satchel. Taniel remembered the fight at Kresim Kurga and the power she had shown.

"It won't be enough this time, Pole."

The dolls kept coming. Ten. Fifty. A hundred. A thousand.

An impossible number rose out of the satchel and spread out evenly in the air surrounding them.

The Kez soldiers had come to a stop twenty paces away and were watching her sorcery, perplexed. A Kez captain lifted his hand. "Load!"

Taniel ignited their powder with a thought. Muskets ripped apart and powder horns exploded and the air filled with the scent of spent powder and the sound of screams.

"A powder mage!" someone yelled. The call went on through the camp as soldiers discarded their muskets and scrambled for swords and knives. More men came running—first a trickle, then in force. Taniel gripped the barrel of his musket and prepared for the fight.

It started as a small, out-of-place movement in the corner of his eye. A Kez soldier stopped in the middle of the camp and rammed his bayonet into the neck of the man beside him. The soldier seemed perplexed at what he'd just done before he suddenly turned and cracked his musket butt across the teeth of another Kez infantryman.

Another soldier suddenly held his powder horn up to his flint-lock and pulled the trigger, blowing himself and three of his companions to the pit.

Fistfights broke out, and the tide of Kez soldiers heading toward Taniel and Ka-poel began to ebb as they turned on one another.

Ka-poel stood, legs braced, eyes on her dolls as if she were examining a chessboard. Around her, the dolls were moving of their own accord. Some of them fought each other, while others tumbled and stabbed at shadows. Taniel felt a terrible fear grip him. She was controlling an entire army, thousands all at once!

An unoccupied infantryman charged Taniel.

Taniel slapped aside the thrust of a bayonet and rammed his own through the infantryman's eye.

"We should go," he said to Pole. "You can't keep them forever."

Ka-poel caught his sleeve and made the shape of a gun with one hand, pointing at her dolls.

"You want me to shoot them?"

A nod.

Taniel dropped the butt of the musket to the ground and quickly loaded it. Lifting it to his shoulder, he looked to Ka-poel for confirmation.

She made a hurrying motion with one hand.

Taniel aimed at her field of dolls and pulled the trigger.

A sound like thunder cracked out of the late-morning air, sending Kez soldiers diving for cover. A nearby soldier suddenly splattered across a tent like he'd been hit by a cannonball. Taniel could hear the cries of dismay, and someone shouted, "Artillery fire!"

Ka-poel threw her head back in a silent laugh.

"That's sadistic," Taniel said. He grabbed her by the hand. "Let's go."

They raced through the Kez camp, heading toward the eastern mountains that lined Surkov's Alley. Ka-poel's dolls kept pace with them, floating, fighting shadows. By the time they reached the edge of the Kez camp and began to climb the nearest hill, the number of dolls had diminished.

Ka-poel panted heavily as they climbed. Taniel looked behind them. No one was following, but it wouldn't be long until they did. He pulled on her arm and felt her sag to the ground, her eyes suddenly cloudy from exhaustion. Taniel swung his musket onto his shoulder and then lifted Ka-poel in his arms, continuing to run.

The hill grew steeper, and Taniel soon found himself climbing more than running. He was forced to set Ka-poel on a large rock in the scree and pause to rest, turning to look at the valley.

They weren't being chased.

The entire Kez camp was in an uproar. Brother fought brother. A weak Privileged was slinging sorcery in a panic. Wardens were trying to restore order by killing "ringleaders" in a perceived uprising among the troops—it only added to the chaos.

All because of Ka-poel's dolls.

Taniel uncorked his powder horn and poured a measure onto the back of his hand. He snorted it. The immediate danger may have passed, but the Kez could still send infantry or even riders after them. There'd be no getting away if they did. He could feel fatigue circling him, like a pack of wolves around a wounded deer.

The burning flame of his powder trance would go out soon. No amount of fuel would keep it going, and then he would be useless.

He and Ka-poel would need to walk the steepest part of the scree north for over three miles to get even with the Adran camp.

Then there was the matter of the traitor Hilanska.

Near the front line, the chaos seemed the least pronounced, and plenty of the Kez soldiers were still watching as Kresimir and Mihali spoke alone between the camps. The two gods faced each other, no more than a few feet apart. Taniel would have given a fair amount to read their lips. Neither seemed to notice or care about the confusion in the Kez camp.

Mihali reached out, resting a hand on Kresimir's shoulder.

Kresimir shrugged it off.

Mihali spread his hands in a calming gesture. Kresimir raised one hand in the air, pointing at the sky, shouting something.

Mihali kept speaking. His lips barely moved and his face was serene.

It was several minutes that Mihali spoke. Much to Taniel's surprise, Kresimir seemed to listen. The god's hand fell to his side.

Back at the camp, chaos continued. Ka-poel's floating dolls had dwindled to no more than a few dozen. She sat up, looking haggard and bruised, but a victorious smile played on her lips. Her attention seemed to be focused on the last dolls, and they were not disappearing as quickly as the earlier ones. She was fighting hard to keep those last few puppets alive.

Taniel watched the two gods. Kresimir and Mihali had edged closer to each other. Mihali was pointing to his opposite hand as if explaining something. Kresimir listened, brow furrowed.

Mihali appeared to finish his explanation.

Kresimir shook his head adamantly.

Mihali frowned. A sad smile crept onto his face and he opened his arms.

Taniel suddenly felt his heart beating faster. He lifted his musket to his shoulder and sighted down the barrel at Kresimir. Two miles. Not a hard shot for him, but the bullet was a regular ball and it would take far too long to reach Kresimir. Taniel could only provide a distraction.

Kresimir suddenly threw his arms wide. For a brief moment, he looked as if he was ready to embrace his brother.

Taniel clutched his hands to his face and stumbled back, falling to the ground as a light brighter than a thousand suns erupted from Kresimir. Taniel braced himself, waiting for a shock wave and the deafening boom of an explosion.

Neither came. The light blazed on so brightly that though Taniel covered his face, he still felt as if he was staring into the heart of the sun.

A hand touched him. He reached out, grabbing Ka-poel. What did she see? Was there anything *to* see? She had to be as blind as he was. He pulled her to him and clutched her to his chest, trying to protect her eyes from the blaze. Sweet gods, what was this sorcery?

Taniel felt the brightness begin to fade after what seemed an eternity. Fear crept through him when he opened his eyes and saw nothing. Had he been blinded?

It must have been twenty minutes before shapes began to manifest themselves in his vision. He blinked rapidly, trying to dispel pools of color, trying to grasp what he'd just seen. That blaze—so bright and intense, but without heat or sound. Not an explosion.

Taniel tried to recall his knowledge of Privileged sorcery. What had Kresimir done?

Slowly, it dawned on him.

Kresimir had opened the Else itself to the world.

Taniel's returning sight began to show him that both the Kez and Adran camps were in chaos now. It seemed that no one could see. Hundreds of thousands of men crept on their hands and knees, wailing and crying out.

In the center of the field, positioned between the two camps, Kresimir stood alone. Mihali was completely gone, not even ash where he'd once stood. Kresimir's mouth was open, his face frozen in a silent scream.

Taniel watched as Kresimir's shoulders slumped. Kresimir stared blindly for a moment at the spot where Mihali had been. Then the god dropped to his knees and wept.

Taniel sagged against the mountainside, overcome with exaustion, his body racked with the pain of his wounds. A few minutes passed in silence before he looked down at his bloody, vomit-stained shirt. There was a rushing sound in his ears, and his hands shook with sudden excitement.

"Pole," he said. "My shirt is soaked with Kresimir's blood."

Adamat couldn't take his eyes off Lord Claremonte as he finished his speech. He'd worked the crowd perfectly. There weren't cheers or shouts—no, not even Claremonte would have expected that.

There were grumbles. Murmurs of discontent. Someone near Adamat told the woman next to him that Claremonte had a point. A rising sense of indignation washed through the assembled masses, and Adamat knew that Claremonte had convinced them. Maybe not all of them. Maybe not now. But the few screams of protest when Claremonte's Privileged destroyed the Kresim Cathedral had been stifled quickly.

All up and down the Ad, Brudanian soldiers pushed their long-boats up onto the riverbank and disembarked. At quick glance they seemed to be working in teams of about fifteen, each one accompanied by a Privileged. They carried bayoneted muskets and barrels of black powder, and Adamat saw the first team reach a church on the other side of the Ad and begin pushing people away.

They were preparing it for demolition.

If Adamat wasn't so horrified he'd be impressed. Claremonte

582   *Brian McClellan*

had arrived with reinforcements and supplies, given a brilliant speech for his ministerial candidacy, and now he was setting about destroying the religious buildings of Adro. He'd taken the horror of the people—the fear of the Brudanians invading the capital—and turned it on its head. Everyone would be so relieved that Claremonte was not pillaging the city that he could do just about anything he wanted.

Adamat wasn't a religious man by any stretch, but he wanted to rush to the nearest church and stop the soldiers from destroying it. These were historical icons, some of them close to a thousand years old! He had the feeling that any move to stop the soldiers would see him killed.

Less than forty paces away, Claremonte's longboat was pushed onto the bank. Ricard was already hurrying toward it, his assistants and bodyguards following cautiously. Adamat shouted at him to stop.

A sailor helped Claremonte onto the muddy ground and then up the shore and onto the street.

Adamat knew from the set of Ricard's shoulders that he was about to do something stupid.

"Fell! Grab him!"

It was too late. Ricard cocked his fist back and punched Claremonte in the nose, dropping him like a sack of potatoes.

Brudanian soldiers surged forward, and Claremonte's Privileged raised a gloved hand, fingers held together as if about to snap them. Adamat's heart leapt into his throat.

"Stop!" Claremonte climbed to his feet. He laid a calming hand on the Privileged's arm. "No need for violence," he said, holding his nose with two fingers.

"What the pit do you think you're doing?" Ricard demanded, cocking his arm back as if about to swing again.

"Doing?" Claremonte said as he tilted his head back to keep his nose from bleeding. "I'm running for First Minister of Adro. You are Ricard Tumblar, I presume?"

"Yes," Ricard said icily.

Claremonte stuck his hand out. "Lord Claremonte. It's a delight to meet you."

"That delight," Ricard said, "is not shared."

"Well, that is too bad." Claremonte let his hand drop. "I assumed we were friends!"

"Why would you assume that?"

"Because," Claremonte said, "you brought out half the city to greet me and hear my speech. That's the kind of thing friends do." Claremonte's smile had dropped on one side—only slightly, but it now came across as a leer. His eyes swept past Ricard and Fell and over the other union bosses and came to rest on Adamat. The corner of his mouth lifted back into a full smile. "Really," he said, still speaking to Ricard, "I must thank you for that. Now if you'll excuse me, I have an election to win."

Tamas felt the familiar jolt and rocking of a carriage as he fought his way back to consciousness.

It brought a panic in him. Where was he being taken? Who was driving the carriage? Where were his men?

Memory of the battle outside of Alvation, of finding Nikslaus's body, and of trying to stop the explosion of thousands of pounds of gunpowder all came back to Tamas at once.

He was on his back, and when he opened his eyes, he stared up at the roof of a stagecoach. It was light outside, so he must have been out for some time. The air was cool and thin, and that brought another wave of worry to Tamas's muddled mind. Was it winter? Had he been out for months?

His arms wouldn't move on his command. After fighting down yet more panic, he decided that yes, his arms could move but they were restrained, and it was a struggle just to shift. Had he been taken captive by the Kez?

The first face that Tamas saw was not one he expected.

It belonged to an ebony-skinned Deliv man with gray hair curled tight against his scalp. He wore a kelly-green Deliv uniform without epaulets or insignia. The man leaned over Tamas, regarding him contemplatively.

"Good. You're awake. The doctors were beginning to think you might be out indefinitely. We're almost to the summit."

Tamas closed his eyes again. Perhaps his mind was too foggy to hear correctly. Had the Deliv said "summit"?

"Who the bloody pit are you?" Tamas asked. The face seemed familiar in a long-absent way, like a painting seen above a mantel-piece or a figure from his childhood. One of Sabon's relatives? No, he didn't look a thing like Sabon.

The Deliv bowed his head. "I am Deliv."

"I said who are you, not where are you from. Bloody fool." Tamas's brain pounded inside his skull like a military parade. He flexed his fingers and tested his bonds. Wait. He didn't have any bonds. Then why couldn't he move? He lifted his head and looked down at the tight-fitting blanket wrapped around his chest.

A little wiggling and Tamas was able to pull his arms free. He pushed the blanket aside and sat up.

He was wearing his spare uniform—at least, he thought it was his spare. This one wasn't soiled from the battle outside Alvation.

The carriage came to a stop suddenly, pitching Tamas to one side. The Deliv reached out a hand to steady him. Tamas waved him off.

"What do you mean, 'summit'?" he asked.

The door to the carriage opened to reveal Olem standing out-side. He snapped to attention and his face split into a grin at the sight of Tamas.

"Sir! Glad to see you awake. How is your head?"

Tamas felt a wave of relief. He was still in the hands of his own men, it seemed, and Olem was still armed. He cast a glance toward the Deliv and stepped out of the carriage.

"Feels like I was thrown off the top of Sablethorn and landed on my face," Tamas said.

He looked to either side and noted they were in the mountains. Well, that explained "the summit."

"Are we past the Alvation Mountainwatch?"

"We've passed the first Mountainwatch post, sir." Olem pointed up the path. "The main Alvation Mountainwatch fortress is up ahead. We'll spend the night there before resuming the march."

Tamas felt emotions flow over him like the surf on a windy day. His legs were already weak, and news that he was already on Adran soil nearly made him fall. He pushed away Olem's offered hand and began to walk up the path. He thought through the calculations in his head. This time of year the pass would be quite clear and likely dry. They could descend back onto the Adran plains and head toward Surkov's Alley. They'd be back defending the country in a week and a half of hard march.

"Sir, you should continue to rest."

"I can walk fine," Tamas said, though his legs had more than a little wobble to them and his head was dizzy. Up ahead, the Alvation Mountainwatch fortress looked tall and imposing. The doors had been thrown open, and Mountainwatchers were cheering at the soldiers marching up the pass. "The fresh air will do me good. Now report. How long have I been out?"

"Two days, sir."

"The battle?"

"It went..."—Olem hesitated—"well enough."

"Our losses?"

Olem plucked a cigarette from his the curl of his jacket cuff and stuck it in his mouth without lighting it. "We have less than two thousand men in fighting condition left between the Seventh and the Ninth."

"That's it?" Tamas came to a stop and turned to Olem. He looked back down the path and noted that their baggage train led far beyond his sight. Where had that come from? They'd not had a baggage train in their march north.

"Gavril?"

"Recovered by Demasolin."

Tamas felt relief wash over him. "My powder mages?"

"Vidaslav took a bayonet to the stomach. We don't know if he'll survive. Leone was killed defending Vlora from a Warden."

"And Vlora?" Tamas felt his heart stop.

"She's wounded, but alive."

Tamas sagged against Olem. It was several moments before he regained his composure and stepped away.

He noticed that the old man from the carriage was following them up the path.

"How are we going to make a dent in the Kez army in Adro with just two thousand men?" Tamas asked. He couldn't help the annoyance in his voice when he jerked his head at the old Deliv and said, "And who the pit is this?"

Olem took his cigarette out of his mouth and twirled it between his fingers. "Please excuse the field marshal," he said to the old Deliv. "He's not in his right mind."

The Deliv seemed amused by this. "I hope he gets into his right mind before we go up against the Kez." He bowed his head. "I am Deliv," he said, "but you may call me Sulem the Ninth."

Sulem the... "Oh. My lord." Tamas inclined his head, shaking off the urge to drop to one knee. His mouth had gone dry. Sulem IX, king of Deliv, and Tamas had sworn at him for being a bloody fool in the carriage. "I meant no offense. I didn't realize..."

"None taken, Field Marshal." The king raised an eyebrow and glanced toward the ground as if expecting Tamas to kneel, but did not pursue the idea further.

Tamas didn't know what to say. How much did the king know? Why was he here, marching along with Tamas and a brand-new baggage train?

"I'm sorry, my lord," Tamas said, "but I am very much out of touch. I'm not sure what has gone on in the days while I was out."

The king clasped his hands behind his back. "Colonel," he said to Olem, "do you mind if I give your report?"

"Not at all, Your Eminence."

"Shall we?" the king asked, extending his arm toward the fortress rising above them.

"Yes," Tamas said.

They continued walking up the mountain road, past the remnants of Tamas's cavalry, with Olem trailing a few feet behind.

The Deliv king said, "Let me tell you how things have come from my side, and then later you can finish your conversation with Colonel Olem. I came to Alvation expecting an Adran army, but instead found two. The day after your battle with Duke Nikslaus's troops was a little confusing, but between my generals and your Colonel Olem and Colonel Arbor, everything got sorted out." Sulem paused for a moment.

"I'm sorry for Alvation, my lord," Tamas said.

"Sorry? What for? You saved a Deliv city, Tamas. I am greatly in your debt."

"The gunpowder?"

"You and your powder mages stopped it before too much damage could be dealt. There were casualties, of course, but the city remains and with it a debt of gratitude."

"I see"—Tamas glanced over his shoulder at the baggage train—"that you've supplied us for our journey. For that, *I* am grateful."

There was a twinkle in Sulem's eye, and for the first time since the carriage, a smile crept onto the old king's face. "Supplies and more," he said.

"More?"

"Field Marshal," Sulem said, "this is the vanguard. We're coming

588   Brian McClellan

over the mountains with fifty thousand men. There would be more if I hadn't sent the better part of my army down the Great Northern Road into Kez. You have my soldiers at your service, and I intend to see you through this war. The kind of treachery plotted by Nikslaus and Ipille does not befit a brother king." Sulem's smile disappeared, his voice gaining a dangerous edge. "You may have sent Manhouch to the guillotine, and I do not approve, but Ipille made an attack upon my people."

Fifty thousand Deliv troops! *That*, Tamas knew, could send the Kez reeling. Tamas felt his heart soar. This would turn the tide of the war. Adro had more than just a chance now, they had an ally.

For the first time in weeks his step was light. He neared the Alvation Mountainwatch feeling as if a great weight had been lifted off his shoulders.

There was a clamor on the walls of the Mountainwatch fortress, and a horseman suddenly burst through the gate at a reckless speed. The messenger saw Tamas and sawed at the reins, bringing his mount to a stop in a spray of gravel. The man leapt from horseback.

"Sir," he said. His cheeks were red, frost-burned from navigating the cold heights at great speeds, and his hand trembled as he saluted.

"Breathe, soldier," Tamas said.

"Sir," the messenger gasped, "we have word from one of our posts on the eastern side of the mountains. Adopest, sir. It's burning."

EPILOGUE

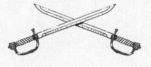

Privileged Borbador stood on the front step of a medium-sized house in the Adran suburbs and wondered when the last time was that he'd asked someone for help. It wasn't something most Privileged were accustomed to doing. They either did everything themselves or they gave orders.

An explosion rocked the evening air, causing Bo to flinch. Another church. Those Brudanian bastards had been demolishing religious buildings all over the city. They'd dragged priests out into the street and beat them to death in public, and the Adran people had just stood by and watched it all happen. They were too shell-shocked by the war, too relieved that the Brudanians hadn't sacked the city, to do anything to stop it.

Some had even joined in.

Bo didn't like the Kresim Church very much, but he hated the idea of standing by and watching while a foreign army destroyed

590 Brian McClellan

the cultural icons of the city. He'd been in the crowd, watching while they tore down the Kresim Cathedral. He'd listened to Claremonte's speech and seen the Trading Company army come onshore, unopposed by people who should have been defending their city.

It made Bo nervous for the Trading Company Privileged to be in the city. He'd spent every day since their arrival going to great lengths to avoid them. At best, they'd try to press him into service, thinking he had no allegiances left to Adro. At worse, they'd see him as a loose end and do their best to kill him.

Bo might have thrown his all at them the day they arrived, sinking several of the ships—maybe even killing Claremonte—before being put down by the Brudanian Privileged. But he was finished with other people's crusades. He had his own problems to worry about now.

A friend and brother to save.

The sound of children's laughter reached him from inside the house. It almost made him pause. Almost.

Bo rapped on the door. The laughter stopped.

"Stay here, children," a nervous voice commanded. Floorboards creaked as someone came down the front hall of the house. Bo's third eye told him it was the very Knacked he was coming to see. He could sense someone peering through the eyehole at him, and then a deadbolt was turned. The door opened a crack.

"Privileged Borbador," Adamat said.

Bo bowed his head. "Inspector Adamat."

Adamat's eyes searched the street, slightly wild, as if looking for a trap. "To what do I owe the pleasure? I didn't think I'd ever see you again."

"I brought gifts," Bo said, indicating the paper-wrapped packages beneath his arms. "May I come in?"

Adamat scanned the street once more. Conflict raged across his face. He was a nervous man these days, it seemed. Bo could relate.

And nobody wanted to invite a Privileged into their home.

"Love," a woman's voice came, "who is it?"

"Privileged Borbador."

The door opened the rest of the way and Bo saw Faye standing in the hallway. She looked somewhat better than that day in Vetas's manor. She'd gotten some sleep, and though Bo guessed from the red in the corner of her eyes that she'd been crying recently, she hid it well.

"Privileged," Faye said, "please come in."

Bo brought his bundle of packages inside with him and deposited them in the living room. "Call me Bo," he said. "I brought gifts for your family."

"You shouldn't have," Faye said, giving him a gracious smile.

Adamat looked less pleased with the idea. There was a wariness in his eyes. He didn't trust Bo.

Bo couldn't exactly blame him for that.

"Did you feel it?" Bo asked.

Adamat seemed taken aback. "Feel what?"

"It would have been an unexplained shock," Bo said. "Like being alone in a room and a cold glass of water thrown in your face."

Adamat slowly shook his head. "I don't know what you mean."

Strange, Bo thought, that Knacked couldn't sense it when a god died. Mihali—Adom reborn—had been murdered six days ago. It wasn't the same as when Taniel had shot Kresimir in the eye, though. This had felt more...permanent.

"Nothing," Bo said. "No need to worry yourselves over it."

"We were just having dinner," Faye said, giving her husband a warning look. "Would you join us?"

"Thank you, but no. I was hoping to talk to your husband alone."

Adamat cleared his throat. "Faye can hear anything I would," he said.

Bo could tell at a glance that Faye wasn't going to leave the room. So much for divide and conquer. He wondered if he should have brought Nila and Jakob inside with him. Bo had asked them to wait in the carriage, but now he thought their presence might have helped put Adamat at ease.

He still wasn't sure what he was going to do with that girl. She was a Privileged, it seemed. A Privileged who didn't need gloves. Bo didn't think that she understood the gravity of what she really was. No Privileged in all the Nine could touch the Else without gloves. Not even the Predeii.

Only the so-called gods could do that.

"I need your help," Bo said.

"I'm not for hire," Adamat said, glancing at his wife. "My family has gone through greater trials the last few months than any family ought. I will not leave them for anything."

Faye narrowed her eyes at Bo, her gracious welcome suddenly gone. To Bo it felt as if the warmth had been sucked out of the room.

"Two things," Bo said, holding up his hands. He'd left his gloves off for this. The last thing he needed was for Adamat to think he was trying to threaten him. "First, I need you, Faye, to watch over Jakob Eldaminse for a time."

"The boy's alive?" Faye asked.

"Second," Bo added, "I need Adamat to help me rescue my best friend—my only friend. I have evidence that condemns General Ket and her sister of selling army property for their own profit. I need you, Sergeant Oldrich, and Oldrich's men to come with me to arrest General Ket and get Taniel Two-Shot released."

This whole thing made Bo nervous. He'd not heard a word from the front since finding out that Taniel was being court-martialed. Taniel could be in prison, he could have been hanged. Bo cursed himself for not acting fast enough on this, but he'd had to find evidence before he could do anything about it. He should have left for the front as soon as he'd found evidence of Ket's involvement a week ago, but he'd had to gather more evidence than just one dead noble's records.

"Arresting a member of the General Staff during wartime?" Adamat scoffed. "That's suicide. No. I won't do it. As I said, I have a family to care for and protect. I am not for hire."

"Please," Faye said, her jaw stiff, "we'd like to get back to dinner with our children now."

Bo ignored them. He hated himself, sometimes, for the things he had to do. For the killing, the lying and stealing. For having to manipulate people. "In exchange for your help, Adamat, I will give you one favor from myself."

"What could I possibly . . ."

"One favor!" Bo said, holding up a finger. "Anything you want from the last living member of the Adran royal cabal."

Faye frowned. Bo could see her mind working behind her eyes.

"No," Adamat said. "I don't think—"

"Love," Faye said, tugging on Adamat's arm.

Bo took a deep breath. "One favor," he said again. "Anything you want. Even if it means I have to slaughter my way through Kez to find your missing son."

There would be protestations. Arguments. They would try several more excuses, but Bo could see in their eyes that he had them.

ACKNOWLEDGMENTS

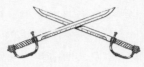

Thanks to my fantastic agent, Caitlin Blasdell, for her editorial advice and her willingness to talk it out when I was having problems with the book—and of course for selling the book in the first place. To my editor, Devi Pillai, who had the patience and faith to let me work through the book at my own pace and kept pushing out the deadline so I could be truly happy with the final product.

My wife, Michele, was great during the whole process. She is always my first brainstormer and editor, and nothing gets to either Caitlin or Devi without Michele's grudging approval.

Thanks to my parents, who have always been incredibly supportive of my writing and were no exception during the writing of this book. My dad was the first "fan" to give his stamp of approval on this book, reading most of the final draft in a single afternoon.

Thanks to Isaac Stewart, who did the maps and interior art for *Promise of Blood*. He not only did a fantastic job on yet another map for *The Crimson Campaign* but updated the old ones to better fit the narrative.

Thanks to all the awesome folks at Orbit for their support with Book One and Book Two: Susan Barnes, Lauren Panepinto, Alex Lencicki, Laura Fitzgerald, Ellen Wright, and everyone else. These books wouldn't be the success they are without all their editing, artistic, and marketing wizardry.

Thanks to Ethan Kinney, who forced me to think about things from a different perspective due to all his damn questions about the powder mage universe.

Of course, thanks to all of my friends and family who supported me along the way, especially Sunny Morton for listening to me chatter about the process and gave great advice to a newly published author.